WAX FRUIT

GUY McCRONE was born in 1898 in Birkenhead. After his parents' return to their native Glasgow, he was educated at Glasgow Academy, going on to read modern languages at Pembroke College, Cambridge, and then studying singing in Vienna. On his return to Glasgow, he organised the first British performance of Berlioz's *Les Troyens* at the Theatre Royal in 1935. He was also one of the founders of the city's Citizens' Theatre.

Glasgow provided the main inspiration for McCrone's writing, and the novels *Antimacassar City*, *The Philistines* and *The Puritans*, begun in 1940 and published as *Wax Fruit* in 1947, are widely regarded as his finest work. Two more sequels followed: *Aunt Bel* (1949) and *The Hayburn Family* (1952). His other novels include *The Striped Umbrella* (1937), *James and Charlotte* (1955) and *An Independent Young Man* (1961). Guy McCrone retired to the Lake District in 1968, where he died at Windermere in May 1977.

Other B&W Titles by Guy McCrone

AUNT BEL
THE HAYBURN FAMILY

WAX FRUIT

GUY McCRONE

B&W PUBLISHING

First published 1947
First published by B&W Publishing Ltd 1993
This edition published 2012
by B&W Publishing Ltd
29 Ocean Drive Edinburgh EH6 6JL

1 3 5 7 9 10 8 6 4 2 12 13 14 15

ISBN 978 1 84502 417 8

A CIP catalogue record for this book is available
from the British Library.

Typeset by RefineCatch Limited, Bungay, Suffolk
Printed and bound by Nørhaven, Viborg

CONTENTS

BOOK I	ANTIMACASSAR CITY	1
BOOK II	THE PHILISTINES	209
BOOK III	THE PURITANS	397

To Glasgow Readers

No. You must forgive me. But I did not have the impertinence to draw for you portraits of your grandparents and their friends.

ANTIMACASSAR CITY

Chapter One

WHY were the dogs whining?

It was Doon and Nith that were making the noise. Clyde, who was the oldest and was most attached to her father, must have trotted off after the trap when her mother and he had driven off this evening.

The strong moon, coming through the skylight, made a dazzling oblong on the wall opposite the little girl's bed. Although she herself lay snug, the attic room was so cold that she could see her breath when she puffed in the direction of the beam of light.

"Haud yer tongue, Doon! Keep quate, Nith!" That was her brother's voice. She could hear his heavy boots cracking the frozen puddles of the farm close.

What time was it? Nine or ten o'clock? Late for Ayrshire farm folks, anyway. Her instinct told her that her parents were not yet come home from their visit. There was still a sense of waiting. That must be why the dogs were restless.

She knew all the farm's lightest sounds. She could tell their meaning. She could hear the movement of hoofs as the Clydesdales shifted the weight of their great resting bodies from one leg to the other.

But the lighter taps of the pony's hoofs were wanting.

A suppressed excitement took hold of her. It was not quite anxiety, though she was beginning to feel that too. This odd child of ten was beginning to hope, almost, that something was coming to her. For, though she did not know it, she was of those strange people who must have experience, even though it be tragic—who, even in catastrophe, are able to stand back and appraise.

She climbed out and threw some bedclothes about her. Dragging the one chair in the room beneath the skylight, she climbed upon it and pushed the glass frame wide open. The air, cold as a knife, met her round warm cheeks, but she did not care. She could now get her head through.

She could see the shape of the buildings—the barn, the cart-shed, the stables, the byre. And beyond, the stacks in the stack-yard, then the gate to the road. In the strong moonlight, and rimed with hoar-frost, everything was colourless. Everything had been reduced to planes and angles of velvet blackness and silver-white.

But for the occasional shuffling of the beasts in the stables and the cowshed, there was silence now. The collies must have followed her brother, wherever he was.

No, there they were, back again, wheeling about the yard like phantoms. Now they were whining the low, restless whines that had awakened her.

"Nae sign yet?" A farm-hand's voice was speaking.

"No' yet." Her brother's voice again.

"Whit time is it?"

"Ten."

So they *were* late. The farm usually went to sleep at eight. This tension was exciting. There were little thrills all over her. It wasn't just the cold creeping up from her bare feet.

II

Were these the steps of a pony now? She listened intently.

Her brother and the man emerged from the shadows and, crossing the yard, hung over the gate.

Were these the familiar hoof-claps? They must be. But she couldn't understand. She knew the weight and ring of them. But she could hear no wheels, and the hoofs clattered together at times as though the pony were dancing hysterically on a leading-rein.

Where was the trap? And where were her father and mother? She could feel her heart thumping in her body.

The dogs had run forward to the gate too, barking excitedly. Her brother turned on them and again shouted at them to be quiet. Suddenly something ran through them. It was her father's dog Clyde. Paying no attention, he came down to the centre of the yard. In the strong moonlight she could see the handsome long limbs of the old collie trembling. His bushy tail was clapped down tight over his thin buttocks. His ears lay as though he were in pain. For a moment he stood shivering, turning his long, elegant muzzle this way and that, looking about distractedly; then, balancing backwards, one thin front paw off the ground, he threw back his head and uttered a long, low howl.

The child had never heard anything so heartbroken. The other dogs seemed to get his meaning, for they were circling round him now, copying his low-sung note of woe.

Her brother paid no attention to them, for the pony, impatient at being led by a strange hand, was dancing sideways through the opened gate.

The three men were talking together excitedly. Suddenly her brother broke from them and ran towards the house. Now, inside, she could hear him calling, though she could not catch what he said.

She jumped from her chair and listened at her door. The house seemed to be stirring. She could hear the door of the servant-girls' room bang.

All this was very exciting. It was horrible to be missing anything. Should she go down to ask what it was? She did not dare. Her brother would order her back to bed, for he was strict with her, as their father was.

Now she could hear heavy steps coming to the foot of the attic stair. They began to ascend. She jumped into bed and covered herself up, ready with the pretence of sleep.

In another moment the catch was lifted and her brother stood in the doorway. Was it the moonlight that made him look like this? His aspect gave her a sensation of intense interest. So people looked like that if something dreadful had happened. He was struggling to seem calm. She could see that his deliberation was merely to give himself time.

She sat up abruptly as though she had been shocked out of a deep sleep.

"What is it?"

His voice was even stranger than his looks as he told her.

Chapter Two

MR. AND MRS. ARTHUR MOORHOUSE, of Ure Place, in the City of Glasgow, were already half-dressed by seven o'clock.

Arthur was standing in his best trousers pouring out his shaving-water from a shining copper can. For though, in this year 1870, hair on the face of the male was considered more ornamental than in later days, there was still a certain amount of shaving to be done. Arthur limited his natural decoration to mutton-chop whiskers. He was wise, for their blackness lent his strong features, his black eyebrows and the natural paleness of his skin an added distinction.

"There was no need for ye to get up so early, my dear. It's a bitter morning." Arthur drew out his razor and tested the edge.

Bel Moorhouse, wrapped as well as was possible against the Arctic chill of the bedroom, was running her comb down through the thick ripples of her hair. Its waved fairness shone bravely in the light of the two gas-jets above her head.

"Nonsense, dear. You've got a long, cold day in front of you. I must see that you get your breakfast properly."

Bel went on with her combing and Arthur took up his shaving-brush.

These foregoing words do not seem, in themselves, very pregnant, but their overtones were many, and to each of these young people betokened more than a perfunctory demonstration of affection on a cold morning.

Bel should stay in bed and take care of herself, Arthur was implying, because she was his precious wife, only lately acquired after many tedious years of looking after his own none too thankful family. And in addition—and of still greater importance—he was delicately reminding her that her body was a frail casket bearing within it their first child, to whose birth both were looking forward with the keenest pleasure. In his heart Arthur knew that Bel was as strong as a horse. But the strength of horses is not romantic, except perhaps in the horses themselves. Certainly it was not considered so in a twenty-four-year-old matron of mid-Victorian days. Politer to assume that any puff might blow her away, though you knew perfectly—and were thankful for it—that her agile young body would stand a hurricane.

And Bel's answer had been just as full of meaning. "You must be fed and tended, my dear husband," it implied, "by the only person who really knows to a hair's-breadth all your needs, physical and mental. You must be fortified against all discomforts of the body and of the mind. Today you are to be with relatives who for the past fifteen years have done nothing but worry and annoy you. You are going to bury your old father—for whom I personally never cared—and with him, a second wife twenty years younger than himself, whom he should never have married. It has all been very sudden and annoying, coming in this the eighth month of our marriage and just before Christmas. But I am much too fine a woman to complain. With my charm, my profound affection and, above all, my great good-sense, I shall throw myself between you and your annoyances. In a word, I shall be to you the perfect wife."

Each comprehended the meaning of the other perfectly. Which all goes to show that Arthur Moorhouse and his wife were on excellent terms.

By half-past seven Arthur was warming himself before a crackling fire in their pleasant red-plush dining-room. The breakfast-table looked cosier than ever from the fact that the room was still in gas-light.

Bel, all pride and importance behind the teacups, was looking up at her slim, thirty-three-year-old husband, more dark and effective than ever in his long black coat. And Arthur, looking down upon his glowing wife, decided that black suited her fairness almost better than anything else.

"When is your train, dear?" Bel asked as he took his place.

"Half-past eight."

"Then you won't be going down to business first?"

Down was the right word, for on their marriage the Arthur Moorhouses had set up house here in Ure Place, a quiet and pleasant little square with trees in the middle, set on the side of a steep hill. Up there they were in the City of Glasgow, but not quite of it. Yet in little better than five minutes Arthur's long legs could drop him down Montrose Street and into the Candleriggs, where he conducted with diligence his business of wholesale provision merchant.

Arthur finished his last spoonful of porridge and held out his hand for his plate of ham and eggs.

"No," he said, "I've no need to go down. David is going to let me know if there's anything."

"That's good," was all Bel said, but in her mind she wondered if Arthur's young brother would really trouble himself to go. He was such an unreliable creature.

"There's time to send one of the maids for a cab," she said presently.

"Nonsense. I'll walk across the town. If I leave at eight I'll have lots of time."

But Bel was insistent this morning. She even went the length—Junoesque though she was—of pretending, a little, to be pathetic, and thus, conquering her lord and master, she succeeded in having the cab ordered.

II

At five minutes to eight, Mr. and Mrs. William Butter arrived.

Mrs. William had been Sophia Moorhouse. Before her marriage, some eight years ago, she had kept house for Arthur. Arthur at the age of eighteen had left his father's farm and come to Glasgow to make his fortune. One by one his brother and sisters had followed him, with the exception of the oldest brother, Mungo, who remained a farmer. Sophia had been the first.

Sophia was not perhaps one of Bel's favourites. For, of all the family, she exploited Arthur with the least shame. Even now—from habit—Bel wondered for a moment what Sophia and her stolid husband could be wanting that they should call in on their way to the station; for they lived in a flat in Grafton Square, further up, across Cathedral Street, or the Stirling Road as it then was, and there was no reason whatever why they should come to Ure Place.

"Good morning, Bel dear. What a cold morning! How cosy

you both look! Could William and I possibly have another cup of tea? Or would it be a bother? We were so hurried at breakfast. Little Wil and Margy were so sure we would be late for their grandpapa's funeral, they kept running with gloves and things. William nearly died laughing."

As their sister-in-law pulled the bell—with the shallowest appearance of hospitality—to have more teacups brought, she could not help wondering what William looked like dying of laughter.

For, although William was only thirty-three, he was fat and square, and as much of his face as possible was covered with hair. Her gay young brother-in-law David had once described William Butter to Bel as a fat, hairy man who stood. You might as well connect the expressing of emotion with the Tolbooth Steeple as with William. Perhaps it was the hair, Bel pondered. But after all he could emit sounds. And this he didn't do either, much. No, if you shaved him clean, there would still be little or no movement of his facial muscles.

"Not that they aren't very sorry about grandpapa's death," Sophia was going on. "But as they've only seen him twice—or was it three times, William?"

William said nothing.

"Yes, that's right, three times, and then only for a little; they can't remember him very well. This tea's putting new life into me, Bel dear. We must get some like it. Mustn't we, William?"

William said nothing.

"It's time we were getting to the station," Arthur said, pulling out his watch.

"What about your bonnet, Bel dear?"

"Bel's not coming," Arthur said irritably.

"Why? Oh, of course. How wise. I was forgetting." She patted Bel's hand knowingly, then apropos of what appeared to be nothing, looked about her and said: "Delightful to think—"

"I've arranged to go to the station in a cab. Would ye like a lift?" Arthur said, with no attempt at grace in his invitation.

"That would be a great help, wouldn't it, William?"

William did not seem to hear.

And at last it broke upon Bel why these two had come down to them this morning. Young David had christened them the

Emperor and Empress of Cadge. David, Bel reflected, was not far wrong.

It was bitterly cold as she opened the front door for them. She saw her husband into his thickest overcoat and tied a woollen muffler of her own knitting about his neck.

Arthur went down the front steps, said "Bridge Street Station, please," and got into the cab without further ceremony.

Sophia bade Bel an effusive goodbye and regretted not having her company in the train.

Bel, having decided that William's hand was a little inclined in her direction, grasped it and shook it.

Holding the cab door open, Sophia turned. "Bel dear, as you're not coming, could you *bear* to send over for the children today? After all, it *is* Christmas-time. Poor wee mites. We can hardly expect them to feel our sorrow very deeply. They looked so forlorn when we said goodbye."

Bel succeeded—just in time—in looking vague and saying something about devoting the day to her mother.

"Well, anyway, if you can— Come along, William, don't keep Arthur waiting. Do you know what the time is now?"

But William did not bother to tell her the time. He merely followed his wife into the cab.

III

As they drew up at Bridge Street Station, they could see the slim black figure of Arthur's younger brother, David, turning into the entrance. His hands were deep in his overcoat pockets and his shoulders were hunched against the cold.

The noise of the car attracted his attention and he turned with a beaming smile to hold the door for its occupants. David was always delighted to see everybody.

Arthur bounced out, paid the cab, then turned to David, saying: "Anything from the office?"

"I didn't go in this morning."

"Why the devil didn't you? I told you to. Have you got your ticket?"

"No."

Arthur said no more. But, going to the ticket office, bought his own and his younger brother's. By this time Sophia was hovering.

"Come on," he shouted. "I've bought your ticket."

Sophia's gentle expostulation, "But, Arthur dear, William didn't mean you to," was cut in two by Arthur saying: "I haven't got your tickets, Sophia. Just David's and my own," as he disappeared into the inner station.

His second brother-in-law George was pacing the platform. George McNairn Esquire, as David always called him, was a large, elderly-looking man of thirty-five. If ever a stomach was made to support the chains of office—if ever shoulders were made to carry municipal ermine, these belonged to Mr. McNairn. He seemed infinitely large as he moved, slow and important, up and down.

He did not go to meet his brothers-in-law, but rather allowed his stately progress to converge with their more abrupt steps. He shook their hands with ceremony and, looking beyond them, spoke impersonally as though he were addressing the back gallery of the City Hall. His words could be heard all over the station.

"Good morning, Arthur. Good morning, David. Well, this is a melancholy duty—a melancholy duty."

Arthur returned his handshake quickly. "Good morning, George. Where's Mary?"

"At the fire in the waiting-room. She's feeling this very badly, poor girl—very badly."

Arthur hurried on to find his younger sister.

Mary was sitting solitary on a hard chair before a new-lit fire that was, as yet, giving out no heat. Her wide black dress was all about her and a thick veil hung over her face. Her hands, in their black gloves, were folded on her lap.

Arthur went to her and greeted her in a business-like way.

"Hello, Mary, how are you? Cold, isn't it?"

Mary raised her veil to allow her brother to kiss her.

"Good morning, dear," she said, in a voice that was controlled and gentle. You could never quite determine just how much this tone was assumed and how much of it came naturally to her.

Mary Moorhouse was a beautiful woman of thirty. Her face

was oval, her brows clear and serene, and her eyes da Vinci-like and candid.

Mary was in danger of becoming a saint. Consciously, that is. For there was a conscious, thought-out quality about everything she did. Like most saints, she was not above staging herself a little. And, again like most saints, she was quite devoid of humour.

At this point Sophia flooded into the waiting-room, embraced her sister and gave her good morning.

"And how are the boys, Mary?" she gushed to her sister, who was settling down again like a lake after a sudden squall.

Mary knew that Sophia was only asking after the children that she might make for herself an opening to begin talking about her own, but she put this unworthy thought from her. Besides, she had something to tell Sophia.

"Georgie and Jackie are having a little tea-party this afternoon, dear. Not anybody in, of course, but I baked some cakes. I felt that they should be happy at Christmas-time. They're too small to understand about their grandpapa."

Before she could say more, Sophia had broken in. "Mary, I wish I had known! My children could have gone there today. Their Auntie Bel wants them." (In the background Arthur grunted at this.) "But still, it would have been nice for the children to be all together."

"I've arranged for a cab to go for them, dear," Mary went on serenely, knowing in her heart what she was saving Auntie Bel and not feeling the less saintly for the knowledge. "One of George's clerks had just been down to take any orders we might have to give him, so I told him to see to it."

In the matter of worldly gear, Mary had done better than her sister. She lived in a neat, front-door house at Albany Place, near Charing Cross. And her husband conducted a flourishing manufacturers' agency in Queen Street.

Sophia, to do her justice, was not really jealous of her sister's greater prosperity. But her motto in life was: If there's anything to be had, then have it. And there was so much to be had from and in connection with Mary.

She turned to her husband, who was standing mute behind her. "William, aren't you delighted? Wil and Margy are going along to tea at their Auntie Mary's."

At this point Arthur, who had been looking out of the doorway, shouted, "Hurry up and get into the train."

So William Butter did not appear to feel it necessary to add to his wife's expressions of rapture. Or perhaps he was just standing.

IV

They were all in the train now and settling down to a melancholy, and what promised to be a cold, journey.

George, by dint of impressing with his majestic presence the man with the trolley of warming-pans, had two put into their carriage instead of one. But these, they reflected regretfully, would not remain hot for long upon so cold a morning.

The train jogged slowly out towards Paisley. In these days all trains going to central Ayrshire went by Paisley, for the direct line to Kilmarnock was not yet available, and the journey, for this reason, was more than an hour longer.

Arthur sat huddled, trying to read his newspaper, but the constant chatter of Sophia—about her children, about her house, about her maids, about a misunderstanding with a lady in the church—became too much for him and he set it down, thrust his hands into his coat-pockets and looked at his brood, pondering.

For in a very real sense they were his brood. He had put them all where they were. In a sense he had taken the place of their father.

Fifteen years before, feeling that life at the Laigh Farm could offer him no future, he had taken himself to the City. The first years had been hard. A man with whom his father dealt had taken him in as a clerk. Pay had been meagre for the eighteen-year-old lad, but Arthur was country-bred and wiry. His health had stood up to long hours, airless quarters and none too lavish food. Presently he had found himself with better wages and more responsibility. It was inevitable, for he had health, character and a sound village education, and his own mother, though a farmer's wife, had been anything but crude. The others had not come to Glasgow until their father's remarriage to one of his own servants eleven years ago had scattered them. The girls had felt their situation worst. Sophia had come to him almost at once. For a couple of years he had made a home for her; then, to the satisfaction of all, the high-mettled William Butter had lost his head at a church *soirée* (or perhaps Sophia had taken matters into her own hands) and claimed her for his own.

It was then that Mary came. For much the same length of time she had been with him. She had always been calm and distinguished. Though she was country-bred, she took on the refinements of the town at once. It was as though its gentler, more genteel ways had called to something in her blood. Arthur had been sorry, a little, when George McNairn had taken her to his majestic bosom. For Mary, in her quiet, self-conscious way, was a highly capable person.

That left only David to come—for Mungo, the oldest of them all, remained a farmer. At the time of his father's remarriage, David was a child of twelve.

He had better make himself responsible for David, Arthur had decided. He didn't want the boy to live in a house where he might feel himself a stepchild. And so, for David's sake, he had persuaded their aunt—a sister of their own mother—to put herself beneath his roof, to keep house, and to bring up his youngest brother.

As he sat now looking at David, he doubted if he had done the right thing. Would it have been better had the boy been brought up in the country? He had been delicate and their aunt had spoilt him. And now that he was twenty-three he was all too well acquainted with the town's ways.

David was slack.

Arthur had him in the business now and was trying to knock some kind of discipline into him, but it was uphill work. He might have done better to leave him to his father and his stepmother.

Why had they taken such a hate to this Highland woman that their father had married? After eleven years they still knew nothing against her, except that she had been a hired servant and was almost illiterate. Mungo, the only one who really knew her, had liked her well enough. Had they been unfair in keeping away so much from the old man? They had felt it, perhaps, a desecration of their mother's memory. But had that been reasonable? And now, they hardly knew their little half-sister

Phœbe. Bel had asked what was to become of her. She had even suggested she should be brought to live at Ure Place. He wondered if he ought to let her come. His habit of taking responsibility for everybody told him he should. Bel had maintained that the child could not stay on at the farm with only Mungo and a household of crude farm-women.

V

The train was jogging on through the frost-bound country. He looked out across the wide Clyde valley. The Kilpatrick Hills and, further away, the Campsies stood peppered with snow. In the rosy-morning distance a white cone stood out. That must be Ben Lomond. He and Bel must make a trip to Loch Lomond sometime. And there were the buildings of the new University on Gilmour Hill at the extreme west end of the town. In the far distance they looked almost completed. He had heard about the difficulty the builders were having with the spire and wondered what they intended to do about it.

Yes, it had been nice of Bel to think of taking in his little half-sister. But he felt reluctant. He felt he had done enough for everybody. Or was he the kind of person to whom everybody would always turn for help? Would he never be able just to lead his own life, be able just to look after his wife and his children and bother about nobody else?

He had hoped he had come to an end when, before his marriage, he had seen David settled in rooms, sold the flat where they had lived alone together—for their aunt had died—and, with the help of his wife-to-be and her mother, had furnished the pleasant house in Ure Place.

That was only eight months ago. And now suddenly his little half-sister was an orphan.

Well, they would all have a look at her today. And this evening, back again at tea in his own house and with the help of his sisters and their husbands, the future of Phœbe would have to be thrashed out.

The carriage jingled on the points and came to a standstill.

"Dear me," Sophia was saying, "this is only Paisley!"

Chapter Three

PUNCTUALLY to the minute, old Mrs. Barrowfield was roused to consciousness by the housemaid re-laying her bedroom fire.

This began every morning on the stroke of eight. Old Mrs. Barrowfield saw to that.

"A body's not much worth, if she's come to the age of sixty-five and still lets her girls get the better of her."

Mrs. Barrowfield's two girls had not sought to get the better of her for a long time now. They had been with her for more years than any of them cared to remember, and the discipline of the old lady's much-betasselled and upholstered flat in Monteith Row had long since ceased to chafe. Time had been when they had not been above an exchange of wit with young men at the door on the back lane. But their hair was grey now and their bodies had long since lost the fluidity of youth and had, like the body of their mistress, turned unalluring and rotund. And young men had, somehow, ceased to be witty.

Mrs. Barrowfield awoke with a sense of uneasiness. She had fallen asleep worrying over her only daughter Bel.

She raised herself on her pillow a little and looked about her.

"Wipe yer hands, Maggie, and draw back the curtains."

The respectful, respectable woman rose to her feet and did as she was bade. From her bed the old lady looked out on the slow winter dawn.

"Is it still frosty?"

The maid at the window cast her eyes over the wide expanse of Glasgow Green—to the winding banks of the Clyde—to the belching chimneys on the further side. On the south-east, the rising day was still red, made redder than it should be from particles of smoke. One or two stragglers, huddled in overcoats, were hurrying quickly along the carriage-way in the park. Distant buildings loomed indistinct in the morning haze.

"Aye, it's still frosty, Mam."

Mrs. Barrowfield let Maggie go back to her work and lay watching her get the fire going. She did it deftly and quickly, according to minute instructions long since given and long since learnt.

Bel. Bother the girl with all her high falutin nonsense.

Mrs. Barrowfield was proud of her twenty-four-year-old daughter. Indeed, it would not be too much to say that she lived for her—that is, when she was not living for her own, immediate and highly organised comfort. But, as Bel's mother often assured herself, she would be no proper parent if she were blind to her child's faults. And to high falute was one of Bel's worst ones.

Mrs. Barrowfield lay considering. Of course, the girl had got it direct from her father, the lamented Doctor Barrowfield. A little decorative pomp had been no bad thing in a doctor with a good-class practice, where bedside manner was everything. But it was merely irritating in the doctor's daughter. Besides, Charles Barrowfield had always managed to high falute without incurring obligation. Which was just precisely what his daughter was not doing. She was threatening to take on a responsibility that might be a trouble to her for years. That might, indeed, threaten her married happiness.

But here Mrs. Barrowfield's sense of comfort intervened. This worry was spoiling the nicest hour of her day. The crackling fire. The newspaper. Tea, toast, and ham and eggs (the eggs just soft and no more, or cook would hear about it).

She would try to dismiss Bel until she had got up.

The maid was standing now, scuttle in hand, preparing to go.

"Bring up my *Herald* now, Maggie. And you'll have to light the gas. It's dark these mornings."

Maggie was surprised. The old lady usually lay contented until her breakfast came up punctually at half-past eight. But she did as her mistress told her, helped to arrange her in bed, found a shawl for her shoulders, and gave her spectacles a rub.

Mrs. Barrowfield—to show defiance, perhaps, to her own uncomfortable thoughts—snapped the paper open.

II

The *Glasgow Herald*, Saturday, 24th December, 1870.

It was her habit to look through the paper systematically. This morning she started fiercely at the top left-hand corner of the front page.

The *Glasgow Weekly Herald* was advertising itself. Special Hogmanay Stories. "A Loveless Marriage", by A Young Lady. "The Fate of Baby Daisy, the Village Beauty." How could people read such trash? People, that was, who had business to attend to. For herself, seeing that time lay in plenty on her hands, she might go the length of a penny to see just in what respect the marriage had failed, that it had become loveless.

The new Theatre Royal, Hope Street. The pantomime, "Sinbad the Sailor", the cast including King Wangdoodle of the Chickorybony Islands. Pity Bel had to be in mourning for her father-in-law, otherwise she might have taken the young couple to see this. Not that she approved of theatre much, but of course the pantomime was different.

Hengler's Circus. Herr Holtum would exhibit his wonderful powers of juggling with cannon-balls. The circus was for children. She laid down her paper smiling and looked about the much-upholstered room, which was becoming lighter with the growing day. Well, Bel was making a start. In May there would be a grandchild.

And say in five more years he—she was determined it should be a *he*—would be ready to go to the circus. The prospect of this grandchild enchanted Mrs. Barrowfield. She would, she pondered, be able to give the little boy lots of good advice.

If only Bel didn't go and—Mrs. Barrowfield snapped up the paper and went on reading.

Pretty Baby Things could be had at Mrs. Fyfe's shops in Argyle Street and in Sauchiehall Street. She must remember that for Bel. She would look into the Argyle Street shop. There was no need of her dragging up into the West End where things were bound to be dearer and not a whit better.

Great Bargains! Smart clothes for genteel assemblies. She was past genteel assemblies and Bel didn't feel like them just now.

The Argyle House was overflowing with French and German

fancy goods. Just imagine that now! With the Germans and the French fighting each other as hard as they could! You would wonder that they had time to send fancy goods anywhere.

Wine advertisements. She could do with a bottle or two of that Marsala for odd guests on New Year's Day.

She turned a page.

Reviews of Books. They all looked as dry as dust.

Letters to the Editor. Women's rights. Dear me! What was making them start that nonsense? Signed "Dejected Brother". Did you ever? What was he dejected about? Because these modern hussies expected all the chivalries from the male sex and yet expected to be on equal terms with them. Rights had never worried Mrs. Barrowfield much. She didn't know what they were talking about. But there would be nothing dejected about *her* treatment of these shameless besoms. A good skelping from their fathers was what they were all needing. That behaviour like this should be happening in what was nearly the year 1871! She would just like to know what the Queen thought of it all!

Criminal Judge of London Court deprives two pickpockets of their Christmas dinner. And quite right too.

War Victims' Fund. A Glasgow meeting to raise funds to help the women and children of France in their terrible plight had met with discouraging response. Poor things! It was terrible for them. Mrs. Barrowfield immediately forgot them as Maggie appeared with the breakfast.

She sat up yet higher, buttered her toast, poured out her tea and took a sip.

Serious Railway Accident at Port Glasgow. Dear me! That was terrible too!

Nice ham they were getting just now.

The War. Great Battle in the North: Sortie from Paris. What was a sortie? Additional details. This war news was really very difficult to follow. Besides, she was perfectly certain the newspapers exaggerated it just to get more sales.

The Mont Cenis Tunnel had been completed for a distance of 12,215 metres. (Why couldn't they say yards or miles or inches?) And only five now remained to be pierced. A banquet was to be held in the tunnel to solemnise the completion of the event. Fancy! In a tunnel. Had they no nice hotels at one end or the other where they could sit down in comfort? But you never knew with foreigners what they would be up to.

The stock market was very quiet, but prices were steady. That was good. Consols were at 91¾ per cent, Railways were firm.

She took a last look through the pages.

Last Days of the Art Union Draw. She had three tickets. It would be nice if she got a picture. She would give it to Bel for her new house. Young marrieds couldn't afford things like pictures.

Mr. Charles Halle, pianist, and Madame Norman Neruda, violinist, were giving a recital in the Queen's Rooms. Well, she would *not* be there. No one would catch her going right away up to the very edge of the town to sit among the hoity-toities from Park Circus and Royal Crescent. She liked a bit of music you could tap your toes to. But these devil's trills were not for sensible people. Bel and her husband had gone once or twice when they were courting. It was nice to think of them going. For her Bel could hold her head as high and look as fine as any of your new-fangled ladies in the West End! And very plain porridge they had come from, some of these very ladies! Mrs. Barrowfield smiled to think what some of them would have thought of their grandfathers.

III

While she was dressing comfortably before her fire, a note was brought by a messenger.

"Dear Mama,

"The funeral is today, as we expected. Arthur and all the others have just gone. I offered to go too, but Arthur wouldn't hear of it. He said it would be much too exhausting for me at present. I have invited them all to come here for tea, but I shall be alone all day before they get back. Would you like to come up and have dinner with me—just the two of us alone? Or are you still busy with your Christmas shopping? Try to come.

"Your loving daughter,

"Bel."

Mrs. Barrowfield had had every intention of going to her daughter this morning, but the letter pleased her. It was affectionate and, from its tone, she judged that Bel would be amenable to reason.

And it said nothing about her husband's little half-sister, Phœbe Moorhouse, who was the cause of all the trouble. Perhaps Bel was now taking a less emotional view of the child's situation. After all, children had been left orphans often before. And in much less pleasant circumstances.

Mrs. Barrowfield hurried into her clothes, intent upon walking across the town to Ure Place where her daughter lived.

At ten o'clock she was out on the pavement in front of Monteith Row, wondering which way she would take. There was bright winter sunshine now. The Green was white with hoar-frost. Windows here and there glittered in the sunlight. Mrs. Barrowfield stood for a moment looking up and down the Row itself—that handsome block of flats and front-door houses—that had, when she was yet a growing girl, been built to be the most exclusive terrace of Regency Glasgow, overlooking Glasgow's Hyde Park. But now the prestige of the Row was sinking. The industrial princes had forsaken it twenty years ago, escaping into the prevailing west wind from the smoke of these, their own factory chimneys. And the famous Green itself, that had played so great a part in Glasgow's story, was sinking too. Covered with smuts, it was fast turning into a mere lung in the centre of an ever-growing mid-Victorian city.

But Monteith Row had not yet fallen to nothing. For middle-class people who liked a well-built place and were not too snob-bish—for people like old Mrs. Barrowfield, in short, who put comfort and convenience before an exclusive address, it was, at this stage of its history, just the right place.

On this bright morning, however, many uglier corners of the town had taken on a glamour. The frost and the sunshine had, for the time, obliterated all suggestion of smoke and squalor. In spite of her preoccupation, Mrs. Barrowfield's spirits rose. She set off briskly. She was a big woman who had, as yet, lost none of her vigour. Iron-grey curls and a bonnet tied with broad flying ribbons. Rather too pronounced, masculine features. Large hands thrust into a small, tight muff. Swaying crinolines, for she refused to be new-fashioned. A sealskin jacket, elastic-sided boots. She moved along the pavement, a galleon in full sail.

At the end of the Row she wondered if she should continue along London Road and thus go direct, but sunshine like this was rare in winter, so, deciding to remain in it longer, she turned along Greendyke Street.

No. She had made up her mind to talk to her daughter straightly. Why should Bel rush to take little Phœbe Moorhouse into her home? She wasn't even her husband's full sister. Indeed, Arthur hardly knew her. It was after he had left the farm to come to Glasgow that his father's second marriage had taken place. And, so far as she knew, none of the Moorhouse family had ever liked their stepmother. Arthur had told Mrs. Barrowfield what he knew of her. She had been a wild Highland woman of forty—handsome, lithe and silent—who had come to the farm as a housekeeper. In a year she had married old Moorhouse and in a year more had borne him this daughter.

And now, only on Wednesday, driving home from a neighbouring farm late in the night, old Moorhouse's pony had bolted and hurled the couple to disaster. The old man was killed at once. The woman had lived until Thursday.

And Bel hearing of the disaster in her mother's presence—and what to Mrs. Barrowfield was much more serious, in the presence of her brother- and sisters-in-law—had exclaimed: "This is terrible! And poor wee Phœbe! Listen, Arthur, I won't hear of anything else. Phœbe's to be sent up here to me. I won't allow the child to be without a mother."

Mrs. Barrowfield had known it was no use talking at the time—indeed, it would have been unseemly—but she considered that Bel's heroics had been simply ridiculous. Moreover, she had seen the momentary glint in Sophia Butter's eye. As though to say: "Bel, dear, that's the kind of high falutin that takes a lot of getting out of!" And Bel's mother knew that Bel hated climbing down, just as Bel's father had done.

IV

Old Mrs. Barrowfield stamped furiously along Greendyke Street. Why should Bel take the child? The farm would go to Mungo, the oldest brother, of course. The child could go on living there. What was to stop her? He was thirty-five and a bachelor, but probably he would marry now, and his wife would have to look after the child. Why should her handsome daughter Bel, for whom she had every ambition, be worried by a gawky farm-child? It was all very well being sympathetic. But there were limits. She preferred to think of her daughter sitting fragrant and Madonna-like, awaiting the advent of her firstborn. Not fagging round after what might turn out to be a very troublesome girl of ten.

She had left the Greendyke now and had come into the Saltmarket. So intent was she upon her thoughts that she was quite unaware that a barefoot urchin had emerged from a vennel and was following her, begging.

"Gie's a ha'penny, lady. Gie's a ha'penny."

At last she noticed him. Barefoot on this cold winter morning and filthy. The people in this neighbourhood were almost beasts! Drunken, brutish and undersized. It was, indeed, only on bright mornings such as this that she would venture up the Saltmarket. On rare occasions when she spent the evening at Bel's or elsewhere, she took care to come home in a cab—or at all events accompanied by a man. Ladies always avoided the wynds and vennels, of course. It was not genteel to know much about them. But this old woman's husband had told her. A doctor must go where others did not.

"Gie's a ha'penny, lady."

She walked on.

Suddenly a memory flared up vividly in the mind of this rather smug, not very imaginative woman.

She saw her husband sitting exhausted and beaten after a long and indescribably squalid midnight confinement in one of these terrible places. It was not his custom, as an established doctor, to take such work, but this time—to help an overworked younger colleague—he had gone.

"I tell ye, ma dear, it's an abominable blot on the honour of the town. It's a wonder the Lord God doesn't strike all the well-to-do folks of Glasgow with His thunderbolts of wrath!"

"Gie's a ha'penny, lady."

Well, it was Christmas. And, when you came to think of it, this child beside her must be human too. She took her purse from her muff and gave him a sixpence. Without a word, he snatched at it, thrust it into a filthy little waistcoat pocket, turned a cartwheel with the agility of an ape and disappeared.

Mrs. Barrowfield walked on, indignant for a moment at the conditions that should bring such a gruesome little creature into existence, only to become a danger to more worthy people. Why did they allow these places? Glasgow was rich!

But the conscience of this comfortable Victorian city was stirring. The City Improvements Trust had come into being and was taking thought. And more potent still than conscience, perhaps, vested interest, in the shape of a railway company, had thrown a bridge across the Clyde and was continuing its arches over the Briggate and through the very worst of these dens, forcing much to be pulled down that should long since have gone. The Royal Hand that signed away the old College of Lister, Watt and Kelvin to make a drab goods station, was also signing the death-warrant of scores of these earthly hells. And now there was talk of a great terminal station on the north side of the Clyde, with an hotel of a luxury unparalleled in Scotland, facing St. Enoch's Square. That would inevitably demolish a great many more of these places.

At the Cross the old lady halted, looking about her. The clock in the Tolbooth Steeple stood at the quarter past. People were lounging about in the sunlight. As there was but little traffic, she crossed over to look at the Christmas display in the windows of Millar's warehouse on the corner of the Gallowgate and High Street. Presently she turned and looked up, wondering if, on her way to Ure Place, she should go on up the hill past the doomed College, or along past the Tontine and up Candleriggs. She took the latter course. There were shops in the Trongate she might have a look at. As she passed the equestrian statue of King William III, she smiled to herself, remembering that her son-in-law's brother David Moorhouse—who thought himself a wag—had told her that the King's horse was a wise beast, that, bronze though it might be, it knew to wag its tail at every Irishman.

But presently her thoughts were on Bel once more. No, it was preposterous. The child might have a very bad influence over the grandchild who was coming. Country children were so coarse and uncontrolled.

"Guid-day, Mum."

She was in the Candleriggs now, passing the business premises of her son-in-law.

"Oh, good morning." She cast an appraising eye through the open door. Everything very neat, she must say. The stock was carefully arranged and tidy.

"Mr. Moorhouse would not be here this morning?" she said, to make a moment's conversation with Arthur's man.

"No, Mum. It's terrible aboot his faither."

"Yes, terrible. The funeral's today, of course. Good morning."

"Guid-day."

At first she hadn't much liked the idea of Bel, a doctor's daughter, marrying a wholesale cheese merchant. But Bel had been twenty-four and it was time she was marrying someone. She, her mother, had had to suffer all the disgrace of spinsterhood until she was thirty-nine (she still regarded it as an intervention from heaven that she had emerged triumphant in the end), and she had had a horror at the thought of her daughter being among the unwanted. She herself had known everything there was to know of patronage from the securely wedded and copiously fecund.

Besides, the Moorhouse boys, although they were farmer's sons, had a strange air of breeding. As though a lacing of blue blood flowed in their honest Ayrshire veins. Perhaps a young aristocrat a generation or two back. But if there was a story Mrs. Barrowfield had never heard it. Victorian propriety forbade.

V

At the head of the Candleriggs she crossed over to the pavement in front of the Ramshorn Kirk, reflecting for an instant that her own parents were buried over there in the churchyard. In a second or two more she was in Montrose Street and making her way up the hill.

She was breathless as she rang her daughter's door-bell. For the upper part of Montrose Street was very steep and Ure Place was almost at the top of it. It had once come into her mind that her son-in-law had fixed his house in a place that was difficult of access to an elderly woman so that he need not see too much of her, but her common sense told her that Arthur's mind could not jump to such subtleties. He was much too straightforward.

Five minutes more found her sitting by the fire in her daughter's pleasant plush parlour, sipping a glass of sherry wine and eating a piece of black bun. Her bonnet, with its dangling ribbons, was laid aside with her sealskin jacket and muff and she was looking pleasantly about her.

"Well, dear, it's nice to have ye to myself for a day. What a terrible hill that is! I'm all peching."

"Yes, Mama. But it's convenient for Arthur up here. He can drop straight down to his work. The steepness is nothing to him."

Mrs. Barrowfield smiled at the bride's pride in her husband's vigour.

Bel was looking wonderful. Her tall fairness was enhanced by the unrelieved black of her mourning. In her wide, unrevealing dress she was still elegant. Admiration and ambition for her prompted her mother's next words.

"I hope before long you'll can move out to the West."

Bel, though she was fully at one with her mother, merely said: "It's very far away for Arthur."

"Nonsense. I hear Menzies is running his Tartan Buses to the Kirklee now. I'm not suggesting as far out as that, of course. But you could go out to the Great Western Road somebit near the Kelvin Bridge. You could even go up the hill into the Hillheed. And with the new University being nearly finished out there, it's bound to turn out a very nice district."

A vision of polite calls and pleasant, intellectual converse in professors' drawing-rooms rose for a moment in Bel's mind.

But "We'll have to make more money first," was all she said as she settled down on the opposite side of the fire from her mother. "Besides," she went on as she took up her sewing, "the people out there would be much too grand and brainy for Arthur and me." She did not say this because she believed it for one moment. For Bel had a fine conceit of herself. It was merely to fish from her mother a little comforting praise.

But all she got was a complacent "Not them."

Mrs. Barrowfield had no fears for her daughter's social abilities when they should be put to the test. Had not Bel been sent for years to a very reputable establishment for young ladies in St. Andrew's Square? If she herself still held in part to the speech and homely manners of earlier days, she had seen to it that her child should speak pure English and observe the modern elegances.

She noticed that Bel was making something for her baby. A good moment to appeal to her, perhaps. But she approached the topic warily.

"So the funeral is today?"

"Yes."

They spoke of this for some moments. How the accident had happened. How the pony had stumbled, then, frightened, had dashed ahead, out of control, along the ice-bound road. Arthur's stepmother had been able to explain before she died.

Mrs. Barrowfield listened to these things with perfunctory interest. Old Moorhouse and his wife were nothing to her. At length, at what she deemed to be the right moment, she said:

"You didn't mean to take Phœbe, did you, Bel?"

"Yes, Mama, I think so."

"What way, can she not stay at the farm?"

"I can't allow Arthur's sister to grow up like a farm-servant."

Her mother's inward comment was fiddle-de-dee, but she said:

"She's got her brother, Mungo."

"He's a single man. Besides, although he's the oldest, Arthur and I are really at the head of the family."

There was Bel at it again, giving herself airs. Her mother looked across at her severely. "Bel, mind, you've got yourselves to think of. And what's more, you've got your own bairns to think of. For all you know, Phœbe Moorhouse may be a thrawn wee besom. Have you thought what you're doing?"

"Yes, Mama. I've thought. And besides, the old man made

Arthur her guardian because he was a businessman and knew about money."

The old woman pricked her ears. "Money? But the bairn has no money."

"Well, of course, it would make no difference if she hadn't, Mama, but as it happens she has. It won't be much, but enough to educate her, we expect. The old man had little outside his farm stock, but what there was goes to her."

Mrs. Barrowfield was deeply interested. Perhaps Bel was nearer her house out West than it might appear. All her worry had, perhaps, been over nothing! With the girl's money—

"And you see how it is, Mama. Arthur has the responsibility for her anyway. It would be much better if we had her here under our eye."

A benign smile suffused Mrs. Barrowfield's features.

"You're your father's bairn, my dear. Aye thinking about doing good to somebody else," she said.

"Actually, it's to be settled this evening when they all come back," Bel said.

Chapter Four

IT was all strange and very unnatural. Yet little Phœbe Moorhouse was by no means struck down by her double bereavement. As was the custom, her elders thought it right that the child should be taken to look upon her dead. The first time, her oldest brother Mungo had taken her by the hand and led her into the eerie, familiar room where her parents lay. Her father's face frightened her at first. He looked so old, so pinched, so yellow. But her mother lay like serene marble, with her white, well-shaped face and her raven-black hair parted in the middle as she had always worn it in life.

Phœbe had clung to Mungo's hand.

But soon she had gone back into the room with her friends, the women servants, Gracie and Jean, who had wept a great deal, and, Phœbe could not help thinking, with a contemptible lack of control. And presently she found herself taking those who came to pay their respects into the chamber of death without any emotion other than a feeling of importance.

The physical aspect, the appearance of her parents as they lay there, quickly came to have no effect upon her, for already, at the age of ten, this country child had seen the death of so many animals, just as she had seen their birth, and she had long since accepted both phenomena without being unduly stirred.

In life, her father and mother had been so remote, so for each other, that the pulsing existence of the farm, with its friendships and quarrels, had, for the great part, gone on without them. Even their daughter had not broken through the invisible ring that seemed to be about them.

Phœbe had grieved more bitterly when the beloved servant into whose charge she was given as a baby, who had tended her in her first years, had finally married and gone away.

Now, in the darkened farmhouse in her new black dress, she tiptoed about, feeling her consequence as the chief mourner, and accepted all the abnormal petting and notice she was receiving with pleasure and complacency.

Then Mungo told her that these other half-brothers and sisters that she scarcely knew were coming to the funeral.

She had only had fleeting looks at them, and that, not for a year or two. What each looked like was half-imagined, half-remembered. It would be exciting to see them again. She had caught herself wondering recently why they did not come often. Indeed, she had gone the length of asking her mother, but the Highland woman had merely laughed, a remote, wry laugh, the meaning of which this child of ten could not guess. But now she was to see them and she was all agog.

II

They arrived. Some with Mungo in the trap, some in the only cab that served the village station. She had pushed back a lowered blind and watched the two vehicles coming in the winter sunshine up the ice-bound road. By the time they had gained the top of the hill and were rounding the farm buildings to come into the more convenient yard, Phœbe, if she had dared do anything so unseemly, would have danced with excitement.

Then, suddenly, she felt shy.

"Here, they're comin'. Come on."

Jean had come to look for her. Phœbe was glad to take the dairymaid's large red hand as they both went together to the door opening on the yard.

Arthur and David were in the trap with Mungo. They were all jumping down. A farm-hand was holding the pony's head. How pale and distinguished these brothers from the city looked, with their shining top-hats, their long black overcoats and black gloves!

Arthur looked like a white-faced, fine-boned Mungo, with his prominent, well-cut features and his mutton-chop whiskers. Mungo's muscles were lusty and developed from a life of labouring in the open air. His body was burly and strong, with no claims to elegance. Sun and wind had given his face a dark enduring tan. Yet his likeness to this brother, two years younger than himself, was very definite.

David was quite different. At twenty-three he still looked boyish. Phœbe noticed that his light hair curled pleasantly beneath his black hat, and when he took this off and bent down to kiss his little sister, she saw how clear his skin was and how attractive his eyes.

Arthur kissed her too and said: "Well, Phœbe, how are you?" Then seemed to think of nothing else to say. But the awkwardness could not last, for all three brothers must turn to help the ladies from the cab.

Her half-sisters were very grand ladies indeed. Far grander, say, than Miss Smith, the retired schoolmistress in the village where Phœbe, along with a dozen other well-to-do children, was sent for morning lessons in preference to the rough-and-tumble of the village school. Far grander than the banker's daughters, who helped with the singing in church. Grander, even, than the minister's wife, who was old and—for a little girl—intensely uninteresting.

Sophia got out first and came straight across to her.

"And is this wee Phœbe? How are you keeping, dear? You know, the last time I saw you, you were only half the height. About the height that Wil and Margy are now." Sophia bent down too and kissed her little sister. It took Phœbe a moment to remember who Wil and Margy were.

Mary pushed back her black veil and bent down too, putting her arms round her. How calm and blue her eyes seemed! And she smelt of lavender. "Well, deary? Here are your big sisters to look after you."

Mary was so elegant in her well-made black clothes and her furs. And indeed—by what Phœbe knew of elegance—Sophia did not come so far behind her.

She suddenly became acutely conscious of her black serge dress, hastily put together by the village dressmaker, her home-knitted black woollen stockings and her sturdy country boots.

But the child's steady little mind was not long in summing up her sisters. Sophia was big and fussy and chattered without ceasing about her own children. But somehow she seemed more spontaneously kind than Mary, whose more ostentatious goodness appeared to be so consciously controlled.

Of their husbands, Phœbe took little note. They were just stolid male things in black that you shook hands with, then dismissed from your mind.

There was hot soup for all the travellers and a "dram" for the men, for the midday meal would take place late, after the funeral. But before they had this, the brothers and sisters requested to see the last of their father.

The child, lynx-eyed and curious, followed them into the room. Mary and Sophia were weeping dutifully, bending over his face as he lay ready in his coffin. Arthur and David stood solemnly by, with set faces. Mungo, accustomed, stood behind merely waiting.

Suddenly a flame of resentment flared inside Phœbe. They were all looking at her father. Not one of them was thinking of her mother as she lay there so quiet, calm as she had always been, and, to her thinking, beautiful. On the woman's breast lay a posy of very pearl snowdrops, grown under a frame in a sunny corner of the minister's garden. The minister's wife had sent them to Phœbe, who had tied them up together with some ivy leaves and put them where they lay. It seemed an affront to herself that they should appear to take no thought for her mother. She was still too young to understand their embarrassment.

Tears sprang into Phœbe's eyes—tears of pride and resentment. For a moment she stood alone beside her mother's coffin, weeping.

It was Arthur who noticed first. He took her tears for uncomplicated childish sorrow. But he came to her, put his hand in her own, and thus remained beside her until the others were ready to go.

From this time on, it was to be Arthur Moorhouse who was to be first of all the family in his half-sister's strange affections. Even before Mungo, whom she had known all her life.

III

People were coming for the service now, and presently the minister and the laird, Sir Charles Ruanthorpe, were there.

The service took place in the Room. This was the sitting-room of the farm—a room of tassels, horsehair stiff chairs, antimacassars and Cupid ornaments. Unlike the other rooms of this prosperous farmhouse, the Room did not pulse with life. It was merely a dead ceremonial chamber where, in the days before their father's remarriage, the two sisters had given occasional formal tea-parties for such friends as were too genteel to eat in the much more welcoming kitchen. Where, if the laird or his lady called, they were thrust to sit uncomfortably looking about them, while the farmer's wife went to tidy herself and to look hastily into her supplies of cake and wine. For years it had given Phœbe much quiet rapture to tiptoe into the darkened Room—the blinds were always down to keep things from fading—and to stand solemnly admiring its aloof splendour.

But now the Room was full to overflowing with black-coated, white-tied men—most of them neighbouring farmers and known to her.

She felt herself wanting to run about to see everything that was happening, but Sophia and Mary sat by the kitchen fire and seemed to expect her to do the same.

At last, when all were there, they rose and, each taking one of her hands, led her into the Room, where places had been kept for them. But Phœbe did not want to sit between her sisters. She wanted to sit between Jean and Gracie, who were wiping red eyes with the backs of their great hands. So, ignoring the chair that was set for her, she wedged herself between her two friends, and, as this was no time nor place for remonstrance, succeeded in remaining.

Except that the minister kept talking about "these, our dear brother and sister" or addressed the Divinity concerning "these, Thy son and daughter," Phœbe decided that the whole thing was rather like church, only at home.

Yet, when the service was over and the child, watching once more from a window, saw the coffins borne out, the procession of mourners forming up and the whole beginning solemnly to move away she ran to her room, threw herself down on her bed and wept bitterly.

Chapter Five

BEL had sent her mother home in a cab as it began to get dark, which at Christmas-time in Glasgow is before four o'clock in the afternoon. In these days there was no question of an elderly or, indeed, any lady walking alone at night in any of the streets that converge at Glasgow Cross. The wretched creatures from the wynds and vennels poured themselves forth from their dens, and, as something like every third shop in such streets as the Briggate and the Saltmarket was a drinking-shop, most of them were drunk. Some of them roaring, some fighting, some of them collapsed in huddled masses in the gutter—men and women.

The better people tried not to think of them. And succeeded on the whole very well. You did not go near a sewer. Why be contaminated? It was the passionate, imaginative few who tried to effect changes for the better. It was those afflicted with highly uncomfortable consciences who could not but see these poor victims of a too hastily improvised industrial era as the possessors of bodies and intellects that nature had once intended to be sound and wholesome like their own. These conscience-ridden people, pointing the way back to the most elementary common sense, have since done away with the worst of Glasgow's slums and raised the descendants of these human vermin to something nearer decency and normality.

Bel was quite aware that her mother was not too anxious for her to take her brother's little half-sister into her house. But she had been careful not to say a word that would tie her in one way or another. Her mother and her sisters-in-law had heard her first, quite unconsidered outburst of pity for the little orphan. And she was determined to leave it at that meantime.

On the doorstep, the old lady, remembering that Phœbe's future was to be discussed by the Moorhouse family that evening at Bel's, and tortured to know whether the amount of money coming to the child would make it worthwhile Bel taking her or not, had kissed her daughter and said: "Now don't do anything in haste, Bel."

"Do you mean about Phœbe?"

"Yes."

"I'll do whatever's right, Mother. Goodbye, dear. Arthur and I will come down in the morning and bring you your Christmas present before we go to church. Don't keep the poor cabman waiting. It's so cold."

When people—especially high falutin people like her own daughter—said they were going to do whatever was right, there was no use talking to them, old Mrs. Barrowfield reflected, beaten. Whatever was right left a vast margin for doing what you, personally, wanted to do. You could, she reflected further, call almost anything right, if you argued hard enough.

But Bel was quite determined not to be dominated any more by her old and domineering mother. It was much pleasanter to be dominated by a husband. She had had twenty-four years of the first kind of domination, and was determined to have no more of it. She was still recently enough married to feel a pleasant feminine thrill—a subtle flattery of her womanhood—when Arthur laid down the law to her. It was, she felt, as though she were fulfilling a wifely function.

She stood at her open door now, looking after her mother's cab. In a few seconds it turned back up into the Rotten Row, for the driver could not trust his horse to go down the steep, slippery cobbles of Montrose Street, and had determined to choose one of the streets further west, where the incline was less abrupt. She took a few paces along the pavement and looked down Montrose Street itself. The hum and lights of the City came up to her. The noise and traffic of George Street. The view of endless roofs. The roofs of the Athenæum. Hutcheson's Hospital. The roof of the hotel on George's Square where the law lords lived when they came to Glasgow. The spires of the Ramshorn Church and Free St. Matthew's, and, further over, the Tolbooth Steeple. Yet further the spire of the Old Merchants' Hall. It was getting dark, and there was some fog. She hoped the train from Ayrshire would not be held up by it. With a little shiver she turned back and shut her front door. The house was cosy and pleasant. It still gave the eight-month bride a little thrill to feel it was her own—

its decoration, its arrangement, everything—for Arthur was a busy man and had left things in her hands.

She must go and see what the maids had done about the tea-table, for in these days—as indeed still, for the greater part of middle-class Glasgow, though its social status keeps ever sinking—high tea, elaborate and triumphantly lavish, is the focal point of the day.

The table was groaning with bread, several kinds of scones, cakes, large and small, fancy and plain, a variety of jams, and much else, all of which were to follow two sumptuously rich cooked dishes.

Bel cast an appraising eye about her. Well, it would be as good a tea as ever Mary produced out West at Albany Place, and certainly more lavish than Sophia's efforts across at Grafton Square. She had no intention of being outdone by her sisters-in-law.

She felt very pleased with herself. It was nice to remember that she was a doctor's daughter, and that Sophia and Mary were the daughters of a mere farmer. It was nice for her to think that Arthur had certainly taken no step down by marrying her. What if her mother was a little downright? You didn't expect your parents to have the polish they had been able to give you. And when it came to the education of her own children, she would see to it that their advantages would well exceed what her own had been.

Like all middle-class Glasgow at this time, Bel—like a thousand other Bels and Arthurs in the City—was on the up-grade.

II

Mary and George arrived first with Arthur. They came direct from the station, since the McNairns had decided that it would take too long to go out to their house at Albany Place and then come back again into town. But, on the platform, Sophia announced that she would be quite unable to touch her evening meal, until she knew her children were back home from their visit to the McNairn cousins and safe. There had, she said, been so many cases lately of children being waylaid and robbed of their clothing. So, in spite of protests from Arthur that nothing could befall them in that quarter of the town, and escorted as they would be, and that there was no possible reason for keeping waiting several people fatigued by cold and hunger and the emotional trials of a long day, she went, taking her inarticulate husband with her.

"I won't really be any time at all, dears," she had clucked. "And it would be a comfort to you too, wouldn't it, Mary dear, to know that Wil and Margy had left your children well and happy?"

Mary felt that, somewhere, there was the sting of a reproof hidden in these words—a hint that she was showing a lack of interest in her own children, but though she was exhausted like the others, and a little out of temper, she controlled herself, merely smiled with that saintly smile of hers, and said with a voice that was all kindness: "Of course. But don't be any longer than you possibly need to be, dear. The boys are hungry. Besides, I don't think we should keep Bel waiting," and thus, having re-established herself as the soul of consideration for everybody, she preceded two impatient brothers and her own large, portly boy into the cab that was to take them to Ure Place.

"We might have taken Sophia and William part of the way," she said, when once the four were fairly started.

Her own husband said nothing. But Arthur snapped: "Not at all. It'll do the Butters no harm to pay for themselves once in a while. Besides, it serves Sophia right for being a fool."

So, apart from drawing David's attention to the reflection of the moon on the river as they crossed Glasgow Bridge, Mary said no more. If the poor boys were tired, she, the most understanding of women, would certainly be the last one to worry them with talk.

Bel, all concern for their comfort, received the four of them with roaring fires, and, what was better still, she had mixed a bowl of toddy which was fragrant and hot, and which did wonders in soothing everybody's bad temper. Even Mary was persuaded to have a sip or two, and as the colour came back into her beautiful calm face, she was pleased to find herself thinking how, in spite of minor defects, perhaps her new sister-in-law was just the very wife for Arthur, and was turning out splendidly.

Her husband, George McNairn, taking rather more than his share, actually revived enough to joke ponderously with his sister-in-law, and determined that Bel was a damned fine looking young woman, full of life and mettle. He regretted himself a little that his own wife—while flinching in no way from her duty—should always be so passive and saintly in their more conjugal moments.

David put his arm round Bel's shoulder, kissed her and said she was a dear, and Arthur glowed with pride and satisfaction.

In other words, Bel's toddy quite dissipated the exasperation these tired and hungry people were beginning to feel at the prospect of being kept waiting by Sophia's over-developed feelings of maternity. Indeed, its success was such that Sophia and William—themselves exhausted and breathless—were finally shown into a room where, though all, of course, was decorum, a distinct atmosphere of conviviality reigned round an empty bowl. And their annoyance was not lessened by the fact that no sooner had they arrived than the starched housemaid, Sarah, rang the tea-bell in the hall, and Arthur said: "Come on, everybody, there's tea," giving Bel no opening whatever to make amends for the toddy being finished.

"Wil and Margy enjoyed themselves very much, Mary." Sophia looked at her sister coldly as she took her place at the table.

"I'm glad, dear." Mary was positively benign.

Sophia waited in a condition of extreme self-righteousness to see if Mary would really not bother to ask after her own children and, finding that she did not, she said triumphantly: "Jessie, my new girl, who went with them, said that your children were looking splendid, Mary."

"They were looking very healthy this morning, Sophia—vulgarly healthy," George McNairn said, wolfing his food with relish.

But Bel, detecting wisps of venom floating in the air, called upon Sophia to decide upon the relative merits of tappit hen and steak pie—and if she cared for neither of these, then the cold ham was on the sideboard—and thus succeeded in clearing the atmosphere for the time being.

III

"Do you know, it's funny to think," she began presently, when her guests had emerged from their meal a little, the first hunger sated, "but I've only seen Mungo once, and that was at my wedding, when I wasn't in a fit state to notice anybody very much. And little Phœbe was ill then, and didn't come. It's queer that I should know you all so well, and yet that you should have a brother and sister I don't know at all."

"Mungo's coming up in the first week of the New Year. He's bringing Phœbe with him. They're coming here," Arthur said.

"I'll be delighted to see them," Bel said, knowing well that two pairs of feminine Moorhouse eyes were upon her.

"We would have been delighted to have them, Bel dear. Are you sure—situated as you are? Arthur hasn't said anything to me about this," Mary interposed.

"No, of course they'll come here. I expect you've family business to discuss with Mungo, haven't you, Arthur?"

Arthur said, well, yes—there was some business to discuss.

"Of course, any of us would be delighted to see them." Sophia came in comfortably at the end of the race.

But all the reply she got from Bel was: "Now try one of these sponge cakes, Sophia, they're very light."

"I thought Phœbe wasn't very well-behaved today. Didn't you think so too, Mary?" Sophia said, having embarked upon a sponge cake as she was bidden.

"A little unfriendly perhaps," Mary answered—agreeing, but softening the accusation.

"Well, considering what was going on, you could scarcely expect her to behave as usual," David said.

"It wasn't that," Sophia continued. "No. She didn't seem particularly upset, which was queer too, now I come to think of it. But there were Mary and I, her own sisters, ready to be a comfort to her, and yet she seemed to be always trying to get away from us."

"She struck me as rather a cold child," Mary added. "But of course it may have been shyness."

"Why should she be shy of us?" Sophia said.

"Because, if you had any sense, Sophia, you would see that

sisters or not sisters, you were perfect strangers to her," David snapped.

Sophia ignored this. "Do you know," she went on, turning to Bel, "she wouldn't sit with us during the funeral service, although there was a place for her, of course."

"And where did she sit?" Bel asked. She had been listening to this conversation with great interest.

"I don't know," Sophia said aloofly.

"She stood between two of the servants—byre-women, I think they were," David said. And as Bel seemed to want him to say more, he added: "One of them had an arm round her. The other was holding her hand."

A look of gentleness on Bel's face thanked David for making the situation clear. Her young brother-in-law had given her a vivid, moving picture of the little girl. Why had the Moorhouse men so much more intuition than the women? Had Mary, with all her ostentatious goodness, been unable to see that the child was trying to find comfort from familiar people, to steady herself in the face of the great change that had come into her life?

"The bairn was feeling it. Don't you make any mistake," Arthur said.

"Well, I would be sorry to think that Wil and Margy would behave like that if anything happened to William and me. While we were waiting for the men to come back from the cemetery, she went to her own room and wouldn't come out of it. They could scarcely get her to come and say goodbye," Sophia went on.

"When *my* father died,"—Bel's voice sounded a little tart—"Mother tells me I missed him very much, and the way I showed it was by being very naughty."

"Our stepmother was a strange, cold sort of woman." Mary felt she didn't quite see the point in Bel's naughtiness being put forward in defence of Phœbe's.

Bel was angry now. Mary was just as lacking in understanding as Sophia. There were moments in life when you had to take definite steps—whether they turned out rightly or wrongly. Moments when the hand had to be stretched forth to a fellow-being without counting the cost. This child was needing mothering—needing understanding—more understanding than her two smug half-sisters could give her. Bel's impulsiveness got the better of her once again. The colour was high in her face when she spoke.

"Well, at any rate, I've been thinking about Phœbe," she said. "I don't see how the child can stay at the farm without a woman of her own kind to look after her. If Arthur wants it, I'll be delighted to have her here."

Old Mrs. Barrowfield would have called this more high falutin. She would have said: "Let the child go to a sister." "Let her stay with her farmer brother." Mary and Sophia, because, perhaps, they had been made to look mean and cold through their sister-in-law's offer to undertake a duty that both of them were determined to avoid, called this speech of Bel's—in their hearts—a mere piece of show-off.

But Arthur was glad that his wife should show his family that her blood ran redder and warmer than theirs, that prudence did not block the channels of her sympathy.

So Phœbe's future was settled without any discussion, after all.

Bel had taken the plunge, everybody felt, and good luck to her. Another five minutes of steady, reflective munching persuaded the McNairns and the Butters to drop any rancour their hearts might still hold, and decide that everything had been settled for the best.

"What perfectly delicious black bun!" Sophia said presently. "Do you think, Bel dear, I could have a wee bit cut off to take home? William's old uncle and aunt are coming in for tea to see the children tomorrow and I haven't a scrap of black bun in the house. I don't know why we've been too busy to make it. But you know what old people are. They expect, at a time like Christmas, just to find all the usual things. Perhaps if you could spare—?"

Chapter Six

THE winter afternoon was getting on as the train containing Phœbe and Mungo beat its way along the last lap of the journey towards Glasgow. Phœbe had never been in a train before. The nearest she had got to it was when she went in the trap to the station to meet her father or Mungo coming home from the markets in Ayr or Kilmarnock. She had asked her mother if she might not go with them one day, and her mother had put her off by telling her that they would take her soon. But soon had gone on receding ahead of her and nothing had happened. Once she had driven in the trap some ten miles to Ayr, and her mother had taken her down to wade in the sea, while her father had bought a new cart-horse. That had been her furthest and most thrilling journey.

Now she was on the way to Glasgow, large, magic and unknown, and she could not sit still for excitement. It was fortunate that they had the carriage to themselves, for now that they had passed Paisley and were speeding across the flat to the great City—where her grand half-sisters and brothers lived, where, she had been told, you could walk and walk and never get to the end of the streets—she kept running from window to window, looking at this and that, as her train went by. Distant spires. The boats on the Glasgow-Johnstone canal—this house—this building—everything excited her. Mungo sat staring a placid farmer's stare out of the window, his handsome, weather-tanned face lighted by the setting sun, and let his little sister jump to her heart's content.

Phœbe had left the farm with a mixture of feelings, but by far the greatest of these was curiosity at what lay before her. She was a child avid for experience, and she had so far known little of fear. Gracie and Jean had packed her little black tin box for her. Her simple and few things were washed and mended to perfection. For, decent souls, they were determined that that Mrs. Arthur to whom Phœbe was going should find nothing amiss in the way they had tended her.

The child had hopped about, watching them. She kept asking them endless questions. What would she do in Glasgow? What kind of school would she go to? Would meals be at the same time? Would she have to help Arthur with his business? That would be fun—she would like that. Did it rain in Glasgow? No, they told her. There was a very large umbrella that the Lord Provost put up every time it rained, so that the town was always dry. She laughed at that. But who was the Lord Provost? And so on her questions went.

Strangely, she seemed to think little about the familiar things she was leaving. She had asked if she could come back on holiday, and Mungo had assured her that she might. That appeared to satisfy her. It was Glasgow that engrossed her.

But at their early midday meal today she had scarcely eaten anything. And when her box was lifted into the trap and she had made to jump up after it, suddenly the sight of Jean and Gracie weeping at the door into their drugget aprons had touched her, and she had run back to them as they stood there and clung to them one after the other, inhaling from them the familiar farm smells of cows and chopped winter feeding, of soap and their own wholesome bodies.

Yet presently she was done with all that and was waving to them valiantly as the pony clattered along the road, causing the farm to shrink into the distance.

II

Now she was at the station. Mungo was buying tickets. Third-class tickets. One for himself and—oh, unbelievable thrill—one for her. What were the glorious people like who travelled first- and second-class? Now the porter had rung his big brass bell. Now the great engine was bearing down upon them. Now the carriages came alongside. This time she was to have a place and was to be allowed to climb in. Now they were off! Trees and houses were rushing past her. Suddenly everything was wiped out. Darkness! The Mossgiel tunnel! The railway tunnel that pierces the rolling uplands of a farm that once was ploughed by the hand that wrote "The Cottar's Saturday Night". But to

Phœbe it was just "the tunnel" she had heard them talk of. In the darkness she sat close to Mungo. Now another station, a different porter, a different bell. Now Kilmarnock where the men came to market. How busy it was! How anxious people seemed to get themselves into the train! There was another girl of her own age. What nice clothes she was wearing. Phœbe wished she would come in so that she could have a look at them. "Looking for the first-class, Mum?" A porter spoke to the lady who was with her. "Further up the train, Mum." So it was people like that who went first-class. Should she herself be looking like that? Would Bel, whom she had never seen, object to her wearing such a plain black dress? But she liked Arthur. She felt Arthur wouldn't mind. Besides, Arthur had seen her in this very dress at the funeral. Here was another station. There was a sheet of water. What was that, Mungo, a loch? Yes. A loch. Now Paisley. Busy and much like Kilmarnock. Now they were away again. They would soon be in Glasgow. Was the station at Glasgow bigger than the ones at Paisley and Kilmarnock? Yes. Mungo thought it was. Now houses and streets and endless backyards. There was fog a little and endless strings of lighted lamps. Was this Glasgow now? Yes. The train was slowing down. It had stopped. A porter was running along opening all the doors. A big porter with a bushy beard shouting in an accent that was Highland, like her mother's, "Bridge Street." He offered to help with the box, but Mungo paid no attention. He reached up and got it down for himself.

Everybody was getting out. Was she to get out too? Yes, of course. Jean had told her to see that she kept her gloves on. That it was more genteel. She had taken them off, but now she hauled them on again over paws that were dirty from the carriage. Little black ones that Jean had knitted herself. She jumped out. What crowds! What a noise of puffing, of steam! What shouting! A fat lady had come to meet another fat lady! What a fuss they were making! *There* was the child she had seen at Kilmarnock! Yes. Her clothes *were* nice. But her face looked petted—or, as Jean would have said, thrawn. Here was Arthur running up the platform! He was all hot with running.

III

"Hello! I thought I was going to be late." He was giving Mungo his hand and bending down to kiss her. Once more she liked the look of this brother, and felt reassured at the thought of going to stay with him.

A porter had seized her black box and was marching down with the main stream to the entrance. Phœbe looked up at the flares of gas burning in the station, although the daylight was not yet altogether gone. Suddenly she realised that she was walking under great roofs of glass! She could count three of them! She was walking in a great glass-house! They were through the barrier. What a wide stair leading down into the street! And what a busy street! Arthur said it was Clyde Place. And there was the Clyde! He called her attention to two great steamers, their paddle-boxes gleaming with golden paint, lying against the other bank. That was the Broomielaw, where the steamers were. One of them, he said, went all the way to Ireland. Behind them were high houses. She read the words "Lord Byron Hotel". Why did people go to hotels? Because they had no friends to stay with?

But Arthur was debating with Mungo what to do with Phœbe's box. "We'll have to get a cab for this," he was saying.

But Mungo seemed annoyed with the extravagance. "Not at all. We've good legs. Can ye not get a barrow? There's a laddie there."

A boy no bigger than herself but much older-looking came forward and tugged at the glossy skip of his dirty cap. He pointed to a little flat hand-cart. "Tak' yer trunk, sir?"

Arthur nodded, and Phœbe was amazed to find with what agility and apparent strength he swung it up and on to his little cart. Arthur waved a directing hand, said "Across the town," and away he went, keeping to the street just in front of them, while they followed on the pavement. In a few moments he was turning to the left over Glasgow Bridge.

Phœbe was glad that her brothers had so much to say, for she was enraptured with what she saw and wanted to be left alone. There was the great river stretching away to the west, the water glittering in the sunset. A steamer was turning round. Churning her paddles in midstream. And down beyond on both sides the shining waters were fringed by forests of sailing-ship masts, interspersed here and there by a steamship emitting clouds of smoke and steam. Distant tugs and ferries and even rowing-boats looked like water-beetles against the light. She had come indeed to a place of magic. The very bridge she was walking on was lit by handsome lamps, set high on the balustrades on either side. The gas-flares inside them looked like pale jewels against the fading eastern sky.

She made to dart across to look at the river on the other side. Mungo caught her shoulder. She was to stay where she was! Now she was in the town, she must learn to be careful. Did she want to get herself kicked to pieces by the bus horses as they rushed past? Phœbe walked on, sobered for a moment. She did not like to ask which were buses, for she was not sure. But presently she decided to ask Arthur. Was that big thing with three horses in front coming up to the crown of the bridge a bus? Yes. That was a bus. She watched it as it passed. How funny! She would like to have a ride on that, especially on the top, where things like two summer seats were arranged, back to back. People were sitting sideways, huddled in their winter coats. She was surprised that they did not appear to be enjoying their exciting position. And how funnily the sides of the buses were painted, with criss-cross colours to represent tartan!

Now they were on the other side. The shops were beginning. First, right on the corner, facing the bridge, Thomson's, clothier and outfitter. The boy with the barrow was well ahead of them now, hurrying up Jamaica Street, so that they had no option for the moment but to take the way he had gone—for the brothers had no intention of letting him out of sight. So Phœbe was able to enjoy herself, casting hurried glances at the lighted shop-windows, as they passed up.

Now they were at the crossing of Jamaica Street and Argyle Street. They halted for a moment, shouting to the barrow-boy to turn to the right, along Argyle Street. Phœbe had never seen anywhere so busy. She counted four of these tartan buses crossing in different directions while they stood. And there were several cabs, two or three men on horseback, a huckster with a donkey, and endless people. Where could everybody be going to? It was getting darker now. To the left, beyond Anderston, the sunset was deepening to a lurid crimson.

Argyle Street, as they went along it, was gay and busy. Phœbe wondered that so many people dare walk about in the middle of the street, with so much traffic on the move. The sound of horses' hoofs was never out of her ears. The shops were ablaze with gas-flares and most of them still had their Christmas and New Year display of goods and decorations. As they passed the opening to St. Enoch's Square, Arthur pointed out to Mungo the position that the great new railway station and hotel were to occupy.

IV

And now, after much walking, they were going up a narrower street. Phœbe was able to read its name on the corner. It was called Candleriggs. She had heard them talk of the Candleriggs. She asked if that was the same thing. They told her it was. It was a cheerful street. Through open doors men were working in the gas-light, moving boxes and bales, or perched at high desks writing in books under a single flare. This was the street where Arthur worked, she was told. Here he had his business. She would like to come and work here too. Would Arthur allow her?

The brothers laughed heartily and said here was Arthur's warehouse. Phœbe, a little sulky, said nothing more. She looked up and read: ARTHUR MOORHOUSE AND COMPANY. What was there to laugh at? She had always worked about the farm, and liked it, for she was a managing little body. Besides, her elders had seemed to expect her to help.

Inside the place was spotless. Great cheeses were ranged on scrubbed shelves. Packing and expediting was in full swing, for though it was four o'clock and almost dark, there were still several hours of work before the warehousemen. Phœbe walked about with her hands behind her, concealing her intense interest under a business-like air.

Suddenly, in a little gaslit den at the back, she came upon the backs of two men perched up, writing. A fire burnt in a little black iron fireplace, making the place hot and stuffy. The men were working with their jackets off and their sleeves rolled up. One of them wore a wide black tie encircling a high collar. Over the edge of this crept the thick chestnut hair of her brother David. Phœbe walked primly round to the side of his desk and said: "Hello, David."

David looked down upon her, smiled quizzically, and shut one eye.

He was untidy, his face was dirty and his fingers were stained with ink. He was not at all the grand young man she had seen on the day of the funeral. She liked him much better as she found him now.

"Jimmie," he said to the elderly clerk at his side, "this is my sister."

"The Maister wis sayin' ye wis comin' tae Glesca, Miss." The man climbed down and shook hands.

Phœbe had never been called "Miss" before. For a moment it made her feel very important. Presently she said goodbye with dignity and went out again, bent upon seeing anything else there was to see.

Mungo and Arthur seemed to be having an endless discussion with Arthur's head man on the subject of cheese. Finding nothing further of vital interest, Phœbe went to the door.

The boy was sitting on his barrow beside her trunk, waiting. He looked a thin, depressed sort of boy, Phœbe thought, but quite good enough to have a conversation with.

"What age are you?" she said, sitting on the barrow beside him.

"Seeventeen."

"Yer ower wee fur yer age. Are ye no' weel?" she said, looking at him critically.

"A'm fine."

"Dae ye get enough tae eat?" she said presently, still unconvinced.

"Whiles," was the fatalistic reply.

She was quite unconscious that she had fallen into the broad Scots of the Laigh Farm. It was natural, for the boy's replies to her were in Scots too. But while Phœbe spoke with the clear, as yet uncontaminated, peasant accent of Ayrshire—little changed, probably, from the accent of the poet Burns—her companion's tongue had all the slovenliness of the Glasgow underworld. This difference, however, went unremarked by the two young people sitting on the barrow. Indeed, the boy wondered that such a well-put-on little girl should speak a tongue so like his own.

They were great friends, exchanging many confidences, when her two elder brothers re-emerged from the warehouse.

"Well," Arthur was saying, "you know the way. I'll be up in about an hour." And, giving the boy directions how to go to Ure Place, Phœbe and Mungo set off behind him up the Candleriggs.

Chapter Seven

BEL realised at once that her mother was merely being naughty when she called at four. She knew that old Mrs. Barrowfield had for once let her native inquisitiveness get the better of her. For, on this particular afternoon, little Phœbe Moorhouse was expected to arrive, escorted by her brother Mungo. Bel felt that her mother might have had sense and seen that her hands would be full.

The child's room had to have its last touches—you couldn't leave everything to maids—and the best room had to be got ready for Mungo.

Besides, Bel was just a little defiant about Phœbe. Her mother and even her sisters-in-law—though much more cautiously, lest they themselves should become involved—had felt it their duty to warn her more than once that the child might be far from easy to put up with. But Bel's honour was already committed. There was no getting out of it unless, of course, she hauled down her colours—a thing she never even thought of doing. So, by way of retaliation, she had high faluted and insisted that she would stand by Arthur's sister, whatever she turned out like.

No. She felt her mother had come out of sheer curiosity, to see the child whose arrival she was prepared to resent. And she could very well have done without her.

But Bel was a woman of quick resentments and just as quick repentances. She chided herself for an undutiful daughter and rang for a cup of tea.

"When are you expecting them?" the old lady asked, pouring her tea into her saucer and sitting complacently with both elbows on the parlour table, holding up the tea and blowing upon it.

This habit of her mother's was a great cross to Bel, who considered it vastly ungenteel and did not like even her maids to see her do it.

"Any time now," she said with that gentleness in her voice that goes with controlled annoyance. "Arthur must have taken them round by the warehouse or they would have been here long ago."

"Bel dearie!" The door had burst open. "I just dropped in for two minutes to see wee Phœbe!" It was Sophia.

Bel, for a bewildered, ashamed moment, had an idea of standing between her mother and Sophia, so that Sophia should not see the old lady in the act of saucering her tea, but Mrs. Barrowfield, who hotly resented that Sophia should have come at this moment to bother her daughter, finished her saucerful at one gulp and, placing her teacup upon it, got up and said very stiffly:

"Good-day, Sophia. Phœbe's not here."

"Never here yet? Oh, well, anyway, I'm not sure that I can stay. I promised Wil and Margy to be back." Then, looking about her: "I couldn't have some tea, could I, Bel dear? I've been down town trailing round the Polytechnic. I'm nearly dead."

Bel went to the embroidered bell-pull and gave it a convulsive, irritated tug.

"You haven't been up to see us for such a long time, Mrs. Barrowfield. Wil and Margy were just talking about Auntie Bel's mother the other day. What did you think of their wee thank-you letters for your Christmas presents? I showed them to William. He said he thought they were lovely!"

Wil and Margy's letters had each betrayed signs of having been written by grubby little paws that had been shakily guided by their mother's hand—the only really original additions being inky fingermarks and a blot or two. But Mrs. Barrowfield, downright though she was, dared scarcely remark on this. Besides, she was waiting for Sophia to say that it was very kind of her to think of sending toys to Wil and Margy at all. For, after all, her connection with them was slight. But as Sophia said nothing more on the subject, and as the pause was becoming noticeable, she said:

"They're wee to be writing letters." This, at least, she felt, was a remark.

But Sophia, who was still ranging the room, did not appear to hear her. The door-handle turned. "Ah!" she exclaimed. "Here's my cup!"

But instead of the parlourmaid, Mary McNairn came in. Her

calm demeanour and her gentle, controlled tones were almost more exasperating to Bel than Sophia's fussiness.

"Bel dear, just for a moment. I brought these little books for Phœbe. I know she's coming to the dearest sister-in-law in the world. But the child will be lonely and have a sore heart sometimes. No matter how good you are to her, and no matter how brave the wee body is. So I thought perhaps these might help her. They're little books of comfort and good conduct and things."

Bel was far from feeling the dearest sister-in-law in the world. There were moments when Mary's saintliness made her sick. And this was one of them. Besides somehow, as often with Mary, her words had left a sting. The very use of the word "sister-in-law" had somehow implied that the child was coming to a house where inevitably she would be unhappy and misunderstood.

But now she felt beaten. Let them all come! It was a pity, she told herself, that she did not have another dozen sisters-in-law and another half-dozen mothers to see Phœbe's arrival.

Her maid had followed Mary into the room with Sophia's cup. She bade her bring another for Mary.

As the girl returned with this, she turned to Bel. "I think that's them, Mam. There's a gentleman like Mr. Moorhouse comin' up the brae. I looked out for a minute."

"Was there a little girl too, Sarah?"

"I didna see right. There was a barrow wi' luggage."

"She must be there." Bel got up. At her own front door at least she herself would receive them.

II

"Listen! We'll all go to the door and give them a grand welcome!" Sophia exclaimed.

Bel gave up. The spark that had dared to revive within her was immediately extinguished. It was no use trying to be a separate person this afternoon. So everyone trooped outside the door to where they could see the travellers coming up the steep incline of Montrose Street.

"Where's Phœbe?" Mary asked.

In the light of the street lamps they could discern Mungo coming up on the pavement, carrying his own carpet-bag. His strong body was inclined forward against the hill. His natural farmer's stoop was accentuated by the effort. Out in the middle of the street a little hand-cart with a black box was being pushed upwards. On one side they could discern the face and ragged cap of the youth to whom the cart presumably belonged. They could see his shoulders rise and fall with his steps as he pushed it upwards. Suddenly a little girl's head appeared from behind the box. She was shoving and pushing just as hard as he was. It was Phœbe.

"Good gracious! There's Phœbe, and look what she's doing!" Sophia exclaimed.

"Mungo ought not to let her. If the boy has a barrow, surely he must be able to push it himself," Mary said.

Bel didn't like it either. After all, if Phœbe were coming to live in a refined quarter like Ure Place, she must learn to behave with dignity. Bel, at this stage, was very much of that social cast that allows its life to be ruled by the nameless critic lurking behind the neighbouring lace window-curtains. She was mortified, too, to feel that the eyes of her sisters-in-law were emitting furtive gleams of triumph.

"I can see you'll have to be firm with her, Bel dear," Sophia said with relish.

"I'm sure your little sister means to help the poor boy," Bel retorted with the shadow of stress on the words "your" and "sister".

But the old lady, who had had her beginnings in an age that was much less genteel, when prim refinement had not been at such a high premium, was pleased with the little girl. She liked people to have what she called "smeddom". And this child obviously had it. The box had to be pushed up the hill, so, without thought of dignity, Phœbe was giving a hand. She could not have chosen to do anything better to put herself into old Mrs. Barrowfield's good graces.

And yet, if Mrs. Barrowfield had stopped to think, it was precisely this unfashionable straightforwardness that she had striven to eliminate from the behaviour of her own daughter. She had paid high fees at an establishment for young ladies, so that Bel should be taught to seem—in public at least—as frail and useless as possible.

Now they had arrived and were standing before Bel's front door under the lamp. After all, perhaps, it had not been such a bad idea of Sophia's that they should all go out together and greet the newcomers. It was cheerful and fussy and it helped to cover up shynesses. She was pleased to see Mungo, whom she knew so little. He was a shy man, but he had that placid force about him that is to be found in many farmers. He was very like her husband, but bigger, ruddy and physically stronger. But his mind seemed slower, and he did not have the quick, appraising eye of the merchant and townsman.

"Bel, this is our little sister Phœbe," Mary was saying.

Bel bent down and kissed this child about whom she—and all the others—had thought so much. She seemed a well-grown, sturdy little girl in her black country-made clothes. Her round apple cheeks were glowing with the effort of pushing the barrow. Her blue Highland eyes were large and penetrating. As the little girl looked up at her, Bel could see shyness and curiosity in them.

"What a lot of people all at once, isn't it, Phœbe?" Bel said, keeping her arm about her. "It's terrible to have your sisters and brothers all so old that they might be your uncles and aunts!"

Phœbe's face relaxed into a vague smile. It was impossible to make out what the child was feeling. Had her words—said at random—conveyed the goodwill that she, Bel, had intended? Or had Phœbe thought them a little silly? She couldn't tell. Nor could she say whether she liked or disliked the child in these first moments.

Phœbe's eyes kept turning towards the boy who was waiting with the little hand-cart. She seemed anxious that he should get whatever was due to him. Mungo was standing talking to his sisters and Bel's mother, paying no heed. At last, breaking away, Phœbe went to him and touched his arm.

"Mungo, the boy's money."

Queer little thing. She seemed almost worried over a slum waif who could mean nothing to her. Was it kindness of heart? Was it self-importance? Was it a premature habit of responsibility?

Presently they were all inside the house.

III

Phœbe had taken off her little round black hat. Her sister-in-law was better able to examine the child's face under the light.

Apart from an impalpable family look, the child was unlike her brothers and sisters. Her face was round and undeveloped. But her eyes were fine and set like a foreigner's, as Bel thought to herself, meaning that strange, high-cheeked, almost Tartar look that you meet here and there in the Highlands. Her colour was glowing and vivid, though a little too countrified to Bel's way of thinking. Her hair was raven-black and glossy.

Bel insisted that everyone should come and have tea before Phœbe and Mungo should be settled, as she put it. She wondered at herself a little for doing this, considering her annoyance at her mother, Mary and Sophia ten minutes ago. But the truth was, perhaps, that she wanted to postpone for a little longer being left alone with these unknown relatives of her husband. The slow, ponderous farmer and the puzzling little girl.

But in a very short time Mary stood up. "Sophia, we've taken too much of Bel's time. But you can understand how much we wanted just to get a glimpse, Bel dear. You'll come to see us of course. Bel, when can you and Arthur bring Mungo?"

Mungo hastened to say he would only be staying two nights. Bel protested politely at the shortness of his visit, then Mary went on: "Well, tomorrow for tea at six. And we'll arrange for you to come and see the children very soon, Phœbe."

Phœbe didn't say anything. She was not used to being kept apart with other children. She had always eaten with her elders in the big, cheerful farm kitchen. And when Mary finished by saying: "Now, dear, remember to be a good girl, and do everything Bel tells you, for it's very kind of her having you here," it made her feel infinitely bleak for a little, and somehow her feelings towards her elder sister did not grow any warmer.

Sophia was able to regret with a clear conscience that there would be no time, then, for Mungo to come and have a meal with herself and William. William could not be counted upon to come to their midday dinner, so *that* was no use.

Sophia and William must come to them too, then, Mary the Saint insisted.

Might they? Was she sure it would be all right? Mary was sure it would be all right. Thereupon the sisters prepared to go. Mary kissed Phœbe and told her how pleased she was to have her where she could get to know her, and Sophia likewise kissed her fussily, arranged for her to come to see Margy next morning, and to everybody's amazement gave her half a crown.

And Phœbe's ten-year-old summing-up of Sophia was that she was stupid but quite nice.

In another ten minutes Mrs. Barrowfield's maid, Maggie, acting on previous instructions, arrived to see her mistress home. Maggie, breathless and not so much younger than the old lady herself, was allowed by Bel's young and smart housemaid to sit and wait for her mistress on a chair in the hall. At which she was furious. For a cup of tea in the kitchen would have made all the difference. Arrived home, she reported to her neighbour this discourtesy of Miss Bel's girl—said that servants nowadays were new-fangled besoms, and opined that that one would come to no good anyway.

IV

It had been a strange day for Phœbe. Later in the evening, hand-in-hand with Bel, she climbed to the top of the house to the little bedroom that was to be her own. For Bel, even though she had not entirely given her heart to Arthur's little sister—she was not a child who responded with quick, open warmth—was, after all, a womanly woman. And it would have taken someone much less motherly than she, to be insensible to the fact that the little girl should, at this time, want some show of affection and sympathy. Bel, like everybody else a person of mixed motives, was determined to do her duty. But the motive that moved her to her duty at this moment was one that made her duty easy, and its name was kindness.

Phœbe, although she did not show it, was very impressed with Bel. There was much about her she could not understand. Bel's quiet voice. Her restrained way. Her—as it appeared to the child—lack of insistence in everything she did. In the country her elders had behaved quite differently. At the farm, if you had guests, you fussed, you insisted on them eating, insisted on them having the chair at the kitchen fire. You talked and laughed, often about nothing, until your voice boomed loud and heartily all over the kitchen and resounded on the stone floor and scrubbed pans in the milk-house.

Here it was different. Everyone was quiet in comparison to the Laigh Farm people. They seemed to try to make as little noise as possible. And Bel was the most restrained. She wondered at first if it was because they were in mourning, then decided it must be the way people behaved in Glasgow.

As for Bel herself, she was the most beautiful person she had ever seen. Her shining fair hair, her neat, well-cut mouth, that now and then expanded into a smile that was charming. There was something so elegant about Bel's smile. Phœbe made a mental note to practise smiling like that before the mirror. And she had sat so well-poised and splendid in her beautiful black dress at the head of her own tea-table, saying in that curiously quiet way of hers, things that seemed incredibly suitable and right to Phœbe, who was used to abrupt manners.

She had seen at once that Bel was going to have a baby. The wives of the two ploughmen at home were forever having babies. The little girl was perfectly used to it. The cow had babies; the mares had babies; the ploughmen's wives had babies. This child, even in these mid-Victorian days, looked upon the births one and all as things of great interest, rejoiced and asked questions.

Now she was enchanted to think that this glorious person who was sitting on the edge of her bed watching her undress was also to have a baby. It would be a very special baby, she decided. And she would be here to help to nurse it. The idea took hold of her. Bel, helping her now to brush out her almost blue-black hair, saw her reflection in the mirror and wondered why, suddenly, she looked so pleased.

Finally she was ready for bed in her long flannel nightgown. It was not very elegant, but it was new and clean, Bel decided, and highly suitable for a little girl.

Bel bent down and kissed her. "Now I'll put out your gas and you can say your own prayers and go to sleep."

Phœbe was grateful to her. She had said nothing about being

good nor about trying to be happy. And it would have been embarrassing to be "heard" her prayers.

Yet Bel waited for a moment. There seemed to be a question hanging on Phœbe's lips. It came.

"Bel, will you allow me to nurse the baby when it's born?"

Bel, brought up to genteel reticence like every other young woman of her class and period, was so taken aback at such words coming from a ten-year-old girl that she could only say, "What baby?"

"Your baby, of course!" Why not? Young things at the farm had always fascinated her. This young thing would be the most enchanting of all.

"But who told you, Phœbe?"

"Nobody."

For a moment Bel actually felt angry. But her fundamental sense came to her rescue, though of necessity she must remain a woman of her time.

"Phœbe," she said, "you mustn't say things like that."

"Why?"

"Because it's wicked." What nonsense Bel knew she was talking.

"Wicked?"

"Well, no, not wicked. Unsuitable."

"But I don't see—"

Bel, fast getting out of her depth, must use her wits.

"Well, come here and I'll tell you something. There *is* going to be a baby in May, and if you don't say a word about it to anybody between now and then, I promise you'll be allowed to nurse it sometimes." And with that she turned off the gas and quickly took herself out of the room.

Phœbe pondered for a long time, sitting on her bed. Why? It would have been nice to think and talk about the baby.

Truly Glasgow was a strange place.

For a moment she leant from her window, looking out across the town. The glow of the street lights had caught the smoke hanging over the great city, giving it a luminous, dusky cover. Endless roofs. And did all these spires mean churches? What a lot there must be! In the near distance she could see indistinctly the shape of Sir Walter Scott's statue standing silhouetted in the haze. She could see a part of the column too, although she could not see its base in George's Square. Who could that be? She must remember to ask Arthur.

She turned back, filled with curiosity and excitement and with an avid desire to go on living. Yes, it had been a strange day.

And now her bed was strange. Not at all like the bed at the Laigh Farm. Her room was strange. Bel and Arthur were strange. But what, on this first evening of her new life, was not strange? She must lie quiet, listening to these strange town noises, and think about everything.

But in five minutes more Phœbe was asleep.

Chapter Eight

IT was just dark as Mungo said goodbye to Bel and Phœbe at the Arthur Moorhouses' front door. In the morning Phœbe had asked Arthur if she might cross the town to see Mungo off, but she had been told no.

Now he had turned to raise his hand to them for the last time and was striding giant footsteps down the incline of Montrose Street. A few drops of rain fell upon his face.

Neither Phœbe nor he had shown any emotion at parting. But his thoughts as he paced quickly downwards, impelled by the slant of the hill, were with his little half-sister. On very few nights of her life had he and she failed to sleep under the same roof. For he had been scarcely ever away from the Laigh Farm, and she never. He was fond of her, he supposed, as he was fond of any of the other young creatures growing up about the farm. He wondered vaguely how she would settle into this new existence. Then he reflected that all the rest of his brothers and sisters had done so, and that they seemed busy and happy.

For himself, two days of it were about enough. He wasn't built for all the fripperies and politenesses of the town. Bel had been very kind and had left no stone unturned in her anxiety for his comfort. But he had felt the constraint of her braw house and her starched housemaid. He had, indeed, been afraid to be left alone with his sister-in-law. For their thoughts and interests were such poles apart. Very quickly he had found conversation hard going. It wasn't that he couldn't get on with fine ladies on occasion. Finer ladies than his own relatives, if it came to that. Miss Ruanthorpe, the daughter of his laird, often hung over a gate and talked to him for half an hour on end, when he came across her, which, now he came to think of it, was not infrequently. And she never made him feel ill-dressed or awkward as he stood in his rough clothes. But then she talked his own language. She could talk of ploughing and reaping and sowing. How the young beasts were promising. She had a good idea of prices. Once or twice she had come to beg his advice about her ponies or her dogs. This had flattered him, for it showed that she considered his advice of more weight than the advice of the grooms or the keeper. And Mungo was well aware that she was right. He knew that he had a growing reputation as a farmer, that his help was of value.

But Bel and Sophia and Mary. They lived in a world of gentilities for which he could raise no enthusiasm. He supposed all town ladies must be like that. Endless tattle about dress. He had heard a great deal about bustles, which were just coming in about this time. What was to be got in the shops. Meetings of this, that and the other kind in connection with the church, at which so far as he could gather—especially from Sophia—you had as many misunderstandings as possible with other ladies. Indeed, the church seemed to be the hub of their universe. Sewing meetings. Missionary meetings. Prayer meetings. Tea meetings. He caught himself wondering just what good all that did. He had always thought of church as a place to go to at twelve o'clock every Sunday. Where you sat in peace and reverence. Not as cockpits of social strivings. Well, he supposed it kept town women out of mischief and prevented a great number of them—especially the unmarried and therefore unwanted—from turning into those sluts who were so much to the fore just now; who claimed that women should have votes and stand equal with men in the world; who had the effrontery to call themselves the New Women.

He had taken his way down the Candleriggs in order to bid his brothers goodbye, and now he was at their door. Arthur was hard at it, directing his men. David was in the back office, sucking the end of a pencil.

He gave them both a hurried farewell, for he saw that Arthur was preoccupied. And he invited them both to come and see him now he was to be by himself. Especially David, for he thought he looked none too robust in his stuffy little counting-house.

No. He didn't want their kind of life. He knew that Arthur was building up a good business, and he admired him. He knew that his brother's name was one which was slowly gaining respect in the City, and he honoured him for it. But he had no desire to stand in Arthur's shoes. The very thought of eternally working in the Candleriggs was abhorrent to him. Packing-cases. Straw. Gas-flares. Account books. The never-ending clatter of dray-horses' hoofs. The oaths and the shouting. No. Never.

It was raining more heavily as he hurried along Argyle Street. The muddy street was shining in the lights. Several times the wheels of the passing buses splashed him, for in his hurry he tried to keep to the less-crowded outside of the pavement. Filthy urchins were calling an evening paper. Hucksters of various kinds were calling their wares. Fresh herrings. Mussels. Caller oysters. Here and there at the turn of a side-street, a barrow of vegetables. John Anderson's Royal Polytechnic was a blaze of light.

Now down Jamaica Street and across the Glasgow Bridge. It was raining heavily. He bent his head as the rain struck against his face. A steamer boomed in the darkness. Above the sound of the traffic he could hear the beat of paddles as another steamer pounded itself against the force of the black, muddy river into position along the quayside of the Broomielaw. Its bow was almost under the bridge.

But here was Clyde Place and the Bridge Street Station steps. In a moment more he was under shelter.

In a few minutes he would be out of it all. And a good thing. For he was a countryman, and he was going back to the country.

II

The rain lashed in bitter bursts against the windows of his carriage whenever the train was free from the covering protection of the station. The raindrops glistened and sparkled on the panes as the train, working its way outwards across the points, moved past street lamps and lighted shops and houses.

Two stout women, with large, uncomfortable bundles on their knees, sat and stared before them in the pale gas-light, bothering neither to speak to one another, though they were obviously together, nor yet to place their bundles on the seat beside them or on the rack above. But Mungo did not think this odd, for, without actually considering them, he rightly took them to be country-folk like himself. And it is the habit of such when on the move to sit clutching their belongings. Indeed, all three of them now sat forward, swaying with the lurches of the railway carriage, in that almost inanimate state of waiting that belongs to peasant people of all lands. It is impossible for townsmen to tell whether they are patient or impatient—whether, indeed, they have sensations of any kind.

At a side-station after Kilmarnock, the two stout women bundled themselves out. Mungo came to life enough to help them with their packages.

He did not move again until the train had roared through the Mossgiel Tunnel. Then he stood up stiffly and got down his bag.

The rain was falling, soft and steady, as he stepped out on the station platform. Here he halted—alive again, breathing familiar air and bidding one or two local people good-evening. This rain was good after the coldness. It would take the frost out of the ground and let him get on with his ploughing.

Outside the station, one of his men was waiting with the trap. The pony, standing in the wet with hung head, suddenly came to life at this known step, shook himself in his harness, put forward his ears and screwed his head round to look at Mungo. Mungo passed his hands down the front of the animal's nose and over his quivering nostrils. Then he greeted his man, jumped up and took the reins. The high-mettled little beast, pleased with the feel of its master's guiding hands, stretched his back and trotted sharply off on the road homeward.

Mungo was happy now. The country round about him was shrouded in darkness. By the help of his own gig-lamps he could see the road a little. That was all. Yet he and his beast knew every turn by instinct. If a black shape passed over his head, he knew it was a certain branch of a tree, which tree it belonged to, and how it looked in the daytime. The very echo of his pony's hoofs told him where he was.

He chatted in a desultory manner with his man. Everything was, of course, as he had left it two days ago. There was nothing to tell. Yet it was pleasant to speak of his own things after the trivialities of the town—to smell the wet, wintry earth and horsey odour from his pony.

In his own farmyard the two dogs, Nith and Doon, were circling and baying with joy. They followed him barking into the glowing firelit kitchen, where Jean welcomed him with a quiet show of country pleasure.

How was Phœbe? she asked. Phœbe, he told her, was fine. Was she going to be happy in the town? He said he thought so. The woman was bursting with questions. About Phœbe. About Mrs. Arthur's grand house in Glasgow. About Glasgow itself. For to her it might just as well have been Paris or St. Petersburg and almost as remote. But Mungo looked thoughtful and she dared not bother him.

It was queer to see only one place laid. For so long there had always been at least four. And often too the inside servants, if they were at liberty, had sat with them. There had always been his father, his stepmother and Phœbe as well as himself. Often, apart from his father calling for a blessing on their food, little or nothing had been said. If Phœbe had been talkative sometimes, she had been told to be quiet. For a mealtime is not always a social event among those who labour heavily. It is a time of rest. Now they were all gone, he missed the strong sense of companionship.

But for his own dogs, he was alone. It pleased him to be at home again in these surroundings, yet he was lonely. He found himself wishing that his little sister were with him.

When, after he had finished and had taken down his pipe and filled it and seated himself in his father's chair, the woman came in to clear away, he was glad to exchange a word or two with her—even to tell her a little about Glasgow—although he had scarcely ever bothered to speak to her in his life before.

Presently everything had been taken away, washed, brought back and put in its place on the shelves of the scrubbed dresser. His heart was strangely empty tonight, but it was pleasant to sit again with his jacket and collar and tie off, and his sleeves rolled up at ease in the Laigh Farm kitchen.

Nith and Doon had settled down in peace in their own separate corners of the room. They were never allowed nearer to the fire than that.

Mungo did not know how long he had sat thus ruminating over his pipe when he heard a thin whine at the door. He got up with slow deliberation and opened it. It was his father's old dog Clyde, gaunt and shaky on his legs, for now, since the loss of his master, he would not eat. The animal showed no pleasure; he merely cast his cloudy eyes about the kitchen as though he were looking for someone. Mungo bent down and patted him. In two days his ribs had become more prominent.

One of the men had said: "That dug'll no' dae nae mair guid, wi' yer faither awa'."

He had been quite right. The dog was doing no more good.

"He's no' here, Clyde. He's no' here, lad." Mungo ran his hand over his ears.

The old dog looked about him stupidly. Mungo tried to bring him into the warmth, but he whimpered and wanted to go out again, so he let him go. He himself came back to his chair by the fire.

No. They were not here.

On a sudden impulse he called his other dogs. They sprang to their feet and came to him. He laid down his pipe and ran his hands down their sleek, long muzzles. This was unheard-of spoiling for creatures who must work for their living. But dogs are tactful beasts. One soon had stretched himself across Mungo's feet and the other sat, resting his head on his master's knee beside his hand.

And so they remained for a long time. Long enough, indeed, for coals to fall in the great open fireplace, and for the cheerful glow from the ashes to sink and dwindle.

But Mungo Moorhouse did not notice. He was asleep.

Chapter Nine

BEL set David's small white tie with all the care of an arch-conspirator.

"There. Now let me look at you."

David straightened himself, and tugged at the front of his brand-new tail-coat.

"Now turn round slowly."

He turned. When he could see himself full length in Bel's bedroom mirror, he halted.

The reflection showed him the picture of a handsome young aristocrat, with a wealth of chestnut hair and side-whiskers trimmed with restraint and refinement that afternoon by Glasgow's Greatest Tonsorial Artist.

"You don't think they've cut my waistcoat too high?" David looked down dubiously at his trim black waistcoat.

Bel cast her mind back to a recent performance of "Astonishment" at the Theatre Royal and to the aspect of the handsome Mr. Kendal who had, in flawless evening clothes, so brilliantly led the company, in partnership with his talented wife. Bel and Arthur went very seldom to the devil's playbox, but an influential customer had kindly given Arthur cards, which, presumably, he could not use himself. Thus, much to Bel's delight, pleasure had, for once, become a matter of business. For Arthur could not dare tell anyone so important that he had not cared to profit by his kindness.

But Bel did not say anything to David about her mental picture of the brilliant Mr. Kendal. She wanted rather to give her brother-in-law the impression that she was more than used to that kind of thing, to convey to him that she was a woman of the world. That David—as a near relative—knew all about her did not damp this hope. So she looked at his waistcoat critically and said, "No, I think it's just right as it is."

She was pleased with the appearance of David. To her eye, at least, he looked as though he might be anybody. In things social

Bel and David were allies. They both had ambitions. David's—to rise in the world generally, not so much by hard work as by getting to know the people whom he considered to be deserving of that elusive qualification right. Bel, while quite approving of the right people, was directing her aims at a handsome house situated out West. The increasing unfashionableness of Ure Place and the increasing prosperity of her husband had created within her the desire to move.

It was Arthur's stubbornness and lack of understanding that had driven Bel and David into this alliance. Couldn't she be happy where she was? her husband asked every time they touched upon the subject. There were moments when really he was infuriating. Couldn't he see that this quarter of the town would, in time, become impossible? Now that he was the father of a boy of three, and a little year-old girl, he really ought to think of a suitable environment for them. And there was Phœbe, nearly fourteen. In a year or two she would be a young lady. She knew Arthur wanted to do well by his sister. She did too, if it came to that. Were they only to have Mary McNairn to depend on for getting to know nice people? (Mary's possession of a wide, if somewhat pious circle, did not increase Bel's affection for her.)

But now, a month ago, David had come to her with a beautiful, gilt invitation card asking him to a Dancing Party in Dowanhill. What should he do?

Bel looked at the card. "Mrs. Hayburn and Messrs. Stephen and Henry Hayburn request the pleasure of Mr. David Moorhouse's company", and so on. "Dancing."

" 'Dancing' means that it's a full-blown dance," David said uncertainly.

Bel turned the card about, admiring but thoughtful, and said "Yes."

"That will mean full evening dress," David said, feeling his way. In the Moorhouse circle none of the men had evening dress. (Except Mr. McNairn, of course, who, now one of the City's Baillies, was really forced to get it. Mary had explained: "You see, we have so many wearisome official functions, dear!") No, they were entertained and returned entertainment—the ladies in what might be called semi, the men in a dark suit.

Bel still went on twisting the card and pondering. It had ceased to be a card in her hand. It was the thin edge of a wedge.

"Who are the Hayburns, David?"

"They're very rich. Their father died last year. Hayburn and Company. Something to do with iron. I know Stephen. There are two sons. They live with their mother near the Botanic Gardens."

"Where did you get to know him?"

David was ready for this. His first encounter with Stephen Hayburn had been at the White Bait Music Hall in St. Enoch's Wynd. They had struck up a friendship, and finding, like many another pair of sparks, that they had frivolity in common, had met there again or at Browns Music Hall Restaurant or some other convenient free-and-easy. Then, in the summer, while the house in Dowanhill was closed and Mama Hayburn and her maids were by the sea, David had invited his friend to share his lodgings for a week or two. He knew that he dare not say the words music hall, even to his ally Bel, nor could he say that he knew Stephen in business for any business David did was from Arthur's office.

"As a matter of fact," he said, "he had rooms at my digs in the summer, when his mother was at Kilcreggan."

"It's queer you never told us about him."

"As a matter of fact, I've really got to know him better since then. I meet him sometimes."

"Have you been to his house?"

"No. But he introduced me to his mother last week. We met her coming out of Wylie and Lochhead's in Buchanan Street. She was just getting into her carriage."

David had, knowing and sharing Bel's weakness, aimed the carriage direct at it. It hit its mark.

She tried to look as matter-of-act and sensible as possible. "Well, David," she said, "I think it's perfectly ridiculous that a young man like you with a steady position in a good business should not have the proper clothes to wear when nice people invite him to things."

And so it came about that David was standing, in full war-paint for the first time in his life, turning himself about, in front of Bel and her mirror.

"Yes. Very nice. Have you got your gloves?"

"Yes." He produced them—white and immaculate kid.

"Wait a minute," Bel went to a drawer and produced a white rose from a little paper bag. It had cost her a bit, for the month was November. And hot-house blooms were hot-house blooms in these days. It was a perfect half-opened bud too, set in maidenhair fern, wired and finished off with silver paper. She showed David where and how it should be fixed when he arrived, and returned it to its paper bag.

David grinned a little sheepishly and thanked her.

II

"Are you saying goodnight to the children?"

"Of course. Arthur's not back, is he?" He looked a little anxiously at the little bedroom clock.

"No. No. Of course not. He had a church-meeting, otherwise I wouldn't have asked you to come and show yourself off." Church-meetings had other uses than merely religious ones. But if Arthur would be so stubborn and silly about the uses of polite society, what could his wife and his brother do?

Firm, still childish, purposeful tinkling was coming from the drawing-room piano. Phœbe had finished practising and was amusing herself playing a waltz David had bought her. It was called "Come to my Pagoda". He had heard it first at Brown's, and Phœbe's innocent strummings evoked memories of the spangled, if a little overblown, charms of the lady who had sung it. He had thought it better to buy an edition with the words left out.

"Hello, Phœbe!"

Phœbe spun round on the stool, and said "Hello!" She looked little different for her four years in Glasgow, except that she was bigger. There seemed nothing of the woman about her so far. And yet you felt that she was approaching the borderline. That any time now she would take a fit of growing, and, before you knew where you were, you might have a slim and elegant young lady for a sister.

"Like that tune?"

Phœbe nodded.

"Some day I'll sing the words to you."

"Why not now?"

"Oh, I don't know—I've got to go away. Goodnight."

She came to David and took his hand. "Come upstairs and look at Arthur the Second."

"I couldn't possibly."

"You must!"

"Don't tease her, David," Bel said, coming in and overhearing this last piece of talk. "And don't wake the babies up."

All the family knew that Phœbe had a passion for her little nephew. Every moment she was allowed to give to him, that she gave. Perhaps it was that she felt she had established a special claim upon him on that very first night that she came to Ure Place, and forced Bel to tell her that the baby was coming. Perhaps her heart had seized on the tiny newcomer and filled its empty places with him, in that first difficult year in Glasgow.

For it had been a difficult year. Both for her and for Bel. There were many times when Phœbe had been naughty, and Arthur and Bel were at their wits' end. At moments it had only been pride and fear of the derision of her sisters-in-law that had kept Bel from asking Arthur to send her back to the Laigh Farm. Often she had to remind herself of what she had said to Mary and Sophia—that a child could show its sense of bereavement by being ill-behaved.

But now in four years she had settled down to be a quiet child—strangely reserved, observant and impartial. One wondered what went on behind those quick, deep-set eyes. She seemed to care little for any of them, even Arthur her brother, though for him she appeared to have respect. The single exception was the little boy, for whom she had this extraordinary attachment.

Bel had never been sure if she liked her little sister-in-law much, but, being on the whole a sensible woman and quite unmorbid, she had long since accepted Phœbe as part of her duty, and left it at that.

David was dragged tiptoe into the nursery where Arthur Moorhouse, junior, slept in one cot and Isabella Moorhouse slept in another.

"Look at him, David," Phœbe leant over the little boy.

Arthur had all the enchantment of any pretty, sleeping child of three. There was nothing more. The strange thing to David was the intensity of Phœbe. She seemed as though she could devour him. He crossed over and looked at his niece, Isabel. To him she was just as pleasing in her way. But Phœbe scarcely bothered to look at her.

David turned and came out of the nursery.

"Goodnight, David."

"Do you know what about you? You're a curiosity. Goodnight."

Phœbe did not know what he meant. Nor did he bother to explain.

Bel was holding the handle of the front door. At the carriage-stone a cab was waiting.

"I'm treating you to this cab," Bel said. "There and back. It's all arranged."

"Bel, you're too good to be true."

"Goodnight, David. Have a good time. And come in whenever you can and tell me all about it." She kissed him and patted his shoulder, as one might pat the bread one is about to cast upon the waters.

She stood on the step and laughed to herself, a little, as the cab disappeared round the corner. A cab from the middle of the town all the way out to beyond Botanic Gardens! When there were excellent horse-buses running, that would take you at a mere fraction of the cost! This was an expense that would have to be discreetly sunk in her house-keeping money! But, after all, David was a nice boy; why shouldn't she stand him a cab? Bel did not care to own up. Even to herself.

It was a good thing that Arthur was now an elder of the kirk and had to attend meetings!

III

The cab jogged its way westward. Cathedral Street, Bath Street, Bath Crescent. The further end of Sauchiehall Street.

David, though he was now twenty-seven and considered himself a man about town, was beginning to suffer from social panic.

Each street, as he watched, sitting forward in his seat, seemed to have become incredibly short. The very outline of the new University seemed majestic and forbidding; seemed to belong to a world that was not his. Now he was outside the boundaries of the City of Glasgow.

What was this strange compulsion that made timid, sensitive people drive themselves into company that knew nothing of them? What was this strange determination not to be left out of things? Stephen Hayburn was familiar enough to him now—and good fun. But why hadn't he left it at that? Why should he, David Moorhouse, force himself to enter Stephen's house? Because Stephen would be offended if he didn't come this evening? Perhaps. But that was the mere shadow of a reason. And David knew it. No. It was something that went much deeper. Down into the roots of him. Meanwhile the damned cab was bringing him remorselessly nearer. And as the distance lessened, the hollow weakness that occupied that part of him where his stomach was usually to be found, seemed to grow in magnitude.

The Hayburns occupied one of the many new-built mansions in Dowanhill. This pleasant preserve of the wealthy was coming into being. It took the cabman some time to find the house. For Dowanhill was then no less confusing than it is today. David, paralysed with shyness, hoped he would have to go on searching for ever. But at last the house was found. Now he must descend, preserving as best he might the outer semblance of a man of the world.

The door was standing open. Flaring gas-jets cast their mellow light. Discreet and pretty parlourmaids directed him onwards and upwards to the gentlemen's bedroom. A handsome room, with a fire burning in a large iron fireplace, littered with black overcoats and scarves. There were a number of other young men. All, David thought, looking intolerably self-assured and appearing to know each other unnecessarily well. One of them, with a cascade moustache, was, he gathered, staying in the house for the night, as his home was so far out in the country. He came from somewhere near the village of New Kilpatrick. He had a great deal to say about the duck-shooting in the ponds not far from his home. He was giving the others in the room pressing invitations to visit him.

David, having said good-evening, and having received in return very formal good-evenings back, left it at that. He picked up the great silver brushes on the dressing-table, and brushed his already perfectly macassared hair. He brushed his shoulders and his sleeves. He sat down and adjusted his brand-new elastic-sided boots of glacé kid. In every way he could think of he did things to himself so that he might remain behind by himself in the bedroom. Up here he was far from comfortable, but the thought of it was heaven to facing the people downstairs.

The young men went, leaving him alone. Then he wondered if he ought to have followed them down. It would have been easier, perhaps, to have gone in and been received with the crowd. He hung about, looking at the bedroom pictures.

There were two handsome engravings of stags and mountains, taken from the work of Mr. Landseer, hanging against the rose-trellised wallpaper. Another of a Greek lady embracing an urn. They were very striking and interesting, David told himself falsely.

Strains of music came up from down below. So they had a violinist and some wind instrument as well as a pianist! The sound of the several instruments increased his panic. It would have been easier—less alarming—if there had been only a piano. His throat was very dry. He remembered a little box of perfumed cachous Bel had given him, and took one.

IV

He was leaning on the mantelshelf gazing into the fire, when a "Hello" behind him caused him to jump and turn round.

A tall, spare boy of nineteen or thereabouts with big, puppy bones that made his clothes look ill-fitting came forward.

"Hello, are you David Moorhouse?"

"Yes."

"I'm Henry Hayburn."

David had grasped this from the family likeness to his friend, Stephen. Though Stephen must be quite five years older, and was handsomer and more mature.

They shook hands.

"Stephen said he thought he had caught sight of you going upstairs. Are you all right?"

"All right?"

"Yes, I thought you were looking a bit seedy when I came in just now."

"Oh, no. I'm all right." David smiled into the boy's pleasant pug face.

"Perhaps you were just feeling like me, that all this kind of thing is just an awful nuisance."

David did not know what he meant. "What kind of thing?"

"All this dancing and nonsense. Turning the whole house upside down. It's not as if we were a family of girls, and had to set to work to find husbands."

David could find nothing to say to this. He smiled vaguely.

The boy seemed to take for granted that he agreed with him. "But there you are, Mother and Stephen are so infernally socially minded. And as usual there were far more women expecting to be asked than men. If you only knew the hunt we've had for anything in trousers!"

It was fortunate that the exact meaning of this remark in so far as it applied to himself did not penetrate to David's flustered reason. For he liked this boy. He was friendly and unaffected.

"Well, come on down, will you?"

David followed. At least, it was not so bad having this approachable, if rather cross, creature to go down with.

The drawing-room was L-shaped and enormous. Or so it seemed, and its size was increased by the fact that all the furniture, except the large cottage piano, its stool and the musicians' chairs and music-stands, had been taken out of it. Only one or two narrow benches, hired from a caterer, were set close against the walls. The main floor was entirely covered by a large, tightly stretched white cloth. The handsome gilded gaselier, and the gilded wall-brackets were, every one of them, lit. Each flame—shaped like the eye of some fantastic peacock's feather, the outer part golden, the inner part next to the jet transparent purple—shed a mellow, flattering light on girlish shoulders, wasp-waists and elegant bustled dresses, on the one hand; and sleek, black, bewhiskered correctness on the other.

Most of the guests were standing up to make sets of quadrilles.

There were four sets and the room would certainly have held a fifth. David's friend Stephen was running about among the guests, getting them arranged.

"Hello, Moorhouse. Glad to see you. Do you mind staying out of this? There's not enough people for five sets." He was gone before David could reply.

"Have you seen Mother, by the way?" Henry said, still beside him.

"No, I haven't."

"You'd better come then."

Henry led the way out of the drawing-room into what was in reality a little study next door.

A stout, elderly lady was sitting by the fire. She looked a very important lady, David thought—partly, perhaps, because he was in a state of mind to be impressed and partly because this lady herself was determined that he should think her so.

She was dressed in black. A handsome cameo brooch held a white silk shawl about her shoulders, and she wore a snowy cap on her plain parted hair. At her hand was a table with tea-things, for it was then the custom to offer newly-arrived guests tea and cakes even at such a formal entertainment as this. Most of the other guests had been offered cups of tea from large silver trays, but Mrs. Hayburn liked to preserve the illusion, even tonight when so many were present, that she was still the reigning queen of her own tea-table. And thus she had had these things arranged beside her.

For the moment she was sitting alone in the room.

"Mother, this is Stephen's friend, Mr. Moorhouse."

She stood up to greet him. "Good evening, Mr. Moorhouse. It's very kind of you to come." Then with the typical Scots belittlement of one's own efforts at entertainment, she added, "The boys thought they would just have a few friends in to make a little dance. It was kind of you to think it worthwhile. Sit down and let me give you a cup of tea."

David murmured as suitable a reply as he could think of while his hostess bent over her tea-table.

Her welcoming speech had been everything that was insincere. She did not think it was kind of him to come. She considered it was an honour for any young man—especially one she didn't know—to enter her house. It was she, not her sons, who had decided to have the dance; for she considered it was time, for prestige's sake, that she should make some kind of social demonstration. The only use David could possibly be to her was that he helped to make up the right number of men.

But now that she had him here she was not averse to finding out something about him.

"Go and see if there are any more people to be looked after, Henry dear," she turned to her long, gawky son who, having offered David cake, was munching a piece himself.

Henry went, leaving David alone with his mother. The music of the quadrilles started up in loud earnest. Even in the little adjoining room with the doors closed they had to raise their voices.

"Stephen said he had got to know you in business, Mr. Moorhouse," she said conversationally.

That would do excellently so far as Stephen's mother was concerned, so David said, "Well, yes." David was grateful to fate and Stephen that his hostess should thus unwittingly have framed this difficult question so that he could answer it.

"He didn't say what you were?"

Her question was impertinent. But David was not to be caught out.

"I'm a merchant, Mrs. Hayburn." That sounded all right. Steel merchants, coal merchants, East India merchants were the lords of Glasgow just at this time.

She was not brazen enough to probe further. Mrs. Hayburn was a snob, and snobs are, as a rule, fairly stupid even at their own game. David was very new and very nervous, but he was naturally gifted socially. To an almost excessive degree he possessed the instinct to make the rough places plain. It was by chance a part of him, just as his handsome, distinguished and rather delicate face was by chance a part of him. As he sat there facing this rather formidable woman, and with the relentless beat of the quadrille in his ears, without ever lying, David gave his hostess a very suitable impression of himself. He had been brought up in the country. Mrs. Hayburn jumped to—or rather was gently led in the direction of—the conclusion that he was a younger son of the Ayrshire county, not very rich, perhaps, who had come into the City to make his fortune. He was very sensibly living in rooms right in the centre to be near his work. That he was distinguished, her own eyes could tell her for themselves.

No. This was a nice young man Stephen had got to know. About the nicest he had brought home so far. She thought of several others and liked David the better.

The music of the quadrille ended. There was the sound of laughter and talk.

The door of the study burst open and Stephen Hayburn put his head in. "Hello, Moorhouse. We haven't seen much of you. What are you doing?"

"Mr. Moorhouse has been talking to me for a long time, Stephen. Which is very nice of him. I only hope you bother to be as polite to *your* friends' mothers."

"Well, come on now."

V

As no one else seemed to be coming into her sanctum, Mrs. Hayburn put her arm through David's and led him into the drawing-room. She was doing this entirely to please herself, but the effect she created for David, little as he realised it, was excellent. The dancers, most of them, had not noticed David when first he had looked in. Now they turned to look at this distinguished young man, basking in the sunlight of that old dragon Mrs. Hayburn's favour. People, especially the women, asked who he was. They learnt he was a young Ayrshireman, come to live for reasons of his own in Glasgow.

These sons and daughters of industrial prosperity were very ready to be impressed. Was this someone really of the county?

David, in a strange, unreal sort of way, was now enjoying himself. His feelings were those of a highly nervous actor, stepping in to improvise with little rehearsal, and finding to his surprise that he is doing well—that the part suits him.

There were one or two middle-aged women sitting round the walls, mothers of girls who were also there, personal friends of the hostess.

Mrs. Hayburn introduced him to these. David had the natural

breeding to give them attention. There was a feminine streak in his make-up, and it gave him little trouble to talk easily with women, whatever their age. In turn, they too were pleased with him. They were not averse therefore to see him stand up with their daughters and go through the movements of the lancers, quadrilles and the country dances. Everything he danced seemed to be danced with good taste and decorum. He was so unpossessive seeming, so unfamiliar. His bearing was one of remote, distinguished shyness. Even when he danced the polka, his almost sad, indulgent smile to his partner seemed to say, "What is this nonsense to either you or me?" And in the waltz, about which more than one mother had strong views, he appeared to dance with nothing more than a carefulness for the swinging steps, and with none of that abandon that maternal hearts deplored. For had not their husbands—as men of the world—assured them, as stays were laced and beards combed out in the privacy of conjugal bedrooms, that this waltzing was the kind of thing that would do neither young men nor young women any good?

David would have been surprised had he known what was in the minds of all these people. And he would have had sense of fun enough to laugh, and say, that, well, anyway a man couldn't help his face. Yet on the whole he was deliberately, if unconsciously, building up this social picture of himself. He didn't know, really, whether to like these people or not, and yet this playing of a part, or rather this instinctive selection of the right facets of his personality, amused him. He had a feeling that up to now he had been missing something. That somehow he was filling an essential want.

It was with the young women that, naturally, he had most to do. He found that they all said much the same thing. The Italian Opera was now in Glasgow. What did he think of Titiens and Trebelli-Bettini? The Tuesday concert in the City Hall. Didn't he think it was a pity that they were playing so much of this German Wagner's music? "The New Music! My father says it's the New Noise. And they say London's mad about him now! We'll be having his operas up here next!" Wasn't it exciting that Herr von Bülow would be in Glasgow shortly? David made a mental note to put his deficiencies in this kind of knowledge right.

There was another type of conversation that was more difficult to deal with. Women were not so prone to it. But when, now and then, he found himself standing against the wall with a man, it was never long before it started up. You had only to establish a show of geniality, then it began. It was what he quickly came to call (when talking these functions over with Bel) "the do-you-know? game".

"Do you know So-and-So?"

"No, I don't."

"Don't you really? But you see him about *everywhere*."

What did the fellow expect you to say? "Oh, but then I'm not exalted enough to go everywhere . . ."? But again you replied meekly in the negative.

"I can't think how you've missed him. You know, he's just become a member of the Western Club. Very young to get in, isn't it? His uncle's Sir So-and-So, the shipbuilder. His mother was a sister of Lord Here-and-There."

"I can't say I've come across him."

Coldly, "Oh, haven't you really? Well, you *must* know . . ." and so the game began again.

David could not understand what was the use of this kind of conversation. It was senseless and hollow, and certainly not conducive to friendliness. Was it to prove to you that the speaker had impeccable connections? Was it to prove to you that you were nobody at all? Or was it merely vapid talk? He decided it was that.

VI

But the evening on the whole continued successfully. Towards its end David felt quite normally jolly. It was, in other words, a dance that had "gone". As people became less punctilious he felt more at home. At its end, like the others, he was reluctant to go. Two of the mothers, quite determined not to let a new and useful young man slip through their fingers, mentioned little dances their daughters were insisting upon giving, and wondered if they wouldn't be too tedious for Mr. Moorhouse. They received his card. A note to his rooms would get him any time. In the course of the evening, David's lodgings or digs had turned into rooms.

At last it was time to go. Even up in the gentlemen's bedroom the atmosphere had lost its chill. David got into conversation with a middle-aged man who came from Edinburgh. He was staying in the George Hotel in George's Square. David offered him a lift back into town in his—or rather Bel's—cab.

They had bidden Mrs. Hayburn goodnight in the drawing-room. The others were saying goodbye at the garden gate. For though the month was November, the prevailing west wind was blowing up the river. Even if it was damp, it was warm. As they stood about waiting for the succession of cabs to take their place, David was conscious of the rustle of the breeze through branches overhead, and the smell of wet country earth. Although it was dark, he was reminded that he was on the extreme edge of the town. But for a terrace or two on the Great Western Road there was nothing further west, only green fields. An incoming ship sounded strangely close. It must be passing near the village of Partick. He thought of Bel and her ambition to live out at this end of the town. He agreed with her. It was not only the right end, it was fresh and pleasant.

The cab arrived. He said goodbye to his friends Stephen and Henry. This last, running up like a great undeveloped colt, assured him it was awfully good of him to come. David felt that the boy really believed what he said. That he regarded things like dances as unpleasant visitations from on high, inflicted through the agency of a restless, self-important mother.

His fellow-passenger mounted too, and they drove off.

"Have you known these boys for long?" he asked him.

"Only Stephen."

The man did not speak for a little. He sat looking out of the window, as the cab unwound itself down out of the maze which is Dowanhill. When it was safely on Byres Road he went on as though talk had been continuous.

"The young one's the better of the two."

David could think of nothing better to say than "I liked him."

"You would. Anybody with sense would. He's like what his father was. Did you know his father?"

"No."

"One of the men that made your Glasgow for you. And made a pile of money too. As clever as you make them. A man that wore himself out with his own enthusiasms. A 'driver', with a streak of genius."

David remembered that there had been a good many drivers with streaks of genius in Glasgow in the last hundred years or so. The more money these amassed, the more they were admired and held in awe. He had actually read in a Glasgow weekly paper recently that "money was the one pass-key that invariably opens the door to success and distinction." He had wondered. It didn't seem right, somehow, although that certainly was the creed of this wealthy city. No. Glasgow's great inventors, saviours of life, leaders of thought, had not built up their city merely by the money they had earned. It was the spirit that burned within them, surely, that had done that. Besides, he was much too easy-going to like drivers, either with streaks of genius or plain.

"And is Henry Hayburn very clever too?" David asked. Somehow he could not think of that great loose-jointed creature as a genius.

"They say so. They say he's sweeping everything before him. He's at the Anderson College. You'll see. He'll do something." David's companion said nothing more for a little, then he added as though to himself: "It would have been better for a boy like that if there hadn't been all that money for him to play with."

Somehow David gathered that this man did not think much of his friend Stephen nor yet of Mrs. Hayburn.

"I don't think Stephen bothers to work much," he said.

"I dare say not. Their mother doesn't want either of them to work. She wants them to be gentlemen." He tapped David's sleeve. "Between you and me she's a bit of a fool. But if Henry didn't work that brain of his would burst. I dare say your friend Stephen's doing everything his mother wants him to do. He's got looks, manners, swell friends and all the rest of it."

David began to wonder in what category this man was placing himself. But now suddenly he felt very sleepy. Reaction from strain had come, and it was late. For the rest of the way he answered the man in monosyllables.

University Avenue, Woodlands Road, past Mary's house in

Albany Place, along a deserted Sauchiehall Street, then finally down the hill and into George's Square. Mid-Victorian Glasgow was asleep. Their own wheels and the horses' hoofs seemed to make the only sounds in the city.

"Here's the hotel. And thank you."

"Goodnight, sir."

"Goodnight, Moorhouse."

Chapter Ten

THE last Saturday in the same month.

It began cheerfully enough. Phœbe, as was her custom, had gone into the nursery several times in the course of dressing. Her nephew and niece had shown due appreciation of her visits. Sarah, who had been with Bel since ever she had set up house in Ure Place, was now promoted from being merely housemaid to nurse-housemaid, receiving some slight addition to her income and occasional help below stairs. Sarah was bleak this morning. With that determined and defeating bleakness that only servants who are beginning to consider themselves indispensable seem able to assume. It was not, however, a manifestation that troubled Phœbe. She was a child who was very little affected by other people's moods. If people showed joy or sorrow, cheerfulness or moodiness before her, as likely as not she would find herself considering them with curiosity, wondering detachedly how they had come to be thus, and how they were likely to behave next.

She took an academic interest, therefore, in Sarah's crossness. But as Sarah was determined to be untalkative, she could not for the moment discover reasons.

Bel, coming down a moment before Arthur, found his little sister sitting on a stool in front of the dining-room fire.

"Good morning, Phœbe dear," Bel bent down and kissed her with business-like brightness. Bel's attitude seemed rather to imply, "I am firmly determined that my house is going to be a pleasant house, and to keep it up to scratch I myself shall be the brightest thing in it."

"Take your porridge while it's hot, dear. There's nothing like porridge for making you a big, strong girl."

Phœbe felt big and strong enough. Besides she loathed porridge, as most Scots children do. But she had learnt long since that resistance was useless. And as the fragrance of ham and eggs, rising from the dish set on the brass stand before the fire, was doing all it could to tempt her to reach the other side of her ordeal, she bravely poured milk over her porridge and began.

Bel watched Phœbe. She was growing up a sensible sort of girl on the whole. She didn't give much trouble. If she saw the point of what you told her to do, she did it. And as she was very intelligent, it was easy to make her see the point. But, although Bel was ready to defend her strange independence to Mary and Sophia, she deplored it rather in secret. She believed now that the girl liked her well enough—she had never known her disloyal or thankless—yet she would have been grateful for a show of warmth. For Bel was by nature a warm, pleasant person herself.

Bel sighed a little and poured herself out a cup of tea. She would take her own ham and egg when Arthur came. No. A queer child. But with any luck she would be a beauty in four or five years' time. And the small amount of money Phœbe had from her dead father, that was educating her now, would go to buying a nice dress or two and getting her off. Bel hoped that Phœbe would not be difficult about her help when the time came. Getting her off would put her into good practice for getting her own daughter off. She smiled to herself at the thought of the little year-old Isabel. Goodness knew where they would all be by the time Isabel was looking for a husband. Times were good and looked like getting better. Life was secure. Still—you never knew.

Bel sipped her tea reflectively, forgetting Phœbe's presence now. The idea of getting a sister-in-law and a daughter off had started a train of thought. Ure Place would not be a good centre for the campaign. Why wouldn't Arthur come to realise this? Why wouldn't he go further out? They were putting down tram-lines all over the city now. They said it would make it much easier for the horses and that the new trams would be much faster than the old buses. The family could live perfectly well in one of the new terraces in Hillhead. Arthur could come down to his work in half an hour. And it would be so much more healthy for them all. Now that they had children, she loathed the thought of being so near the slum quarter. Only last night she had turned away a wretched, evil-looking fellow begging at he door. She was certain Arthur could afford to move. Of course, he never told her what he had, husbands didn't, but he was free and open-handed—and grudged her nothing within reason. The business must be doing well.

And now the new friendships that David was making. He had come, of course, and told her all about the dance at the Hayburns'. He had put it all very amusingly. He had made her laugh like anything over this and that. Still, the fact remained that David was making his way. He had already accepted two other invitations of the same kind. She was glad she had helped the boy. And already so far as she dared she had put into practice several little household customs which, she had gathered, the better people always followed.

No. High time they were out of here. They were—all of them—worthy of a better background. She must brace herself once more and have it out with Arthur.

Phœbe stood up to put her empty plate away. Bel's thoughts came back to actuality.

"Finished, Phœbe? I hear Arthur. Put the ham and eggs on the table, dear."

Phœbe did so, then went over to the window. Bel thanked her and set about her task.

"I hope it's not raining," she said as she divided out. "It's dull enough." She turned to look on her own account, then turned away again. "You've got to go to your music and your dancing, and little Arthur's going out."

Phœbe's interest heightened at once. Her nephew's name was enough to do this at any time. "Where are you taking Arthur?"

"Sarah's taking him to see his granny. He's to stay for his dinner. She's in bed. I promised to send him to cheer her up."

Old Mrs. Barrowfield, sixty-nine now, was suffering from rheumatism. On Friday Bel had called and found her in poor spirits. As a very special treat she had promised the old lady she should have her grandson all to herself next day at her midday meal, on condition that she did not ruin his sturdy little stomach by giving him this, that and the other. The old lady having given her promise, fully intended to break it. For what did a young girl like Bel know about feeding children? Still, better to humour her. Or the child would not be sent.

It was now that Phœbe understood Sarah's gloom. Sarah hated the old lady's officiousness. But she hated more the treatment that was accorded her by the ageing, bad-tempered maids in the Monteith Row kitchen. Bel's young maids and her mother's old ones were in a state of perpetual warfare. Phœbe, now familiar with both camps—for old Mrs. Barrowfield continued to like her, and she went there often—heard the point of view of each with interest, and was filled with a detached contempt for all.

II

Arthur seemed preoccupied. He had a sip of his tea, and took up his letters. He looked quite his four years older. His face was, perhaps, a little more set, but his hand, quick and sure as it slit open his letters, showed assurance and vigour.

"Here's a letter from Mungo," he said presently. "What's he writing in pencil for?" And then again after a moment. "He's in his bed. He's wrenched his leg."

"Mungo? Good gracious. How, Arthur?" Bel exclaimed.

Arthur read aloud: "I was in the loft of the cartshed looking at some old iron that was up there. I knew there was an old plough and some old chains, and one thing and another. Phœbe will know where I mean. I don't know when they were put there. A scrap-iron man said they might be worth a shilling or two if he could see them the next time he came. Anyway the whole floor was rotten and gave way, with me and the plough and everything else. The old plough half fell on the top of me. I was badly cut and scraped. And a leg was twisted. The boys got me out, and went for the doctor. He got me all cleaned up, and he brought the new assistant and they did what they could between them. That was on Wednesday. But it is just today that I feel like writing. I am all right but if you could manage to run down I would not be sorry. You could arrange some things for me." Arthur folded the letter.

"I think you should go, Arthur," Bel said. "You could stay and come up on Monday."

Arthur pondered. He hated being put out of his routine. Besides he was now an assiduous kirk elder. But all common sense, every consideration of brotherliness pressed him to go.

"You must go, Arthur. You must see for yourself how he is.

We'll be all right here. I'll pack your bag and send it down to the warehouse."

"All right. There's a train at Dunlop Street about twelve o'clock." Being Saturday made it easier from a business point of view.

Mungo now had his special place in the family. As farmers go he was becoming comfortably off. Old rule-of-thumb methods were going one by one at the Laigh Farm. With no one dependent upon him he was able to put back what he earned year by year into his stock. If he were allowed to buy his farm, Arthur did not doubt that he certainly would do so. But so far the laird, although he was on very friendly terms with his tenant, had shown no wish to let him do so. Arthur would certainly have helped Mungo with the purchase. It would be a brotherly act and an excellent investment, for Mungo in his way was as solid as himself.

During the four years that had elapsed since he had been left solitary it had been Phœbe who had remained in closest contact. She had always gone for part of her school holidays. They had considered it right that she should not be cut off from her old home. She had always come back with her accent broadened and an inclination to be noisy, but Bel had sense enough to see that these were only surface faults, and with a little checking Phœbe lost them again in a week or two. The women servants Gracie and Jean were still there, and Mungo had assured Bel that they were good girls who would not let Phœbe come to harm. Last summer Sophia had implored Mungo to take her children for a fortnight while Phœbe was there. Wil was now eleven and Margy nine. But every day she had sent him letters telling him how to feed them, when they must go to bed, when they must change their clothes, asking if blankets were well aired, and heaven knew what else, until at last Mungo, in a rage, had sent them home. Mary's children, and, of course, Bel's were as yet too young to be an affliction to him.

The consensus of opinion in the family was that Mungo and his surroundings were excellent in their way, but roughening and coarse for those who had profited by the refinements of town life.

Now it was decided that Arthur should go. The bag was to be

packed, and in addition, Bel was to make an expedition down to the shops to have a special parcel of delicacies made up for the invalid.

Having a few minutes more before she must go to her Saturday morning dancing class, Phœbe sat down and wrote the following letter:

"Dear Mungo,

"This is terible news. You should not have gone up there. If I had been there I would have told you, because I knew these boreds were rotten with the damp and the rats. I have climed up often, so I know. Is your suffering terible? If so, remember we are all thinking about you. Jean and Grace nevertheless will be a very present help in time of trouble. We are all splendid here. Arthur, the second, is going to spend the day with Mrs. Barrowfield, and I am very angry, because I wanted to play with him this afternoon. How are Nith and Doon and the new poney doing? If you want me I will come down to you at once. Bel will just have to give me a line to get off the school. Trust in God and your affectionate sister,

"Phœbe Moorhouse."

She put this in an envelope, addressed it, and sealed it carefully so that Bel should not read it. Great as her secret admiration for Bel still was, Phœbe hated people poking into her affairs.

III

Old Mrs. Barrowfield sat up in bed watching her grandson. The child was her greatest joy in life. She kept insisting to everybody that he was the very image of his Grandpa Barrowfield. This may or may not have been true, but the old lady would have it so, for she could not endure to think that he should bear any likeness to his Grandpa Moorhouse, who had been nothing but a farmer. At all events the child had Bel's fine, fair colouring.

She was feeling better than she had felt for some days. For, in addition to her rheumatism, she had been suffering from acute loneliness and boredom—a complaint often to be found among the elderly—and for the time little Arthur had succeeded in banishing this.

The clock on the mantelpiece of her large and comfortably upholstered bedroom overlooking the Glasgow Green chimed two.

"It's time Sarah was coming for you," she said to the mite, who was hunting lions and tigers at the foot of her enormous bed. She had promised to send the little boy home, to have his afternoon sleep, for it was essential that he, with Sarah, should get home in safety in the daylight. And she herself, comfortable and happy now, would be quite content to drop over until tea-time.

No sooner had she spoken than Sarah appeared. Sarah was grim and purposeful, having just eaten her dinner in the enemy's camp. She began packing Arthur into his little velvet coat, gaiters, muffler, gloves, sailor hat and all the rest of it. His grandmother watched him with sleepy approval. There were not many little boys so well dressed as her grandson. That little coat had been a gift from herself. (In secret Bel thought corn-flower blue a little over-bright, but wear it he must when he went to Monteith Row, or there would be no plumbing the depths of the offence her mother would take.)

Affectionate goodbyes were said, and Sarah and her charge set to. The sun was shining through a gap in a wintry sky, but as November sunshine is precious the woman determined to make the most of it. She would take her way across the Green. Probably Arthur would run for some distance, and for the rest she could carry him, for she was strongly built and well able to lift and carry a child of three. For a time after they left the Row it was very pleasant sauntering at a child's pace in the open, grassy expanse, but as they neared the Saltmarket it became unpleasantly crowded with slum children. Sarah picked up Arthur and hurried on into the Saltmarket itself. She was glad she had not come any later in the day, for already this street, famous for its disarray and squalor, was beginning to show signs of living up to its reputation. Men and women—their newly received weekly earnings already being quickly spent in the numberless drinking-shops—were showing signs of becoming boisterous.

But Sarah's honest stomach was not easily turned. You couldn't be brought up in Glasgow, if you were of the working class in however decent a family, without having seen a thing or two. She continued, therefore, cheerful and undaunted, up the Saltmarket.

It was outside O'Reilly's Oyster Rooms that the thing happened.

A younger sister of Sarah's, Peggy by name, suddenly emerged from a provision shop. She was a child of about fifteen. Sarah was annoyed to find her down here, for her family did not live in this low quarter of the town, but in a respectable quiet cottage up at the Monkland Canal. Their father had work in one of the many woodyards by its banks. She stopped to ask what Peggy was doing. Their mother had sent her out to get something, she replied, but she had failed to get it further up the town.

Sarah would not believe this. The girl had reasons of her own for being down here. Sarah decided to find them out. She was filled with what she considered was a just and righteous fury. She set down Arthur and pitched into her. Peggy defended herself badly, for she was a weak sort of girl, but Sarah's reproof was long and heated. Peggy must remember that she came from decent folk. Saturday afternoon was no time for her to be by herself in the Saltmarket. For some moments the sisters became engulfed in their quarrel.

One or two people, hearing, wondered what it was all about. Who was this decently dressed woman talking to this girl? She must be a servant. The rich-looking, golden-haired child in the blue coat, who was wandering round them, must be in her charge.

Two or three entrances up, a hag who dealt in old clothes—and other things bent down and picked up a kitten that was playing at her feet. She came down towards them, and dropped the kitten near Arthur. He saw it and pattered towards it. She leered at him, picked up the kitten and dropped it again further off. He still followed. She did this a third time. Still he followed. Now he was opposite her own entrance. Again she picked up the kitten and again Arthur followed.

Sarah turned: "Where's Arthur?"

She could not believe he was not by her side. She refused to believe. She shrieked.

A passing urchin pointed. "The wee boy went in there."

She rushed to the doorway. It was merely a passage-way leading through to a narrow close, known as "Hughie's Yeard". There were a dozen doors leading up filthy stairways to rooms above. He might have been taken up any of them. There was no one in the yard. She tried one stairway, but it was blocked by two drunken men. She tried a second, tripped and fell on her face, while half a dozen hags yelled abuse and laughed at a decent girl making a fool of herself. At a third a man put his arms about her. She had to struggle to force him to let her go. Out in the middle of the yard again, he stood at the door and smiled a drunken smile. Slowly he withdrew one hand from a pocket. It held a razor.

Again she shrieked and ran out through the passage into the Saltmarket. She had quite lost her head now. Her sister tried to speak to her, but she could get nothing but "What'll the mistress say? What'll the mistress say? It'll be the jail for me!"

Poor Sarah started to run. Out of the Saltmarket into the High Street, up Kirk Street, past the Royal Infirmary in Castle Street and beyond. In her hysterics she did not think what she was doing, but her instinct was taking her home to her father's cottage.

IV

After her midday meal Phœbe had sat herself down in the nursery. Bel had established herself in Sarah's accustomed place while her daughter had her afternoon sleep. Phœbe, lately promoted to serious knitting, was making a pair of socks—black and unspectacular—for Arthur. Her feelings of self-importance were just managing—and no more—to keep boredom at bay. For black is not an interesting colour for fourteen years to knit.

The sound of voices, quickly distinguishable as those of Sophia and the two children, were not, then, entirely unwelcome to her.

"Go down and say I'll come in a moment, Phœbe. I'll send Bessie up here." Bessie was the cook.

Phœbe went down. Pompously holding her knitting. Determined that Wil and Margy Butter should see how important she had become.

Sophia's children had settled down to play an improvisation for four fists at the piano.

"Hello, dear. How are you? I've come across to hear about Mungo. William met David. Children, would you stop it! Aren't they awful! I can't hear what Phœbe's saying! Is it true Arthur's gone down?" There was a crazy kind-heartedness and warmth of feeling about Sophia that had always made Phœbe rather like her.

Phœbe walked over to the piano. For the moment, perhaps because of her knitting, she was feeling very much their aunt, even though she was only two years older than Wil. She put a hand on the back of each of their necks and shook them until the din stopped. "Be quiet," she said firmly, but without temper. "You'll waken Isabel."

Wil and Margy were normal and spirited. A fact which never ceased to astound those who thought about it. For were they not the offspring of a hen and a deaf-mute? Sophia's fussing had made them intolerably impertinent to herself. But apart from that they were much like other people's children.

The three young folks settled down to entertain themselves with Phœbe's scrapbook. Bel came in and greeted Sophia. Her face was a little anxious.

"Do you know," she said, "I've just realised it's after three, and Sarah is never home with Arthur yet?"

"I thought Arthur had gone down to Mungo." It was typical of Sophia to make such a senseless remark. Even with a light cloud of worry blowing up in her mind, Bel could not help seeing this funny. The thought of her serious husband having a day out with Sarah.

"No, Sophia, I mean little Arthur." She went to the window for a moment. "I do think it's too bad of Mother to keep him so long. Old people are dreadful. You can't get them to be sensible. And she promised faithfully to send him back after dinner. The streets down there get so nasty on a Saturday afternoon."

She came back to the fire, however, and talked of Mungo and his accident, showing no more worry until it was after half-past three. At last she called to Phœbe, "Go and look through the house and see if you can see any sign of them."

Phœbe went, and returned to say they were not anywhere to be seen.

"Well, I'm not going to worry seriously until four o'clock. After that it begins to get dark."

"Mrs. Barrowfield will send them home in a cab now, surely," Sophia said, trying to be comforting but arousing all kinds of horrors in Bel's mind.

Phœbe was hanging about. Scraps had lost their interest. She had left Wil and Margy to squabble by themselves.

The hands of the clock came, after what seemed an eternity, to four. It was raining slightly, and the light was going.

Bel was now frankly upset. Bessie came with tea, but she could not touch it. "I wish Arthur was here; I must go across to Mother's. Bessie," she said to the girl who had come back with little Isabel, "go and look for a boy to fetch me a cab."

Bessie went. There was usually a corner boy hanging about in the Place ready to run errands.

V

Phœbe followed her to her room. Watching her in mute misery as she put on her outdoor things, she saw that there were tears in Bel's eyes. For once she did not despise the sight of them. They must be for Arthur, and they filled her with an apprehension such as she had never known before.

Bessie came to say that the cab had come. Phœbe followed Bel downstairs and hung about dejectedly at the open door after she had driven off.

For quite ten minutes she stood gazing into the drizzling rain. When at length she turned to go, she noticed a figure of her own size hanging about the corner. It was Sarah's little sister Peggy.

Peggy was rather a friend of Phœbe's. The girl often came to visit in the kitchen. Phœbe was very fond of her—or rather of her visits—because Peggy was a silly child and allowed herself to be dominated, which Phœbe much enjoyed doing. She shouted to her now.

"Hello, Peggy, what are you standing there for?"

The child came forward. Phœbe could see that she was crying.

"What's wrong with you?"

Peggy's father being a coward himself had sent her down with the news of Arthur's disappearance. Sarah, still hysterical, was quite unfit to come herself. Seeing Phœbe, Peggy took heart. It was easier for her to tell Miss Phœbe than to tell Mrs. Moorhouse. Through her tears, and prodded on by Phœbe's increasingly excited questions, the news came out.

Phœbe was appalled.

Arthur stolen! She had heard of such things. When she was younger Sarah and Bessie had told her tales to frighten her. But of course it was a thing that could never really happen to anyone you knew! She hadn't even believed in the stories much.

And Arthur! Her own particular Arthur! Had she not staked her claim upon him on the very first night she came here, months before he was born? Had she not lain in bed on some of those first homesick nights telling herself that there was a baby coming, who would make up for everything she had lost? She stood trembling. What was to be done? Her contempt for Sarah was measureless. Fancy leaving the place before she had got him out! She told Peggy so roundly.

Peggy, protecting her sister, told her that the people in those places were terrible. Phœbe could have no idea.

Phœbe almost spat back at her. No, she had no idea. But that had nothing to do with it! Sarah would have to go to jail!

But she must think what to do. She told Peggy to come in and wait in the hall. The elder child obeyed.

Sophia too was appalled at the news. But for once she became quite calm and sensible. She called for Bessie—told her to take her own children home at once, and bring back her husband and David, wherever they had got to. She would stay here and look after Isabel and Phœbe.

Bessie went with Wil and Margy as she was bidden.

When they were gone, Phœbe, hanging about miserably, felt herself in the very pit of dread.

Arthur—what could they be doing to him? Why had they stolen him? She had heard that rich children had been taken for their clothes. But that might not be the end of it! This child who despised tears found herself choking back bitter, shocking sobs.

No. She must do something. *She* must think of a plan too!

Couldn't she go and try to get him herself? She daren't tell Sophia. Sophia would tell her she was mad, and trot out the usual tales that only slum people could go into these places with safety on Saturday nights.

Very well. She would be a slum child. She would disguise herself. Only last Hallowe'en she had dressed as one and gone across with Sarah to Grafton Square. They had all been taken in. And when she liked she could talk like any of the beggar bairns that came to ask a piece at the Laigh Farm back door. Suddenly, in her innocence, she was enchanted with the idea. Peggy was here and could show her exactly where Arthur had been taken.

She found Peggy still sitting, miserable, in the hall.

"Come up to my room, Peggy."

The child followed her.

"Now take off your dress and give it to me, I'll give you this one."

"Whit are ye goin' tae dae, Miss Phœbe?"

"Never mind, give it to me. This is a better one for you anyway."

Peggy was the most easily cowed creature in the world. In a few moments they had exchanged dresses. She was standing in Phœbe's little braided serge school dress, and Phœbe was in her plain stuff one. But this was not the end of it, for Phœbe had taken a pair of scissors and ripped Peggy's into rags.

Peggy began to cry again.

"Don't be a silly, Peggy. You can keep my dress."

Having taken off her own shoes and stockings, Phœbe told Peggy to come. She led her down to the kitchen. As they passed to go out at the back door, Phœbe took down the old sacking apron that Bessie put on when she washed the front steps of a morning. She would wear this on her head as a shawl. In the back green she rubbed her legs and face with mud. It was raining now, so she bared her head that the wet might take the curls out of her hair—curls nightly re-made by Bel with the help of screws of newspaper.

"Now come on."

"Where are we goin'?"

"Along the Rotten Row." Phœbe's tone cowed any further questions.

Now that she had burnt her boats she began to feel that this escapade might after all be regarded as a piece of naughtiness. For the moment she was not so sure of herself. Could the people be so awful as they said? What kind of awful? If it was only drunk—well, she had seen the farm-hands drunk often. Still, she felt a little afraid. Arthur, her brother, when he heard about this, would be furious. But she could not turn tail now. She could not appear frightened before this silly girl crying beside her. And then suddenly she thought again of the unaccustomed sight of tears in Bel's eyes, and again the thought of Arthur the Second and what they might be doing to him made her sick at the stomach. No. She didn't mind about these people that everyone said were so terrible.

They were at the end of the Rotten Row now. At the Bell o' the Brae.

She turned to her companion.

"Listen, Peggy. We're going down into the Saltmarket. You're going to show me where Sarah lost Arthur."

"No' the night, Miss Phœbe!"

"Yes, tonight. If you don't come, I'll see that Sarah gets taken straight to jail." And Peggy thus once more frightened into obedience turned to come with her down the hill.

VI

It was now about six o'clock, damp and foggy, but the rain was stopping.

The High Street was tumbling with humanity as the two children made their way downwards. The wynds and vennels, it seemed, had emptied their inmates into the main street. Filthy children, their sharp white faces already old and cunning, fought, played, snatched and howled in the gutter. Women hanging round close entrances, many already staggering, enfolded dirty babies in their drab shawls; others shrieked harsh greetings at passing friends, calling obscene pleasantries; again others, though it was still early evening, were already sitting or lying huddled against walls, rendered senseless by whisky. Men stood about in knots, their afternoon's dram causing some to appear lifeless and stupid, others to quarrel fiercely. Younger people of both sexes were parading up and down, thronging the street—pushing and jostling. The shops were busy with their Saturday-evening trade, small shops most of them, their windows lit by one gas-flare. Only the packed public-houses seemed to have enough light. High over their window-screens could be seen gaseliers with lavish clusters of white frosted globes. The children kept to the middle of the street. There it was less crowded, for walkers had to dodge hoofs and wheels, as the buses came and went on the hill. And the drivers, losing patience, were not above lashing out with their whips.

Strangely, perhaps, Peggy was more afraid than her companion. She had had many a stern warning from her parents about these quarters at certain times of the day and week and she was ready to be terrified. For there was a gulf fixed between respectable working folks and the depraved creatures here.

Phœbe did not understand the meaning of much that she saw and heard about her. She could see the wretchedness and squalor. It was a platitude to her that abominations existed in the slums. But there was no reason that she should know more than this. She was fourteen and from a genteel, Victorian household. In addition, her mind was moving on a single track. Her passionate purpose made her, at this stage, almost unconscious of her surroundings.

They had reached the hurly-burly of Glasgow Cross now. Here the crowd and the tumult were greater than ever, but the lights of the larger shops, the flow of the traffic and the sight of more than one policeman, was, for the moment, reassuring. Peggy would have paused beneath the Tolbooth Steeple but her companion turned to her relentlessly and pointed across to the Saltmarket.

"Is it down that way?"

"Yes, Miss Phœbe."

The children crossed over, pushing through.

A little way down the Saltmarket two drunken sailors were fighting. The face and beard of one of them streamed with blood. Peggy screamed, and fresh tears came. Phœbe turned to look at her, and saw that she was again on the point of retreat.

"Come on, Peggy. You can go home in a minute. Where was

it they took Arthur? If I get Arthur, Sarah won't have to go to jail." She seized Peggy's arm and marched her forward.

In a few moments more the older child stopped and pointed.

"It was in there."

"All right, you can go away now."

Phœbe loosed her grip on Peggy's arm.

Peggy turned and ran.

Phœbe hesitated for a moment, then she crossed to the other side of the street to have a look at where she had to go. In the foggy gas-light she could see a group of women standing gossiping and cackling at the close mouth. One, very drunk, was leaning against the wall, her bonnet on one side. The others were laughing at what she said. Yet another kept performing vague reel steps, hitching back and forth as though she had a kind of St. Vitus' dance. Another, perhaps younger than the rest, with some attempts at dilapidated finery, and with an unnaturally white and pink face and yellow hair, would catch a passing man by the arm now and then and try to stroke his face. This was greeted by howls of laughter from the others, though the woman seemed angry when the man shook himself free. Phœbe did not fully understand, but all her instinct told her she was looking into the abyss of degradation.

She stood pondering. How was she to get past these terrible women? For a moment fear took hold of her. But resolutely she forced it back.

Arthur was hidden away somewhere behind them. If she were feeling afraid, what must he be? No. She could not afford to be frightened.

She must use her wits again. She had already made herself look like a slum child, and she could assume a thick country accent; it was indeed a second language to her. She had gone thus far unnoticed. She must have patience and wait her time.

Another couple of sailors were coming up on the further side singing. The yellow-haired woman danced a step or two before them as they passed. The men shouted, seized her, and, one on either side of her, marched her, screaming with laughter and emitting oaths, off up the street. The other women followed, howling gibes. Only the drunken woman was left, supporting herself against the wall.

The entrance was free. Phœbe had seen the hands at the Laigh Farm drunk. She didn't like it, but she was not afraid. She could get herself past this woman without much trouble. She crossed the street, paused for a moment to look in. The woman gazed at her stupidly, blinked and said, "Guid nicht tae ye, dochter."

Phœbe returned the "Guid nicht", and passed through the dark passage into "Hughie's Yeard".

VII

If the place had looked disgusting to Sarah this afternoon, it was worse now. Phœbe's eyes had to become accustomed, for it was lit merely by one lamp and by such light as percolated through one or two dirty windows. It seemed to be entirely enclosed, its only entrance being the one through which she had come. She had to go warily, for her feet, though they had often gone unshod in pleasanter places, were sensitive to the garbage upon which she trod. More than once she avoided a broken bottle or tin can. After the rain there was a heavy stench. Several times her feet slipped among that which caused it.

There were a number of people, men and women, in the courtyard and one or two children. Some windows were thrown open, and women were shouting to each other. There was a constant wailing of infants. Yet, for it, Hughie's Yeard was fairly empty. Most of its inhabitants, and many of them were women of a certain trade, were out of it now having their Saturday's fling in the drinking-shops, or walking the streets for business. The people paid no attention to Phœbe. Her childish look and the rags she had assumed were ample disguise. She stood some minutes bewildered by her surroundings. But noticing she was unheeded, she took courage and began to think what she would have to do. People were going out and in through the dark doorways that surrounded the yard. She would try them, one after the other. She began with the one nearest to her.

From the entrance on the ground floor itself several single rooms opened off. Most of their doors stood open. In most of them, too, fires were burning in curious primitive fireplaces, built into one corner of the room. Women were working about, some of them cooking. It was Saturday night and there was money to buy food for the pot. By the light of the fires she could see other men, women and children lying on dirty mattresses or on straw, or merely on the floor, which was bare earth. She wondered how so many people could live together in one room. She did not know that the rooms were comparatively empty.

Through each door she peered as far as she dared. For Arthur must be somewhere. Strangely, it never struck her that he might have been taken elsewhere.

This first place was useless. She decided to ascend the stair.

The steps of the stair were littered with the same obnoxious filth as the yard outside. It was not only damp oozing through ill-maintained roofs that made the woodwork cracked and rotten. There was one landing, and yet another. The rooms that opened off them and the people inside repeated very much what she had seen below, except that people lay on boards instead of earth. Some rooms had beds. But beds in Hughie's Yeard were places of luxury—and of business.

With a doggedness that had become almost mechanical Phœbe tried stair after stair. Once she was struck aside by a drunken man. Once she had to leave out a top landing because two harpies were locked together, fighting like she-devils, tearing out handfuls of each other's hair. It was amazing how little these things had come to affect her. The more appalling the horrors the greater grew her determination to find Arthur.

She had one more stair to try when a boy spoke to her. He might be her own age, but it was difficult to tell with stunted slum creatures.

"Whit are ye goin' up an' doon a' they stairs for?"

Phœbe started. This boy had been watching her! It was the first time, in what had actually been more than an hour, that she had been addressed directly. At other times she had merely been cursed out of the way. But she must go on keeping her wits about her.

She told the boy in her broadest Ayrshire that she had come up that day from Kilmarnock, and had been told that she would find her aunt here.

What was her aunt's name?

Phœbe invented one.

He did not know it, but then there were so many people here. What did her aunt do?

Phœbe looked blank and said she didn't know.

The boy leered and said something to her that she did not understand. But she thought it best to smile.

At any other time or place Phœbe would have run from this white-faced, undersized creature, but the fact that he seemed to be friendly gave her courage and set her wondering if he might help her in some way. Should she ask about a well-dressed little boy being brought into this yard today? Then fear that she might give herself away overcame her.

He offered to help her to find her aunt on the last staircase. Again it was fruitless. He pointed out to her a corner of an upper room which he said was where he lived. Phœbe made him stare by asking if every family did not have a room to itself. He asked her if they had as much space as that in Kilmarnock, and she had the wit to say they had. But after that she was afraid, and asked no more questions.

Being a helpful sort of boy, it seemed, he offered to try all the yard with her again. Although, as he said, her aunt would probably be out in the streets. Phœbe accepted. But after further endless weary plodding they could discover nothing. He tried several doors that were locked. He told her that when women were having babies they always tried to have them behind doors that locked, for then they would lock the door on the doctor, and the others could force him to give up his money before they let him out. He considered it a good joke. Did they do the same in Kilmarnock?

At the end of his journey he became affectionate and laid his hands on Phœbe. With a brute temper that she did not know was in her she struck him full in the face. Under the lamp she saw his nose was streaming. But, having called her names, the meaning of which she had no idea, he left her.

VIII

A numb bewilderment settled on her. But she would not leave Hughie's Yeard. She could not give up the idea that Arthur was behind one of those doors. She had no idea what to do now. She crouched down in a corner near the entrance and waited.

A bell somewhere, tolled nine. . . . Now and then she could hear the trains roaring on the Union Railway viaduct that cut its way through places such as this to connect with the new College Station. Still she crouched and waited, it seemed for an infinite time. The distant bell tolled ten. The courtyard was getting noisier and fuller. There were endless fights—sometimes between a couple of ill-built, ape-like men, sometimes between drink-inflamed women. Blood flowed freely. But she was past caring. For she was stupefied now with dejection, sick with anxiety and disgust, weak from cold and want of food. Yet even now this child's iron will would not let itself be broken. She must wait here in this terrible darkness. Wait until she could take Arthur with her.

All at once there was a cry at the entrance and a rush of policemen. There were half a dozen of them, of the small, stocky type that at that time Glasgow put on slum night duty. There was a hush in the court. The squabbling stopped and the ranks closed against the intruders.

A raucous voice shouted to ask what they wanted. Phœbe was electrified by the reply.

"Is there a stolen wean in here?"

There was a shout of laughter. "Ye better come and look." The yard knew that six policemen would not, in common prudence, dare. The number of scoundrels against them was unlimited.

But Phœbe's heart was bursting her body. So Bel or David had informed the police! All the windows above were filled with heads. The mob standing back in the yard and the police by the entrance stood glaring at each other. There was a no-man's-land between them. Phœbe, near the policemen, could hear what they said. They were not going up "they bloody closes the night". It was sure murder. Even if they all went into one together they would be trapped like rats. It would be impossible to fight their way out again. They had obeyed orders and come into the yard. More they could not do. Toffs should look after their own weans.

The people began taunting them. A woman threw some filth

from a window that knocked off a policeman's top-hat, covered his face and ran down his beard. The yard applauded. Another, at a window, showed a child.

"Is it this yin?"

There was yet another roar. A woman carrying a second child danced across the no-man's-land from one close entrance to another. The thing became a game. Women danced across with children or showed them at windows.

At a top-floor window opposite to where Phœbe crouched, an old hag and several young women were leaning out, enjoying the spectacle. They seemed, most of them, very drunk, as they howled down abuse in their imbecile delight.

Suddenly the group parted and a child was held out. Its face was smudged and scared. It was wrapped in what looked like a piece of sacking. The woman, seemingly less drunk than the rest, held him up.

"Here! Is it this yin?"

Phœbe's scream was lost in another shout of animal laughter.

It was Arthur.

The numbness had left her. She must decide at once what to do. Should she tell the policemen beside her? Or were the chances of getting him out better if she acted by herself? She had heard them say they would not let themselves be trapped. No. She would act by herself.

There were more howlings, more taunts, more children held up, but at last the policemen went. The inmates of the yard settled down to discuss the affair. From what she could hear, they did not know of the stolen child.

She must go and reconnoitre. She went up the stairs to the top. From its window, it was quite easy for her to decide in which room Arthur must be, although the loathsome landing was almost in black darkness. She pressed against the door gently. It did not give. Presently a woman came out and went downstairs. The door was at once closed, and Phœbe could hear a key being turned. But she had caught a glimpse of a brightly burning fire, a number of women and on one side a bed.

She settled down to wait. She was very excited now, and felt a strange tension in her head; but she felt no fear. People came and went from the other rooms on the landing. She had constantly to be jumping to avoid them. But they were used to crouching children, and they let her be.

Gradually she became conscious of increasing noise in the yard below. There seemed to be more roaring and drunkenness. She did not know that the public-houses closed at eleven, that those who had been turned out were coming home. Several people came up and staggered into the other rooms. At last two women came up dragging two reeling men with them. She had to press herself hard against the oozing wall to let them pass. She could not understand why the women were using words of coarse endearment. They banged on the door, giving their names. The door opened. One man was so drunk that it took a long time to get him through. Phœbe was given ample time to examine the room. Men and women were lying about on straw. Another couple were in the bed. The beasts of the Laigh Farm had taught Phœbe life's straightforward facts. She could have no knowledge of these more terrible ones. It was lucky that her eyes could only look for Arthur.

IX

He was there near the fire, sitting on a heap of straw. His eyes were bewildered. Once he made to move. But the old hag that she had seen at the window struck him. He whimpered, but did not cry. Phœbe felt herself trembling.

The door closed again. It had been no use going in just then, among these furies. But business was becoming brisk, more men and women came up the stair. The door opened and shut many times. Sometimes, indeed, it was allowed to stand open. Whisky went round freely. They did not bother to turn the key any more. The room was littered with people—stupefied beasts. But still the hag sat on a box by the fire, keeping watch, controlling in some measure her dreadful trade. At first she refused pulls of whisky when they were passed to her. But later Phœbe saw her take one or two.

At last a man came up by himself. Two women greeted him. Each seemed to think him her special property. They began to fight, tearing each other's hair. The room went into an uproar.

Foul bodies were exposed but Phœbe did not see. She was nothing now but an instinct, calculating its chances to snatch. A little, predatory animal, lurking outside in the darkness.

Now in the turmoil she saw what she wanted. The old woman had risen to interpose. In the fight she was thrust screaming against the wall. For the moment Arthur was forgotten. It was lucky he was near the fire. Even in drink they knew to keep away from that. Phœbe slid into the room.

Several times she was crushed by the onlookers as they swayed out of the way of the fighters.

She picked up Arthur and, shielding him as best she might, carried him from the room.

Down the stairs, as quickly as she could. A broken bottle had cut her foot, but she did not feel it. Into the yard. The passage was blocked with people, but she pushed past them. She did not hear their senseless oaths. To them she was merely a slum child carrying another. The pandemonium of the Saturday night Saltmarket was at its height, but she did not notice. Several times she tried to speak to policemen, but their hands were full. They would not stop to listen to this filthy girl with the dirty, white-faced child.

Now she was at the Cross. For an instant she halted. Arthur was very heavy for her. She set him down for a moment to think. She would make along the Trongate until she came to a quiet part. At length she came to Glassford Street and turned up. In Ingram Street it was peaceful. She set down Arthur again. His weight was killing her. For the first time she became aware of her foot. She saw it was bleeding freely.

"Walk, Arthur. Walk with Phœbe." It was the first time she had spoken to him.

But the child merely gave bewildered whimpers and held up his arms.

A policeman passed. She crossed to speak to him, planning to use her usual voice, to tell where she lived, and so prove that she was not what she seemed.

But he turned upon her. "Away hame. Away oot o' this." He had had enough of slum rats and their stories.

There was nothing to do but summon all her strength and try to pick up Arthur. Now she was on the low, flat part of Montrose

Street. Now at George Street. She set him down once more and looked up the hill. How would she ever get him up there?

She stood, leaning against the wall for what seemed an eternity. She made attempts to encourage herself. Had she not done what six policemen had failed to do? Arthur had said that there were places where no respectable man dare show himself. She had dared. But her pulsing head was past encouragement.

They would be so angry with her for going. . . . Still she had had to go for Arthur. . . . She couldn't help it. . . . She had had to go. And now she must just collect herself and try to make Ure Place. She took Arthur by the hand and dragged him. He began to howl, but she paid no attention. At least, she was getting him to walk. Here was Richmond Street. That was half-way. All was dark. Respectable folk were asleep. She sat down with Arthur on a doorstep to gather strength for the last effort. Arthur's little teeth were chattering as he cried, for he was wrapped in nothing but a bit of sacking.

And now the last effort. Up. Up the steepest part of the hill. She must get there even if she went mad. Now the lower side of Ure Place. Everything was dark but their own house. She could see it through the shrubbery that filled the middle of the square. Its windows were blazing. The door was open, too. Restless figures were haunting the threshold. She moved to get a better view. Against the light she saw the shapes of Bel and David.

With a final effort she gathered the remainder of her strength to shout as loudly as she could.

"Bel! Bel!"

In a moment more her brother David had lifted her up from the pavement, senseless.

Chapter Eleven

IT was Christmas Day, an event which was then given little importance by the country folks in Scotland, for New Year's Day was—as indeed, it still is—the winter feast day. It was the towns, less traditional and less grim, that first became infected by the cheerful spirit of the English Christmas.

But on this dark morning the Laigh Farm was an exception to the rule. Its kitchen, at least, was filled with the Christmas spirit. The great fire, re-lit hours ago, flamed red and cheerful, glowing into every corner and defying the frosty, half-hearted daylight outside. The plates stacked on the scrubbed dresser, on the opposite wall, glittered and blinked. And there was holly about. Along the top of the dresser. Up beside the plates that were put there for ornament. In a white jug on the high mantelshelf. Between the pair of china dogs and the pair of tea canisters, bearing portraits of the young Queen and the Prince Consort. Over the large new portrait of the middle-aged Queen, that last summer Phœbe had persuaded Mungo to buy from a traveller at the door—simply because he had looked tired, and had appealed to her feeling for lame ducks. Over the grandfather clock that placidly ticked out the life of the Laigh Farm in another corner. The farm-women called all this holly Phœbe's nonsense. For it was Phœbe, versed now in the customs of the town, who had put it about.

Phœbe was an indulged young lady these days. A cloth was laid over one end of the great scrubbed table and breakfast was laid—still awaiting her august arrival, though it was almost nine o'clock. There were parcels, too, by her plate—Christmas presents from the family in Glasgow.

Jean bustled in from work outside. She was a stout, pleasing figure now, with her glowing cheeks, her coats kilted for work, her drugget apron, and her Annan clogs. She took down a frying-pan from its hook and began to bang about.

"Guidsakes," she said to herself, "is that lassie never up yet?"

She opened a door to call, but was met by Phœbe coming in.

"Good morning, Jean."

"Guid-mornin'. A wis comin' tae look for ye. It's nine o'clock."

"Well, here I am." Phœbe was a little spoilt and pompous, for she had been ill. Her face was still pale a little, and now and then a nervousness in her movements, a haunted look, betrayed the fact that she had passed through an ordeal beyond her strength.

"They things are fur yer Christmas," Jean said, indicating the parcels.

Phœbe, forgetting her dignity, ran to the table. She looked through the parcels and the names of the givers. She had never had so many. Why were they all making such a fuss this Christmas, she wondered. Everybody seemed to want to give her something. All the brothers and sisters. And here was a parcel from Jean and Gracie. Tactfully she opened it first. A box of "Edinburgh Rock", several pink and white sugar mice with string tails, and a little hymn book.

"Oh, Jean, these are lovely!" And the inevitable Scots remonstrance, "You shouldn't have bothered."

"Och, they're jist some bits o' things," Jean said self-consciously as she took Phœbe's porridge from the fire and poured it into a bowl.

"Is Gracie in the milk-house?" Phœbe ran to thank her, and brought her back into the kitchen.

The two devoted women were all eagerness to see the other presents as Phœbe undid them. A beautiful workbox from Bel with wools and canvas for a sofa cushion, already "begun" to indicate the correct colours. Books from Arthur. Indoor games from Sophia and William, and a new book to hold scraps from Wil and Margy. An expensive, handsomely illustrated book of religious stories from Mary and George. A book of quadrilles and lancers and a bottle of scent from David (Phœbe was to spend the remainder of her holiday drenched in this).

The women went into greater raptures than Phœbe did, especially over the coloured wools.

Phœbe sat down to her porridge feeling very important indeed.

As Jean changed her plate, and set her ham and eggs before her, Mungo came in, and the two women left the kitchen. He was still very lame and used crutches. He lowered himself down into his big chair by the fire. His two dogs curled themselves up under the table at Phœbe's feet. She wished him a Merry Christmas, and pointed to her presents.

He smiled good-naturedly. "Aye, ye've done very well." He thrust his hand in his pocket and drew out an envelope. "And that's from me," he said, adding, "Ye see, I couldn't get to buy you anything."

The envelope contained a gold half-sovereign. Phœbe thanked him, pleased but embarrassed.

"That'll do fine for your bank." A rather bleak suggestion, Phœbe thought. But he tempered it by saying: "Unless there's anything particular you're wanting."

Controlling herself, Phœbe said demurely that she thought there might be, but she would keep it and see; then settled down again to her breakfast.

II

"I've got something else here for ye," Mungo said presently, pulling out a neat little parcel and holding it out to his sister. "They said I was to take charge of it and give it to you myself."

Phœbe came across and took it from him. "What is it?"

"Open it and see."

When she had taken off the wrapping-paper she came upon a small cardboard box, bearing upon its lid the name of a well-known Glasgow jeweller. And inside this was a still smaller black-grained box. Phœbe took it out and opened it. There, mounted on a red-velvet mount, was a handsome lady's gold watch, surrounded by coils of fine golden chain and handsomely engraved with the initials "P. M."

She looked bewildered. "Where did this come from?" she asked her brother, who had been sitting watching her.

"Open and see."

She opened it. On the inside were the words: "From Arthur Barrowfield Moorhouse to his Aunt Phœbe. Saturday, 21st November, 1874."

Phœbe said nothing. She turned the watch about, examining

it closely. But her brother could see a deep flush. Bel and Arthur must have bought this for her. At length she put it back into its case, twined the long chain into place, and closed the lid.

"It's a nice watch, isn't it?" Mungo hazarded.

"Yes."

He could not tell what was going on inside her head. She must realise, of course, that the date marked the day on which she had brought her nephew back from Hughie's Yeard. He tried again to make her speak. "Will I keep it safe for ye?"

"Yes." She came over and handed it back to him.

They had all been puzzled, even the comprehending Bel, though the family was, in fact, behaving strictly according to her orders. Phœbe, indeed, was living in the middle of a conspiracy of silence.

When she had come to her senses again on that November Saturday night, she had found herself in her own bed with Sophia and the family doctor standing over her. Sophia, who was holding her hand, smiled when she opened her eyes. "Yes, dearie, it's me."

Phœbe looked about her wildly. "Is Arthur all right?"

"Yes. Yes. His mother's with him. He's all right."

After they had got her clean and made her drink hot milk, she lay restless. The cut in her foot was pulsing. She could smell carbolic. Sophia sat by her watching. "Are you all right now?" she asked presently.

Phœbe turned her head and looked at her sister. "I would like to speak to Bel."

"I'll get her."

Bel came, bent over Phœbe and kissed her. The child could see tears in her eyes. "Do you want to say something to me, Phœbe?"

Phœbe nodded, then raised herself to look about.

Bel, grasping her meaning, reassured her. "It's all right. There's nobody here but ourselves." She shut the door.

"Bel, will you promise to tell nobody where I've been?"

"But, Phœbe, why?" Bel was utterly bewildered.

"You see," Phœbe went on, "I had to get Arthur. The more bad things I saw, the more I knew I had to stay till I could bring Arthur with me."

"Of course, dear. You should be proud. Why not tell people?" But she could not get Phœbe to respond.

"I saw—I saw—" Phœbe's voice trailed off. But her look and her tone opened up vistas.

"Don't tell me what you saw Phœbe, unless, sometime, you feel you want to. We'll all forget about it. I'll tell Arthur. Nobody else. And we'll never talk to you about it again."

Phœbe looked relieved. "Does Sophia know where I've been?" she asked presently.

Bel nodded. "I think perhaps she guessed. But she won't tell anybody either."

These promises seemed to calm her, and it was not long before exhaustion called her into uneasy sleep. Bel stood by her bed wondering. What kind of mark had the experience of the night laid upon the spirit of this strange child whose wilfulness had so often sorely tried her? And now in a burst of mad courage she had paid her back for her trouble a thousandfold, without, it seemed, even realising that she had done it. There was nothing, Bel told herself, that she would not do for Phœbe for bringing back her son safely.

But in the days that followed, the days of getting well, Phœbe continued to puzzle her sister-in-law. She kept imploring Bel to keep people away from her. She would see no one. It was as though the child had submitted to some shame in order to rescue her nephew. A shame which even such a motive could not wipe out.

The little boy, apart from lingering night fears and a bad cold, was very little the worse; but Phœbe's was a much more difficult condition. It seemed, at first, as though the slums had laid their blight upon her. Her round face was pinched, and her steady Celtic-blue eyes seemed almost shifty. If she heard a visitor in the hall below she got out of bed and locked her bedroom door.

Bel and Arthur, passionately anxious now to do their best for her, were at their wits' end. But when the time came for her to be about again it was Phœbe herself who solved their problem.

"Bel," she asked, "am I to go back to school?"

"Not until after Christmas. And only if you feel well enough."

"I would like to go and stay at the Laigh Farm." And then,

scrutinising Bel's smiling and much-relieved face: "You haven't told Mungo, have you?"

Bel continued to smile. Without hesitation she lied to Phœbe, placidly and radiantly. "Of course not. What would I tell Mungo for? I think the Laigh Farm would just be the very place for you."

And so it came that Arthur took her down in a few days' time, cautioning everyone who was likely to come into contact with her against making mention of her exploit.

The entire Moorhouse clan buzzed with talk, of course. Mary agreed that Phœbe had been splendid, but added that no doubt little Arthur would have been quietly turned into the street on the next morning and been little the worse as other children who had been kidnapped for their clothes invariably were. Sophia told Wil and Margy that Phœbe was a heroine, then realising that she had gone too far, refused to say any more and was forced to tell them she would whip them if they kept on asking questions. There were many discussions, too, about Phœbe's curious shame over the episode. Sophia said indiscreetly that she could just imagine what Phœbe must have seen. Mary looked so shocked that Sophia should claim any such powers for her imagination that Sophia squirmed a little and said, "Well—not exactly." At which Mary looked at Bel and said, "We hope not." Then Mary said she thought it would be a good idea if they all three prayed every night that their little sister's soul should be cleansed. Bel nodded a pious acquiescence, but felt in her heart that the air of the Laigh Farm was probably having much the same effect.

III

Jean came back to the kitchen and began to clear away. Phœbe came over and sat herself opposite Mungo. He watched her as she busied herself with the wools and canvas Bel had given her.

"Why are ye taking out the bit that's done already?" he asked presently.

"Because I want to do it my own way."

"But that's to show ye the right colours."

"I want to decide my own colours."

Queer, dour wee thing, with her black hair sternly controlled, her curls pushed back by the large round comb, her wide, braided serge dress spread about her, and her feet crossed on the hassock. There were a lot of things she would want to decide for herself as she grew up.

All at once the dogs got up from beneath the table and began to grumble. "There's somebody coming in. See who it is, Phœbe," he said, regretting his lameness.

She rose and went to the window, looking into the farm close. "It's a lady, with a brown dog, carrying a basket."

"It'll be Miss Ruanthorpe."

"Miss Ruanthorpe of the Big House?"

"Aye." Mungo shifted restlessly in his chair.

"Why is she coming here?"

"She comes often. She'll want me to tell her what to do with some o' her ponies."

In a moment Gracie came back, followed by a lady and a brown spaniel, at which Doon and Nith continued to show fangs, until they had to be ordered from the kitchen. "Here's Miss Ruanthorpe," she said. And Phœbe, with the innocent lynx eyes of a child, saw Jean and Gracie exchange the ghost of a smile.

She was rather an authoritative lady, Phœbe thought, as she took in her strong muddy boots, her rough tweed clothes and her rather mannish hat of the same stuff, skewered to her thick brown hair with several hatpins. Her skin was weather-beaten, but she had fine eyes and flashing teeth.

"Don't get up, Mr. Moorhouse. I haven't come to disturb you. How's the leg? Getting on? That's good. I've just come in to wish you a Merry Christmas."

Phœbe moved to give Miss Ruanthorpe her chair, and herself took the wooden one that Jean had pushed forward.

"So this is the little sister I've been hearing about. A Merry Christmas, my dear. My father has sent you this bottle of Napoleon brandy, Mr. Moorhouse—more than sixty years old—and here are some sweets that cook has been making. We mustn't forget our invalids, must we?"

She settled herself and beamed all around her. She was a queer lady, with her booming voice and her "English" accent, but nice, Phœbe decided, as she opened the package of sweets.

"You see, Sir Charles is English, Phœbe, so that gives us an excuse to hold Christmas, and my mother is Scotch, and so we have to hold New Year too." She laughed amiably.

Queer, reserved little thing, Margaret Ruanthorpe thought, looking at Phœbe. Was she shy? Or was she merely undemonstrative? That she had character and courage, she already knew: for Mungo Moorhouse had told her.

She sat looking about her, laughing and chatting in the glowing friendly kitchen. This only child of the laird and his lady had left a house full of guests because she could not help herself. Christmas Day was merely an excuse to come across and visit the man who sat there with his crutches beside him. She could not keep away. She looked at him now, his face lit up by the firelight. His accident had taken some of the robustness out of it; it was paler than usual, a little thinner and more distinguished. She had heard the legend of the Moorhouse family's beginnings. She could well believe it. Mungo Moorhouse's natural breeding and dignity came from somewhere. He was an honest Ayrshire farmer, but he was neither obsequious nor arrogant; his poise seemed a part of himself.

From time to time, since he had been left alone, he had helped her with her dogs and her ponies. Their friendship had ripened, mostly in and around her father's stables. At first, she had determined to regard him as an agreeable and obliging tenant. But growing feelings would not hide, and she had come to realise that she had started up more than a casual friendship. She had spent many a sleepless night wondering what to do about this handsome forty-year-old bachelor farmer. She kept inventing endless excuses to bring him to her or to come and see him herself. His accident had been a godsend. She was assailed now by the full passions of a woman in her middle thirties desperately in love. His respectful politeness maddened her. Her situation and his made it more difficult. Could there be no way out? If only she had been the man!

Now she was inviting Phœbe to come and spend the day at Duntrafford. But Phœbe looked troubled, and Mungo excused her on account of her illness. It was always the same. Things conspired to baffle her.

"Well, perhaps you'll both come when our guests have gone and we're by ourselves again." She got up. "No, don't, please, Mr. Moorhouse."

But Mungo struggled to his feet, saw her to the door, then hobbled off to talk to his men.

IV

From the kitchen window Phœbe watched Miss Ruanthorpe and her spaniel go out through the back gate. She caught herself wondering vaguely what the smile that had passed between the two farm-women had meant. She must ask them. What was the joke about Miss Ruanthorpe? It couldn't be that she was in love with Mungo, she decided complacently, nor Mungo with her, for she was much too different. Phœbe was still too much of a child and a provincial to realise that even people who had strange, foreign ways might have feelings just like herself.

She gave up thinking about the visitor, and came back to the fire. On the ledge of Mungo's pipe-rack was the case containing her gold watch. Mungo had left it there, forgotten, when he had gone out. She must give it to him to lock up when he came back.

Now that she was alone she could examine it unself-consciously. She took it out, dangled it, looked at its inscription, put the chain about her neck and slipped the watch, where it should be, beneath her belt. She stood up on a chair to examine the effect in a small square of mirror that hung by the window. Having done this she jumped down, and put it carefully back into its case. She looked at it long and thoughtfully before she closed the lid.

So they had considered it worth while to give her that, because of what she had done for Arthur? Even though she had run away to get him without their permission? She tried now, for the first time, deliberately to cast her memory back into the terrors of that night. She had not understood all, but she had understood enough. And her sensibilities, poised between girlhood and womanhood, had received a bewildering shock. But in these quiet weeks at the farm, her firm will, like her strong little body, had already in great measure come to her rescue. Already the pictures of

Hughie's Yeard, the yard itself, the terrible fighting women, the nightmare room where Arthur had been, were becoming unreal—were beginning to haunt her less and less as she lay at night in the darkness. And perhaps in time the strange, unexplained sense of shame would leave her too.

She put the watch-case back where she had found it, and settled down once more with her canvas and her wools. Anyone looking through the window would have seen a rather prim little girl of fourteen sewing as though her life depended upon it, a girl who had seen nothing more than other children of her age.

Phœbe was well on the way to recovery. Now for the first time she dared to return to her habit of detachment—to view herself as the leading figure in what had been a very unpleasant experience—to prod, indeed, her wounds a little, to see just how sensitive they still might be. And as she sat there examining her feelings coolly, a conviction began to form itself. Hughie's Yeard had scared and terrified her. It had sickened and revolted her with named and unnamed horrors. But it had not driven her from her purpose. It had not broken her passionate will. She, Phœbe Moorhouse, had, even at the most terrible moments, managed to be strong.

Chapter Twelve

THERE was little that Margaret Ruanthorpe did not know of the doings at the Laigh Farm. Since, in the middle of January, she had heard that Phœbe was not yet gone back to Glasgow, she determined that Mungo and she should pay their visit to Duntrafford. She announced her intention in a roundabout way to her father and mother as they sat at breakfast.

"Now we've got everybody away, I'm thinking of sending someone over to the Laigh Farm to fetch Mungo Moorhouse to see Jupiter. He's not right yet. He ought to be by now, but he isn't."

Sir Charles looked at his daughter. He was an abrupt old man of seventy-five. "What does Johnstone say?"

His daughter shrugged. "Oh, Johnstone! You know what kind of a vet he is."

Her father reflected. He had an excellent idea of what was in her mind. As a family the Ruanthorpes prided themselves on their lack of subtlety. You said what you thought. You did what you liked. You showed what you felt. And Margaret had shown what she felt about Mungo Moorhouse. He didn't object. When she had been younger he and his wife had thought of her in terms of good marriages and likely young men. And Margaret, not lacking looks, had had such a young man at one time, but he had been killed in a skirmish somewhere out East. And after that she, too, had become a little loud-voiced and abrupt. And she had become louder and more abrupt after her only brother was killed in the hunting-field; an event that had nearly broken the heart of the handsome, tight-lipped woman of seventy sitting at the other end of the table. But they were all tough. Charlie's death had turned poor Lady Ruanthorpe into an austere woman, interested in social conditions. Thus had she managed to go on with life.

"Johnstone isn't bad," she was saying now as she plunged a knife into the corner of an envelope. "He was very good with Pansy when she had distemper. I wish he wouldn't drink so much." Having made this contribution to the breakfast-table conversation, she withdrew the contents of the envelope, flicked it open, and began studying what proved to be a fresh call upon her philanthropy.

Her husband drank his coffee thoughtfully, supporting the cup in his hands, both elbows on the table. No. If his daughter could bring off this strange affair of hers, let her. After all, she was getting on. It didn't matter a curse what the county thought. Damn it, she was a Ruanthorpe, and Ruanthorpes did what they liked. Moorhouse was a fine young man (forty is young to seventy-five), and as straight as you make 'em. She might do much worse. She couldn't have looked anywhere for better, cleaner blood. He was a countryman, and they were country people. Her interests were passionately for the land, and so were his. Good luck to her. But she had better hurry up if she wanted to produce a brood of Ruanthorpe-Moorhouses. And, besides, he didn't want to be too senile to enjoy them. Indeed, the thought of all this warmed you vastly. You wouldn't feel so old and dried up, so discontinuous. If Charlie had lived, of course—still, that was milk spilt long ago now. Sir Charles laid down his cup and looked out of the window. For a moment he saw a young man's set, white face with a streak of crimson oozing slowly over his brow from underneath thick dark hair. For a moment he felt again the agony of trying to tell himself that those eyes that stared up at him were not turning lifeless and glassy, as he held the boy, kneeling there, regardless of the mud in that new-ploughed field. Yes. A brood of children to run about and make a noise before you were too old to care who did what.

"The little sister is still there. A strange kind of child."

"Is that the child who has been ill? Who went into the Glasgow slums?" Lady Ruanthorpe asked, suddenly pricking her ears.

"Yes; I thought I might ask them both to lunch."

"Do. I shall ask her exactly what she saw."

"You can't do that, Mother. It's not allowed."

Lady Ruanthorpe grunted. "Ask her to lunch anyway." She took off her steel spectacles, held them in the light, puffed at them, and rubbed them up firmly with her table napkin, much as her own butler did the spoons. Thereafter she stabbed another letter and was again lost to her family.

II

This time Miss Ruanthorpe persuaded Phœbe to come to Duntrafford. All her life, of course, Phœbe had heard of the people at the Big House, and she had all the awe that still lingered among the country people when they came into contact with the laird and his family. It was strange to her now to find Sir Charles's daughter bothering to be so friendly. There was something canny in Phœbe that put her on her guard against people who were too nice. But Margaret's habitual abruptness breaking through, now and then, her intense desire to please, had the effect, strangely enough, of reassuring her.

The winter-morning drive to Duntrafford was everything that a fine January morning in Ayrshire can be. Farm steadings, crowning rolling hills, shone white in the brief sunshine. Old trees stood up around them, every twig and branch adding to the pattern they made against the duck-egg blue of the sky. Ploughs turning up the long purple-brown furrows, behind the sleek fat buttocks of the giant Clydesdale horses. Seagulls, flapping greedy white wings, following after. On the horizon a piled-up white cloud. Everywhere the smell of the fresh turned earth and rotting leaves—the smell of winter. As they came into the Avenue of the great house, rooks rose from high trees above them. Once there was that heavy scent of a fox.

Miss Ruanthorpe had been wise enough to extract no promise to stay to lunch from either of them, for she knew that Mungo was shy. But when the Moorhouses were driven round to the front of Duntrafford House, unexpectedly—for Mungo thought he was being taken direct to the stables—a man was there with a tray and decanter, and Mungo, unable to refuse, had to take what was offered him, while his sister, bidden to jump down, was taken in charge by Lady Ruanthorpe and led inside to eat cake and drink milk.

Phœbe looked about her. She felt strange, in this great padded room, dangling with tassels, hanging with pictures, and glittering with Indian brass pots filled with hothouse plants. And before her the lady she had so often seen of a Sunday, sitting in the Duntrafford pew in the Big Kirk. Indeed, the very thought of church suggested, in her mind, a musty smell of Bible, coconut matting, a hassock your short legs couldn't comfortably reach, and Lady Ruanthorpe in the front of the gallery. Phœbe didn't believe she was real, that she had an existence elsewhere. When Mr. McMinn the beadle dusted the pew and brushed the cushions, he must surely give Lady Ruanthorpe a dust and a brush-down too. Now here she was sitting in a room at Duntrafford, being given plum-cake and milk by the lady from the front of the gallery. Still she was not quite real to Phœbe. She seemed a creature from another world, but the child realised that in spite of her severe expression, and her formidable old-fashioned iron-grey curls and cap, Lady Ruanthorpe was trying to be kind.

"I'm not taking you out to the stables, Phœbe, because I hear you've been ill," she said.

"I'm quite well now, thank you," Phœbe said demurely. "The doctor said I could go out if I kept warm."

"You'll keep warmer here."

Phœbe was disappointed. She had hoped to see the Duntrafford ponies. She said so a little timidly.

Lady Ruanthorpe smiled. "This won't be your last visit, I hope, my dear. Then you can run about everywhere and see everything."

And so, Phœbe had to stay and talk to this downright lady. She told Phœbe about the dogs and the horses, and insisted that she must come back when it was spring and see the foals and the puppies at the kennels. Phœbe, having formed anew her ideas of what one talked about from Bel, was surprised that the old lady should tell her so much about stud doings. According to her town code it was not ladylike. And yet if Lady Ruanthorpe were not ladylike, who would be?

But the old woman knew that Phœbe was, after all, a daughter of the land and treated her accordingly.

Funny little thing this, with her gentilities of manner, and a slight Glasgow twang in her pleasant voice. Life had written little on her smooth childish face. And yet there was a firmness about her mouth, and her blue eyes were quick. So this was the child who had disappeared for many hours into the worst of the Glasgow slums—the worst in Europe, as she had learnt from missionary pamphlets and special commission reports—and re-emerged triumphant, late in the night, with her stolen three-year-old nephew, safe. What had she done while she was there? What did places like that look like? What had happened? Margaret had said she must not be questioned. Stuff and nonsense. She would ask the child about it now. She was interested in that sort of thing.

It was not extraordinary, perhaps, that an old lady, who counted upon always getting her own way, should ask Phœbe the forbidden question, but it was extraordinary that Phœbe should tell her all the story of her adventure from end to end, answering and amplifying, on being questioned, all that she had already said. When she came to look back on this, as a grown-up woman, she could not explain it to herself. It was not merely that she was well again and able to think of her experiences without nervous revulsion; for when she returned to Arthur and Bel and found that they made no mention of it, she did not attempt to break the taboo. Perhaps it was that Lady Ruanthorpe was nearer reality, was less a creature of her time than Bel. That, somehow, even in the short half-hour Phœbe had known her, she had created about the child an atmosphere of directness—of spades-spadishness—that naturally chimed with Phœbe's own nature; chimed better than the rather stuffy gentility of Ure Place with its polite carefulness. But whatever the reason, there it was. And Phœbe felt much the better for the telling. This odd, over-frank old woman had the effect somehow of a confessor. And when the recital was over and when she seemed to think that what Phœbe had done was not only right but brave, the child felt that something had been washed clean again, that a puzzling inner disarrangement had been set straight. Looking back she was always grateful to Lady Ruanthorpe for inducing her to talk.

III

Their day out was indeed an experience for both the Moorhouses.

Mungo, hobbling about, said his say about Margaret's colt. He looked at the other horses and ponies. He spoke to the grooms whom, in the everyday traffic of the district, he knew well. He had a word for the keeper at the kennels. When he said he must go to find his sister and return home Miss Ruanthorpe laughed and told him that her mother was keeping Phœbe for lunch, and wouldn't he stay too?

There was nothing for it. No way out. He had been brought hither in Sir Charles's gig and could only get back when he was taken. So Mungo and Phœbe found themselves in the large, heavy dining-room of Duntrafford House, lunching with the laird and his ladies.

His bearing was shy, but he was direct and simple. His manner had no gentilities. The talk at the table was entirely within his range. Sir Charles was an eccentric, as many landlords were; for in these not very democratic days they were little kings and behaved accordingly—but on the whole he was a good laird. His interests went with those of his tenants. And so the meal passed for Mungo in a pleasant exchange of familiar ideas, and—although he did not define this—in an atmosphere of respect and flattery to himself.

Phœbe sat through the meal reserved and quiet, collecting, detachedly as usual, many impressions. At last, in the early afternoon, the gig was sent for and they were allowed to think of going home. She was surprised when Miss Ruanthorpe bent down and kissed her as she said goodbye.

Mungo had limped round to the horse's head to have a look at him. Presently he found Margaret Ruanthorpe's hand in his. In a way, they were, for the moment, isolated from the others.

"Goodbye, Mr. Moorhouse." Mungo's strong, farmer's hand, crushing her own, made Margaret a little reckless. She went on, "You will come again soon, won't you? Remember, it will always give me a great deal of pleasure." Her tanned face was scarlet, and the sober farmer's face suddenly caught fire from it. With a little awkward laugh he said goodbye and turned to manœuvre his lameness up into the gig.

On the drive home Mungo Moorhouse sat utterly dumbfounded. Phœbe, and the groom who drove them, wondered why they couldn't get a word out of him. So the laird's daughter was in love with him? There could be no mistaking her meaning! Strange though it may seem the glaring fact had just occurred to this steady, unimaginative man for the first time. He had no vanity to tell him sooner. Now he was thunderstruck!

What was he to think about it? He didn't know. He simply had no idea. He would have to consider a great deal. He was not in love with her. He had never been in love with anybody, really. He was in his fortieth year, and he supposed he had forgotten to fall in love.

And yet—No, he must think about it. Of course, a man was all right up to forty, but after that it was a dreich kind of life with no woman and no bairns about. Why hadn't he thought about it before? Why had he let things go? Now the laird's daughter! And what would the laird think? And would he, Mungo, have to change his way of life? He couldn't do that at his age. No. He would have to think about it. He would have to think about it a great deal—give the matter great consideration!

Chapter Thirteen

IT had taken Bel some time to take stock of things. Arthur the Second, and, even more, Phœbe, had given the household in Ure Place much anxiety and much to think about. By the time the little boy had been nursed back to his cheerful, baby normal, and Phœbe had been dispatched to Mungo at the Laigh Farm, Christmas and New Year were upon her. Presents, black bun, plum-pudding and the pantomime with Sophia's and Mary's children, who were now of an age to enjoy it, had put an end, for a time, to her favourite hobby of planning.

Bel, ever the most advanced, announced that this year the Christmas dinner would be given by herself. Mary McNairn claimed the New Year dinner, after the weakest of protests from Sophia, who remonstrated feebly that her emotionless husband, William, would be terribly disappointed that the family weren't coming to Grafton Square.

This arrangement pleased everybody. It was more fashionable to entertain at Christmas—that pleased Bel. It was old-fashioned and kindly to entertain at the New Year—that pleased Mary. It was nice after having protested suitably to have the trouble and expense of neither—that pleased Sophia.

At this point Bel, determined to have everything up to date, had called in her ally David, who was becoming familiar with the uses of society. He had been to two or three more dances in the intervening weeks—and, most impressive of all, he had been to an evening dinner-party. They had actually dined at seven o'clock! In matters of decoration and dress, David was of the greatest use. For such detail his memory was a dry sponge. Though for business detail—as Arthur had pointed out more than once tartly—his memory was much less absorbent.

And so it came about that Arthur took the head of a restrained and elegant dinner-table on Christmas afternoon, while George presided over an old-fashioned and lavish one at the New Year. And at each Sophia, a little guilty at having got out of everything so easily, privately told the hostess that her dinner was the only one to which she had been looking forward.

It was well into the New Year, then, before Bel could really take time to think. But having at last done so, she found herself perfectly clear about one thing—that the Arthur Moorhouses could not go on living in Ure Place. Her motives this time, she told herself, were altogether reasonable, and had nothing to do with worldly ambition. In other words, it came to this: Ure Place was becoming much too near the slum quarter of the city. The children simply must not again be exposed to the dangers through which little Arthur and Phœbe had passed. Arthur, her husband, must think at once of buying a house out West. She said so to Mary, to Sophia and to her mother; and they, all of them, having no responsibility in the matter, and no reason to contradict her, agreed with her heartily.

She decided, therefore, to open the campaign. The best thing she could do, she felt, would be to make an expedition or two out to Hillhead and Kelvinside, where new terraces were going up steadily; and, having found a suitable house, insist that Arthur should go to see it. He would then be unable to retort—as he had already done—that she would have to find a house first.

But it was to be four years more before Bel succeeded with her stubborn husband. One warm day in February she and old Mrs. Barrowfield made a first expedition Westwards. On the journey out she had felt stuffy and overloaded with clothes, and the familiar enough, horsy smells in the tramcar had made her feel sick. Once arrived, she and her mother had trudged about in the sunshine of the early year, noting the clusters of crocus and snowdrops growing before the high terraces above the Great Western Road; had heard the birds chirping in the Botanic Gardens, the cawing of the rooks in its high trees, seen the sparkle of the sun on the glass of the Kibble Palace, which was one of the newest additions to this fashionable private park. But Bel had felt limp and enthusiasm was lacking. On the way home she was overcome again with nausea, and, once arrived at the tram terminus in St. Vincent Place, she had found herself strangely feeble and had been forced to sit on while they changed the horses to the other end of the tram. When at last she had had to leave, her mother had sent an urchin for a cab, and thus had got her back to Ure Place.

A fortnight later Bel knew that she was going to have another child. During most of the time of the child's coming she was ill, and, indeed, for nearly a year afterwards. Thus her hopes had suffered, if not eclipse, at least delay while she established her own health and the health of the newly arrived Thomas Moorhouse.

Then Arthur struck a bad patch in his business. Not a very bad patch, but bad enough to plunge a solid Victorian household into deep gloom. The book-keeper of Arthur Moorhouse and Company had pocketed the money of a few accounts paid to him and disappeared. Arthur said it was a disaster. It would take years to repair. The household must save in every way possible. And therefore his loyal wife had held her tongue and saved.

But, as time went on, Bel began to notice that Arthur himself was in no way cutting down. He was giving freely to charity. He had joined the Traders' Club. He did not carp at bills. It was difficult to assess Arthur's prosperity for he was anything but personally extravagant. That he should frankly tell the wife of his bosom how they stood for money was, of course, quite unheard of. Yet there seemed always to be money to help outside things.

At last Bel asked David. David replied that Arthur Moorhouse and Company were booming. Even discounting David's congenital optimism she must believe him.

And so once more the push Westwards began.

II

Bel had hoped to enlist Phœbe's help as she grew up—she was nearly eighteen now—but Phœbe continued in her strange detachment. She was, indeed, ready to believe that Phœbe had come to like herself and the family at Ure Place. Had she not—well over three years ago—shown amazing devotion in rescuing little Arthur? And had she not in return been overwhelmed with the family's affection and consideration, to an extent that would have drawn love from a stone? But—well, you just had to take Phœbe's affections on trust, and that must be the end of it.

The girl went about quietly, living her own life. Her school-days had come to an end, but she had some small talent for drawing, and embroidery. She studied music with a master, but made little of it. For the rest, her days were spent learning to dressmake, to cook, to dust—to learn, in short, to be the head of that household of her own which every young lady was then taught to expect. When Bel had tried to fire her with enthusiasm over the prospect of a new home in a fashionable quarter, Phœbe had gone no further than saying that it would be very nice, then seemed immediately to lose interest. Bel sighed and decided to fight the battle alone.

At first Arthur confronted her with all the usual retorts. Had she been unhappy here she was?

No. She could not say she had been. But the character of the locality was now changing.

Did she not realise that a man had to be near his work?

There were endless trams running West now. He could come and go in no time.

Did she not realise that everything would be more expensive out there—schools, and shops and everything else?

She replied that if they were dearer they would be better. And in any case such things, when a man could afford them, were not to be set against the benefit to his family.

And so it went on. Such bouts usually being wound up by Arthur declaring with finality that at any rate he could not afford it, so not to worry him.

Bel had to be content with promising herself that she would return to the attack later.

III

But suddenly, on the same day, two things happened. One sent Bel into a fit of hot rebellion. The other she did not even hear about. But both combined to be decisive.

It was again a bright, early spring morning when Sophia bounced in upon her.

"Good morning, Bel dear. What do you think has happened?"

"Good morning, Sophia. What?"

"I've suddenly decided to move out West!"

"I've been decided for a long time, Sophia; that hasn't helped me much, but—"

"Oh, but we've got a house!"

"You, what?" This was really too much!

"Yes, North Woodside Road! The first terrace there, Rosebery Terrace. Overlooking the Kelvin at the bridge. Facing west and everything! They're talking of rebuilding Kelvin Bridge. And I wondered if that would make dust and mess, but both Wil and Margy insist it would be so interesting. Just like children, isn't it? And then it's splendid for the children getting to school. Nothing for Margy to go to the Park School in Lyndoch Street. And the new Glasgow Academy is to be across the bridge, just opposite, for Wil!"

Bel was thankful that Sophia babbled on. It gave her time to hide her intense chagrin. She had had no idea that William and Sophia had wanted to go Westward too. Probably she herself, with all her talk, had put it into their heads! Bel looked at Sophia's thick, rather untidy, forty-year-old figure—and hated her.

The other thing happened to Arthur. That same morning he stepped over from the Candleriggs to the Traders' Club where he had an appointment with an important business acquaintance. Their affair finished, they remained to smoke and talk, for Arthur felt he could not, at once, leave anyone of such consequence. And presently someone of yet greater consequence hailed them, and asked permission to smoke his pipe beside them.

"You know Moorhouse, Sir William?"

"Fine. Fine."

Sir William was genial. He set his tall hat, upside down, on the carpet beside him, sat down heavily with his feet stuck out in front of him, his fat hands with the gold signet ring folded over his stomach, his bland face and several layers of clean-shaven chin framed all round by grey bushy hair, and began to suck his carved Viennese meerschaum steadily.

He talked at them continuously, waiting for no replies. Of business. Of the Stock Exchange. Of City Improvements. Of Lord

Beaconsfield. Of Russia and the Turks. Then he talked of his garden in Kelvinside, and what his gardener was doing about spring planting. Finally, having sucked his pipe to the end, he got up, lifted his top hat, and put his meerschaum back into his pocket.

"Well, I've enjoyed my crack. Good-day. Where are ye staying now, Moorhouse?"

Arthur actually felt a little ashamed to have to say Ure Place.

"Tuts! Get out o' there. Bring yer missis and the bairns out my way. The centre of the town's no place to bring up a family. It's time a solid young man like you had a house that gave you some standing."

And following on these words, Sir William's fat legs and square feet tripped their way among spittoons and leather chairs across the Turkey carpet and out through the double doors.

IV

As he made his way up the hill for his midday meal, Arthur was given over to reflection. When Sir William had called him solid he had referred to his bank account, not to his body. And as for being young, well, he was now forty-one—and though he sometimes felt less, he usually felt much more. At all events, Arthur was flattered by the attentions of the great and the rich, as embodied in the square figure of Sir William. And he was respectfully impressed by his advice. This might, then, be just the time for him to move. It would not be overstretching prudence—and it would vastly please Bel. He thought of his wife now with affection. Indeed, he had seldom done anything else, in spite of having opposed her dearest wish for many years. Yes. She was a fine girl, Bel. At thirty-two she was a grand, upstanding woman fit to grace any fine house. He must think of some way of hauling down his flag over this business of moving out West—of some way which would be dignified and not look too much like capitulation.

But Bel made the matter easy for him. For he found her in their bedroom weeping bitterly, face down on the bed.

This was terrible. Arthur had not the faintest idea what to do about it. He was quite unused to Bel making him scenes. This was something quite new. His wife, he had often said with pride, was the steadier of the two of them. Her nature was strong and dependable. He jumped to the worst conclusions. Disaster might have befallen the household. Was it one of the children? Phœbe?

He went over and laid his hand on her shoulder. "Bel! What's wrong with ye, my dear?"

He received no reply. Bel continued to sob bitterly.

He tried to force her to turn her head, but instead she sat up and looked at him. Suddenly it was borne in upon him that his pleasant, even-tempered wife had become, for once, a flaming fury.

The story of Sophia's visit and her new house out West was flung at Arthur with a force that took him quite by surprise. So the Butters were to have a new house? It had even got through *their* thick heads that they were living in a ridiculous part of the town. It had been all very well living here, even eight years ago. Glasgow was smaller. But now there were modern tramcars running in every direction with the speed of the wind! You could get to the pleasant outlying parts in no time. And now the Butters! Where would Sophia Butter have been if Arthur hadn't brought her to Glasgow and turned her into a lady? Washing out milkpans in the Laigh Farm milk-house. And Mary too? And David—who was for that matter already in lodgings near the University. Arthur seemed willing enough to do everything for his brother and sisters. It was time he thought about his wife and children.

Arthur bore the storm with a very good show of patience and lordly toleration. He was grateful to his wife. For he saw that she had put him into the exactly right position in relation to herself.

"Calm yourself, Bel. Calm yourself. And listen to what I've got to say to ye."

For a reply Bel threw herself down on the bed again, and went on howling.

Arthur contemplated her back for a few moments, then addressed her once more: "It may surprise ye to know that I was just thinking about a new house as I was coming up the brae."

The sobbing diminished a little.

"Ye see, I was looking at the books this morning, and I find that the last year has not been so very bad. I know ye've had the idea in your head for some time, my dear, but I haven't been just able to see my way."

Bel sat up again, still weeping, and asked her husband if he really meant that. Her husband assured her that he did. After all, the little story about the books wasn't much—even for an elder of the Ramshorn. Besides, if it came to that, he was an excellent merchant, and knew fairly well the position of his business from day to day.

Bel sobbed a little longer. Indeed the impetus was such that she had to have time to let it die down. But now her husband was sitting on the bed beside her, his arm lovingly about her as though they weren't married at all. And she was going to have her new house. And she was feeling very happy. And surely it would be bigger and grander than anything William Butter could afford. And she might even be into it before Sophia was into hers. And, anyway, it would be very much prettier, for Sophia had terribly bad taste.

Thus Mr. and Mrs. Arthur Moorhouse sat together on the edge of their humdrum marriage bed, enjoying the amazing tranquillity of a quarrel just made up. Tender and gentle towards each other, as they had been when they had sat together on the edge of another bed, some nine years before, a newly married pair, come to spend their honeymoon at the Bridge of Allan.

It was Sarah who, all unwittingly, brought these raptures to an end by ringing the dinner-bell loudly in the hall downstairs, and thereafter coming upstairs to the middle landing and shouting on Arthur the Second and Isabel to hurry down, while she looked to the baby.

V

But Bel's day of pleasure was by no means ended. For after the meal, her husband, having looked out of the dining-room window, and having seen that it was going to be a fine afternoon, told his wife to get on her things, because—since he would not have much business to do this afternoon—they might as well take the green car out Hillhead and Kelvinside way and have a look round.

And so the part of the town that was to know them for so many years to come took note, perhaps for the first time, of a lean, distinguished man, clean-shaven but for his greying side-whiskers, discreetly dressed, with his black frock-coat, his grey waistcoat, his black bow tie and his shining tall hat. And on his arm a handsome woman in her early thirties, with a good, maturing figure in a well-fitting bodice and flowing skirt. A smart hat with a piece of white veiling falling elegantly behind set on a fine, fair head. A mouth whose continual smile betrayed dazzling white teeth, and fine eyes that looked steadily about her.

They had come, these two, to find their new home, and they found it in Grosvenor Terrace. A Victorian row, "commanding a beautiful view of the brilliant parterres of the Botanic Gardens, with the umbrageous woods of Kelvinside beyond", set back from the placid, easy-going traffic of a Great Western Road, where once in a while a green car rattled past on its way to and from Kirklee; where handsome equipages with their freights of silks and parasols glittered by on fine afternoons; the solemn, liveried flunkies, sitting high above the spanking horses as they flew past brave, new terraces, built of the famous Giffnock stone—cream coloured, and not yet blackened by the smoke of the encroaching city; where milk-carts jingled in the early morning, as they came from the country or passed back in the forenoons out to the green farmlands that lay so near at hand. A Great Western Road, where there was a good deal of mud in winter; and where—in the autumn—fallen leaves lay thick.

It was settled very quickly. Almost that afternoon. For Bel knew that when Arthur had set his heart on something he would not halt until he had got it. And if he wanted this dignified terrace house with the For Sale board, he would do everything, that prudence allowed him, to obtain it.

She was so sure, indeed, that as their tramcar crossed over Kelvin Bridge on its way back to the City, and she looked at the house her sister-in-law would occupy, she felt she could afford to say to Arthur that that was where poor Sophia was going to be, that it was a pity they hadn't found somewhere nicer, for, after all, it *was* the wrong side of the bridge. But that, at any rate, it was nice to think that the families would go on being near each other.

Arthur, well pleased with himself and his wife, merely contented himself by smiling a vague smile of approval. And when he felt the pressure of Bel's hand, as he sat ruminating behind the trotting horses, he thought of his morning encounter at the Club, and decided it would be better, on the whole, not to mention even such august and flattering advice as Sir William's, but to let her think that the decisions of the day had had their source only in his deep affection for herself.

Chapter Fourteen

ALTHOUGH the house in Grosvenor Terrace came to be theirs in February, it was May before Bel and her family moved into it. For anyone so house-proud as Mrs. Arthur Moorhouse a shorter time than this would have been utterly impossible. The house had been bought from wealthy owners, and was in excellent condition. Most of the paint, even, was fresh. But all its four floors had to be painted anew, from the children's flat beneath the slates to the maids' basement bedrooms. As Bel said, "We can't have the name of going into a house that isn't perfectly fresh, can we?" And then there were endless discussions over furniture. They couldn't have furniture that would make a fool of them. Everything must have the label solid or good. The word beautiful was not often uttered.

Arthur and Bel were at one in this. Their house must be a complete expression of their stability of outlook and circumstance. A house in the West End of Glasgow of that time need not be lightsome or gay, but it must be substantial. Or what would all the other people think? All the other people who were sitting round conventionally in similar houses, wondering, in turn, what people thought of them. All of them equally determined not to be thought arty or trashy.

Bel toiled ceaselessly. It was not all pleasure, by any means. She was haunted by the fear that what she bought or what she had decided to take with her from Ure Place might be considered vulgar. And the Arthur Moorhouses mustn't have the name of being vulgar. She spent a night entirely sleepless over a walnut china cabinet that had cost much, and that Arthur had decided was a very handsome piece and would just make their drawing-room. She had not been too sure of it at the time, and now that it stood in its place she had just discovered a thin line of gilded metal inlay. Was that bad taste? What would people say?

Phœbe noticed that Bel was worried. At breakfast she asked the reason.

"It's about that drawing-room cabinet, Phœbe, I'm not sure if I like it. And it's about the most expensive thing we've bought."

"I think it's beautiful," Phœbe said, more to reassure her than because she had bothered to think about it.

Bel did not say any more. Phœbe's opinion was of no value, she considered.

Phœbe, really, was perfectly aware of this. But as her sister-in-law went on looking worried to death, she decided to drop down to the warehouse to see David.

David was a creature of great distinction now. Even in an old office jacket he had the art of looking quite special. Sometimes Arthur felt proud of David's appearance, at other times his younger brother's cool svelteness maddened him. But, on the whole, David had now shaken into a niche in Arthur Moorhouse and Company, and was quite a good businessman. He had stood so long in awe of Arthur and been so much forced into regular habits and methodical ways, that his own rather weak character had settled into quite a creditable groove. In other words, Arthur the downright had been the making of this aristocatic young man.

David looked at Phœbe. He hadn't seen her for some time. As a connoisseur he was delighted to note how slender and elegant his eighteen-year-old sister had become.

"Hello, Phœbe, how are you? What have you come down about?"

"David, I want you to help me with Bel."

"Why? Is she ill?"

"No, but she will be if you don't do something. Could you possibly drop in to Grosvenor Terrace and have a look at the china cupboard in the drawing-room? Tell her how beautiful you think it is. That you admire her taste. And that your friend Mrs. Hayburn has got one exactly like it."

"But that's probably not true."

"Never mind. If you don't do what I tell you, Bel won't be fit to live with. Remember you're the swell of the family. She thinks you know all about these things."

David accepted this statement without remonstrance. In the main he agreed with it, though he felt Phœbe was perhaps getting blunt a bit as she grew up. However, he did as she asked him.

He met Bel in the new house as though by chance, raised the cabinet extravagantly, and told her that his friend Stephen Hayburn's mother had one very like it. Thus Bel was successfully guided past yet another crisis.

David was not particularly enthusiastic about his family's coming out West. For some years now he had himself been in rooms near the University, where he conducted his discreet and highly selective bachelor existence. Indeed David was now one of the most respectable of young men. His early visits to music-halls and free-and-easies had merely been to him a reaching away from the humdrum. Grandeur was now his one hobby. No. He felt that his comings and goings might be watched over by the family rather more than he cared about. Not that he had anything to hide except, perhaps, a few conceits of dress—a few little affectations of manner, which he had the sense to shed each morning on his way to the Candleriggs. Still, he would be only one of the Moorhouses shortly, not the unique and special Mr. David Moorhouse. For he had, by this time, quite lived down cheese. The portrait he had constructed of himself might suffer a little alteration here and there from having the others about. But he was, of course, too honestly fond of them to be anything more than a little apprehensive. Even a snob has his moments, when it is pleasant to sit with his mental waistcoat unbuttoned in the warm company of relatives who love him, even though these may be quite indifferent to the altitudes to which he has soared.

II

Phœbe's attitude to the removal annoyed Bel a little. She kept on being so remote about it. It was not that she was unhelpful—far from it. She was forever in and out of shops. Running errands. Matching hangings with carpets, chair stuffs with hangings—this with that. But through it all her aloofness persisted. What was the girl thinking? Was she laughing a little? When Bel said how nice it was going to be for them all, Phœbe would smile and agree how good it would be for the children to be near the country. The word "nice" was never off Bel's tongue these days, she simply couldn't get rid of it. And yet when she used it in Phœbe's presence she always felt self-conscious. Couldn't the child see that she was taking a step up socially, just at the time in her life when such a thing was most important to her?

Yet another annoying thing. She seemed just as interested in Sophia Butter's removal as in the change of her own home. She spent whole days, when Bel did not need her, sewing and making for Sophia. Sophia's plans, like all the rest of her, were in a perpetual muddle. And muddles—especially other people's—can be cheerful things. People who are in a state of confusion usually allow their helpers to do what they like. And Phœbe being strong-minded and clear-headed did exactly what she liked. While the most august of painters' men were applying the very best of paint from garret to basement of the house in Grosvenor Terrace, Phœbe spent several blissful days with paint all over her hair, applying it at random to rooms that didn't matter—such as the maid's room and the children's bedrooms at Sophia's. She did not show much skill, perhaps, but the work was done amid peals of laughter.

But on most counts Sophia's removal at the same time as her own was a blessing to Bel. For one thing it was the lever that had, at last, dislodged Arthur from Ure Place or so Bel believed. For another, now that things were in train, it gave her a continual sense of her own superiority in matters of taste and generalship. And for yet another, although she would not admit it even to herself, Bel was a little timid of her new surroundings, and it gave her a feeling of support that her silly, warm-hearted sister-in-law was to be near at hand.

At this time scarcely anybody remembered the existence of the McNairns. Mary's attitude to these upheavals was, throughout, one of indifference. She had no wish, she confided to her husband, to live further West than Charing Cross. It was essential, she said, for children to spend all their growing-up days in one house. It stamped them with the right feeling of permanency. George McNairn agreed—not having bothered much to understand what she meant. But the word "permanency" was very much in the air and greatly approved of in these days, so George felt that, without unduly agitating his fast-congealing brain, he could agree with his wife wholeheartedly.

George and Mary McNairn had put on weight in the last year or two. George, a fully-fledged baillie now, pursued his platitudinous way greatly respected. Respect, indeed, kept accruing to his character in much the same ratio as fat kept accruing to his waistline. Nor was his wife a skeleton. Her hands were as white, her face was as smooth, her features as good as ever. But none of these could any longer escape the charge of being chubby. Mary kept a good table—and that not merely as a demonstration to the world of her prosperity. The McNairns all liked their victuals. There were twin four-year-old girls now, in addition to Georgie and Jackie, and these likewise, especially the babies, were more than comfortably padded.

George and Mary were on excellent terms with everybody. They were too complacent to quarrel. And they did not see much of their relatives now. The house in Albany Place was pleasant enough if you were really hungry and wanted a square meal well cooked. But if you were in search of spirited talk, then it was a place rather to be avoided. Shafts of wit seemed to bounce on impervious cushions of platitude and to return to you like boomerangs bearing the label "silly". The McNairns indeed were kindly enough. But they did not make you feel a success. There was, too, an atmosphere of don't-tell-about-yourself-listen-about-me, which, to say the least, was defeating. In other words, they were just dull.

On the first Friday of May, Sophia moved out. Wil and Margy were given a holiday from school to help, and it was a day of blissful picnicking amid incredible confusion. A meal eaten on Oberon's bank of wild thyme would have given them nothing like the rapture they got from sitting with Phœbe, dangling their legs from a newly-arrived kitchen table, surrounded by straw, packing-sheets, old newspapers and the remains of Phœbe's paint pots, eating sandwiches. The rush of talk that came from the lips of their over-excited mother was no less constant than the rush of the waters of the River Kelvin as it fled through the bridge that spanned the gap that lay before their front door. It was, indeed, a great affliction to get themselves tolerably clean and go down in the evening to Albany Place to their Aunt Mary who had risen to the occasion and had invited everyone, no matter in what condition, to come and have a good filling meal. Later on

David looked elegantly in and asked if he could be of use, but he looked so frail and impeccable that Phœbe told him no, and sent him away again—much to his relief; though he felt a little worried in case the young woman before him with a black smudge on her face should be growing up too unconventionally. For she would, sooner or later now, have to be presented to his friends.

III

But he need not have worried. The next time he saw her she was cool, immaculate and lovelier than ever he had seen her before.

It was on a perfect Sunday afternoon in the latter half of May. He had eaten his midday meal with the Hayburns. It was warm for the time of the year in Scotland, and on Stephen's proposal, he and the two brothers dragged wicker chairs out into the garden. All three young men spent the early part of the afternoon drowsing. At last Henry stirred his loose-boned frame—grown bigger and more mature, but much as it was four years back when David had first known him—and proposed that they should go and have a look at the great hot-houses in the Botanic Gardens which were then being reconstructed. Stephen was still too sleepy, but David, always polite, agreed to go.

The Botanic Gardens of Glasgow were then owned by a private company of select gentlemen. On Sundays only these shareholders and their friends had the right of a key to their paradise of privilege. And thus on this balmy, indolent afternoon David and Henry found themselves strolling around beds of late spring flowers, among bursting pale green leaves, past rare trees covered with blossom. Clumps of common lilac hung heavy with perfume. It was pleasant to raise a beige top-hat to girls you knew, as they went by wearing spring dresses frothing with frills that had, perhaps, been taken from their boxes for the first time this very day.

As usual Henry was talking about himself—his plans for Hayburn and Company—his work. His pug face was all animation. David knew him well now, and he realised that a mere show of interest was all that was necessary. You need not worry unduly about Henry. He was a bit of a genius—and geniuses, it seemed, were intense people who talked overmuch about themselves and their interests. On an afternoon like this you could dream along casually, feeling pleased with yourself—the flowers and the sunshine, the spring, and your own elegance. Henry's talk did not do much more to David than the buzzing of the one or two early bumble-bees.

But suddenly Henry received a resounding clap on the shoulder. Both young men spun round. It was Sir William, Arthur's friend of the Traders' Club, and with him, much to David's surprise, were Arthur and Phœbe. He knew they had just moved in, but had seen nothing of them. He had not expected they would be out and about yet awhile. He ought to have known that Bel, when she did come to move, would advance in perfect order—that the thing would be done with the minimum of fuss or inconvenience to her household. And so, on this their very first Sunday, they were in the Gardens, sunning themselves under the tutelage of Sir William, who had met them by chance at the gates.

David was delighted with the encounter. He knew Sir William by sight, of course, and it was most gratifying to be able to exhibit his sister and brother under such august wings. And there was no denying that they did him credit. Today, feeling the weight of his new possessions, perhaps, Arthur presented an appearance that was gaunt, distinguished, and very unvulgar. And as for Phœbe, he had never seen her like this before. Her dress of fine grey stuff lay with extreme elegance to a figure that spoke at once of girlishness and maturity. Her close-drawn waist was small and flexible, and its grace was accentuated by the suggestion of a bustle. A fashionably small hat was set on her small graceful head. Eyes, strangely set and devastating, looked out on the beauty of the spring from under a straight-cut fringe.

"So this is a Moorhouse, too," Sir William was asking. "You talk to the young lady, Henry, and I'll see what this young man's got in him."

So David had to submit to a genial examination, and Phœbe was left to Henry Hayburn.

Queer excitable young man this friend of David's, Phœbe thought, as she sauntered along, beneath her parasol, at Henry's side. There was an attraction about his odd face with its young black beard. She noted, too, his gesticulating engineer's hands. She guessed his age to be about twenty-three or twenty-four. But, good gracious, couldn't the creature stop talking? He was telling her all about himself at an incredible rate. He didn't make you feel of much importance. She tried to stop him once or twice—to draw his attention to some of the beauty about him—but he gave her only the attention of an instant, then off he went again. What he said was not stupid, she had no doubt, but there was so much of it! She had heard that one of the Hayburns was very clever, and she began to wonder if this were he. She came to the conclusion that it must be; he was so peculiar.

At last there was a shout from behind from Sir William. She held out her hand. "Goodbye, Mr. Hayburn!"

Strange creature. His face fell as though he were a puppy that had been whipped.

"Oh, goodbye, Miss Moorhouse. I've enjoyed our talk tremendously." Then, perhaps because he saw a flicker in Phœbe's eyes, "Look here, I've been doing all the talking."

He looked so ridiculously like a little boy that had been scolded that Phœbe found herself feeling sorry for him. "Not at all, Mr. Hayburn, I put a word in here and there, you know."

"Now you're laughing at me."

"Nonsense."

"Shall I see you again sometime?"

"I suppose so. We've just come to Grosvenor Terrace, you know."

All Henry said to this was "Goodbye", then he turned and trotted off after David as though David were his nursemaid.

Chapter Fifteen

MRS. ARTHUR MOORHOUSE was vastly proud of her new house. It was a source of endless delight to "have things just so", as she expressed it. When Mary and Sophia called during the first days to ask how things were going and to offer help, she was careful that they should not see too much, for she was determined to have a house-warming and to let the full and finished effect burst upon them. She mentioned her plan to Sophia, who was delighted.

"What a good idea, Bel! You see, your house is so much bigger and grander than mine, that a house-warming out here will do beautifully for both of us. But, of course, you must let William and me help with the expense."

There was, perhaps, a trace of coldness in Bel's voice as she thanked Sophia for her offer. Arthur, she said, would no doubt want to provide all the entertainment himself.

Sophia as only too prompt in replying genially that—oh, well, she dared say he would. That the notion had just then come into her head—she hadn't really thought it out. But anyway a house-warming at Grosvenor Terrace would be lovely for everybody.

There was no further talk of entertainment on her own part, either jointly or independently.

But Bel's entertainment was not to happen for a week or two. By then she would have time to draw her breath, everything would have found its place, and the last french polisher would have given the last inch of mahogany its final rub. She hoped to invite everybody—even the enigmatic and seldom-to-be-met-with Mungo.

For in the last years Mungo had certainly become both of these things. Bel couldn't make him out. He was turning into a different kind of person. It was only at New Year time that Mungo could be counted upon to make his appearance. And last New Year she had noticed a very marked change in him. To the rest of the family he was the same old Mungo, with his sturdy farmer's ways—and his slow Ayrshire voice. And he still seemed not to know, quite, how to behave towards herself and his own sisters. But there were several odd things about him. You would have thought that a bachelor living by himself with no one to tend him would have become more careless in his ways, to show more of the recluse in his manner. But the exact reverse had happened. He seemed to have gained a quiet authority. He still wore the rough clothes of a farmer, but they were well made and unslovenly. His linen, now, was always spotless and of a finer quality than before. And—a detail that she noticed specially—his flat farmer's hands were always clean, and though he still kept his nails cropped, they were neither broken nor in mourning. And yet you couldn't quite put your finger on the real difference. Perhaps it was that Mungo was behaving much more as though he were a person of some consequence in his own circle. But what kind of consequence? What more was Mungo now than he ever was? A bachelor farmer who was prospering. Phœbe, who went most often to the Laigh Farm, reported that things were much as usual. But Phœbe was the worst gossip in the world. She seemed to notice nothing. Perhaps Mungo went about a bit more, that was all. He had taken to breeding a pony or two. The common interest of pony breeding took him, it seemed, to the stables of Duntrafford, and even, sometimes, she had heard, to meals in Duntrafford House. But surely, Bel pondered, there could be no equal friendship between the laird and his tenant. And the shy Mungo was the last person in the world to try to force himself into a friendship above his station. No. Her own husband and David might, in their way, be ascending the social ladder, but when all was said, and whatever change was taking place in Mungo, he would always remain just a plain Ayrshire farmer, without frills.

And frills were the things that counted with Bel. Frills. Any amount of them. A grand house expensively, solidly furnished. A financially solid husband, who went to a financially solid business—it was more genteel not to specify what kind of business—every morning in order to provide more frills. Clothes made by the best dressmaker. Well-fed children at the best local school taking all the extras, getting all the frills. Good, solid accounts in equally solid banks. Accounts that were never, never drawn to their limit. Seats in a well-built Victorian-Gothic church, where the minister delivered splendid sermons that told you where the unfortunates went who weren't as honest and solid as yourself.

One regret she had, and that was that her mother, Mrs. Barrowfield, was left by herself in Monteith Row in the middle of the city. She was as snug and comfortable and—but for occasional attacks of rheumatism—as hearty as ever; but it was bleak for her, Bel felt, to have her only daughter the better part of an hour away from her instead of ten minutes. She never said so, and she was vastly proud of her daughter's fine house, and additional consequence—but she was now a lonely old woman. Bel knew it, and forced herself to make many a trip into town when she would gladly have rested.

As time went on she was to have great reason to be grateful to Phœbe, who, strangely, had always been a favourite with the old lady. There was a downrightness about both of them that seemed to find an echo each in the other. Mrs. Barrowfield's pre-Victorian outlook pleased the young girl. Phœbe found she could talk to Bel's mother with less reserve than she must use with Bel. The old late-Georgian seemed to meet her on a commoner ground. At the time, too, Mrs. Barrowfield had been greatly stirred by the Hughie's Yeard incident. Had her eldest grandson been any child she would still have applauded Phœbe's smeddom, as she called it, for she accounted courage the first virtue. But that the girl should have rescued her own eldest and quite special grandson was enough to place her on a pedestal for ever. And so it came about that Phœbe paid many visits to Monteith Row in Bel's place, and always found a warm welcome.

II

On the Friday evening following his chance meeting with Phœbe in the Botanic Gardens, David came to call at Grosvenor Terrace. Phœbe ran down into a nearly completed drawing-room, smelling of furniture polish, to find him with Bel in conversation which, however, stopped when she came in. For a moment, as she greeted her brother, she thought she detected a glint of intrigue in Bel's eye, a glint she was well used to, for Bel was by nature an intriguer.

"Hello, Phœbe," David said, looking approvingly at his—there was only one word for it now—lovely young sister. He bent down and kissed her solemnly.

"Peculiar young man you had with you on Sunday," Phœbe said.

"Henry Hayburn? Why peculiar?"

"He seemed very excited."

"Perhaps he was," David said, then he seemed to think better of this and added, "No, I don't suppose he was any more than usual. He's a great talker, Henry. What did he talk about?"

"Himself."

David laughed. "He's not really conceited," he said.

"I didn't think he was."

"David says the Hayburns are very rich," Bel said. She was sewing rings on a curtain.

"Then he ought to buy himself a suit of clothes that fits him."

"Didn't you like the young man, Phœbe?" Bel's head was bent. She was stitching diligently.

"Yes. Quite. Why?"

"Oh, I don't know. You seemed—well—David says he's brilliant."

"Yes, I've heard all that," Phœbe stood up again, and, crossing to the window, looked out. The new green leaves of the trees on either side of the Great Western Road looked so virgin, so tender that, for a moment, they laid the restlessness of the spring upon her. The street lamps were already lit, although it was not yet dark. Two hansoms, one following the other, raced past towards the City. A young workman and his girl went by laughing. She watched them until they were gone. People were out and about—doing things. She sighed and came back to Bel and David. "What a beautiful night it is! It makes me homesick for the Laigh Farm. I would like to go for a walk in the country."

"It's just what I've come to ask you to do," David said. "But not tonight. Tomorrow afternoon."

"I can't go tomorrow afternoon. I'm taking little Arthur to see the animals at Balgray Farm. I've promised."

"The children are going to their Granny tomorrow," Bel said firmly. "They haven't been to see her since we flitted."

This was the first Phœbe had heard of the arrangement, which, she thought, was strange. And it was new for David to be troubling about her. Still, perhaps, it was natural. "All right," she said, "I'll come."

And so it came about that she found herself setting out on the following afternoon.

III

They took the right-of-way known as the "Khyber Pass" that skirted the west side of the Botanic Gardens and served as a short cut from the Great Western Road through to the Three-Tree Well and the wooded banks of the River Kelvin. There were mills here and there at the water's edge, but the gorge of the Kelvin was still beautiful in parts, though building to the north was in progress. The little industrial village of Maryhill had not yet crept down to the edge of the wooded gulf.

David proposed that they should follow round until they came to the high aqueduct which carries the waters of the Forth and Clyde Canal across the valley of the Kelvin. The great water-bridge and the chain of locks were, he said, things to be seen. Phœbe was very willing to follow.

It was a surprise to her, however, to find Henry Hayburn and a young man, whom she took to be his brother, hanging over the parapet of the Canal Bridge idly looking about them. For a moment she wondered if David had arranged a meeting with these two young men—then she dismissed the idea. Why should he?

"Hello, fellows," he was saying, now that they were within earshot. "Out enjoying yourselves? Phœbe, this is Stephen Hayburn."

Stephen Hayburn was as carefully dressed as his brother Henry was the reverse. He wore fashionable English flannels and a straw boater. In his sporting tie was fixed a gold horseshoe, and he had an eyeglass. Henry gave the impression of being dressed in any old thing.

He flushed as he greeted Phœbe, hat in hand. Stephen's manner was controlled and elegant. He adjusted his eyeglass and tugged at his drooping fair moustache as he greeted her amiably, and said suitable things about his delight at getting to know David's sister. But his eye kept running over Phœbe appraisingly as he talked. She decided that she liked Henry better, stuttering and boyish though he might be.

Which way were they going? David asked.

They had planned to have look at the locks, then return across the aqueduct upon which they now stood, follow the tow-path for a bit, turn up over the hill and eventually come to the Great Western Road again at North Balgray Farm. They would be pleased if Miss Moorhouse and David would walk with them, if it were not too far.

Phœbe assured them that she was well used to long walks in Ayrshire, and so they moved up towards the locks. Stephen and David went in front, while Henry followed with Phœbe.

Phœbe, in so far as she must choose one or other of the Hayburns, was best pleased with this arrangement. She would have been glad merely to continue her walk with David and let the brothers take their separate way. But all three men seemed determined that they should return home together.

If Henry had spoken overmuch at their first meeting, now he did the reverse. It was left to herself to make desultory conversation as they went along. Now and then she exclaimed at the canal—what a labour it must have been to cut it right across Scotland—building waterways across deep gulleys such as the one they had just crossed. She exclaimed at passing ships. Barges carrying coal or wood to the City woodyards, towed by little smoky tugs. At the Maryhill locks they stayed behind to see a boat go up through, for Phœbe had never seen such as this happen before.

And during all these happenings Henry continued to say little. Now and then he would explain a point to her—usually in highly technical language—as one engineer to another, using terms that Phœbe couldn't possibly know. The working of a tug's steam-engine. The principle of the rise and fall of water in a canal lock. How the level of the canal was maintained. And yet it all seemed as though he were holding himself in. As though he were a little boy who had too much to say, and had been told to remember to let others talk. To every word of her own he gave intense, blushing attention. But there was no ease about him. Only in the shortest possible words did he reply to her questions.

A queer person. She couldn't make him out. Other men she had met talked when they wanted to, and held their tongues when they didn't. And after the torrent of speech on Sunday in the Botanic Gardens! Yet, on the whole, she rather liked him. He seemed such a simple creature.

At last they had regained the Great Western Road, and were coming to the parting of their ways. Again Henry put the question he had put at their first meeting. Would they see each other soon again?

She smiled. "Well, we're very near you now, you know."

He blushed again and relaxed a little.

"I didn't talk too much this time, did I?"

"I never thought. No, I don't think you did. Why?"

"Because I talked far too much the first time I saw you—"

"Did you?"

"Yes, I fairly chattered my head off."

This was really absurd. He couldn't really be grown up. "I didn't notice. I talk just as much as I feel inclined to. Don't you?"

"Yes, usually. But I can be terribly tedious. You see, I get so interested that I forget people are not so interested as I am."

She gave him her hand. "Well, the next time we meet just talk as much as you want to, Mr. Hayburn. Say whatever you like. I like people to be themselves."

"Do you really mean that?" Why did his eyes shine so boyishly?

"Yes. Of course. Goodbye."

And when Phœbe and David had turned and gone away, leaving him to his brother, Henry could hear nothing but her parting words ringing in his ears. And into these words he read all kinds of meanings that Phœbe had in no way intended.

Chapter Sixteen

STEPHEN HAYBURN dropped in upon his mother in her little sitting-room as she sat drinking tea and reading *Good Words*, her practice on Sunday night when she was alone after dinner. She was pleased to see him.

"Will you take a cup of tea, Stephen?"

"Thanks, Mother. If you'll allow me to smoke."

She smiled. "I don't mind fresh smoke. But I hate the smell of stale tobacco hanging about in a room afterwards. Still, for once. I'll ring for a cup." She pulled the china bell-knob.

Stephen returned from his smoking-room with his cigar and a box of vesuvians. He was also wearing a tasselled smoking-cap embroidered in gold and a dark red smoking-jacket. He took his teacup from his mother's hand, thanked her and set it on a little brass Indian table beside his armchair.

"Where's Henry?" Mrs. Hayburn asked, looking up at her elegant son.

"Upstairs working, I expect. Or thinking about Miss Moorhouse."

"Miss Moorhouse?"

"Yes." Stephen stood watching his vesuvian fizzling, then he lit his cigar with it, settled himself luxuriously opposite to his mother, crossed his feet, which were encased in embroidered house-slippers, on a hassock in front of him, and continued: "Henry has asked me to talk to you."

She sat forward. "About what, Stephen?"

"About Miss Moorhouse."

"Is this girl the sister of David Moorhouse?"

"Half-sister, I believe."

"Well. And what about her?"

"Henry has fallen in love with her. Very badly, I should say."

Mrs. Hayburn said nothing. She sat looking into the fire (for like most Scots she insisted upon a fire even on warm spring evenings). She had always told herself that when Henry fell in love he would fall heavily. Everything he did, he did with intensity. So far as she knew he had had none of the tentative, lesser affairs of most young men. Affairs that served perhaps to give them some sense of proportion. With her younger son it would be head over heels or nothing. Now it had come. And not very conveniently.

"Where has Henry seen her?" she asked presently.

"He met her last Sunday in the Botanic Gardens, while he was walking with David. She was with her other brother, the one who is David's partner, and Sir William."

"Sir William? They know him?"

"Yes."

That helped a little. Still—the sister of cheese merchants. David was socially established now. Cheese or no cheese. He was an old friend—and quite unstamped by his occupation. Besides, for some reason he had got himself accepted everywhere. And with him the question of marriage didn't enter, nor up till now had he obtruded his relatives. But now this half-sister—?

"Have you seen her, Stephen?"

"Yes. We arranged with David to meet them yesterday."

"Arranged? Did this girl know it was arranged?"

"No. We made it look like an accidental meeting."

"Why hasn't Henry talked to me himself? Why does he ask you to tell me this?"

"He thinks I can persuade you better than he can."

"Persuade me? Persuade me to what, Stephen?"

"He wants you to invite her here."

"How can I?"

"She lives with the Arthur Moorhouses. The brother's family who have just come to Grosvenor Terrace. He wants you to leave cards on Mrs. Arthur Moorhouse."

"I don't know that I want to." Leave cards on a provision merchant's wife? Her own grandfather had been a crofter in Argyle, but that was two generations back, and merely made her the more jealous for her position now. "What have you said to David Moorhouse about this?"

"Very little. I don't suppose his family would object if anything came of it."

"No. I don't suppose they would." Object to marrying her son? The son of a family that was established, of excellent standing and rich? Stephen and Henry could look to drawing a handsome income from Hayburn and Company all their days. If Henry insisted upon working for his living that was his affair. He didn't need to. (She had already offered to settle him in a country estate. His queer ways would look better in the country, she had thought.) Object? Not very likely. But she was aiming higher than Phœbe Moorhouse for her sons.

"I don't want Henry to marry this Miss Moorhouse," she said presently. "I know David's a friend of yours; and I've never discouraged him coming here. I knew you liked him, and I thought he was quite a good friend for you. Even when I discovered what his business was, I didn't let that make any difference. Still, you must see, Stephen, that it's another thing when there's a question of marriage."

Stephen sucked his cigar and nodded. It made no difference to him what happened. He had merely given way to Henry's importunings in speaking to his mother.

"Besides," Mrs. Hayburn added, "it's just the sort of marriage your father would have hated." This was quite untrue. For her husband had been in temperament very like his son Henry—a quick, eager man, over-trusting, uncritical and affectionate. But his widow had a way of dotting her i's and stroking her t's by invoking his memory.

Even Stephen saw this last remark a little ridiculous, and said, "Oh, I don't suppose he would. Father wasn't like that."

She did not, however, bother to reply. Instead, she sat gazing into the fire. At last, the gradual twilight of the north was beginning to make itself felt. The room was growing dim. A flame found glossy reflections in this elderly woman's plain-parted hair. It lit up her prosperous, wrinkled face and the innumerable transparent frills of her snowy cap.

"What do you advise me to do?" she asked him at last.

Stephen considered. Damned handsome girl. He wouldn't mind seeing her about. The old lady was being unduly fussy. And it was not at all likely that Henry would ever be attracted to anyone so presentable again. If she came into the family, at least she would be something to look at.

"Better ask her with David to dinner, Mother," he said. "Then you can have a look at her."

"I can't do that. At any rate, I hope, for her sake, that she's not the kind of young woman who would accept such an invitation. No, I'll have to call on Mrs. Arthur Moorhouse first, and I suppose Mrs. Moorhouse will have to call here. That means beginning with the Moorhouse family, whether I want to or not."

II

At this moment Henry came into the room looking as self-conscious as possible. His mother came to the point at once. "Stephen is suggesting I should call on Mrs. Arthur Moorhouse, Henry. He has told me you want to see more of Miss Moorhouse."

Henry's face flamed. He tugged his unfledged moustache and plunged his hands wildly into his pockets, then took them out again. "I say, Mother, it would be awfully kind if you would," he said.

"I don't know whether I am going to or not, Henry. There's a lot of things to think about. I wish your father was here to advise me. I'm sure Miss Moorhouse is a delightful young lady, but, after all, you haven't seen much of her, have you?"

"Twice."

"Twice is nothing at all."

"Oh yes it is, Mother. I've quite made up my mind."

Mrs. Hayburn laughed. "Nonsense. How can you have made up your mind? My dear boy, you're only twenty-three. You'll meet a great many more young ladies before you really have to decide."

Henry, who was leaning his back against the heavily draped mantelshelf, shuffled with embarrassment, kicked the hassock upon which his brother's embroidered feet were disposed, was reprimanded, apologised, then finally said, "Well, anyway, you *will* call on Mrs. Arthur Moorhouse, won't you, Mother?"

Mrs. Hayburn was not inhuman. And there were moments when her younger son reminded her sharply of her husband whom, on the whole, she had loved. He was reminding her of his father now—the young, vivid engineer she had married, not the platitudinous ogre it was her pleasure at moments to invoke.

"Do you really want me to, Henry?" she asked, softened.

"Please, Mother."

"And have you any idea if"—how was she to understate her question tactfully—"if Miss Moorhouse wants me to leave cards with her sister-in-law?"

If it was possible, Henry turned a brighter scarlet. "Oh, no, I don't know anything about that, Mother. How can I?" And then, as his mother did not reply immediately, he added anxiously, "but you will call, won't you, Mother?"

After all, Miss Moorhouse might not be so interested in Henry as he was in her. The affair might be quite one-sided. Though she could hardly hope for that considering the obvious advantages of the young man. Still, her heart might be given elsewhere for all any of them knew. That would be best, perhaps. At any rate, unless she were going to estrange him, she must do as he asked.

"All right, Henry, I'll go."

"Will you really, Mother? That's splendid." And her youngest son bent down and gave his rather forbidding mother a gawky, embarrassed kiss.

Thus it was that Mrs. Hayburn came to call on Mrs. Arthur Moorhouse. And really she couldn't have done it on a more awkward day. For having got the impression somehow that Mrs. Arthur Moorhouse was settled in Grosvenor Terrace much longer than she actually had been, she decided to call at once. Besides, a burning curiosity to know what kind of young woman had succeeded in attracting so violently her callow recluse of a son had begun to take hold of her.

Chapter Seventeen

IT was three o'clock in the afternoon. Bel was standing in the middle of her new kitchen wearing one of Bessie the cook's aprons and conducting operations with the decision of a general. For on this night she had decided to have her first real dinner-party. Her mother, Mary and George, Sophia and William, and, of course, David, were all to be invited—all the Glasgow clan. She had even made Arthur write to invite Mungo, but they had received no reply. It was to be a gesture. She intended, when she saw fit, to entertain formally after this. She was not going to stand free-and-easiness from the others any longer. None of those terrible droppings in of the wrong relatives that can so effectively ruin the pattern of carefully planned hospitality. And it was to be a dinner-party. No high-teaing or nonsense. The better people out here were going over to evening dinner now. And Bel—so help her God (and her brother-in-law David)—was not going to be left behind. In addition, the house was at last to be thrown open for show—to be the envy of everybody.

But at the moment it was three o'clock, and she was in the kitchen directing a nervous but intensely loyal Bessie in the opening preparations. A young and yet more nervous housemaid, specially engaged for Grosvenor Terrace, was standing beating together much flour and many eggs. Sarah, the reinstated criminal of Hughie's Yeard, now a stout, dignified person well into her thirties, was not to be seen.

One of the long line of bells above the kitchen dresser began to jangle and dance on its spring. It was the bell belonging to the front door.

"Who's that?" Cook said, bending over her work.

"I wish the message boys would learn to come to the back door," Bel said.

At this moment Sarah, who had been dressing in a maid's room facing the front area, and didn't know that Bel was in the kitchen, burst in, "Losh, Bessie, it's a cerrige-an'-pair!"

Bel's heart stood still. But she let none of her maids know it. She clung frantically to a show of firmness. "Go up at once, please, and see who it is. If it's anyone calling, then I'm not at home."

Sarah started. "Not at home?"

Bel coloured, but stood her ground. "Yes. Please. It's what you say if you're not ready to see people."

Sarah turned and went. After all, who was she that she should question the morality of the best mistress in the world? The memory of a pardon, amazingly granted less than four years ago, made a constant background to Sarah's devoted service.

When she had gone up, Bel left the kitchen and, tiptoeing into a maid's bedroom, stood on a chair behind the net curtain, thus managing to get her line of vision on a level with the pavement.

And there, sure enough, the sparkling wheels of a carriage, and eight shining, well-groomed hoofs!

Sarah, more than realising that the full pride of the Arthur Moorhouse household was, for the moment, in her hands, opened the front door and presented to the critical old woman peering from her carriage the picture of a crisp, sedate and thoroughly superior maid. She regretted that Mrs. Moorhouse was not at home, received cards and closed the door. And her mistress, perched on the chair, saw the polished top-boots of a lackey re-cross the pavement, go round to the other side of the carriage, and climb up out of view by the side of, presumably, the coachman.

Bel was standing in her kitchen again, a smothered fire of curiosity, when Sarah came down.

"Who was at the door, Sarah?" Her voice was a model of casualness.

"A Mrs. Hayburn, Mam. She left me her cards for ye."

"Thank you, Sarah."

David's Mrs. Hayburn! What did this mean? She had always understood that Mrs. Hayburn was a stiff, exclusive old woman. And yet she had called upon her before anyone else had done so! Were her sons pushing her into a friendship? Was Phœbe the reason? Phœbe! David had hinted that perhaps—! That would be very exciting for everyone! And such a splendid connection. She would take Phœbe with her when she returned Mrs. Hayburn's call. She must find out from David which was the exactly correct day.

"Are ye just havin' the potatoes boilt plain, Mam?"

Was it possible that Cook was putting this question to her for the second time? First things first. She must carry through this dinner-party successfully. Mrs. Hayburn must be dealt with in her proper order.

Bel drew herself up. "Yes. Yes, Bessie. I heard you the first time. I was thinking about it. No. I think you'll have to do potatoes in two ways for tonight."

But having saved her face by giving Cook further minute instructions, human flesh and blood could not wait any longer. So she took herself up the kitchen stairs into the hall, and hanging over her brand-new card-tray she allowed herself to gaze in ecstasy at Mrs. Hayburn's cards.

II

By quarter past seven, Bel, in a fashionable and most becoming dress, was to be found serenely, if a little purposefully, putting the finishing touches to the card-tables in her drawing-room. For she had decided that after their meal her guests should play whist. She had thrown embroidered cloths over two tables of suitable size, and was arranging at their corners packs of cards—new, their wrappers still unbroken—and little dishes of sweets, very special ones bought down town, and also, for those who preferred something not quite so fancy, a special make of Russian toffee.

Phœbe and Arthur, severely cautioned not to be late, and consequently unnecessarily early, were standing before the fire watching her. Arthur was looking grave and dignified in his tail-coat, and Phœbe, in white as became a young girl, was looking like a lily.

"Man, Bel, ye think of everything," Arthur said, stretching out his hands behind him towards the fire.

Bel looked up at the brother and sister for a moment, then went on with her arranging. She wondered if she had detected a glint of amusement passing between them. Members of the same family often possess a telepathy which comes, perhaps, from having the same blood in their veins—a telepathy that even beloved wives do not share. Bel felt that now and resented it a little. For a moment she felt a wave of defiance. Very well. If they were laughing, let them. She was doing her duty by her husband and her children. What did Arthur want them all to be? A family of nobodies? And Phœbe? Who had looked after her and mothered her for the last eight years?

There was the sound of horses' hoofs.

"See who that is, Phœbe," she said, a little tartly.

It was Mary and George. Both looking more portly than ever, Phœbe thought, as she watched them descend carefully from their cab. And her opinion was not altered when, announced some minutes later, Mrs. George McNairn, clad in regal red velvet, came in followed by the baillie.

"Bel, I think your house is very nice," Mary was saying in her flat, unemotional tones. Then having greeted the others and looked about her she went on, "You know, I once had to go to a committee meeting held in a drawing-room in this terrace. It was just the same shape as this. Of course it would be, wouldn't it? Now what *were* the people called? Anyway, they must have been very well-off. It was a wonderful room. Still I do think you've got this awfully nice, really. Hasn't she, George?"

Mary was prevented from saying more by the arrival of Sophia and William.

"Bel dear! This *is* fun! Do you know it's my first real dinner-party in the West End? William's been so excited about it that you would hardly have known him." (Bel reflected that she certainly would not have known an excited William.) "And as for the children, they've been perfect little abominations! Do you know they wanted to drive out here in the cab with us and walk back! I said it wouldn't do at all, and their father had to give them a good scolding. How do you like my dress? It's the one I had last year, with new lace and cut lower. Margy says I'm to be careful it doesn't fall off my shoulders altogether. Isn't she awful? William was just saying the other day he didn't know what present-day children were coming to. Didn't you, William?"

Mr. Butter said nothing.

Sophia rattled on. "Oh, here's Mrs. Barrowfield coming in. How are you? Aren't you proud of Bel living in all this grandeur?

We could never attempt this kind of thing. As William was just saying the other day—'It's plain Jane for us, Mother. We're not fashionable people, and it's no good pretending to be. We'll leave that sort of thing to Bel.' Didn't you, William?"

Again William said nothing.

As David appeared in the doorway at this moment Sophia went on, "David! How are you? Looking as if he lived in his tail-coat. Of course, so you do. I always forget you're such a social light! And here you are coming to have dinner with all your old dowdy relations!"

Bel was glad that Sarah came up to announce dinner at this point. For she was feeling a little ruffled. First, Mary had struck a wrong note by assuring her how much grander a neighbour's drawing-room was than her own; then next, Sophia had struck so many wrong and unnecessary notes that her performance, even for her, might almost be classed as a virtuoso one.

It was altogether too much. She gave up her original idea of pairing them off in the drawing-room, and allowed them to huddle downstairs to the dining-room as best they might.

III

As she came down the staircase she could hear the front-door bell ringing. Against the frosted panels, with its key-pattern border and its design of an urn of ferns, she could see the vague shape of a man. Who could it be? Anyway, Sarah and the new housemaid, now starched and waiting in the dining-room, couldn't possibly go to find out until the party was arranged and seated.

Arthur being a business-like man said a long, business-like grace. His wife might be getting grand but he was damned if he was going to let her get irreligious. And so, in quiet, authoritative tones, he pointed out to his Maker at some length that what they were about to partake of would be eaten to His glory, and with humble feelings of thankfulness. Scarcely was the Amen out of his mouth than Sarah swooped down upon the lid of the large and handsome soup tureen, which was standing, ready, in front of her mistress. Clouds of savoury steam ascended, and for a time nothing was seen of Bel but a capable, elegant hand wielding the soup-ladle.

Gradually through their chatter the party became aware of frenzied ringings and knockings.

"There's somebody at the door," Arthur said to the new housemaid, who happened to pass near him. "Go and see who it is."

"The girls can't do everything at once, Arthur," Bel said, through her cloud of steam. "It can't be anything important."

Arthur, as he was at the head of the table and near the dining-room door, got up and went to the front door himself. To his wife's intense annoyance. She must stop Arthur doing this. It was all very well when it was just the family. But this—in her mind—was a dress rehearsal for other, and more important, dinners, when such casual conduct would never do.

The next happening did not serve to soothe her rising irritation. For the party heard loud, brotherly helloings in the hall, and the voices of Arthur and Mungo could be heard greeting each other. In another moment Mungo was ushered in smiling; grubby from his journey, and delighted to see all his relatives, who showed equal pleasure at seeing him. This was really too bad! It smashed the careful formality of this entertainment that Bel had been planning for weeks! The table which, in great measure, she had decorated herself, had to be pushed about and rearranged, to allow another place to be laid. Mungo, who was looking rougher and more tweedy than ever against the evening clothes of the others, went out again with Arthur to have a wash. They took what seemed an eternity to come back. The carefully timed courses were all at sixes and sevens. She could hear them gossiping and laughing, quite forgetful that they were keeping a roomful of people waiting.

Bel, behind a set smile, felt very much like bursting into tears. Everyone was saying what a lucky chance for Mungo to find them all together like this.

It was Sarah who saved the situation.

"Will I set Mr. Mungo's place beside you, Mam?"

Bel raised troubled eyes to Sarah. Suddenly she realised that Sarah was just as upset as she was. There had been sympathy and a full understanding in the woman's honest Glasgow voice.

It gave Bel back control of herself—re-established her common sense.

"Yes, of course, Sarah. I must have Mr. Mungo beside me. You won't mind pushing round, will you, David?" No. Tonight it seemed she must do with things as things did with her. Formality, for the time, must go.

And when Mungo came back and took his place she was able to welcome him warmly.

IV

But after his first burst of greeting, Mungo, it seemed, was even for him—surprisingly tongue-tied. Bel, David, his sisters plied him with questions. How was he? What of the Laigh Farm? What was the Ayrshire news?

At last, Arthur, looking down the table, said: "If I were you, Mungo, I would just tell them and be done."

"Tell us what?" Sophia cried. And all eyes were on Mungo's face, turned many shades redder than his country life warranted.

But Mungo, who was contritely hurrying through his soup, shook his head.

"Go on, man, they'll have to know sooner or later."

"You can't refuse now," Bel said.

"Oh, well then, you can tell them, Arthur."

Eyes went to the head of the table.

"Mungo's going to be married."

"Married!" Mary and Sophia exclaimed together. Mungo? At the age of forty-three Mungo was getting married! It would be one of his farm-girls. The old story over again. It was too bad. Just when their children could do very well with a well-to-do bachelor uncle. Sophia had been planning pleasant, endearing little spells of housekeeping for Margy at the farm whenever she was old enough.

Mungo looked up embarrassed but good-natured. "Well, what's wrong? Any objections? Are ye not marrit yerselves?"

"But tell us who the lady is, Mungo," Bel said

It was Arthur who spoke. "It's Miss Ruanthorpe of Duntrafford."

"Miss Ruanthorpe!" Again Mary and Sophia exclaimed together, and thereafter sat quite dumb, saying nothing whatever.

It was hardly for Bel—a mere town sparrow—to appreciate the shock of surprise to the two sisters. She had never known, like them, a country child's reverence for the Big House. A reverence which was planted deep in any farm-child's breast. In days gone by Sophia and Mary had hidden frightened, shy little faces in their mother's skirts when Sir Charles, calling at the farm, had bent down to say a word to them.

And now their brother Mungo, the least genteel, most clodhopperish of all the boys, was going to marry Sir Charles's daughter! No. They sought about for some link that would make this possible, and found none. And typically they did not seek to attribute it to any special qualities in their brother. Mungo was just Mungo. And Miss Ruanthorpe must just be very eccentric indeed.

But it was very exciting. By themselves in the drawing-room after dinner, Mary, Sophia and Bel got their heads together. (Phœbe had gone up with Mrs. Barrowfield to visit her nephews and niece.) It would be a great upheaval in Mungo's life. He was to be married quietly in two or three months' time, and he and his wife were to occupy the Dower House of Duntrafford. His elder ploughman was to be put into the Laigh Farm house, but Mungo fully intended to go on looking after his farm, for it was his life's work.

Mary, roused out of her customary placidity, did not really see how this arrangement could possibly work. Sophia agreed with her.

But there were other aspects. Mungo would shortly be as good as laird of the whole of the Duntrafford Estates for Sir Charles was seventy-nine—and therefore rich! Much richer than any of them. It was a little hard, Bel thought, now adding her theme to the trio, considering how the other boys had worked and how well they had been supported by their wives. Still, she said angelically, it was nice to think of anyone so worthy as Mungo having such good fortune. Apropos of nothing, Sophia said, "Mungo told me she was thirty-nine. They may have no children, of course."

All three sat and pondered this for some time. Each working out its implications in relation to themselves and their children.

Presently Bel asked, "Do you know if she has any near relations?"

"I don't think she has anybody at all," Mary said, and added, "I remember when I was a girl, Father and Mother saying so when her brother was killed at the hunt."

"Was he killed at the hunt? That must have been terrible," Bel said, but her voice seemed considerably brighter as she added, "Still, that's all the more reason, dear, to hope they *do* have children. After all, thirty-nine isn't too late."

And then, as Phœbe had come back into the room, and you couldn't possibly suggest that marriage might result in children before a young girl, she was reluctantly compelled to drop that aspect of the situation.

But, from her point of view, there was an even more immediate, and—though she would never admit it—alarming aspect of this new alliance. They would have to make contacts with their new sister-in-law. They would have to meet her. She would have to come to stay. How would she expect to be treated? As the wife of Arthur she must ask her to stay at Grosvenor Terrace first. They had moved out West just in time! As she thought about it, courage returned. Yes. In this house she would be able to face the daughter of a baronet. David was always such a help—you could always go to him, socially naked and unashamed, and say to him simply, "What do I do next?" and he was much too sympathetic and good-natured ever to mock.

When the men came upstairs they were all in the best of spirits, thanks to the excellent claret that David had said was the right thing to drink at a dinner-party. And also thanks to a good deal of port, which he had also said was the right thing to drink *after* one.

If they were all very homely and affectionate, and very much their old selves, without formality or anything else, and did nothing but hang about and chatter, leaving the women to their own devices, Bel did not really mind much now. The family was the family. And she supposed she must let them go on being just that. With the prospect of further social advances to be made, social positions to be stormed in the near future, it was, perhaps, a comfort to her to find herself, for this evening at least, among those for whom she really need make no effort whatever.

Chapter Eighteen

AT exactly the right moment of exactly the right afternoon, Bel dressed herself in what she considered to be exactly the right clothes and, supported by Phœbe, set out to return Mrs. Hayburn's call.

The door was opened by a decorous maid—no detail of whose behaviour or dress escaped Bel—and they were requested to follow her upstairs.

Bel was glad that they were left by themselves for a moment in Mrs. Hayburn's large drawing-room, since it let her have a good look round. So this was the room where David had danced upon his first memorable visit? There was much that was old-fashioned and restrained, Bel thought. For Mrs. Hayburn's idea of furnishing had been formed when fashion had not yet run to the riot of heavy German drapery and tassels, to the rich, meaningless ornamentation that marked the late 'seventies; formed when decoration had not quite moved away from Georgian simplicity. Bel liked the room. Much of it appealed to her natural good taste. She found herself determining to eliminate this and that in her own too modern house, and wondering how she could do it without offending Arthur who, of course, had had all the paying to do and was indiscriminately proud of all his new possessions.

Presently the door opened and Mrs. Hayburn came towards them.

Her manner was several degrees more genial than it would have been some days ago. For, since she had left her cards at Grosvenor Terrace, David had been here to see the boys, and had let fall the information that his brother—the Ayrshire one—was to marry into the county. Up to now the existence of David's country brother had never been stressed, but in the sunshine of his astounding alliance, Mungo, simplest of souls, had budded and bloomed into a social asset.

Still, all that was very well. Henry's mother, however, was

not yet by any means sure that she wanted Henry to marry Phœbe. Like a good and tactful parent, she must, of course, avoid all appearance of placing obstacles. But—well—it was surely her first duty to examine the young woman before her and decide for herself. Certainly his taste was excellent. Miss Moorhouse was a beautiful creature. She had never thought that Henry would have eyes for this sort of girl.

Indeed, the two women before her made rather a splendid pair. Miss Moorhouse, dark and slender, with fine tempestuous colouring, and also that indefinable air of distinction that her brother David possessed. And her sister-in-law, fair, elegant and mature—her taste in dress a little too good, perhaps, a little too careful—and yet withal, impeccable.

"It's very kind of you to come to see me, Mrs. Moorhouse," she said, begging them to sit down. "You see, we've known David for such a long time now. Yet it almost seemed as if he had no relatives."

Bel replied pleasantly that there were her own family, and the family of two married sisters in Glasgow.

"Yes. He did mention you, of course. But for a long time I had no idea that some of your husband's family were still left in Ayrshire. David only told us recently."

"Oh yes. The oldest of all. And it's so amusing to think—at his time of life! We all thought he was a confirmed bachelor, of course. And now he's just got engaged to be married to the daughter of an old friend, Sir Charles Ruanthorpe." There were times when Mungo's impending eminence filled Bel with envy. But here, in Mrs. Hayburn's presence, she could only be obliged to him.

Mrs. Hayburn, who was nothing if not curious, was delighted that Mrs. Moorhouse looked like gossiping. She put her hand upon the bell-rope. "You'll stay for tea?"

Bel, who had heard it was not smart to drink tea upon a first visit, held up an elegant glove hand: "No, thank you. I'm sorry. We're going on."

Phœbe vaguely wondered where Bel thought they were going on to, but dutifully held her tongue.

"I'm sorry," the old woman was saying; then she added: "The Ayrshire Moorhouses will go on staying in the country, of course?"

At this moment the devil entered into Phœbe. Or so, at any rate, it seemed to Bel.

"Oh yes, of course, Mrs. Hayburn. You see, my brother is just a working farmer. He says he won't let his marriage make any difference to his work." Too much play-acting had a strange effect upon Phœbe. It made her feel as though she were in an overheated room where she must, cost what it might, throw wide the windows. Bel coloured, but said nothing.

A violent sort of girl this, old Mrs. Hayburn thought. She could see that Phœbe had embarrassed her sister-in-law. Why had she done it? Through sheer coltishness? Or was it by intention? Strangely, the sight of Bel's confusion aroused within her a feeling of friendship. She so hated violence. And after all, why was the girl making a fuss? Her brother was going to marry a baronet's daughter. He couldn't just be a ploughman.

And as they went on talking her liking for Bel increased. Mrs. Arthur Moorhouse was highly personable and unvulgar, and she seemed anxious to play the social game. She would not mind seeing her from time to time.

But she was not so sure about Phœbe. This child spoke her mind much too frankly. Perhaps that had appealed to Henry, but she, for her part, did not approve of it. There was a fearlessness about the girl that she did not like. No. If it were at all possible she must steer her dreamy, unpractical son safely through this shoal. He had much better take one of the young ladies she had planned for him instead of this odd, stormy creature.

II

But Henry had other views, and Phœbe was to learn them very quickly.

One evening, after a meal at Sophia's, Phœbe found herself with the Butter children on the old Mill Road, down by the waters of the River Kelvin. She had decided to try to go home this way. It was a pleasant walk, she had heard. Wil and Margy had promised to come with her as far as the Flint Mill. A curious little road it was, down there in the gully. High above, on both sides, crescents and terraces were springing up—or stood, already built. But here, down out of it all, the rural past still lingered. It was June and you were in the country, if you didn't raise your eyes. Here there were fresh leaves, the rushing river, and nothing but a white cottage and the mill. And though City sounds were shut out by the flow of the water, you heard the notes of the thrushes and the blackbirds in the bushes nearby. There was no traffic on this little lost road, which was, every day, becoming more engulfed in a thriving Victorian city. It was secluded and remote.

Wil and Margy skipped along by Phœbe's side showing her this and that. A robin's nest. The wild hyacinths. A flowering lilac bush. Phœbe frisked with them. It was nice to have a rest from being grown up. When they came to the mill they hung about watching; for the men were working late.

Suddenly a voice called: "Miss Moorhouse." She turned round. It was Henry Hayburn. He was bareheaded, and carried a book in his hand. His black hair was shaken anyhow over his brow and his eyes were excited. With his dusty coat, his loose black tie, and his boyish beard, he looked, she thought, like the conventional picture of a poet.

She held out her hand. "I didn't expect to find you down here. What are you reading? Poetry?"

He looked at her solemnly for a moment, surprised, as though he were not quite sure whether she was real, then he grinned. Colour came suddenly into his freckled white face. "No," he said. "It's not poetry. I never read poetry. I can't be bothered with it." He laid his hand on the pocket into which he had thrust his book and said with sudden earnestness: "No. This is a book about steam-pressure."

The difference was ludicrous enough. At another time or said by anybody else Phœbe would have laughed. But the tone of his voice, the lack of any sign from him that he was aware of having said anything comic, the fierce glint of enthusiasm in his eyes, suddenly gave the young girl a glimpse of that strange passion which was Henry's heritage. That fierce, creative obsession. With iron, coal, water-power, electricity, expanding steam. It gave her a glimpse of the importance of these things to this young man. In a flash of unwonted insight—for her peasant blood was not particularly quick—she saw how much it meant to him to be numbered with the old and famous brotherhood of Glasgow's engineers.

Somehow she felt embarrassed. She looked about her. Wil and Margy were hanging over the fence by the mill-stream gazing at the water as it flowed into the mill. She called them.

"Have you seen my nephew and niece before? Wil and Margy Butter. This is a friend of your Uncle David, Mr. Hayburn."

The Butter children shook hands. It amused them to see Phœbe suddenly grown up again. For a moment they stood grinning awkwardly before the unkempt young gentleman, then shortly they turned back to the mill and left Phœbe with him.

"I suppose it's possible for me to get home this way?" Phœbe said conversationally. "I don't quite know where I am."

"Yes, it is," he said. "But you have to go a bit farther up. Look here, I can take you."

Phœbe protested. "Oh, no! Please don't let me bother you. I know there's a footbridge somewhere."

He had become solemn again. He was looking now like a disappointed child. "I would like to show you the way. You can cross by the footbridge at the Three-Tree Well." And as he was still looking at her like a spaniel who wants to be taken for a walk, Phœbe accepted.

"All right. It's very kind of you, Mr. Hayburn."

She called the children and they said goodbye.

III

The evening was warm. But the walk through the trees by the riverside was cool and pleasant. Henry paced along by her side, still saying little, though at their last meeting she had laughingly given him permission to talk. But she did not mind. It pleased her to imagine that she was out in the country far from the encroaching city. She could understand why in past days the valley of the Kelvin had been renowned for its beauty. Even now there was much left. They came to the bridge at the old ford. When they stood in the middle of it she stopped and, leaning on the rail, looked down into the water. The young man halted beside her. Midges were dancing. Birds were calling in the wooded bank on the farther side by the Three-Tree Well. Neither of them spoke for a time.

Presently Phœbe looked at her companion. He was not looking down into the water any more. He was looking at herself intently. She smiled at him. "You can talk to me, you know. I gave you permission the last time I saw you."

"I remember," he said bashfully. "It was very nice of you."

She tried to read his face, then laughed—a little defensively, perhaps. "Oh, don't be too serious about it. It wasn't much, really."

"Yes, it was."

She did not know what he meant, so she turned way and again gazed into the water as it ran beneath them.

Once more he hung on the rail watching her. Her face was rosy with leaning.

Still looking down, she spoke. "I've spoiled your evening for you," and as he made to answer, "Yes I have. You came out with your book to read up something and enjoy yourself, and here you are seeing a young lady home because you think you ought to."

He was incapable of fine speeches, but he cried, "Oh no, Miss Moorhouse, I wanted to."

Suddenly she was touched. "It's nice of you anyway. I'll tell you something. When you told me what your book was about I realised just how much all that kind of thing—I mean your work, engineering—matters to you."

His eyes gleamed at her. "Did you, Miss Moorhouse?"

"Yes."

"How could you possibly?"

"I don't know. Just a sudden look. Something."

This was wonderful. It was more. It was of great and exciting importance. That she, of all people, should know by instinct what his own people could not, or would not, grasp.

"Mother and Stephen never would have, you know."

"What a pity!" she said simply.

"I'm glad you do."

She looked at him quickly and straightened herself. "It's nice of you to say that, Mr. Hayburn, but why you should care what I think, I don't know. We'd better go on—" She was very young and, except in her own virgin thoughts, perhaps, the lands of tenderness were still hidden country, yet the tone of his voice had told her to be careful. She crossed the remainder of the bridge quickly, walking a little ahead of him But there she had to stop, for she was not sure how next to go. "Which way?" She turned to him smiling, determined to be pleasantly normal.

"That way. It doesn't matter."

Without waiting she turned and began going up the hill. Presently she stopped, panting for breath. It was strangely quiet here. Quiet and secluded. Queer to think that it was a stone's-throw from Glasgow's most fashionable Gardens. She stood still and looked back. He was coming up behind her. His face was flushed and troubled as though he were unravelling some conundrum in his mind.

IV

When he came level with her he caught her hand and said, "Miss Moorhouse, I want you to marry me."

It was said so absurdly simply, with so little seeming emotion, that Phœbe was seized with a mad feeling that she was acting charades—that presently they would have to go back to the beginning, and Henry would be told to put much more expression into it. But she couldn't stand here, her hand in Henry's, thinking about charades. She drew it away and said, "Mr. Hayburn, you're talking nonsense."

He had turned his back, and saying nothing, was looking out through the leaves across the river.

Phœbe had a strong desire to laugh. It was all so sudden and ridiculous. And she felt she was behaving quite wrongly. As a well-brought-up young lady she ought to have fainted. Bel had fainted the first time Arthur had "sought her hand", or so, at least, she had once said. But even Bel, even in moments of great stress, always made a point of doing the correct thing. Or if she, Phœbe, hadn't fainted, at least she should have exclaimed that the suddenness of his proposal had taken her completely by surprise—as indeed it had. But instead of causing her a proper maidenly agitation it had only made her want to laugh. The thing was so abrupt, so ill-timed.

She stood for a moment watching his back. Suddenly he turned and faced her.

"Well?" His voice was almost savage. It was gloomy here in the evening woods, but she could see the distress in his face. For a moment this wealthy young man, this spoilt child of fortune, had turned into a lame duck.

"What do you want me to say, Mr. Hayburn?"

"I've asked you to marry me."

"Please, I don't want to marry anybody. You or anybody else. Quite honestly I haven't thought much about that kind of thing. You see, I've only just grown up."

"Will you promise you'll think about it, Miss Moorhouse?"

"No. I don't think so. Please don't get upset, Mr. Hayburn. But why should I?" He was standing looking so miserable, that she added, "There's a seat by the well, isn't there? Come and sit down." He followed her, and they sat.

"I wanted to marry you whenever I saw you. You're never out of my mind now."

"Nonsense. Admit you think a great deal about your work."

He turned to her, his eyes shining with eagerness. "But that's it. Don't you see? Down there on the bridge just now, when you told me that you understood about my work, it was wonderful that you, you of all people, should understand what it means to me! When even my own mother and brother—"

"If you don't mind me saying so, I think it's possible that neither your mother nor your brother may be very quick in the uptake. You'll find many people, besides myself, who would realise it quickly enough."

He shook his head. "No," he said. And then, after a long pause, "Please, Miss Moorhouse."

Phœbe shook her head. She turned on the seat and looked at him. "You know, Mr. Hayburn, I'm not such a nice person as you think I am. I want to be fair to you, you see. That's why I'm talking about myself. No. There's a hard core to me."

"I don't believe it."

"You needn't bother to say that. There is. Sometimes I think I haven't got real affections at all. I find myself standing back and looking at everything and everybody interestedly, as if I was watching—oh, how can I put it?—well, looking at people as if they were goldfish swimming about on the other side of the glass. You'll see what I mean, if you try."

He nodded.

"It makes me frightened sometimes. It's not a nice thing really, to feel quite cold when people expect you to feel glad, or sorry, or excited about something. But there it is. I even look at the people I live with and wonder if I really like *them*." She stopped for a moment, then went on, more to herself than to the young man. "And yet—yes, I suppose I do. I've done things for my nephew Arthur. . . . And I still have a kind of schoolgirl's hero-worship for my sister-in-law, Bel. But do you know, I'm looking at you just now, and a bit of me is saying to itself, 'That's what a young man looks like when he imagines he's in love.' " She put her hand over the large, capable hand that was resting on the seat beside her. "Oh, I'm nasty and callous, Mr. Hayburn. Forget about me."

He said nothing, but grasped her hand and held it. It was he who spoke first again, after a pause. "Perhaps your feelings are not developed yet."

"Perhaps not. Perhaps someday I'll turn into a real woman."

"For God's sake, don't talk like that, Miss Moorhouse."

She got up. "I don't think this talk's leading us anywhere, anyway. I don't know why I began it. Unless maybe to show you how little use I can be to you. At least you can forgive me. Will you?"

He got up too. "I don't see what there is to forgive. I spoke too suddenly. I believe I've frightened you."

"Not in the faintest. I wish you had! That would have been something!"

He could not make her out as he followed her up the road to Kirklee. There he said goodbye to her, feeling how desperately unsatisfactory life was, how much he was always bungling things, and how inadequate he had been.

And as Phœbe crossed the Great Western Road and went down towards Grosvenor Terrace she was, perhaps, not far from having the same feelings.

Chapter Nineteen

PHŒBE'S first proposal of marriage left no deep impression on her mind. When she did think of it—which, in a very short space of time, was not often—the incident seemed a little ridiculous, even a little pathetic. Henry Hayburn couldn't, after all, really care much about her. He had met her only twice before in his life. That his proposal had been, at the moment, sincere, she did not doubt. All his behaviour, its very ineffective gaucheness, had shown her that. Yet his feelings couldn't have deep roots.

But, of course, she just didn't want to marry Henry or anybody else. She was only eighteen. On the whole, her family made a pleasant pattern about her; and if she was not conscious of strong attachment to them as individuals, she knew she was, at least, attached to the pattern. Bel and little Arthur were perhaps exceptions. For her sister-in-law, Phœbe's first childish admiration was not diminished, though at times she found herself smiling at Bel's intense preoccupation with the correct thing. Her nephew Arthur was, somehow, a part of herself. He was the one being on earth, herself not excepted, whom she was unable to see objectively.

Now that the excitement of settling in to Grosvenor Terrace was, at last, beginning to subside, it was Mungo's coming marriage to Margaret Ruanthorpe that held everybody's interest.

Bel, dutiful, a little tremulous, but firmly determined to do the honours, asked Miss Ruanthorpe and Mungo to stay. Margaret replied to Bel's letter with great friendliness, and duly arrived for two nights to see her future husband's family. Somehow she filled the house. Bel could make little of her, but what little she made she could not dislike. Even though she stamped through the house in boots made by a village shoemaker, wore rough-cut tweeds from a village tailor, and mannish shirts with collars and ties, she had an indefinable quality that Bel recognised and valued beyond rubies, and wondered how Margaret achieved it.

"I can't tell you what it is," she said to her mother one

afternoon shortly after the future Mrs. Mungo's visit, as they sat comfortably together over their cups of tea in the Monteith Row parlour. "You know, if I wore the same clothes as Margaret I would be ready for the pantomime. But she seems to manage to carry everything off. And when she puts on her dress for the evening—and, mind you, I wouldn't give two-pence for it—you would say she was a very nice-looking woman."

But somehow—perhaps because Miss Ruanthorpe was "English"—Bel could not approach her very closely. She boomed about with her "English" accent, was scrupulously polite, impersonal and cheerful, in a manner that defeated Bel's burgher understanding.

There was no sitting down with her and having a good heart-to-heart talk. Margaret, Bel felt, did not make conversation. She issued statements. Not unpleasant statements, but statements nevertheless. It never occurred to Bel that Margaret might in her turn be feeling shy and strange too, and showing it by her abrupt behaviour.

Phœbe and Arthur, having the country in their bones, got on much better. Phœbe, indeed, was of real use to Bel, as she consented to be dragged out by Margaret for a long walk into the neighbouring country, thus giving Bel an afternoon of freedom from her baffling guest. Even Mary and Sophia had more in common with Miss Ruanthorpe, for there were many old interests, memories of their country days, that they were able to recall with the help of this sister-in-law to be. Margaret, being about Sophia's age, remembered their own mother well, as a kindly body in the Laigh Farm kitchen, and she was able to remember pleasant things about her that even they did not know.

It was now high June. The wedding was to be in the early autumn, she said. It was to take place in the drawing-room at Duntrafford, for Sir Charles was no longer young, and it would be too much of an effort to get him to church. She was putting the Dower House into order as quickly as possible. They had allowed it to stand empty for some time. There was to be some building, and much putting right. When this was done there would be nothing to wait for. She turned to Mungo with a smile and asked him if there was. It was obvious that she was very fond of him.

And Mungo's family smiled to themselves. It was clear, Arthur said to David, that he had his young lady well in hand. He was letting her do everything. After all, it was being done with Margaret's money. But it was not hard to see that what Mungo said went. There was evidence of affection, even a little complacency on his side. On Margaret's there was evidence of much more. The brothers agreed that, in the circumstances, it was a good thing; and long might it last for his sake.

II

But Margaret Ruanthorpe was very well pleased with her bargain. It had taken a long time—four years indeed—to break down the barriers between herself and this solemn intelligent farmer who was her obsession. During all that time she had known she was following an instinct that was right. The country was in the blood of both of them. They had, fundamentally, common interests, which were bound to make their union, should it come about, successful. And so, without loss of dignity be it said, she had persisted. If Mungo had accepted her enthusiastic friendship slowly, and with extreme caution, at least he had not drawn away from it. Her parents, old and preoccupied with their ailments and each other, let her do as she pleased. She had the sense to move slowly, digging herself in at every new move. He and his little sister had been persuaded to come to Duntrafford to lunch. Later he was induced to come alone. Now that he knew her parents, she consulted him about them—about her father's health, the management of the estate. His advice was invariably good. When she heard Phœbe was back at the Laigh Farm, she came to see her. She made herself familiar and pleasant with the workers on the farm, who, on the whole, came to like her. She stayed for pleasant simple meals in the glowing firelit kitchen. On the first occasion, when Mungo came and found her sitting with Phœbe, waiting for him, he went to put on his jacket. But she protested. She would take it as very unfriendly of him if he made any difference for her.

Thus things had gone on. So gradually indeed, and over such a space of time, that their closer relationship seemed a natural sequel, a growth rather than a thing of violent feelings. But underneath Margaret was steadily determined.

And thus, some weeks ago, the inevitable had happened.

One of Margaret's fillies, a very valuable hackney pony that was not thriving as she should, had, on Mungo's suggestion, been sent over to him at the Laigh Farm. He would keep her in a field nearby and watch over her himself. She would be the finest beast Duntrafford had ever bred, he said, if only he could bring her to a flourishing maturity.

He had had her for some weeks. In addition to improving Margaret's very elegant little animal, he had given Margaret ample excuse for coming across every day. They were on such terms now, however, that this went without remark.

Suddenly disaster fell. The pony entangled a hoof in a coil of barbed wire lying rusty and hidden in a deep patch of grass. The creature, finding herself caught, had danced in a frenzy, wounding herself terribly before they could free her. Round the top of her hoof the flesh was badly torn.

The man who had seen this happen and had eventually succeeded in freeing the pony, was afraid to tell Mungo. The farmer of Laigh Farm was slow tempered, but they, all of them, knew his temper was there. But told he must be. Mungo went white with rage. It touched his honour, that this animal he had taken into his care, to bring her to her full beauty, should be ruined by mere stupid carelessness. That the beast was not his own made it worse. And that it was Margaret Ruanthorpe's made it worse still. In addition, the idea of the creature's agony tormented him.

For a moment he lost control. Was this a place to look after horses, if the louts about couldn't keep their eyes open for rubbish like a bit of wire? It must have lain there all winter. Surely someone could have seen to it. The man, knowing his master, let him storm; and at last, with a grunt meant to be an apology, Mungo turned and ran.

The pony's condition was as bad as possible. He sent one man for the vet, another to Duntrafford. Margaret and the vet arrived from different directions almost at the same time.

Margaret greeted Mungo. She had never seen him so much moved before.

The hysterical pony, soothed a little by Margaret's voice, allowed some kind of examination. The vet shook his head.

"I'm sorry, Miss. She would 'a' been worth a lot."

When Margaret was excited her voice went high and harsh. "You mean she'll have to be shot, Mr. Johnstone?"

He nodded.

"Is it no use fighting?"

"The beast's in terrible pain, Miss! An' I doubt—a rusty wire. There'll be poison."

"Couldn't we try?"

"Well, Miss—" Again he shook his head.

She turned abruptly to Mungo. "Mr. Moorhouse, couldn't we fight with her? For tonight at least?"

Mungo looked at Margaret sorrowfully.

"The beastie will not let ye touch her."

"She'll let me touch her." She crossed the box, and standing beside the trembling pony, ran her hand part way down the injured leg. The movement was womanly and gentle. It was not lost on Mungo. The creature threw back its head, its nostrils were wild, but it stood quiet. She held the injured hoof up, painfully tipping the puddle made by the blood that was dripping steadily to the floor.

"Mr. Moorhouse, we must try." Margaret's voice was trembling.

Mungo turned to Johnstone. "What is it first then? Get it clean? Plenty of rags and boiling water? You stay with her, Miss Ruanthorpe; I'll go an' tell the lassies."

And thus the battle had begun. All through the first night, Margaret and Mungo—fanatics for horseflesh, both of them—stayed in the box together, scarcely leaving it, dressing the terrible gash, striving to calm the pain-stretched nerves of the high-strung animal and keeping her from doing herself harm. What devotion could do, that they did. Sleep hardly occurred to either of them.

In the late evening Margaret sent a scribbled note back to Duntrafford, telling them briefly what had happened, saying she could not come home. In reply the old woman who had been her nurse arrived with clothing and instructions from Lady Ruanthorpe that if Margaret stayed at the Laigh Farm, she, her nurse, must stay too. And so, propriety having been upheld, the fight for the pony's life went on.

For the first days they did not know if the wound had been poisoned. With expert help they did everything in their power to get it clean. But gradually, as time went on and healing showed itself, their fears began to diminish. They would not be able to tell for long, however, if she would be permanently lame. The two discussed the chances endlessly. If the animal had been a brilliant child whose intellect might be permanently injured, and they had been its parents, they could scarcely have been more intense. Whatever happened now, Margaret was determined not to have the filly destroyed. Even if she could never be broken in she might hand down her elegant proportions as a brood mare.

But the leg would be stiff for weeks. How long would it be before they could tell? There was consultation. Endless talks. Animals that have been nursed become affectionate and petted like delicate children. And they tend to forge a bond between those who have struggled with them.

At last there came a day when there was no further chance of the pony losing its life through poisoning. There was no possible reason, therefore, why Margaret should stay longer. She left the Laigh Farm. But she left it as the promised wife of Mungo Moorhouse.

So it had come. And neither of them knew in the end how it had happened.

Margaret had returned to her own home tired out, but satisfied. It was the fulfilment of a long hope.

And Mungo, too, was pleased. Long familiarity with the Ruanthorpes had broken down his timidity and doubt. He would be at home with this woman he was to marry. For a long time now he had been well aware that Margaret wanted him. But, emotionally slow as he was and uncertain of the wisdom of the step, he had let things take their course. Now their course was taken, and he was content. He could look forward to companionship with a wife of whom he would be genuinely fond.

III

As she said goodbye, Margaret Ruanthorpe invited Arthur and Bel to come for a weekend to Duntrafford. Bel, she said, must get to know her parents, and Arthur must renew an old acquaintance. Bel, curious "to see how people like that did things", was sorely tempted to accept, but even with her spirit the battle of getting there, going to the trouble of having the right clothes, and being on her P's and Q's for more than two solid days was too much for her, and she was forced to decline. The labour of getting herself and everybody else into Grosvenor Terrace had been enough for a time.

And now it was nearly July, which meant, if you were a proper matron of the City of Glasgow, that you collected your forks and knives, table and bed linen, the entire supply of old clothes belonging to the household, and heaven knew what else, and locked or corded them into trunks or hampers. Then, on the first of the month, you (and whoever you could get to help you—in Bel's case, Sarah and a man sent along from the warehouse, and at the last moment, a porter) got everything on to the deck of the Bute steamer, or the Arran steamer, or the Kintyre steamer, at the seething Broomielaw. You then sat upon it stoically watching your children, eating sandwiches and listening to the German band until you reached your destination. Whereat you disembarked and lived in extreme primitiveness—and usually, for your children at least, in extreme rapture—for the months of July and August.

For the last years Arthur had insisted upon their going to Glen Rosa in Arran. It was a beautiful place, of course, but there had been times when Bel had thought that it would be nice to have a smart house at Cove, and, as she put it, "meet people". But this year the idea of Brodick and their house in Glen Rosa which, like most Arran houses, was simple to the point of crudeness, filled her harassed soul with balm. Grosvenor Terrace was very well and she was delighted at last to find herself established there. But now, for a blessed two months, she could do and look precisely as she liked. Her time would be pleasantly taken up, running to the beach with the children. Pulling off and on shoes and stockings, drying little brown bodies and unpacking chittering bites. And in Glen Rosa there would be the smell of bracken and bog myrtle, of burning peat, the sound of running water; and of a morning, as she lay in bed, the cackle of cocks and hens. And sometimes, in the evening, she would see the

Duke's deer moving on the shoulder of the mountain, frescoed against the sky.

No. A visit to Duntrafford would be too much for her at present, so she thanked Margaret and regretted that she must wait to know her parents until later.

But Phœbe was to be at the Laigh Farm for the summer. Now that she was grown up she must take her share of family responsibilities. On every count it was right that she should be there. She was the only woman of the family who was free to go, and the only one to whom the farm was now familiar. Even in the country she managed to conduct her own very personal existence and live within herself, bothering no one—very much indeed as her own parents had done before her. The farm-hands liked her; she did not interfere. Mungo too was pleased, for Phœbe's independence kept her from being in the way. Indeed, her presence was of great use, for she made it possible for Margaret to come and go without seeming bold.

Chapter Twenty

PHŒBE arrived at the Laigh Farm this summer with great plans for improving her mind. She had been reading in a ladies' magazine—a truly genteel periodical, with no sympathy for that abhorred creature The New Woman—just how important it was for the refined lady to be well read. There was no reason, it said why, for instance, a woman of average good intelligence should not grasp the works of Mr. Ruskin and Mr. Carlyle. A little determination was all that was necessary. Mr. Dickens was, of course, a great author, but he was a little helter-skelter if it came to the question of forming style in addition to being well read. Besides, there were moments when he could scarcely be freed from the charge of vulgarity.

Perhaps it was better to leave Mr. Dickens to the gentlemen. And talking of style, Miss Austen's books were, as everybody knew, excellent, but on other counts they were a little tame and old-fashioned, perhaps, and lacking in romance. Still, they were the works of a gentlewoman and could safely be recommended. Books like *Jane Eyre* the contributor could not recommend. If a young lady must be romantic, there was always Sir Walter.

Again, before leaving her music-master for the summer, Phœbe had suggested to him he might set her some holiday work. He had perhaps noticed that her practising had not been so regular of recent months, but she had been tremendously busy helping her sister-in-law. Now, however, she was going to bury herself in the country for the whole of the summer, and had every intention of more than making up for lost time. The piano at her brother's farm was an old one, having been bought for her sisters years ago, and perhaps, now, its tone was rather tinny, but she would write to her brother to have it put in order by a travelling tuner. At this point she had looked at her music-master. Would an indifferent piano, did he think, spoil her touch? Knowing her, or rather her youth, better than she knew it herself, he assured her that he thought it would not.

So down into Ayrshire Phœbe came, arrived with many improving books, a fat bundle of pieces and exercises, and a fair amount of fancy sewing, with which she intended to decorate her own bedroom in Grosvenor Terrace.

All of which she at once forgot in the superb July weather. Besides—she lamented later to David who had the temerity to tease her about it—there was so much she found she simply had to do when she got there.

Margaret was always wanting her over to Duntrafford to do this and that. They were forever in the Dower House watching and instructing joiners, plasterers, paperhangers and painters. There was no end to it. And though Margaret had a sewing-woman, of course, there were always little odds and ends that she, Phœbe, found herself promising to do. Then there were all Mungo's clothes to be gone through. She really couldn't let him be married without seeing that he had everything necessary. She had never realised, she said importantly, just how negligent men could be. So David needn't sneer.

Indeed, she built up a very effective picture of herself slaving her way unselfishly through these summer months for her brother and his wife-to-be; the very personification of thoughtful sisterliness, when she had much rather, of course, been sitting in seclusion improving her mind and her fingers.

But she did not tell him of a litter of collie puppies, shocking wasters of time. Nor of the long, solitary walks that took her over field and moor, or across the green holmes and by the wooded banks of the River Ayr—expeditions that she came to make daily.

Almost every evening, too, when Phœbe and Mungo did not dine at Duntrafford, Margaret came across to look at her pony. They were walking the injured leg daily now, very carefully. An ailing animal was a lame duck to Phœbe, and she had become as interested as the others. Would the beautiful little creature yet fulfil its first promise? A pony by the same stallion had gone to America, sold, it was said, for a thousand guineas, to pull the governess-cart of a Vanderbilt. Mungo, who had seen this animal, declared its proportions were not so fine as those of the Duntrafford filly. Would she too come, after all, to be of great value?

Or was she to be nothing now but a brood mare? When Phœbe saw her first the filly was still hobbling, hardly putting her hoof to the ground. But by dint of much tending and rubbing the limp began to go. At first she would allow only Mungo's and Margaret's hands upon her. But later Phœbe, having made herself familiar, was allowed to tend her too. Steadily the limp diminished. At last, one afternoon towards the end of August, a farm-boy was given the halter rope and told to trot her. The lad called encouragement and began to run. Margaret, Mungo and Phœbe stood watching. The pony was petted. At first she would only walk, dragging back on the rein. At last, finding this uncomfortable, she hurried her pace and in a moment more her enraptured audience saw her set her elegant neck and begin to trot "high and disposèdly" round the yard, like the aristocrat she had first shown promise of becoming.

Mungo turned to the women. "She's all right," was all he said. Which, to anyone but a Lowland Scot, may seem inadequate for more than four months of constant anxiety and labour.

II

A pleasant summer for Phœbe, most of it, and if she didn't carry out the scheme of education she had planned for herself, she received, perhaps, some education of another sort. For her constant association with Margaret Ruanthorpe and her parents gave her a glimpse of a different world, a different point of view from the climbing provincialism of Bel's house in Kelvinside. As ways of living, there was not much to choose between them. Sir Charles and Lady Ruanthorpe held to their view of life just as complacently as the Glasgow Moorhouses held to theirs. But their code of life followed a wider tradition, the code of Victorian Britain's lesser gentry; whereas Phœbe's own family, only just emerging—by their own honest effort—from the peasantry, had their outlook sharply limited by that all-absorbing occupation known as "getting on". At all events, the world of Duntrafford was something new for Phœbe, and helped her, perhaps, towards finding her own perspective.

The wedding, Margaret had decided, was to be at the end of

the first week in September. The holiday-makers would be home again by then. The bridal pair wanted as little ceremony as possible, a fact which suited Phœbe admirably, for thus, until the last moment, she was left free to go her own ways. Late August was lush and beautiful, and her long rambles in the wilds had become more of a rapture than ever.

But her last days were destined to be disturbed. She had called a dog and was setting out one afternoon when, suddenly, as she opened the front door of the farmhouse—a door which had to be unlocked, for it was little used—she was confronted with Henry Hayburn. She drew back surprised.

"Mr. Hayburn!" She held out her hand. She was confused, and she knew her face showed it.

He looked hot and tired. He must have walked the three miles from the railway station. He was wearing the same black clothes. The same loose tie. He took her hand.

"I hope I haven't surprised you too much. David told me you were down here."

So he had come to see her. "Come in and have a rest," was all she could think to say.

He shook his head. "You were just going out. Don't let me stop you. Perhaps I could walk part of your way with you."

He looked so tired and apologetic now that Phœbe laughed, and laid her hand on his arm. "Don't be ridiculous. I was only going for a walk by myself. You must come in and sit down. I'll get you something to eat."

"Really—I don't want—"

"If you've come from Glasgow you must be hungry. Come in." She led him into the cool kitchen.

"You mustn't give yourself any trouble," he said lamely.

"I won't." She fetched some bread, new-baked scones and cheese from the dresser, brought a jug of milk and a pat of fresh butter from the cold milk-house, put them on the scrubbed table, and set a chair. "There," she said, "that wasn't much trouble, was it?"

She sat watching him while he ate and drank, running her hand over the muzzle of the collie who sat waiting beside her, and playing with its ears.

Strange, gawky young man this, with his hair all about as

usual, and his black beard making his cheeks look absurdly young and boyish. There was something appealing about him today, something that pulled at her heart-strings. She felt, somehow, as though she had taken in a beggar man and was giving him food. What else could she do for him to send him happily on his way? That depended on what he had come to beg for. She felt it better not to ask.

She saw that he ate little, but he drank most of the milk she had given him, for he was hot and thirsty. And while he was eating and drinking he said almost nothing. Answering her merely that, yes, he *had* seen David lately, and that he looked well. And again, yes, his mother and Stephen were in the house at Kilcreggan. Stephen had been yachting. No, he hadn't been there much himself. He had been too busy at Hayburn and Company, working on a new idea.

"You look as if you needed a holiday, Mr. Hayburn," she said.

He did not reply directly to this. He rose, struck the flour of the scones from his hands, and asked her if he might come with her on the walk she had intended to take.

III

She was uncertain what to do with him. She did not want to ask him, right out, why he had come. And yet it seemed odd, to say the least, that he should want to make a train journey, then walk for miles through the dust, just to go for yet another walk when he had arrived. She was not really afraid of what he might say to her, but it was a peaceful, sunny afternoon, and she had no wish to be emotional, if emotional he intended to be. Besides, what she had to say to him, if he opened up the topic of their last meeting, would only hurt him. For her mind was not changed.

"Well, shall we go?" he was saying.

"If you want to." What else was there to do? How else deal with him?

She led him by fieldside paths that skirted hawthorn hedges, untrimmed and high, and with scarlet autumn berries already formed in clusters against the dark green leaves. By Mungo's fields of corn, ripening fast, as it stood up motionless in the still afternoon sunshine. Then further up to the moorland, across a rough stone wall or two, through beds of rustling brown bracken and seeding dry grasses. Here and there a sheep, with her half-grown lamb, started up, taken unawares.

Phœbe was becoming conscious now of a growing exasperation. She realised that she was hurrying on ahead of Henry out of sheer annoyance with him. And all he did was to tag bleakly after her in his untidy town clothes. What right had he to intrude like this? These Hayburn boys were rich and spoilt. Because they had money and an indulgent mother they thought they were the lords of creation.

Presently she halted and turned round to look at her companion. No. She had to admit it. At the moment the last thing he looked like was a lord of creation. He looked more tired and hot than ever. His hair was over his eyes, and sweat was glistening on his face.

She laughed, and her own laugh, for some reason, sounded to her a little hard.

"I'm sorry to race you along like this, Mr. Hayburn. You look desperately hot. But you wanted to come, you know."

He looked at her—irritatingly, feckless, she thought—and said, "Yes, Miss Moorhouse, I did."

"Look. Here's a burn. Lie down and have a drink of water. That'll cool you." She stood over him contemplating his back, his thick black hair and his long legs, spread apart as he lay flat on the turf by the burnside, putting his lips to the clear surface. She noticed that the seat of his trousers was shining, and felt sure that his mother would disapprove of this careless shabbiness.

Suddenly Phœbe's irritation evaporated. He was such a child. Like a good little boy, he had dropped down on his knees the moment she had suggested it. He seemed prepared to do everything she told him. She knelt down beside him and, cupping her hands, dipped them into the stream, and drank too. Then she shook the water from them and turned, smiling, to look at him.

He turned too, still prostrate over the little pool, and looked up. His face was red with stooping. Water dropped from his beard and from the point of his nose. A slow smile dawned, in response to her own. He crawled back into a kneeling position, and thus they remained for a moment, both of them, kneeling by the stream, as though they were performing some obeisance.

"Feel better?" she asked presently.

He seized her hand and bean speaking rapidly.

"Miss Moorhouse—Phœbe, I still want you to marry me."

She started, angry, and tried to drag her hand away, but he would not let it go. "I've been miserable ever since I spoke to you in the springtime. I can't work. I can't do anything."

She wrenched her hand away and sat back looking at him. "I told you I didn't want to marry anybody."

"I thought perhaps you had changed your mind. I spoke to David about you and he said you were down here."

"Did David send you?"

Henry said "No," but Phœbe suspected a hesitation. David would hear about this the next time she met him. What did he know about it? A cool, genteel bachelor who cared for nothing but his clothes and his dinner-parties. He was pushing Henry at her, because he considered him a good match. He had no right to encourage this poor boy to come to her once more, merely to be made miserable. Her rage had turned on David. She was sorry for Henry now.

"No, Henry. It's no use. I'm sorry."

"I can't go on."

"Of course you can. I'm no great prize, I assure you."

"I think you're the most beautiful girl in the world."

She laughed. "Thank you, Henry," she said.

"You won't take me seriously." He complained lamely. "You don't seem to care if . . . if you break my heart." His voice broke.

She looked at him quickly and saw that his eyes held tears. Suddenly her sympathy was touched. She was moved to an extent that frightened her.

"Oh, Henry! Please!"

"Phœbe!" He held out his hand to her.

"No." She stood up, came to him and drew her handkerchief from her belt. "Look, your face is all wet still, you silly boy. I'll dry it for you."

He was still kneeling. She bent over him, purposefully polished his face, and put back his hair, as though he were her nephew Arthur.

"Now, promise you won't go on making yourself miserable. It's ridiculous nonsense, you know." She stuffed her handkerchief back into its place and shook the grass from her skirt. "Now get up and behave yourself."

He got up and stood looking down on her. His eyes were burning. Again she was moved strangely. For the first time she became aware that she was standing beside a man. "When am I going to see you again?" he asked.

She was surprised at her own lack of coolness. "I don't know. I've no idea."

"When are you coming back to town?"

"In week or two, after my brother's wedding."

"Will you allow me to see you?"

"You're a friend of David's, aren't you?" Then, fearing her tone had been tart, she turned to him. "Henry, I'm not refusing to see you. I want to be friends. But anything more is hopeless. Please. That's my last word. If you keep bothering me, we'll only be miserable—both of us."

"Then I suppose I'll see you when you come back?" He was calm now, and somehow, perversely, his returning poise, if anyone so callow as Henry could be said to have poise, irritated her.

"Yes, I suppose so. I think we should go back. The farm folks have their tea at four, before the milking. You'll meet my brother Mungo." She turned to lead the way home. Henry turned and followed her.

IV

Yet to Phœbe that was not the end of it. After Henry had asked her to marry him in early June, she had not bothered about it further. She thought of it merely when something brought it to her mind.

But now this second happening by the burn kept invading her thoughts. It came of its own accord, forcing her to give it endless reflection. She had been sorry, troubled, angry. She tried to puzzle out to herself why he had so stirred her. But she could find no answer. Was it a quality of fecklessness? An appeal to something protective in her make-up? The family told her she ran after lame ducks. Was Henry a lame duck? In a sense perhaps. But then he was said to be very clever in his way. Brilliant, she had heard said. At all events she didn't know. But certainly, whatever her feeling, she was not in love with him she told herself.

Now, as though the thought of him were not enough, he had taken to writing her letters. Long, rambling things, mostly about his work. It was quite plain to her that when she and what she stood for were not obsessing his mind, it was a mind that ran on a single track. Engineering was not only his calling. It was his passion. What would happen to the woman who married him? Would she find herself, shortly, a mere piece of furniture in his house? A creature, scarcely noticed, who was there to look after his comfort—to liberate his mind from distracting instincts that it might continue upon its own brilliant way? There were many self-effacing women who, if they loved him enough, would accept these conditions considering their lives fulfilled. She was made of different stuff. Often, recently, she had felt purposeless. Had asked herself, indeed, why the Almighty had seen fit to create her. But she was certainly not self-effacing. She kept turning over these things, but her thoughts could find no rest.

The first days of September passed, and now there was the wedding. The family came flocking down, all of them. Mary and George, fat and placid, with their fat, placid children. The Butters. Sophia excited and talking her head off. Wil and Margy, brown and sprouting after their holiday, and looking really quite handsome children. Their father, William, as silent as usual. David, the ever correct and immaculate. And then Phœbe's own people. Arthur, Bel and her nephew Arthur (the younger children had been left behind). Phœbe was delighted to see them. Little Arthur sulked at first and complained that she had never come to Glen Rosa, but he clung by her all through the day.

Bel was beautifully dressed. A little too beautifully, too carefully, Phœbe thought, comparing her with the one or two Ruanthorpe guests. Indeed her own family looked, somehow, a little over-prosperous, too defensively confident, too urban, for their surroundings. Now it was Mungo, still countrified, but calm and solemn, who was in place. But the ceremony was a pleasantly simple one, performed, as had been arranged, in the Duntrafford drawing-room before the two families and the men and maid-servants of the estate. This suited Sir Charles and, somehow, it seemed right that these two should be united in the surroundings to which they were to belong.

And in due course when all was over the Moorhouse clan trooped back to Glasgow, related now, by the bonds of holy matrimony, to a real live baronet, the owner of quite extensive lands. A matter for much secret complacency to most of them, though wild horses would not have dragged this from them. But Providence they felt had been kind to them in many ways, and was repaying them even more than they deserved for their devotion to the things that mattered. Such things as the common-sense practice of a good, sensible brand of religion and a strict attention to business.

Chapter Twenty-One

"WHERE are you going to, Aunt Phœbe?" Arthur the Second, large enough to be promoted to the breakfast-room, and with a napkin tied round his neck, stopped for a moment from shovelling porridge into his manly mouth. He was a schoolboy now, Bel having sent him to the newly-built Kelvinside Academy which had just opened its doors "to enable pupils to qualify for the University and for commercial and professional pursuits". It was to be, Bel understood, the most select establishment in Glasgow for the education of gentlemen's sons.

Arthur looked up at his aunt for an instant. He resented that she had come into the room wearing a hat and outdoor things. It meant that she was going to do something he wouldn't be able to share in now that he must go to school.

Phœbe slid an affectionate hand over his round head as she passed him on her way to look out of the window. "I'm going into town with your Papa," she said. "I've got some shopping to do. Then I'm going to see your Granny. I've been home for nearly a fortnight, and I haven't been to see her yet."

It was a fine autumn morning. The trees in front and across the Great Western Road in the Botanic Gardens had turned to brown and gold.

"Finish your porridge, Arthur," Bel said reprovingly.

"Couldn't you go on Saturday?" he asked anxiously.

"No, dear. She's going today. Hurry up, son."

"I'll take you somewhere on Saturday. Where would you like to go?"

Arthur smiled. "I don't know. I'll have to think," he said, and attacked his porridge plate once more.

Phœbe, still wandering about, bent over the still empty chair belonging to the master of the house and glanced casually over his folded morning *Herald* to see if there was anything in the way of shop announcements worthy of her interest. The first outside quarter page yielded nothing. Births and marriages of people she didn't know. Bank notices.

She picked up the paper, and held up the front page fully opened out. Wednesday the second of October 1878. An announcement of a new story beginning in the *Weekly Herald*: "Marguerite: or A Woman's Wit." A romance from Spanish History. "The story is essentially modern in spirit; antiquarian research has not been suffered to impair the action of the narrative." She might spend a penny on that if she remembered. On Monday the seventh October, a return visit of the Comedy Opera Company. They would play "HMS Pinafore: or The Lass that Loved a Sailor" by Mr. Gilbert and Mr. Sullivan. She might try to tease David into taking her to that. Royal Botanic Gardens. In the Kibble Palace, Mr. Cole's Splendid String Band. Tomorrow from seven to nine." She would keep away from that. She didn't want to run into the Hayburn boys. She had not seen either of them since she had come back. If Henry had written, the letters had not been forwarded. She had, these days, a nervous desire, almost, to shut him out of her thoughts.

This was better. "Mr. Copland of the Caledonian House in Sauchiehall Street is just home from Paris, and has made a happy selection of Rare and Beautiful Costumes, the surpassing beauty of which exhausts the vocabulary of ecstatic imagination." And Millar's at the Cross, and the Polytechnic had autumn shows too. She must really have a look round all these. She had better have her midday meal with old Mrs. Barrowfield and make a day of it. It was nice to be back in Glasgow again in this crisp autumn weather, to have all kinds of things to look at, and to be eighteen.

She folded the *Herald* as she heard her brother's step outside the door, and put it back by his plate.

II

The man of business was preoccupied. He was never at his most talkative in the morning. He greeted everybody curtly. Bel hurried to pour out his tea. Phœbe served his ham and eggs. While this was going on he stood warming himself in front of the fire.

When he saw that his breakfast was awaiting him, he said, "Thanks," and sat down abruptly. He took his first sip of tea, his first piece of ham, then put out his hand for his morning paper.

"The City Bank?"

Phœbe and Bel stopped to look at him as his quick hands folded the sheets to the news page.

"What is it, dear?" Bel asked.

Arthur read: "The City Bank of Glasgow has stopped payment. For some time past rumours have been in circulation unfavourable to the position of the bank; and these have been only too well founded." He dived deeper and went on reading without comment.

"Is that a very serious thing? What does stopping payment really mean, Arthur?" Bel asked.

He paid no attention.

"I hope we've got no money in it," Phœbe said.

"If it's a serious thing, that would be dreadful. Arthur, you must tell us! Arthur!"

"What is it?" He put down his *Herald* querulously.

"Have we got any money in the City Bank?"

"No. We haven't."

"What a good thing!"

"Yes. This may be very serious." He took up the paper again.

"Will people be ruined?"

"Very likely. There'll be some fun in the town today." He folded it up and pushed it into a pocket. "I'll read the rest going in," he said. He snapped up the remainder of his breakfast with lightning speed. Finished, he pushed himself back and got up. "If you're coming with me, Phœbe, you'd better come," he said. "This bank affair is going to be terrible," he added. "It'll affect trade. It'll be a bad autumn for everybody. By the way, I believe David's Hayburn friends are in, up to the neck. Somebody mentioned it at the Club the other day."

He did not give his sister time to ponder his words, for, in an instant more, he had seized his hat and was out on the pavement waiting for the tram. Phœbe hurried after him, well-used to this treatment. Arthur was the best brother in the world, even if he hadn't time to wait for his ladies.

When they had mounted the tram, however, he remembered he had his sister with him. For instead of swinging himself agilely up the little stairway to the roof, he came inside. This was occupied mostly by elderly men. The conductor rang the bell, the horses were off, and brother and sister settled down to the morning journey into the City.

Presently Phœbe found herself wondering why everybody was talking to everybody else. Tram passengers were not usually so free with their talk. On the few occasions upon which she had had to go into town at this hour she had invariably found herself in the company of a tram-load of solemn, bearded, bewhiskered gentlemen; murmuring, perhaps, polite greetings to a newcomer, but for the most, sitting staring in front of them, their hands crossed stolidly over the ivory or ebony handles of their large umbrellas, pondering no doubt the matters of weight which the day held in store for them. But today all was animation and talk. The man next to Arthur had begun talking to him. He was talking of the City Bank. The two gentlemen on the other side of her were talking about the City Bank. Those opposite were talking about the City Bank. What a terrible thing it was! What had brought it about? What would be the extent of the damage done?

To Phœbe, being a well-brought-up young woman, most of this business talk was Greek. The other banks were accepting its notes, one man said. That seemed to be a good thing. An old gentleman shook his head and said *that* wouldn't last long. He had heard talk last night. The Exchange had been humming. He wouldn't be surprised if the affair reached the criminal court. He turned and addressed a passenger sitting on his other side who, so far as Phœbe could tell, had until now said nothing. "What do you think, sir?"

"I hope it's not as bad as it looks, or I'll be a ruined man." For this man's benefit the old gentleman immediately became falsely cheerful, but no one who was listening—least of all Phœbe—was convinced by his tone.

As she sat swaying behind the trotting horses, she found herself staring at the gentleman who had said he might be a ruined man. She regarded him with her usual impersonal interest. He must be racked with anxiety. Did people express so little when they were faced with ruin? Did they merely sit quietly and look before them? Was she really hard, that she could not feel more for this stranger? Was there something left out of her make-up? Had she a limited supply of sympathy?

The tram rattled on. Now the brakes were screaming as it descended Renfield Street. Now it had reached its terminus in St. Vincent Place. People were getting out. They were preparing to change round the horses.

III

Arthur asked her if she were going direct to his mother-in-law at Monteith Row—in which case she might accompany him by George's Square and the Candleriggs. But Phœbe thanked him and said that she had promised herself to go down Buchanan Street, then by Argyle Street and the Trongate, so that she might see what was showing in the autumn shop-windows. Arthur bade her a hasty goodbye and hurried off.

In Buchanan Street, too, there was an air of excitement. Phœbe, having been in the country for so long, set about examining each window display with immense relish. But presently she found her attention continually caught by the excited voices of passers-by. The City Bank. Always the City Bank. It was now long past nine. In front of the *Glasgow Herald* office there was a small crowd of people. She crossed over and asked a boy who looked like a young clerk what the crowd meant. They were trying to get further news of the City Bank. As she reached Argyle Street, morning passengers were pouring out of St. Enoch's Square from the great, new-built railway station. Urchins selling late editions of the morning papers were doing a roaring trade.

She took her way along Argyle Street. Here in the rush of Glasgow's busiest street the excitement seemed swallowed up.

For a time Phœbe let such windows as were worth looking at engross her. Her aim in coming into this undistinguished part was to spend some time in the great emporium known as the Royal Polytechnic, to have an entertaining and profitable look round.

As she came opposite to it she stopped and crossed over. For some time the display in its many windows took all her attention. "Modes from Paris", "The very latest from the City of Fashion." What it had worn at its Great Exhibition this summer. The Polytechnic had sent its buyers, and nothing had escaped their notice. Glasgow's ladies need consider themselves in no way behind in up-to-date elegance. They had merely to put themselves into the hands of the Polytechnic buyers. In one window there was a lithograph of the Prince of Wales and his lovely Princess Alexandra being shown round the Exhibition by deferential Frenchmen.

Phœbe was enjoying herself thoroughly now. She took each of the many windows in turn, gazing her fill. At last she decided to buy some small thing as an excuse for going inside to see the still greater wonders there.

She was turning to go back to the main entrance when she became conscious that people were hurrying along in excited knots on the other side of the street. For a moment she stood looking, and then, anxious to miss nothing, she picked up her skirts and ran over to see what it was all about. Presently she found herself at the corner of Virginia Street, a street which, in the ordinary way, was quiet, business-like, unobtrusive and without interest for a young girl. Some little way up there was a large crowd of people standing. All of them were gazing up at a doorway. In a moment more she had joined them. She saw now that those about her were very excited, pressing forward, it seemed, towards this door. She craned her neck to see better and was able to read the words "The City Bank of Glasgow, Head Office."

She spoke to a woman by her side. "Why is everybody waiting here?"

The woman, poorly dressed in black, turned. "A don't ken whit *everybody's* waitin' for. A jist ken A'm waitin' till it's ten o'clock, to let me get ma money oot o' that place," she said acidly.

A man in front of them looked round. "You'll get no money out o' that place."

"Aye. A'll get it oot." The woman's voice broke hysterically. "It's ither that, or gang to the puirshoose."

"It's ten now," the man said, and as he spoke a clock somewhere could be heard striking out ten strokes. The hour when upon a normal day, all honourable banks threw open their doors and looked the world square in the face. But this one it seemed could not. Voices became more high-pitched and excited. Women began to weep. The special staff of police, who had been sent against serious trouble, kept shouting not to block the street entirely. Their continual cry of "Move on, please!" could be heard above the din. Here and there a sympathetic policeman could be seen telling a weeping woman to go home; that she was doing no good by standing here, that if she had City Bank notes in her possession she could turn them into coin elsewhere. From time to time people called out that they were ruined. They shouted the words "Robbers! Thieves! Scoundrels!"

Now the police were forcing the crowd to make way. Phœbe, firmly wedged in now, was swept backwards. "Keep back there, please! Let these gentlemen through!" Suddenly the crowd went silent. Was the miracle to happen? Was the bank after all to open its doors, just as though it were an ordinary morning. The solemn, black-clad men succeeded, with the help of the police, in pushing their way forward. But the door was merely half opened as they passed inside. The crowd did not like this. Why should these men be the only ones to get inside. Why shouldn't they, too, be allowed to go in and ask for their money? There was a rush forward. Before the police and those inside could quite control them one or two slipped through.

But almost at once the door was forced shut and the people were left murmuring.

At last Phœbe decided she had had enough of it. These people would probably stand here all morning. There would be nothing more for her to see. She turned and began to extricate herself, shouldering her way determinedly among anxious faces. She could not help smiling a little to herself at the thought of how disapproving Bel would be at her boldness in allowing herself to be pushed about in this seedy crowd.

IV

She had wormed herself free and was in the act of setting straight her hat and her dress before walking off, when she saw a private carriage swing round out of Argyle Street, and come to a standstill by the edge of the pavement a little way down. A glance at the shining harness and the handsome, well-groomed horses told her it belonged to someone of consequence. Now, as she came nearer, she could see it was in some way familiar. Another step towards it brought complete recognition. It belonged to Mrs. Hayburn.

Her brother's words came back to her. "By the way, I believe David's Hayburn friends are in, up to the neck." Had they sent someone to find out? She would have turned and gone in the other direction, since, if the carriage contained a Hayburn the meeting would be awkward, but retreat was blocked by the throng. There was nothing for her but to go on. Just as she came up, Stephen and Henry jumped out, and began advancing towards her. Stephen was the first to recognise her.

"Miss Moorhouse!"

Phœbe guessed that both the brothers were very excited. She did not know what to say. She weakly said: "Good morning." Then, feeling she must explain herself, she added, "I'm just in town shopping. I came up the street to see what all this was about."

Henry was looking at her dazedly, as though he were trying to remind himself of something. "We're all here," he said hoarsely. "Mother too. She's in the carriage. She insisted on us all coming to see if we've been turned into beggars or not."

Phœbe noticed the toneless ring of his voice. "I hope it's not as bad as that," she said lightly.

"It's just as bad as it can be, Miss Moorhouse," Stephen said, adjusting his eyeglass with a very good show of calmness.

Phœbe admired him. She had never liked Stephen Hayburn much, but now, in this moment of stress, he was doing well.

"I don't think you'll be able to get any news this morning," she said, preparing to move. "The policemen were telling people not to wait."

"We had better go up, just to please Mother. It was she who

made us come here." Stephen pulled Henry's arm, and they raised their hats and went off.

Having no other choice now but to pass Mrs. Hayburn's carriage, Phœbe began to wonder what she could possibly find to say to the stiff old lady in her distress. As she passed, however, Mrs. Hayburn took no notice of her. She was sitting forward in the carriage, staring before her, in a terrible trance of suspense. Could worldly possessions really matter so much to anyone? Phœbe wondered, as she gazed at the wide-open, unseeing eyes and the set face suddenly turned frail and marbled with unnaturally blue veins. She wondered if she ought to make herself known and offer to stay until the sons came back, but at once she decided against this. She felt that she would receive no thanks for breaking in. If Mrs. Hayburn fainted—as judging by her appearance she might very well do—her coachman could look after her.

Chapter Twenty-Two

IN Phœbe's mind the City Bank collapse was inextricably tangled up with the Hayburns. When people talked of it—and for the next month not only Glasgow but the whole of Britain talked of little else; even *Punch* had a cartoon of an erring bank manager awaiting judgment with other common thieves—Phœbe could think only of the two anxious brothers and the terrible white face of their mother as she sat there alone in her carriage. For many days, however, she heard nothing more of them. She knew, of course, that Hayburn and Company had crashed, "succumbed" (as the papers put it) "to pressure of money matters." And this made her wonder. But David, who could, at most times, have told her, had not seen them either and had not liked to obtrude.

Meanwhile the disaster kept piling up. On the first day the depositors had been kept calm by the action of the other banks in accepting City Bank notes and by the exhortations of the newspapers. On the second day the books went into the hands of the auditors. And from then onward the news became more and more sensational. The further the examination went the more shameful was the tale of swindle and deceit. Mouths were full of expressions of contempt. "Banking run mad", "Utterly rotten", "Reckless plungers", "Cooked accounts". One newspaper reported that you could hardly go a dozen yards without meeting a friend who had lost everything. Shareholders had not only to pay up in full to the extent of what they held but had to do this six times over. The burden, in most cases, was unbearable. Charity lists were opened for the unfortunate. People like Arthur Moorhouse gave lavishly. In less than three weeks the directors were arrested.

On the day following the arrests, Arthur, scanning his morning paper, read out the announcement of the death of Mrs. Robert Hayburn. Phœbe's comment, at the time, was merely that she was not surprised. But as the days went by, this news haunted her. She found herself taken by a strong desire to see Henry and know how he was getting on. She felt he would be defenceless before the blows that had fallen. She did not know whether he had loved his unamiable mother or not. But she rightly guessed that he was one of those who do not bother much about the routine in which they find themselves, so long as it does not interfere with their own intense interests, but who are utterly at a loss if that routine is broken.

At last on the evening of the funeral day, Phœbe, certain that David would have been among the mourners, felt herself impelled to call upon him to hear news of Henry.

II

She found Henry alone by the fire in David's sitting-room. She had expected David and Stephen too, for the landlady had said they were all there. He was sitting forward, his feet on the black, iron fender. His head in his hands.

He looked up casually, for he was expecting the other two. His eyes looked haunted in his white face.

He sprang to his feet. "Miss Moorhouse!"

Phœbe drew back. She felt she was intruding. "I'm sorry, Henry," she said, using without noticing his Christian name, "I thought David was here. I've disturbed you."

"No, no. You're not disturbing me. Come in. David and Stephen went out for a walk. They'll be here any time."

Phœbe came into the room and gave him her hand. She was distressed to see how crushed and ill he looked. Whether she would or not he had been so much in her thoughts during these last days.

But in her mind she had not seen him so red-eyed, so weary as this. If ever there was a lame duck, it was Henry Hayburn now.

He shook hands formally and they sat down.

"Henry," Phœbe began. "You don't look well."

"I'm all right." He smiled wearily.

"I was going to write to you," she said gently, "but—well, you see, it was perhaps a little more difficult for me than for—most people."

He nodded.

Phœbe went on. "Still that wouldn't have kept me. I would certainly have written if I hadn't met you here." She waited for a moment, then continued, "I was really shocked to hear about your mother's death. In a way I wasn't surprised. I had seen her, not so many days ago. You remember? She looked ill."

"Yes. The morning we all drove down to Virginia Street to make sure that we were ruined."

"It was a shock to me to hear about Hayburn and Company too."

He appeared to wince at this, but he did not reply directly. He merely asked, "What were you doing there?"

"I had gone up the street to see what the crowd meant."

"Your folks had no money in the City Bank?"

"No, Henry. We were lucky."

"So you had just gone up to see what ruined people looked like? Just as a matter of interest?"

She was not angry with him. She had after all told him she was that kind of person. He was stating now what had been perfectly true. She did not reply, and he went on:

"I suppose you're doing the same now?"

She got up and laid her hand on his shoulder.

"I'm going to speak the truth to you, Henry. You've never been out of my mind since that morning. You may think this queer of me, but I've been really pleased that I could feel so badly upset—over a friend. You see it's not nice to keep on feeling a—a kind of fish with no feelings." She turned away and leant against David's betasselled mantelshelf, with its black marble clock, its pipe-cleaners, its photographs and the gilt mirror stuck at the edge, with half a dozen cards of invitation, requesting the pleasure of the company of that eligible bachelor Mr. David Moorhouse at this ball and that conversazione. Looking down on Henry Hayburn's black mop, she was struck, for the first time, with the eternal see-saw. Henry had been up. Now he was down. It was her brother David's turn.

"You're a queer girl, Phœbe," Henry was saying.

"I've never hidden from you that I was. Have I?"

"No." Then after a pause, and with a voice that tried to be hard, but only succeeded in being heartbreaking, "You needn't bother defending yourself against me now. Beggars don't ask young ladies to marry them."

Phœbe laid her hand on the mantelpiece. Something told her she was at the parting of the ways. She must get out of here at once if she did not want to be caught—trapped for ever by her own unaccountable self. She saw this so clearly that she felt a little giddy. She had only to turn his last thrust aside, tell him again how sorry she was about everything and go. But after a moment, a moment that seemed to her to stop and hang motionless in eternity, she found herself still here in David's room, looking down into Henry Hayburn's eyes.

But even yet she did not give up the struggle. "What will happen to Hayburn and Company, Henry?" she said, as though she was attempting to ignore his last words.

She looked down at his engineer's hands. He was wringing the fingers through each other, nervously. When he spoke he seemed to her to be speaking to himself.

"Hayburn and Company was the whole of my life. My father, Robert Hayburn, made it, built it out of nothing. He was an inventor. Other people had to look after the money for him—and you know now what that has led to—but he was the brain, the heart of it all. Stephen and Mother didn't understand about Father's work. What it had meant to him. They weren't touched with the—fire." And after a long pause, "If they had given me time I would have taken up his work where he had laid it down." He turned aside as though to hide his face from her. Again he had tried to harden his voice, and again its tone came near to breaking her heart.

III

She stood looking down upon him fascinated. It gave her a strange, passionate pleasure to hear him say that "Hayburn and Company was the whole of his life." Who was she, Phœbe Moorhouse? A strange, not too sensitive young woman who lived without purpose in and for herself. And here was a young man whose mind might be warped and broken by what life was now forcing upon him. She had courage and strength if she had nothing else. At least she could bring him these. It was in her power to save him, to help him to pick himself up and go on. She saw it now indeed as a sacred duty, the reason why she had been sent into the world. She felt now as she did when, a child of fourteen, she had been impelled to go down into the desolation of the slums and rescue her nephew. She had just the right toughness, the requisite lack of feeling, to stand between life and this brilliant, sensitive creature. She alone could let him go on with his life's work.

She was terribly shaken by the decision she had made. Her tears were falling as she bent forward and turned his face up to look at her. She put her arms about his neck and kissed him full on the mouth. He sprang to his feet.

"You *are* going to take up your father's work where he left it off, Henry. I'm going to be with you and see that you do. We'll build up another Hayburn and Company."

He stood, stupid and speechless, holding her two hands. When he spoke it was to say: "But don't you see, Phœbe, I'm a beggar!"

"So am I. But we're both strong. Your father started from nothing, didn't he?"

"I can't allow you—"

"Of course, if you don't want me."

"Oh, my dear!"

He took her into his arms. The faces that came together were both wet. She could feel his beard on her face, smell tobacco, the faint smell of the macassar on his hair, of his linen, of himself. And still, far away, the silent, waiting Phœbe, the Phœbe Moorhouse who had nothing to do with this excited overwrought girl, sat waiting and wondering.

They came apart. His eyes were shining, and his cheekbones were red. She had made him happy. She had given her life a meaning. She would be happy too.

"Henry," she said, at length, "I want to ask something of you."

"What is it, darling?"

"Let me go home now. You can come and see me tomorrow."

He kissed her again. Then she turned and hurried away.

Chapter Twenty-Three

BEL came back to consciousness with an odd feeling that someone somewhere in the house was not resting. For a moment she wondered what time it was, and then, as though in answer, the clock on her bedroom mantelpiece struck one. She lay listening. Beside her, Arthur lay peaceful, breathing steadily. A faint autumn night wind caused the lace curtains by the open window to stir now and then. The pale light from a lamp outside made reflections on the ceiling. The clock ticked hurriedly, quietly persistent. She too began to feel restless—on edge. What had happened to wake her up?

She had gone to bed wondering about Phœbe. The girl had come in from David's rooms. She had asked her how David was and if he had had any news of the Hayburn boys. She said she had not seen her brother, but that Henry Hayburn had been there. Bel had ventured to ask how he was and what his plans were, and Phœbe had answered her casually that Henry didn't look up to much and that she didn't know what his plans were. The girl was in one of her remote, moody fits, so Bel had let her be. She had drunk her evening cup of tea in silence, wandered about the drawing-room aimlessly, played a bar or two standing in front of the piano, then said goodnight and gone off early to bed.

Bel lay wondering now, as she had wondered then, if something had happened.

Above her a board creaked. That must be in Phœbe's room, for it was directly overhead on the top floor. Had she got up for something? Wasn't she well? She would wait a little to see if it went on. Was that another creak? Or was she imagining? Was that the handle of a door turning quietly? It was difficult to tell in this solidly built house even in the dead of night. Was there movement now on the upstairs landing? Or were these simply imaginings, born of this unpleasant midnight alertness?

Bel tried to persuade herself that it was nothing. That she had better get off to sleep again. For a long time she lay, trying to make her mind a blank. But it was no use. When the bedroom clock struck two she had to admit that she was wider awake than ever. Should she get up and satisfy herself that all was well upstairs? If it had not been for Arthur she would have done so now, at once. But it seemed unfair to risk wakening a tired, busy man just for a mere whim. In a little time, surely, she would begin to feel sleepy again.

What was that? No. She must go upstairs and see that all was well. Perhaps one of the children—? But if it were one of the two smaller ones, Tom or Isabel, their nurse was with them in the nursery. And if anything was unsettling little Arthur, who was now promoted to a bedroom of his own, he had a way of coming straight downstairs to her or going across the landing to Phœbe.

She slid to the edge of the bed with great caution, listening at every move that her husband's breathing kept steady, and finally found herself standing on the floor beside her bed. Noiselessly she stretched out her hand for her dressing-gown and felt with her bare feet for her slippers. The handle of the bedroom door turned without noise. Like a ghost she slid through.

As she came up the stairs to the top landing she bent close to the bottom of Phœbe's door to see if a light was burning. She could find no sign of one. Over on the opposite side, Arthur's door stood open, and his gas was burning at a peep, for he was a nervous child, and did not like to feel he was shut away in the darkness by himself.

She crept forward and looked in.

II

There in the semi-darkness, in nothing but her white night-dress, Phœbe was sitting by the sleeping boy's bed, silent and motionless, holding his hand.

Bel drew back, alarmed for a moment, as though, almost, she had seen an apparition. The girl had looked so pale and still, with her long, black plaits of hair falling down in front over her shoulders. What did this mean? Had she come there to comfort Arthur, or in search of comfort for herself?

But Bel's practical mind came to the rescue. It was nonsense whatever it was. The girl would catch her death of cold. She looked into the room again, and said quietly:

"Phœbe dear, what are you doing?"

Phœbe started.

"Come back to your room. You'll catch cold."

Phœbe disengaged her hand gently and came out of the room after her sister-in-law.

Bel lit Phœbe's gas, turned back the bed, and made her get into it before she said:

"Is Arthur all right, Phœbe? Did he want you?"

Phœbe merely shook her head and said, "No."

"What were you doing there, dear?"

"I don't know. I just went."

Bel stood looking at her, puzzled. It had been a rule with her never to break into Phœbe's confidence. She had always let her tell her what she would. Never forced her. But now it was clear that something was troubling the child. If only she would talk. She looked at her to see if she had been crying. But the eyes that looked out of her lovely pale face shone hot, and strangely clear, like the eyes of a trapped animal.

Bel sat on the edge of the bed beside her and did something that she had never dared do since Phœbe had grown up—she put her arms about her and kissed her.

"Phœbe, my dear, I would like you to tell me what's wrong. You know I don't bother you often, but I would like to know now."

Phœbe still said nothing. And Bel, holding her, wondered for a time if the girl in her arms resented this show of affection. Presently, however, she felt Phœbe's hand over her own. And thus they remained for some minutes. But things couldn't stay like this.

"I think considering all I've done for you, Phœbe, you might tell me. I don't know whether you're fond of me or not, you've never shown it very much"—Phœbe was amazed at this, though she said nothing—"but I'm very fond of you. It makes me miserable to see you like this. Did something happen in David's rooms tonight?"

Again Phœbe did not speak. But Bel saw that she was going to now, and waited.

"Yes," Phœbe said at length, speaking with strange evenness. "I promised to marry Henry Hayburn."

Bel withdrew her arms and sat up looking straight at her. All kinds of thoughts crowded in. Henry Hayburn? She would have thought differently of this before the Hayburns had been ruined. But Bel's snobbery was skin deep; like the snobbery of most women when it is set against the happiness of those they love. She dismissed Henry's fall from prosperity. After all, he was young and clever. But why wasn't the child happy? She herself, at the same stage, had been upset, and wept and laughed and been so unreasonable that her mother had been driven to lecture her roundly. But at least she had made some show of emotion, of happiness. She had not gone into this still, dry-eyed trance.

"Phœbe dear, do you *want* to marry Henry Hayburn?" she asked at last.

"I suppose so." The girl was incomprehensible.

"But Henry Hayburn's a very nice young man. Aren't you happy?"

"I think so. At any rate, I'm going to marry him."

It was useless. She bent forward and kissed her again. There was nothing else to do.

And now it was Bel who found herself crying. And through the tears she saw the fourteen-year-old Phœbe, ragged and bleeding, carried senseless into the house in Ure Place in her brother David's arms. No. There was nothing she wouldn't do to make up to her for that night. But it was so difficult, so baffling.

Now the girl was speaking. "Bel, will you do something for me?"

"My dearest, anything."

"Will you stay with me for the rest of the night?"

Phœbe had no idea of the happiness this gave Bel.

"Of course. If it will help you."

A minute later they were together in the darkness. She was allowing Bel to hold her hand as they lay.

"Phœbe," Bel said presently, "I want you to make me a promise."

"I'll try."

"If ever you're very unhappy—any kind of unhappiness—it

doesn't matter what or where, will you come, as quickly as you can, back home here to me?"

"Why do you say that, Bel?"

"I don't know, dear. But tonight, somehow I feel I must. Will you promise?"

"Yes. Of course I promise."

"I'm glad, Phœbe. Now try to sleep."

Neither of them said any more. But, after a time, Bel was pleased to hear Phœbe's breathing come quietly, rhythmically. She did not withdraw her hand. She was afraid to wake her.

THE PHILISTINES

Chapter One

FOR a few moments David Moorhouse did not realise that the play was over. The tension still held him. It was only when the curtain had swept down into its place, its golden fringe bouncing a little in the glow of the footlights, that he began once more to be conscious of his surroundings. Suddenly the storm of applause broke. Men and women were standing up in their places clapping their hands. There were whistles and shouts from the pit and the gallery. For a time the roar continued. At last the curtain trembled. The storm changed to a tempest.

Irving, lean and exhausted, was standing before them, modestly bowing his thanks.

David had never seen him before. A classical actor in a classical play wasn't much in his line, really. But he had been told that, to be in the swim, he must see Irving's Hamlet. It would be a solemn, stately affair, he had expected. He would buy a ticket for himself and go to have a look at it. After that he would be able to tell his friends he had been, and duly and suitably agree how wonderful Mr. Irving was. And now he was standing up in his seat like the others, clapping his hands off in thanks to the strange, pale creature down there in front of the footlit curtain. His equipment for judging Irving's art were his own placid emotions, a certain natural refinement, and a shallow, provincial sophistication. But that had been enough for Irving to work on.

David had gone to take part in a social ritual. Instead, he had been forced to share, and share acutely, the feelings of another young man, troubled and wearied, groping his way through indecision and corruption to a merciful death. It had all been intensely human—the last thing that he had expected. He had heard that Mr. Irving could be terrifying; that he could freeze a theatre with horror; that he could be cold, aloof and regal. But this heart-breaking, noble intimacy, this pitiless exposure of the raw places of a wounded mind, was something beyond David's experience.

As he stood in the hot theatre looking down, he found himself wondering what possible kind of person this Mr. Irving could be. What were actors like? How did they live? He had never had the slenderest contact with the world Irving belonged to. Actors and artists were strange, erratic people. That was a commonplace. And, in Glasgow at least, solid, well-doing people didn't want to know them. But now in his enthusiasm David could not help asking himself what Mr. Irving had done to prepare himself for this performance. Had he learnt the words and trusted to his exceptional emotions? Or did he discipline himself in some way?

Irving was standing now hand in hand with his Ophelia, Miss Brennon, acknowledging the endless applause. What kind of life did that girl lead? She looked frail and gentle and not any older than David's own sister Phœbe. He had been solemnly told that actresses were exposed to all sorts of moral dangers. He could well believe it of the girls who sang in the Scotia or at Brown's. Nobody expected a girl in a free-and-easy to be a paragon. But this girl who had so well set forth for him the anguish and gentle madness of Ophelia?

David Moorhouse was hopelessly Philistine, but he belonged to a tribe whose emotions were by no means overworked and blunt. He had been much moved by a great actor in a great play, but it would have been quite beyond his powers to tell why.

II

It was late when he found himself standing at last outside the new Theatre Royal in Hope Street. There had been flurries of snow during the day. But now, though it was cold, it was dry. A long chain of cabs waited to take the wealthier of the audience home. One by one, as the doorman called out their numbers, the muffled cabmen pulled the rugs from the backs of their horses and moved to the brightly lit entrance.

Under the blazing gaselier, David had recognised more than one friend who might have offered him a lift. But he had avoided everybody. The play had thrown him into a strange, unaccountable excitement. He wanted to be left alone. For a moment he looked about him, wondering if he should go down into

Sauchiehall Street and pick up a cab for himself. But almost at once he decided to walk. The theatre had been hot. The fresh air would do him good. He wanted to think. He turned into Cowcaddens and made his way towards New City Road.

He was now passing through one of the slums of the city. It was only Tuesday night, and he would have only himself to look to. Towards the end of the week, when wages came in, drinking and riot made this district impossible at so late an hour. Even tonight, as he hurried along, he passed one or two wretches staggering and roaring. Many dirty, barefoot children were still about. There was filth and squalor everywhere; and not a little misery. For in November of 1878 Glasgow was deep in trade depression. In this she was like the rest of the Kingdom. Businesses were failing everywhere. Banks were collapsing. The City Bank of Glasgow had been the first and greatest British Bank to go. Its shareholders and depositors had been the victims of fraud as well as bad times. Unemployment was mounting. There were rumours of war. Depression bred depression. And meanwhile the people suffered; just such hungry, haggard people as David was passing now.

But as he hurried along, his hands deep in his pockets and his coat-collar upturned, his thoughts were far from the people around him. One became used to the sights of everyday. The play had set his brain racing, sharpening consciousness, stimulating thought. As he paced along, he found himself living again the hours he had passed in the theatre. The wonderful traffic of the stage, with that extraordinary man at its centre. The packed auditorium; a great tribute to Mr. Irving in these bad times. The people sitting near him—well-dressed, comfortable people, taking life easily. And then, inevitably, life in general, and his own in particular. What did it all come to?

Where did he, David Moorhouse, stand? Where was he getting to?

He was pounding along New City Road now. For a long distance in front of him, beyond St. George's Cross, he could see the chain of street lamps stretching, as it seemed, to infinity. A sharp wind was blowing in his face. He bent his weight against it and pushed on.

He was thirty-one, unmarried, prosperous. Indeed, the whole

Moorhouse clan was prosperous. The family business in the Candleriggs might be slow this autumn, but it was steady. These farmer's sons, Arthur and David Moorhouse, dealt in the produce of the farmlands; and people must eat, even in bad times. It was possible to wait for better times before commissioning a house or an Atlantic liner, but it was less easy to wait for a pound of cheese.

The foundations of his life, then, were sound, thanks to an older brother who had built the business and taken him into it. Time was when he had resented Arthur's guiding hand, but for years now he had been quite settled and able to spread his wings. The family in its increasing prosperity, had moved out West. The Moorhouses were beginning to have standing. And his, David's, social success had been greatest of all. He was reasonably handsome. He was young and he was eligible. People invited him.

He stopped for a moment at St. George's Cross, to allow traffic coming up from St. George's Road to pass him. The breath of the horses showed as puffs of white vapour in the cold air.

Yet what did it all amount to? He was just an ordinary, well-disposed young man with a facile, pleasant way with him. Nobody at all, really. But why should that matter?

David stared, taking stock. Tonight he had looked into the face of great achievement, and although it was of a kind for which he held no yardstick, it had left him dissatisfied and self-critical.

The theatre. Irving. The applause. His tangled train of thought brought him to the love of Hamlet for Ophelia, and from there it went to the question of love as it affected himself. Was love the solution of his problem; the answer to his restlessness? Would it close this void, this emptiness? Many women had asked him why he didn't marry. He had told them quite truthfully that he didn't know.

Marriage presented itself to him as a house in a terrace, a starched parlourmaid, calling-cards and a carriage. But the strange being who would have to share the carriage with him? What about her? On this strange night of quickened sensibility, David looked into himself sharply, and had to admit that he did not want to share a house, or a carriage—or a bed, for that matter—

with anyone. At any rate, not permanently. And, now that he came to think of it, he never had done.

This last aspect of it troubled him. He had never been in love. No nineteen-year-old passion, even, had crushed his hopes of happiness forever. Was he abnormal? He had reason to know that he was not. Abnormal emotionally, perhaps? Too self-analytical, too apt to stand aside and note his own feelings?

III

He was coming to Kelvinbridge now. On his right hand was Rosebery Terrace, where his sister Sophia Butter and her family lived. There was still a light in a downstairs window. Should he go in and say "Hello", just before he went back to his own bachelor quarters? Sophia at least was the family. One of his own. But he decided against it and pushed on. Sophia was a good-hearted chatterbox. But she was the last sort of person to soothe him in the mood in which he found himself tonight.

On the bridge he could hear the waters of the Kelvin rushing over the weir in the darkness below him. On the other side a third horse was being joined to a late tramcar to help to pull it up into Hillhead. In five minutes David would be home.

Did it come to this, then, that he had better get himself married, whether he was in love or not? Would it turn him into someone? Develop him? In a year or to he would be one of the old young-men-about-town. Not a fraternity he wanted to belong to. If only he could fall in love, everything would be easy. Or so the more sentimental of his married friends told him. He had never quite trusted the people who had hastened to offer him this information. People who could talk about these things tended to be shallow. Still—perhaps.

Near the top of the hill he took a street on the left, and in a few minutes more he had reached his lodgings. He let himself in with his key and turned up the gas. There was still a glow among the ashes of his fireplace. He bent down, raked the bits together and coaxed a flame from them. As he straightened himself and took off his overcoat, he examined his reflection in the great gilt mirror that filled the wall above his draped and tasselled mantelpiece. His face had more colour than usual. Wind and exercise had put it there. He pushed back his thick, chestnut hair and stroked his discreet, boyish whiskers. It was not the first time David had looked into a glass, and it was not the first time he had been pleased with the reflection. But now, tonight, it was the first time that he had caught himself wondering what kind of effect that reflection might have on the young woman, whose face as yet he could not see.

Suddenly his lips broke into a smile and he turned away. No, he didn't look so bad. Men with worse faces than that had got themselves married. So far as faces went, his chances were quite good.

But now a thought had struck him. He would go and ask Bel Moorhouse about all this. Bel would help him. Bel was pleasantly, comfortably worldly, and quite prepared for any amount of pros and cons. He would look in at Grosvenor Terrace, sometime during the coming weekend.

David pulled off his boots and thrust his feet into his embroidered slippers. Getting up, he went to his sideboard, poured himself out a tumbler of whisky and water, and settled himself by the fire. Yes, Bel was the one to discuss this. If he could make her realise that he was in earnest, perhaps she could help him.

Chapter Two

THIS Saturday evening Bel Moorhouse was enjoying the luxury of absenting herself from where she had decided it was proper for her to be. She had taken tickets for Herr Julius Tausch's orchestral concert in the New Public Halls in Berkeley Street. The Arthur Moorhouses were not very musical. But it was time, Bel felt, that, living as they now did in one of the smartest terraces in the West End of Glasgow, they should be seen among people of consequence and taste.

But she had been busy. Already this week they had been to see Mr. Irving in "Louis XI", to a church social, and to spend a dull and dutiful evening with Mary McNairn. This afternoon, as she stood at one of the long windows of her pleasant first-floor drawing-room, looking out across the Botanic Gardens, cheerless and dank, she decided that home was the only place this evening. Her spirit for once had failed her. No. Her mending-basket and a seat by the fire.

She turned to find her sister-in-law standing beside her. "Hullo, Phœbe dear."

The sight of the young girl gave Bel pleasure, as she stood there, glowing in brown velvet and fur.

"Where have you been?"

"In Hillhead, shopping."

A beautiful creature really, this slender child, with her slanting Highland eyes and her jet-black hair. And she had promised to marry a strange young man who had lost all his money. Pity, in a way, although Bel liked Henry Hayburn well enough.

Bel became all friendliness and briskness. "Phœbe dear, I feel that you and Henry ought to go to the concert tonight."

"We're too hard up."

"But I was going to offer you our tickets. There's a new singer tonight."

"Who?"

"An Italian name. I don't remember." Bel looked at the

window as a blast of sleet struck the glass. "Anyway, it's bound to be very interesting," she added.

"I would quite like to go. At least it's something to do."

"Very well, that's settled. You and Henry are just at a time in your lives when you should be enjoying everything you can. Arthur and I have had our fling."

Phœbe had thanked Bel, wondering what kind of fling her hard-working brother had ever had. And so, having duly fed and packed Phœbe and her affianced husband off to the New Public Halls, Bel settled down by the fire with her sewing. There was only one thing lacking for her immediate contentment, and that was the presence of her husband. Arthur, an elder of the Ramshorn Church, was downstairs in the parlour (which Bel was trying to induce the younger members of the family to call the library) having an interminable interview with a dissatisfied church member.

It was right, of course, that anyone so upright and dependable as Arthur should be a church elder. But really, there were limits. Arthur was forever receiving calls from stuffy church people in whom she couldn't possibly be interested. And it was wonderful what they could go on being dissatisfied about. If only Arthur would stop being so conscientious. Bel rooted crossly in the mending-basket. She had arranged a quiet Saturday evening for him. Now it was being spoilt by dissatisfaction.

The solution was, of course, for Arthur and his family to leave the Ramshorn and join a church in this new and fashionable suburb of Kelvinside. It was tiresome to make the long journey into the City every Sunday. Especially when you might be going to a smart church not ten minutes away; a church with a bright, modern minister, who would keep your ideas abreast of the times, and bright, modern members who bought their wives entertaining hats, and had other, more up-to-date hobbies than dissatisfaction.

There was the sound of someone moving in the hall downstairs. It must be Arthur's visitor going. That was better.

She did not even turn her head as the drawing-room door opened, but merely said: "Dear me, what was the trouble this time, Arthur?"

"It's not Arthur, it's David."

II

Bel turned round in surprise. She regretted the darning-basket a little. David and darning, she felt, didn't quite go together. But it was too late to put it away and take up her embroidery.

"Oh, David, come in! I'm glad to see you. Arthur's downstairs in the library having his evening ruined with some church squabble."

"He's too conscientious."

"That's what I say."

David settled himself on the chair Bel had hoped to see her husband occupy. She was genuinely pleased to see him, though she wondered that he should come thus unannounced on a Saturday evening. For David's bachelor existence was full. But something was worrying him. She knew the signs.

"Well, David?"

David looked about him. The pleasant, richly furnished drawing-room. The stacked-up, flaming fire. The handsome, fair-haired woman opposite him, who was giving the whole a core of agreeable femininity. Here was the sympathy for which he had come.

"I thought I would look in to see you," was all he found himself saying. "I hadn't seen you for a day or two."

Bel looked up from her work and smiled. "You can smoke one pipeful here if you like."

"No, thanks. I wouldn't dare to contaminate this room."

Bel smiled again. David was sensitive and considerate.

"Phœbe and Henry have gone to the concert," she said conversationally.

"How are they getting on?"

Bel looked at David. Here, perhaps, was her clue. "What do you mean? As separate people, or as an engaged couple?"

"I suppose I mean as an engaged couple."

Funny question for a man to ask. Any woman might ask it, of course. "Quite well, I suppose. Have we *ever* known what Phœbe was thinking?"

David got up, put his hands in his pockets and took a pace or two in the room. "But do you think she's happy?"

"I don't see much difference in her." Bel wondered at this. What had prompted it? She put out another feeler. "But I'm certain it's made all the difference to Henry, after what has happened to him this autumn."

David thought of his friends Stephen and Henry Hayburn. The loss of their fortune in the City Bank crash, and the death of their mother.

"Yes, I dare say it's a good thing for him." And then, after another silence: "Do you think Phœbe is in love with him?"

"My dear David, I don't know." Did all this somehow apply to David himself? What was his problem? He was striding up and down in a way quite unlike him, trying to ask her something.

Suddenly he stopped. "Tell me this, Bel," he said. "Do you think it's better for a man to be married?"

"Of course."

"But he's got to fall in love with somebody first?"

"Yes."

"Would you say it was a lonely business later on, not being married?"

"Certainly."

"The trouble with me is, I can't fall in love."

"Nonsense."

"It's true."

Bel put down her work and sat, gazing away from him into the fire. She genuinely wanted to help him. Something had stirred him and made him very much in earnest about this. He was not just a boy. The great loneliness of the unmated had overwhelmed him, and he didn't know what to do about it. It was so difficult to help a man, to know a man's feelings.

David was attractive and lovable, but she could well believe he had never been in love. He was agile-minded, quick to discover his own reactions, and not, she guessed, more than normally sexed. He would laugh at his own little susceptibilities too quickly, refuse to take his feelings seriously. And he had far too many pleasant friendships with women; understood them too well, to be easily borne off his feet.

Still looking into the fire, she spoke. "Are you anxious to be married, David?"

"I don't want life to slip past me."

"You can afford to wait. Arthur was your age when he married me."

"Yes; but he knew he wanted to marry you for years before that. That makes all the difference."

"Yes. I see what you mean." Bel let him pace about for some moments more, then she asked: "Do you know of anybody that you think is interested in you?"

"Interested?"

"Well, in love with you, then?"

"What a queer question to ask a man! Women don't show their feelings."

"If a woman was in love with you, you would know. You're that kind of man. She would be clever if she hid it from you."

"I don't know if that's a compliment."

"I'm not trying to pay you compliments, David; I'm trying to help you."

"There have been two or three."

"I thought so. Is there anybody now?"

"Yes."

"And what kind of feeling have you about her?"

"I like her. But since I've seen she was—well, like that, I've been keeping away."

"Go back and have another look at her." Bel took up her mending again. "You know, David," she said, "there are some people who fall in love only after they're settled down and married."

"Do you mean I'm one of them?"

"Maybe."

"But it's very important for me to know."

Bel did not reply at once. This was the strangest conversation she had had for a long time. She was very fond of David. He had been a very young man when she had married his brother. And of all the family, perhaps, she had stood nearest to him; nearer than his own sisters. There was a fastidiousness about him, a niceness, that had always appealed to her.

"I don't really know how you feel about this, David," she said at length. "How can I? Many women marry without love, and it turns out all right. They say it doesn't happen so often with men."

"Would you risk it, if you were me?"

To give definite judgment was too much responsibility. Bel

hedged. "Go back and see your girl, anyway, David. Give your feelings a chance."

Arthur Moorhouse's appearance brought this talk to an end, the church member having taken himself off. It was just as well, Bel felt. Confidences such as these tended to become dangerous. Arthur's wiry, vigorous presence brought things back to normal. He stood on the rug, his back to the blazing fire, warming himself.

"I want a cup of tea, Bel," he said testily. "I'm sick of folks and their blethers."

III

Phœbe, followed by Henry Hayburn, jumped from the cab that had brought them to the New Public Halls in Berkeley Street. Inside, the auditorium was quickly filling with people. Bel had obtained the seats intended for herself and Arthur in the front of the gallery, half-way down the long hall. They ascended the main staircase, found their block in the steeply graded rows, and climbed down into their places. Sitting now, beside the eager, boyish young man who had but lately engaged himself to become her husband, Phœbe looked about her. Glasgow's large new concert hall was still a novelty to her. She looked with interest at the sea of seats in the area beneath her; the people finding their places over there in the gallery opposite; at those—scarcely to be distinguished, so great was the distance—who were filing up into the high gallery at the back.

Phœbe and Henry had no intense interest in music. But young people, so alive, could not fail to feel the latent excitement in the waiting audience. They consulted their programmes. They hung over the gallery, picking out acquaintances. They twisted themselves about to see who was near them.

Now the orchestra was coming in. The platform was becoming busy. The harpist was plucking odd strings. One player nodded greeting to another. Musicians were placing their chairs to a nicety. The right positions for music-stands were being found. There was a constant tuning of the fiddles and their like. Wood and wind instruments emitted fragments of scales. Up at the back, the drummer was adjusting the tension of his drums. The air was filled with the sounds of preparation. Phœbe and Henry were enjoying themselves.

Sitting on Phœbe's other side, a young woman was making much fuss with herself. She was telling friends how she had studied recently with this very Julius Tausch who was to conduct his first popular Saturday concert in Scotland tonight. To enhance her own importance, she was doing her best to impress upon them what a singular man Herr Tausch was. He was a pupil of Mendelssohn, she said, and had succeeded Schumann to a musical post in Dusseldorf. Phœbe, avid of life herself, listened with interest, and envied the young woman her education abroad.

The noise of tuning stopped, as the first violin came in to take his seat. A hush of interest swept the halls. Late-comers tiptoed hurriedly to their seats. Now the side-curtains were held aside by an unseen hand and the new conductor, a heavily-bearded, shaggy-haired, energetic German, hurried in to take his place before the orchestra. For a moment he stood, acknowledging the welcoming applause; then he turned, tapped his desk with Teutonic vigour, and the concert had begun.

It was a Saturday concert, and the music was not, in everything, strictly classical. A popular overture. Next, an arrangement of tunes borrowed from many sources, entitled "Melodious Congress", in which the leading instruments of the orchestra had solos to perform as an exhibition of their skill. To Phœbe it was entertaining enough. But, even so, she was not sorry to note that when the "Melodious Congress" had been given, a certain Signora Lucia Reni would delight them with her singing. At least one could look at the singer's dress, wonder how young she really was, and if her hair was all her own.

Now the second piece was ended. Herr Tausch had laid down his baton, and gone beyond the curtain to return at once gallantly leading the Signora, who came, smiling and bowing with professional coquetry. As she took up her place at the front of the platform, Phœbe scrutinised her with interest. The singer looked thirty or thereabout. Her aspect was Parisian rather than Italian. Her skin was fair and Gallic, though her abundant hair was black. The white satin dress sat severely plain on the plump bust, the hour-glass waist and the carefully corseted hips; it was only when it had come below the knee that, after the fashion of the day, it broke into lavish loops and frills. Her long kid-gloves added to the effect of whiteness. The only colour the Signora permitted herself was a red rose admirably set in her hair, killing any austerity in her dress, and somehow adding sparkle and gaiety to her features. A splendid concert appearance, Phœbe decided. But that was not all. Why was her face familiar?

Now Signora Reni was standing, charmingly serious, listening to the orchestra as it played the introduction to her aria. Now she was singing with a clear, trained, concert soprano's voice; filling the great space with a practised ease. No. Phœbe had seen this woman somewhere before, though she had never heard her perform. A long time ago, perhaps. This imperfect remembrance baffled and maddened her. Now the singer was bowing and smiling acknowledgment at the end of the song. Now she was going off. Still Phœbe could not place her in her mind.

She turned to her companion. "Henry, have you ever seen that woman before?"

"No, never."

"Doesn't she remind you of anybody?"

"No, I don't think so."

The orchestra was playing again. Henry was no help, then. She couldn't have known her when she was a little girl in the country, could she? She had never known any Italians. Yet, she had heard that public singers often gave themselves Italian names. She turned to the programme once more. Lucia Reni. About a mile from the Laigh farm there was a farm called Greenhead. Its farmer was called Rennie. One of his daughters was called Lucy. Lucy Rennie. Lucia Reni. Now she was getting somewhere. The light was breaking. Yes, she had seen Lucy Rennie once or twice, when she was a little girl at the Laigh. Lucy Rennie had been, if she remembered aright, about the same age as her brother David. They had been schoolmates together. And she had seen the other Rennie sister and her father quite recently. She must, in part, be recognising a family likeness. She would have another look at her when she came back to sing again.

Phœbe gave her future husband a joyful dig. Henry, whose attention had been caught by the music, turned reluctantly to see her smiling in triumph.

"Henry! I've guessed who she is! She's no more Italian than I am!"

Henry responded to her joy with impatience. "All right. You can tell me later," he said, turning indignantly again to the music.

IV

David was still at Grosvenor Terrace when Phœbe and Henry Hayburn came back. In the light of his conversation with Bel and his own preoccupations, he found himself watching the young people closely. Henry, coltish and uncouth, was quite obviously very much in love with Phœbe. There was something still schoolboyish in his attitude towards her; although he was twenty-three and Phœbe eighteen, he seemed very much the younger of the two. Towards Henry, Phœbe, as usual, betrayed nothing. She was cool and friendly. Nothing more. Perhaps Moorhouses were not like other people, David pondered.

"Well, children," Bel was saying, "did you enjoy yourselves? What about the singer?"

Phœbe turned to Arthur and David. "Do you know who the grand new singer was?"

Arthur looked at his youngest sister with fatherly benevolence.

"Don't ask me, my dear. I don't know about these kind of people."

"Does the name Lucia Reni sound like anybody you know?"

"It sounds to me kind o' Italian or something."

Phœbe's eyes shone with triumph. "It was Lucy Rennie of Greenhead!"

"Do you mean to tell me that? Old Tom Rennie's daughter?"

"Yes."

All this was Greek to Bel. Who was Lucy Rennie? Where or what was Greenhead? Why the surprise? She asked questions.

Greenhead, it was explained to Bel, was a neighbouring farm to the Laigh. This prima donna with an Italian name was none other than the neighbouring farmer's daughter. The Moorhouse boys and Phœbe had known her family all their lives.

"I knew one of the Greenhead lassies had gone to London. She would have been better to stay at home," Arthur said presently. The Moorhouse roots went deep into the Lowland peasantry. And, like most peasants, they were suspicious of artists and their like—seers of visions and dreamers of dreams. If you had made your fortune, walking all the while in due fear of the Lord, then perhaps you might spend some of it in buying their books or their pictures, or even in watching their performances on stages or platforms. But there contact must end.

Phœbe and David took Arthur's meaning perfectly. They were of his blood. But Bel was anxious to hear more of this woman.

What did she sing?

Phœbe had brought home a programme. It all looked very professional and high falutin.

Had she sung well?

Phœbe and Henry thought so. She had made a success and been recalled several times.

What did she look like?

She was elegantly dressed in white, and seemed pretty in the distance.

"She'll be thirty if she's a day," was Arthur's comment.

Bel sensed the hostility in his voice and was at a loss to account for it. Arthur was usually so fair-minded. She could not understand that, in addition to his inborn dislike of artists, he had struck upon an old family rivalry. There had been courtesy and even help between the farms, as is necessary among those who must close the ranks every now and then in their battle with Nature. But the Rennies of Greenhead had always been sharp and opportunist; while the Moorhouses of the Laigh Farm had been plodding and industrious. Now a Rennie, true to her type, had appeared and scored a point in a most unexpected and, to Arthur's thinking, none too admirable a way. And, little as it concerned him, Arthur didn't like it.

Chapter Three

IF there had been a woman in the office of Arthur Moorhouse and Company, she would have noticed the difference in David's appearance at once. But these were not yet the days when women clerks were to be found everywhere. Arthur would strongly have disapproved of the idea. He had said often enough that the Candleriggs was no place for a woman. By which he meant that it was no place for a woman who was unused to the coarse oaths and obscene badinage of the carters and warehousemen as they loaded and unloaded their heavy goods, or roughly elbowed their way in this narrow, straw-and-paper-littered street where the distribution of Glasgow's food-stuffs took place.

But as it was, all the hands being male, none of them noticed that Mr. David was more meticulously dressed than usual. His old office coat was put on, of course, when he came in of a morning, but the one he hung up on the peg behind the counting-house door was new, and before he put it on again to go out it was brushed with the office clothes-brush. His waistcoat, his linen and his trousers, always careful, were even more careful these days.

In other words, David had made up his mind, and—never at any time averse to a little forethought—was laying his plans. Bel had told him to have a look at this girl again, and he had made up his mind to do so. But, careful and practised bachelor as he was, he was quite determined that this meeting should not seem deliberate. It must look casual, at all hazards. There was nothing for it, then, but to wait for an encounter. David knew the movements of his world. The chance would not long be delayed, if he put himself in the way.

It was a late November morning, bright and sparkling, with the first touches of frost. The sun, striking for a time down the narrow canyon of the Candleriggs, lent even this humdrum street a passing glory. A morning for everybody to be out. David turned back into the darkness of the warehouse. He had tried Buchanan

Street several times. He would try it again, making some excuse for half an hour of escape.

He guessed, as he turned into it, that it would be full of carriages. Women of consequence would have come into town to shop. He was right. There were equipages from the West End and the country. Most of them were halted by the kerb on either side of the broad, handsome street. Cockaded flunkeys stood by impatient, high-bred horses, holding their heads or adjusting their rugs, while their stylish mistresses made their purchases, gazed at their leisure at the windows, or merely walked and talked with each other, enjoying the sunshine.

David was preparing, not for the first time, to make a detailed examination of the carriages and their occupants, when his arm was caught and firmly held by an elderly man.

"Hullo, Moorhouse. Are ye looking for somebody? Ye haven't seen my wife and girl, have ye?"

"Oh, good morning, Mr. Dermott."

Old Robert Dermott wondered why David changed colour. "They should be here, somewhere. They were coming in, if it was a fine morning." It would have surprised him to know that the young man he was good-naturedly holding was there to look for them, too. They stood looking about them for some moments.

David Moorhouse, the farmer's son from Ayrshire, was not sorry to be seen thus affectionately held by one of the princes of Glasgow's shipping world—a prince who, like so many of his kind, had begun life with nothing. Nearly fifty years before, the young highland giant, who was Robert Dermott, had come to a rapidly expanding Glasgow. Now he owned a fleet of merchantmen and a house in the country overlooking a deepened Clyde. From his windows he could watch his great steamers, as they moved carefully in the narrow waterway; arriving from, or setting out for, the other side of the world.

David looked up at the grand old man beside him. As he stood there, he seemed to dominate his surroundings. There was something patriarchal about his flowing beard and his bushy eyebrows. The eyes beneath them were arrestingly gentle in all this ruggedness, as they ranged the street looking for their own.

"By the way," he said conversationally, "I've taken somebody you know into Dermott Ships Limited. Young Stephen Hayburn.

I don't know what he has got in him, but I am doing it for his father's sake. His father was a friend of mine. We learnt our ABC from the same dominie at Ardfinnan."

David found himself saying that it was kind of Mr. Dermott.

"Kind? It's not kind if the boy has got anything in him. I hear the young one is to marry yer sister."

"Yes, they—"

But Mr. Dermott's thoughts, still running in their own groove, went on aloud, "Terrible smash that City Bank business. Ye know, Moorhouse, the amount of poverty and destitution up and down the country, and in this City of Glasgow this winter—"

But the amount of poverty and destitution did not at this moment prevent a particularly handsome carriage and pair making its way round from Argyle Street into Buchanan Street, the stepping horses shining with moisture after their long run into town from the country. The carriage was dark green, as was the livery of the men up in front. There were discreet monograms "R.D." in yellow on the doors.

Robert Dermott opened his giant's throat and bellowed: "Here, MacDonald, stop!" People turned round to look. The nearest horses waiting by the kerb threw up excited heads and had to be controlled. But those in the carriage in mid-stream, for whom it had been intended, had heard, too. The footman turned to tell the coachman. Two ladies were seen to lean forward and look about them. The pace slackened, and in a few moments more the horses were standing, steaming in the crisp, frosty air.

Robert Dermott, still holding David's arm, marched him forward. "Here's the wife and Grace," he said, beaming with pleasure. "Come and say hullo."

No, David pondered, as he moved forward, the thing could not have been more suitably accomplished, nor with a more casual seeming.

II

The footman was handing the ladies from the carriage. Grace Dermott sprang out first. She was a slim, fair young woman of nearer thirty than twenty. Her mother was large and commanding like her father, and some ten years younger than he. She greeted David warmly in a loud, West of Scotland voice. People turned in the street and said "Oh, there was Mrs. Robert Dermott." Her daughter, too, gave David her hand.

"Well, Mr. Moorhouse, we haven't seen you for a long time. Where have you been?"

David told Mrs. Dermott he had been busy. As he stood talking he found himself watching Grace. She was pleased to see him, but, quick to go on the defensive, he wondered now if there was more than that. He thought so. Indeed, it was to see these signs that he had put himself in her way.

In the sunshine, they walked up the street together. The horses, over-warm, had been driven on, for they must not stand in the cold. David, although he had been the guest of the Dermotts a number of times, looked at them anew this morning.

He liked them. They were effusive and kind, with that easy, enveloping kindness of simple people who had become very rich. The world had treated them well. Robert Dermott's days of striving were so far behind him that, although he talked much of his boyhood and his struggles in a bragging, old man's way, prosperity and ease had long since wiped out their bitter reality from his mind.

David's friend Stephen Hayburn had first taken him to visit them. They had accepted him at once as Stephen's friend.

He was walking between the two women. They talked of Stephen.

"Mr. Dermott has just told me that he has taken him into Dermott Ships Limited," David said.

"Yes, Robert felt he ought to, Mr. Moorhouse. His father was an old friend. We felt it was the least we could do," Mrs. Dermott said. She spoke as though nobody had any reason to be uncomfortable; but if there was any difficulty, they, the powerful and benevolent Dermotts, would see to it.

"I hear that Henry Hayburn is to marry your sister, Mr. Moorhouse," Grace said.

"Yes."

"Is she like you to look at?"

"Not in the least."

Mrs. Dermott laughed. "I nearly said what a pity."

David acknowledged the compliment and held out his hand. "Look here, it's time I was getting back to work. I'm not as idle as I look, you know." This last was aimed at Robert Dermott. Shipping princes did not approve of young men who appeared to have nothing to do.

"Can't we arrange for you to come and see us soon, Mr. Moorhouse?" Mrs. Dermott said. "What about Saturday. There are trains at all kinds of times. Or perhaps it's asking too much?"

No, it was not asking too much of Mr. Moohouse. He was merely, indeed, receiving what he had come for. "Go back and have another look at her." Bel's words came into his mind as he turned across Exchange Square making for Arthur Moorhouse and Company. Grace Dermott was a handsome girl, and everything that was good. He would go and have a look at her as he had been told to.

He liked her. Without knowing it, David slackened his brisk townsman's pace, and sauntered slowly along the pavement thinking. Obviously Mrs. Dermott wanted him to come. What did Grace feel about him? Was he perhaps, after all, imagining that she loved him? But then, Bel had said he was the kind of man who would know. David thought he knew.

III

When they had finished their business, Grace Dermott and her mother ate their roast beef before the fire, in the comfortable, well-padded dining-room of one of the many hotels in George's Square. Her father, having gone back to his office for an hour, had joined them. Although they had seen each other at breakfast and were to meet again in the evening, this affectionate trio were pleased to eat their midday meal together. None of them spoke much. Robert Dermott sat enjoying vast quantities of beef, potatoes and cabbage, his glass of claret, the prosperous looks of his wife and daughter, and the blazing fire. These immediate things occupied his mind. His thoughts, for the moment, dwelt neither upon the state of British shipping, nor upon the young man they had chanced to meet this morning.

Mrs. Dermott, having attended a committee formed to relieve the present distress in the city, sat nursing her annoyance over a decision that had been taken against her wishes.

Grace alone thought of their meeting with David.

Early in the afternoon the carriage came to fetch them home. It would take them over an hour to get there. In the yellow November sunshine they took their way along the road that follows the Clyde to Dumbarton. It was getting colder. Already a thin fog was rising from the river, rising to meet the sun hanging low and wintry in the sky, turning it to a luminous disc of pale gold. The misty smoke and the tenements of Glasgow, caught in the light, made a magic of their own.

Snug among their wrappings, the Dermotts discussed their day. The provoking Distress Committee. Grace's visit to a dressmaker. The fine gold watch that had been dropped so unaccountably, that the man had said would be so difficult to mend. A new design for embroidery. The talk of those whose business it is to spend, to be pleased and receive respect wherever they may go. But presently, lulled by the beauty of the evening, the steady trot of the horses, and springing rhythm of the carriage, they sat back saying nothing more.

They were passing Kelvingrove, with the new, ornate University towering high on the hill above it. The green slopes of the park and the clumps of bare trees were lit by the dying sunshine. From the River Kelvin, too, a white mist was rising.

So her mother had asked him to pay them another visit. Grace was glad. She would see him again. At the same time she was afraid. Would the visit merely bore him? Caught up suddenly in the upsurge of her feelings she found herself twisting her gloved fingers together under the great fur rug. She knew quite well why her mother had invited David. No confidences about him had ever passed between them. But there are a great many things that women do not need to tell each other. They were passing through the village of Partick—now a busy, industrial suburb. Here and there they caught glimpses of the Clyde's busy waterway; of fussy river steamers belching smoke and churning the water with their paddles; of the many high masts of the clippers. Across the water a great iron hull stood uncompleted in the stacks, black against the sun.

If he had wanted her he would have come on his own account. He wouldn't have waited to be asked. Men were like that.

They didn't need encouragement. There would be someone else. Why had her mother bothered him? They would lose dignity over this. She would tell her she did not want to see him. No. That would be absurd.

Now they were driving between farmlands. Fields of green pasturage and yellow stubble spreading over the flanks of rolling hills or stretching flatly towards the river.

But Grace, as she sat forward clasping her fingers, did not see what was around her. She saw the face of David Moorhouse, handsome, serious and, somehow, remote. And again she saw it as it was when, some weeks ago, he had bent down to pick up some trifle she had dropped on the harness-room floor, flushed and laughing, with a thick strand of chestnut hair over his brow. A woman never should give her heart until she was asked for it. She could not help herself. It had happened like that, and there was nothing to be done.

A sudden glimpse revealed the widening river in the sunset, a sheet of angry copper. Presently they had turned from the main road, passed a gatehouse and were between the trees of their own drive.

Mrs. Dermott looked at her daughter. She saw that her eyes were full of tears.

Chapter Four

LITTLE Arthur Moorhouse had had his hair cut. And by way of recompense for stern self-control during the cutting, he had received his reward. The barber had given him a balloon. Now the seven-year-old stalwart, one hand in his mother's, the other grasping the string of his prize, was being towed about Hillhead, while Bel did her weekend shopping. Progress was not easy; for everybody else was out, on this, the last Saturday morning of November; and, as Arthur refused to look in front of him, but kept his head turned round watching the large, sea-green sphere that floated behind him, he was continually colliding with other little boys or their mothers; much to the annoyance of his own.

"Come on, dear; you can play as much as you like with your balloon when you get home."

"Mother, would it be very unselfish of me if I gave this balloon to Tom when I get home?"

"Very."

"Too unselfish?" Should one ever do so much for a brother? Bel looked at her son's troubled face and laughed. "Tom's very wee, he's only three. Perhaps he would just burst it."

"Yes; I think perhaps it would be wiser not to give it to him."

Arthur now looked pleased and comfortable.

For a moment Bel was stricken. Was she teaching her elder son to be selfish? But really, with her mind so full of tomorrow's roast beef, and fish for tonight, and the baker and the florist, child psychology (although it was not yet known to her by that name) was too much for her this morning.

"I've not spent my Saturday penny yet," Arthur said, suddenly stopping dead and refusing to move.

"Well, come on, dear; you'll have time to do that if we hurry. Don't dawdle."

Arthur trotted along, meditating deeply. Now here prestige was involved. If he had only his own tastes to consider, he would buy Slim-Jim, or broken chocolates—you got a lot of that. But, on the other hand, as a man of the world and a Kelvinside Academy scholar of some three-months' standing, perhaps he owed it to himself to buy liquorice straps. The boy who arrived on Monday morning with straps of liquorice was popular and important. You flogged all the dirty, perspiring paws of your friends with the liquorice, then gave them torn-off pieces of it to eat in return for having unflinchingly allowed this sadism. No. On the whole, liquorice straps would be best. He would give them to his Aunt Phœbe to keep until Monday morning. Otherwise infirmity of purpose might overcome him, and he would eat them before they could be used to increase his glory.

So in the sweetie-shop Arthur bought his liquorice. And, as she happened to be on the spot, his mother bought materials to keep him—and herself—contented in church on the morrow. As they left, tragedy occurred. Bel, quick and over-purposeful, shut the shop door behind her too soon. There was a loud report. She had crushed Arthur's balloon. On the pavement outside there was threatened lamentation.

"Now, remember, you're a big boy, Arthur. You know your mother didn't mean it." Arthur was uncertain of his emotions, and had to be further reminded that the boys at school would think him a great baby if he cried about a silly thing like a burst balloon.

Using a child's very effective blackmail on his harassed but tender-hearted mother, he thought he might feel better if he were allowed to go down to Kelvinbridge and look down at the water rushing over the weir. Bel was not strong enough to refuse him.

II

Arthur cheered up as his mother held him to look over the parapet at the rushing Kelvin beneath him. There were great moving islands of foam and autumn leaves. He even recovered enough to spit several times and watch the result descending.

"Come along, Arthur; we really must go." She had him on the pavement again, and was striking the dust of the parapet from him, when she came face to face with Sophia Butter, accompanied by a young woman.

"Bel, dear! And Arthur!" Sophia always made a great deal of noise about nothing. "And look who I've got with me! Of course, you don't know her, because, of course, you haven't met. This is Lucy Rennie! This is Arthur's wife Bel!"

Bel turned to the young woman with interest. Fashionable herself, she took in her appearance at a glance. So this was the singer they had been discussing the other evening!

Miss Rennie was small, dark, rather plump and very well dressed. There was a quickness and sparkle about her manner that might have belonged to a Frenchwoman.

"I used to know your husband, Mrs. Moorhouse, although I knew David better." She was a little affected; but that too, Bel thought, was charming. Her speech held no trace of Scotch.

Bel couldn't help being interested. The very fact that Arthur disapproved of her gave her a tang. She seemed a harmless enough sort of young woman.

Sophia had never stopped chattering. "It's too silly! I met Lucy wandering about in Hillhead. And I knew her at once after all these years! Not a bit different! Terribly smart, of course. And very grand! That's what comes of being so much in London. I am taking her in to have a cup of tea and tell me all about herself. Come along too, Bel. And Arthur will see the children—at least, if they're there. They're so awful, I never know where they are."

It was not often that Bel went to Sophia's house. First, because she was seldom invited; and second, because its untidiness embarrassed her. Like many very orderly people, the untidiness of others made her ill at ease. But now, busy though she was, she could not refuse.

They crossed to the east side of the bridge. A few steps more took them to Rosebery Terrace. Sophia's house smelt of cooking. The little maid, who let them in, glided off in carpet slippers to get them tea. Seated in the back parlour, Bel could hear cups being indignantly banged on a tray. There was a quarrel going on between the son and daughter of the house somewhere upstairs.

Sophia poked up the fire. "I think I hear the children," she said. "Come with me, Arthur, and we'll go and look for them.

I won't be a minute. But they must be told Arthur's here. I would never hear the end of it if they didn't see him." And Sophia went out of the room, leaving Bel and Miss Rennie altogether.

"Oh, I know Sophia of old!" Lucy Rennie said. "She was always terribly kind." She laughed. Gaily and intimately. As one woman of fashion to another. She gave Bel the impression that she had stopped herself just in time. That the adverb "terribly" had been intended to qualify some adjective quite other than "kind". "Funny" perhaps, or "idiotic".

Bel was delighted with her. Everything about Miss Rennie appealed to her. Her alertness. Her knowledge of the world. Her "English" accent. Her poise.

"I can't believe you came from the farm next to my father-in-law's."

"Why?"

"You don't strike me at all as being a farmer's daughter."

Lucy smiled. "I dare say. I have been in London for the last eight or nine years. It's a long story, but a simple one, really. Someone heard me singing when I was twenty, and offered to give me a year's training. I accepted. Soon I did some teaching, myself, to keep me going, then I began to get engagements as well as teaching. And here I am."

"Wasn't it very hard?" Bel asked innocently.

"Abominably."

"Weren't you very lonely?"

"Very—at first. Later I made friends, of course." Miss Rennie allowed her eyes to twinkle. "I'm a self-made woman, I'm afraid, Mrs. Moorhouse."

For a moment Bel sensed that she was merely presenting her with a façade. That a quite different person might be there behind this charm. No young girl that she knew would have the hardihood to do what Miss Rennie had done. She had, surely, taken great risks. And yet Bel liked her none the less. She saw no reason to question what Lucy Rennie had told her, nor did she stop to think that this might not be quite the whole story.

"Is your home in London?"

"Yes. I have nearly all my work there. I do a certain amount of public singing, but most of my engagements are private."

"Private?"

"Yes. People with handles to their names, and so on, give musical parties and pay me to sing at them."

III

Further talk was interrupted by Wil Butter, a large, gawky, good-natured boy of fifteen, who burst into the room carrying Arthur pick-a-back, and followed by Margy, his sister, a long-legged girl in a pinafore. Arthur was screaming, delighted and hysterical. It was not every day that he had large cousins devoting themselves to his amusement.

Sophia followed them. "Children, shake hands with Miss Rennie and your Auntie Bel, then go away at once. We can't hear ourselves speaking. Here's tea. No, children, you're not to eat the biscuits. They're for the visitors. Arthur, you have one, dear. That's right. That's a nice one. Wil, Margy, what did I say? Hand them to Miss Rennie at once. Margy, ask Jenny for the sugar. She's forgotten it. Lucy, how do you like your tea? Weak? Well, that's all right. It's pretty weak as it is. Sugar's just coming."

As Bel watched Lucy, sitting easy and self-possessed in the midst of all this good-natured uproar, a scheme was forming itself in her mind. Smart people gave musical parties in London, did they? She wondered if she dare. It would be so very up-to-date, so very interesting. But, then, how did one go about it? And what did one pay?

"I'm sorry to say I didn't hear you sing at Mr. Tausch's concert in the New Public Halls the other Saturday," she said.

"I didn't either," Sophia broke in, or, rather, deflected the ceaseless stream of her talk in their direction. "William, my husband, and I meant to go. Then I can't remember what it was kept us. Anyway, a lady in the church told us you were just wonderful. She said you brought tears to her eyes. Now—what was it you sang she said was so beautiful? Anyway, she said she had never been so touched by singing in her life!"

Miss Rennie smiled. Even this flattering nonsense was grist to her mill. She sang for her bread-and-butter. And it did her self-esteem no harm to know that even that kind of person liked her work.

Would she be singing in Glasgow again? Bel asked. Not in the meantime. But she was in private rooms for a week or two, using the City as a centre. There was a piano where she could work, and give odd lessons. Thereafter, she was going back to Ayrshire to spend New Year with her family.

Bel rose to go. Sophia went to find Arthur for her. He had been carried off again by the larger children. Miss Rennie said she must go, too. She would leave with them.

As they said goodbye to the Butter family, Bel's mind was working. Should she ask this woman to her house? Arthur seemed to object to the entire Rennie clan, but that was ridiculous. After all, she had met this woman at his sister's. She was interesting, clever and different. Why be stodgy?

"You must come and see me, Miss Rennie," she said as they stood at the end of the little terrace.

"I should like to." Mrs. Arthur Moorhouse, after all, looked a woman of some consequence.

IV

A little group of ragged children, wheeling a dirty baby in a soap-box, scuttled past them. A white-faced mite, who looked two or three, but had the sharpness of six or seven, detached himself from them and held out a filthy paw to the ladies.

"Gie's a ha'penny." His black eyes were pitiful in his little sharp face.

The ready emotion of a performing artist brought tears to Miss Rennie's eye. She drew her purse from her muff and gave him a sixpence.

Bel, not to be outdone, gave Arthur the same to give to the urchin.

"Poor little things!" Lucy Rennie said, as she watched the child scamper back to the others.

"My husband says there's terrible distress among these people this winter, Miss Rennie. There are subscriptions and charities being organised for them everywhere."

"It's bad in London, too. I've sung at one or two charity evenings." She looked after the ragged children. "If you have a large drawing-room, Mrs. Moorhouse, I should be glad to do it for you. It's quite a good way to raise money."

Bel was enchanted. But she must go warily. After all, there was Arthur.

"It would be wonderful, Miss Rennie. Come and see me next week, and meanwhile I'll discuss it with my husband. There is nothing I'd like better."

She fixed a day, and bade Lucy Rennie a cordial goodbye. This was amazing! And for charity! Arthur couldn't be such a bear as to refuse. He couldn't be so narrow-minded. Sometime this weekend she would await her opportunity and ask him.

"Come along, Arthur; we're going to be late."

Arthur the Second trotted home behind a mother who was carried forward on wings of delight and determination. As he had no such wings but merely his own sturdy enough little legs to depend upon, he found it hot work.

Bel was set upon having her evening. That it be charitable, was very proper; that it be smart, was imperative.

Chapter Five

THERE are certain strong, elderly women who work off their energy interfering with other people. Mrs. Robert Dermott was one of these. But as her interferences were on the whole benevolent, and as, in the case of the poor at least, they were accompanied by cheques of her own signing, she seemed to make strangely few enemies. If she were not interfering in person, then she was writing letters of interference. Of such are the convenors of committees.

Mrs. Dermott wrote letters all over her large, ugly and comfortable Clydeside house. At Aucheneame, her bedroom and all the living-rooms had a desk with pen and paper waiting ready to her hand. Even in the large conservatory full of palms, maidenhair fern and chirping canaries, there was a slender bamboo table waiting to creak beneath her weight as she leant upon it writing. Her spectacle-case, attached to her person, was kept full of stamps, for, as she would have told you, she hated to have to be hunting for things.

A purposeful, though not dislikeable lady, if you could stand up to her, with much of the strength and drive belonging to her husband. It was no wonder that this couple had long ago reduced their only daughter to meekness and docility. And yet, between her letter-writing and committee-attending, and after her own fashion, Mrs. Dermott was very fond of Grace. She had been thinking about her recently, and she was worried. Grace was twenty-nine and unmarried. It was high time she was. What was wrong with the young men? She was reasonably pleasant to look at, gentle and feminine, and not half-witted. What more did young men want? What kept them away?

It had never struck Mrs. Dermott that her husband's wealth, and the crashing personalities of both of them, had tended to push suitors to a distance.

On the early evening of her return from Glasgow, Mrs. Dermott sat at the writing-desk in her bedroom sucking the end of a pen and thinking. She thought of the strained look and the tears in Grace's eyes as they had driven home that afternoon. She had noticed such symptoms before. Putting two and two together, she was almost certain that the girl loved David Moorhouse. This morning, Mrs. Dermott had asked him to visit them, just as she would have asked any young man, or indeed any pleasant person who would have been willing to come. For what was the use of all the paraphernalia of hospitality if you were inhospitable? Grace, for all her seeming passiveness, had betrayed excitement at the prospect of David's visit. She must, then, take the young man seriously, and do what was best for her daughter.

What about this David Moorhouse? What sort of person was he? He had already been four or five times in Aucheneame, and Mrs. Dermott, in so far as she had thought about him at all, had liked him.

Neither she nor her husband were highly critical. They were too intent upon themselves. They met many people, and took them as they found them. He made his friends in the business world, and she in the world of philanthropy. Like most successful public people, their friends were those who worked well with them.

But now, Mrs. Dermott pondered, it was time she found out more about this young man. She must ask Grace about him. As casually as possible, of course.

II

As she rose to find her, Grace's father came into the room.

"Hullo, Robert," she said. "I didn't know you were home."

Her husband stood warming his back at the bedroom fire.

"I have been thinking about Mr. Moorhouse," Mrs. Dermott went on, "and I've taken an idea that Grace likes him."

Robert Dermott merely stroked his patriarch's beard with an enormous hand and said: "Is that the way of it?"

"He seems a nice sort of young man."

"Aye."

"I wish you would find out something about him, Robert."

"I know a lot about him already. I thought things might be taking a turn that way. So I took some trouble to find out."

"And do you mean to say you never bothered to tell me?"

"It wasna verra important."

"Then why did you bother?"

"I bother about every young man that comes here. I've a daughter in the house."

"She's my daughter, too, Robert."

A smile slowly lit up Robert Dermott's eyes. "Sir William knows him and his brother," he said.

"And what are they?"

Dermott told his wife. Three Ayrshire farmer's sons. The eldest still a farmer, but, rather surprisingly, married into the Ayrshire county. The other two brothers, Arthur and David, were prosperous cheese merchants, who somehow managed to have the bearing of professional men. Two sisters, who had made everyday marriages. And the young half-sister who was engaged to Henry Hayburn.

"You seem to know all about them. You're a sly old rascal."

"D'you want your lassie to get married to a cheese merchant?"

"Yes. If it's going to break her heart if she doesn't, Robert."

Dermott turned and looked into the fire. "You took me. I was only the son of a herd."

Mrs. Dermott rose and kissed her husband—an indulgence she did not often permit herself. The Dermott's were built on a scale too imposing somehow to do much kissing.

A housemaid came in with gleaming copper cans steaming with hot water. She saw to the room and laid out such clothes as they might want for the evening. And as he stood watching her, Robert Dermott thought of a cottage fifty years ago, where the peat smoke had found its way out through a hole in the thatch. It was a far journey from there to here, but he had made it. He was not the only one who had made this journey—and with dignity—in Victorian Glasgow.

III

It would seem an impertinence that a young man, situated as David Moorhouse was, should coolly plan a visit to the only daughter of a shipping prince, to find out if he could possibly like her enough to ask her to marry him. That was the exact purpose of this visit he had arranged for himself. And yet to state it thus is somehow to misstate it. For the worldly aspect of an alliance with Grace Dermott did not greatly influence him.

David Moorhouse belonged to a rising family. But none of them were narrowly mercenary. Each and all of them had a fundamental, peasant dignity. If David had come to visit Grace, it was to seek the answer to a question that he was earnestly putting to himself. Trimmings had little to do with it. In no way could he be called contemptible. He was handsome. He was quite straightforwardly kind. He had good manners, and a certain fastidiousness. He was quick to adapt himself to the ways of those about him, because he had been born sensitive. In other words, he was socially adroit. He must not be labelled a common schemer. There was nothing of that about him.

And yet it was a very collected sort of young man who gave his name to the man-servant that winter afternoon at the door of Aucheneame. He had a complete hold of his emotions, for the good reason that he had no strong emotions to take hold of. And when, some moments later, he stood in the open doorway of Mrs. Dermott's drawing-room and caught a glimpse in a mirror of himself standing with a smile on his face, ready to be welcomed by his hostess, the elegant cut of his frock-coat and trousers reassured him. He would be able to give his usual easy performance, and from behind that, he hoped to be able to make up his mind.

Grace and her mother were in the room. Mrs. Dermott, advancing upon him in a way that was somehow reminiscent of one of her husband's ocean-going steamers, conducted him to a chair by a heaped-up fire, speaking at the same time words of welcome, regret at the coldness of the day, and assurances that tea would be here immediately, all in her loud, assured voice.

Grace's colour had risen and her eyes were shining. Surely he had guessed aright her feeling for him. It was for him now to search for his own.

It was bleak outside the large windows, but the bright leaping fire seemed to gather the little party into its friendly glow. Darkness was falling quickly now, but the shadows, as they deepened in the great tasteless room, merely served to make their circle more friendly.

Tea came, and the master of the house was called. The Dermotts could not help themselves. Their warm-heartedness towards each other was easily extended to take in their guest. If they had had no deeper interest, if he had merely been a passing visitor, it would have been much the same. Grace's parents had much to say. He could sit, eat his buttered toast and observe. Grace seemed quite unembarrassed. She poured out tea and looked after everybody, smiling indulgently at him as one young person to another, when the talkativeness of her parents clashed; or when, as happened frequently in their vitality and enthusiasm, they fell into argument with each other.

David, trying to be pleased, assured himself that she was more appealing than he had ever known her.

"Are you very anxious to be married?"

"I don't want life to slip past me."

His conversation with Bel. He was honestly seeking the answer. Could this gentle young woman hold on to life for him? Keep it from slipping past him? Allow it to unroll itself richly and naturally before him? Prevent it from drifting on to the end, arid and aimless, a thing of unsatisfied instincts, a barren passing of the time? David was beginning to think so.

He felt happy and at ease. If Grace really wanted it, her parents, surely, would not make it difficult. She was not in her first youth. Marriage might easily miss her now. Rightly he guessed that the way would be made plain for him to find his place as the prince consort in this shipping dynasty.

The fine china and solid silver were being removed, blinds were pulled down, curtains drawn. Robert Dermott had gone off to see to some business. His wife rose.

"You will stay for a meal tonight, Mr. Moorhouse? It's nice to have you all to ourselves."

David was pleased to accept.

"I have a letter to go to the post, if you'll excuse me. You must just try to put up with Grace by herself for a little. Do you mind?"

No, David didn't mind. So they were throwing her deliberately in his way, were they. Very well. So much the better.

IV

Grace Dermott had repose of manner. Perhaps it came from having to live with stormy, energetic parents, having to keep calm in the centre of the turmoil they created around her. This quality stood her in good stead. Even now, when the storm raged in her own senses, she continued to seem at peace.

Left alone with David, she rose, stirred the fire, and bade him take the great chair that her father had quitted, regretting the while that it was grown too dark and cold to be outside.

David, too, seemed at his ease. In this atmosphere the couple talked. Of trivialities. Of the terrier lying on the rug in front of the fire. Of the people they knew. Of books. Of recent visits to the theatre. Of themselves. Of what does any civilised man or woman talk, when the battle of sex is being fought out between them? Any talk is a revealing of the one to the other. Its subject does not matter.

Grace's sensibilities were not any less quick than those of the young man who sat before her. Like herself, he was restrained and friendly. They had let themselves fall into a pleasant adult intimacy. There was no callow boy-and-girl self-consciousness. Yet each was intensely conscious of the other.

She had no doubts about herself. If this young man who was bending forward, his face aglow in the firelight, wanted her, she was his for the taking. Quite ridiculous things moved her. A way he had of putting back his thick chestnut hair. The set of his mouth and eyes when he smiled. Certain inflections of his voice. In other words, she was prepared to adore David Moorhouse in the most normal way possible.

But when she came to try to read his mind towards herself, Grace was baffled. As his good-mannered talk flowed on, she was puzzled. What had brought him here? Love for herself? She had no idea. She could find goodwill, pleasure in her company, a sincere attempt to make himself attractive to her. But further than that she could not yet penetrate. Suppose he were thrown thus intimately together with any other young woman? Would he behave in the same good-mannered way? She could not tell.

Meanwhile she must be glad she had him by her; take what she could from this hour; encourage him, in so far as dignity would permit, to visit her again.

Grace sat late before her bedroom fire that night. She was not unhappy. At parting he had given her his hand and asked if he might come soon again. It might be difficult to guess his feelings, but in doing this he had, at least, given a sign.

Chapter Six

ARTHUR MOORHOUSE saw his foreman turn the key in the main door of Arthur Moorhouse and Company. "I'll go up to the Infirmary myself, James, and I'll meet you at the Cross at three." He turned in the direction of the Traders' Club. He was glad to find the sombre dining-room empty, though indeed he had expected this, for most members ate their midday-meal at home on Saturdays, or snatched food quickly elsewhere before they went to golf—a game which, at this time, was beginning to be fashionable. He sat at a table by himself, glad to eat his chop in peace. It had been a distressing morning. There had been an accident to one of his packers.

The man was a raw Highland crofter, who, like so many of his kind, had been driven to the City to make a living. A startled dray-horse had suddenly backed, and a wheel had passed over his foot. Arthur had seen the man and his foot before they had been able to have him taken to hospital. It had been a sickening and pitiful sight. As he sat waiting, numb and patient, afraid to stir lest he increase his pain, the Highlander had reminded Arthur of a wild thing in a trap.

"Have ye a wife, McCrimmon?"

"Aye."

"And weans?"

"Aye."

"I'll go and see yer wife and take yer wages to her."

Tears rolled down the man's cheeks. That had been thanks enough for Arthur. After his meal he took himself up the hill to the Royal Infirmary, and was told that the foot had been amputated. Sorrowful, he turned from the door, and made his way down towards the Cross to break the news to the man's wife and give her a week's wages.

Arthur had arranged with his foreman to meet him; for this part of the city, small in area, yet with more than one-quarter of its inhabitants thrust together into its stews and slums, was a labyrinth to anyone who did not know it. The High Street was waking up to its usual Saturday orgy. Hungry, barefoot children, drink-sodden men and women, tired and struggling humanity. The dark side of this great, successful city. Arthur was well used to the look of these people. As a rule he accepted them, telling himself, as all his like did, that do what one would, poverty and squalor would always be. But today the sights about him weighed upon him more heavily. There were plans, he knew—plans and passionate appeals on behalf of the victims of this slumdom. But even if they bore fruit this afternoon, they would be too late to save that consumptive drab, that little group of undernourished children. He hurried on, comforting his conscience with a promise to give as much as he could to charity.

His foreman was waiting for him. Together they set off down one of the nearby wynds. He was glad to have protection. For, as the man knew this region of "ticketed houses", and had, indeed, been to the injured man's quarters, he was able to show the way. No easy matter. For in this part of the town a policeman, tracking a criminal, would receive such an address as: "Crawford's Wynd, No. 21, Back Land, stair second on left, three up, left lobby facing the door." Such directions were keys of labyrinths—labyrinths of crime and disease, indecency and death. Arthur followed through a filthy entrance, across another narrow wynd, up stairs rank with humanity, and along a passage where they had to strike matches to see their way. Everywhere they were followed by eyes—dull eyes, over-bright eyes, pitiful eyes, bewildered, childish eyes; the eyes of those to whom the great revolution of the nineteenth century, the triumph of iron ships, the expansion of industry, had been cruel.

Their luck was in. They found McCrimmon's wife at home. That is, if a part of a room partitioned off by thin wood can be called home. A low fire was burning, and by its light and such as came through the small window, Arthur saw a young woman and two little children. From what he had seen of the denizens of this place on his way up, he was surprised that the woman was normally tall. Though she was pale, she was neither ailing nor wasted. There were two chairs, a table and even a bed. An attempt was made at cleanliness—a difficult feat this, where water had to be fetched up several flights of stairs.

The sight of the black-coated gentleman threw the woman into a dumb agitation. It could forebode nothing but trouble. She stood in the middle of the room, her children clutching her dress, waiting for Arthur to speak.

"Are you Mrs. McCrimmon?" he asked.

"Yes, sir. Mrs. McCrimmon. Hamish McCrimmon's wife. Are you being Mr. Moorhouse?"

"Yes."

"I was after seeing you before once in the distance, sir." She twisted her rough apron in her hands. Her voice had the soft beauty of the north. She spoke carefully, this English language that she had learnt. Arthur was moved by her dignity—a peasant dignity, that any Moorhouse could well understand.

"I brought yer man's wages, Mrs. McCrimmon," he said.

"Oh, thank you, sir." She took the envelope, and looked about her, as though she were looking for the answer to some question in the dark corners of the room.

"Yer man's had an accident, Mrs. McCrimmon." Arthur had to force the words out of himself.

"An accident?"

"Sit down at the table and I'll tell ye."

The woman went rigid. A more imaginative visitor than Arthur Moorhouse might have guessed that she was drawing on the immense reserve of pride that was her birthright. "I'll be standing where I am, Mr. Moorhouse, please."

"A wheel went over his foot. They had to take it off at the Royal Infirmary this afternoon."

She stood, still saying nothing. The fingers of each hand kept moving in the hair of the two infants that clung to her. That was all.

Arthur did not fully comprehend that the dry eyes were staring straight into the face of starvation, but his robust companion knew.

There was nothing to be done but go on stammering out details: what they had said at the hospital; when she might see him if she went. The woman stood saying nothing.

If she had lost control and screamed, as indeed they could even now hear a drunken woman screaming in another room, it would have been pitiable. But somehow it was more than that.

This woman was on a level with himself. She and these children had no right in this place. He must get her out of it to a place where there was air and light and decency. How had she and her husband come to occupy this room? How had they come to set upon themselves Glasgow's special stigma, as inhabitants of "ticketed houses"?

But she was not to be talked to. He held out his hand. She did not seem to notice it. "You know where my office is, Mrs. McCrimmon. If you come next Saturday morning at twelve o'clock I'll give you yer man's wages again."

A strain seemed to go out of her face. She managed to look at him. "If you pay me money, I'll be working for it, Mr. Moorhouse."

Arthur foresaw a battle with her pride. He became brusque.

"Well, anyway, I've got to go now. Goodbye. And come and see me if you're in any trouble, Mrs. McCrimmon." His sharp, purposeful tone was too much for her.

"Yes, sir. God bless you, Mr. Moorhouse."

Arthur turned and left her, followed by his man. He was shaken by this meeting. In a voice that was still abrupt he bade him good-day, thanked him shortly for troubling to come with him, and walked off in the direction of the Kelvinside tram. His stocky foreman stood watching the lean, striding figure until it was lost in the Saturday rabble.

II

Bel wondered, as she sat at her midday meal with little Arthur and Phœbe, if it would be worthwhile to talk to her sister-in-law about the charity concert. Her enthusiasm decided her.

"I met Lucy Rennie this morning at Sophia's," she began.

"Did you?" Phœbe went on with her soup.

For the last eight years she had had the upbringing of Phœbe, and, with very good reason, she loved her husband's youngest sister. But every now and then in these eight years Bel had been overcome with a strong impulse to smack her. Why couldn't she settle down to a good gossip once in a while? Why couldn't she ask what Miss Rennie looked like at close quarters? If she was pleasant to speak to? What kind of clothes she wore? Why she was at Sophia's? How long she was to be in Glasgow? In fact, all the pleasant trivialities of normal feminine intercourse.

Bel should have known better. At more serious moments than this, Phœbe had, maddeningly, held her tongue.

"Do you remember her when you were a little girl at the Laigh Farm?" Bel persisted.

"I saw her once or twice in church."

"Did she sing in those days?"

"I don't remember. Yes. I think she was in the choir."

"Did she never come to the Laigh Farm?"

"I don't remember."

No. It was too hard going with Phœbe. And yet the girl had bounced in from a concert two weeks ago to tell David and Arthur that this young lady with the Italian-sounding name of Lucia Reni was none other than Lucy Rennie of Greenhead. Yes. Phœbe was quite unaccountable.

Bel gave it up. She had been seeking some clue to the Moorhouse dislike of the Rennie's—a clue that might help her to overcome Arthur's expected resistance. But it was no use. She would have to plan the campaign by herself.

Arthur was brusque and businesslike, but beneath, as his wife very well knew, there was a sympathy that could be quickly touched. Before she had told him anything of Lucy Rennie and the concert, she would tell him about the ragged children. And from there she would lead through easy stages to the meeting with Miss Rennie at Sophia's, and how they had planned a drawing-room concert to help the suffering in the city. To this, Bel hoped, Arthur could not but respond.

But as she sat, later that afternoon, giving a cold and dejected husband tea, Bel wondered. Arthur had not yet told her what had kept him in the City. His mood was dark. It would be folly to trouble him now. She must have patience.

There was a real understanding between these two. In the nine years of their marriage each had learnt of the other where it was possible to lean, where to go lightly. Goodwill, intelligence and a fundamental respect, each for the other, had brought together a man and a woman who were widely dissimilar. Bel saw that Arthur was preoccupied and weary. She knew that he would snap her head off if she mentioned the concert. But likewise did she know that this would pass; that this thing, whatever it was, pent up inside him, would have to be told, and told to herself as Arthur's inevitable confidante.

Arthur was therefore allowed to drink his tea in peace, and when it was done to sit on the other side of the fire from a comfortable and untroublesome wife, who seemed wholly intent upon her embroidery.

III

"Well, dear, were you busy this afternoon?" she ventured presently.

"One of the men in the warehouse got his foot smashed."

"Our warehouse, Arthur?" Bel put her sewing in her lap.

"Aye. They took his foot off."

"Oh! Poor thing! Do I know him?"

"No. I don't think so. His name's Hamish McCrimmon. He's from the Islands. He's just been in Glasgow a week or two."

"Has he got a wife?"

"A wife and two weans. I had to go and tell her, poor body."

Bel took up her work again. Here was her husband at his best. Taking responsibility upon himself. Shelving nothing that was disagreeable, merely because he didn't like it. "Poor Arthur!" she said. "What a thing to have to do!"

Arthur gave a grunt of self-depreciation.

"Is she Highland, too?"

"Aye."

Nothing more was said for some moments. Suddenly Arthur sprang to his feet as though he had been stung. He stood on the rug in front of the fire looking down at her. "She was in one of those terrible rooms off the Briggate. I've never seen anything like it!"

By hearsay and description Bel knew very well what these places were like. Had not her elder son at the age of three had his clothing stripped from him in some such den? Were not reformers and social workers telling those who had ears to hear what such places were like?

"Was she a slum woman, Arthur?" she asked.

"No. She seemed to me a decent Hielan' body, that didn't know where she had landed. She was like a—a bird that was taken and put in a cage."

It was not often that Arthur took to poetry. Bel did not need to look up to realise that what he had seen had moved him to a great pity.

"What did she do when you told her, dear?"

"She just stood—stood with her bairns hanging on to her." Arthur let his voice steady itself for a moment, then he exploded savagely, "Dirty, stinking place!"

Bel said nothing. She merely bent her head over her work. Her own frivolous scheme had faded. Her mind was filled with the picture he had shown her.

As he stood looking indignantly about him, Arthur saw a tear fall upon her hand. Neither of them spoke for a time.

"What are you doing to help her?" Bel asked.

"I'm not sure yet. She's to come to the office next Saturday anyway and get his wages."

"I'll come down and see her."

"I would like if you could." Arthur sat down again. His feelings were relieved. He had come very near to Bel. For a moment he sat thinking. "That's a terrible place where she is," he went on. "It'll be the death of them. I was thinking, maybe, we could get the coachman's house cleaned out and give it to them."

Bel looked up. "When the man comes out, couldn't you send them all home to the Islands?"

"He came from the Islands to get work."

"Times are bad here, Arthur."

"They're worse there."

Bel had been biding her time about the coachman's house. She had been delighted when Arthur had bought a house that had one. They had been only six months in the West End, in this fine house in Grosvenor Terrace. That was expense enough for the moment. But, inevitably, if you had a coach-house, sooner or later you would have a carriage. Especially when everyone else around you had one. Unless, of course, you filled the living-quarters with lame ducks, and were unable to house a coachman. And here was Arthur suggesting they should do just that thing.

There might be no getting rid of the McCrimmons. Bel and her family were of the sort that attracted hangers-on, and she knew it. Her prudence told her that they might be burdened with a useless, lame Highlander, a feckless wife, and an ever-increasing number of children, who took her charity and house-room, and thwarted her ambitions to have a smart carriage like her neighbours.

Arthur wondered at the silence his wife had fallen into. The idea of having a carriage of his own had not yet entered his mind. "Well, my dear, do ye not think it would be the right thing to do?"

"What, Arthur?" Bel brought herself back from her own thoughts.

"The coach-house is standing there doing nothing."

When Bel capitulated, she had the great merit of capitulating fully and handsomely. She had done it in her life before, and she made such a capitulation now.

"Of course, Arthur; we'll get the rooms cleared out and tell the poor woman to come when she can."

"You're a good lassie," Arthur said, looking at his wife as she rose to put away her sewing.

Bel laughed, a little emotionally. "Yes," she said, "I sometimes think I am. I must go and see what the children are doing."

And on her way upstairs to the nursery it came to her that instead of winning her difficult battle about Lucy Rennie and the concert, the war had been carried into her own territory and she had lost disastrously.

Chapter Seven

BUT not irretrievably.

The Lucy Rennie affair was bound to come up again. For the remainder of the day Bel was content to bask in her husband's goodwill. They were busy people. They had little enough time to water the plant of connubial tenderness. And, like a sensible woman, she knew that when it blossomed afresh, it would be vandalism to break down so delicate a blooming. She was happy to let matters be.

But on the following day things developed. Arthur had now obtained a family ticket to the Botanic Gardens—that select outdoor club of Western Glasgow. It was their custom to join the after-church parade of wealthy citizens there. They did this on fine Sundays to give themselves an appetite for their roast beef, to display Bel's smart clothes, to see and be seen.

There was a snatch of November sunshine as they took a turn or two in front of the great glass-house, watching the passers-by and greeting friends. Suddenly Bel became aware of a hand lightly laid upon her arm. She turned round to see Miss Rennie standing beside her.

"Good morning, Mrs. Moorhouse. I have just come across to ask you to introduce me to an old friend." She smiled at Arthur.

A little flurried, Bel made the introduction. Arthur was gravely polite.

"I don't believe you remember me, Mr. Moorhouse," she said, giving Arthur her hand.

"Aye. Fine. Many a time have I helped yer father to tie corn," Arthur replied, kindly enough.

"I mustn't keep you," Miss Rennie said. "I must go back to my friends. But I just wondered if you had thought any more about a drawing-room concert, Mrs. Moorhouse?"

Bel felt caught. "I haven't had time to discuss it properly," she said quickly. "But I'll let you know when you come to see me."

With a goodbye, Miss Rennie turned and went.

"So that's old Tom Rennie's girl, is it?" Arthur said as they moved on. "Plenty of airs and graces. And plenty of the Rennie cheek. But how do ye know her?"

"I met her yesterday at Sophia's, Arthur. I forgot to tell you." Forgot was perhaps not the right word, but how else was Bel to explain it?

"What's all this about coming to see you?"

She would have to tell him now. And perhaps it was all for the best that it happened so. She told Arthur of the ragged children, of Lucy Rennie's quick sympathy, and her offer to sing.

Arthur grunted, but Bel did not read discouragement from this and continued: "She's been doing it in London. I said I would talk to you about it." She looked at her husband. "I feel perhaps it's our duty to help."

"I don't like the Rennies. And I don't like public singers."

"That's a little old-fashioned, dear. You know, we might make thirty or forty pounds."

Arthur merely grunted once more.

But Bel was determined to have her concert. She must use whatever means came to her hand. "No, I don't think she's bold or heartless," she said after a moment. "In fact it was Miss Rennie who first thought of giving money to that poor little child, Arthur. I don't think you are being quite fair, dear."

"Maybe not, but I can't help it."

Bel tried her final shot. "After all, the child we gave the money to might have been one of the poor little children you saw in that terrible place."

Arthur said nothing to this. She took it as a good sign. She tried again. "Surely you must feel that we should do all we can, dear."

Arthur had retreated inside himself. He looked at the crowd of well-dressed people as they milled about in the wintry sunshine, elegant, slim-waisted ladies in their furs and finery, smilingly acknowledging the greetings of frock-coated, bearded men politely raising silk hats from sleek, macassared heads. A world that was taking little heed of the tragic world that was so near them. The balance was wrong somewhere. But it was difficult, this, unless you had seen the other side of the picture for yourself. No. It would be wrong if he stopped his wife's generous impulses. A fashionable drawing-room concert did not seem a very effective way to attack the problem of the slums. But, after all, what could a nice woman do about it? Women could not leave their homes like men. Women didn't go into the world, or at least only those brazen "New Women" did. And he had no wish for his wife to be one of these. Yes, he supposed she had better go on with it if she wanted to. She was a good girl, Bel, and had shown great understanding about the McCrimmons. But he didn't want her to be permanently mixed up with this Rennie girl.

"Is the Rennie lassie to be in Glasgow long?" he asked presently.

"No. Only for a short time," Bel said, anxiously trying to follow the train of his thought. "That's why I was hoping we might decide about this at once."

Arthur considered the matter for a step or two further. "Well, if ye can manage it, I dare say ye had better do it," he said.

Bel was delighted. But she knew better than to show her delight. She received her husband's permission as though he had conferred upon her a solemn mission.

"Who will ye get to help ye?" he asked.

Bel considered. "I think I'll ask Mary," she said, with a fine show of thoughtfulness. After all, his sister Mary was safe. None of them liked her much. But she was pious, and would give the occasion all the sanctity it needed. Besides, she was lazy, wouldn't interfere, and her husband, George McNairn, was a baillie of the City.

As she stood at her own front door waiting for her husband to find his latch-key, Bel felt uplifted. There was nothing like a walk in the Botanic Gardens to give you an appetite for roast beef.

II

Bel's relationship with her husband's married sisters was made up of some affection and much criticism. On the whole perhaps, she liked Sophia best, because, at every point, she felt herself

Sophia's superior: house, management of her children, personal looks—everything. And Sophia, good loquacious creature, would have been the first to admit it. Indeed, she would almost go out of her chattering way to tell Bel how well she looked, how well-run her house was, and however did she manage it? And that she, Sophia, somehow never seemed to have the time to keep herself and her possessions properly straight. She would even admit her own parsimony with an easy, flustered laugh. "Well, perhaps William and I *were* a wee bit mean about the special collection, dear, but with growing children it takes us all our time." No, Bel could hold Sophia in comfortable, complacent contempt, and really quite like her.

With Mary McNairn it was more difficult. She was the wife of a baillie of the City of Glasgow. Thirty-eight, still good-looking in a plump, smooth sort of way, and, Bel considered, unbearably smug. Yet Mary had her uses. Bel couldn't quite do without Mary. For Mary and her husband, the baillie, represented official Glasgow. George McNairn had, in certain directions, influence; and the presence of himself and his wife would, at least, stamp any function with respectability. And it was just this that Bel wanted now. You had to be careful of your reputation when it came to associating with women like Lucy Rennie, who had actually, she gathered, stood upon the stage of a theatre. It was Bel's ambition to be considered smart, but she abhorred the thought of being considered fast.

And so in the week following the Sunday walk in the Botanic Gardens, Bel set out upon a visit to Albany Place.

Mary was, as Bel had expected, enjoying her three o'clock tea. Enjoying was the word; for Mary saw to it that such means of enjoyment as toast dripping with butter and cakes dripping with cream should not be wanting. The McNairns were piously thankful to Providence for making so many good things available, and they were not slow to avail themselves of them.

Mary was, on the whole, pleased to see Bel. Like most people who sit about and eat too much, she had a tendency to find life savourless at times. And this dull, early December day was one of these times. She was quite by herself. Her little twin daughters were out with the nurse-housemaid, and the boys were not yet home from school. Besides, Bel, she felt certain, was taking care of her figure, and would not sensibly reduce the supply of toast and cream sandwich intended for herself.

"Well, Bel dear," she said in her flat, pleasant voice. "This is a great surprise. We never see you, these days." She presented her sister-in-law with a smooth, plump cheek.

Bel settled her elegant self down in Mary's snug, over-furnished little parlour. It was ridiculous for Mary to be wearing the black of middle age already. After all, she was only six years older than herself, Bel reckoned. In a calm, Madonna-like way, Mary used to be the beauty of the family. She should go for walks and eat less, and she would look as handsome as ever.

Bel drew the gloves from her well-tended hands and accepted a cup of tea. She declined a succulent slab of toast. "No, thank you, dear. I'm not eating between meals. I read in a magazine that it's very bad for the digestion." But seeing something that might easily be offence in Mary's eyes, and feeling her reproof had been too pointed, she changed her mind. "Well, dear, may I have one piece?" Bel was glad to see that Mary looked happier now.

She made the proper inquiries. Mary's children, she found to her intense relief, were all much as usual. The baillie was finding his business slow on account of the bad times this autumn. But as a member of the Town Council, he was very busy and, Bel was given to understand from the tone of Mary's voice, his services were of the first importance to the welfare of the City.

Bel said what was expected of her, and agreed that George McNairn must be very busy and important indeed. She even went so far as to say she couldn't imagine how he did it all; although she was firmly convinced that her pompous, platitudinous and slow-moving brother-in-law did as little as he possibly could. Concord being established, however, she came to the reason of her visit.

"I want your advice, dear, about something," she began. "You see, I felt that as you and George went to so many official functions, you would be the best ones to help me."

Mary took up a fine lace handkerchief and wiped some melted butter from her fingers. If Bel had not been there, she would have licked them. It was a pity, she reflected, to waste good butter. She would be very glad to give Bel advice. Like many people who are too inert to pursue much activity themselves, she and her husband felt fully qualified to advise in the activities of others. She indicated, absent-mindedly helping herself now to an ample slice of cream sandwich, that if there was any point upon which she could advise Bel, Bel could count upon her so doing.

"Well, dear, I suppose Sophia will have told you that Lucy Rennie, the daughter of an old neighbouring farmer of your father, has been singing in Glasgow. She became a professional singer. Wonderful, everybody says."

"I haven't seen Sophia for a week or two. It's time she was coming to see me," was Mary's only comment.

Bel had to stop herself from feeling annoyed. Was Mary so self-centred that she could not be stimulated by this not uninteresting piece of news? News about someone she must have known as a girl.

"Did you know Lucy Rennie?" she asked.

"Yes; we knew all the Rennies."

And as Mary merely went on eating, Bel continued: "Well, Arthur and I think it would be such a good idea if Miss Rennie gave a little charity concert in our drawing-room. There have been so many appeals for the poor this winter."

Mary managed to catch some of the cream that looked like falling out at the other side of her cake by biting it just in time; then she asked: "How much will you have to pay Lucy Rennie?"

"She's offered to do it for nothing, dear."

Mary showed no surprise at this. She merely examined her cake to see that no more cream was eluding her. "At least you'll need to pay a pianist," she said.

"Even if we have to, that won't be much. Arthur would be glad to pay that. No, thanks, Mary. But I'll have some tea. So we thought, perhaps, that you and George would help. Ask some well-known people to come. George might even approach the Lord Provost. You see, if it's made important like that, you can really make something with a silver and gold collection."

Mary swallowed the last of her slice and again applied the lace handkerchief to her plump white finger. She had no objection to doing things that made her feel important. "I'll speak to George about it, dear. His time's very taken up just now, but he'll help if he can."

"Miss Rennie's coming to tea tomorrow, Mary. Would you care to come and meet her?"

"No, thank you, dear. Our family never liked the Rennies."

"I can't understand why."

"I don't know, Bel. It's just an old feeling. You say you met her at Sophia's?"

"Yes."

"Sophia should have let her be."

"She seems a very bright, good-mannered young lady," Bel insisted.

"I dare say. But I don't know. Anyway, George and I will do our duty, when you tell us what you've arranged. It's the charity that matters."

Really, Mary was maddening, Bel reflected as she made her way home. It was as though Mary had said to her: "We can't touch pitch ourselves, dear, but we'll do everything to help you if you want to touch it." Oh, the smugness of these McNairns! But, for the moment, she must put up with it.

III

On the afternoon of the next day Miss Rennie paid her visit, and in doing so confirmed the good opinion Bel had formed of her. In the pleasant orderliness of her own drawing-room, Bel gave her tea, and heard her ideas concerning the evening of charitable music. A musician whose name was a household word in refined Glasgow would be her accompanist and would himself play pieces on the piano. She had, she said, persuaded him also to give his services for charity. Bel was delighted. It remained to fix the evening and the details of the entertainment. She would let Miss Rennie know.

Looking in that evening, David found Bel in high feather. She was bursting with her project. She took him aside, wanting his advice about everything. What did he think about it? Wasn't it a good idea? The McNairns were helping. They would bring some of official Glasgow. How many did he think the room would hold? Where did he think the piano ought to be? What about refreshment? What would be right and proper? David was the member of the family who went about. He must tell her. But as she talked, she began to feel a lack of enthusiasm. He seemed worried and anxious. By degrees it was borne in upon her that she was being selfish; that David had, perhaps, his own problems about which he had come for advice. Her mind went back to their last talk.

"Well, David, and have you taken the advice I gave you?" she said presently. They were in the parlour of the house. David was in front of the fire looking down upon her.

David did not answer at once, but colour came into his face.

"Have you, David?"

Again he waited a moment before he answered her. "I wrote her a letter tonight asking her to marry me. I posted it on my way up here."

"David!" She didn't know what to make of all this. "David, sit down and tell me. Who is she? I don't even know that."

"She's the daughter of old Robert Dermott of Dermott Ships. They're friends of the Hayburns."

Of course Bel had heard of them. But how could David have made up his mind so quickly? "Did you see her again as I said you should?"

"Yes."

"And that settled it?"

"I think so."

"*Think*, David? But you've just written to her to ask her to marry you!"

"Well, I'm sure of it, then."

Strange boy. Why all this hurry? And why had he written to her? Why hadn't he gone to see her? They neither of them spoke for a time. They sat, staring at the fire. Yet Bel felt she could not let it go at this.

"But, David, is it all right?" she asked at length. "I feel that there's more to be said. You haven't rushed into this in a fit of—of, I don't know what, really—well, because she's rich, or you just want to be married or something?"

"No. I've made up my mind."

"But are you happy about it? Will you be happy if she accepts you?"

"Yes. I'm queer, Bel. I don't think there's any getting away from that. I'm quite certain that this marriage, if it comes off, will be the making of me. You yourself told me that some people don't fall in love until they're married. I like everything about Grace Dermott. I'm taking a chance."

They were interrupted at this moment, and Bel was grateful. There was nothing more, she felt, that could be said.

Chapter Eight

PRESENTLY David rose, and bidding the family goodnight took himself home. It was a wet, blustery night as he walked across to his rooms in Hillhead. On the corner of his own street was the pillar-box into which he had dropped his letter of proposal. He looked at its black shape. No. There was no getting it out. He turned into his own entrance. Draughts of air, eddying in from the street, were making the gas-light flicker. The scrubbed and whitened stone staircase was unwelcoming and chill. He sat down by his fireside thinking. He had come home from his visit to Grace Dermott pleased with himself and with her. Grace had been so gentle, so sensible. He had felt warmed and uplifted. Glad to find himself thus, he had fanned the flame, putting this warmth he had felt to the front of his mind and thrusting doubts back out of sight. His self-persuasion had been successful. It had ended in the letter he had written this evening. Now that a step that might be irretrievable was taken, he was suffering from the reaction. Alarmed by this crisis of his own making, he had gone round to Bel for comfort and advice. For the first time in his life, he had not found it. Bel could do nothing but chatter about the arrangements for the charity concert she was planning. And then, when he had told her, she had been very surprised and seemed anything but sure he had done rightly. Bel was not usually so obtuse as this. She knew his difficulties. At least she might have shown some understanding.

David got up with a sigh. It had taken him something to write that letter. He thought of the young woman he had asked to be his wife. She was superior in his mind to any other he could think of. Even without Bel's assurances, he felt he had done right.

He turned to his sitting-room table preparing to reach up, turn out the jets in the gaselier that hung above it and go to bed. On the red baize table-cloth lay a clean pad of blotting-paper. He could see it had the reverse imprint of the short letter he had written to Grace. He tore off the sheet. Should he hold it up to the mirror to read again the words he had written? On a quick impulse, he crushed up the blotting-paper and thrust it into the fire. He stood watching the flame spring up and die away, then turned back to extinguish the light. There was nothing more he could do until he had received her reply.

II

Grace did not keep him waiting. After a day's interval her answer came. It seemed to David a cool letter, telling him that she was much surprised at what she had found in his note, that he had given her no sign he had any such feelings towards her, and wouldn't he come soon and discuss the matter with her?

It was a curious thing that this young man, who was not insensitive, should go so far astray in his assessment of her reply. Didn't Grace want him after all then, that she wanted to talk about it? Why discuss anything? What was there to discuss?

He did not see that his proposal of marriage had been accepted; that there was nothing for her to do but answer his own formal letter with a formal letter of reply; that Grace was surprised and disappointed that he should have written to her, instead of coming to her himself to make his proposal; that if she had not wanted him, she would not have asked him to come on any account.

But now this morning he must certainly go and see her. Through the good offices of his landlady he sent some excuse to Arthur for his absence from work, and set out for Aucheneame.

It was unreal somehow, this short morning journey on the empty down-river train. There was nothing remarkable about it in itself, but some of its trivial details were to remain with him. The upcoming trains bearing businessmen to the City. It seemed so unaccountable that he should be going in the opposite direction. The misty Clyde. It was high water and shipping was brisk. A grain clipper had swung across the river and was holding up the traffic. Two steam-tugs were pulling it straight. The railway carriage was cold. The warming-pan was tepid. He would always have a picture of himself huddled into a corner wondering what the day would bring him.

Now he was at the station. It was some distance to walk to the house. A low, chill mist was hanging in the fields. As he walked quickly up the drive, the trees on either side were dripping.

A man in a striped apron answered his ring. Aucheneame did not expect visitors at this time of the morning. Yes, Miss Dermott was at home. What name would he say? David stood before the fire in the morning-parlour for what seemed a very long time. Why was she so slow in presenting herself? Was she afraid of him? After all, she merely wanted to discuss things with him. He went impatiently to the window.

How damp it was this morning! It was becoming so foggy that he could scarcely see the river down there in the distance across the fields. He turned his head quickly. The door had opened and closed. She was standing with her back to it, her hands behind her. Her face was flushed, uncertain.

"Miss Dermott!" He moved to meet her as she came forward hesitating. Suddenly David's heart was caught up in a wave of gentleness for this girl. She seemed so unsure, so little the imperious mistress whose favour must be sought. He took her hand.

"I got your answer," he said lamely.

"Yes, I—"

He looked down at her. Her eyes were brimming, though she was trying to smile. Her face was turned to him, expecting his kiss.

He kissed her and held her in his arms, letting her sob away the fullness of her heart. He could feel her body trembling against his, the body that it would be his duty to possess; its yielding contact was agreeable and vaguely stirring. All sorts of things passed through David's surprised and sharply conscious mind. He knew he was not unhappy. Life would go on now. He was holding the mother of his children in his arms. Unmated discontent was behind him. There was expectation now. There would be adjustments, but it would be easy with a gently loving woman. Their joint life would be full and prosperous. They had nothing to do but go forward.

As he stood there holding Grace Dermott, and thinking these thoughts—thoughts that at such a moment had no right to be in his mind—David made himself a solemn promise. He, and he alone, was answerable for this engagement entered into. He had offered himself as her husband, and whatever came now, he would stand by her to the end.

III

And now, this one step taken, it was easy. It was easy to sit by her and watch her happiness unfolding itself; to find her gently, shyly taking possession of him. Did David like this? She was glad, for she liked it too. Did David detest that? She was glad, for she never could bear it. She was joyfully, tenderly exploring his thoughts and his feelings.

It would have taken someone of less sensibility than David Moorhouse to remain unmoved. She loved him deeply and must have done so for some time. That was evident. There was nothing bold in her possession of him, but it was plain that her heart was fixed. He had never realised that anyone could feel so tenderly about another. It shook him to find himself the object of this tenderness. It filled him with awe. And, made as he was, it was not difficult for him to respond. It was easy to tell himself that he loved her and to tell her so in turn.

Presently her mother burst into the room. They sprang to their feet.

Mrs. Dermott's monumental person was covered by a voluminous Inverness cape. She was on the point of going out. She came to a standstill at the door with a loud "Good gracious!"

David's eyes followed Grace as she went to her mother and told her. She hoped that her mother and father would see their way to allow it.

"I don't suppose there's any allow about it, now you've made up your minds," Grace's mother said, advancing genially. "What's your first name, by the way, Mr. Moorhouse?—I forget."

"David." Its possessor smiled. Here was normality; his familiar, everyday world.

"You had better kiss an old woman and get it over, David. I know Robert will be pleased. He's very fond of you. You had better stay to lunch, then go into Glasgow and see him at the office. It's always better to get the business side of things over and done with, and then we can get on with our plans. You'll come back for the weekend. Grace and you will want to see each other, and there will be so much for us to talk about. I'll probably spend Sunday writing letters."

David smiled and submitted. He wondered that Grace said so little. But it was evident to him that Mrs. Dermott's daughter was used to this kind of thing. There was no mistaking the older woman's pleasure, and she was showing it in the way that came most natural to her—by going into an orgy of arranging.

Already he was being made to feel a part of the mechanism of the Dermotts' world. It was something stronger than himself. But he was rather pleased than otherwise. Its restrictions would not chafe. It would suit him very well. He must do now what he was told, and let things take their conventional course.

Sometime during next week polite Glasgow would open its morning paper to read that Mr. David Moorhouse, youngest brother of Mr. Mungo Ruanthorpe-Moorhouse of Duntrafford, Ayrshire, had engaged himself to marry Grace, only daughter of Mr. Robert Dermott of Aucheneame, Dumbartonshire, and Chairman of Dermott Ships Limited. And on the whole this would give David satisfaction. He was taking the road he wanted to go.

Chapter Nine

LUCY RENNIE had her lodging in Garnethill. It may seem strange, perhaps, that a young woman of Miss Rennie's attainments should live in the quarter of Glasgow that has long been assigned to theatrical folks and to undistinguished foreigners, but she was a woman of the world and could very well look after herself. Yet there was nothing of the "New Woman" about her. "New Women" were pugnacious, brandished umbrellas and had big feet—or thus the comic papers of the time showed them. But for all that, Miss Rennie was fully qualified to go her own ways according to her own not uncharming fashion. She had not been a music student forced to live anyhow in London and Paris without learning independence. She knew very well when the polite conventions could be useful. But she had no scruples over breaking them when they were merely a drag. The rooms she occupied were better than most of their kind. They had been recommended to her by a fellow-singer, and they suited her purpose. They were clean, had an air of gentility, and were not threadbare. There was a piano that was usable, and her landlady, a former actress, was a motherly soul who did not bother her with questions.

As she sat by her fire, plump and pink in a warm dressing-gown, drinking a final cup of breakfast tea, and looking very much like the heroine of the novel a French acquaintance had lent her, two letters were brought. The first was in her father's hand—a laborious farmer's hand, one that seldom held a pen. It was a letter in reply to one of her own, and it contained a reproach that although she had been in Scotland for some time now, she had not yet bothered to see her family in Ayrshire. Her father reminded her that bygones were bygones; that her independence would not be criticised, and that those at home were anxious to see her.

She folded the letter thoughtfully. She had promised herself to go at New Year, but that was still some weeks away. She would visit the old man before that. It was only fair, perhaps. She had paid a flying visit when her mother died some three years ago. Since then she had not seen him. It would be more of a duty than a pleasure. The past nine years lay between her and the people at home. She had struggled, and studied, and lived this way and that. Now she had work of her own, behaviour of her own, tastes of her own. She did not intend to change them. Her mind went back to the man who had paid for her first lessons in London. She had been wise to free herself of him quickly, to go on by herself. That episode had been unpleasant, but it had taught her her world.

She brushed these thoughts out of her mind, and settling down once more, she broke the seal of the other letter. It was from Mrs. Arthur Moorhouse. The letter was conventionally kind. She had discussed the matter with her husband and, like Mrs. Moorhouse herself, he was delighted and grateful to Miss Rennie for all the trouble she was taking. They hoped to have some of official Glasgow present, through the good services of their sister, who was the wife of Baillie George McNairn. Miss Rennie would certainly remember her as Mary Moorhouse.

Lucy sat wondering now why she had bothered to offer Mrs. Arthur Moorhouse her services. Because she held it as a rule always to make a good impression when she could? Or because she had been spontaneously moved by the little, ragged children? But it was strange that she should be doing it for the wife of a Moorhouse. Her father had never liked the Moorhouse family much. She had forgotten why. Perhaps it was that they were irritatingly prosperous, working for their prosperity, and in the case of Mungo Moorhouse, the eldest, marrying into prosperity. And now only yesterday she had read in the morning paper that the youngest Moorhouse was to make an excellent match. In childhood, David had been a friend of hers. They had bird-nested and gone to the village school together. But the Moorhouses were so conventional, so cut to a pattern, such complacent, Scotch provincials.

Yet, an appearance in Mrs. Arthur Moorhouse's drawing-room would do her no harm professionally. At all events it was letting her name be known. Mrs. Moorhouse seemed a pleasant sort of woman, and one among whose friends she might later find rich pupils. Lucy got up, took pen and ink, and informed Mrs. Moorhouse that the day appointed would suit her very well. She also wrote to her father that she would be with him at Greenhead Farm the following weekend.

II

Miss Rennie was not a famous prima donna. She was a working musician who had to cut her coat according to her cloth. It was not her custom to buy a first-class ticket for a railway journey, when a third-class ticket would do. But this afternoon it had been very cold, snow was threatening, and she had made up her mind that, for all the additional expense, it would be worth her while travelling in comfort to her father's farm in central Ayrshire.

As she came through from the booking-hall she found herself under the gigantic glass arch of the new railway station of St. Enoch's. For a moment she looked about her with curiosity. It was one of the sights of Glasgow, this great station which was barely yet completed, and its novelty caught her interest.

Her train was waiting. Lucy found an empty first-class carriage, wrapped her travelling-rug about her and sat down. There was a Friday-night animation about other travellers. Week-ending was coming much into vogue. Businessmen who could afford to live in the mansion houses that heretofore had been occupied by the gentry, were beginning more and more to gather their friends about them from Friday night to Monday morning, to forget for two days of the week at least that they were men of business, and to ape the ways of the people whose houses they were increasingly coming to occupy.

Presently, as she sat idly watching the crowd pass her window, hoping, as every railway traveller hopes, that she would be left in peace, her interest was aroused on seeing Mrs. Arthur Moorhouse pass down the platform accompanied by a woman who seemed in some way familiar. The two women passed her, looked in without recognition, then came back, opened the door, and the woman who accompanied Mrs. Moorhouse got in. As the train was on the point of going she laid down her belongings quickly, then turned to the open window to bid her companion goodbye.

As Mrs. Moorhouse had not seen her, Miss Rennie did not feel there was anything to be gained by making herself known. Presently the train moved off, slowly puffing its way out of the great new station into the evening, rounding the old steeple of the Merchants' House, crossing a windswept, leaden Clyde, passing the growing suburbs on the south side of the river, and speeding out into the open country.

Miss Rennie examined her travelling companion with some curiosity. Herself a farmer's daughter, she knew very well, merely from the look of her, that this was a woman of the county. There was nothing of the town about her country clothes, her stout boots, and the air with which she arranged herself and her parcels. Presently she remembered. This was Miss Ruanthorpe, the daughter of her father's landlord, old Sir Charles Ruanthorpe of Duntrafford. She had not seen Miss Ruanthorpe for some ten years. But, of course, now she was not Miss Ruanthorpe any longer. She was the wife of Mungo Moorhouse of the Laigh Farm. Sitting demurely in her corner, Miss Rennie examined her fellow-passenger with interest. So this rather distinguished woman was the new bride? They said in the county that she had pursued the farmer of the Laigh Farm for years.

The train jogged on across the wintry country. Neither of the women exchanged a word. It was evident to Lucy that Mrs. Mungo Moorhouse had no idea who she was. And a tenant's daughter could be of no great interest. The journey was tedious. The train stopped at this station and that. Doors slammed bleakly as passengers alighted on windy platforms. Interest in Mrs. Moorhouse had quickly evaporated. It was too cold to be interested in anything. There was nothing to do but sit grimly, with her eyes shut, waiting for the train to arrive.

Suddenly she became aware that Mrs. Mungo Moorhouse was asking something of her. The request was a strange one on such an evening. She asked if she might let some air in, as she felt the carriage strangely stuffy. Lucy opened her eyes in surprise. She saw that the colour was gone from her companion's face. In another moment Mrs. Moorhouse had fainted. This was alarming. For a moment she did not know what to do. But she was not a young woman who lost her head. She succeeded in laying Mrs. Moorhouse flat along the seat and undoing anything that might constrict her breathing. Presently Lucy saw with much relief that she was coming to herself. That was better. She remembered a little flask of spirits, that, as a person whose calling required her to travel much, she always carried with her.

Now Mrs. Moorhouse was sitting up again, tremulous a little but restored, and apologising for doing anything so silly. It had never happened to her before, she protested. She was sincerely sorry for having caused the young lady any sort of shock.

III

Mungo Moorhouse—or Mungo Ruanthorpe-Moorhouse, as he was now called in deference to the wishes of his eighty-year-old father-in-law, Sir Charles Ruanthorpe, Baronet, of Duntrafford, Ayrshire—stood in the midst of the prosperity he had married himself into, hastily swallowing down cups of tea. He had come back early from overseeing his farm, for in less than an hour he was to meet his wife Margaret at the railway station. As the winter evening had turned very cold, he had come home first to fetch an additional rug or two and a warm wrap, so that Margaret should not be chilled in the open pony-trap.

Mungo was nervous. He was forty-four and his wife was forty. They had been married for some three months. It was late to be starting life. And late for Margaret to be paying the kind of visit she had been paying to a Glasgow doctor today. But they were both country bred and strong as horses, and the hope of an heir, even if his surname had to be Ruanthorpe-Moorhouse instead of Ruanthorpe, was the one thing that old Sir Charles and Lady Ruanthorpe clung to. If Margaret's news was good tonight it would give the old people a new lease of life. He put down his empty cup and, going to the window, pushed back the heavy curtains, trying to look out. In the darkness it was difficult to see anything but the lamps of the trap moving up and down in front of the house, as a groom walked the pony back and forth to keep it warm. Presently he saw that a light powdering of snow was lying on the sill of the window. This was annoying. He turned back into the warm little Dower House parlour. He would have to go at once, to give himself time. The road might be difficult. It would be dangerous to hurry.

The fire was burning well enough, but he lifted the coal-scuttle in his strong farmer's hands and emptied additional coal upon it. Margaret must be warm. She had spent last night at his brother Arthur's house in Glasgow. It was the first night since their marriage that they had been apart. He was as eager as a youngster over his wife's home-coming.

As he struggled into his heavy driving-coat in the little hall, he shouted in the hope that some servant would hear him: "Ye better keep an eye on that fire."

A maid came running, a surprised look on her face. "Is anything wrong, sir?"

"There's a lot of coal on that fire. Watch it doesna fall out."

"Yes, sir."

He was not yet in the way of ringing bells and giving orders to starched parlourmaids. He had shouted to the girls at the Laigh Farm when he wanted them. That had been good enough. He was not like his brother David, who had been caught young and turned into a gentleman. But Margaret seemed to like his farmer's ways, so why should he bother?

On the doorstep he stood looking about him into the darkness. Feathers of snow were wheeling slowly down around him. He shouted to the groom, "Are ye there, Davie?"

The man brought the trap over.

"It's a pity to see that snow," Mungo said.

"Aye. It'll be a cold run home for the mistress."

"I'll need to watch where I'm going." Mungo ran his hand down the neck of his pony, then he climbed in and took the reins. For an instant the groom stood watching the beams from the lamp of the trap as they lit up the snow on either side of the short Dower House drive. Presently there was nothing but the sound of hoof-claps lightly muffled by the new-fallen snow. The man took a short cut through the shrubbery to the Duntrafford stables and the harness-room fire.

IV

The snow was falling thickly as Mungo, having covered his pony as best he could, waited in front of the country railway station. This delay was tedious. It was no night for a beast to be kept standing.

But as Mungo stood at his pony's head, the snow alighting gently upon his shoulders, he was strangely excited. What news was Margaret bringing him? It seemed quite unreal that, at his age, things should have taken this turn. He had gone on for so long working; first, for his father at the Laigh Farm, and then later by himself. He had taken his life for granted. He had been interested and busy. That had been enough. He had no opportunity to marry in his younger days, and had not, perhaps, even thought of doing so. Then, as it seemed to him suddenly, he was the husband of the laird's daughter. And this very night he was standing in the snow, his placid heart beating like the heart of a twenty-year-old, waiting to hear from her if he was to be the father of the laird's grandchild.

Suddenly the night was pierced by the scream of a whistle. There was an increasing roar, and a splash of fiery red in the snowy darkness. The drivers of dog-carts and carriages jumped to their places. There was a rush and hurrying on the ill-lit platform. There was the beat of slowing wheels; the lighted rows of moving windows. The evening train had come to a halt.

Still holding his pony's head, Mungo stood peering anxiously through the lighted arch of the railway station. People for the village came first, chattering with friends who had come to meet them, looking up unhappily at the falling snow, wrapping themselves closer, then hurrying off on foot. Someone came out, hired the village cab, and drove off. Familiar people, business-men and gentry, hurried into their carriages and went off to their country houses. Mungo was becoming impatient. It was time his wife appeared. All the conveyances were moving or preparing to move. All except the Greenhead dog-cart. It was waiting, too, with old Tom Rennie perched up impatiently in the driving-seat.

At last Mungo saw the outline of his wife against the light of the station entrance. She was talking with a smaller woman, who seemed to be carrying her things for her. A moment later Margaret had seen him. Both women were coming across.

"Oh, there you are, Mungo. What a terrible night!" Margaret said, coming up. "This is Miss Rennie of Greenhead, who is being very nice to me." Mungo remembered Lucy Rennie and nodded.

"Are you all right, Mrs. Moorhouse?" Lucy was packing Margaret and her parcels into the trap.

"Quite. Now run away. There's your father waiting for you. And it's a promise that you'll come across and see me when you are here at New Year? Good. Now run. This snow is awful."

This was no moment for ceremony. A second later the Ruanthorpe-Moorhouses, muffled to their ears, were making their cautious way home.

The road led steeply downhill. They were both of them too much of the country to engage in talk while the driver had the very slippery foothold of his pony to see to. The snow had made the road uncertain, and Mungo, however much he might want to hear her news, must give his mind to the pony and the darkness. But soon they were at the foot of the hill and on the level. The little animal was trotting cautiously on familiar ground.

Margaret broke silence. "I did a silly thing, Mungo. I suddenly fainted right away in the train. The Rennie girl from Greenhead was with me in the carriage. She gave me some brandy."

"Are ye all right now?" Mungo was crouched over the reins; his intent eyes were trying to pierce the gloom beyond his pony's ears.

"Yes."

He drove steadily for a moment. He was waiting for his wife to speak again, but she did not. He was driven to speak himself. "Was that—a good sign?"

"Yes, Mungo. It was a good sign."

"Fine." Mungo did not belong to a breed that carries emotion on its sleeve. There was nothing he could do to show his pleasure, here in the snowy darkness. He had no command of words. But a glow was lit within him. He found himself holding the reins in his hands with greater care, straining to use his countryman's knowledge yet more skilfully. He must give his whole mind now to getting his wife home safely.

V

"Charles, what's the matter with you?" Old Lady Ruanthorpe looked down the table of the dining-room at Duntrafford. Even when they were alone, this dogged old couple persisted in dining formally.

Sir Charles, a stringy old man with mutton-chop whiskers, a black stock and velvet dinner-jacket, glared back at his wife. "What do you mean, 'matter', Meg? I'm all right."

"You've eaten practically no dinner."

"Surely I can eat as much as I choose to. Remember I am eighty. It's wrong for old people to eat too much."

There was something that might have been anxiety in her determined, weather-beaten face. Lady Ruanthorpe peered at her husband over the expanse of white linen, cut-glass, hothouse fern and silver. "Fiddlesticks," was all she said. Her eyes weren't too good, and the lights from the candles dazzled them a bit. But Charles had been refusing this dish and that. It was ridiculous.

A man-servant had set the fruit on the table, put the port in front of his master, and was preparing to withdraw.

"Campbell." The old man's sharp voice brought him back.

"Yes, Sir Charles?"

"Look through the curtains and tell me what sort of night it is." Sir Charles poured himself out a glass, got up and, laying one hand on the white mantelpiece for support, sipped his port and warmed himself at the fire.

The man reappeared from the window recess, through the heavy crimson velvet curtains. "It's deep snow, Sir Charles," he said.

"Go downstairs and ask if there's no word from the Dower House, and come back and tell me at once."

As the servant went, Lady Ruanthorpe turned to look at her husband. "What do you think you're up to?"

"I want to know if Margaret's back."

"Margaret's been in Glasgow before and got back safely. She's quite fit to look after herself."

Sir Charles grunted. "How do you know?"

His lady went into a peal of cracked laughter. "You're an old rascal; that's what you are."

Sir Charles did not reply. He merely stood his port on the mantelpiece and warmed both his hands, waiting.

In a moment the man came back.

"Well, Campbell?"

"No, Sir Charles. No message."

"Damn it! They might at least—"

"Charles, what's the matter with you? It's a horrid snowy night. You can't expect—"

But Sir Charles was fidgeting with impatience. "Has the snow stopped falling, Campbell?"

"Yes, Sir Charles."

"There should be a moon. Was there one?"

"Well, it's not Campbell's fault if there wasn't."

"Don't be frivolous, Meg."

"There was a moon, Sir Charles."

"Very well, then. Go and tell them to bring round the closed carriage."

"Charles! You can't bring Margaret across here after a long day and a cold journey!"

"I have no intention. Do as I tell you, Campbell."

The man went.

Lady Ruanthorpe was really alarmed now. She got up and crossed to her husband. "Charles, what do you intend to do?"

"I intend to go to the Dower House, and ask Margaret if she is going to have a child."

"I wondered." She regarded her husband. He was looking like a stubborn child himself now. She must do what she could with him. She put a hand on his arm. "You know you haven't been out at night for weeks now. Remember that we had Margaret's wedding in this house because you weren't well enough to go to church."

"I tell you I'm going, Meg." She wasn't to be allowed to put him off. Ruanthorpes had always prided themselves in doing what they wanted.

She shook his arm affectionately. "I'm terrified for you, my dear. I'll go across quickly when the carriage comes, then come back at once and tell you."

He did not answer, but she could feel his arm trembling. She raised her eyes to his face.

"Good gracious me, Charles! Whatever—?"

"I wouldn't have been making such a fuss if Charlie had been living."

Their boy who had been killed in the hunting-field years ago. An old wound that had never healed. She knew now what this meant to him, or he would never have hurt her with this reminder. She summoned the years of bleak self-discipline to steady her.

"All right, Charles. There's no more to be said. We'll get you wrapped up and I'll come with you."

VI

And so it came about that Mungo had a visit that evening from the most unexpected of guests. This stolid Ayrshire farmer took his parents-in-law on the whole calmly. They had sought him and, by his manner towards them, he never quite allowed them to forget it. Their abrupt patrician ways, so different from the ways of his prim and urban relatives, worried him, usually, not at all. But tonight even he had to admit that their behaviour was unexpected. His wife and he were sitting snugly in the Dower House parlour when the door was thrown open and a bundle of clothes with Sir Charles Ruanthorpe's head at the top of it pushed itself into the room, followed by Margaret's mother. They sprang to their feet. Margaret went to him.

"Good gracious, Father! Whatever are you doing here?"

"Are you going to have a baby, Margaret?"

"You needn't shout so loud, Father. The servants will know soon enough."

"Then you are?"

"Yes. If all goes well."

"You had better kiss me."

Smiling a little sheepishly, Mungo watched his wife embrace her parents. They appeared to him to have forgotten about him, or, indeed, that he had anything to do with it. For a moment he was the farmer of the Laigh Farm again, and here was the laird and his family. They were fond of making a fuss with themselves, the gentry.

"If it's a boy, his name's to be Charles," the old man was saying.

Margaret turned to her husband. She knew there had been a good, peasant line of Mungo Moorhouses.

"What do ye think, my dear?" Mungo asked her.

"Charles has always been the name of the first boy in our family," her father insisted.

Margaret touched her husband's arm. "Charlie was the name of my brother, Mungo."

"Very well, my dear, if yer baby's a boy we'll call him for yer brother Charlie."

Mungo Moorhouse had given Sir Charles Ruanthorpe of Duntrafford his permission.

Chapter Ten

AT St. Enoch's Station, Bel said goodbye to her sister-in-law Margaret with the most affectionate smile she could muster, then trudged wearily down the platform feeling she hated everybody, particularly everybody who was called, or likely to be called, Moorhouse. Yesterday, Margaret Ruanthorpe-Moorhouse had descended upon her suddenly. Then, claiming the intimacy of a married relative, she had asked Bel to accompany her upon her visit to the doctor. Bel wished Phœbe could have gone with Margaret. Phœbe knew more of the Ruanthorpes. She had often been to Duntrafford from the Laigh Farm. But the errand to the specialist was a particular one. A young, unmarried girl couldn't be expected to understand Margaret's hopes and fears. So Bel had had to go with Margaret, and duly express her genteel and knowing pleasure at the coming happy but unmentionable event.

Today was Friday of the first week in December. That meant Christmas looming, with all the fuss of presents and entertainment. Tomorrow she had promised to drag herself down to the warehouse to see that poor Highland woman whose husband had lost his foot. On Tuesday of next week she had invited David's newly affianced bride and her mother to tea at Grosvenor Terrace to be introduced to David's sisters. That meant sweeping and garnishing the house on Monday. No. She had too much to worry her.

She stood at the entrance of the station for a moment grimly wondering how best she could get home. A sudden gust of icy wind made her shiver and draw her furs about her. All at once a thought came to her. She would indulge herself a little. She would call a cab and visit her mother in Monteith Row. From there she could easily get a message to her husband telling him to fetch her later. Tea and a little maternal petting was what she was needing.

The cab was chill and musty and smelt inside of leather, sawdust and horse, but Bel didn't mind. She closed her eyes and thrust her hands deeper into her muff. It was a relief merely to be sitting still. They jolted down the ramp leading from St. Enoch's Station into Argyle Street. Already, gas-flares were lighted in most of the shops. Christmas decorations were appearing everywhere. Windows were brighter and more tempting than ever. There was tinsel and coloured paper everywhere. The very badness of the times seemed to be forcing the shops to make their wares appear more desirable.

As the cab threaded its way through the traffic, Bel, in spite of her weariness, could not help craning forward to see what it was they were exhibiting in this window and that. Presently she was paying off the cab in front of the entrance to her mother's flat in Monteith Row.

Mrs. Barrowfield, who had been feeling dull, was delighted to see Bel. It had been cold this morning, and Maggie her elderly housemaid had, on being commanded to deliver an opinion, duly delivered the opinion expected of her, and advised the old lady to stay in. This may have been safe advice, but a day at home was not entertaining. Mrs. Barrowfield therefore received her daughter with great energy and affection, and sat her down on the other side of the fire.

Almost at once Bel began to be sorry she had come. Her mother, having finished her own tea, was sitting bolt upright in front of her preparing to fire off reproofs, questions and advice.

"Well, my dear, where have ye been? Ye look as if ye have been running yerself off yer feet."

"So I have, Mother, but I can't help it."

"Well, you *should* help it. Nobody'll thank you for doing it. Where were ye today?"

Bel had to go through the entire story of Mrs. Mungo's visit and the probability of her having a baby. The old lady didn't take this news particularly well. She had hoped that the Ruanthorpe-Moorhouses would remain childless. Her daughter's children might then in time have become, in some part, their legatees.

"And what's all this about David?"

That had to be gone through, too. Then Bel had to listen carefully to the story of the rise of Robert Dermott's fortunes. A story that was common knowledge in Glasgow, and had already been recounted to her many times—usually, as now, with the purpose of impressing upon her that her husband's brother was marrying no one of any real consequence after all.

"Grace Dermott and her mother are coming to tea on Tuesday. That means polishing and cleaning the house."

"Ye'll kill yerself," Mrs. Barrowfield said with every evidence of satisfaction. "And you'll only have yerself to thank."

"I won't be able to thank myself, if I'm dead," Bel smiled bleakly.

But Mrs. Barrowfield only fixed her through her steel spectacles and said, "Find out what David wants me to give him for a wedding-present. He's a friend o' mine, is David." Like many old ladies, she was pleased to imagine she had a special understanding of young men.

Bel sighed. She had come hoping to find the old lady sympathetic. She had wanted to confide in her about the Rennie concert, and about her worries over the slum people that Arthur was proposing to put into the coach-house. But it was no use today. She would merely be scolded for everything. Such was her mother's mood.

Presently Mrs. Barrowfield rose and fetched a pencil and paper. "And just when I have ye, my dear, I want ye to tell me what I'm to get for all the bairns' Christmas presents. Let me see, there's your three, and Mary McNairn's four, and Sophia's two. Then I aye give Phœbe something, and there's you and Arthur. I'll not bother with David this year, seeing he's getting a good wedding-present. But there's the minister and the usual folk in the church."

Bel put up a beaten protest. How could her mother feel so well and strong? "Oh, not this evening, Mother! I can't think. I've had a busy day."

"Get away with ye! It'll not take a minute." She got down in front of Bel and began writing, her hard grey curls dangling on either side of her energetic head.

It was no good. Bel had to go through the list, and there were several more that occurred to her mother as she went along. Each had to be considered and argued about, and she had to suffer not a little exhausting contradiction.

Arthur's arrival was as a straw to a drowning woman. Mrs.

Barrowfield greeted her son-in-law in high good-humour, pressed a glass of wine upon him, and tried to make them stay for a meal. But by hidden signs Bel indicated to her husband that at all costs they must go.

So Arthur, like a dutiful husband, much regretted. Everybody would be anxious about them at home. It was a pity, he said waggishly, that they all hadn't these strange American things called Bell telephones that some of the more progressive doctors were said to be getting in this winter, so that they could consult each other in dire emergency without leaving their own houses. But until such a time it was kinder to arrive home when you were expected, or people would jump to the conclusion that you were under the hoofs of a tramway horse.

Mrs. Barrowfield said she didn't believe a word about these distant speaking things, and what would people be up to next? She embraced Bel with energy, thanked her almost pathetically for her visit, and told her to remember that her mother was a worn-out, lonely old woman, who was always grateful when she could spare the time to come and see her.

Well aware that all this last was for Arthur's benefit, Bel kissed her mother affectionately enough, and went off on her husband's arm. She turned to him at the end of the Row. "Would it be terribly extravagant to take a cab home, Arthur?"

"It's a long way. Do ye feel ye need it, my dear?"

"I do." How comforting of him not to ask any more questions! She wouldn't tell him she had wasted money on one today already.

Once settled in the cab, Bel affectionately propped herself against her husband's shoulder and sentimentally held his hand. The regular trotting of the horse made her sleepy. For the first time today she was contented and happy. There was something soothing about Arthur. He wasn't really a bad old thing. Perhaps, after all, she concluded to herself dreamily, Moorhouses did have their uses.

II

On the following morning Bel had all the symptoms of a bad cold. There was nothing for it but bed. This was a nuisance. She had the arrangements for the weekend to see to. And, in addition, she had promised to go down town to see the Highland woman and to arrange, if the woman looked civilised enough, for her charitable sojourn in the coachman's quarters in Grosvenor Terrace Lane. Now Arthur said she would have to allow Phœbe to go in her stead.

Bel was not sure about this. Phœbe was so impulsive. She had no balance when it came to lame ducks. The sight of one was quite enough to rob her of all common sense. There was always some rescued mongrel or kitten in the empty stable at the back being fed and tended by Phœbe. Much to the delight of Bel's own children, of course. But it was all very well. Phœbe did not stop to remember that such animals might carry disease.

Why couldn't he pay the woman her man's wages and let her remain where she was for another week? she demanded huskily of Arthur as he brushed his hair. After the evasive fashion of husbands, Arthur replied that he had better see. See what? Bel demanded. But by this time Arthur was on his way downstairs to breakfast. And when Sarah, Bel's housemaid, brought up her breakfast tray, she told her that Miss Phœbe had gone out with the master. That was that. There was nothing now for Bel to do but feel sorry for herself.

Later in the morning Phœbe came back from the meeting important and excited. She had found lame ducks after her own heart. The woman, she told Bel, was a poor, proud creature, and the two little children were sickly mites. She had arranged for them to come this afternoon. One of Arthur's warehouse men was fetching them and their belongings in a cart.

Bel heaved a worried sigh. If she had arranged this herself, she would, of course, have been uplifted by her own kindness. But as Arthur and his sister had arranged it, she was filled with disapproval. The roses of her bedroom wallpaper danced unsteadily before her eyes. She felt feverish forebodings. These urchins would probably infect her own children with every known disease.

"I'm worried about this, Phœbe," she said. "Did the children look clean?"

"How could they be clean?" Phœbe demanded of her with sudden and surprising passion. "I know what these slum rooms look like. Are you forgetting that once I brought Arthur out of one of them?"

Bel never forgot that. However puzzling, however maddening this girl might be, Bel was never to forget a night four years ago when her world had stood still with horror because her three-year-old son had been kidnapped. She would never forget the ragged, filthy girl of fourteen who had appeared out of the cruel darkness dragging the child to safety. That was a link between Bel and Phœbe that would never be broken. Passionate self-will could have another name even in a difficult half-grown girl. The name was courage.

This was the first time, indeed, that Phœbe had referred to it, and Bel guessed rightly that this slum woman and her children had reawakened echoes in Phœbe's stormy heart.

"What a dirty wee brat you looked!" Bel replied with intentional triviality. After all there was no purpose in allowing Phœbe to excite herself with memories.

The handsome, flushed child, standing at the foot of her bed, did not reply to this. Her colour merely deepened for an instant, and a flicker of contempt showed in her face. "Anyway, Henry can help me with them when he comes this afternoon." She turned and went to join the family at their midday meal.

Bel smiled to herself in spite of a swollen nose and pricking eyes. It seemed a strange sort of love-making that went on between this eager and restless couple. Either they were quarrelling or engrossing themselves in some quite unlikely occupation. And helping a slum woman with her flitting was one of the most unlikely.

III

David had not been looking forward to Tuesday. This perhaps was not unnatural. At almost no time does a young man see his own family in a more critical light than at the moment when he must present them to his future wife. At no time do relatives seem more homely and inadequate. No. Tuesday was merely an ordeal to be got through.

Grace and her mother drove into the City in the morning.

David was asked to join them at their midday meal. He found Robert Dermott with them. The Dermotts were, each of them, warm-hearted people in their way, and their pleasure in David's company was not assumed. Placed between Robert Dermott and his wife, David was compelled to listen to an account of the appalling state of British merchant shipping on one side, and on the other, to hear, minutely and at length, just what Mrs. Dermott's plans for Christmas were, and how very greatly they must now be altered as a result of his engagement to her daughter. David did everything he could to sustain both conversations at once, which was not difficult, as his future parents-in-law were doing all the talking.

When the meal was over he rose to go. He would meet the ladies later and all three would drive out in the carriage to Bel's house in Grosvenor Terrace. Robert Dermott came with him.

Once out in the street, the old man caught his arm. "Ye haven't a minute to come up to the office, David?"

David thought he could find that minute.

"Come away, then." Mr. Dermott said no more, but turned in the direction of the office of Dermott Ships Limited. In some moments they were there, and David was following on the heels of the chairman of the company through the great main doorway. He felt self-conscious as he passed through the large outer office filled with clerks, who, at the sight of the old man, had suddenly been seized with an intense interest in their work. They passed through a smaller office with some three or four senior clerks in it. Among them was David's friend Stephen Hayburn. As he was hurried on, David allowed himself a hasty smirk of recognition, and Stephen shut one eye.

The chairman's private room was like every other chairman's private room in Glasgow. It had a great mahogany desk, a deep, Turkey carpet, an extravagantly blazing fire and composite photographs of various bodies of important gentlemen of the City hanging in faded gold frames against Pompeiian red walls.

"Sit down, boy." David found himself affectionately thrust into a worn leather chair out of which the padding was bursting. For a time the old man fanned out his coat-tails in front of the fire and looked down at him, saying nothing. David waited.

"I want my son-in-law to come into this business," Robert

Dermott fired at him suddenly; then, as many businessmen will, he stood watching the effect of his words.

David's colour changed. "It's very kind, Mr. Dermott," he said lamely.

"Kind? Everything I have in the world will go to you and your wife someday. I want ye to learn to look after it. Dermott Ships Limited is not all mine. But most of it is. And I don't want ye to throw it away."

David stood up. The Dermotts' love and generosity were closing round him in a way that was frightening. The idea of joining Dermott Ships alarmed him. The family did not consider him a good businessman, and he knew they were right. As a boy in his teens, Arthur had taken him, drilled him, and set his somewhat frivolous feet in the ways that a sound businessman's feet should take. The snob within him told him that he would rather be in ships than in cheese. But that was only one side of it. The proposition overwhelmed him.

"I would like to talk to my brother Arthur about this," he said at length. "You see, I owe everything to him, Mr. Dermott."

"I'm glad to hear you say it, David. Ye're a good boy. But yer brother would be mad to refuse ye a chance like this." He put his great hand on David's shoulder. "I'll come across with ye and see yer brother, if ye like."

"I'll speak to him myself first, Mr. Dermott."

"Very well."

"And thank you again." David held out his hand, feeling like a boy who had been to tea with the headmaster.

"Get away with ye. Ye belong to us now, laddie." He struck the young man's shoulder a resounding blow of affection. David was amazed at the warmth of this great, over-emotional Highlander. He was glad to get himself out of the room, to find himself alone in the street.

IV

Bel was forever setting her stage and hoping that everything would run according to her programme. The facts of this afternoon's arrangements were these. She had asked Mrs. Robert

Dermott of Aucheneame to tea, together with her daughter, Grace. And she had asked David's sisters to come and meet them.

Out of this, Bel had painted for herself a picture. On Tuesday afternoon she would be found by her chief visitors, calm and poised and, she hoped, not entirely without good looks, sitting in a flower-filled drawing-room, graciously ready to take her newest sister-in-law to her elegant bosom. They would have a charming talk, with just the proper amount of emotion in it, then she would give them tea from a table spread with delicate lace and covered with glittering silver and fine china. Later, David's elder sisters would appear, drink tea, and be presented. And through all this she herself would move, smiling and holding the social reins. Encouraging here—restraining there. And, though she did not quite admit it, the hope was hidden somewhere within her, that David's future relatives would in due course take their leave feeling that it would be a privilege to be allied to anyone so charming and so accomplished as Mrs. Arthur Moorhouse.

That was the picture as Bel saw it. By Tuesday morning she knew that some of the details at least must be imperfect. For one thing, she herself would not be in her best looks. Her cold was receding, but her nose was still red. And when she had got up yesterday, she had felt weak on her legs and unfit to see to such important things as dusting, sweeping and the buying and arranging of flowers. Phœbe had said she would see to everything, but that wasn't quite the same. She was much too impetuous, and prepared to think that anything would do.

Then, while she was scarcely yet ready to receive her guests, Sophia and Mary arrived. Bel was annoyed. She had asked them to come later, hoping to have the Dermotts to herself at first. Now she had only to enter her drawing-room to feel that indefinable closing of the family ranks.

"Bel, dear, what a dreadful cold you have!" Mary said. "Is it wise to be having a tea-party today? As I was just saying to Sophia and Phœbe, I think it's wonderful how you keep yourself on the go."

Sophia, who had been chattering to Phœbe, turned the flood on Bel. "I hope you don't mind us coming a little soon, dear. But you see we've heard so little about all this. It's been so secret.

But, then, these things have to be secret till the last minute, don't they? It wouldn't really be suitable if they weren't, would it? But, as I said to William just last night, 'Trust Bel. She'll know all about this!' "

Bel had no intention of telling David's sisters anything of his confidences to herself. As she sat looking at Sophia, she noted with some satisfaction that she had left her muff to dry too near the fire, as some of its hair was singed, and it had lost its lustre. "It's all been a great surprise, hasn't it?" was all she said.

"And Phœbe tells me that Margaret Ruanthorpe is going to have a baby," Mary said with a conventional show of pleasure.

Bel winced a little. Young girls like Phœbe shouldn't be talking about such things. Even to their own married sisters. That was what came of being a farmer's daughter, she supposed.

But Mary had thrown a stone that was bound to cause ripples.

"Of course, we think it isn't wise," Sophia said. "After all, Margaret must be forty. Well—I mean forty is not quite the age to be having a first baby."

Bel took the precaution of sending Phœbe downstairs to see after something quite unnecessary, then the three married ladies got their heads together. She had much to tell of Margaret's visit. What the doctor had said. In what respect she must be careful. How she had taken the news. Bel couldn't help enjoying the telling. Nor could she think so ill of Sophia and Mary as she had done a moment ago. After all, they were comfortable, familiar creatures to gossip with. They had forgotten she had a cold, and were exposing themselves to it freely in their eagerness to catch every detail of this important family news, as it fell from Bel's still-swollen lips. And so Bel, Mary and Sophia had quite forgotten appearances, and were deep in talk, when Mrs. Dermott, Miss Dermott and Mr. David were announced. Hurriedly Bel rose to receive them, feeling all too acutely that her reception of them lacked the poise and graciousness she had planned.

David did not enjoy this women's tea-party. As was natural, he was very conscious of everything his relatives did. He had counted on Bel to maintain an atmosphere of refined distinction. But she had, it seemed, a bad cold, and appeared ridiculously fussed as she poured out tea.

Mrs. Dermott's habit of talking loudly made, for those who did not know her, the easy interchange of polite and suitable ideas a difficult matter. Grace, instead of behaving as the honoured guest, was apologetically handing round bread and butter. And as for the others, David decided it was no use expecting the family to be anything else than the family. At last, however, they settled themselves down in some sort of way. Grace and Phœbe beside Bel at the tea-table, and Mary and Sophia with Mrs. Dermott.

As he moved about he saw that Grace's eyes were upon him. It was strange how little confidence she had in herself, how often her look was asking for his approval. She was a gentle creature. He was fond of her.

He wandered for a moment to the window and looked out. The offer he had received from Robert Dermott worried him. What was he to say to Arthur? His brother had done everything for him. He felt that if Arthur wanted him to stay in the business in the Candleriggs, he was bound to do so. Yet he could not deny that it would be great advancement to be one of the firm of Dermott Ships. And he knew that it would please Grace.

David stood uneasily gazing through the bare December trees out into Great Western Road. An almost empty tramcar, its mud-bespattered horses trotting dispiritedly, was making its way to the Kirklee terminus. A couple of hansoms, their wheels casting a spray of snowy slush, were flying downhill into town.

Over there across the road in the white Botanic Gardens there was no sign of life. The gas-jets in the street lamps shone pale in the fading daylight.

Yes. It was all bound up with Grace. Everything was bound up with Grace now. He could never escape that. He was never free now from an unnamed feeling, an unnamed compulsion. He must keep compensating—making up for something he was unable to give her. He had not defined this even to himself. But it was there, influencing all his plans.

"I've been sent to tell you to come and talk to us." He felt a hand in his own, and turned to find Grace beside him. He came back with her, recalled to his duty. He was pleased to see that Grace had made friends with Bel, and that even Phœbe, who could on occasion be so withdrawn that there was no understanding her, had unbent, and was telling her of some slum family that had become her latest hobby.

Sophia and Mrs. Dermott in their group were happily talking simultaneously.

"And you see, Mrs. Dermott, in a family like mine," Sophia was saying, "it's very difficult to have meals at regular times. You see, my husband never will tell me when he's coming home, so he just has to be fed when he appears. And the children are worse. I was just saying to the servant this morning—"

And through all this Mrs. Dermott was explaining: "So I had to tell these women that if they were taking that attitude there was nothing more to be said. Of course admittedly it was annoying for me. I had given a lot of my time and money, and the gardener had sent several bunches of greenhouse flowers to decorate the platform first, and be sold to help the funds afterwards. But then it was silly of me to expect—"

Mary was sitting between them pretending to give this rather disjointed conversation some kind of cohesion, but in reality she was making the most of a particularly delicious chocolate cake that was one of the specialities of Bel's kitchen, the recipe for which Bel was—Mary suspected by intention—always forgetting to give her.

This was not the kind of meeting David had foreseen, but they all seemed to approve of each other, and everyone seemed happy. He went back to the party at the tea-table.

"I've just been telling Bel," Grace said, looking up at him, and blushing to find herself using Mrs. Arthur Moorhouse's first name, "that I don't think she should have this charity concert she's telling me about until after Christmas. She's got a terrible cold, David, and, as she says herself, she's got all her Christmas things to see to." She appealed to Phœbe. Phœbe, who had never really troubled to think about it, was quite prepared to agree.

"But Miss Rennie will have left Glasgow after Christmas," Bel protested.

"Perhaps not immediately after. Write and ask her at once. David, couldn't you take Miss Rennie a letter this evening, after we go?"

"Yes, of course."

Bel allowed herself to be persuaded. It was nice of Grace to show this thoughtfulness. Grace, she felt, was going to be on her side of the family camp.

The carriage was announced. Mrs. Dermott rose to go. She held out her hand to Sophia, but Sophia did not take it.

"No, my dear, I'm coming down to see you off at the door. We'll all go!"

Bel was amazed at the state of easy familiarity between her least presentable sister-in-law and the forbidding Mrs. Robert Dermott. Sophia's suggestion seemed to have pleased her. Etiquette was being flaunted at every turn. They all trooped downstairs and waved the carriage off. Everything was friendship and goodwill. Sophia even offered Mrs. Dermott her singed muff as additional comfort against the coldness of the journey.

Chapter Eleven

IT was quite dark when David left Grosvenor Terrace bearing Bel's letter to Miss Rennie. His sisters had waited just long enough to express their approval of his choice—an approval that was not altogether conventional; for Grace Dermott had been anxious to please.

Bel's note was short. It was better, she had determined, for David to try to see Miss Rennie himself and explain to her how things really stood. Bel knew that she could depend upon David's tact. If Miss Rennie were not in, he had promised Bel to go back at a time when he should find her.

It was damp and cold as David stood, huddled in his greatcoat, waiting for a tramcar to come down from the turning place at Kirklee. He felt dispirited. After years of bachelor freedom, of few obligations, of easy friendships, responsibility was gathering itself around him.

At last a car was approaching. He signed to it to stop. He settled himself gratefully, as the horses resumed their measured trot. It had been, after all, a day of strain. And tomorrow he must speak to Arthur about Robert Dermott's wish to have him in Dermott Ships.

At Hill Street he got down and began making his way up into Garnethill. The street was not well lit. He had to peer about in the darkness, seeking the number. Once, thinking he had come up too far, he asked his way of a young woman standing beneath a street lamp. She directed him eagerly, offering, indeed, to come with him. He noted her "English" voice and her too ready laughter, as he protested that he could find his destination very well by himself.

Miss Rennie's landlady assured him that her young lady was at home, and that, although Miss Rennie had just come back from the country, she was sure she would see him. He stood in the dim little hall, lit by a single gas-jet, which for economy's sake had been turned down to a peep, while the woman opened the door, went inside and shut it behind her. David was kept waiting for just such time as it takes a self-conscious young woman who has thrown aside her outdoor things to make herself hastily tidy.

II

"David Moorhouse!" Lucy Rennie came forward and gave him both her hands. The landlady closed the door behind them. "I would have known you anywhere, David," she said, bringing him to a seat by a cheerful fire. "Would you have known me?"

"Of course, Lucy." David was surprised at himself. In the stress of events it had not somehow occurred to him that he was coming to meet an old friend. She was not much changed after fifteen years. Her face was still round and gay, and her eyes still danced with mischief. Maturity, womanliness and a pleasant, cultivated voice were added. That was all.

They sat, as people in a like situation will, gazing at each other with frank, unaffected curiosity, their thoughts going back to such things as hunting for peewit's eggs in the high Ayrshire furrows, or standing hand in hand, two frightened little children, as the "otter hunt"—pink coats, baying hounds and yapping terriers—made their alarming way past them as they played by the river.

"You're a very grand young man now, David!"

"You're a very grand young woman, Lucy."

Lucy laughed. "No; not very grand, David. I've got to work for my living. I've learnt my way about. That's all."

David brought out Bel's letter. While Lucy broke the seal and read it, he sat looking about him. The little sitting-room was warm and comfortable. In addition to its cheerful plush-covered furniture, it was made gay with innumerable knick-knacks, a painted tambourine, feathery pampas grasses dyed in bright colours, painted fans, silk bows on velvet picture-frames; the random decorations of some unselective, feminine mind. There was a silk-fronted piano piled with music. Supper was laid. Lucy must just have come in. Furs and other outdoor things topped by a smart little hat and veil were lying on a chair to one side.

His eyes turned to re-examine the girl who was living thus independently. It was unthinkable that his sister Phœbe should live unchaperoned like this. And yet what was there that was wrong about it? Why should it be unusual for a man to be sitting here, the one visitor in the rooms of a young woman who was, after all, a childhood's friend?

The vague feeling that in some way he was overstepping propriety, amused and stirred this very conventional young man with new and not unpleasant sensations. Somehow it touched his manhood. Lucy Rennie, he felt, was putting full dependence on his chivalry. The situation was novel. As she bent over Bel's note, she looked different from the women he was accustomed to. She was plump, and her dark hair was piled up on her head like a Frenchwoman's. As she looked up, folding the paper at the same time, the expression of her round face was quick and responsive.

"I'm sorry about Mrs. Moorhouse, David. I like her so much, you know."

David explained about Bel. Earnestly excusing her, hoping that Lucy would understand and forgive, and in the end, daring to hope that when New Year was over, she would still be in Glasgow long enough to make it possible to give her recital of songs.

Lucy understood everything. She would be at home in Ayrshire over the New Year, but thereafter she would try to spend a day or two in Glasgow in order to fulfil her promise. She would write a note to Mrs. Arthur Moorhouse to reassure her. David thanked her and rose to go.

"David! Already? It's so nice to see you. Must you go away? There was so much I wanted to say to you." Lucy stood up and put her hand on the bell-rope. "Look, David, I was just going to have supper. I don't know what there is to eat, but as you've dared to penetrate into Bohemia, why don't you stay and share it with me? I wanted to tell you I had seen your brother Mungo and his wife. I'm just back from Greenhead. And I want to have a look at you just for a little longer." Her smile had a whimsical appeal in it.

David was tempted. It was pleasant here. For the first time today, he did not feel that all the cares of the world were pressing close about him. This, after all, was an old and harmless friendship. If Lucy's manner was flattering, if she was intensely feminine—that was how she was made, and it could have no significance.

She saw his hesitation. "David, I believe I am being too unconventional for you! Really! It wouldn't be the first time we had picnicked together, would it? But perhaps I've been a gipsy too long. Perhaps I am forgetting what's proper. I must leave it to you."

The landlady was standing by, awaiting orders. It would be churlish, David felt, to walk out—churlish and gauche. He turned gaily to the grey-haired woman. "Will you allow me to have supper with Miss Rennie?"

The woman was surprised at his flushed face, his refinement, his air of innocence. This young man was a gentleman; an unusual type for hereabouts. "I think we might allow that, sir. I'll bring another cup."

"I'm so glad, David. I'll show you where to put your coat."

The meal was cosy and gay. They told each other what they had done with themselves since they had parted in their teens. David was surprised to find how much more Lucy had seen and done than he had. She spoke French fluently, she told him, having spent some time as a student-governess in Paris. She had sung in many famous London houses. Although she had been only a paid musician, she had been in some kind of contact with many celebrated people, and had used her eyes and her ears. She was able to give him many amusing impressions of them. It was a world beyond the provincial climbings of David Moorhouse.

Presently they talked of the old days, when the little boy from the Laigh Farm had waited at the end of the road for the little girl from Greenhead, and together they had trudged the mile or so to the village school. There had been no great friendship between the families, but the children gave each other companionship and a sense of protection in the winter roads. Lucy, although she was younger, had seemed the elder and more responsible then. As they grew older there had been pranks in which Lucy had always been the leader: getting lost, bird-nesting in some remote wood; bathing together, contrary to injunction, in the innocent indecency of childhood. David spoke of his mother's death, and his father's remarriage to the Highland housekeeper who had become Phœbe's mother. Lucy had been his boyish confidante in these difficult years. He had forgotten that no one knew so much about him. She had taken him back into another world. It was strange to be sitting now in theatrical lodgings in a great town, hearing again so many long-unheard echoes; hearing them from a sophisticated young woman whose mode of life would certainly be open to the criticism of his friends.

"But, David,"—suddenly Lucy stopped—"I quite forgot I read last week that you were engaged to be married!"

David had forgotten, too.

"Tell me about her."

David told her about Grace. Who she was. How he had come to know her. As he told her, he found himself wondering why Lucy should be putting so many questions, watching him so closely.

"She sounds to me just the very wife for you," she said at length.

"I must have thought so, too, when I asked her to marry me." David laughed. Yet the disloyal overtones of his joke seemed wrong somehow.

"She's a lucky girl, David."

"Thank you, Lucy."

"No. I mean it."

But the carefree atmosphere of this meeting had changed. It was no more pleasantly intimate, innocently clandestine. She saw that David was ill at ease, and, now that their meal was at an end, she was not surprised that he should remember some duty and plead that he must be gone.

"Of course, David. It was kind of you to stay so long, to talk about old times." She watched him get himself into his overcoat in the little dim entrance hall, and waved him goodbye as he turned downward out of sight on the gaslit stone staircase.

III

In the two hours or so that David had spent in Lucy's rooms the weather had grown colder. As he made his way down Hill Street he found himself slipping in ruts of frozen snow. Above him the sky was clear and there were stars.

He wondered now why he had so suddenly invented an excuse to leave Lucy. It had been a queer little visit, he told himself, smiling into the darkness, and one that for all its unusualness had done no one any harm. It had been pleasant to recall the past with someone who had once been a playmate; to laugh at little, long-forgotten things.

He thought of the odd, friendly room where he had found Lucy, and of Lucy herself. The little pinafored girl had turned into a creature of much charm. She had easiness of manners, quickness of wit, tact—all accomplishments that David valued highly. There was something gallant about her independence.

Presently he found himself at the foot of the hill pondering which way he should take. He wondered now that he did not feel tired, as he had done earlier in the evening. It had been a strange day. Lunch with the Dermotts. Robert Dermott's too generous offer. Grace's formal visit to Grosvenor Terrace. And then, this unexpected visit to Lucy. Now his day was done. He could go home, write a letter to the girl he was to marry, and rest. But somehow he was restless. As though there were an important question forming itself in the hidden places of his mind. A troublesome question that would sooner or later take shape, rise to the surface, and have to be answered.

The air was crisp and frosty. It was pleasant and refreshing. He would walk about the lighted City to stretch his legs and think. This decision taken, he pushed on hurriedly, noting very little where he went. Now his thoughts were taking him back to his boyhood at the Laigh Farm. He had been the youngest. His sisters had petted him when he was little. They had laughed at his natural gentilities and encouraged him in them for their own amusements. His mother had made as much of him as was possible to a busy farmer's wife. Childish pictures rose before him—things that had not crossed his mind for years. A secret clearing in the wood that he had called his kingdom. A cave by the river's edge that he had always hurried past because of the giant who lived there. A pond rimmed with bulrushes and yellow irises, where the prince of all the frogs lived. The imaginings of an ordinary, sensitive child, set alight from the few picture-books that had found their way to the children of the Laigh Farm. He had not told his brothers and sisters about these things. He had shrunk from their laughter. But he had always told the little girl, as together they clattered stockily along the road to school. Lucy was quick in the uptake, and could be depended upon not to laugh in scorn.

Jets were being turned out on the long brass gas-pipes in the shop-windows as David made his way down into the centre of the town. Shutters were going up. In front of one or two shops the pavement was being swept clean of snow, and ashes thrown down. In Renfield Street horses were straining uphill with their loads, clapping their labouring hoofs on the sanded track and puffing jets of steam into the frosty air. On the steeper parts of the hill the brakes of descending tramcars were screaming.

Why this muffled excitement? Was it because he must tell Arthur of Robert Dermott's offer? Or was it over-sensitive of him to worry lest he should seem ungrateful to the brother who had done so much for him?

David was perplexed. The world had been too good to him. He had nothing to complain of. And now it looked as though by the mere fact of having chosen a gentle and desirable girl to be his wife, a fortune was to be handed to him. Why, then, this inward dispeace? For one strange moment he had an impulse to turn back to Lucy Rennie's lodging; to ask her as an old friend what was the matter with him. No; that was ridiculous. Whatever she had been to him as a child, she was, to all intents, a stranger to him now.

Without noting what he did, he had come down as far as the Clyde. He was crossing Glasgow Bridge. The lamps on the balustrade on either side stood up like pale jewels, strung out against the glowing darkness. The tide was in. On the right he could distinguish the gilded figurehead of a clipper. In the river further down there were dim shapes of masts, and moving lights. At the far end of the bridge he turned into the Georgian quiet of Carlton Place. Here there was a sudden peace, an absence of traffic.

Was this marriage he was making just an impetuous mistake? Had he rushed into it unnecessarily? He remembered how, not so many weeks ago, he had raged along the night streets on his way home, inflamed by Irving's Hamlet, thinking excited thoughts even as he was doing now. Was it all a mistake, then? It couldn't be. What of the feeling of emptiness, of all the sorrow of a young man's loneliness that he had felt on that night? Was he not far better now?

He was in the traffic again, crossing the Stockwell Bridge. The river stood full and high beneath it, sending up slow, zigzag reflections from its black, glassy surface. Now he was in the bright rabble of the Stockwell itself. Even on this cold night there were barefoot children. There was laughter and drunkenness, misery and rough good cheer. There were barrows with flares set above them. By one of these a powerful Irishwoman with raven hair, gipsy ear-rings and harsh, weatherbeaten good looks, called, "Rosy apples". She picked up an apple, breathed upon it, and quickly rubbing it on her apron, held it out to David. Hungry urchins stood gazing up, their faces white in the light of her flare. Further on, a second woman, leading a donkey-cart, was calling, "Caller herring". A cold trade on such a night. An old man standing at the kerb kept muttering quickly, "A penny, a penny," to no one in particular. David saw that he was selling cotton pocket-handkerchiefs. The doorman, in splendid gold braid, was ordering ragged, half-grown boys from the lighted entrance of the Scotia Music Hall. They were shouting back obscene impertinence. A locomotive on the viaduct overhead puffed out a fountain of steam and red ashes, making a display of fireworks against the night.

David found himself making in the direction of home; pounding along, his feet crackling the frozen snow as he went. He had some distance to go, but he did not think of this. There was bright moonlight now. That made it easy to cut quickly through quiet sidestreets.

What was this, then, that had taken hold of him? What did he expect of himself? Was he to go to Grace and tell her that, after all, their engagement had been hasty and foolish. That was unthinkable; an idea that could not be taken seriously. And yet, here he was, striding along as though this very thought had taken upon itself a horrid shape and was following in the darkness behind him. Everything within him shrank away from the pain that such an avowal must cause. To say such a thing to Grace? Never!

The mere thought of that had, for a time, quickened still more his pace, but now at length he began to feel exhausted. He looked about him. In ten minutes more he would be home. Since he had left Lucy Rennie's rooms he had tramped down the hill, made a circle of the inner City, then walked some miles west without noticing. This was senseless. He must not let himself become so overwrought.

He took out his latch-key at the top of his stairs and let himself in. His sitting-room had been warmed by the fire that was now burning low. He held a taper to the gas, then looked about him. Here was a bleak, bachelor sort of room. There were none of the absurd, frivolous knick-knacks that made Lucy Rennie's lodging so cheerful. He threw off his overcoat and drew a chair to the fire. His feet were beginning to ache. He pulled off his boots slowly and held out the soles of his feet, one after the other, to the fire. The familiar surroundings were beginning to calm him. After a little while he even felt drowsy. The clock on his mantelshelf struck eleven. He had no idea it was so late. Better go to bed. Surely, after all this walking he would get some sleep.

Chapter Twelve

GRACE DERMOTT had put the Moorhouse clan in her pocket. That a daughter of success should at once command the respect of a homely family in this city, where material prosperity was the common yardstick, is not, perhaps, a matter for wonder. Grace had gained everything by her engagement to David. She was beginning to have a life of her own. Hitherto she had spent her time as a pleasant, timid absorber of shocks. Between the personalities of her parents, when their strong wills threatened to clash together. Between her mother and the members of her mother's committees. Between her parents and the servants. Between one servant and another. Spasmodically, she had made the pretence of having interests of her own—working in Berlin wool; painting on china; and even, once, going the length of taking lessons on the guitar. But too often she had felt in her heart, as many a rich young woman of her time felt, that her days were gapingly, needlessly empty.

Now all this was changed. David and his family were everything. Before many mornings she was back in the carriage at Grosvenor Terrace to see how Bel's cold was getting on, ladened with conservatory grapes and flowers. She had just dropped in on her way to town, she said. Taken unawares and informally, Bel's conventionality had no choice but to break down. Grace was quite simple and direct. It was plain she had come back so soon because she liked everybody, and was making haste to know them better. She got to know Bel's children, and offered to take the two elder ones, Arthur and Isabel, to Hengler's Circus. She promised little Thomas, who was scarcely four, and who showed immediate displeasure at being left out of the party, that she would take him to Aladdin's Cavern at the Argyle House, where Aladdin would give him a toy all to himself.

Even Phœbe was forced to respond. Grace remembered the Highland woman and her children in the coach-house. The man, Phœbe told her, had left hospital and was with them now. Grace asked to be taken to see them. She stayed with them talking for some time. Phœbe could see that she was used to such people, hurting none of their quick pride with a sympathy that was blunt or heavy-handed. Grace Dermott was not, after all, perhaps, the sweet-faced nonentity Phœbe had taken her to be.

Returned from the coach-house, Grace gave Bel her hand and said she must be gone, as she wanted to look in on Sophia. Bel said goodbye with apprehension, wondering what kind of confusion she would find at Rosebery Terrace. If she had known, her apprehension would have been greater. The entire Butter family were at home. Wil and Margy had been given a skating holiday from school, and were clamouring noisily for an early meal, as they wanted to go off to skate.

Sophia was fussing round in the steam of cooking, wearing one of her little maid's aprons. "Be quiet, children! I am being as quick as ever I can. Margy, go and lay the table. Katie, did you forget we needed salt? It's too silly having no salt in the house. Wait. Here's some salt spilt on a dresser shelf. I'll scrape it together and use that. Wil, there's the bell, dear. Go and answer it. Katie's busy."

The door was opened to Grace by a lanky boy of fifteen with some of the Moorhouse good looks. He looked at the smart young lady in the fur jacket, then at the carriage behind her, and waited, saying nothing.

Grace smiled. "Are you Wil Butter? I'm your new Aunt Grace. Can I come in?"

A sheepish grin spread on Wil's face. He opened the door wider, and Grace followed him. "I'll get Mother," was all he said, leaving her standing in the hall. A moment later she heard voices, presumably in the kitchen.

"Mother, that's Aunt Grace."

"Aunt who?"

"Grace. Uncle David's young lady."

"Dear me! Run and tell her I'm coming. Where have you put her?"

"Nowhere."

"Silly boy. Why didn't you show her in beside Father? I must come at once." Sophia came into view undoing the apron. "Grace dear, I'm delighted to see you! I'm hurrying up dinner because the children want to skate. They're so impatient. It's awful! Do come in where it's warm. William, this is Grace. This is my husband."

A black, hairy man was sitting in the stuffy little parlour in an embroidered smoking-cap and slippers, reading the newspapers. He got up ponderously and gave Grace his hand.

As he did not offer a remark, Grace said it was very cold. Sophia said it was indeed cold, and please to sit down and warm herself.

"I only looked in to leave a brace of pheasants. Mother said she thought you might like them."

Nothing pleased Sophia better than to receive something for nothing. "Oh, how kind of you, dear! What a nice present!"

The dinner-bell clanged harshly. "Oh, there's the bell. Grace, stay and have something. We all want to see you." The words were out of Sophia's mouth before she could take them back.

So Grace sent the carriage away, and stayed to eat shepherd's pie and mashed turnips from cracked dishes laid on a stained table-cloth. Her hirsute host was expressionless and speechless, but, Grace decided, not antagonistic. With Sophia and her constant talk, flowing rather from the lack of ideas than from the possession of them, Grace was already familiar. But she was interested in the two untidy, handsome children. Like herself, they were direct and friendly, and prepared to make her one of themselves. And so, this most unlikely of luncheon-parties was a success. Grace said goodbye to William and Sophia in a cloud of goodwill. The pheasants, still lying in the hall, had been duly admired, and Grace drove off towards the fog-threatened city accompanied by Wil and Margy muffled up and carrying their skates. She had undertaken to drop them at St. Vincent Pond, which was, like so many other ponds in and about the city, being advertised as having its ice in prime condition.

In the carriage she extracted a promise from them to come down to spend the day at Aucheneame on Saturday. Their Uncle David would be there, and, if it was still freezing, they would all go skating on one of the lochs in the Kilpatrick Hills. By that time the ice would be safe even on deep water.

As they sat fitting on their skates, the Butter children agreed with each other that their new aunt was a bit fussy, perhaps, but not too bad. And that they had expected their la-di-da Uncle David would want to marry more of a fool.

II

Since her first visit to Bel, two days before, Grace had not seen David. But this morning she had received a letter from him telling her that he had consulted Arthur about quitting the family business in the Candleriggs, and that all was well. She had replied by electric telegram bidding David come down to Aucheneame for the night, if possible, in order to talk things over. He would find Grace at his sister Mary's house at Albany Place where she had been invited to take tea. They could drive back together.

Having left the two Butter children at St. Vincent Pond, Grace spent the intervening time shopping. In spite of the cold and the threat of fog, she went about the town with a light heart. The shops were warm, and gay with Christmas tinsel, and Miss Dermott of Aucheneame was a welcome customer. Several times Grace found herself humming little snatches from sheer pleasure, as she trod the wintry pavements, stopping every now and then to examine the contents of a window. In the light of her own happiness, the Moorhouse family seemed a grand lot. The Grosvenor Terrace household. Sophia's family. She was glad that half-grown boy and girl, who had driven part of the way into town with her, were to be her nephew and niece. Their gawky eagerness warmed her. She wondered how they were getting on with their skating, and found herself wishing she were with them. But there was this visit to be paid to Mary, where she was to see the McNairn nephews and nieces. Yes; she liked the Moorhouses.

And at the centre of them all was David.

And now presently it was time to meet the carriage and make her way west once more. This time in the direction of Charing Cross and Crescents.

III

Baillie George McNairn had pompously announced this morning at breakfast that he was coming home specially to do the honours at tea. The occasion, he said, demanded it. His new sister-in-law must be received with all respect. If Grace had not been the daughter of one of Glasgow's shipping princes, if she had been the mere daughter of an empty purse, the baillie might not have felt so strongly the compulsions of politeness. But at all events, there he was with his wife, ready to receive the child of Robert Dermott with every manifestation of decorous approval.

As Grace appeared in the doorway of the snug, over-furnished drawing-room in Albany Place, it was George, plump and imposing, who advanced heavily to meet her. "Come away, my dear, come away. Very pleased indeed."

George did not make the reasons for his pleasure more precise, but it was nice for Grace to know the mood of her host and hostess. She advanced to Mary, and was received with calm affection, remarked how foggy it was becoming, and was bidden to sit close to the fire.

For once, Grace found herself doing most of the talking. Didn't they think it unusually cold for early winter? Did they think the fog would really settle down? Wouldn't it really be a pity if it were a cold winter, when there was so much distress about? It was hard going. She was almost grateful to George when, cutting in upon her own somewhat forced efforts, he began a long panegyric on the merits of her own father, on his great brilliance as a man of business and as a leader of men. It was embarrassing to listen to, perhaps. Especially as George had so many of his facts wrong. But at least it was less of an effort than having to pump out conversation on her own account.

"And to think that he rose from nothing—nothing at all!" George was winding up his discourse on a note that a quicker, less well-disposed daughter might have found necessary for her father's sake, to qualify, when two very fat little girls of four or thereby, in much-starched white dresses, large red sashes and red buttoned boots, were pushed into the room by a hand that did not belong to any discernible body.

"Come along and see your Aunt Grace," Mary said placidly, without getting up to bring them.

"What little darlings!" Grace exclaimed.

The darlings were very slow in coming to be presented. The tea-table, groaning with every kind of cake, rich and ornamental, lay across their path, and drew their interest much more surely than any aunt, however agreeable, that they were ever likely to acquire.

Grace went to them and knelt down before them. "What are your names?" she asked.

"Anne," said one. "Polly," said the other. They both then turned away and went on examining the tea-table. They were both exactly alike, fat and round-faced, with hair cut close, like little boys. Both were so intent upon the glories to come, that Grace burst out laughing.

Their parents smiled benignly. If Grace had not been a daughter of the exalted, they might have wondered what she was laughing at.

Presently tea arrived, and with it the two elder children of the family. Georgie McNairn was fourteen, and, in so far as a beardless boy can look like a fat, middle-aged man of forty-three, George's rather heavy, undistinguished features resembled his father's. Jackie, a boy of eleven, was, on the other hand, a thin distinguished child whose features seemed entirely Moorhouse. Like their Butter cousins, they had been skating. It did not take Grace very long to guess that they had been commanded by their father to come home in time to meet her, and that this had not pleased them very much. To put herself into their good graces, she invited them to come on Saturday with the Butters to Aucheneame.

Their parents were pleased about this, and accepted for them willingly. As George said to Mary after Grace was gone, you never knew what visits to places like Aucheneame might lead to. Mary was too lazy to bother thinking out what her husband meant. But, somehow, it would have pleased her better if her own children had been invited by themselves, and not together with Sophia's quicker-witted son and daughter.

But Grace's visit was a great success. During tea, the baillie's tongue was loosened enough to tell her at length about a long and intricate misunderstanding he had had with another member of the Town Council. His narrative was, perhaps, difficult to follow, interrupted as it was by the clatter of tea-things, the constant cross-talk of the children, the continual necessity of passing cakes to them, and of refusing cake herself. But from it all Grace understood enough to grasp that George's sound common sense had triumphed; that if it had not been for Baillie McNairn, the entire civic policy of the City of Glasgow would have taken the wrong turning. She therefore did her best to show approval at the right moments, and, when he had finished, to tell him how fortunate it was that he had been there to arrange everything so wisely.

The cup of even George's vanity was full. David, when he arrived, was surprised at the amount of joviality that his stiff and humourless brother-in-law was displaying. He was even more surprised when, as Grace and he rose to say goodbye, George slapped him on the back, and told him that there wasn't another girl in the West of Scotland that he would prefer as a sister-in-law.

IV

"Well, David, are you pleased to see me?" Grace and David, buried in rugs, were settling themselves for the long, cold drive to Aucheneame.

For reply, David turned to Grace and kissed her. She had looked forward to having him in the carriage all to herself. She took one of his hands and drew it inside her muff.

At the McNairns', David had seemed unusually solemn. It was a mood she did not yet know. "Are you all right, David?"

"Of course. Why?"

"Oh, nothing." She must not be a fussy wife. Men, she had read somewhere, detested that above all things. Yet she imagined he had looked preoccupied, and even a little strained, as he had come into Mary's drawing-room. But David was so much in her thoughts, that she was over-quick to imagine things about him.

"Tell me about Arthur, David," she said.

"Oh, Arthur was very good." He told her about his interview

with his brother. How Arthur had expressed his pleasure that David should have such good fortune. He had made no difficulty whatever about David's going. Trade was bad, and the slackness of the times made it easier. David had promised to remain until the end of the year, when he would be ready to come into Dermott Ships.

There was animated talk about all this. Grace was pleased to see that, as David sat talking to her, the sense of strain seemed to go from him. Her presence seemed to soothe him. The shadow of the cloud that had crossed her happiness passed over and was gone. David was himself again. And more affectionate than ever he had been. With the affection, somehow, of a child. This again was a new mood, but not one to trouble her.

She told him of her visits to the family. How she had seen Phœbe's Highlanders. Her unexpected lunch with Sophia. How she had invited the children to skate at the weekend. They laughed together over this and that. The impatience of the Butter children. The comic appearance of Mary's little twin girls.

Presently, after a pause in their talk, he turned to look at her. "Grace," he asked, "when are we to be married?"

She felt the colour rising in her cheeks. It was the first time he had asked this of her.

"Do you want to be married soon, David?"

"Yes. As soon as ever we can."

"It won't be long, my darling." She had dropped her voice to a whisper. She wished that she were clever, that she could read the mind of this man who was all the world to her. Something told her it had not been a conventional lover's question. There were unmistakable overtones of appeal in his voice, overtones that baffled her. She wished she knew what he meant. She wanted to talk about it. To ask him why. But what could a brotherless, cloistered young woman know about the make-up of men?

He was sitting now, looking before him in the dusk of the carriage. Grace could not see his face distinctly enough to tell if the look of strain had come back. But something told her it was there. Instinct prompted her next words.

"We would be happy and safe if we were married, wouldn't we, David?

"Yes, Grace. We would be safe."

The hand she had drawn inside her muff grasped her own hand tightly. It was time for them to get down before its grip was relaxed.

Chapter Thirteen

IT was in the morning of the last day of the year, a Tuesday. Margaret Ruanthorpe-Moorhouse had written to Grace Dermott inviting her to spend New Year with them, along with David. It was disgraceful, her letter had said, that all the rest of the family should be getting to know her so well, while she and Mungo, marooned as they were in Ayrshire, had not yet met her. Could they come on the Saturday before New Year and spend a week, or the better part of it? Phœbe, who was a favourite with her mother, Lady Ruanthorpe, was coming to Duntrafford House, with Henry Hayburn. Together, they would all make a pleasant New Year party.

Grace showed herself loath to leave her own parents at this time. It would, she protested, be her last unmarried New Year with them. On being scolded by Mrs. Dermott, however, for working up a deal of sentimentality about nothing, and reminded that her first duty was to her man, Grace gave way at once. It would give her great pleasure, she wrote, to come to the Duntrafford Dower House to get to know everybody and to see David's calf country.

But David and Grace were prevented from going down into Ayrshire on the day arranged. To add to the poverty and the evil times, the year 1878 closed with a bitter frost lasting four weeks, the longest period the West of Scotland—a region of wet, south-west winds—had known for twenty years. In the poorest quarters of the city the suffering was intense. But those who were young and had some money spent all their leisure perfecting their skating. Local trains were filled with cheerful young people making their way to nearby lochs and ponds. Such places, lighted late into the night, and provided with coffee-stalls, were being advertised among the places of entertainment in the daily papers together with the pantomimes, Hengler's Circus, the music-halls and the demonstrations of Pepper's Ghost at the Coal Exchange.

On the Friday after Christmas, however, there were heavy

snowfalls up and down the country. To begin with, long-distance trains could not come through. Then even local traffic came to a standstill. On Saturday night the west wind brought the rain in torrents. Sunday was a day of flooding and confusion. By Monday communications were beginning to reopen. The snow was being washed away. On Monday evening David and Grace, accompanied by Phœbe and Henry, reached Duntrafford.

Now this following morning Grace was standing with Margaret, waving to David as he drove off with Mungo in the pony-trap. Mungo had his usual business at the Laigh Farm, and Margaret had instructed him, when that was finished, to drive across to Greenhead to find out if Miss Rennie were there. She had not forgotten Lucy Rennie's kindness to her in the train. Remembering that she would be at Greenhead over New Year, she was sending a note asking Miss Rennie to come to see her.

"Have you met this Rennie girl?" Margaret asked Grace as they set off on foot to Duntrafford House, where Grace was to be presented to Sir Charles and Lady Ruanthorpe.

Grace had not yet met Miss Rennie.

"You would be surprised if you knew her people. Very ordinary farm folks. Not that there is anything extraordinary about that," Margaret hastened to say, remembering, perhaps, her own husband. "But Lucy Rennie herself has turned into something so very different. She might be an Englishwoman. You would never guess she was an Ayrshire farmer's daughter."

Grace expressed her interest in Miss Rennie. She had, Grace understood, spent a long time in London, and no doubt that accounted for the change which had taken place.

Margaret said, "No doubt." And they walked on in the direction of the Big House in silence.

Grace wondered about Margaret herself. She belonged to a type with whom the Dermotts, as yet, had little contact. Robert Dermott's fortune had put him among the locally important. He lived in a large house in a country place, and allowed himself servants, and, when he could, a country life. But he and his kind were not yet of the county. The industrial great of Scotland had not yet, to any extent, taken to educating their children in England, thus levelling their manners, their speech and their habits of thought with their like across the border, as would happen a generation later. They had not yet begun to mould them to the English county-squire pattern.

And thus, Sir Charles Ruanthorpe, an Englishman, with his lady and daughter, seemed as different to Grace Dermott as an American might have seemed. Their controlled good manners. Their English accent and turn of speech. Their habit of distinguished understatement. Their large hospitality, which was, unlike Scottish hospitality, never pressed. Their sureness of their own point of view. Their quick responsibility for their dependents. They belonged to a world that was trained to authority. She did not define these things, but she felt them, and like many another who uses the English language but does not possess English blood, she had to adjust. But their goodwill was unmistakable. So, quick to blame herself for any lack of warm feelings, Grace decided that Mungo's wife and her parents were everything that was admirable.

But how Mungo Moorhouse, an Ayrshire farmer, had come to marry Margaret Ruanthorpe was a mystery to her. How these so seemingly different people had come to make a match of it was beyond her understanding. She must get David to tell her, when she had him to herself.

II

It was many years since David Moorhouse had found himself in Ayrshire for any length of time. He had not made a stay even of four days, as he was now doing, for quite ten years. As he sat beside Mungo, looking about him, this came to his mind. It struck him as odd. There had been nothing much to bring him back to the Laigh Farm house, he supposed. Mungo's bachelor existence had been all work and no play. To a young man who had welcomed the town and its ways, the farm had little attraction. Even before the accident that had ended the lives of his father and stepmother, he had come home very little. Where Arthur was, there was David's anchorage.

But now it was pleasant to be driving in country that was stamped on his first memories. He was surprised at his quick familiarity with the twists of the muddy lanes, the gates and thorn hedges, the clumps of high trees on the round hill-tops, the shape of the green, rolling fields. They were there as he remembered them. This midwinter Ayrshire had its own beauty. The torrents of rain at the weekend had washed the fields clear of snow. It lay now only where there had been deep drifts, sodden and stained with red mud. In contrast, the wet fields seemed in the morning sunshine to have taken on a greenness that gave them, almost, the freshness of spring. Furrows and ditches were full. Streams were raging torrents. The placid River Ayr, as they crossed the bridge, had run wild, and was dashing itself against the sandstone cliffs—a boiling, red-brown cataract. There was a newness, a promise about this Ayrshire of the Winter Solstice; a purging, a washing of the fertile lands, that again in proper season they should be clean and waiting to receive the seed and bear the annual harvest.

David, alert just now, and oddly sensitive to impression, had eyes for everything. His mind, unsettled and quick, kept darting hither and thither. Why did he find himself so much uplifted by the country this morning? It was said that as you grew older you began to put back your roots—try to touch back to your beginnings. Now he was approaching middle age. Perhaps these feelings were beginning to awake in himself. He must come to Ayrshire more often. No. They must come. He and Grace. He had been unhappy and restless in the last weeks. So unhappy and restless that he had even mentioned it to Bel. But she had given him to understand that, in her opinion, this was what being in love did to a man. That when at length he held his wife in his arms, his unhappiness would be resolved, his body and mind would find their assuagement and their peace.

Well, it would come soon. At the beginning of March. Neither of them wanted a fuss, but, when it came to the point, a fuss there would no doubt be. If it were merely as an exhibition of Mrs. Dermott's organising talent.

There was the Laigh Farm now, over there, with the high trees in the stack-yard. There were still rooks' nests in the upper branches. They had all been born at the Laigh—all the Moorhouse brothers and sisters. And that was the road-end where he had been used to meet Lucy Rennie on the way to school. They had cut part of the wood there, further down where they had gathered wild hyacinths in the springtime. The Bluebell Wood, they had called it.

Lucy Rennie. Mungo, who was busy, had asked David to set him down at the Laigh Farm and drive over alone with Margaret's message. She would be glad to see Lucy at any time. But—and David was to put this tactfully—Lady Ruanthorpe had suggested that Lucy might come across to the Big House, dine with them on New Year's night, and sing to them all. He was to put it that they knew this was asking much of a professional musician, and of a daughter who was so little at home; but that it would be giving great pleasure to two old people who had no other means of hearing real music.

As they turned into the yard of the Laigh Farm, Phœbe and Henry Hayburn appeared at the back door of the farmhouse.

"Hullo, what are you doing here?" David shouted.

Phœbe shouted back, "Showing Henry round."

"Did you walk across?"

"Yes."

"You must have come early."

Mungo was jumping down. His two old collies, Nith and Doon, rushed out to meet him. The old ploughman who had been promoted to be farm grieve came out. He spied David and called to him by name.

"Oh, it's you that's up there, Davie? How's yersel'?"

"Fine, James. How are you?"

"Fine, Davie. Man, yer a great stranger! Are ye no' comin in?"

"I'm going up to Greenhead. I'll come in when I come back."

A sudden mood had taken David. He wanted to be away from it all. This place was a memory, with his mother and father, his sisters and brothers, all of them there. Its present reality offended him. The stones had no right to be standing any longer. It should have no existence but as an image in his mind. That shed was new. It didn't belong. That door was the wrong colour and had hinges he didn't know. They had made a new window in that wall. These things didn't really exist. They were not to be found in the records of his mind. For so many years he had turned a snobbish, adolescent back on the Laigh Farm. Now it must be taking its revenge.

He took the reins from Mungo a little uncertainly. He had not driven a horse for many years.

"Wait a minute. We'll come with you. Come on, Henry."

Phœbe and Henry were up beside him. For some reason undefinable, his heart became lighter. He was glad they were coming to Greenhead too.

III

Lucy Rennie also had been going through the experience of coming back. This experience, indeed, was sharper than David's, because she had left her home in Ayrshire as a rebel. Now her father and elder sister were treating her with as much forbearance and tact as their peasant manners would allow them. But she did not like being treated as a brand snatched from the burning. If she had been a little scorched, and if she chose to risk being scorched again, that was her own affair. Yet she could not but be touched at the anxiety of her family to please.

She was sitting in the best room of the farmhouse—a stiff, red-plush room, seldom used, that had been dusted and warmed against her coming—when her sister Jessie, a stocky country woman, came to tell her that Davie Moorhouse of the Laigh was there with his sister and a young man. They were talking to her father in the stack-yard. Lucy roused herself, went downstairs, and out by the farmyard door. Advancing across the yard, she made an incongruous figure as she held up her elegant skirts to avoid the mud and the puddles. When she came within speaking distance, she called to draw their attention.

"Good morning. Why aren't you coming in?"

"We're only here for a minute or two. It's just to deliver a message. Your father has asked us in already," David shouted.

Old Tom Rennie, squat and graceless, grunted assent.

She had a moment more before she came up to them. David was standing hatless in his dark clothes. His sister was standing beside him, bareheaded too. Where had these Moorhouses got their good looks? The morning sun was striking down on David's warm chestnut hair and his long, distinguished face. Phœbe's black hair was wind-blown and untidy, but her cheeks were glowing. And, as everybody must, Lucy marvelled at her strange, Highland eyes. They might have stepped out of Raeburn canvasses, both of them.

"So that's what little Phœbe Moorhouse grew into!" she said, holding out her hand admiringly.

Phœbe did not attempt to make any easy reply to this. She merely gave Lucy her own hand in return.

Lucy turned to the second young man. He was wearing country tweeds in a large trellis check. His thin, bony body was buttoned up in a tight, shapeless jacket, and his long legs were in narrow trousers. He took off a hat of the same cloth with a skip back and front. He seemed a pleasant, pug-nosed sort of creature, and bestowed upon Lucy a boyish smile. David introduced him as Henry Hayburn, a future brother-in-law.

"You are a very lucky young man, Mr. Hayburn." She looked towards Phœbe, who had turned aside to pat the nose of a cart-horse that had put his head over the fence.

Henry grinned, and went to join old Tom Rennie, who was on his way across to Phœbe.

"And how are you this morning, David?" Lucy asked, giving him her hand. She wondered why the colour had flooded up over David's face, why he looked at her as though she were hiding something from him. He had not been like this when he had called on her in Glasgow.

"Oh, I'm all right, thank you."

Why was he embarrassed? There were men, she knew, who could not talk to a young woman like herself without immediately becoming conscious of her sex. But she never would have guessed that David Moorhouse might turn into one of these.

As he stood giving her his message, Lucy wondered. After all, within his own narrow range, he was rather a sophisticated young man. What, then, was there about her to embarrass him?

Yes, she told David, she would be glad to visit Mrs. Ruanthorpe-Moorhouse. No, she was doing nothing this afternoon, and would be glad to come across for tea. It was very kind of Mrs. Ruanthorpe-Moorhouse to ask her sister too. She would tell her, but she did not think she would be likely to come. The Duntraffords would readily understand that Jessie's duties at the farm would not allow it. When David and the others had gone,

Lucy picked her elegant way back across the farmyard smiling with satisfaction. Her stay at Greenhead, then, was not to be so dull, after all. At their midday meal she was pleased to see that her father and sister seemed glad that the Big House should be taking notice of her. Here was her achievement in terms that they could understand. For in those days, the landlord, if he had any sort of dignity, was still held in honour, and regarded with some awe by his tenants.

Lucy looked forward to her visit to Duntrafford with pleasure and no sense of shyness. There was nothing to overawe her about Margaret Ruanthorpe-Moorhouse, and just as little, really, about old Sir Charles and his wife. Did she not, after all, earn much of her living teaching the daughters, and singing in the drawing-rooms, of personages much more important than they?

Chapter Fourteen

GRACE had looked forward with pleasure to meeting the remarkable Miss Rennie. From everything Margaret had said, she seemed an unusual young woman. This afternoon she would see this farmer's daughter who had disappeared from her home and reappeared a polished, accomplished and independent young lady.

And yet, when Grace came to look back on this visit to Duntrafford, it was clear that things had begun to go wrong for her on the afternoon of Lucy Rennie's call at the Dower House. It was difficult to tell just in what respect the savour had gone out of things. Grace was not a worldly person, neither was she particularly quick-witted, nor, least of all, had this gentle daughter of indulgence had cause in her life to learn the cruelties of jealousy. But she was head over heels in love with the man she was to marry, and her tenderness towards him was open to every wind that blew across it.

Miss Rennie came. And Miss Rennie was charming. Miss Rennie was quite obviously enjoying herself.

Lucy, sitting in the midst of stiff respectability, and pleasantly friendly—but very definite—condescension, found herself being given tea by the laird's daughter. Yet, from Margaret's manner to her, she was made to feel that, whatever she did with herself she would never rise to the level of the Ruanthorpes. And here was Mungo Moorhouse of the Laigh, safely high and dry, and out of the struggle, having joined his blood to the blood of the Big House. And these young people. So very much now the children of privilege, all of them. They were all very sure of their complacent, northern world. There was just enough of the street arab in Lucy to see the fun of it all. She had known the artist quarter of a Paris that was settling down after the Prussian occupation. There, respectability, she remembered, had been so very much a matter of ready cash. It had been as fragile a thing as that. And as for the airs the Ruanthorpes gave themselves, she was accustomed to sing in houses of people of vastly greater importance; to rub shoulders with snobs who would have looked down their noses at old Sir Charles and his lady.

But she liked David. And he seemed to like her. From her memory of him, he had been a gentle, but rather self-possessed little boy. She had wondered this morning at his obvious confusion when he spoke to her. It was the same again this afternoon. What did he think of this sweet, rather limp young woman he was going to marry. Why had he chosen her? But of course! She was rolling in money, and David was, after all, a Moorhouse. And quite right, too. Money perhaps wasn't everything. But, look at it as you would, it lifted you up, out of the battle. She dared say David would do very well with Miss Dermott.

David had come to her side. She turned to him.

"I heard Margaret speaking to you about dinner tomorrow," he said.

"Yes, I'm coming. It was very kind of Lady Ruanthorpe to ask me."

"I'm glad. We'll all be there. I hope you're going to sing."

"Of course. If they want me to. What kind of songs do you like?"

"I'm not particularly musical."

"But you must like some songs. All men do. If they know no other kind, they say they like simple, old-fashioned songs."

"I think these are the kind I *do* like."

"Oh, David! David!"

Grace, who was near enough to hear this conversation, wondered what there was in all this to cause Miss Rennie's laughter.

"Do you never sing simple, old-fashioned songs?" she heard David asking.

"Of course. A great many of them. I sing for my living."

No, Grace Dermott did not like Lucy Rennie. She seemed to be able to play on that instrument which was David Moorhouse, to strike notes that she, the owner of the instrument, was unable to touch. Miss Rennie was quick and gay, and had a mass of small talk. She was not superficially vulgar. She was neither loud-voiced nor pushing. Her behaviour was perfect. But Grace, too, had noticed David's changing colour, his betrayal of dispeace in Lucy Rennie's presence. She was glad when Miss Rennie rose to go.

On the doorstep, when they had waved Lucy out of sight, Grace turned from the others to David.

"How warm it is. And moonlight! Come for five minutes' walk. Just as we are."

They sauntered arm in arm through the Duntrafford shrubberies. The moonshine was making silver and black velvet of the shining path and the wet leaves of the deep rhododendron bushes. They found themselves at a viewpoint on the cliffs looking far down on a sharp bend of the river Ayr. There was a churning eddy where the flood was forced to change its course. The moon had caught the water where it boiled. They could see the angry river emerge for a moment into the light of the whirlpool, turn itself into a cauldron of cold, white metal, then plunge on, roaring into the darkness. They bent over the balustrade hand in hand.

"It's wonderful, isn't it, David?"

"Yes. Shall we go back now?"

"Yes."

They wandered back to the Dower House. It was Grace who kept hold of David's hand.

II

Lady Ruanthorpe's dinner-party was for ten. Herself and Sir Charles, along with the party from the Dower House, made eight of them. In addition to that there was, of course, Lucy. And, with great forethought on her own part, as the old lady considered, she had invited a shy young man who made his living as a piano-teacher among the daughters of the county. Thus, Miss Rennie would not have to accompany her own singing. The two musicians were made the guests of honour, Grace having already been given her place on the right hand of Sir Charles on the previous evening. The shrinking young man was placed on the right hand of Lady Ruanthorpe while Lucy sat to the right of Sir Charles. Though these people were mere entertainers, she saw to it that they suffered no discourtesy.

The timid young man was petrified when he saw what his position at table was to be. But a glass of sherry with his soup did wonders. And he quickly found that Lady Ruanthorpe either did not hear, or did not pay attention to a word he said. She kept delivering a monologue at him. The songs she sang when she was a girl. What a wonderful voice her father had had. So good, indeed, that he might have been a professional singer, if he had not been a Lieutenant-General. How she had been piped into dinner, when she was staying with friends in the Highlands. How she had been staying near Glasgow, when her daughter was a little girl, and her host had pressed her to stay over to hear a pianist called Chopin. She had always regretted she had not done so, for she had since been told that his music had become famous. Was this the case? Or was she talking nonsense? Perhaps Mr. Wilkie could tell her. For a moment Mr. Wilkie emerged from the enjoyment of the best food and drink he had ever tasted, to tell her that yes, Chopin's music was quite well known.

At the other end of the table, Lucy was enjoying herself hugely. Sir Charles, she was amused to note, regarded her as something of a scarlet woman, and was determined, in so far as it could be done at the age of eighty, and under the eye of his daughter—he was safely shielded from his wife by a forest of epergnes, maidenhair, flowers and candlesticks—to prove to Miss Rennie that he, in his time, had known very well what it was to sow a wild oat or two. A mention of the fact that she knew Paris set him off on a long description of a sojourn there as a young man in his twenties, at the gay, cynical time of the Bourbon restoration. He had been sent by his parents to learn French. But he must admit, he said, looking at Lucy with a twinkle in his fierce, bloodshot eyes, that he had learnt more than French, perhaps. Lucy would fain have driven him to bay by asking him to tell her just what he *had* learnt. But this would have delighted Sir Charles too much, and might have led to talk not quite suitable for Lady Ruanthorpe's dinner-table. Besides, demureness, she kept reminding herself, must be the keynote tonight. So, when Sir Charles continued archly to mention the names of resorts of entertainment, and the names of the notorious who entertained there, Lucy found herself replying with gay innocence that she knew nothing of these places or people—as was indeed the case, for Sir Charles had known Paris fifty years before she had. But within the limits of discretion, she succeeded in keeping her host amused. So much so, indeed, that when Lady Ruanthorpe rose to take the ladies from the room, Sir Charles patted Lucy on the shoulder, said she was a capital girl; and where had her father got her? And she must come across and see them whenever she came to Greenhead. Now, immediately under the eye of Lady Ruanthorpe and the other women, Lucy smiled with becoming diffidence, thanked him very much, but rather thought it might be some time before she was back in Ayrshire.

For most of them the remainder of the evening went very pleasantly. As Lucy had guessed, old Lady Ruanthorpe had invited her much more from a feeling of self-importance than from any real desire to hear her perform. The evening was well advanced before Lady Ruanthorpe, who had been enjoying her own dinner-party far too much to remember Miss Rennie's talents, at last begged the musicians to go to the piano. A first song proved to Lucy that she could not trust the obliging young man's playing too far. But it did not matter. They were a party who would only appreciate David's "old-fashioned, simple songs". She had brought a number of these, and all agreed that she sang them charmingly. Especially Sir Charles, who had talked steadily during the performance of each of them. But everyone was pleased, complimented her, and was friendly. For a moment, later in the evening, she found herself beside Grace who, fearful of showing her dislike, set herself to praise Lucy's singing. Lucy was acknowledging Grace's kindness when David came across and joined them.

"Well, David! Are these songs old-fashioned and simple enough for you?"

"I thought they were beautiful. Don't you like them yourself?"

"I've sung them very often."

A servant appeared to announce that a conveyance was waiting to take Miss Rennie back to Greenhead.

"Couldn't you sing just one more song?" Grace asked.

"A song that you really like this time!" David said.

Lucy went to the piano. With a friendly nod to the pianist, saying she hadn't the music, but thought she could remember, she sat down and played and sang. It was a gentle nostalgic sort of song in a foreign language. But it was evident that she loved this music, and her voice was warm. When it was over she swung round in the stool to find David immediately behind her. On his face there was a look of embarrassment.

"Well, David, was that too high falutin for you?"

"No." And in a moment—"What was it?"

"It's called *Nussbaum*, by Schumann."

"Will you sing it again at Bel's concert?"

"Yes, if you want me to."

Lucy said her goodbyes. And as she drove home under the stars, with the soft west wind in her face, she thought of David Moorhouse and wondered.

III

A winter sun, not yet far above the horizon, was shining bravely as Grace came down to breakfast next morning. She found Margaret alone behind the teacups. A bright fire was burning. The little dining-room of the Dower House was warm and cheerful.

"Good morning, Grace. How did you sleep? There's your porridge and ham and eggs. You'll help yourself, won't you?"

Grace was getting used to Margaret's matter-of-fact, English voice. She made everything she said, to Grace's West of Scotland ears, sound cut-and-dried and official. It was not a voice crammed with overtones of sympathy, but neither did it contain any overtones of spleen. It was the voice, Grace had decided, of a person you could depend upon; the voice of a woman who had solved her own problems quite straightforwardly. The bright sunshine and Margaret's crisp friendliness cheered Grace. She had not slept well. The New Year's party at Duntrafford House last night should have been pleasant enough, but somehow, for her at least, the evening had fallen flat. Quick to blame herself, she had lain awake in bed telling herself she was a fool. Sir Charles and Lady Ruanthorpe were old, eccentric and wilful. But they had been hospitable and kind. With the others, of course, she was already on familiar terms. Surely Miss Rennie could not matter to her happiness? Or was she troubled because David had shown too much interest in Lucy? Was she, Grace, at last learning what it was to be jealous?

She had lain in bed scolding herself. She was being quite ridiculous. David had known Lucy all his life. If she was going to resent every gesture of friendliness her husband made to other women, what kind of marriage was before her? These thoughts had chased themselves round in her mind until at last she had fallen into uneasy sleep.

But now the sun was shining. And Margaret was sitting, the very picture of reassuring normality, rapping out observations. Where the early snowdrops were to be found. How the gardeners had planted thousands of daffodils under the beech-trees of the park. How the shrubs in front needed cutting down. And now here was David himself, followed by Phœbe and Henry, all saying good morning with pink, new-washed faces, all cheerful, and making plans for the day.

"What do you mean to do with yourselves?" Margaret asked David and Grace.

David turned to Grace. "Have you any ideas?"

"I haven't seen the Laigh Farm, you know."

"We'll go over there."

This was pleasant. She would have David to herself this morning. They would drive out together on this pleasant morning, and her own unhappiness would be forgotten.

It was much as she had hoped. They drove between bare hedges by fields where ploughmen, taking advantage of the soft weather, were at work. Each team looked like the last. A pair of sleek, gigantic Clydesdales. The Argonaut's bow of the plough turning the smooth, red wave of loam. The clank of harness. The cloud of following rooks and gulls. The sturdy figure of the Ayrshire ploughman stepping steadily as he kept his furrow even—stepping in the footsteps of a great poet, who once had tilled the red Ayrshire earth not many miles from here.

David seemed pleased to tell her about familiar things as they passed. The road the brothers and sisters had taken when they went to school. The mill where their father had taken his sacks of grain. A pool in the river where he had learnt to swim. David, a working farmer's son, had known a childhood of interest and variety, such as she, the daughter of a wealthy businessman, had never known.

They found Mungo at the Laigh Farm directing his men. The old grieve was pleased to see David, and shouted to him.

"Ye said ye were comin' back the other day, Davie. But ye didna come."

"Well, here I am now, James."

They descended, and Grace was presented. Presently she was in the farm kitchen, so familiar to the Moorhouses, so strange to herself. She had to allow tea to be made for her by the wife of Mungo's manager as they sat in front of the great kitchen fire. She was taken round the house. She was shown the room where David had slept with Mungo before Arthur had taken him to Glasgow. Phœbe's little attic bedroom. The room David's parents had occupied after they had decided to take away the concealed bed from the kitchen. Where Mary and Sophia had slept as young girls. For David's sake, Grace was interested in everything. She tried to see the beloved ghost of a little chestnut-haired boy in these bare-scrubbed rooms.

They wandered outside. Then through the outhousing, saw this and that, and at last said their goodbyes and drove out of the farm close.

"Are we going back by another way?" Grace asked presently.

"No. Not exactly," David said. "Lucy Rennie left a piece of music, and I told Margaret I would take it to her."

Grace glanced at David sideways. Jealousy rose within her like a flame. "Why didn't you tell me we had to go to the Rennies' farm before?" she asked, keeping her voice even with an effort.

"I thought you knew. Is it so important?"

"No."

"Well, then." David drove on saying nothing further.

Grace looked at him again. The expression of his face was fixed. She turned. "David, I don't want to go up to Greenhead Farm. After all, one piece of music can easily be posted. I want to go back to Margaret."

"But, Grace, that's absurd. There's Greenhead just up there."

Grace said no more. They drove up the farm road and into the Greenhead farmyard. Old Tom Rennie came out for them.

"Good morning, Mr. Rennie. I have brought some music that Lucy left behind last night," David shouted, preparing to jump down.

"She's no here, Davie. She's away tae Ayr wi' Jessie."

Grace saw David's face fall as he handed the old man the roll of music, said goodbye and turned his horse.

They drove back in silence. The colour seemed to have gone out of the morning. It was just a bleak, midwinter day. At Duntrafford a groom caught their horse's head, and David ran round to help Grace down. Without looking at him, she turned away and ran into the house.

Chapter Fifteen

DAVID'S world had tumbled about his ears. He had pushed the knowledge away from him. But he knew now. It was past all hiding. He was in love with Lucy Rennie.

On this, the first Monday of the year 1879, he sat, huddled over the fire in his lodgings, perplexed and miserable. He had brought Grace from Duntrafford on Saturday, taken her to Aucheneame, and spent the weekend there. Today had been his first day in Dermott Ships Limited. This morning he had travelled to town with the chairman of the company, and he had been received as though he were the chairman's son. At Aucheneame, and at the office, he had had to act the part of the happy, fortunate young man into whose lap fortune was pouring everything; not a pleasant part to play, when his senses had been surprised, and when, whatever his behaviour towards the Dermotts, he must feel a cheat and an impostor.

He wondered what Robert Dermott had thought of him in the office this morning. He had been dazed and slow. Had the old man begun to wonder if his daughter had chosen a fool for a husband? And yesterday at Aucheneame. He wondered what Grace thought of him. Had she suspected anything? He did not see how she could. Yet, when he came to think of it, he had thought her manner subdued and a little aloof. And he had been too self-conscious, too self-accusing to ask if anything were troubling her.

David shivered, and picking up the poker, dangled it in his hand, thinking. The frosty weather had come back again. Outside it was very cold. Again skating was in full swing. He stirred the fire.

Grace. His mind went back and forth over the short span of the weeks of his engagement to her. From the beginning things had gone well. He was getting the habit of Grace; getting the habit of her commanding, warm-hearted parents. They had turned, in that short time, into pleasant, sympathetic relatives. He was on the easiest terms with them. This had been a calculated attachment, but he had calculated well. His own measure of worldly wisdom had not, thus far, misled him. He suited Grace admirably, and she suited him. All that was lacking was the spark on his side. In every other sense he loved her. If affection can be called love.

David, his troubled face glowing in the firelight, leant forward and again dug the poker between the iron bars. If only Lucy Rennie hadn't crossed his path; hadn't lit that spark that Grace, with all her love for him, had so far failed to light. The thought of Lucy troubled him. She roused the male in him. Her womanhood was coming, more and more, to obsess his mind; to open up for him a vista of enchantment, the primitive enchantment of holding in his arms the woman who could arouse this fever within him. For the moment he could not bother to determine if the feelings she had awakened were good or bad. At least they were natural. The fact of Lucy Rennie clouded his judgment.

David, a man of thirty-one, belonged to a time, and a people who, however unfanatical their own beliefs, had inherited a strict background of behaviour, where irregularity was abhorred. In other words, David's education as a male of the human species was almost non-existent. And the lack of it now, in his dilemma, was causing him cruel distress.

Although he could not see clearly, this young man belonged to an honourable world. His mind was constantly on Lucy Rennie. At the same time he found himself caught up in self-loathing at his disloyalty to Grace. There was no peace, no rest for him anywhere. How could he go on with his engagement in the present state of his feelings? And yet how could he break it? Could he throw all the kindness of Robert Dermott and his wife back into their faces? And Grace? Was he to take her great tenderness towards him (he knew it now for what it was) and throw this, too, back at her?

As he sat moodily stabbing his fire, he remembered the solemn promise he had made himself on that morning he had asked Grace to marry him: the promise to stand by her and see the thing through. But would it be right to go on? He could not even decide what was the honourable course. David got up and paced his room.

And even if he were free, what of Lucy Rennie? Had she any

interest in him? He could not tell. His infatuation encouraged him to think she was not indifferent. But he had not seen enough of her. She had been friendly and charming to him. That was all. The image of her stood before him. Her elegant person. The faint perfume she used. The moving quality of her voice. Her quick, easy gaiety. Her pleasant good manners.

This room was intolerable. He would go across and wish Bel and Arthur a good New Year.

II

As David was being led upstairs by Bel's parlourmaid Sarah he heard a hum of talk.

"Are they alone, Sarah? Who's with them?"

"Baillie and Mrs. McNairn, Mr. David."

If David could have turned and run, he would have done so. But Sarah would have thought him crazy.

As she opened the door to announce him, he was met by the noise of family voices—what, in a blither moment, he would have called the Moorhouse roar. They all seemed to be speaking at once, and all speaking loud.

The first voice to succeed in disengaging itself from the general din was the baillie's. Possibly because he was used to shouting.

"Hullo! hullo! Here's the shipowner himself! A good New Year to you!" George, dazzled by the eminence to which David was rising, advanced to greet him cordially.

David bade everybody a Happy New Year. He kissed Bel and his sisters, Phœbe and Mary, and shook hands with Arthur and George. After all perhaps the family wasn't so bad. There's something about finding oneself among them; even if, in happier, less care-burdened times, they all seemed utterly commonplace.

"Phœbe says you all had a splendid time at Duntrafford!" George McNairn went on. Phœbe, on being asked, had merely told him that her stay at Duntrafford had been "quite nice". But the baillie's mind liked to dwell on magnificence.

Like Phœbe, David echoed that it had been "quite nice".

"And what about Dermott Ships Limited? They haven't made you chairman yet?" George went on facetiously.

There was nothing for David to do but allow George's gloatings over his good fortune to exhaust themselves—the good fortune that was weighing so heavily on his spirit.

George having finished, Bel was waiting to speak. "I'm very glad to see you," she said, "because I got a letter from Lucy Rennie today. It's about the concert here. She writes that she is willing to sing, but she must be back in London by the middle of next week. She has engagements there. She suggests Saturday afternoon of this week. It's giving us a very short time. That's why I've asked George and Mary here tonight, to try to get people together quickly."

The mere name of Lucy Rennie had thrown David's senses into confusion. He was glad that the baillie was pacing the room importantly, repeating, in what he thought was a voice loaded with modesty, that surely he, with his little bit of influence, could find one or two people who weren't nobody.

"We want Grace and her mother to come. And perhaps they could suggest some people who would care to hear Miss Rennie." It was Bel's secret hope that the Dermotts' friends would, for smartness's sake, outnumber the friends of the McNairns.

David promised to do what he could. What else was there to do? The foundations of his existence might be rocking, but the bright pattern of the surface must, in the meantime, continue unbroken.

Bel now called upon Mary and David to discuss the arrangements for Miss Rennie's afternoon. That is, Bel did the talking while Mary, determined to do as little as possible, sat applauding every proposal that would bring no exertion to herself, and constantly looking round to see if Sarah were bringing tea. David merely sat and gave a dazed assent.

"Well, that's all that settled," Bel ended gaily. "Now the next step is to let Miss Rennie know what we intend to do, and make sure that it suits her. Could you run up and see her, David? You don't mind, do you? Perhaps at lunchtime tomorrow? It has to be at once."

No. David would be glad to do anything to help. The pattern was unwinding itself. He could not stop it. And he could not hide from himself that he was pleased to have this excuse for going to Lucy Rennie again. Next week she would be gone out of his reach—unless?

"Here you are, then, David. Here's a short note to Miss Rennie. Oh, here's Sarah with tea. Mary dear, you'll wait and have some tea, won't you?"

Mary, who was making no move, thanked Bel and stayed where she was. "Just when you are at your desk, Bel dear, could you write me the recipe for your chocolate cake? I see Sarah's brought one up. You've always been going to do it."

But Bel, remembering some other, urgent point about the concert, was in sudden deep talk with David. Phœbe poured out tea, and Mary was foiled again.

III

Lucy Rennie's morning had been busy with pupils, and she was grateful, having finished lunch, to take a cup of coffee to an easy chair by the fire. Outside it was very cold and a little foggy. A letter received this morning had told her it was mild in London. She was glad to be going back.

But it was not only the weather that made Lucy glad to leave Glasgow. It was time she was gone. In London she had found her niche. That was her world. It was a friendly, easy world, with its own standards. And, if you were tactful, were not infirm of purpose, and were a hard-working artist—all of which attributes Lucy, having long since shed illusion, had acquired, you could make a very good life of it. London was her home now. It was there that she could breathe.

She had been glad to leave Greenhead yesterday. She, her father and her sister had made good-natured attempts to reach each other. But Lucy's life had thrust them too far apart. Her ways of thought, the education she had picked up, had set up too many barriers. She was better, really, not to see them very much. The thought distressed her a little. It was dreary to face the truth that the bonds between herself and her relatives had fallen away.

But that was not all the reason for her disquietude. There was David Moorhouse. When she had seen him at Duntrafford she had become aware that he was attracted to herself.

Lucy bent over the fire, thinking. It wouldn't do. She had no intention of starting up a flirtation with David. If it had been someone of her own world, who knew the rules of the game—but with a man of the Moorhouse world, the world she had broken from. . . . No. Besides, David Moorhouse had always been the little boy of her memory, a part of the picture of her not unpleasant childhood. There had been one or two close friendships with men, since she had grown up. But David would always hold a unique place. He had grown into a handsome man, in no way belying the promise of his boyhood. But she did not want to know this man. Much better to leave as undisturbed as might be the picture of the boy—to leave the grown man to the young woman he had chosen, and go her own ways in peace.

The door was thrown open and the man she was thinking of stood before her.

"David! How are you? Come in. What has brought you at this time of day?"

"It's about Bel's concert, Lucy. I can't stay."

"You look cold. Take off your overcoat for five minutes, and I'll give you a cup of coffee."

He did as he was told. "Well, only for a minute. I've gone into a new business, you know: Grace's father is taking me into partnership."

"I know. I heard all about it. Some people have all the luck."

"Have they?"

"Well, aren't you having luck, David? I would call you very ungrateful if you said you weren't."

"Yes, I dare say I am lucky."

But the brightness of David's prospects proved but a flat topic between them. So Lucy took Bel's letter, read it, and discussed its contents with him.

"Well, I think that's about everything." Lucy's contribution to the concert arrangements had not taken long. And now that she came to think of it, she had done all the talking. She expected David to go now, but he stayed on, making disjointed remarks, unable, it would seem, to take himself away.

He asked her what she did in London; how she lived. She gave him suitable answers. There was something very innocent about all this; dangerously naïve. If she had disliked David it would have been easy to show him the door. Young men at this emotional pitch were not unknown to her, and in the past she had dealt with them clear-headedly, as it had suited her. But she couldn't do it with David. He was too much a part of memory. And she was beginning to feel that if she were not careful, her own emotions would be caught.

She stood up. "David," she said, "I'm sorry to have to send you away. But I must go out soon."

He stood up, too, as it seemed to her, reluctantly. For a moment they were together on the hearthrug. Quickly, Lucy moved away and ran one finger over the keys of her piano as though she were impatient to practise.

"Lucy, can I ask a favour?"

She turned and faced him.

"Will you sing the song you played and sang at Duntrafford? You know, the one you said you would sing at Bel's concert."

No. She wasn't going to help him to an emotional scene. She allowed a smile to spread over her face, and permitted herself a little burst of laughter. "What a sentimental old thing you are, David! You want me to sing that song to you, just because that girl of yours liked it."

"No, Lucy, I—"

"Here's your coat, David! I'll sing it for you all on Saturday. She'll be there, won't she?" She held up David's coat for him to get into.

There was nothing left for him to do but to put it on, say goodbye and go. His face, as he went, had the same embarrassed expression as when, in childhood, they had been caught together at the same forbidden prank and he was being roundly scolded.

She laughed as she went to her window and watched him as his muffled figure receded down the hill. But there was wistfulness and self-distrust in her laughter.

Chapter Sixteen

GRACE was quickly becoming part of the family. Bel sat looking at her with approval over a cup of eleven o'clock tea. Only a day had elapsed since Bel had decided to have Miss Rennie's concert on Saturday afternoon, and here was Grace up to Grosvenor Terrace this morning already.

Yesterday David had sent her a note by her father. She had come to find in what direction she could be helpful. A strong sympathy was growing up between Bel and Grace Dermott. They were both well-intentioned women, though Bel's goodness suffered, at times, from a thick overlay of snobbery and petty scheming. Grace was simpler, and had none of that unimaginative unattractive shrewdness, which many comfortable Lowland Scots mistake for common sense. But she had some of her parents' organising instinct, and she was putting this at Bel's service this morning.

She sat at the table in the back parlour, pencil in hand, making suggestions and writing down one item after the other. A carpenter to unscrew hinges. The florist. The caterer. She would make inquiries of all sorts, and come back to tell Bel.

Grace's mother, Bel learnt, had a list of people to whom she was writing at once, telling them that they must attend Mrs. Arthur Moorhouse's concert and give liberally for the distress in the city. Bel knew Mrs. Robert Dermott well enough to know that these people would regard her letters as royal commands and come, unless their excuses for staying away were very solid. Mrs. Dermott's list was large and contained many important names in the West of Glasgow. It would all be very gratifying to look back upon. But the thought of these august people at Grosvenor Terrace, and how they should be treated, fussed Bel. Grace must stand beside her, tell her who was who, and see her through. They were, of course, the people Bel wanted in her house. Much more so than the McNairns' honest City fathers and their wives, who would do well enough if she could do no better. She caught herself wondering if she dare send a note to Mary saying that, very unfortunately, Mrs. Robert Dermott had been over-zealous and had already invited as many people as the room would hold; and would Mary and George please delay inviting anyone until Bel saw how numbers were going. But even Bel's nerve failed her before this culminating snobbery. She must take her chance with Mary's guests.

Everything, then, was satisfactorily arranged, and Bel was settling down with Grace to a final cup of tea when Sophia opened the parlour door and walked in.

"Hullo, dear. How are you? And Grace? This is nice! How are you both? A Happy New Year. I had such a nice bedside book from your mother, Bel, for Christmas. I must write and thank her. I haven't had time yet. *From a Thinker's Garden* it was called. You know. Nice, quiet, wee bits from great writers, just to make you think about life. Splendid to read just before you go to sleep."

Had Bel not been so full of arrangements, and so resentful of Sophia's intrusion, the picture of her fussy sister-in-law in bed beside her speechless bear of a husband, reading nice, quiet, wee bits and thinking about life, would have made it hard to keep solemn. Especially if David had been there to wink behind Sophia's back. But this morning there was too much to be thought about.

"*Could* I have a cup of tea, dear?" Sophia went on.

With the best grace Bel could muster, she pulled the bell-pull by the fire.

The spate of talk continued: "I was out shopping, and I suddenly had a terrible hunger to see some flowers. I get it sometimes in winter. So I went into the Botanic Gardens and walked through the glass-houses. The bulbs are really lovely, dear. You should go. And just as I came out, I looked across here. I could see your house from up there quite clearly. Wasn't it funny? It's because there are no leaves on the trees. And I saw Sarah out at the door. She was polishing the bell and the letter-box. And I thought: 'I'll hurry across and walk straight in, and give Bel a surprise!' "

A third cup arrived at this moment, and Bel succeeded in producing something that looked like a wan smile of invitation as she poured out tea. Sensing danger ahead, she would fain have warned Grace to say nothing of the concert arrangements. But before she knew where she was, Grace had innocently told Sophia of Saturday's doings. The inevitable happened.

"My dears! How interesting! I must tell dozens of people to come! And to think, Bel, that it was through me that you met Lucy Rennie! You remember, on the bridge?"

No; Bel had not remembered that it was through Sophia that she had met Lucy Rennie, and this, having now been pointed out to her, was an inconvenient fact that she could neither deny nor dismiss from her conscience. But with Sophia, what was to be done?

Sophia went on: "You see, I know a lot of nice church people, who would be terribly interested about Lucy, and probably have nothing else to do on Saturday afternoon. I dare say they would be glad to give a sixpence or two; especially if there was a cup of tea."

It was some support to Bel to see that even Grace's guilelessness was worried by the implications of Sophia's offer. Like herself, Grace had no doubt been thinking, not in sixpences, but in five-pound notes. She must rally her forces. As a preliminary, she invited Sophia to have a piece of the chocolate cake of Mary's coveting.

"It's very kind of you, Sophia," she said, assuming what she hoped looked like a grateful expression, "but I have just been worrying about numbers a little, dear. You see, George McNairn is asking some of the baillies and their wives, because it's a town charity. And Grace's mother has been very kind and written several people she thinks might give us handsome donations. So if you wouldn't mind waiting until I let you know—I am so afraid of not having room for everybody. You'll come yourself with William, of course, won't you, dear?"

"Oh, of course. I quite see." Sophia's face fell. She had hoped to repay some casual entertainment not in her own house, but in Bel's. "But you *will* let me know if there is room?"

Like the queen of mendacity she could be, Bel assured Sophia that she would.

II

Presently, and much to Bel's relief, Sophia rose to go. She explained at length that she still had shopping to do, and must be home to see to the children's midday meal. Bel's bad conscience prompted her to kiss Sophia affectionately, and see her with more than usual attention to the door. She opened it with a parting word of guilty endearment, to find Miss Rennie standing on the step outside in the act of ringing the bell that Sarah had so lately polished.

"Lucy! How nice to see you! I'm coming to hear you sing on Saturday! How are you?" Sophia burst out.

Miss Rennie had a bright purposeful smile for both the ladies, and bade them good morning.

For a moment Sophia lingered on the doorstep. It was obvious to Bel that she was considering whether she ought to come back into the house and have a friendly talk with Lucy. But that would be altogether too maddening; when there was so much to arrange; when Grace was there to help with her counsel; and when Miss Rennie had come with the expressed intention of talking business. Bel was well aware that a flicker of an eyelid would have brought Sophia back inside. But guilty conscience or no guilty conscience, her eyelid did not flicker. So there was nothing left for Sophia to do but go down the front doorsteps to the pavement, while Bel's door was closed behind her.

"See who's here," Bel called to Grace as she led Lucy into the parlour and rang for yet more tea. Bel was delighted. She had not expected Lucy; at all events not so soon as this morning. Now they could really push on with arrangements.

Lucy greeted Grace with politeness, trusted she had had a pleasant journey from Ayrshire, and expressed her own opinions as to how pleasant the meetings with old and new friends at Duntrafford had been. "David came to see me yesterday," she went on. "He brought me your letter, Mrs. Moorhouse. And I thought I had better come up to see you as soon as I could to tell you my arrangements and hear what you were doing." Lucy accepted a seat and suggested her programme. They then went upstairs, where Lucy ran her fingers over the piano, was tactfully doubtful if it was just the most suitable piano for her accompanist, who would also play pieces, and received Bel's immediate permission to choose a hired piano and have it sent out from town at once.

Grace had come with them. Bel kept trying to draw her into the discussion. She had been so helpful already this morning. But, somehow, the light had gone out of her. Bel caught herself wondering if, after all, Grace were moody and spoilt. It might be. Though she had shown no sign of it before. As they descended the stairs again, Grace said she must go. She would see to the things she had undertaken to do this morning, and would call back later to let Bel know. Bel did not keep her. But she wondered.

"What a charming girl Miss Dermott is," Lucy Rennie was saying as she came back into the parlour.

"Yes. We think David's very lucky," Bel answered, heartlessly enough.

"Miss Dermott's very lucky, too, Mrs. Moorhouse. You see, I know David quite well. We were great friends as children. It's been quite a—what shall I say?—bit of the past for me to see him again."

"And what do you think of him now?"

"I've always thought David was a darling."

Bel flinched a little at a young woman calling a young man a "darling". Miss Rennie had picked up this unScottish expression in London, she supposed.

"I shall always be fond of David," Lucy went on. "I'm glad he's marrying someone nice."

It would have taken someone much less alert, much less sensitive to overtones than Bel, to miss linking Grace's sudden departure with what Lucy said. Had something happened at Duntrafford? Had David's behaviour to Lucy given Grace cause to be jealous? Or had the mere fact that Lucy claimed the freedom of an old friendship thrown a spoilt only daughter out of temper? But instinctively Bel sided with Grace. Grace was one of the tribe now. This woman was, after all, just a singer—a Bohemian outsider. The Moorhouse family, in addition to David himself, had much to gain from David's marriage to a Dermott. She must give Miss Rennie a tactful warning.

Bel smiled pleasantly. "Yes," she said, "I think I can say

David's a special friend of mine, too. You see, he was just a boy when he came to Glasgow. In some ways I took the place of his mother. He tells me most things. I know Grace Dermott is everything to him now." She looked steadily into Lucy's eyes.

"The Dermotts are very rich people, I hear," Lucy said solemnly.

Bel fell into Lucy's trap. "Very. It's a splendid connection. Dermott Ships, of course. David is to be made a partner."

"So he'll be among the great and the mighty. Some people have everything thrown at them, don't they, Mrs. Moorhouse?" Lucy smiled, looking steadily back at Bel for a moment. Then with a little laugh she added: "While people like myself have to fight for everything." After a moment's pause, and as Bel made no reply, she went on: "Now, you were asking about the tuning of the piano. Well, you see—"

Bel felt, somehow, that it was she who had received the warning, as Lucy, serene and sure of herself, went on with the arrangements that had brought her to Grosvenor Terrace.

III

Bel's concert was arranged for three o'clock on Saturday afternoon. Grace and her mother arrived at two, Grace having promised to see Bel through the final stages of preparation. And as there was nowhere else convenient for her mother to be, she had to bring Mrs. Dermott with her. Grace's mother was an awkward person to have in the house at such a time. She came in, giving loud instructions that no one was to mind her. But the great Mrs. Robert Dermott was the sort of person one had to mind. Her presence filled every house she entered.

Bel's children, Arthur, Isabel and Tom, were gathered together, a rather forlorn little group, in the hall, waiting for their Aunt Mary's nursemaid to call for them and take them to spend the afternoon with their McNairn cousins at Albany Place. Mrs. Dermott demanded of the harassed mother to be introduced to them, asked them their names, and bestowed half-crowns upon them. All of which wasted precious time. For Bel had to make sure that they were being polite, and answering their new Aunt Grace's mother nicely, while caterers were coming in with trays of cakes and drums of ice-cream, and every other kind of tradesman was coming to the front door instead of going properly to the back, and all sorts of last-minute activity were under way.

Having at last finished with the children, and still shouting to everyone not to mind her in the least, Mrs. Dermott said she would just go upstairs and sit quietly in the drawing-room. But Bel had continually to go out and in to see to this, that and the other. And, each time, Mrs. Dermott waylaid her with observations that she had to stop, listen to, and reply to.

"Do you think it's wise, Mrs. Moorhouse, to have the piano so near that window?"

"I do think your flowers look nice. Grace said she was giving you some from our greenhouses. Now, which are they?"

"By the way, Mrs. Moorhouse, do you know if Lady McCulloch is coming this afternoon? I wonder if I remembered to write to her?"

"I do think these are nice town houses. It's not so very long since they were built. Now, will it be as much as twenty years ago?"

Really, dates at this moment! But Mrs. Dermott was so accustomed to making her presence felt, that merely to sit on a chair in an empty room trying to reverse the process was almost killing her.

How much better it would have been had she sent a cheque and good wishes, as Margaret Ruanthorpe-Moorhouse had done.

At half-past two Sophia arrived with her husband. She was nursing a grievance. Bel had made no move about the church people Sophia had wanted to invite. Bel, however, was long past noticing Sophia's grievances. Without telling them that Mrs. Dermott was sitting solitary and ready to pounce, she directed them to the drawing-room, and heard Mrs. Dermott exclaim: "Ah, Mrs. Butter! There you are!" before the door closed. When, some minutes later, necessity forced Bel to look in, Mrs. Dermott and Sophia were enjoying themselves hugely, shouting across William, who sat between them, his fat hands clasped before him on his comfortable stomach, saying nothing.

But now people were really beginning to arrive. Maids were sent to their proper stations, and Bel and Arthur, with Grace to help them with names, had taken up their places in the drawing-room. Bel had every reason to be pleased that Mrs. Dermott had shown interest. Everybody who was anybody, or at any rate the females of the breed, were filing into her drawing-room. After today, Bel felt certain, the Arthur Moorhouses would be somebodies in Kelvinside. And she was glad to see the one or two town dignitaries whom the McNairns had sent. Official Glasgow was there, in addition to fashionable Glasgow.

At ten minutes to three the McNairns themselves arrived. They came upstairs, and standing for a moment breathless on the landing, hoped to make a pompous entry. But the room was so full of the highly important, that nobody took any notice of them. Perhaps it was annoyance at this that caused Mary to turn to Bel and express the hope that Miss Rennie and her accompanist had arrived safely. Bel sent Phœbe to see. No, Miss Rennie was not yet there. Had she got lost? For some moments Bel was thrown into a panic. She turned to her husband, "Arthur, Lucy Rennie's not here! Surely she should be here by now!"

At an easier moment for her, Arthur would have teased his wife. But now, standing close alongside of her, he pressed the hand that was near his own saying: "It's all right, Bel. The lassie knows the time."

And presently, as the grandfather clock on the stair was preparing to strike three, David appeared from downstairs to say that Lucy had arrived with her accompanist, and that they would be ready to begin almost directly.

IV

David, conscious now of his feelings towards Lucy, had come unwillingly this afternoon. He was filled with apprehension, almost fear. Things had passed beyond his control. And he was afraid that, in some way, he might show it. Very quickly now he must make up his mind what must be done. But today, of all days, that surface pattern must still remain unbroken.

When he came to look back, this afternoon took on a nightmare unreality. Bel's packed drawing-room. The pots of greenhouse plants. The heavy scent of Roman hyacinths. The black, shining grand piano, brought in, not to be a decoration in a rich man's house, but as an instrument for hands that could use it. Stray, tormenting details that were to build up memory. Now, as he listened to Lucy's singing, he felt the full force of her. Her disciplined performance. Her self-assurance, that, for him at least, had a certain gallant appeal. Her obvious accomplishment. Her ability to please. And above all her womanliness. There was nothing, it seemed, of the essential Lucy frittered away. All of her seemed to be brought to bear. He no more understood the source of Lucy Rennie's power than he had understood the power of the great actor he had seen as "Hamlet" in the autumn. David was troubled, dazed, conscience-stricken and enchanted.

At an interval in her recital she spoke to him as she moved from the room. "Well, David, I sang your song for you."

"Did you?" He was too stupid to dissemble.

"Oh, David! I sang it with the other Schumann songs. Didn't you recognise it?" She passed on with a laugh.

"David dear, come here." It was Mrs. Dermott's loud voice. "Lady McCulloch, I want you to meet my son-in-law, at least, nearly my son in-law, David Moorhouse. Grace and he are being married at the beginning of March."

It was as though he were acting in a terrible charade, going through movements that were merely mechanical.

But presently the other players would be gone, and Grace, Lucy and himself would have to play out this distressing game to its unrelenting finish.

Chapter Seventeen

BEL sat combing her long fair hair in front of her mirror. Arthur bent over her, tying his white tie. This Sunday morning it was his turn to stand by the plate in the Ramshorn Church. The reflection of his narrow, handsome face, with its high cheekbones, his black hair and his trim side-whiskers, was the reflection of decorum itself.

"Are ye coming to the Kirk this morning, my dear?" he asked, giving the bow of his tie a final tug.

"Of course."

"I thought maybe ye would be tired."

"No, I'm all right." Bel was surprised. Normally there was never any question as to who should go to church and who shouldn't. Arthur's question implied that yesterday's concert had exhausted her. Which was quite the reverse of true. Bel was living in the exhilaration of a real success. The sum she had raised for the distressed children of the city was far beyond what she had expected. And, more important perhaps, she felt she had made a social hit. The fact that certain prominent people had been in her house and had contributed generously did not put her on calling terms with them. But it had made them aware of her existence.

Arthur was pleased with her. She had grasped this from the tone of his voice. He was even prepared to spare her the discipline of Sunday morning worship, a thing almost unheard of in his orthodox Scottish family. But Bel wanted to appear in church. Sophia and Mary would be there for her to queen over. And her mother, old Mrs. Barrowfield, who had declined to come to the concert and mix with grand folks, would be there too, and would have greedy ears for Bel's success.

Bel and Arthur finished dressing, and prepared to go downstairs to their Sunday ham and eggs. As they passed the drawing-room, there was the noise of children's voices. All their three children were jumping about among the rows of caterer's chairs, arranging themselves in the jungle among the welter of flowers and decorative plants, and even daring to touch the notes on the great, strange piano. Arthur commanded them sternly to remember it was the Sabbath Day, and to come to breakfast.

All this morning Bel was floating on air. Her feelings were somewhat those of a young prima donna who, after years of preparation, has made a triumphant debut. There was a wintry sunshine this morning as she, her husband, Phœbe and little Arthur set out on the long journey to church in Ingram Street. As the cab-horse jogged down through Hillhead towards town, she felt like royalty, as though almost it was incumbent upon her to bow her fair and fashionable head from the window, as she went by.

At the church door her mother met her with a "Dear me, Bel, what are ye all dressed up for?"

"Dressed up, Mother? What do you mean?

"Ye know fine what I mean. How did ye get on yesterday?"

"Bel's concert was a great success, Mrs. Barrowfield," Arthur replied, preparing to take up his station by the plate.

His wife herded her mother along with the others into the family pew, smiling the while with regal affection. Having got them all seated, and seen them supplied with hymn-books and Bibles, she raised her veil and, inclining her head to her beautifully gloved hands, said her prayers with great elegance. The sermon, as it happened, turned out to be on the subject of Christian charity—a subject which did nothing to lower Bel's self-esteem.

Everyone, it seemed, approved of her this morning. After the service, Sophia, forgetting her own grievance, did her best to envelop her in the usual flood of talk. Two baillies' wives who had actually been at Grosvenor Terrace yesterday, and had been so much impressed by the augustness of Bel's audience that they had given more than they had meant to, pressed forward to congratulate her. Mary, finding herself included in the aura of Bel's glory, decided to bask in it for the time and to leave some criticism she had been incubating until later.

It was no wonder that Arthur seemed pleased, Bel reflected as, just back from church, she sat once more at the mirror straightening her hair before she went down to the Sunday dinner.

Again she saw the reflection of her husband behind her. "Well, dear?" she said pleasantly, continuing with her toilet.

Arthur sat down on a chair near her. "Something has just come into my head, Bel," he began.

Bel cast him a fleeting smile of encouragement.

"I was just thinking that maybe it was time ye had a carriage and pair of your own."

Bel's heart gave a bound. Arthur had done more for her than he knew. He, the husband of her love, was giving full and final approval. Had she obeyed her impulses, she would have jumped up and thrown her arms about his neck. But she had known him too long to do anything so emotional. It would merely embarrass him. A little resistance, indeed, would fix his purpose more surely, and confirm his opinion of her careful good sense. She turned to him, her comb in her hand, and said: "Oh, Arthur! But in these times? Can we afford one?"

Arthur sat considering. His wife let him take his time.

"Well," he said at last, "ye see, David's not taking money out of the business now, and the papers say things will be better by the summer. And what with you getting to be such a swell and everything."

That was too much for Bel. She got up, told him he was an old silly, kissed him and sat down again.

"But what about the coach-house?" she said presently, "and the McCrimmons?"

"They're decent folks," Arthur said, pondering.

"Surely we could get McCrimmon some work, Arthur. Phœbe says he's getting an artificial foot."

"How can we put the McCrimmons out, my dear?"

"It's not a case of putting them out, Arthur. It's a case of letting McCrimmon himself know that we thought it was time he was looking about him."

"There's not much work to be had," Arthur said doubtfully, adding as a rueful afterthought: "And for a lame man—"

"No. But, after all, we're not turning them into the street. We can wait until he finds something. It's a question of giving him notice. That's all."

"I wouldna like to do that, Bel."

"That's nonsense, dear. I'm going in tomorrow morning to

pay Mrs. McCrimmon for helping in the kitchen during the concert yesterday. I'll tell them."

"Very well." Arthur gave a wan assent. He saw again the quarters from which he had rescued these people. He wished, now, that he had never, in a sudden burst of admiration for his wife, said the word carriage to her. She was doing very well as she was.

II

Bel's aspirations had put her on the rack. If her feet, this morning, had trodden clouds of realised hopes, this afternoon they were weighted with lead. But her purpose held. She would tell McCrimmon first thing in the morning that, whenever he was well enough, he must find employment and take his family elsewhere.

She spent the rest of the day wrestling with her feelings.

Common sense was, as it so often is, on the side of ambition. It was ridiculous, she assured herself, that there should be any difficulty about these people going. She had shown them every kindness. Most of the actual attention had been paid to them by Phœbe, but that was because the girl had less to do than she, Bel, had; and had a mania for lame ducks anyway. But she had refused none of Phœbe's requests for them. The little McCrimmon children had been clad in the cast-off clothing of her own children. She had invented work for the woman to do, so that her stiff, Highland pride should not feel, too sharply, the sting of charity. She had, more than once, committed herself to the laudable fraud of ordering larger amounts of meat than she knew her own household could need, so that the remainder should be taken to the coach-house by Phœbe with the request that the McCrimmons might be so good as to eat it, and thus save waste.

No, Bel assured herself, she had nothing to be ashamed of in her treatment of them. But her first duty was to her husband and her children. Arthur had come out West because he wanted to keep up "a certain position". And very rightly. That he was able to do so was the reward of his industry. And a carriage was part of the paraphernalia this "certain position" demanded. She, herself, was doing what she could for him. Yesterday she had filled his house with the right people—people among whose children she looked, when the time came, to marry her own. Surely the first thing to be done was to live as these people lived.

Thus, for the remainder of this outwardly uneventful Sunday, did Bel struggle with her softer self. She did not dare to discuss the matter further with her husband, and still less with his sister.

Before breakfast on Monday morning she took her purse in her hand, and set forth to carry out her intentions. The earlier the better. There were, after all, times when feelings must be set aside and duty done as impersonally as might be.

The little stone staircase leading up to the McCrimmons' living-quarters was, Bel noted, scrubbed clean and decorated with ripples of pipeclay. There was the piping of children's voices. She knocked. On the other side of the door there was a sudden hush, then footsteps. Bel, as she stood waiting, became aware of her own heart-beats. It was not the ascent of the short stairs that had brought them to her consciousness. As the door was opened by Mrs. McCrimmon, Bel fixed a smile on her face and summoned her resolve. The woman fell back respectfully at the sight of her.

"Good morning Mrs. McCrimmon. I hope I'm not disturbing you too early in the morning, but I have a lot to do today, after Saturday."

"I could be coming across and helping, Mam."

"Oh, no, thanks. The men will be taking away things. But there's nothing the maids can't do by themselves."

The woman made no direct reply to this, but asked Bel to step inside.

Bel looked about her in the bare kitchen. The family were at breakfast. The two little children, in mended clothes only too familiar to her, and their father, in a cast-off suit of Arthur's, were sitting over bowls of porridge. There was nothing else on the scrubbed table but that and mugs of milk for the children. It looked a dull enough meal to Bel, but at least it was filling. The room was warm. Arthur had seen to that. And it was clean. It was furnished with the McCrimmons' few shabby things and some old furniture Phœbe had borrowed. A discarded nursery rug lay in front of the fire. The man withdrew his footless leg from the stool that supported it, and made to stand up in Bel's presence.

"No. Please sit down." But he stood, balancing on one foot, and holding the table. Bel asked how his leg did and when he would be able to wear an artificial foot. She asked for the children, and tried to make them tell her their names. If there had been more to ask she would have asked it, for now she was struggling with her resolution. She opened her purse.

"I just came across to pay you what I owe you for helping on Saturday, Mrs. McCrimmon." She took the money out, laid it on the table, and smiled at the stiff woman beside her. She was surprised to see that McCrimmon's wife had gone red to the roots of her hair, and that there were tears in her eyes.

"I should not be taking this, Mam. You've done a lot for us."

"Nonsense, Mrs. McCrimmon. We can't expect you to work for nothing." Bel stopped. There was nothing now to say, except to tell these people they must leave their place of refuge at the earliest possible moment, so that she, Bel Moorhouse, could install a properly trained and fashionable coachman.

As she stood, hesitating and embarrassed, the two Highlanders looking at her could have no idea of the battle that raged in the heart of this handsome, City lady. It was not the first time that snobbery had assailed Bel's tenderness. And yet, it is perfect truth to say that Bel despised herself for what she next found herself saying.

"McCrimmon, Mr. Moorhouse has decided to have a carriage." She stopped for a moment, but the cloud of apprehension that crossed their faces made her hurry on. "And we were wondering if, when you get your artificial foot, you would like to be our coachman?"

As she crossed the back garden on the way to the house she chid her cowardice for having tied a Highlander, unstylish, uncouth and lame, about her neck, but her step was light, and a weight was lifted from her.

She found her husband alone in the breakfast-room. "I'm afraid I've asked McCrimmon to be the coachman, Arthur," she said, flushing guiltily.

Arthur smiled with offensive complacency. "That's fine, my dear.

It's just what I expected," was all he said, and stirred his tea with what Bel considered was a ridiculously unfashionable vigour.

III

Mrs. Dermott and Grace had taken David back to Aucheneame. He was bewildered and exhausted. He had not wanted to come with them after the concert, but, until he had decided what he must do, there was no excuse for absenting himself. As he sat in the carriage opposite Grace, he noticed that she, too, seemed tired and out of spirits. This was not perhaps surprising. At Grosvenor Terrace she had been running here, there and everywhere.

Neither of them spoke much. Nor were they required to. Mrs. Dermott, stimulated as she was by any gathering of people, talked without ceasing.

"I do think the whole thing was excellently arranged, David. Mrs. Arthur Moorhouse must be a born organiser. I really must ask her to join us on the Indigent Mothers. There's a vacancy on the committee."

"What a beautiful singer Miss Rennie is! She reminds me more of Trebelli-Bettini than anybody. You remember we heard her in London, Grace?"

"I like your sister Sophia so much, David. She seems to me so sincere. Her husband doesn't say very much, does he?"

"Lady McCulloch was asking where you were going for your honeymoon. I said I hadn't the faintest idea. I didn't tell her I had strongly advised you to go to Paris. I didn't see any reason to pander to her inquisitiveness."

David was thankful that the chatter in the carriage went on. And he was thankful, too, that the weekend was filled with the same sort of thing. It was the first weekend since he had entered Dermott Ships, and Robert Dermott was forever making excuses to take him aside and talk business. It was unpleasant for David to go on feeling an impostor. But anything was better than being left alone with Grace. It was easier and less contemptible to be acting a part to her father, than to be acting a part to herself.

But he dreaded the hour or two after the Sunday midday

dinner, for it was then, usually, in the quiet of the afternoon, that he was left alone with her. Even that, however, he managed to avoid. For after their meal, Robert Dermott was seized with feelings of faintness, and David, having with the aid of a man-servant helped him to his room, undertook to go with a groom in Mrs. Dermott's pony-trap to seek out and bring back the local doctor. The process of finding him, bringing him, and hearing his pronouncement, that Mr. Dermott was merely suffering from some slight indisposition such as came to men at his time of life, and that he must remember his age and be careful, filled up the hours till tea-time. And beyond even that, indeed, for Mrs. Dermott kept the doctor to tea, and spent a considerable time, now that her anxiety for her husband was allayed, telling him in detail of an attack of pneumatic fever she had had some years ago, how expert his predecessor had been in effecting her cure, and how sorry the district had been to see the former doctor take up practice elsewhere.

In the late evening David came down from Robert Dermott's room. At the request of the old man, who said he felt well now, but had been counselled to remain at home for some days, David had been sitting, notebook in hand, taking down instructions which he was to carry to the office. He had expected to find Mrs. Dermott with Grace. But Grace sat alone by the fire, a book on her knee.

He went to her, and, as was expected of him, bent down and kissed her. She caught his hand and raised it to her lips. He stood, his back to the fire, fanning out his long coat-tails and looking down upon her. She seemed tired, even a little worn, as she looked up at him.

"Well, Grace?"

"Well, David?"

"Your father's all right. He's been ordering me about as if I was the whole office staff of Dermott Ships put together. You haven't been worrying about him, have you?"

She smiled. "No, not any more. Although anything like that is very unusual with father. I suppose we must accept that he's getting old."

David continued warming himself before the fire for some moments, looking in front of him, occupied with his own thoughts.

"David."

The tone of her voice made him look down quickly. He saw that Grace's colour had risen, that she was trying to say something.

"Grace? Is anything wrong?"

"Sit down, David. I want to say something to you."

He sat down upon a stool at her feet. "My dearest, is anything—?"

"Let me say this quickly—mother may come in. David, I just wanted to say that any time between now and March, if you—well, feel you don't want to go on with our engagement, I want you to know that—that I'm not holding you in any way. I don't want you to feel bound, because—" Her voice stopped, she could say no more.

He rose to his feet and, bending down, kissed her once again. He felt a great tenderness towards her. His sensibilities were tortured by her own. And yet, in the act of reassuring her, he found himself asking what signs she had seen; how she had come to guess? He felt that had he known passion, rather than tenderness towards her, he might have raged; demanding why she wanted to be free of him, why she wanted to ruin his life? But he dare not ask these questions, for the very asking of them would be untruthful.

But Grace seemed comforted by the reassurance he could give her, and when her mother came to them there was no sign that any storm had been.

IV

In the middle of the following morning Bel received a note from David. It was delivered by hand, and read as follows:

> "Please meet me in Ferguson and Forester's restaurant in Buchanan Street today at one. We can have a private room. I must talk to you. I am in great trouble. Don't tell anyone that you are meeting me.
>
> "David."

For Bel, David's request was highly inconvenient. She was setting her house to rights after Saturday's disturbance. But Bel was fond of David. She must go to him somehow.

She called to Phœbe, who was going out: "Phœbe dear, I wonder if you would mind staying in this morning. The men are coming to take away the grand piano. And some chairs are to go back. And all sorts of other things. Sarah will tell you."

Phœbe agreed to remain. Although she could not see what she could do to keep the house from damage if the workmen chose to wreck it.

"I've got to go and call on Margaret's doctor." A white lie never troubled Bel, and this was her best alibi. No one would be so indelicate as to ask questions about Margaret's condition.

Bel was not accustomed to having *tête-à-tête* meals with young men in private rooms of restaurants. She was nothing if not circumspect. The very thought of scandal was abhorrent to her. But every movement and feature of David proclaimed him a Moorhouse, and a brother of her husband. People, if they saw her, might think it unusual, but a midday meal with a brother-in-law could not be accounted fast.

"Well, David? What's all this about?" she said, pulling off her gloves. David, she noted, was looking pale and as though he had not slept.

"We'll order dinner, and then I'll tell you. It was kind of you to come." He pressed the bell on the wall above their table.

"Did you go to Aucheneame this weekend?" Bel asked conversationally, as they waited.

"Yes." He told her of Robert Dermott.

"Grace and her mother would be glad to have you."

"Yes." His tired eyes did not look at her. They seemed to be glad to fasten themselves on the waiter who presented himself.

When he had gone with his order there was silence.

"Well, David? Tell me." She felt she must force his confidence. After all, he had brought her here to confide.

"I'm in love with Lucy Rennie, Bel."

Bel said nothing whatever. She merely sat looking at David, letting the first impact of the words do what they would with her. She must give herself time. Her thoughts turned to Grace

Dermott. She liked everything that Grace stood for. A Moorhouse-Dermott alliance was important to all of them. Yesterday the thought of Lucy Rennie had raised Bel to the seventh heaven. She had allowed her own vanity full scope. But Lucy Rennie was a nobody compared to Grace. Now she could feel nothing but anger and disgust against Lucy. And anger, too, with David for being such a fool. But she must keep her head. For everybody's sake. Not only for David and Grace. Gradually her thoughts began to clear themselves.

Yes, above all, she must keep her head. David would not have told her this unless he had wanted her help. This meant that she had some power with him. She would not dramatise. She would play the whole thing down. She would not fan the flames of his infatuation, either by resisting him or by offering comfort. If she could stifle this, she must do it.

"David," she said, "I don't think you *are* in love with Lucy Rennie."

"Why?"

"Listen, dear. Let me tell you what I think. I dare say you've got—well, a little carried away. You see, Miss Rennie's very nice. But she's the kind of person our family don't know very much about."

"I've known Lucy Rennie all my life."

"Not the part of it she spent in London. You see, it's her stock-in-trade to be attractive. I don't say she's doing it consciously with you—"

"How could she? I knew her when she was a child."

"Perhaps that's made your friendship a little—well, sentimental, David. It's the first time you've met her as a woman. Does she know how you feel?"

"No, not really. But I'm certain she suspects."

"As far as Miss Rennie's concerned, there may be one or two other young men who are 'certain she suspects'. Young men think all sorts of things when they're in your state of mind. Especially innocent ones, David." She saw he did not like this, but she left him to consider for a little, then went on: "You see, David, this isn't a simple love affair. There's Grace."

She saw him flinch, as the waiter threw open the door to bring in their soup. The man wondered at this couple sitting so expressionless and silent. He put the plates down and closed the door behind him.

"Grace offered to free me yesterday evening."

"Grace!" But she must hold on firmly. "David, have you broken your engagement?"

"No, I hadn't the strength of mind. Remember, her father was ill. You can think how I felt."

Again Bel considered. "You love Grace more than you know."

"I wish I thought so. I was weak, Bel, that's all."

"Nonsense, David. I'm glad you didn't. What does Grace know about you and Lucy Rennie?"

"I don't know. She can't know much. There's nothing to know."

"Was there anything at Duntrafford?"

"No, I don't think so. Except—" He stopped.

"Except what, David?"

"Well, except that we saw Lucy there, more than once."

"You fell in love with her there, you mean?"

"Perhaps."

"And do you imagine, David—you of all people—that Grace wouldn't notice?"

He sat thinking, crumbling bread with one hand.

"So that's why she offered to free me," he said at length. And then, with a look of distress, he muttered: "Bel, what am I to do?"

Bel sat considering. It would be so easy to plunge into an orgy of womanish emotion with this young man. But if she did, she would merely be indulging herself. And she must remember her own part in this affair. She had, in a sense, encouraged David to engage himself to marry Grace Dermott. She felt some responsibility. And now that she knew Grace, she was sure they were well suited. Both David and Grace were accommodating, easy people. They would do excellently together in the world where they belonged. The pity was that this ridiculous, boyish flare-up hadn't happened when David was twenty-one instead of thirty-one, just when he was on the eve of being more than suitably settled.

As they stood up to go, she gave him her verdict.

"David, don't make any break with Grace yet. I'll think about this, and see you towards the end of the week. At least you owe it to Grace to wait until her father is quite better. It would be very cruel to do anything else. Will you promise?"

"All right, I'll promise."

As Bel took her way up Buchanan Street, she found herself wondering if a call on Miss Rennie would serve any purpose. But she decided against it. She had had indication already that Lucy would not take her interference. It might, indeed, rouse her resentment and weigh the scales down on the wrong side.

Chapter Eighteen

THE mid-January sun was shining in through the large, revealing windows of Aucheneame this morning, finding its way through chilly, starched lace curtains and between hangings of tasselled velvet into spacious, tasteless rooms. It found very little dust in any of them, nor could it catch many dust-particles floating in its own slanting rays, for this house, set on a green hill above the River Clyde, received none of the smoke of industry, and its mistress, competent herself, saw to it that her many servants made diligent use of brush and duster. There was nothing cosy about Aucheneame. Yet on a morning such as this it was not uncheerful, filled with the sunshine as it was, and catching the sun's bright reflection from the winding silver of a river, spotted with the black dots of fussy river craft, steam-tugs and such, as a forest pool is spotted with water-beetles.

But to Grace Dermott it was home, and as she moved about from one bright room to another, doing her Monday-morning household tasks, she was not unhappy.

It would not be true to say that she was quite carefree. But her talk with David last night had lifted most, at least, of the weight that had lain upon her mind since her return from Duntrafford. She was glad she had offered him his freedom. It had been an effort, such as she had never made in her life, but she would not hold him against his will; however much it might cost her.

There was little doubt that David had been attracted by Lucy Rennie. She had some sort of effect upon him that Grace could not understand. She disliked Lucy, but she was not sure that it was fair to blame her. Grace had watched David at Duntrafford. He had flushed and responded to Lucy. He had appeared unnaturally alert when Lucy was present. He had seemed anxious to be in Lucy's company. Above all, the picture of David's face as he sat listening to Lucy's singing on New Year's night had worried and tormented her. It had driven her to a decision.

If Lucy's spell seemed still to move David at the concert on Saturday, then, Grace determined, she would offer to let him go.

It had been a terrible step, but she had taken it. And she was glad. It would have been easier for her to be weak; to confide in her mother; to confide, even, in Bel. All kinds of aspects of her problem had jostled each other in her mind, but one decision, at least, had resulted. She would do nothing to coerce David, to drive him into the fold beside her. This was a thing between herself and him, and no one else must interfere. She knew all the Moorhouse family were her friends. She had made them so, anxiously and determinedly. But not from any idea of finding support for herself; merely that she should become as quickly as might be one of themselves as David's wife. Moreover, she had come to realise Bel's position among them. She knew Bel's influence was strong. Bel could easily rouse family feeling on her behalf. Join Moorhouse feeling to the outrage of her parents, and a renegade David would be facing something formidable indeed.

But this was the last thing she wanted for him. She had taken her resolve. Whatever happened between herself and David must have the dignity of secrecy.

Bel's concert, then, had brought things to a head, and Grace had taken her decision. Tremulously jealous, she had watched David, and there had been no mistaking his feelings. Lucy Rennie attracted him. She must offer to let him go.

Grace stood at a window looking out into the winter sunshine. A giant grain-clipper was coming up the river in the tow of what seemed an absurdly small black tug. The bare, spidery rigging showed against the green of the hillside on the far bank. The picture misted a little before her as she smiled to herself.

David had not wanted to be free of her. He had treated her gently, assured her that she was his, and that must be an end of it; that she was worried and overstrung by the illness of her father, and had begun imagining things. She had not argued with him. She could not. And he had reassured her. Or at least, she had allowed herself to be reassured. She had been foolish. That was all. The Lucy Rennie affair must be wholly superficial—something outside of David's control. She must remember Lucy was an old friend of David's, and naturally he must have some affection for her. And she was going back to London this week some time. That would end the matter.

Grace turned to find her mother standing behind her.

"Oh, there you are, Grace," Mrs. Dermott said. "I think you might go to your father. He's not feeling very well again this morning. I'm going to send again for the doctor."

Grace turned and went.

II

Bel's day was to be a disturbed one. She had made straight for home after quitting David. Yet, full as her head was with problems, there was still room for worry about that was happening in Grosvenor Terrace. Was Phœbe seeing to the tradesmen properly? Was her precious house suffering no damage?

The tram-horses puffed their way up into Hillhead and stopped at Botanic Gardens. As Bel alighted and turned into Grosvenor Terrace she was surprised to see a carriage standing in front of her own door. A groom was holding the horses' heads; Sarah was standing on the step looking up and down the Terrace. In a moment more Bel recognised the Dermotts' carriage. What was the matter? Had Grace come to pay a call? But why this unbecoming informality at the door? She hurried her step, and called:

"Sarah, is there anything wrong?"

"It's a message from Mistress Dermott, Mam."

Bel was now standing by the carriage. "Good afternoon, MacDonald. I hope there's nothing wrong," she said, conducting herself, in spite of the confusion of the moment, with what she considered was becoming dignity before Robert Dermott's servants.

"The Master is no' so well, Mam. The Mistress said I was to be giving you this. And be waiting for you." There was a look of concern in the man's eyes. He handed her an envelope.

"To wait for me?"

"Yes, Mam."

"I'll read it at once." She broke the seal where she stood, and read Mrs. Dermott's letter.

"DEAR MRS. MOORHOUSE,

"I wonder if I can claim the help of someone who is nearly a relative? My husband was taken unwell yesterday. The doctor came to see him, and said all he needed was rest. This morning, however, he is rather worse than better, and the doctor, who has been here again, says Robert should be seen by a heart specialist at once. Would it be too much to ask you to try to find one for us, and send him back in the carriage? . . ."

Here Mrs. Dermott mentioned the specialist of her choice, but begged Bel if he were not immediately available to find one who would come at once. The carriage was at her disposal.

There was nothing to be done, then, but to accede to Mrs. Dermott's request. A few hurried inquiries as to the state of the house, a quick look round in the hall, an assurance shouted by Phœbe from an upper landing that everything was all right; and Bel found herself sitting in the Dermotts' family carriage, heading once more in the direction of the town.

Ten minutes later she was in the region of Charing Cross and Crescents, and the horses were swinging round towards Newton Terrace, which was then, as it still in part is, Glasgow's Harley Street.

No—Sir Hamish was not at home, a discreet male servant told Bel. At this hour he was, as usual, at the Royal Infirmary. Yes, it would be worth her while if she could drive straight there. But would the lady wait one moment?—and he would ask Sir Hamish's colleague on the Bell telephone; just to make certain of Sir Hamish's movements. Bel stood in the hall wondering, while the man went to a little box placed on a bracket on the wall. He spoke a number, waited, then entered into what seemed to be a conversation, although Bel could only hear his side of it. At the end of this he turned to Bel, and, as though he had merely been interrogating a third person, informed her that she was certain to find Sir Hamish at the Royal Infirmary if she went. He was likely to be there for still another half-hour.

The great man's door, with its glossy green paint and its shining letter-box, closed behind her, as she hurried down the steps, gave the waiting footman fresh directions, and settled back inside.

III

Bel stood in the square in front of the Royal Infirmary, her task accomplished. The name of Robert Dermott had had its effect on Sir Hamish's augustness. He must, he felt, get himself to his dear and influential friend's bedside without delay. She stood watching the carriage swing round into Mason Street and disappear, the coachman whipping up the horses as much as he dare in the City's traffic. She had delivered her message with decorum, and what she hoped was elegant dignity, and, even at this anxious moment, some enjoyment of the sense of her own importance. Sir Hamish had, very civilly, offered her a lift westward. But she had declined it, insisting that she must put no kind of hindrance in his way.

Now, as she stood under the portico of the hospital, she found herself wondering what next she had better do. She had gathered, in the brief moment she stood inside her own house, that Phœbe and the maids had dealt with the ravages of Saturday. There was nothing immediate to do, then, at Grosvenor Terrace. The excitement of finding the doctor and sending him off to Aucheneame had driven David and his problem from her mind, but now, in the blank left by the specialist's departure, her midday meeting had come back to her. What was she to do with David? How was she to help him?

Presently it occurred to her that she might go down to see her mother. It was not far, and she would be glad, now, of the air. She took her way down the Bell o' the Brae, down the High Street and Saltmarket to the gates of Glasgow Green on purpose to walk across the Park to Monteith Row.

Her mother received her with some surprise. She had expected that Bel would be engaged in putting her house to rights. "I didna expect to see ye today," she said, as she sat her daughter down and rang for the inevitable cup of tea.

"No, I had to go to the Royal Infirmary."

"The Royal Infirmary?"

Bel explained. The old lady shook her grey side-curls with much rueful gusto. "If it's heart it's a bad business, I doubt." And then, after a pause, "Will the money go straight to David's wife?"

"I've no idea, Mother. But we all hope the old man will live."

But Mrs. Barrowfield would have none of it. Again she shook her head, and insisted that if it was heart it was sure to be a bad business. Bel was so used to her mother's habit of killing off her contemporaries, that she did not bother to protest further. Tea was being brought in, so she allowed her mother to ply her with questions about the concert before old Maggie.

When the door was finally closed behind them, she came to the reason of her visit.

"I've something I want to talk to you about, Mother. I met David at lunch-time today. He says he's fallen in love with Lucy Rennie."

Bel saw that Mrs. Barrowfield had, after the fashion of the elderly, not bothered to take this in. She poured out tea and merely said, "Now, sugar it for yourself," as she handed Bel her cup. Her daughter knew she must give her time. "Did ye say ye saw David?" she said presently.

"Yes, Mother, I'm telling you. I saw him today. He's fallen in love with Lucy Rennie."

Mrs. Barrowfield stirred her tea. "But surely he's in love with Miss Dermott, is he not?" she said, with what looked like a maddening determination to misunderstand.

"That's the whole trouble, Mother. That's what I've come to talk to you about. He wants to break his engagement."

"Who's this Lucy Rennie?" Mrs. Barrowfield put down her cup.

"The girl who sang on Saturday. David knew her when they were children."

"And he says he's in love with her?"

"Yes."

"And what about Miss Dermott?"

"Yes. What about her, Mother?"

The old lady sat thinking. The facts had penetrated. Bel waited.

"When was the marriage to be?" she asked at length.

"The beginning of March."

Again Mrs. Barrowfield lapsed into silence. When she spoke again, her tone was hot with contempt—the contempt of an old squaw, who cannot forgive disloyalty to the tribe.

"David Moorhouse is a terrible fool!"

"It doesn't help to say that, Mother."

"Fancy jilting Robert Dermott's girl for somebody like that!"

"I don't think he's thrown her over yet, Mother. I've advised him to do nothing until her father's better." Somehow her mother's implication that David was letting a fortune slip annoyed Bel. Had she been quite honest with herself, she would have realised that this aspect of the matter worried her, too. But there was so much more than that. She liked David, and she liked Grace. She applauded what they stood for. David's folly was more to her than a mere business deal going wrong.

"I've always got on with David," Mrs. Barrowfield continued. "He was a bit bee-headed, when he was young. But I thought he had got over all that."

"What am I to do, mother? He asked for my help."

"Is this woman still in Glasgow?"

"She's going away in the middle of this week."

"Ye canna keep him away from her, I suppose?"

"Not if he wants to go."

The old woman thought again for a moment, then said, "He should be down at the Dermotts', where they need him. He'll know Miss Dermott's father's ill?"

"They would send word to the office."

"Ye better go up to his lodgings on yer way home and make sure." Mrs. Barrowfield got up, pulled her fine white shawl about her shoulders and moved about the room. She was furious with David. She stopped at her window looking across the Green, which was beginning to be lost in the growing dusk and the fog rising from the river. She was turning matters over in her slow, but not stupid mind. This Dermott-Moorhouse alliance would be good for all the Moorhouse family, and, therefore, good for her daughter, who was one of them. At last she turned.

"Well, there's just this about it, Bel," she said. "I've known David a long time, and I've always liked him. But he's not what ye would call a strong character. If ye could just get him married to Miss Dermott, it wouldna break his heart that he hadna married the other one."

"That's what I think, Mother. I got his promise to wait for a day or two, anyway."

"Aye. The great thing is to get him to wait. It can make all the difference. And there's always old Robert Dermott's illness to send him back to Robert Dermott's daughter. Be sure ye see that he knows about it tonight."

Bel called at David's rooms an hour later. As she did not find him there, she asked leave to come in and write him an urgent message.

Chapter Nineteen

ON this same Monday, when so much else was happening, Lucy Rennie spent most of the day packing. She was sick of Glasgow and all it stood for—so sick, indeed, that she had decided to leave it a day earlier than she had planned. She wished, now, that she had not been so obliging as to stay over for Mrs. Arthur Moorhouse's concert. People like the Moorhouses did not deserve to be noticed by artists.

In allowing herself these reactions, Lucy was not quite just. She was deliberately choosing to forget that it was she who had first proposed the concert to Mrs. Moorhouse, with the object of helping, a little, the distress that was at the moment so widely spread in the city. But now she was in reaction from the effort she had put forth, and she was ready to blame, merely for the relief of blaming.

The truth of it was that her vanity as a musician had been hurt. Though, had she been faced with this, she probably would have denied it. She had had success. People had applauded, and called her back to sing more. That was, of course, gratifying, but just what her experience had expected. Her practised eye had seen at a glance that this well-dressed, well-fed, well-circumstanced audience would clap its good-natured, indiscriminating hands at anything which conformed to its conventions. And it certainly was better that they should clap them than not clap them. But somehow, when everything was over, when these noisy, wealthy people had stood about drinking tea and chatting with their acquaintance, she—the singer, the centre of this meeting, who had given her voice, her skill and her forces—had been allowed to stand aside unnoticed.

Wealthy, place-seeking Glasgow had milled about the room, teacup in hand, the lesser seeking out the greater, in the hope of catching a wan smile of recognition or a crumb of conversation.

Or so it seemed to Lucy, who was well used to metropolitan drawing-rooms. She, a Scot herself, had forgotten the Scots' reticence, the fear of addressing an artist, lest the word of praise might seem an impertinence. She could think of other private recitals in the South, where people had come to her, wrung her hand, and talked a deal of flattering nonsense. But for one who had given of her best it was better that way. It let down strung-up nerves and gave a sense of release and relaxation.

Mrs. Arthur Moorhouse should have seen to all this. After all, she, Lucy Rennie, should have been singled out. Instead of that, Mrs. Moorhouse had shown signs of being fussed, of letting the reins slip from her hands. One pompous woman after another had borne down on the hostess, who had lost control, and allowed herself to become enveloped. She had, indeed, bestowed flustered thanks on Lucy when she said goodbye. But that had been all, except for a short and, Lucy thought, gauche little note, thanking Miss Rennie in a perfunctory way, telling her of the gratifying sum collected, and hoping formally that any time Miss Rennie found herself in Glasgow, she would come to Grosvenor Terrace to see them.

And David Moorhouse? Now, this evening, as Lucy sat musing in her gaudy little sitting-room, she wondered if David were not, after all, at the core of her unhappiness. He was so obviously attracted to her. It was absurd and disturbing. After all, the young woman he had promised to marry in some six or seven weeks' time had been there, at the concert, too.

Lucy rose, and drew the heavy fringed curtains to shut out the last of the foggy, dying twilight. The room was warmer so, with no other light now but the flickerings of the fire, as they threw up weird, dancing shadows on the walls. It would be very easy, really, for her to become sentimental over David Moorhouse—to remind herself that they had promised to be sweethearts as children after the fashion of magazine stories. Yet this young man appealed to her. He had no artistic sensibilities. But he was gentle and quick. She had noticed more than once a sudden flush and a sharp question in David's eyes, when he feared for a moment that his talk had been construed wrongly, feared he had given pain. Add to that his pleasant good looks and the springtime memories of childhood, and it would not be difficult to let oneself go. Lucy stared at the flames. Now she was asking herself a direct question. If David were free and asked her to marry him, what would she have to say to him? It was a pity she had not known him as a grown man sooner. They might have done very well together, and it might have saved her from more than one male friendship that she would, by Moorhouse, or, indeed, by any other standards, have been better without.

Now she could hear the little door-bell clanging on its spring in the kitchen. Then footsteps. It must be her landlord home from work. She looked about her and sighed. No. There was no question of herself and David Moorhouse. So why bother to think about it? She had weathered storms enough already. Her heart would not be broken.

II

The door of her little sitting-room was thrown open.

"Mr. David Moorhouse."

Lucy rose. Her training had taught her cool-headedness. But for a moment her face was flooded with colour, and she found herself fighting down confusion.

"David!"

He seemed as perturbed as she was. "I'm sorry if I've disturbed you, Lucy. I had to see you before you went away." He closed the door behind him, and stood for a moment against it, one hand behind his back still holding the handle. The flickering firelight caught lights in his chestnut hair, lit up his face, and flung a fantastic shadow of him on the wall beyond.

She was getting possession of herself. "Come and sit down." She forced a laugh. "Don't stand there, as if I were going to eat you."

He came forward, threw his hat on the table and sat down on the other side of the hearth.

It was Lucy who spoke first, after a moment of bewildered silence. "Shall I light the gas?"

"The fire's all right." He was tense, unnatural. He might say anything.

She had had declarations before. If he must speak, he had better do so. She bent down and stirred the fire. "There," she said, "that's a bit brighter. Take off your overcoat."

He paid no attention to this invitation. He merely sat, fumbling with the gloves he held in his hand. "When do you go?" he asked presently.

"Tomorrow morning, David. I have nothing to keep me. And I've work waiting in London."

"I'm glad I came up this evening."

There was nothing to reply to this. She would neither help nor hinder what he had to say. She allowed her eyes to wander back to the fire.

"Lucy."

She turned towards him. He was trying with difficulty to say something.

"Yes, David?"

"Lucy, if I were free to marry you, would you marry me?" He spoke the words explosively. She saw that his eyes were great with excitement; that his hands were wringing the gloves he held until they looked like pieces of rope.

She stood up and began to pace the room. He rose, too, as though to follow her.

"No, David. Stay where you are. Let me think." She came back to the mantelpiece, and stood looking down upon him. "Have you broken with Grace Dermott?" she asked presently.

"No. I promised I wouldn't do anything for a day or two. Her father's ill."

"Promised? Promised whom?" She could see that, with the sharpness of her question, he regretted his last words already.

"I've been very unhappy about this, Lucy."

"But have you discussed me with Miss Dermott?"

"Oh no. With Bel. I thought she could help me."

"What had *she* to do with it?"

"Lucy, perhaps you don't understand. I've always been a close friend of Bel's. Ever since I was a very young man."

"So this is a matter for the whole Moorhouse family?"

"Oh no, Lucy. Bel's the only one who knows."

She stood, gazing into the fire, one hand on the draped mantelpiece, one foot on the wrought-iron fender, her other hand catching up her dress as it rested on her knee. She was trembling with anger. So this had already been dragged before the Moorhouses? What did it matter if it were only Bel Moorhouse? She was the distilled essence of all of them—the distilled essence of everything that was complacent and Philistine; of everything that she, Lucy Rennie, had been forced to fight against.

But now, in the lightning of her rage, Lucy saw clearly that she loved this young man, whose background she detested.

When she spoke, her voice was hot with passion, with the echoes of old rebellions, with the desire to wound.

"You don't happen to be in love with me, David, do you?"

"Of course! I—"

"Well, you haven't said so."

"Lucy—please! That's why I'm here, against—"

"Against your better judgment, David? 'Your purer self'?"

"You're trying to hurt me."

"But you don't mind hurting me, do you?"

"I didn't know I was ever going to meet anyone like you, when I got engaged."

"And now you want to make the best of both worlds, David?"

"I don't know what you mean."

"You want to make quite sure that you're on with me, before you do anything so rash as to break with Grace Dermott. You've decided all this carefully with your sister-in-law. Oh, you're smug! Smug and hard and cowardly! All of you!"

David stood up in alarm. Lucy had burst into a fit of sobbing, and was standing beside him shaking, her face in her hands.

"Lucy! Lucy! What can I say to make you believe me?"

"Believe what?" She was standing looking up at him with brimming eyes. He could feel her willing him to take her into his arms. He caught her up, and kissed her with such a kiss as he had never given before. It was his turn to tremble now, in the tempest of his feelings. Here there was no room for calculated thought, for solemn promises to himself of honourable behaviour—room for nothing but his staggering senses.

At last she disengaged herself. "David, what are we doing?"

She could have done now what she would with him, and this knowledge staunched, in part, her wounded pride. But a common liaison with David Moorhouse was not her purpose.

"You haven't given me a reply, Lucy."

The tone of his voice touched her. She must thrust this untimely, passionate anger from her, search her feelings, and make her decision with as much coolness as she could. "David, dear—no. Sit down again. Have patience with me. Let me think for a moment."

"Then you will consider what I'm asking?"

"Hush!" She took up again her former attitude by the mantelpiece. No. She must make David jump through every one of the hoops of his own conventionality, in order to come to her. Her pride would allow nothing else.

"David," she said at length, "so long as you're engaged to Miss Dermott, I can't possibly discuss this matter with you. I was wrong to let you kiss me just now. Now please go, before there's any more foolishness."

"Lucy, you're not angry?"

"No, David. I'm not angry."

"Can I write to you?"

"If you have anything to write about." She turned, gave him a card bearing her address in London, then held out her hand. "Goodbye, David. And God bless you."

He took her hand, repeated "God bless you", picked up his hat and went.

III

David made his way down Hill Street without knowing what he did. Last night, Grace. Now tonight, Lucy. And yet he had always considered himself rather more than usually self-possessed. What had happened? He must be mad. Instinct would have taken him back to Bel, but a moment of thought showed him that this way was barred.

And yet, if Bel could have come on David as he stood now, aimlessly at the corner of Cambridge Street, looked into his heart, and glimpsed the depths of his trouble, she would, loving him as she did, have been torn for him as she would have been torn for one of her own sons.

David stood dazed, looking about him in the foggy, ill-lit darkness. Then, as no tramcar appeared, he turned and, thrusting his hands deep into his greatcoat pockets, made his way towards the lights of Sauchiehall Street. Presently he became aware that an arm was being pushed through his own. He stopped to look round. It was his friend Stephen Hayburn.

"Stephen!"

Stephen smiled. "I've been watching you for quite a long time. I even spoke to you, but you didn't notice me. Anything wrong, David?"

David stood still, merely giving Stephen a nod of recognition. "Many things are wrong with me tonight," he said at length, "but I can't talk about them."

"Anything I can do?"

"Yes. Take me somewhere."

"Have you had something to eat, David?"

"No."

Stephen went with David, wondering. Had he broken with Grace Dermott? Was he in debt? Had he got himself into some doubtful tangle? He had known David for the better part of ten years, and he knew that such happenings were much more likely to befall himself than anyone so respectable as a Moorhouse. They had both been frivolous in their early twenties together, but for years now David had been the mirror of propriety.

"Where do you want to go?"

"Anywhere you like, Stephen."

Presently David and Stephen found themselves in a little foreign eating-house at the City end of Sauchiehall Street. It was steamy and warm, and smelt pleasantly of Mediterranean cooking. A dark-eyed waiter, with a white apron round his waist, welcomed Stephen as a friend, and led the young men across the sawdust floor. They settled themselves and looked about them. The little restaurant, with its coarse table-cloths, wooden pepper-mills and toothpicks, was busy with Glasgow's Bohemia. A couple of heavy-bearded German fiddlers were, each of them, wolfing plates of macaroni, and drinking the pale beer of their own country from high glasses: players, probably, from some orchestra. Argentine Spaniards from shipping-offices chattered noisily over their specially cooked tortilla and their raw, Iberian wine. A bedizened lady with saffron curls, talking bad French, was being entertained by a swarthy but fashionable southern Italian, who was managing his macaroni with an elegance that should have put the Germans to shame. The place was ridiculous, cosmopolitan and gay.

Stephen sat back preparing to enjoy himself. But his companion, he saw, was preoccupied and listless. When their friend the waiter returned with his thumbed little menu card, Stephen sent him at once to fetch a flagon of wine.

"There. Put that down," he said, pouring David a full glass from the round, straw-covered bottle.

As he had intended, food and much wine began to have their effect. David was beginning to look like himself. Presently he was even commenting with some amusement on the people about him.

"Well, David, feeling better?"

"Yes. Glad I met you."

"You wouldn't like to tell me what was troubling you?"

David shook his head. "I can't," was all he said.

Stephen tried to read his flushed face, but could discover nothing. "Well, never mind," he said.

Stephen Hayburn's thoughts went back some months to the time when the Hayburn fortunes had gone in the Glasgow City Bank disaster—a happening which had killed his mother. David had been kind then. He would try to help him now.

IV

They were finishing their meal.

"What should we do? I don't want to go home," David said rather surprisingly. No, he was looking almost cheerful.

"You're not drunk, are you?"

"No. But I feel better than I did."

Stephen looked at his watch and considered. "It's after eight. I say—we haven't been to Brown's music-hall together for years."

"We'll still get in. It's Monday night. I forget who's performing, but anyway we'll be in time for the nine o'clock ballet."

The two young men made their way down the hill and across George's Square to Dunlop Street. As Stephen had predicted, there was no difficulty in getting into Brown's, even at this hour. Monday evening was slack. The little music-hall was gay enough, although there was less tobacco smoke and noise than David seemed to remember. He wondered what the family would think of him. In the early days he had received more than one lecture from Arthur for coming here. Places like Brown's were not approved of.

A massive lady in a dress of black sequins, white, elbow-length kid-gloves, and a white rose in her piled-up, ginger hair, was singing sentimentally in a loud contralto, as Stephen and David made their way to the bar at the back, and stood waiting for her turn to finish, that they might order their drink and find a seat. When at length they came down towards the front, the chairman spied Stephen and waved to him with his wooden mallet. Presently David found himself sitting in the chairman's half-circle in front of the grand piano and the little orchestra.

Now the chairman was knocking for silence. He was announcing the next item. This was fantastic, unreal. David was in possession of his wits, but his senses were misted. This circle of boisterous men. Those busy musicians. The curtain with its tinsel fringe reflecting the flickerings of the footlights. And now this ridiculous little street scene, with a jaunty Cockney telling them in his song that he was in love with a lady called "Clementina Angelina Margarita Green", who had unaccountable ways of fainting in situations which became more and more compromising as verse succeeded verse. Fantastic, unreal. But he was laughing with the others. Inside, he was bruised, perhaps, but it didn't matter.

The song came to its first ending in a storm of laughter and applause, and the jaunty comedian, having run out and in to the roll of the drum, at length let himself be persuaded to stay and sing the naughtiest verse of all. Now that, too, was over, and after more clapping the curtain closed and the lights went up once more.

"Have another drink, David?"

David declined. His Moorhouse caution had decided that for the moment he had had enough. Stephen went off to get a drink for himself. Before he could get back the ballet had begun. Six young ladies in black-and-yellow-striped tights and wearing gauze wings representing, presumably, bees, set themselves prettily to pursue six more, who were even more colourful, and represented butterflies. When this dance came to an end, and the Queen Bee and the King of the Butterflies, also a lady, were falling into postures ready to begin their part of the revels, Stephen, who had slipped back into his seat, turned to David:

"There's a lady friend of yours here tonight."

"Here? Who?" David was puzzled. He was not the kind of young man to have lady friends in the half-world of Glasgow. And the women of his family and their like would rather die than be seen in a place like this.

"Tell you after." Stephen was giving his whole attention now to the gyrations of the Queen Bee and the Butterfly King.

The ballet ended at last, and the voluptuously curved ladies minced back more than once to receive the applause that was their due. Again David pressed his question.

For reply, Stephen rose, took his arm and said, "Come on, it's time you had another drink. Whether you want it or not. You'll probably meet her."

And so it came about that David, carrying a full glass in the promenade of the little theatre, came, once more, face to face with Lucy Rennie. At a later time he could not tell why the encounter gave him this sense of shock. Tonight he had left Hill Street, his mind torn with indecision, self-hatred and amazement. Amazement that his senses had driven him to make the offer he had made. By his meeting with Stephen, he had managed to lay his stunned distress aside for a time.

Now, here was the ground in front of him burst open, and the same Lucy, provocative and very much mistress of the situation, smiling up at him. There was nothing extraordinary about her except that she was here, in this place which all Moorhouses regarded as a resort of libertines and scarlet women. Here, taking everything complacently for granted. Her arm was linked through the arm of the man who had accompanied her singing in Bel's drawing-room.

"Well, David? I didn't expect to find you here in this frivolous place." There was sympathy and, somehow, an echo of the intimacy of their meeting earlier in the evening. But no sense of embarrassment.

"This is my friend Stephen Hayburn, Lucy. He brought me. I haven't been here for years."

There were introductions and easy laughter. Lucy explained

how she had felt so dull that when her friend had called to say goodbye, she had asked him to take her somewhere gay.

David did not know what to make of it. Had his conventionality seen Lucy as quite another person? Had it allowed him no understanding? Could the standards of his life offer his feelings no yardstick, that Lucy's presence here so much disturbed him? Or was he just a prig? A fool?

The music had struck up again. The curtain had parted, and a juggler and his lady were getting ready to perform wonders. Stephen and Lucy's cavalier had moved ahead.

Lucy turned to David. "There's lots of room tonight. We can all sit together."

They found places to one side, and sat watching the remainder of the performance. David was glad when it came to an end. He felt unhappy and ridiculous. Why did he so ardently hope that no one who mattered should see him here? What was this unexplained sense of shame? Why did it displease him that Lucy seemed so much at her ease?

At the entrance she gave him her hand, telling him that her friend, who lived near her, would see her to her lodgings. Confused, bewildered and heartsick, David bade Stephen goodnight, and took his way home.

There were two short notes waiting for him on his sitting-room table. One was from Bel saying she had called, and regretting she had missed him. The other was from Grace, delivered by the hand of a servant. They both contained the same message. Robert Dermott's condition had become very serious. David was to go to Grace and her mother at once.

Chapter Twenty

IT was curious that it did not occur to David that he should not now go to Aucheneame; that, with his visit to Lucy, this evening, and with what had happened, he must have given up the right to enter Robert Dermott's house as the promised husband of Robert Dermott's daughter. He sat down heavily in his armchair by the dying fire, crushing the two pieces of paper in his hand. His quick sympathy could feel Grace's present distress, and he was sharply aware of how much she must need him. It was too late to go tonight, but tomorrow morning he would take an early train. His head had become clear, but it had cleared merely to show him his own perplexities. On the one hand he felt as though Grace's eyes were fixed upon him, accusing him of frivolity, and worse, while her father's life was in danger; and, on the other, it was as though he could see Lucy's smile of mockery, that he, a man of thirty-one, could not take himself and his emotions in hand and behave before the world with courage and honesty. Lucy had been right, of course, to refuse to give him an answer so long as he was promised to Grace. Yet Grace's father was ill, and, as Bel insisted, he must not be so cruel as to break with her now. But yet again, he had felt he must speak to Lucy before she disappeared from Glasgow. Now he could well see that it must have looked to her as though he had wanted to make sure of her before he had finally broken with Grace. He could see how despicable he must have seemed.

But was it not more than a seeming? Was it not, indeed, true? Still in his overcoat in the cold sitting-room, David sat forward staring before him. Had his cautious Moorhouse instincts been at work? Or was it that somewhere at the bottom of his heart he had no real intention of giving up Grace Dermott? Yet what had driven him to Lucy's room this evening? And had something changed in himself since he had seen this other Lucy in Brown's, later tonight? A new Lucy, familiar, easy and undisturbed among the light-headed, none too well-behaved men, in a place where even his independent and unconventional sister Phœbe would never have gone. Was he beginning to realise that Lucy Rennie lived by a different code from his own?

It was in the small hours of the morning that David stirred himself from his chair to go to bed. He would lie down, even if he did not sleep. Tomorrow, events must be his counsellors. He would go, at least, and help these two women in their distress. He was, he knew, the only man they had to turn to.

He was actually asleep when his landlady roused him early to a foggy, wet morning. His body was numb and weary and consciousness, as it returned to him, brought with it all the confusion and dilemma of the night. But now, however weary he might feel, he must face what lay before him. Robert Dermott's wife and daughter would already be wondering, indeed, why he was not with them.

He got up hurriedly, shivering, as he poured the hot shaving-water from the polished metal can into his wash-basin. The air, even in his bedroom, was raw with a penetrating January dampness. His landlady, a homely creature with an affection for him, scolded him as she brought him his overcoat. He appeared to have eaten so little breakfast. The notes of last night, she told him, had been left, one by a man in livery, the other by a lady who had asked permission to come in and write; who had said she was Mr. David Moorhouse's sister-in-law. The lady had seemed disturbed. Nothing, the good woman hoped, was wrong. Miss Dermott's father was ill, David told her, as he hurried away.

It was not the first time, David reflected, looking out upon the sodden, misty country from his railway carriage, that he had gone down to Aucheneame in a state of emotional tension. His mind went back to the day of his engagement to Grace, and from that his thoughts went on to review everything that followed. At Aucheneame he had found much happiness, and much contentment; a conventionality that suited him very well, and peace of mind. Grace had spoken his own language, and he had fallen into a well-bred fondness for her, which had promised nothing but good in the closer intimacy of marriage. If only his heart had not been astonished into this folly with Lucy Rennie. In the passionless grey of the winter morning, David sighed and called himself a fool.

The train halted at a half-way station down the river. David became aware that a watery sun had broken through. Wet roofs and roadways were gleaming in a chill January light. His one companion in the carriage, a businessman who had sat throughout reading the morning news, jumped up, asked the name of the station, hurriedly threw down his paper and got out. The train started once more on its way.

David's thoughts had been far from newspapers, but now, seeking perhaps to escape his troubles for an instant, he picked up this one left in the seat, and ran his eyes down its front page.

Thus it was that he learnt that Robert Dermott was dead.

II

In some minutes more the train had reached its destination. David found himself, the only passenger to alight, standing on the country platform. For an instant he stood stupidly looking about him. The stationmaster blew his whistle, waved his flag and the train puffed off on its leisurely morning journey down the riverside. The tide was low. A light western breeze was coming up from the Firth, smelling of mud-flats, sand and sea-wrack. Above his head a seagull wheeled and cried querulously in the pale sunshine.

"Your ticket, sir?"

"Oh yes. Of course."

"Many thanks." The stationmaster, knowing David now by sight, touched his cap to the young man who was to marry Robert Dermott's daughter.

"There's naebody tae meet ye, sir." This was strange, the man thought. Surely the Dermott household, even on this sad morning, must know the movements of so close a friend and send a carriage to fetch him from the station.

"It's all right, thanks. They didn't quite know when I would come."

David set off towards Aucheneame. He let his legs take him in the direction of his duty. Disjointed scraps of thought passed through his mind as he walked. The obituary notice in the morning paper. "Mr. Dermott's sudden death would be a severe loss to the shipping world." "A man of great ability, and a staunch supporter of the City's charities." Discreet, unstressed details of Robert Dermott's humble beginnings. "Mr. Dermott's daughter and only child is engaged to Mr. David Moorhouse, a young Glasgow businessman, who, it is understood, has quite recently entered the firm of Dermott Ships Limited." Scraps from the music-hall performance of last night. His hurrying footsteps were pattering out the rhythm of "Clementina Angelina Margarita Green". The absurd, tripping ballet. Lucy's face. "Well, David, I didn't expect to find you here, in a frivolous place like this." The visit to Lucy's rooms. "Goodbye, David. And God bless you." No; events had arranged themselves wrong. Nothing made sense. Perhaps sometime in the future the knots would come out of their tangle, and he would find rest.

There was Aucheneame now, with its blinds lowered in mourning. He gazed up at the great house as it stood up stark among its low shrubberies. He felt as though he wanted to ask it a question. But the lowered blinds made it look like a face with closed eyes; impassive and refusing to respond. He hurried on, his feet crushing the new-raked gravel of the drive. In another moment he had ascended the short flight of steps to the front door and was ringing the bell.

He has received by a man-servant with discreet surprise and pleasure. "We didn't know when you would get here, sir."

"I got back very late last night. I only got the message to come, then."

At David's request the man followed him into a room while he asked him questions. Robert Dermott had died in the early evening, while Sir Hamish was in the house. It had been too late to find David at Dermott Ships Limited, and he was not to be found at his rooms. The ladies, as was natural, were stunned by the event, but Miss Grace had left word that she was to be told at once of his arrival. She was now in her room, but there was no doubt that she would want to see him. She had been awaiting his arrival with impatience. The man went, leaving David alone.

The lowered blinds with the sun upon them made a strange yellow twilight in the room, giving the appearance of things an unreality. David stood in front of the new-lit fire waiting, listening intently. This house of mourning seemed strangely silent: a muffled whisper; the crack of a floor-board now and then. That was all. A sparrow chirped outside in the shrubbery. Now he was aware of his own heart-beats, beating out the rhythm "Clementina Angelina Margarita Green". No. It was preposterous. He would think about all that later—later, when he was not a mere mechanism, here to do what was expected of him.

Presently the door opened softly and Grace came to him. Now that she was here, it seemed natural that he should have come to help her. There were traces of fatigue and weeping, but her pleasure at seeing him had made her almost radiant. Her dress, even, was familiar, for she had not yet had time to secure mourning.

"David, darling. There you are. We've been trying to find you." She was sobbing with relief as he held her in his arms.

Now she was sitting beside him possessively holding his hand and giving him a controlled account of her father's last hours; of Sir Hamish's arrival, and of his inability to do anything in the face of Robert Dermott's condition.

Presently she was leading David to her father's room. The old Highlander lay under a white sheet, his arms crossed on his breast. Grace's mother rose from a chair by the bedside, and embraced David, weeping. Her daughter scolded her gently for not resting and led her away.

Left alone with this man who had accomplished so much, who, for once, would deserve the formal words that would be spoken and printed in his praise, David was surprised to find himself invaded by a sense of calmness. In the quiet immensity of death, his own confusions seemed to recede from him, to fall into proportion. Here, too, it was so still that, as he stood at the foot of Robert Dermott's bed, he could again feel his tired pulses throbbing. But this time the throbbing did not beat out the words of a song. Now Grace, her hand in his own, was standing looking with him at her father. It was almost with a feeling of reluctance that he allowed her at last to draw him away.

"Come, David. We've got things to see about."

III

In the little room where Robert Dermott had been used to conduct his personal business, Grace gave David his keys.

"But, Grace, is it right that I should know about your father's affairs?"

"He wanted it. He said so yesterday. There's a letter for you, in his desk."

David turned the key in the great office desk, and slid back its heavy top. As he had expected, everything was arranged in order. Papers relating to the house, the garden and the stables were neatly docketed and carefully classified. There were receipts and personal correspondence. Together they sought out and found Robert Dermott's letter, the sealed envelope, addressed in a careful, almost copperplate hand: a hand that had been acquired with much diligence by an ambitious Highland boy, whose dream it had been to come out of the mountains and seek his fortune in the City. It bore the words: "To my son-in-law, David Moorhouse. To be opened in the event of my death", and was dated 1st January, 1879. The letter ran as follows:

> "MY DEAR DAVID,
>
> "I am sitting in the quiet of the New Year's morning thinking of my family. I am not a young man now, and in times past I have worried about my wife and daughter. I just want to tell you that your engagement to Grace, and everything I have come to know of you since, has lifted a weight from my mind. It is a great relief for me to know that I now have a son in whom I can have full confidence. I need not recommend my dear ones to your care and your affection. The cashier of Dermott Ships Limited has my will and all instructions locked up in my private drawer in his safe at the office. The key is with the others on my ring. May God bless you all. I hope I shall have lived to see a grandchild, before you open this letter.
>
> "Yours affectionately,
>
> "ROBERT DERMOTT."

David put the letter down. Grace, who had been reading it over his shoulder as he sat, picked it up, and carrying it to a window, re-read it tearfully. With hands clasped on the desk in front of him, David sat staring vacantly at the row of pigeon-holes before him. He was conscious of a great weariness now, conscious that last night his unhappiness had allowed him little sleep. Yet, as he thought of the generous message to him set down in the old man's letter, he could not feel the shackles it was laying upon him, as he might have done yesterday. Something had changed within him. Perhaps, if he did what he conceived to be his duty, his perplexities would begin to fade away and leave him at peace.

There was an early meal, in order that David should get back to the office in the afternoon to seek help in making funeral arrangements. In the evening he promised to be with Grace and her mother once more.

As he made his way back to Glasgow, David lay back in the empty carriage and closed his eyes. The wheels were beating steadily beneath him. There would be wheels beating steadily beneath Lucy Rennie at this moment as the day train to London hammered out the long miles. Yesterday, after he had left her in Hill Street, he had felt certain that, before long, he would be in the train too, following her, seeking her out. But now he was not sure.

He hadn't Lucy Rennie's courage. Her ability to throw away the substance for the shadow. He would never understand that for the Lucy Rennies the shadows are everything.

As he passed up the street to the offices of Dermott Ships Limited, he stopped to buy himself a new black cravat, asking permission to tie it in the shop. Was his vanity stirring to life? Did he feel that he, David Moorhouse, could not escape a gratifying importance in the eyes of the staff as he made his first entrance as a mourner.

At the great swing-doorway of the offices, a senior clerk who chanced to be coming out stood aside, holding it open to let him pass, and giving him a greeting pregnant with condolence and respect. As he passed through to the chairman's room, Stephen Hayburn came forward, gave him his hand, said he was sorry to hear the news, and withdrew tactfully.

The elder men of the staff, some of whom had shared Robert Dermott's struggles, came to shake his hand. He could see that their sorrow was sincere. It had not been difficult to like the old man. David, as he returned their handshakes, was full of understanding, earnest solemnity and dignified regret. He unbent sympathetically and gave them such details of the chairman's death as they might want to have, and told them that the condition of the chairman's wife and daughter was what might be expected. As the seniors of the firm went back to their desks, they agreed that Mr. Moorhouse was feeling this death in a way that did him credit; that he was a fine young man, even if he hadn't anything like the brains and drive of the old man; and they felt, with some confidence, that there was no reason why, with such excellent support as themselves, Mr. Moorhouse and the firm of Dermott Ships Limited should not continue together on their prosperous way.

Late in the afternoon Arthur paid a visit. As he entered the chairman's room, hat in hand, David caught himself wondering if even his downright brother was not now showing him some slight deference. But he was glad to see Arthur, and stepped forward to greet him.

"I came in to see if there was anything we could do for ye, David."

David thanked him, but thought not. Everything, with the help of the excellent people here, had been put in train.

"You'll be going back to Aucheneame tonight?" Arthur asked.

"Oh yes. They need me down there."

"Bel was just saying she hoped this wouldna keep back yer marriage for too long."

"I don't think it will, Arthur. I'm ready when Grace is. It would be best now—for everybody."

Chapter Twenty-One

IN the first days of June, Charles Mungo Ruanthorpe-Moorhouse was born. The event occurred in the morning, and in the evening, before dinner, the baby's grandfather, Sir Charles, despite his eighty years and his indifferent health, eluded the vigilance of his lady, marched across to the Dower House of Duntrafford in pouring rain, broke through the ring of Margaret's attendants, and shook his exhausted daughter triumphantly by the hand. He told her she was a good girl, a credit to her parents, and reminded her with satisfaction that there was nothing the Ruanthorpes couldn't accomplish if they set their minds to it, the little red creature in the cradle before the fire being proof positive of this contention. He assured her that his life's wish had been fulfilled, and that now he was ready to die. Margaret opened her tired eyes for a moment, contemplated her father as he stood over her, saw his jacket dripping with rain, and decided it was very probable that he would not have long to wait. Sir Charles, however, turned on his heel, marched back home through the summer downpour, had a hot sitz-bath before his dressing-room fire, drank his grandson's health in champagne and Napoleon brandy, and settled down to a hilarious evening, declaring he had never felt so well in his life.

On the last Saturday of June the official celebrations were to take place. Tenantry and servants were to have sports in the Duntrafford park and receive a liberal meal in a large marquee set up for the occasion; while relatives of the family and such neighbouring gentry as came to pay their respects were to be given entertainment in Duntrafford House itself. In the evening there were to be fireworks.

The Glasgow members of the Moorhouse family looked to this event, each in a different fashion. On the surface, of course, everyone must appear delighted. But Bel, for one, couldn't help the feeling that a deal too much fuss was being made about the Duntrafford baby. After all, she had safely brought three of her own into the world, sound in wind and limb, without as much as a single match being put to a single squib on the occasion of their arrival. Margaret, of course, was forty, which was a hazardous age to be having a first child, but even so, surely one could be thankful for dangers past without marquees and gunpowder.

In addition, it was the end of June—just the time when most Glasgow matrons were in the throes of packing knives and forks, bedsheets and table-linen, and preparing to transfer their households to some seaside place on the Clyde for the months of July and August. To have to key oneself, one's husband and one's children up to garden-party pitch was altogether too much. Bel decided to have a sister-in-laws' tea-party to feel the family pulse.

"I just wanted to know what you all felt about this Duntrafford visit next Saturday, dears," Bel said, smiling around her with an affectionate assurance, born of the conscious possession of fine eggshell china and the heaviest solid silver. "I wondered if we couldn't just slip down some other day, and see Margaret and take the new baby a present. You see, we ourselves are going off to Brodick on the first of the month, and although, of course, it would be lovely to go to Duntrafford, it would be a dreadful rush."

Sophia's ideas chimed with Bel's. "Just what I was thinking, dear. William was just saying this morning he didn't know how in the world we were going to manage to get to Saltcoats this summer. The new girl I have has turned out so stupid. This year I have to do the actual packing as well as all the brainwork. But I just said to William, 'Well, my dear boy, another year I've no intention . . ."

It took Mary to stem the flood. She looked at Sophia severely. "We can't be disrespectful to Sir Charles." And not for the first time, Bel's town upbringing was at a loss before the almost feudal respect that these farmer's daughters still bore to someone who had been their father's landlord.

"I want to go," Phœbe said shortly. She had, indeed, just returned from Duntrafford that morning.

Sophia laughed. "Oh, you! We all know you. Young birds or beasts or babies. You can't keep away from them." It was on the tip of her tongue to add: "It's time that boy of yours married you and you had some of your own," but she stopped herself in time, fearful of reproving looks from Bel or Mary.

Bel turned to her newest sister-in-law, Mrs. David Moorhouse. "What do you think about it, dear?"

Grace had been looking at Phœbe. This beautiful, restless child had been the most difficult for her to understand of all the Moorhouse family. Good to the point of simplicity herself, Grace had been collecting evidence in Phœbe's favour, seeking to find reasons for liking her. Now it pleased her to hear Sophia say that the girl had a mania for the young and the helpless. Bel's question brought her back.

"I had a very kind letter from Lady Ruanthorpe. She asked mother and David and myself to stay at Duntrafford for the weekend. But you see mother doesn't much feel like being away from home just yet. Still, I feel David and I should go. I dare say we'll get back on Saturday night. The carriage can meet us in Glasgow and drive us back late to Aucheneame."

Bel had to acknowledge herself defeated. Grace, although she was not yet married to David more than three months, was already her favourite sister-in-law. But this daughter of luxury could not be expected to understand the magnitude of an expedition such as the one proposed for Saturday. To see three children dressed in the best of everything, a husband looking suitably dignified, prosperous and impeccable, and oneself in the height of fashion; and to keep everyone, including oneself, looking their best for a long and tiring summer's day—this was an undertaking to tax the wit and purpose of any woman. But she had both wit and purpose. And she knew it. Very well. She would take her family to Duntrafford on Saturday. And she would see to it that they, the Arthur Moorhouses, were the best-dressed and most presentable family there.

II

The day of rejoicing was hot. Sir Charles had spent an anxious week, looking a hundred times a day from the windows of Duntrafford at threatening clouds or actually falling rain. But suddenly on Saturday morning the old man, as he sat up in bed breakfasting, saw that the weather had cleared, and that a hot June sun already high in the summer heavens was causing a steamy mist to rise from the parklands beyond the lawn, and was beginning to dry the sodden canvas of the great marquee. This was better. Sir Charles ordered his man to fetch him the tussore suit he had worn last when he was in India, chose a bright tie, and put them on with much satisfaction. His lady, wearing black spotted foulard and a large leghorn hat, wagged her ebony stick at him and went off into peals of eldritch laughter. Her husband merely growled, muttered something about her not being fit to have a grandchild, and marched out of the house to inspect the preparations, heedless of her cries that he should remember that the grass must still be very wet.

The morning was delicious. In the late Ayrshire June the spring still lingered. The foliage was become rich and deep, but it had not yet taken to itself the dark, glossy green of midsummer. Followed by his two old house spaniels, Sir Charles, his hands clasped behind his back, stumped about enjoying himself. Trestle-tables were being set up in the marquee by caterers' men. He told them that he thought it was ridiculous to be arranging them in this way; that they should be arranging them in that other way; then walked off, feeling he had shown these fellows who was in authority.

At the finely wrought-iron gates of his walled garden, he commanded his spaniels to sit and wait for him, peering back through the ornamental iron tracery at two despondent pairs of bloodshot eyes that looked up as though they had been excluded from Paradise; told them to be good doggies, and went on down the damp scented turf alleys to see that his gardeners had carried out his instructions. Even Sir Charles had little to complain of. This Ayrshire garden was a miracle of luxuriance refreshed. The herbaceous borders were lavishly splashing their colours against the sombre green of the old yew-trees. Early roses, the raindrops still upon them, were sparkling in the sun. Tubs of geraniums and hydrangeas had been brought out from under glass and set about to add to the riot. Fruit was beginning to shape itself on the apple-trees, trained against the south wall. Sir Charles went, exchanging greetings with his gardeners, examining the trimmed edges, and pulling up the odd weed that seems to appear from nowhere after a warm, wet night. With a parting word that the men had better keep their eyes open while the mob walked round this afternoon, he turned and left the garden.

At a distance he could see that luncheon guests were beginning to arrive: Mungo's relatives from Glasgow, probably. This was annoying. Was it that time already? He had meant to go round and say good morning to his grandson, and ask his daughter Margaret how she did. But now these Moorhouse women would be gibbering and swarming all over the place, and making a fuss over a baby who meant nothing much to them. There they were, all silks and feathers and parasols, emptying themselves out of the wagonette and chattering like magpies. His wife and his son-in-law were dealing with them. Well, let them. He would see them all at lunch. Sir Charles stalked round a rhododendron bush in full bloom, hurried down a path in the shrubbery and entered the house by a side door.

He found his butler in the pantry, and told him to bring a glass of madeira to his dressing-room, the only place where, today, his privacy was secure against invasion. He sat down in an easy chair before the empty fireplace, sipping his wine and resting. He felt a little tired. After all, a man couldn't stay young for ever. But this wine was doing him good. Giving him heart, making him feel that life had treated him well. There had been Charlie's death, of course. But on this radiant day that belonged to his grandson, he mustn't feel bitter, even about Charlie. He rose, went to a drawer in his desk, took out a little daguerreotype photograph of his son, and sat down again to examine it. Charlie. . . . Margaret, good girl, had just been doing everything that could be done to staunch that wound.

He still had half his wine to finish. It was comfortable and pleasant here. The warm scents of June were coming in through the open window; perhaps, if he closed his eyes for a little . . .

Lunch was announced, and after some waiting, Lady Ruanthorpe came to look for him. She found him sleeping in his chair.

"Charles! Wake up! We had no idea where you had got to."

He opened his eyes slowly.

"What's that on the floor?" She saw that a little gilt square was lying at his feet, half hidden in the bearskin rug. She bent down, picked up the picture of her son, fumbled for her glasses and examined it silently for a time; then put it back in its drawer.

"Hurry, Charles," was all she said. "You're keeping everybody waiting."

III

On the whole, it was a highly uncomfortable day for Mungo. At any time this bashful countryman loathed pedestals, and here he was on this hot afternoon set up, as he felt, for everyone's approval or derision. He, a farmer-tenant like the rest, had dared to marry the laird's daughter. And here were all the other tenants with their womenfolk to nudge and criticise and wonder. He was proud of his son, but before these strapping countrymen and their wives, some of whom were younger than himself, yet already had eight or nine stocky children to their credit, one single baby seemed no very great exhibition of the virility of a man of forty-four. And inevitably, because of Sir Charles's age, the management of the celebrations must fall on Mungo's shoulders. He was acutely conscious of eyes following him as he moved about gravely greeting friends, directing helpers, and receiving congratulations.

No. His wife was not out yet. But she was doing well, he was glad to say. Sir Charles had pushed on with the celebrations so as not to interfere with the hay-making in July. How were they all "up bye"? And how were the young beasts coming on this year? Yes. There was the baby being carried across the park by the old Duntrafford nurse, Mrs. Crawford. His sister Sophia was with them. They must go and speak to her. They could cut across after the sack race had finished. What was that they were saying? Yes, it was difficult to hear, with the brass band making all that noise. Yes, and there was Mary too. No, no. He had to admit that his sisters Sophia and Mary were not as thin as they had been when they left the Laigh Farm to go to Glasgow. But, then, that was years ago, wasn't it? And they weren't so young, either. Besides, dear me, they were the mothers of growing families now.

In answer to a distant sign, Mungo gave his farmer friends apologetic, friendly nods and moved off in the direction of a great beech-tree beside the lawn. Beneath its shade, seated in cushioned basket-chairs, and with their old spaniels snapping flies at their feet, Sir Charles and Lady Ruanthorpe were holding court. Most of their communication was dumb show, for the brass band, stationed near them, was playing indefatigably with a loudness that made speech inaudible.

Mungo made a detour round the sack race, which was being energetically refereed by his sister Phœbe; pushed his way through another dozen or so of farm children squealing with excitement as they prepared to run the next race, balancing potatoes on spoons; looked into the marquee, where stout countrywomen were sitting gossiping together out of the sun, drinking tea, or feeding their smaller children, before the older and more boisterous ones should rush in after the children's part of the sports was over, and snatch the little ones' share. Seeing that some county people from another great house were bending over his parents-in-law in greeting, Mungo hung back in the shelter of the crowd until they had passed on. Now he was standing beside them, as, suddenly, the band stopped. It had been so loud that for a moment the party beneath the tree found itself unable to speak in the sudden vacuum of silence.

"Mungo," Lady Ruanthorpe said at last, "I don't think it's good for Baby to be taking him about among the crowd in this hot sunshine."

"They want to see him," Sir Charles said, searching for his grandson through a pair of old, race-meeting field-glasses.

"Don't interfere, Charles," Lady Ruanthorpe snapped. "There he is over there. Tell Mrs. Crawford to bring him here, where it's cool."

"It's just because you want him here," Sir Charles remarked, without lowering the glasses.

"Well, there's nothing very monstrous in that, is there?"

They were settling down comfortably to one of their customary bickering bouts, when a fashionably dressed, fair woman came forward, elegantly closing her parasol, as she moved into the shade.

IV

"Now, you're Mrs. Arthur Moorhouse, aren't you, my dear? Come and sit beside me," Lady Ruanthorpe said. "I don't know how you manage to look so cool," she added, surveying Bel's stylish garden-party hat, her frills and her ribbons, and deciding that she was much too carefully dressed.

Bel, feeling like an actress who has endured a harassing day, but who, in despite, is somehow managing to wring a good performance from her frayed nerves, took an empty chair and looked about her graciously. She explained that she had been to see Margaret, and opined that Margaret had been most wise not to make an effort to appear today.

Old Sir Charles was giving her broad smiles of approval. He liked pretty women.

"Now, let me see, how many children have *you* got, my dear? And how many are with you today? I *should* know. I must have seen them at lunch. But I'm a silly old woman."

Bel was preparing to shout a detailed description of her family to her host and hostess, but the band started up again, and there was nothing to do but make a graceful gesture of impotence, sit back, and endure the din. On the whole it was better so. She would, at any rate, have a headache when she got home tonight; but there was no need to add a strained throat to it. At least it was cool here and pleasanter than milling hotly about in the crowd, aristocratic and bucolic, in the park beyond.

Now she could see Mungo coming towards them, pushing his way through, and followed by a stiff old woman in the uniform of a children's nurse; the white streamers of her starched cap floating majestically behind her, as she had in her arms the heir to the Duntrafford estates and all that they stood for. Really, what a fuss these people made about everything! But Bel was impressed. And she was annoyed with herself for being impressed. Charles Mungo Ruanthorpe-Moorhouse was settled between his grandparents amid smiles and signs of admiration, the shattering noise of the band still precluding talk—and Bel was free to look about her once more from her point of distinguished vantage.

Over on the other side of the lawn she could see her husband Arthur deep in talk with an elderly farmer. With him was a sturdy country girl—the old man's daughter, presumably. The girl's looks reminded Bel of someone, for the moment she could not think of whom.

And now here were David and Grace. Their recent marriage had, in consideration of the bride's loss, been a very private ceremony; not even all the family. Although Arthur and herself had been there. David was much as usual, really. Becoming a little more important from being a married man, perhaps; and from the sudden weight of great possessions; showing less tendency, perhaps, to make his old frivolous comment on everything that went on around him; losing his sense of humour a little; becoming stiffer—more of a person; yielding, in other words, to the relentless dictates of the dignified prosperity he had chosen for himself.

Grace, adoring as she appeared to be of the husband on whose arm she was now hanging, seemed tired and a little dispirited, Bel thought. She was glad to see that Lady Ruanthorpe had motioned to Grace to come into the shade and rest. Perhaps there were happy reasons for her fatigue. "And his name will be Robert Dermott-Moorhouse," Bel said to herself tartly, reflecting the while how much more sensible it was that her own sons—at the moment, no doubt, inflating themselves shamelessly with lemonade in the marquee—were plain Arthur and plain Tom Moorhouse.

The music stopped abruptly once more, leaving its vacuum of silence, just as Arthur joined them. He had been renewing an old acquaintance. He smiled a deferential greeting to the laird as he came up.

"Who were you talking to, Arthur?" Bel asked.

"That was old Tom Rennie with his other girl. Ye mind Lucy Rennie, that sang in the house at the New Year? Her father."

Bel started up. "Oh, I would like to meet them." She looked at Grace and David and settled back. "No. It's too hot. Never mind. Funny. You would never think Lucy Rennie would have a man like that for her father. Did he say anything about her?"

"She was back at Greenhead," Arthur told them. "She had been ill, or something, and came home for a rest. She just went away back to London yesterday. They wanted her to wait and come here today, but she didna."

Bel's eyes met David's. Both looked away hastily. Now she was glad that the ear-splitting music had started up again. It made talk impossible. Grace, her straw hat in her lap, was lying back fanning herself. Arthur, Mungo and David stood behind them propped against the silver-grey trunk of the beech-tree. Bel was not surprised to see David presently wander off by himself. It was a good thing Lucy Rennie had not come today. David had never told Bel the end of that story, and she felt she could not press him for it. But she thought she had guessed most of the rest. And perhaps someday, if a confidential moment presented itself, she would ask him. She wondered how much Grace knew. Not much, probably.

At all events David had made the right, honourable and profitable marriage that common sense and the family expected of him, and all was well. That benign Providence that watches over the affairs of the respectable had cracked the whip at the right moment, and he, who had threatened to stray, had been safely headed back into the heart of the prosperous flock. And now, as Bel well knew, David was much too tame, much too conventional, to do anything but stay in the fold.

V

The little path that David followed through the shrubbery was pleasant and cool. The green mosses, the pale, half-curled fronds of fern, the wild garlic and the sprouting grass beneath the rhododendrons, all still damp from yesterday's rain, gave out their woodland perfume.

It was pleasant here among the bushes and under the great trees. The tumult and the noise had become mere rumours. Only the more persistent trumpet notes of the band came to him like far-off echoes. A man could walk at peace here; sense the sharp fragrance of the cool damp air about him; and quiet the smouldering discontents of his heart.

Had she left Greenhead quickly because she had suddenly realised that she must come with her relatives to the Duntrafford celebrations, where she would be certain to meet him? And had she really been ill? And what had made her so? David would have given much to know these things. But he knew he never would. And perhaps it was better not.

His path suddenly brought him to the viewpoint where Grace and he had stood at New Year time watching the River Ayr boiling down there, far beneath them in the moonlight. But, looking down, David's thoughts were on earlier times, when the water was flowing placidly in the bright sunlight, as it was flowing now; taking its leisured ways among those warm, white-baked stones of the river-bed. There would be minnows to catch down there in the warm shallows, and trout snapping at flies in that dark, dangerous pool that was deep, and beyond the depth of two adventurous farm children.

He remembered how Lucy, on one forbidden expedition, had dared him to swim in that pool; how he had been afraid; and how she had sat down indignantly on the bank, stripped herself naked, plunged in, and swum about triumphantly by herself; how he had been shamed into following her. They must both have been about ten then.

But he had not followed her all the way. He had not been wild, like Lucy. It would not always have been cool and easy to plunge after Lucy Rennie, and swim safely in the dangerous waters she had chosen.

Last evening Grace had hinted that they might both, in the natural course, be the parents of a child. The thought had filled his mind with pleasure all this morning.

What, then, had taken him, that he had stolen away from her now to look down on the sunlit river of his childhood? Seeking with regret for the dreams he would not clothe with reality, even if he could?

There was holiday laughter from the bushes behind him. A young ploughman and his lass came forward hand in hand to look over at the view. As they caught sight of the fine young gentleman who looked so like the more homely Mr. Moorhouse they well knew by sight, they dropped their hands and stood respectfully to one side.

David smiled, bade them a good day, and went to see if his wife was still sitting under the beech-tree.

THE PURITANS

Chapter One

"WHAT do ye mean, Hayburn?"

There was no reply.

Had Henry Hayburn understood people as well as he understood machines, he would now have realised that his employer was very angry.

Not that the chairman showed it. He took his time. He straightened the large pad of fresh blotting-paper that lay in front of him. He set his pen-tray exactly symmetrical with it. He took up the holders to see that fresh pen-nibs had been put into them this morning. He flicked open the lid of his inkwell to make sure that there was the proper amount of ink. He pushed his letter-basket away from him as though to give himself space. Having done these things, he rested his elbows on either arm of his revolving office chair, brought the tips of his fingers together, looked for a moment through the window at a yard labourer who was wheeling a barrowful of smoking, burnt-out ash to the slag-heap; then, turning his eyes again to the young man on the other side of his desk, watched him without speaking.

The older hands in the office would have understood the signs. When the chairman did these things, something was coming. It was a long-learnt trick of his, this arranging of everything around him. Thus only could he master himself; avoid saying what was rash or ill-advised. He looked at young Henry Hayburn steadily. That was a trick, too. The chairman knew that his personality was strong; that his gaze could be disconcerting.

The young man stood, ungainly and confused, his hands behind his back, looking, in spite of his beard, like an unrepentant schoolboy. A dark, untidy strand of hair fell on his brow, and his snub, sulky face was crimson. But there was no sign of yielding in the moody eyes that returned the domineering, practised stare of his employer.

The old man had had enough. Hayburn was refusing to take orders. At last the chairman spoke.

"Ye mean to tell me that ye're not going to do what ye're told in this office?" His voice was quietly controlled.

"Not when I know it's wrong, sir."

"How do ye know it's wrong, Hayburn?"

"I worked it out for myself last night."

The chairman parted his hands and trifled once more with the things on the desk in front of him. "How old are ye, Hayburn?"

"Twenty-four, sir."

"Well, I'm nearer seventy-four. And I don't need to be told what's right and what's wrong by boys. It's cocksureness that's your trouble. How long have ye been here?"

"About six months, sir."

"I've been here nearly sixty years."

Again there was silence, and again, after a time, the chairman broke it.

"Well? Are ye going on with that job, Hayburn?"

"No."

The old man jumped up. It was a long time since his authority had been flouted like this. "Get your money from the cashier and get out of here!" He spoke through shut teeth. He turned away from Henry, striking his hands together behind his back, striding to the window, and gazing out fixedly.

Henry went. Presently, the chairman was surprised to find himself trembling.

At his age it wasn't good to allow himself to get so angry. He came back to his chair and sat down heavily.

"Impertinence!" he muttered to himself. But, as he formed the word, he knew it wasn't quite that with young Hayburn. There had been a clash of wills, and he had not succeeded in making the young man's will yield to his own. No. Young Hayburn might be headstrong and foolish. But this was not common impertinence. He was brilliant, and his brilliance, untempered by experience, made the boy arrogant.

But, if only for his health's sake, he must banish his anger. And he must make his peace with the son of his dead friend, Robert Hayburn.

He bent forward and banged the brass bell on his table. "Is Hayburn there?"

Henry came back into the chairman's private room. He carried his hat.

The old man held out his hand. "Ye're the son of a very old friend, Henry," he said, using the young man's first name again now that he had ceased to be an employee. "It would be a bad business for us if we didna part friends."

There was a childish, almost appealing look in Henry's face as he took his hand, mumbling: "Thank you, sir."

"I thought I was doing you a good turn taking you in here. I thought that maybe—" The chairman had meant to say things about taking Henry's father's place; about helping Henry back to prosperity. But he realised in time that anything he might say would have an air of falseness to this strange young man with his strong opinions. There was nothing to do, then, but shake the hand that Henry gave him, wish him well, and repeat his hope that what had passed would make no difference to their friendship.

Henry stammered assurances. But as he turned and went out, each of them knew that they had merely thrown crumbs to appearances; that their ideas were flatly opposed; that there could never be any question of Henry's remaining in the employ of the established and unprogressive firm of which this old man was the chairman.

Chapter Two

BEL MOORHOUSE sat on the rocks, awaiting the arrival of her husband on the weekend steamer. From where she sat near the new-built pier, Brodick Bay stretched away from her in a crescent of summer loveliness. The sweep of golden sand. The little Highland village. The green woods. Above them the moors and hills, turning purple, here and there, with the first of the bell heather. And, assembling all this, giving shape to the picture, the elegant cone of Goatfell, basking up there across the bay in the July sunshine.

But Bel was not particulaly in tune with all this beauty, as she sat, too carefully dressed for this, the least conventional of islands, absently digging the point of her parasol into a crevice of the rock. From time to time she looked up from her thoughts to assess the size of the squat black dot out there on the diamond horizon. The dot was her husband's steamer as it paddled its way across the breezy, sunlit Firth on its Saturday afternoon run to the Island of Arran.

No. It was all very well. Brodick was beautiful, of course, and the children liked running wild. But there were limits. After all, the Moorhouse family were turning into somebodies, and would have to live accordingly. Exactly a week ago, they had all spent the day at Duntrafford. Arthur's brother Mungo, by virtue of his marriage to its heiress, was, however simple his ways might seem, a man of substance. And David, Arthur's younger brother, had married another young woman of wealth. David was no countryman. He had poise to unite to the fortune his marriage had brought him. Bel had no doubt that he and his wife, Grace, would fly high before they had finished.

She did not suffer from any narrow jealousy, but she had no intention of being left behind. Were Mungo's and David's children to be allowed to grow up looking down their noses at Arthur's children? Not so long as the mother of Arthur's children had any say in the matter.

In the concentration of her thoughts, Bel dug her parasol into the crevice of the rock with so much force that when she drew it out again, she found, to her irritation, that the point had lost its metal ferrule. She turned it round, examined it ruefully, then laid it down by her side.

Out on the sparkling horizon the dot was beginning to increase in size. Bel experienced a quick, compensating emotion of pleasure that soon her husband would be with her. She leant forward and plucked a little posy of sea-pinks that were growing primly out of a compact cushion of green, wedged among the stones beside her. Neat-handed in everything, she began to shape these into a formal little bouquet which, perhaps, she would tie up with grass and give to her six-year-old daughter Isabel. Down there just beneath her, out of the wind, a glassy sea was rising and falling, breathing among the rocks. Looking into it, she could glimpse a waving garden of seaweed, and, now and then, the silver belly of a fish.

Bel continued with Isabel's posy, thinking. Was it wrong to have social ambition for one's children. She could not think so. It was someone like Sophia Butter, who was inept with the mere mechanisms of life—remembering to pay the butcher and baker, inducing kettles to boil and pots to stew—who would tell you, piously, that her only ambition for her children was to have them become good and wholesome members of society. Bel could see no reason why riches and privilege should not be added to goodness and wholesomeness.

She was glad that Sophia and her family had not taken a house in Brodick this summer. Their extreme homeliness, and the fact that Sophia was forever borrowing things she had forgotten to bring, would have annoyed her. Mary McNairn and her family were bad enough. But if, as relatives, they were without distinction, at least they were not without competence in conducting their lives. You could always reckon upon Mary providing her share of cosy, if pedestrian, hospitality.

This very afternoon, for instance, she had taken the whole of Bel's family to picnic and bathe in Glen Rosa. Phœbe, little Arthur and the two McNairn boys had had to walk; while Tom and Isabel, being younger, had gone with their Aunt Mary, the little twin cousins, a nursemaid, and much good food, in a farmer's wagonette. Bel sighed a little at the thought of Mary's picnic.

A little breeze had sprung up, rippling the plume in Bel's straw hat, and setting her wondering if strands of her fine, fair hair had come loose, thus making her untidy to meet her husband. Out in the sea the black dot had transformed itself into a midget paddle-steamer with a wisp of smoke blowing from its tiny funnel; and with little flashes of white showing, now and then, as the bow and the paddles encountered the waves that must be running out there beyond the bay. Bel turned towards the pier. People were beginning to move down to its end, for at Brodick the arrival of the steamer was ever an event of importance. Waiting at the gates of the pier were one or two farmers' traps and a cart. She stood up, shook the grass from the folds of her dress, made sure that it lay smooth on her waist and hips, adjusted her hat and hair as best she could, and picked up the damaged parasol. As she finished doing this, she was surprised to hear Mary McNairn calling her.

II

"Bel! Bel dear! Hullo!" Mary's flat voice was doing it's best to make itself heard.

Bel gave Mary a little wave of surprised recognition, as they advanced to meet each other across the natural lawn of short sea-grass which lay between the shore road and the rocks. How matronly Mary was becoming, Bel could not help thinking, as she took in her sister-in-law's plump figure, her too easily fitting black dress, the coloured shawl on her shoulders, and her flapping straw hat. After all, Mary was not yet forty; and Bel did not like to feel that her contemporaries were beginning to look old.

"I thought I would find you here," Mary said as they wandered back for a moment to where Bel had been sitting.

"But how did you manage to come, Mary? I thought you were with the picnic in Glen Rosa."

Mary explained that a friendly crofter had stopped his little cart to ask after the family. She had begged him for a lift. "You see, I was worrying about George. I felt I wanted to come to meet him."

"George?" Bel turned to her sister-in-law.

"Yes. He's not quite well. I've been worrying dreadfully."

Bel looked at Mary, and received what almost amounted to a shock. For a moment a quick look of terror had risen to the surface of her plump complacence, then died away again as she took control of herself.

"But you haven't told me anything about this, Mary. George isn't really ill, is he?"

"I don't know. I hope not. He was to be examined this week. There's the steamer coming in. We'd better go." Mary did not seem to want to speak of George's threatened illness further.

Bel followed her, wondering. The McNairns had always been so smug. Hopes, fears and tremulous uncertainties were things you simply couldn't connect with the McNairns. They weren't quite human. That they could have any possible spark of passion for each other, in their squat, well-fed bodies, was the last thing that would ever occur to anyone about George and Mary. But now, surprisingly, Bel had caught a glimpse. People could love each other, then, even if they were fat and self-centred.

The steamer was in full view now. In a moment or two she would be slowing down. They could see the Saturday evening crowd from Glasgow leaning over her railings, eager to catch their first, close glimpse of the beloved island.

Bel took out the necessary coppers to pay for their admittance through the wicket gate of the pier, and they continued down its short length, preparing to meet their menfolk.

"Is anyone coming besides Arthur?" Mary asked presently.

"Henry Hayburn."

"Did Phœbe know he was coming by this boat?"

"I don't know, Mary—yes, she must have known."

"It's queer she didn't want to come down with me to meet him. There was room in the cart," Mary said.

"I've never the least idea what's going on between these two. They don't seem to me to behave like an engaged couple."

Now the *Ivanhoe* was in the bay, swinging round in order to take the pier at a proper angle. Daring spirits were out in rowing-boats, waving in the gaiety of their holiday mood to any passengers on board that would bother to wave back to them; waiting to row into the white foam that the steamer's paddles would presently leave in her wake.

"Do you think their marriage will ever come off?" Mary asked as they stood waiting.

Bel shook her head thoughtfully and shrugged.

"Do you think he's good enough for Phœbe?"

The picture of Phœbe's radiance, as she marshalled the children to take them off to the picnic today, came to Bel. A beautiful creature; and only nineteen. Why should she waste her loveliness on this graceless, talkative young man? And she didn't even seem to care much about him. If Henry still had his father's fortune, then, of course, it would have been different. But now he had nothing. He was, so far as Bel knew, a mere employee. And, as she had just been reminding herself as she sat there on the rocks, the Moorhouse family were turning into somebodies.

"No, Mary. I don't think Henry Hayburn is good enough for Phœbe," she said at last. "People say he's very clever, of course," she added, her eyes still on the incoming steamer.

"It's time he showed some of it," Mary's flat voice said beside her.

"That's what I say."

"I don't think you should worry, Bel. If she hasn't even bothered to come down to meet the man she is supposed to be engaged to, the affair won't last long."

The *Ivanhoe* had come alongside now. There were the ringings of bells and the thrashing of paddles as she manœuvred into position. Coils of slender pilot rope were thrown up from the deck, and the heavy hawsers to which they were attached were dragged up by powerful Highland hands that seized the giant loops and slid them over over the stanchions of the pier.

Wives waved to husbands; hosts to weekend guests. There was shouting in Lowland Scots and Arran Gaelic. A rattling of gangways. Those who were coming off stood waiting on the deck, in conventional City clothes, holding handbags and overcoats, and bringing with them a breath of the town from which they were escaping. The horn was sounded, emitting a jet of pure white steam which rose for a moment to make a contrast with the cloud of black smoke issuing from the funnel; then was lost, as together, black and white, the smoke was blown down the wind. There was tumult, laughter and the bumping of luggage; and as a fitting background, a German band that Bel recognised as one that played in the streets of Hillhead at other times of the year, kept pumping out the notes of the "Blue Danube" waltz from a sheltered corner of the deck.

III

"There they are!" Mary had spied the three men among the crowd that waited while the gangway, which had now been slid across, was adjusted to its proper position on the paddle-box.

Arthur was looking up at Bel, a smile on his lean, handsome face. As her eyes caught his, he raised a hand in a friendly salute. Bel was filled, for a moment, with a feeling of keen pleasure. After a day or two of separation, the sight of Arthur meant protection, permanence and the completion of herself.

Baillie George McNairn was standing, stout and apparently unemotional, looking very much as usual, Bel thought. He, too, allowed a glint of recognition to rise up to them from his plump face.

"I hope George is all right," Mary was saying beside her.

"I'm sure he is, dear. I wouldn't worry if I were you." And then, to change the subject, perhaps, Bel added: "What strange clothes Henry Hayburn seems to be wearing."

Henry was wearing his suit of large, trellis checks, and the cloth cap of the same stuff, which it was his pleasure to affect when he came into the country. It gave him an odd, buttoned-up appearance, that seemed to accentuate the lanky gracelessess of his body. As though he knew his name was being mentioned, he suddenly turned in the direction of Bel and Mary, and his plain, boyish face was lit up in a quick smile.

Bel felt a stab of compunction. There was, after all, something disarming about Henry. She caught herself feeling annoyed with Phœbe that she had not come back from the picnic in time to meet him.

Henry wriggled his way through the waiting crowd to the side of the steamer, and shouted a friendly "Hullo" to the ladies above him. Bel wondered if the absence of Phœbe had even occurred to this strange young man.

"Hullo, Henry!" she called back to him. "They seem to be taking a long time to let you off."

"Yes. Some of the hands are helping over there." Henry cast his eyes along the side of the boat.

Bel's eyes followed them. "Somebody getting a new cart?" she asked.

A gangway of planks was being laid at another part. Half a dozen deck-hands were standing ready to drag across them a brand-new farm-cart, which had been brought from the mainland. The cart looked like a giant toy, Bel could not help thinking. It was new painted, bright red and green, and the metal parts were shining.

"There we are now!" Henry wriggled back to his place beside Arthur and George.

The passengers, struggling with their belongings, had begun to come, one at a time, up the gangway. Presently the two husbands came, carrying neat weekend gladstone bags, and followed by Henry carrying a small and shabby carpet one. The elder men bestowed the responsible, conjugal kisses that husbands bestow upon wives in public, while Henry gave the ladies a hearty handshake, then began looking about him anxiously.

Again Bel felt a pang. "I'm sorry Phœbe's been kept at a picnic, Henry. But she ought to be back by the time we get home."

Henry merely said "Oh," and went on looking about him. "I've brought my ordinary with me," he said, using the customary name for the penny-farthing bicycle of the period, and adding: "I suppose they'll bring it with the rest of the luggage after they get the cart off. Just go after Mary and George, and I'll follow you. Good heavens! Look what's coming!"

The main gate at the end of the pier had been thrown open, and a giant Clydesdale horse was being led towards them by a brown-skinned Highland lad with bare feet. The boy was grinning broadly as he came.

"It must have come down to take away the cart," Arthur said, looking towards the animal.

"But look who's on its back!" Henry was laughing and waving wildly.

No, Bel couldn't think this funny! There was her husband's sister Phœbe, and her own son Arthur, perched high on the great creature's back, coming down the pier in front of all the people! Was Phœbe mad? Had she forgotten the meaning of the word propriety? For a young lady in her position to be sitting up there, hatless and dishevelled, making an exhibition of herself, was something of which Bel could not approve! And little Arthur was only eight, and might fall off and be seriously hurt! Indeed, if the horse started suddenly, they might both be thrown from the pier into the water.

"Arthur, tell them to come down at once! This is disgraceful! Mary, speak to Phœbe at once! She's your sister."

"Come down, Phœbe," Mary called placidly, looking up. George had had time to tell her that his doctor's report was good, and Mary could not feel angry, now, with anybody. And as Henry and Arthur laid down their bags and ran forward to help them to descend, Mary added: "Her mother was a Highland tinker. She looked very like her sitting up there."

But Bel was in no mood for family history or romantic likenesses. Besides, if anyone in the family had low connections, it was time they were forgetting them. When at last they stood before her she merely said: "Phœbe and Arthur, I'm very disappointed with you," then marched off down the pier on her husband's arm.

"Well-put-together young woman, Phœbe is, now," George remarked to Mary as they followed after.

"Time she was learning sense. Bel was quite right to be angry!" Mary said. Now that she had George's assurance that his health would allow their smooth life to continue as usual, she did not in the least see why the baillie should be encouraged in his altogether too easily aroused interest in the slenderness of waists and the shapeliness of feet. The small eyes in George's fat face were over quick, Mary knew, when it came to feminine perfection. "Like Henry the Eighth's," she had said to herself angrily on a more dangerous occasion.

As the two married couples made their way along the shore road towards their rented houses, leaving the young people to their own devices, they were startled by a bicycle bell, and shouts of "Get out of the way!" They turned to find Henry, perched on his penny-farthing bicycle, steering with one hand and carrying his carpet-bag in the other. He was going as slowly as possible so that Phœbe and Arthur could pant along beside him. He nearly fell off through trying to wave his handbag at the others as he passed them.

"Phœbe came down to meet Henry, after all," Mary said to Bel when the three had passed on in front.

Bel merely said "Yes." But now she was fixed in her resolve. These free-and-easy Arran holidays must come to an end. Nothing was to be gained from this ridiculous unconventionality. Next summer the family would find themselves in some resort where convention must be observed.

Chapter Three

MRS. BARROWFIELD was one of those women who don't need to look at their knitting. Her hands seemed to be leading a busy life of their own as they fashioned stockings for her elder grandson. The rest of her was at peace, as she sat in a wicker chair in the little front garden of the farmhouse her daughter had rented for July and August.

Though it may seem strange on a Scottish island, Mrs. Barrowfield was sitting under a palm-tree. Strange, but not impossible, for, as the shores of Arran are washed by the waters of the Gulf Stream, and the mountains catch the rains and winds from the warm south-west, frost is no great menace. It was a little unkempt garden, with an odd flower or two springing up, rather from among the uncut grass, than from any discernible plot. But it was surrounded by a low hedge of fuchsia now in full bloom, and the view from it swept the beauty of the bay.

The late afternoon sunshine caused the old lady to contract her almost masculine features now and then. A starched cap, spotlessly white, was set upon her grey curls, and her best shawl was on her shoulders. It was only right that she should receive her son-in-law with proper dignity.

Although she could not see the pier from here, she had heard the beat of the steamer's paddles, caught odd, drifting music, and seen black smoke blow down the wind. Bel would be coming back with Arthur; and, by the way, there would be that queer Hayburn boy. She had almost forgotten him. She didn't quite know what to think about Henry. But Phœbe had engaged herself to him, and Mrs. Barrowfield liked Phœbe. It was too bad that he had lost all his money. Or perhaps not—at his age?

But her hopes and fears for Phœbe and her future were presently interrupted. A piping voice said: "Hullo, Granny," and her granddaughter Isabel opened the little garden gate and came in, leading her younger brother Thomas by the hand.

As grandmothers will, Mrs. Barrowfield found herself re-examining her descendants with critical affection. She was pleased to note that, in so far as six can be the image of thirty-three, Isabel was the image of Bel. Little Thomas, a gentle little boy of four, reminded her more of David Moorhouse than of his father.

"Well, bairns? Have ye had a nice picnic? Come here to me, Isabel." The child went. "Ye've got hair like yer mother." Her grandmother took the round crook comb from the child's fair hair, combed it a little, then pushed it back into place over the front of her head. Having smoothed down her little, braided serge dress, and adjusted her pinafore, she said: "There now. Tell me what you saw."

"Glen Rosa," little Thomas said, looking at his grandmother solemnly.

"Tell Granny who spoke to you in Glen Rosa," Isabel said, prompting.

"A Duke." Thomas did not approve of wasting syllables.

"A Duke? The Duke of Hamilton?"

Isabel filled in the details breathlessly. A gentleman on horseback had spoken to Aunt Phœbe, Thomas and herself, as they were fetching milk for the picnic. He had been talking to the farmer's wife, and had bent down to ask them if they were visitors from Glasgow, how they were enjoying their holiday in Arran, and if their father and mother were well and enjoying Arran too? Aunt Phœbe had said they were all enjoying themselves very much. And Isabel, and even little Thomas, had said: "Thank you, sir."

"Where were the rest?" Mrs. Barrowfield asked.

"Getting sticks for the fire," Isabel said. "He didn't see them."

The old lady purred as she took up her knitting again. She was, of course, a staunch partisan of her own grandchildren. That the landowner, using the kindly formula of greeting he was known to keep for summer visitors to his island, had greeted Bel's children, and not Mary McNairn's, couldn't fail to give her satisfaction.

Presently, Sarah the housemaid, rather less starched than at Grosvenor Terrace, but still strangely impeccable for these rustic surroundings, appeared at the farmhouse door and led the children away.

But Mrs. Barrowfield was not to be left in peace. For now

there was a rattling at the gate, the sound of voices, and Phœbe, Henry Hayburn and her elder grandson came in. They were flushed and hot from coming up the hill. Phœbe, dishevelled and glowing, was in one of her moods. Her queer-set eyes were smouldering. Giving the old lady the merest recognition without bothering to smile, she passed on into the house. Henry, having successfully pushed his ungainly bicycle into the garden, came forward and gave Mrs. Barrowfield his hand.

He saw the enquiry in her eyes as they followed Phœbe. "She's fallen out with Bel," he said by way of explanation.

"Dear me, Henry. What about?"

"Aunt Phœbe and I rode down from Glen Rosa to the pier on one of the cart-horses, and mother was very angry. She said it was no way for a lady to behave," Arthur chimed in pertly.

His grandmother looked about her placidly, her fingers continuing independently with her work. "Yer mother's getting very genteel," she said at length. And added: "When I was yer Aunt Phœbe's age, I often had rides on cart-horses."

II

When Henry had passed into the house, Mrs. Barrowfield was left once more by herself in the garden. She smiled a little. Her beloved, beautiful and successful daughter Bel was inclined to be pompous these days; to keep remembering what she was pleased to call her position. And, as the years went on, and the tide of prosperity rose round her, Bel, her mother was afraid, would become more and more so. The old woman thought of Bel's father. The lamented Doctor Barrowfield had been a very self-important sort of man. But she had loved him. And she could not love their daughter any the less, when she showed herself like him.

Still, it was comic, Mrs. Barrowfield could not help thinking, how, every now and then, something happened to shatter Bel's sense of propriety. And usually it was Phœbe who was responsible for the shattering. Queer how she, Bel's mother, always found herself siding with Phœbe and not with her own daughter. She wondered why. But here were Bel and Arthur coming up the hill.

Bel merrily made a sign of greeting to her mother, asked if the others had arrived, announced her intention of seeing to things, and passed into the house. Arthur dropped his bag and packages on the grass beside his mother-in-law, and bent down to kiss her.

The old woman patted his shoulder. Ten years of affection, begun as a duty, had ended in a relationship which was close, unforced and warm.

"Ye'll be tired?" she said as her son-in-law stood, hat in hand, looking at the beauty about him.

"It was warm coming up here," he said, still looking into the distance. "Where are the bairns?" he asked at last, turning.

"Getting their faces washed. Sit down and rest yourself."

Arthur picked up an empty wicker chair that his wife had been occupying earlier in the afternoon, and sat himself down beside Mrs. Barrowfield. For a few moments he would rest and let Arran sink into him.

The smell of the sea, of the farmyard, of the tangle of moss-roses growing wild in a corner of the garden; the smell of bog myrtle and heather borne on the breeze from the hills above them. A golden quality was coming into the early evening light. The sun, striking lower, had begun to clothe the mountain across the bay in warmer tones; and, lighting it from one side, was throwing boulders, craggy outcrops and the sunken bed of a stream into black relief. The little herd of cows belonging to the farm were lowing as they passed the garden gate, driven in by the farm-girl to the evening milking.

Arthur continued to look about him, sighed with satisfaction and said: "This is fine!"

Mrs. Barrowfield's needles clicked with satisfaction. She liked having a man to herself. Doubly so, if the man were Arthur. "What's all this about Bel and Phœbe?" she asked presently, dropping her voice that it should not reach the open windows.

Arthur gave his version of the story of Phœbe and the cart-horse. He was inclined to agree that Bel had made too much of it. "But that's not what's bothering Bel now," he went on. "Ye see," he said, dropping his voice still further, "last week Henry Hayburn got the sack."

"The sack! From his work?"

"He was sent away."

Mrs. Barrowfield laid down her knitting, rested her hands on her lap and turned to Arthur. "Did Henry tell ye this, Arthur?"

"Yes. On the steamer coming across."

"And was he not ashamed to tell ye?"

Arthur considered for a moment. "No," he said. "He was quite joco."

"He looked joco when he came in here a minute since. He didna look up nor down." She thought for a moment, then asked: "And what does he think he's going to get married on?"

Arthur shook his head. In Moorhouse circles it was unheard of to be dismissed from one's work.

"What does Bel say?" the old lady asked presently.

"She's not very pleased."

But now Bel reappeared herself, to make a third in this whispered colloquy, and to express her own displeasure.

"The plain fact is," she said, sitting on the grass between their chairs, that she need not raise her voice, "the sooner Phœbe and Henry decide to give up their engagement the better. I don't believe either one or the other of them knows what the word responsibility means! I don't believe they're even in love with each other! Like grown-up people, I mean. I think Phœbe was just sorry for Henry, when she promised to marry him last autumn. I remember how queer she was on the night it happened." Despite her indignation, Bel, turning to gaze out to sea, let memory take hold of her. Yes, on that night Phœbe had been very strange.

"But can anybody make them break it?" her mother asked, bringing her back.

Bel shrugged. "Well?" she demanded in a whisper which was hot with desperation. "What is it to be? He's crazy and she's crazy! And the one encourages the other!"

"I've always been told he was clever," her mother said.

"And is he to keep her waiting, while he goes on being clever? I don't think being sent away is at all clever! And all the time she'll be getting older! And maybe at the end they'll find they don't want each other! This kind of thing may go on wasting the girl's life for years!"

Mrs. Barrowfield laid a hand on Bel. "Don't excite yerself,

my dear. Don't excite yerself! They're good bairns. Both of them." She turned to Arthur. "Did he tell you what he was sent away for?"

"Some job he refused to do."

"Refused?"

"In his opinion the calculations werena right, or something."

Bel, who had been dabbing her eyes, sat up and demanded fiercely, "What right has he to have an opinion?" She stared indignantly before her and added: "And then he arrives down here with his bicycle, and behaves like a clown!"

Nobody answered this. They sat in silence looking at the view before them. The light on Goatfell had become still more golden. The wind was quite down. Smoke from the chimneys of thatched cottages was rising up perpendicularly against the dark woods. They could hear hens cackling in the yard behind the house as the farmer's wife called them to be fed. Boys with a dog, far away on the sands, were throwing sticks into the water. In the stillness, they could catch, even at this distance, the animal's excited barking. Far out on the horizon a ship was moving.

Mrs. Barrowfield took up her knitting. Once again she found herself siding with the young people against her daughter. If Henry and Phœbe had the spirit to be crazy and to behave like clowns, perhaps, after all, it might be no bad thing. There was more to this story than had yet been told her. Bare facts were not enough. She would make an opportunity to question Henry, herself.

Little Isabel came out of the house to greet her father and tell them their meal was ready.

III

The face of the old minister, people said, resembled nothing so much as the face of an eagle; a pleasant eagle, most likely, if you met him out walking on any other day but Sunday. Now, however, there was no pleasantness in it. He had a flock to save, and that, if anything could be, was a matter for deadly earnest. He paused, transfixing for a long instant a worshipper who had dared to cough. Then, taking in all the ladies of the congregation with a sweeping glance, he delivered one of the broadsides for which he was famous. "And as for you, with your flowers waggin' in your bonnets. They'll no' be lasting long where you are going! They will all be burnt up!"

Arthur the Second looked up nervously. The poppies, cornflower and wheat-ears surrounding the crown of his Aunt Phœbe's straw hat would not stand a chance, he was afraid. And the curling lime-green ostrich plume which, along with the lime-green veil, drooped so elegantly at the back of his mother's fair and shining head would be inflammable too, he feared. Probably his granny, with her tight little black bonnet, would do better. The licking flames would find less to catch hold of.

He was surprised how calmly they were taking it. His mother and his Granny had not moved a muscle. For a moment he wondered if his Aunt Phœbe's eyes had begun to dance, but a second look found them cast down and prim as ever. His father and Mr. Hayburn did not seem to be unduly troubled either. So perhaps it was all right. Perhaps this Arran minister, with his strange Highland accent, did not mean everything he said. Besides, anyone so calm and radiant as his mother, or so friendly and indulgent as his Aunt Phœbe, were far too nice to have the trimmings burnt off their hats.

Arthur's mind sought refuge in the basket of strawberries his father had brought with him from the Glasgow fruit market yesterday evening, and the bowl of thick farm cream that was to accompany them to the midday dinner-table, when the family had arrived back in church.

The sun streamed through the plain glass windows of the little, unadorned church. Dust particles, floating through its slanting rays, turned for a moment to silver, then were lost again against the shadows. Outside, a corncrake was sounding his ratchet among the green corn. Somewhere a bee was buzzing. Now they were all standing up to sing the last hymn, trying to catch the tune from the slow, toneless voice of the precentor. Now the service was over and they were standing outside the little church, talking with acquaintances, and basking in the July glory about them.

As the church was some way out of Brodick, Arthur Moorhouse had borrowed his landlord's gig, and now was gone to fetch it at the nearby farm where it had been left. Although at Grosvenor Terrace his wife had a carriage of her own and a coachman to attend her, this Arran unconventionality was pleasant to Arthur. Like many another countryman who had found fortune and formality in the City, he liked to remember at times that he himself was a farmer's son and could harness a horse to a gig and drive it with the best of them. It was, perhaps, one of the greatest charms of Arran that it allowed the striving and successful to give up the struggle for a time, to touch back to their own simple beginnings.

The gig had been overloaded during their coming. Henry announced his intention of walking back. Bel promised to delay their meal for half an hour. Phœbe declared she would join him.

The weekend had not, so far, gone particularly well for this temperamental couple. They set out in the direction of home, saying nothing, pleased to be alone together. Henry seemed as disinclined for talk as she was, so Phœbe left him in peace. The Arthur Moorhouse atmosphere had been noticeably chilly. The clash of Phœbe's high spirits with Bel's propriety had only been the beginning of it. When it was known that Henry had been forced to relinquish an excellent business opportunity, specially made for him, merely because he, Henry, had chosen to set what looked like nothing more than his own wilfulness against greater experience, then the temperature had dropped steeply.

It is not pleasant to feel oneself regarded as the single failure in a family of successes. And it was just this feeling that was beginning to penetrate. Yet, rightly or wrongly, Henry felt confident that success was in him. He knew he was quick, educated and diligent. If, outwardly, he seemed undisciplined, it was merely because he could only acknowledge a sharp, unforgiving inner discipline. But, for the success-mongering Moorhouses, this, it would seem, was not enough. But how could he make them understand?

Life, until the collapse of last autumn, had been handed to Henry to play with. A dangerous toy. But he was one of those young men an assured fortune would not have spoilt. He would merely have put what he needed of it to the uses of his calling. And, unlike his own brother Stephen, have continued on his way, quite heedless of the privileges that money might have bought him.

He had been awakened early this morning with the crowing of cocks, the cackle of laying hens, and the other, pleasant farmyard noises. He had lain across the hills and valleys of his lumpy Arran bed, staring at the crude, faded roses of his wall-paper, thinking.

Last night, made tactless, perhaps, by her smouldering annoyance, Bel had talked much about the doings of the family. David and Grace were now taking over Aucheneame. Mrs. Dermott had determined to come into Kelvinside, buy a suitable house, and devote herself to her committees. Her daughter and son-in-law were planning to extend the garden and build on a nursery wing to the house. Mungo Ruanthorpe-Moorhouse had bought a tiny and very valuable Shetland pony against the time when his son should be able to sit on its back. The baby's grandfather, Sir Charles, Bel understood, had already transferred a substantial block of Consols to his grandson's name. Every word she uttered seemed so pointedly to refer to the success of the others, and their power to spend lavishly, that even Henry's indifference had begun to do more than wonder if her talk were deliberately aimed.

IV

The couple walked briskly along in the sunlight. It was strange that lovers should have so little to say to each other. But these were strange lovers and they were well accustomed to long silences together.

Henry was dismayed and puzzled. He had never been pressed about his doings in the old days. Indeed, his mother had not wanted him to take up any work seriously. She had wanted Stephen and himself to occupy their time being gentlemen. That was ridiculous, of course. Still, the scramble for fortune and position had never, until now, seemed a necessity to him.

All about them were fields of growing corn, studded here and there with poppies; fields of fresh-cut hay, of rich green pasture. Down on the right the sparkling sea. And in the distance in front of them the peak of Goatfell and the rugged splendour of the castles. White butterflies were dancing among the seeding grasses, the harebells and the dandelions by the roadside.

What did Phœbe think about it, he wondered? In his life there was Phœbe, and, far behind her, everybody else. And yet there was not much love-making between this odd couple. In times of normal happiness they fed on each other's eagerness like two schoolchildren. If there was passion, it flowed deep, almost beyond the consciousness of either. Bel had often said of them that neither was quite adult. In one sense she was right.

"Your folks don't like me, Phœbe," he said suddenly.

She was accustomed to his breaking in like this. She took a moment to take in his words. "They don't like me either," she said. "After last night Bel thinks I don't know know to behave myself like a lady." Her face darkened for a moment. Then she laughed. "She'll get over it."

Henry plucked at a long grass that sprouted by the wayside, and sucked its tender end, reflecting. "She'll get over anything you do. But I'm different. I'm just a stranger," he added, using the last word in its Scotch sense, meaning someone who is not a relation.

"How can you be a stranger, if you are going to marry me?"

"I'm not sure that she wants you to marry me."

"Nobody's asking her what she wants."

"They don't think I'm good enough for you."

"Good enough, Henry! A Hayburn not good enough for me!"

"It would have been all right last year, when mother was alive and we had our money."

"That's rubbish. What difference does that make?" Yet even Phœbe knew there was a difference. She could not be unconscious of it. She knew the Moorhouse yardstick. The thought roused a feeling of rebellion.

"It's sensible enough," Henry went on, almost as though he were thinking aloud. "After all, we can't be married till I can earn a living."

"You know perfectly well I can wait."

"Do you want to wait, Phœbe?"

"Not for ever." She turned to look at him. Their eyes met.

For an instant Phœbe caught a glimpse of the sudden, almost pitiful defencelessness that could weave itself so strangely into the texture of Henry's indifference. And the quick of her sympathy was cut almost as it had been cut on that night of his despair; the night upon which she had promised to become his wife.

She gave him her hand.

V

Mrs. Barrowfield spent August at home. This happened every summer. Bel always pressed her mother to stay with them for as long as they should be by the sea, but much as she liked her daughter and her grandchildren, the old lady felt that a month of improvised comfort, of smoking peat-fires, of Arran downpours, of cramped rooms, was as much as she had any taste for. She began to long for the ordered quiet of her own flat in Monteith Row.

Besides, town was not unattractive to her in August. Most people were away, and such social obligations as the remainder of the year laid upon her did not exist. Her son-in-law, Arthur, who always had his holiday at the fair in July, and was, in consequence, left to himself in August, came frequently to see her. David Moorhouse, before his marriage, had often visited her at this time too. She liked these masculine attentions. It amused Bel to tease her mother about her August "young men". This year David's bachelor life had, of course, come to an end. But now it would seem that Henry Hayburn was beginning to take his place.

She had invited him to visit her when they were together in Brodick, and Henry, sensing sympathy at the core of Mrs. Barrowfield's downrightness, had come. A sudden, lively friendship had sprung up between them. The strange, erratic young man had taken to dropping in of an evening. She enjoyed his excitable, self-revealing talk, his regardlessness of convention, his quick confidence in herself. She realised his great loneliness; the loneliness of someone young and eager who has not yet found his place in the scheme of things. She was flattered that he should come to her, an old woman, for understanding and support.

It is not to be wondered at, therefore, that Mrs. Barrowfield had become Henry's partisan. He had explained to her, with much technical and quite incomprehensible detail, just why he had to leave his last employment. Loyally, she declared that she quite saw, and was convinced that there was nothing else for him to do. She believed that there were great potentialities in Henry. Either for good or ill. His ardour would either make or break him. If he were headed in the right direction, then he would do great things.

He told her about Phœbe: how Phœbe was everything to him. But Mrs. Barrowfield sometimes wondered. Phœbe was so much a bird of the storm herself. How would these two unstable creatures fare together?

This summer of 1879 was long and dragging for the young man. World trade continued in the doldrums. Henry could suddenly appear at Monteith Row and declare that he was finished with Scotland; that nothing was any good; that he had determined to emigrate. Thousands were going to the New World. Why shouldn't he? Mrs. Barrowfield's experience knew not to take these outbursts at their face value. He had merely come to draw strength from her sympathy, to let off steam.

Usually he found her in an arm-chair by the open window, busy with her work. She would command him to sit down, order tea to be brought, and listen while he talked himself out. With a brisk, cheerful tact she would counsel patience. She would strive to renew his faith in himself; to remind him of his abilities. The right employment would presently present itself. It was merely a question of time. What about Phœbe, if he chose to emigrate? Did he imagine for one moment that her brothers would allow her to follow him into the wilderness?

Sooner or later peace would descend. If it were evening, there would be birds chirping in the trees outside the window. Beyond, couples could be seen in the distance, wandering across the wide, cool expanses of Glasgow Green. Presently the lamplighter would come, and the branches near the lamps he had lighted would take on the vivid look of painted scenery. In later August the gossamer mists of approaching autumn would rise from the distant Clyde and wreathe their wisps across the darkening Green. There would be the tap of an occasional step on the pavement beneath them; the voices of children playing in the gloaming; the sounds of far-off laughter.

And now Henry's talk would be changed from shrill expostulation to comfortable commonplace, while the old woman sat sewing, saying nothing. But she would smile in secret, tell herself that young people needed their elders sometimes, and assure herself that once more she had given back to her young friend the strength to continue with the highly arduous occupation of being young, impatient and eager.

Chapter Four

MUNGO RUANTHORPE-MOORHOUSE was a miracle of good temper—or so, at least, his parents-in-law, Sir Charles Ruanthorpe and his lady, were constantly heard to declare. But on this fine September morning it was taking Mungo all his time.

The harvest was in full swing, and Mungo was busy. Arrangements of all kinds had to be made at the Laigh Farm. And, in addition, as a progressive farmer, he had purchased one of the new combined reaping and binding machines, that not only cut the corn, but actually, as it went along, forced it into sheaves, tied it with hemp string, and cast it to one side ready to be set up in "stooks". Everything needed his attention, especially the new reaper and binder: for if this turned out to be a failure, he would be confronted by the unpleasant fact that he had been wasting good money. In addition, he knew that his fellow farmers would smile, and, in their blunt country fashion, inform him that they could have told him from the beginning that these new-fangled, mechanical devices were never any good.

Now, as he stood among his cornfields, in the yellow sunshine of this Ayrshire September morning, a messenger came from Duntrafford bearing a letter in Sir Charles's hand. Mungo opened the letter apprehensively. Had something gone wrong? Was someone ill? Margaret? Or his three-months-old son? He was not accustomed to having messages sent to him thus while he was in the fields.

But the letter, disdaining apology or explanation, informed Sir Charles's son-in-law that Sir Charles was sending a foreign gentleman to see the working of the automatic reaper and binder, and would Mungo be so good as to show everything and explain everything the gentleman wanted to know. He would perhaps ask young Henry Hayburn, who happened to be staying along with Phœbe at the Dower House, to bring the gentleman over some time this afternoon while harvesting was in progress. The stranger was an Austrian banker and had connections with Sir Charles's stockbrokers in London.

The stable-boy, who had ridden across with the letter, saw Mr. Moorhouse crush it roughly in his hand and thrust it deep into his trouser-pocket. But he could not see how Mr. Moorhouse had to crush as roughly his quick annoyance at this needless interruption. What possible right had a banker, of all people, to come wasting a busy farmer's time? What interest could this binder be to a foreigner? Margaret's father was country bred. He should have known better. But he was eighty years old and very petted.

Mungo Moorhouse, however, was by nature restrained and moderate. "Ye can tell them it's all right for the afternoon," he said none too graciously; and the stable-boy rode off to deliver the message.

II

It will never be known whether Sir Charles had bidden Henry Hayburn to lunch with the intention of finding employment for him. It is not improbable. For, as Mungo's sister Phœbe showed no sign of giving Henry up, his lack of employment had become a family problem. Besides, there was something about Henry's spirit and quickness that appealed to the old man. A command had come to the Dower House. Henry was required by Sir Charles to come across and meet an Austrian gentleman.

Who was he? Margaret Ruanthorpe-Moorhouse did not know. Was Phœbe expected along with Henry? They did not say so. Henry went alone.

He found the old laird of Duntrafford and Lady Ruanthorpe in the great drawing-room of the house. Although the autumn sunshine was pouring through the festooned lace curtains of the long windows, filling the pleasantly rich and padded room with warmth as well as light, a bright fire was burning. Margaret's parents sat on great chairs on either side of it. Sir Charles's old house spaniels lay on the rug. At his elbow was a decanter of sherry. There were Michaelmas daisies, late roses, and yellow beech leaves. A country room that could belong only to subjects of the Queen.

But now, at once, a different note was struck. The rather swarthy gentleman who was being presented to Henry did not belong to this picture.

Sir Charles was doing the honours. "Come along, Hayburn. Glad to see you. I see you didn't bring Phœbe." Whether Sir Charles was pleased or sorry about his, Henry could not discover, as he gave his hand to his hostess, then to the old man, who went on talking: "By the way, how is my grandson, Hayburn? I haven't seen him for two days. I must go round after tea."

Lady Ruanthorpe expostulated. "Really, Charles! How can you expect Henry to take an interest in a baby?"

"I don't see why not."

"Hadn't you better stop arguing, and introduce Henry to Mr. Hirsch."

Henry gave Mr. Maximilian Hirsch of Vienna his hand, noting the while, in his not very far-travelled mind, that Mr. Hirsch looked like a piano-tuner. But if Henry's parochiality could only think of a piano-tuner, his common sense quickly told him that the stranger, with his bowing and smiling, his shock of black hair, and his bushy side-whiskers, cut in accordance with the fashion set by his Emperor, was much more a man of the world than he was himself.

Mr. Hirsch spoke English with an accent, but almost without fault. He knew London intimately, he said, and had many business interests and friends there. His chief occupation was banking, but it was banking in the Continental sense, which meant that he was not excluded from the practical direction of several manufacturing ventures. He was always, he said, on the outlook for new ideas to exploit. He had been sent to Glasgow by a friend in London to obtain information that would be of use to him in connection with steam river-craft on the Danube.

As Henry was sipping his sherry, he began to regard the foreigner with awe. This man had been received by the heads of many famous Glasgow firms. He talked with intelligence, much more intelligence than old Sir Charles, who was obviously bored, and impatient for his lunch.

The young man became interested. Had Mr. Hirsch seen this

at such a shipyard? Had Mr. Hirsch seen that at such another engine shop? Henry's eyes kindled and his tongue wagged. He did not know that he was revealing himself. That this intelligent cosmopolitan had come to seek after such a one as himself.

Sir Charles had become more and more testy. He did not like torrents of talk he could not understand; could not even hear properly. He grunted. He offered more sherry. He demanded of his wife when she had told Campbell to announce lunch. He adjusted his stock. He dragged his gold watch out of its spacious pocket in his waistcoat, and snapped it open and snapped it shut.

The visitor stopped, smiling. "But we are talking too much Mr.—? I do not think that I heard your name?"

"Hayburn." Henry, brought to earth, looked about him a little abashed.

Mr. Hirsch said the name after him. "Hayburn?"

Henry repeated it.

For a moment the stranger seemed to be seeking about in his mind. "Hayburn," he said presently, and added: "It is strange that I should know your name." He stopped again, then exclaimed: "Ah! Robert Hayburn of Glasgow! A famous engineer. I have heard of him many times." And suddenly: "Your father?"

"He was. My father died some years ago."

"But you are in his famous Company, of course?"

Lady Ruanthorpe, gruff and old though she might be, felt that here was a situation with which she had better deal. She saw the blush on the young man's face.

She interposed with resolution. "You know, Mr. Hirsch, I think it would be such a good thing if Henry drove you over to see my son-in-law's reaping machine this afternoon. I feel you have got all sorts of things to talk about." And then with relief: "Oh, there you are, Campbell. Thank you. Come along, everybody. I expect you're all starving."

And Mr. Hirsch could not at all understand why the old woman had thus cut into his conversation. Like every other Continental, he found himself marvelling at the bad manners of the Islanders.

III

Maximilian Hirsch, urbane, highly civilised and intellectually curious, was enjoying this, his first visit to Scotland. This northern land was so different, its customs so apart. When he got himself home again to his comfortable and expensive first-floor apartments in the Inner City of Vienna, with its windows overlooking the Minoriten Church, he would have something to tell his friends of the strange, rigid ways of life, and the sombrely prosperous town, where he had just been spending his Sunday. The outward appearance of the London Sunday was sober enough. But, after all, London was a great, cosmopolitan city. There was plenty of amusement to be found by a sophisticated foreigner who knew where to look for it.

But yesterday, Glasgow had been quite dead. He had walked out from his hotel to look at the City, as it lay, quiet and resting, in the September sunshine. The sound of church bells. The earnest Protestants hurrying to church. Heavily bearded, black-coated men raising their tall hats and smiling seriously in greeting, as, together with their wives, their sons and their daughters, they hurried to foregather in tasteless yellow pine vestibules and passed on out of sight into their austere places of worship.

And yet they seemed a prosperous, well-fed people, and their faces, on the whole, appeared contented, even complacent. But what did they do to amuse themselves, to exercise their intellects, to feed their minds, on this, their day of freedom? Even the workpeople—those of them who could be seen about—seemed not to expect amusement. They roamed the traffickless thoroughfares, or stood at street corners in knots, gossiping.

He came from a city where amusement was deemed a necessary food for the spirit. He could see no attempt at light-heartedness here. At home, on an early September Sunday morning, the workpeople would be streaming to the open spaces of the Prater, Vienna's popular and fashionable park. Or the young and enterprising would be crowding the horse-trams and singing without self-consciousness to the accompaniment of trotting hoofs and tinkling bells, as they rode towards the suburbs to spend their day eating and dancing in the gardens of one of the many restaurants, or wandering happily in the Vienna Woods.

And the fashionable world—or such of it as had already come back from the country—would have its ceremonial carriage parade in the afternoon in the Prater, and later make its appearance at the opera or in the theatres.

In Glasgow, throughout the afternoon there was nothing, it seemed, but stagnation, and in the evening another dose of church.

But they were not uninteresting, these people; so long as one were not condemned to spend one's life among them. In his business interviews he had met much forcefulness of character, much agility of mind. He had found them resourceful, eager and shrewd, beneath what seemed to be a universal pose of slow-wittedness and pompous courtesy. A baffling species, even for a fine-taster of peoples and places like himself.

He was glad Lady Ruanthorpe had given him this young man to drive out with. He was of the species, but divergent from it. For young Mr. Hayburn was without pompousness. He was boyish, quick and candid. And, it would seem, far from stupid. Yes, Henry might be of use.

He sat up on the high seat of the Duntrafford gig, looking about him, as his companion drove in the narrow Ayrshire farm roads; between beech hedges, which, here and there, were beginning to turn from dark green to yellow; between hawthorns hanging with crimson berries. He marvelled that beyond them in the fields the corn was still waiting to be cut. In his own, more southern country the oat crop had already been gathered weeks ago. Here in this northern land the year's cycle was later. But it was a beautiful, mellow country, well tended and eloquent of a healthy peasant life; unspoiled by the industries that had ruined so much of the Island.

"Have you seen this reaping and binding machine, Mr. Hayburn?" he asked his companion presently.

Henry, who was not a practised driver, did not take his eyes from the horse's head. "No, I haven't," he said.

"It should save a great deal of labour in the fields. Yes?"

"I suppose it does."

"It must be a very clever invention. To cut and tie at the same time."

"Yes."

"Do you understand the principle?"

"I've never tried."

"But you are an engineer. I would have thought . . ."

"Oh, I dare say I would understand it quickly enough, if I had to."

Strange young man. His answers were almost rude; yet the Austrian could see that they were not so intended.

Suddenly, after successfully negotiating a corner, Henry turned: "Do *you* understand it?" he asked unexpectedly.

"No. But I'm very interested. I may try to get the patent, and open a factory for reapers in Vienna. You see, in my country, or rather in Hungary, corn-growing is the most important industry. We could make them in Vienna and send them down the Danube." Mr. Hirsch waited for Henry's comment.

But he only said: "I don't know whether it's any good or not," and went on driving.

IV

If this morning Mungo had felt annoyance at the prospect of having to receive a visitor sent by his fussy, self-important father-in-law, the happenings of the early afternoon had done nothing to lessen it. Just after his men had returned to work, the new reaper and binder broke down.

Mungo was a good farmer, but he was a bad, impatient mechanic. Like peasants all the world over, he was inclined to believe that a complicated mechanism has some strange, magic life of its own. That, if it goes wrong, it must be propitiated, rather than painstakingly understood and set aright. The workers stood by waiting, uncomfortable at his displeasure. They were well aware that Mungo was loathing the enforced idleness for which he would have to pay them.

The harvest field was in a state of angry tension when Henry and his companion arrived. Henry called to a man to open the gate of the field to allow him to drive in, then begged him to hold the horse's head. This done, the visitors alighted. Mungo, perfectly aware of their coming, made no sign. He had not wanted to be bothered with Sir Charles's foreigner this morning, still less did he want him now.

Mr. Hirsch had heard that the Scots could be ungracious. He was to get a demonstration of it now. He crossed the expanse of stubble—where the reaping machine had already done its work—hat in hand, ready to greet Sir Charles Ruanthorpe's son-in-law. But Sir Charles Ruanthorpe's son-in-law did not bother to raise himself from his crouched position. He merely presented Sir Charles's visitor with his back.

This rudeness might have been disturbing. But Mr. Hirsch, being a man of many worlds, did not allow it to be so. He had not come here to worry about hurt feelings. He turned to his young companion, and waited. The young man made no attempt to effect an introduction. He was intent upon what Mungo was doing. Presently Henry spoke.

"What's the trouble, Mungo?"

"I wish I could tell ye," was flung back over Mungo's shoulder.

"Have you been stuck for long?"

"Since dinner-time."

"Let me have a look."

Mr. Hirsch was astonished at the change in Henry; his sudden excitement before a mechanical problem. Now he was down on his knees, regardless of his clothes, having pushed Mungo and his assistant aside.

The Austrian did not mind that Mungo, standing up stiffly and slowly from his crouched position, did not bother, even now, to greet him. The sudden animation of this strange boy fascinated him.

"Look, Mungo. A nut has come loose and got lost there. And therefore that thing has come out of its place. Oh, and good lord! Look at that! If you had tried to drive any further you would have smashed the whole machine! For heaven's sake unharness the horses now, before they move and do any damage!"

The young man was in control. The others were doing as he told them. As the horses were led forward out of harm's way, Henry was flinging off his coat and rolling up his sleeves.

"What have you got in your tool-box? Yes, I want that spanner. Oh, and good—there's a spare nut the right size! It'll do for the one that's got lost. Now, what happens here?"

His hands were strong, deft and trained. They seemed to be leading a life of their own; quick, with mechanical understanding. There was education, skill, and a great, urgent talent.

He worked rapidly and with fanatical concentration. For him there were no white clouds in the sky, no golden landscape, no calling moor birds; no field-workers, impatient to get on with their harvesting. His hands, his clothes, his face even, were smeared with grease, as he crawled hither and thither, beneath and around this piece of dead mechanism it was his passion to bring back to life.

At last he rose, oily and grinning. "There. That should be all right. Put the horses back and try it." And presently he was running, cheerful and dishevelled, shouting instructions to Mungo in the driving-seat, as the reaper cut its way successfully down the next stretch of standing corn, throwing out at rhythmic intervals the finished sheaves.

When the cavalcade had returned triumphant to the point at which they had started, it suddenly occurred to Henry to introduce Sir Charles's guest. Mungo, more mellow now, regretted that his hands were too dirty to be shaken; but he expressed his pleasure at seeing Mr. Hirsch, and told him he would be pleased to show him his new, and altogether excellent combined reaper and binder.

V

They had, of course, to consult the family. The family came into everything. A strange, foreign gentleman, who went by the name of Maximilian Hirsch, had offered Henry an important post in a new factory in Vienna. If there had been anything for him at home, Henry and Phœbe would not have considered the proposition for a moment.

But there was nothing. The summer had dragged on, nerves had been frayed, and things had looked hopeless. Now there was this man offering a sum which, if Henry took pencil and paper, and turned things called *Gülden* and *Kreutzers* into pounds, shillings and pence, seemed really quite a lot. Quite enough to live on, perhaps even to marry on; if, when Henry got there, he found that Vienna was a place suitable for a properly-brought-up young lady.

Vienna. Round the fireplace of Bel's drawing-room in Grosvenor Terrace they got out Arthur's atlas and peered at the dot on the map. It did not tell them very much. They knew it was the capital of Austria, and appeared to be situated on the Danube, which, according to the waltz, then in high popularity, was beautiful and blue. That was all very well, but were the people on its banks God-fearing and civilised and fit for a Hayburn, and possibly a Moorhouse, to mix with?

They were simple people, these, who gazed at this black dot in the centre of the map of Europe; none of them many generations away from the peasantry. And what education they had, had been gained as an aid to their advancement in the world. They had not yet had time for foreign travel.

Mr. Hirsch had given Henry a week to decide. If he accepted, then he was to travel to London, and thence continue his journey in his company. Henry was unsure of himself. Now he was being asked to cast his moorings and set his course for the unknown. Besides, he did not particularly want to work in a factory for making reaping machines. His interests lay in the heavy industries that ran in the veins of his own city.

But Phœbe kept urging him. Her sense of adventure was kindled. Let him go, she said, get things started, and she would come to him. Or, if that were not allowed by Bel, he would, surely be given time to come home and fetch her. Let him think what fun it would be for them to be alone in a strange, new city, making new friends, finding a new life.

Upon a suggestion of Phœbe's going at once with Henry, Bel put down her foot. No; Phœbe could not possibly go until Henry had found out what sort of place Vienna was, and established a settled and comfortable existence for her. If he could not do without her for a time, then he must stay at home.

But staying at home meant having no work to do, and Henry did not want that. It was very difficult.

What had Sir Charles thought? Sir Charles had thought the offer an excellent one. Just the very thing. He himself had been in Vienna once as a young man. He could not remember the year, but it was before he was married. It must have been a long time ago, because he had gone through Switzerland in a stage coach sort of thing. And Phœbe had better pack her bags and go with Henry, for, if his memory served him right, there were one or two handsome young women in Vienna.

All of which, being in substance reported to Bel, was not particularly reassuring. Sir Charles was very well, and in their burghers' hearts they were proud to be connected with him; but, with some justification, they were none too sure of the oats Sir Charles must once have sown.

During this week of indecision, discussion raged furiously in the Moorhouse family. Stephen, Henry's elder brother, feeling himself confined and prospectless in the offices of Dermott Ships, urged Henry to get away at all costs. Stephen's advice meant much to Henry. David, who had never put forth any effort beyond keeping his place in the procession of prosperity, told Henry from the safety of his pedestal that he seriously thought Vienna would be the making of him. Sophia bustled in to say that William had read that the Viennese were all Roman Catholics and went to the theatre on Sunday; and she would not at all approve if it were Wil or Margy who thought of going. Mary, who happened to be calling on Bel at the same time, felt that home was the best place for all young people, and that she and George had always done very well just staying quietly in Glasgow. Mrs. Dermott wondered what kind of schemes there were for social betterment in Vienna; and hoped Henry would have time to look round and write her about them. And Bel and Arthur, who were the only ones who were genuinely troubled, did not know what to advise, and worried their heads off.

In the end, it was old Mrs. Barrowfield who weighed down the scales in favour of Henry's going. She had learnt much about the young man during the many visits he had paid her in the dog-days of the summer. Anything was better for him than these last two months of unhappy idleness. Frustration and a growing suspicion of his own futility might begin to undermine his splendid eagerness. This offer would stop all that. And it would develop Henry, turn him into a man, to find himself pitched headlong into new responsibilities, new labours, a new world. In some ways he was immature, boyishly dependent on sympathy, lacking in the confidence his abilities seemed to warrant. Nothing could be better for him than that he should go to this strange city to find his feet, learn to depend upon himself, and make his mistakes away from the criticism of those who knew him.

And so it came about that, as an eastward-bound express flew on its way relentlessly through the pale mists of a late September dawn, an odd-looking young man, homesick and dishevelled from the long night journey, peered from the window at the eddying, clay-coloured waters of the River Danube, at the unfamiliar reds and browns of the autumn vinelands, at the odd little wayside stations that rushed past him, all of them painted in the official black and yellow of the Austro-Hungarian Empire.

Chapter Five

JOSEPHINE—known among her intimates as Pepi—Klem, only child of Joseph and Martha Klem, of the new-built and very unfashionable Quellengasse in the Favoriten suburb of Vienna, was often described by her good-natured and pleasantly sentimental parents as the light of their lives. But if Pepi was a light in the lives of her adoring parents, she was a light that gave forth sparks. And there had been sparks this Monday morning before her father, a bank clerk, had taken himself off to his duties. Indeed, if her parents had addressed any remark whatever to Pepi during the weekend, sparks had been the result.

Now she was banging about the little flat in the Quellengasse, viciously punching up the feather-beds, and putting them to air at the window, rubbing up the hardwood floor as though it were the face of a prostrate enemy, and wringing washcloths as though they were the necks of her foes. Before this tornado her meek and kind-hearted mother had fled to do the morning shopping, leaving Pepi and her displeasure shut up and alone in the apartment. She knew from experience that her daughter would probably do the housework in half the usual time out of sheer bad temper. And she prayed that when she got back Pepi should have become more calm.

It was Pepi's father who had raised the storm again this morning, over their rolls and coffee, by asking, well, what was he to say to Herr Pommer? Pepi had exploded. Herr Pommer? The Pommer had nothing to do with her. What did he mean, Herr Pommer? He could say what he liked to Herr Pommer. The Pommer did not exist so far as she was concerned.

Her mother had tried to interpose. Pepperl must not talk to the Papa like that. The Papa was thinking of her future. The Papa wanted her to become betrothed to a nice, steady young man, who had a nice steady post in the bank like the Papa himself. And Herr Pommer was being so steady. The Papa said that in no time at all he would be able to marry her, and install her in nice apartments just like these ones here. And who knew, perhaps in a year or two there would be a dear little baby to take up her interest, when the good Pommer was at the bank?

At this, Pepi, who was not perhaps so innocent as her childish pug nose and her surprised brown eyes might indicate, said the Viennese equivalent of "Bosh!" and dissolved into tears of fury. She would get something better than the Pommer, with his apologetic cough and his worn, grey-cotton gloves. And if she didn't get that, she would stay as she was! And a nice apartment like this one here? Out in a suburb, within pleasant reach of the meat market, the goods railway station and the gas-works? And even that was too expensive for them. Were they not, even now, trying to rent one of their rooms to a suitable tenant? The Pommer was not yet thirty, and the Papa was fifty-five. When, she asked, would Herr Pommer come to achieve the Papa's magnificent income?

By this time her father had got himself into his short Viennese overcoat, set his soft hat upon his blond, distracted head, opened the door of the flat and fled.

It was after this that the child said something that somewhat alarmed her mother. Pepi dried her eyes, fixed them, gimlet-like, upon the older woman and said: "I don't care. I'll go and ask Lisa Fischer to find some work for me to do!"

Even Frau Klem's mildness was shaken. "You'll what?"

"You know very well I want to be a singer."

"Not that kind of singer, I hope."

Lisa, a young second cousin of Herr Klem, had shaken the family dust from her elegant shoes, and taken herself into the chorus of comic opera. But though her relatives had now little opportunity for talk with Lisa, it was obvious to all of them that more than the pay of a lady of the chorus supported her magnificence.

Vienna was an important capital city. But in certain respects it had the gossipy qualities of a market town. In the Inner City, or in the great main carriage-way of the Prater, everybody kept meeting everybody else. Only yesterday afternoon the Klem family had seen a very fashionable Lisa indeed, tricked out with feathers, parasol and gloves, driving in a glittering private phæton beside an officer of the Hungarian Guard, pass over the Aspern Bridge on the way to the Prater. Her older relatives had dropped their eyes discreetly. But a glimmer of recognition had passed between Lisa and her young cousin.

Having gained a sufficiency of composure, Pepi's mother managed to ask: "Have you any idea what kind of woman Lisa Fischer is?"

"A singer. What else?" Pepi was perfectly aware of the right answer. But she knew her mother, and enjoyed driving her into corners.

Frau Klem rose from the coffee-table troubled. "Well, if you don't know the answer to that question, I dare say it's just as well," she said, hedging. "But let me tell you, my child, any thought you have of following Lisa's example is playing with fire." And having thus, not quite honestly, quieted her conscience, she put on her hat and went out to buy blood sausage and sour cabbage.

II

Having done everything else in the house that she intended to do, Pepi went back to the open window to take in the feather-beds. As she did so, she stopped to look out. It was a pale, late September morning. A light fog hung over that part of Vienna which could be seen from her window, high up in the Quellengasse. Far on her left she could just make out the slender spire of the Cathedral of Saint Stephen—an insubstantial fretwork ghost, hardly distinguishable in the morning haze above the Inner City. Down there, much nearer and more distinct, were the solid towers of the Imperial Arsenal. And over there, in the distance, beyond the houses of the Landstrasse district, stretched the great expanse of the Prater.

Beneath her the street was depressingly autumnal and silent. What little traffic there was seemed to be strangely hushed. The leaves on the newly planted trees beneath her were limp and colourless. She could hear the barking of a dog, coming from a distance. Having put the feather-beds back, she returned to the window and sighed dispiritedly.

She felt low and frustrated, as only nineteen can. Here she

was, young, pretty, a creature of endless potentiality, and all the future was to be allowed to hold for her was Willi Pommer. A tear dropped on the window-sill. Pepi looked at it ruefully. Another splashed beside it. Let them all come! She was no longer angry. Her spirit was gone. She was nothing more now than a poor, tragic child! Let them go on falling until they made a waterfall down the front of the building, splashing first on old Frau Wolfert's window-sill immediately below, and then next into the geraniums of the Linsenmayer's window-boxes before they finally flooded the pavement.

Taken now with this tragic fantasy, Pepi leant a little farther out of the window just to look down to see what exact part of the pavement the waterfall would strike. In doing so, she received a sudden shock. For there on the pavement, immediately beneath, with every appearance of making to ascend, were two young men. She drew in her head abruptly; but almost at once, that she might not be mistaken, she thrust it out again. As she did so, a soiled, grey-cotton hand pointed out the number. Yes, it was the Pommer himself.

It is a strange fact that young women on the point of meeting suitors it is their firm intention to reject should rush to their mirrors before they meet them. But this was what Pepi did. And when, at last, the door of the Klem's flat was opened to Herr Pommer and his companion, they were confronted by a little lady who was the ultimate expression of provocation and off-hand charm. Herr Pommer, shabby Viennese bank clerk though he was, bent over Pepi's hand with a reverent elegance that would have done credit to an Esterhazy, a Trauttmannsdorff or a Dietrichstein, his shock of mouse-coloured hair falling over his brow as he did so.

Was Fräulein Pepi's gracious Mama at home?

Fräulein Pepi regretted.

Because he had brought this English—no, Scottish gentleman, on the suggestion of Fräulein Pepi's honoured Papa. This gentleman was on the outlook for a room in the house of honourable people, where he might be one of the family and practise his German. He had come all the way from Scotland to organise and manage a new factory in the Neubau district. In the meantime, Herr Pommer, pleased to impress upon Pepi his accomplishments, told her somewhat off-handedly that he had given himself up to acting as this gentleman's interpreter, the great Maximilian Hirsch having decreed that he should do so.

Fräulein Pepi permitted herself some show of interest. The gentleman from Scotland was formally presented to her. He was a bony sort of young man with an abrupt handshake, queer English clothes, and no discernible manners. But he had white teeth, a disarming smile and did not look unfriendly. And, putting him at his lowest, at least he was a novelty. So she hastened to say that although she was the only one at home, she was sure it would be all right to show the gentleman the spare room, as he had been sent by the Papa.

She allowed herself to remark, however, that it seemed strange for him to be seeking rooms in the Favoriten district when his work lay in the Neubau. Secretly, Herr Pommer gave Pepi a bad mark for this. Although he hoped to make her his wife, and although she spoke in a tongue that was quite incomprehensible to the stranger, she must learn that in business—even if it only be the letting of a room—one did not as much as breathe of disadvantages at the moment of negotiation. He said nothing, however, but followed her along, with his companion, into the house. Pepi, remarking that her mother was due to appear at any moment, left the front door open.

III

There were endless peculiarities about the young "Englishman" who had taken a room at the Klems' in the Quellengasse. And one of the chief of these was that he kept insisting—at first by means of Pommer, his interpreter—that there was no English blood in him whatever; that he came from Scotland. Had not the Klems heard of the land of Mary Stuart, of Shakespeare's Macbeth, and of Sir Walter Scott?

Of course they had! Were not Schiller's "Maria Stuart" and Shakespeare's "Macbeth" on the repertoire of the Hofburg Theatre? And Walter Scott? Who had not read Walter Scott? In this City of culture even humble people like the Klems must not admit any ignorance.

But indeed this young Islander was a strange, incomprehensible being. Old Frau Kummer, farther down the Quellengasse, had once had an Oriental medical student who had come to Vienna to study under the great Billroth. And dark though his skin had been, and fantastic his garments, he had seemed to adjust himself much more easily to the life of Vienna. He had been gay and erratic. He had spent hours pleasantly wasting his time in suburban cafés, or in the large coffee-houses on the Ring. He had had several private adventures more or less publicly; and had, in other words, behaved in a way that was normal and understandable. But he had paid well, and old Frau Kummer had been fond of him. Although, indeed, she had been compelled to return a niece, who was in Vienna learning millinery, to her home in Pressburg. The Oriental gentleman was taking her for more rides on the switchback in the People's Prater than Frau Kummer considered wise.

There was nothing of this about the Klems' "Englishman". Apart from the fact that he paid regularly, he was different in every respect. Yet no one could say that he wasn't an easy lodger. He was almost no trouble. He was the most serious young man the Quellengasse had ever seen. He took morning coffee at an early hour, then set out on one of the new safety bicycles; bicycles with both wheels the same size—in Vienna the best-known make were "Kangaroos"—to pedal his way across to his factory in the Neubau. Much to the interest of the Favoriten district. By means of Herr Pommer, he explained that it saved his waiting for the infrequent horse-trams. In the evening he came back for his meal, and thereafter took himself to his own room, where, on certain nights, Herr Pommer came to give him lessons in German.

In his absence, Pepi took much interest in the foreigner's belongings. It was a way of finding out about him. He had begged for a larger table at which to work, and this was now strewn with technical books and drawings, engineer's blueprints, a German grammar, notebooks containing hieroglyphics connected with his work, and German exercises written out for Willi Pommer.

There were two little photographs. One of a rather forbidding old woman in a white cap, to whom he bore some resemblance, and another of a girl about Pepi's own age. Pepi spent much time wondering about this girl. She was stiffly posed, and wore a fur bonnet that was dowdy by Viennese standards, but, in the picture at least, she was beautiful, with eyes that slanted a little in the same way as the eyes of a Tartar gipsy who had once told Pepi's fortune in the Prater. Was he betrothed to this girl? Married to her? Was she his sister? Had not Pepi been hotly determined to keep Willi Pommer at a distance, she would have begged him to find out.

But, as the weeks passed, the barrier of language began to dissolve. Herr Pommer had reported at once that his pupil was very intelligent, that, in the factory, his quick mind and his practical good sense were combined with a surprising creativeness. Maximilian Hirsch had shown astuteness in employing this young man. Some time in the beginning of the New Year he would have the little factory running. And it was the same with his study of German. Before many weeks Henry was giving directions to the men in the factory. Here and there Pommer would catch him using their own homely, uninflected speech. He told him that this was not German, but that he was in good company, as the Emperor Franz Joseph, too, spoke Viennese. Henry replied he did not mind what he spoke, so long as the men obeyed him.

Pepi's interest in Herr Hayburn grew as his ability to express himself increased. Now he went out of his way to talk to all of them, begging them to set him right when he went wrong; which was continually. There was laughter at this, and friendliness, and the warm-hearted, suburban family began to like the stranger who had come among them.

At this time Pepi Klem was happy. Her ambition to be a singer had, strangely, ceased to trouble her. Although Willi Pommer came continually to work with Herr Hayburn, she managed to keep him at arm's length, and her parents seemed prepared to let things be.

The young foreigner occupied her mind. She helped him with his stumbling German. She corrected his exercises. He was so unlike other young men, that it was possible, somehow, to treat him with camaraderie, like a schoolboy; to scold him and laugh at him; to forget he was a creature of the opposite sex. And yet he seemed to like her; to turn to her ready friendliness when he was lonely. It was not quite without a pang that Pepi learned that Henry was betrothed to the young woman in the photograph; that he intended to marry her whenever it was possible. But everything about him was so strange, so unreal, that Pepi felt she need not quite believe it.

On Sundays, now, when it was fine, the Klems took him sightseeing. To any Viennese, there is nothing so well worth seeing as Vienna. He seemed to enjoy himself, but his enjoyment had an austerity, an odd, Puritan self-consciousness, that would not be shaken off.

At this time the building of the Ring was in progress. The walls and ramparts of the Inner City had been thrown level to make the most spectacular boulevard in Europe—a spacious circle round the inner town, with trees and gardens being planted and many public buildings nearing completion.

Herr Hayburn's interest seemed caught with all this planning and laying out. What was the purpose of this great building? And that? It was awkward to be made to feel ignorant about these things by a foreigner. Pepi and Frau Klem were not quite sure which was the new town hall, which the new university, which the new parliament buildings, which the new museums. They had sometimes to refer these questions to the Papa.

But why bother about solemn, unimportant things like public buildings, in this, the capital of elegant pleasure?

IV

Now, in less than a week it would be Christmas. Emerging from the overheated atmosphere of the bank, Willi Pommer dug his gloved hands deep into the pockets of his short overcoat and looked apprehensively at the sky. It was the colour of lead. The snow was late this year, but now it looked like coming. A sharp gust of wind from the east blew papers and straw along the street. Piled-up mud, swept to the side, was frozen to solid iron.

Willi turned up the fur collar of his coat and started off up the street. Somewhere a clock struck the quarter before midday. He had not realised the morning was so far gone. He had been given a note from Maximilian Hirsch to deliver to Mr. Hayburn at the factory in the Neubau, but he decided he would have a walk to rid his lungs of the stifling air of the bank, have lunch somewhere, and deliver the message thereafter. That would be time enough. He was in no hurry to see Mr. Hayburn this morning.

Willi Pommer was depressed, and Mr. Hayburn had much to do with his depression. When the Scotsman had come at first, everything had looked so promising. The study Pommer had made of English had, at last, turned to his advantage. On his return from London, Maximilian Hirsch had enquired among the clerks if any of them knew English well enough to act as interpreter for a young Scotsman who had come to Vienna. Willi had offered himself. It had given him a sudden importance in the eyes of his fellow clerks; it had also allowed him much greater freedom; for, of necessity, his time as an interpreter must be irregular. He had attached himself to this young man from Scotland with an interest almost amounting to passion. In every way he was so different; so incomprehensible, yet so fresh; so far removed from the humdrum of other young men in Vienna, with their favourite cafés, where they sat for hours playing tarock or dominoes, their adventures that were so commonplace that they were scarcely adventures at all, their talk of horse-racing in the Freudenau.

His new duties had made him feel a being set apart; had raised him up into that world of intellect which counts so much with the Viennese. Had he not been such a styleless creature, Willi would have begun to give himself airs.

As he walked from the Bankgasse towards the Franzensring, he came on the staging and partially built walls of what was destined to be the new Imperial Theatre. The intense cold had brought work to a standstill. Scaffolding and stonework alike were rimed with frost. Smoke was rising from the braziers of the crouching watchmen. An itinerant Slovenian peasant in a shaggy sheepskin coat was trying to sell roast chestnuts from his little, wheeled charcoal oven.

Yes. And the culmination of his good luck had come when Mr. Hayburn, tiring of his hotel—or its cost—had begged him to find rooms. Or luck at first it had seemed. Willi's senior at the bank, Joseph Klem, had always been his friend. So much so, indeed, that Joseph and Martha Klem had smiled upon his application for the hand of their daughter. With his pupil settled in the Klem household the advantage to everyone would be great indeed. The foreigner, who seemed quite overwhelmingly respectable for so young a man, would have pleasant lodgings. The good Frau Klem would receive a welcome addition to her housekeeping money. And he, Pommer, in his capacity of English tutor and interpreter, would of necessity be constantly received in the flat, and thus be able to press his suit with the desirable but rather too high-spirited Pepi.

But as the autumn moved into winter, things had not seemed to get better. Mr. Hayburn's apparent boyishness, his immaturity, seemed to appeal to the young woman. Were they genuine? Or was this yet another example of Albion's perfidy? They had struck up a great friendship, it seemed. She was forever helping him with his German; trying to tease the solemnity out of him.

Slow, single feathers of snow were falling out of the sky as Willi Pommer turned from the Franzensring into the Burgring. By the afternoon, Vienna would wear her winter mantle. Over there, before him in the distance, a company of the Imperial Guard had swept through the Burgtor, their splendid, nervous horses dancing in the sharp cold as they crossed the wide expanse of the Ring on their way to the Imperial stables. It must be after twelve. The Palace Guard was changed.

Somehow the sight of them gave Willi confidence. Pepi was young and wilful. But she was a lovely, gay little creature. Things must take a favourable turn soon.

Deep in this thought, Willi did not notice that a long, striding figure enveloped in a rough Inverness cape was coming towards him. Henry Hayburn hailed him with a shout: "Hullo, Pommer."

Willi jumped. The Hayburn was the last person he had expected just then. He was annoyed to find himself returning Henry's greeting almost with an air of guilt.

But Mr. Hayburn certainly noticed nothing. He was radiant, friendly and bursting with news. "Do you know where I've been?" he demanded gaily, taking the Austrian's arm.

"Where, Mr. Hayburn?"

"I've been down in town arranging my ticket. I've been given leave to go home at Christmas. I'm getting married. I'm going to surprise them."

"Ach! But I did not know you had . . ."

"Yes, well, I have. And I am going to bring her back with me. Come and have lunch."

Herr Pommer was led away expressing congratulations that came from his heart.

Chapter Six

BEL MOORHOUSE was enjoying herself as an invalid might enjoy convalescence. It was no unpleasant thing to feel that the battle was over, just for the moment; that there need be no more gathering of her forces, no more steeling of the nerves.

Bel had given the customary family Christmas party at Grosvenor Terrace two days ago, and it had been a tiring business. Her sense of hospitality, her sense of importance, her vanity and her kindness of heart had joined themselves together and forced her to ask everybody. And so, in addition to the usual McNairn and Butter families, there had been Mungo and Margaret, and David and Grace; and as Grace's mother, Mrs. Dermott, could not be left solitary, she, too, had received an invitation.

But now, on Saturday evening two days later, Bel's troubles were behind her. The house, except for the still hanging Christmas decorations, showed no trace of the recent upheaval. Exhausted maids had been placated, and she, herself, could rest. She sat by a blazing fire in the pleasant drawing-room of Grosvenor Terrace, her feet on the embroidered hearthstool, occupying herself with needlework. Her husband, Arthur, relaxed for once, sat opposite to her reading his newspaper. Upstairs her children were sleeping. The only member of the family who was not safely beneath the roof was Phœbe, who had gone with the Butter children to the orchestral concert in the New Public Halls, or Saint Andrew's Halls as they were coming to be called. Bel had wondered at her bothering to go. The night had been so wet and stormy.

Even now, as she sat here in the warmth, she started a little, as a particularly sharp squall burst against the drawing-room windows, causing them to shudder in their frames, and driving the rain against the glass.

"Listen to the storm, Arthur," she said, looking up from her work.

"Aye. It's wild," was the complacent answer.

"I wish Phœbe had stayed at home."

"She'll be all right."

"I hope so." Bel settled back. She supposed there was nothing to be alarmed about really. And Phœbe had been determined to keep her promise to go with her cousins to the concert.

Yes, she reflected, she had had her troubles with the immense Christmas party. That was the worst of being in a family at all kinds of social levels. The Butters were so homely. The McNairns were so smug. Bel's own mother, old Mrs. Barrowfield, could be so outspoken, with the habit of flaunting her opinions in broad Scotch to make them sound yet more downright. Set against these, there were David and Grace, who were becoming more and more distinguished as time went on; Grace's mother, who met lords and ladies on her various committees, knew what was what, and did not scruple to say so. And Margaret Ruanthorpe-Moorhouse, a daughter of broad acres, who had genuine, blue blood. An appalling hotchpotch of a family really!

Sitting here at peace, Bel wondered how she had ever had the courage to bring them together. And yet, in spite of awkward moments, it had been a friendly gathering, with much goodwill and a display of affectionate indulgence that did everybody credit.

Bel's besetting sins were her preoccupation with the trimmings of life and her obsession with social compatibility. She had worried that William Butter had not been properly dressed; that her mother's speech was abrupt; that the McNairn boys had seemed rude. But she had not taken account of the sense of security and family good-feeling that existed among them, even among the newer members; of the consciousness of each that, should things go wrong, all the others would be there to give support.

There was another shuddering gust against the windows, and, following it, a metallic crash on what sounded like the private carriage-way of the terrace.

"Good gracious, Arthur. What's that?"

"Somebody's chimney-can."

"What a night!"

Arthur rose, parted the curtains of a window, and looked out. Street lamps were dancing and flickering. Some of them had been extinguished. A torrent of rain was lashing a traffickless Great

Western Road. He fancied he heard a branch crack and break off over there in the Botanic Gardens.

"It's as bad as I've seen," he said, turning back into the room.

Bel looked up at the clock. It was after nine. She felt a genuine stab of apprehension now. "I wish Phœbe was at home and safe," she said.

"She'll take a cab."

"Do you think a cab will dare to bring her?"

"Of course. It's scarcely time yet."

Bel went on with her sewing, thinking of Phœbe. She had seemed quieter this autumn. Quieter and more contented. She got letters from Henry in Vienna, but said little about them. Bel had begun to think that her interest in Henry was on the wane. But with Phœbe you never knew. When she asked her how Henry was getting on, Phœbe usually said, "All right," and left it at that. But she was well accustomed to Phœbe's queerness. She could do nothing but leave her alone.

There was a momentary lull in the storm. They could hear the sound of horses' hoofs, and presently the slamming of a cab door.

Arthur was at the window again. "It's stopped here," he said. "I'll go and let her in."

II

"Henry! Where have you come from?"

Henry, still in his Inverness cape, stood grinning at Bel.

"From Vienna. From where else do you think? Can I stay here tonight?"

"Of course." When had Bel's hospitality ever been appealed to in vain? "But why didn't you tell us? Phœbe is at a concert."

Momentary disappointment clouded Henry's grin. He began to unwind his thick scarf. "It's a terrible night," he went on. "I thought the cab was going to be blown over when we were crossing Kelvin Bridge. I hope she'll get home all right."

"Of course she will. Have you ever known Phœbe stuck?"

Another fierce blast struck the house and roared in the chimney. Henry replied with a doubtful "No", and stretched out his hands to the fire. "I've never seen such a storm," he said. "My porter at St. Enoch's told me that a lot of the glass roof of the station had been blown in. I'm glad I didn't try to cross from Hamburg to Leith. The porter said word had come through that there was trouble on the East Coast. The Tay Bridge. He didn't know yet whether it was true."

Arthur joined with Bel in pressing Henry to stay at Grosvenor Terrace, which Henry had fully intended to do. But why was he in Scotland, and what was the purpose of this surprise visit? Henry avoided the answer to this question. He had things to see to at home, but he must return to Vienna within the next fortnight.

As he sat with them talking of his work, Bel and her husband could not help noticing that, in so short a time as three months, Henry's character had undergone many not quite definable changes. He was more of a man. The lines of his face were more mature. It was the old Henry who, gesticulating and excited, was telling them of his struggles in the strange, far-off city where his calling had now taken him; of his difficulties with a strange language; of his troubles with the kindly, almost Oriental lethargy of the Viennese workmen—a lethargy that the people of Vienna themselves, prepared to excuse everything, especially their own and everybody else's shortcomings, dignified by the name of *Schlamperei*. It was at once obvious to Bel and Arthur that Henry was developing. He had been given authority, and he was able to take it. He had said do this to this one, and do that to that other. People had taken his orders as an expert, and neither he nor they had questioned his right to give them. This was fixing his character. Was it also colouring his eagerness with tinges of conceit?

"And what kind of place is Vienna? Is it as wonderful as they say it is?"

What was the meaning of the smile that flickered in Henry's face? Was it the smile of a cosmopolitan, who has returned for a moment to the ignorance of his native province? Was it a faint smile of patronage?

And yet, what had he done in the last months? Gone to Vienna and lodged in a workman's suburb with a family who were less educated than he. Schemed and laboured to set up a factory for harvesting machinery. Studied the German language. Gone for walks, written letters home, suffered from sharp fits of loneliness. The real life of the City had scarcely touched him. He had been quite unaware that a part of the cultural history of Europe was being written under his nose.

He had seen the Emperor Franz Joseph make one of his paternal appearances at his study window at the midday changing of the Palace Guard. He had seen him wave to his people. He had, here and there, caught glimpses of military splendour. But that was all. He had viewed such happenings with little curiosity, and no sense of romance.

And yet the Imperial City had worked a change in him. It had given him a consciousness that lay beyond the horizons of his boyhood. Of lands that took notice of neither his cults nor his creeds; yet seemed to do very well in their ignorance of them, and rise, after their own fashion, to a glory of their own choosing.

The door was suddenly thrown open with the words: "What a night! We couldn't get a cab and decided to walk." Phœbe was standing framed in the doorway, dripping and dishevelled.

"Phœbe, dearest, see who's here!"

She stood where she was, looking at Henry, who had risen from his chair. For a time neither of them moved.

Fascinated, Bel tried to interpret the emotions of this strange, unpredictable girl. She saw the colour flood up from Phœbe's neck and set fire to her face. For a moment it wore an expression of softness that Bel had never seen before. Her gipsy eyes shone. Her lips seemed to be exclaiming the word "Henry!" In an instant it was over, and Phœbe was advancing into the room to shake Henry warmly by the hand, and to kiss him in all friendliness, as though she were his sister.

"Hullo, Henry. What on earth are you doing here?"

"I've come to take you back to Vienna with me."

The colour began to rise in Phœbe's face again "What do you mean?"

"To get married, of course. We've only got a fortnight."

Phœbe said nothing. She crossed to the mirror over the fireplace and fingered the strands of wet hair that straggled on her cheeks. More, even, than the others, she had already felt the new force that Henry had brought back with him. "I'm soaking! I must go and change at once. I won't be a minute." She left the room.

"You never told me!" Bel said as they sat down once more.

"I wanted to tell her first."

"But, Henry, Phœbe is only nineteen! And you would be taking her so far away! I don't quite see how we can allow it!"

But now Bel remembered how Phœbe had looked a moment ago as she stood in the doorway.

III

Everyone was out at church next morning. The fury had gone out of a wind that had dropped to little more than a breeze. As the Moorhouse carriage, containing Bel, Arthur and their elder son, together with Henry and Phœbe, made its shining way towards town and the Ramshorn Church, a watery sun found strength, for some moments, to pierce a fissure in the low-hanging cloud, filling a wet rain-washed city with a sudden flood of diamond light. Streets were littered with slates and chimney-pots. Shattered glass lay here and there on pavements. Trees, hoardings and wooden fences lay torn and broken.

Already there was early morning talk of a great railway disaster. It was, perhaps, to hear of this that so many people had come out this morning. Being Sunday, there were no newspapers to tell them, but telegrams had been coming from the East Coast. The great middle span of the Tay Bridge had collapsed before the fury of the storm, taking a trainload of some two hundred people with it. Glasgow, along with the rest of the Kingdom, was horrified.

People stood on their church steps, talking of it; declaring it could not be true. And what was the world coming to?—With this dreadful happening; the depression in trade; and last year's collapse of so many banks up and down the country, beginning with the collapse of the City Bank of Glasgow. They shook their heads and agreed that the times were indeed terrible, and that things couldn't be much worse. It was only when the bells showed signs of stopping that they remembered where they were, and turned to hurry inside. In many churches, prayers were offered for the bereaved. And when the service was over, worshippers lingered once more to discuss the disaster further, to tell their friends how their own washing-house door had been torn from its hinges, how a chimney-pot had smashed the glass of garden-frames, or how a tree had fallen on the rose-plot in the front lawn.

Like many another returned traveller, Henry felt himself detached. Those of the family who had come to church this morning expressed momentary surprise at seeing him; then seemed to take him for granted; to forget all about him. He put this down to the all-engrossing news. But in this he was wrong. The imaginations of the Moorhouse family, as of most people, could not stretch beyond the circle of their own experiences. The appearance and customs of the Austrian capital in no way aroused their curiosity; except when they fell to considering if it was wise or foolish to allow one of their number to follow him thither as his wife.

Even on the church steps, Sophia, hearing from Bel that Henry proposed marrying Phœbe and taking her back to Vienna almost at once, was quick to express an opinion. "But, Bel dear, Phœbe's only a child! Now, if it was my own Margy, I would never think—and I read somewhere that Vienna was a fearfully wicked place! Oh, Henry Hayburn's quite a nice boy, dear; I don't mean he . . . But you remember we always used to think that his brother Stephen—you know, in David's office—was just a little bit—well, dear, light-minded. Of course, I'm sure he's quite settled down, and all right now, what with his mother's death, and having to work, and everything. Still, the family has a wild streak—and we couldn't have Phœbe . . ."

At this point Arthur had hurried Bel and their elder son into church, where they found old Mrs. Barrowfield comfortably ensconced in the corner of their pew; her elastic-sided boots on the highest and most comfortable hassock; her special, large print Bible and hymn-book conveniently placed in front of her; and her gold spectacles polished, ready to begin. She was smiling delightedly at Henry and Phœbe, who were already in their places, and she was addressing Henry in loud, unnecessary whispers.

Somehow, Sophia's chatter had stirred up Bel's anxiety. Was she to let Phœbe go? How could she hold her against her will?

Was not Phœbe much too young to marry this impetuous, strange young man, and go to live with him in a great, unknown city? For one of the few times in her life, Bel wished she were better educated—better informed.

Standing, sitting, praying, going through the actions of worship, with elegant, automatic reverence, Bel took in nothing of the service. She was worried by love and anxiety. Phœbe would want to go. Her behaviour last night had shown Bel that.

What, then, had stung Bel to apprehension? Sophia's silly talk? The sense of disaster that hung in the air this morning? But now Bel remembered that Phœbe had once promised to come back to her if she were in trouble. Surely there was comfort in that? Bel stood up for the benediction. For the first time during the service, she found herself receiving some comfort; some quieting of her fears.

IV

"Well, Phœbe? Are you coming back to Austria with me?"

"I think so."

They had been given possession of Bel's parlour on Sunday evening. For the first time, almost, they were left to themselves.

Henry took her into his arms and kissed her, with a force, a lack of apology, that Phœbe had never met in him before. His former love-making, when, indeed, there had been any, had been boyish, tentative, and virginal. These were the embraces of a man.

"No, Henry. Go over there and sit down. That's better. Did you miss me when you were away?"

"Yes. Did you miss me?"

"Of course."

It was impossible for these two to be arch or oblique in their utterance, the one to the other.

"You know, you've changed," Phœbe went on, looking across at him.

"For the worse?"

Phœbe considered this for an instant. "Not for the worse. I think you're a bit older. That's all." And then after a moment: "No. I'm glad you went. It's been good for you."

For reply, Henry allowed a flicker of indulgent amusement to show itself upon his snub features. She had never seen this look of masculine patronage before. Yes, Henry was changing.

"Tell me about everything."

There was much of the old Henry left. Indeed, now that he was in full cry, chasing his ideas, following his plans, the old Henry seemed livelier than ever.

She was accustomed to these outbursts. Henry, she knew, was launched. A semblance of listening, a word or two of assent, and he could go on like this for hours. And meanwhile she would sit, hearing his voice, basking in his enthusiasm, testing the strength of the bond between them, seeking the answers to the questions of her own unquiet heart.

What had brought her together with this strange young man, who sat here gesticulating happily before her? An uprush of emotion, when, that night two autumns ago, she had seen he was at breaking-point?

She sat watching him, summing him up behind the mask of her smiles. The attitudes of his body. The eagerness of his voice. The graceless expressiveness of his gestures. That was Henry; the Henry she knew now through and through; the Henry she had defended hotly; the Henry she had sometimes quarrelled with childishly; the Henry whose fears she had stifled; whose resolution she had steeled. There was little more now of Henry to know, until she came to know the unknown Henry who was her husband.

Was she ready to go thus far with him? Was she ready to join hands with the unknown Henry, and follow him confidently into an unknown world?

But now, as she sat watching him, his body bent excitedly towards her, it came to her clearly that should Henry leave once more for Austria without her, he would be tearing away a part of her with him. For better or for worse, Henry Hayburn was her own.

"But tell me a little about the *town*, Henry. What does it look like? In what kind of house shall we have to live?"

The will to adventure had never been lacking in Phœbe. And now that she had settled essentials, she was prepared to let excitement do what it would. Henry could tell her that Vienna was a great, important city; a city of spectacle, consequence and glitter. When they got back it would be lying under the white, mid-European winter. But while they settled in, it would be moving forward towards the spring. And people had told him that there was nowhere comparable to Vienna then.

She tried to see Vienna in her mind. But she could not. She had never been in London, and, like so many people in the West of Scotland, only once or twice in her own lovely capital. But she allowed the prospect of living in this far-off City of enchantment to take hold of her. Life would be new. She could not believe that it would not be beautiful. And now that she felt sure of her heart, her doubt was banished. This passionate girl could look to nothing but adventure and fulfilment. Her lover saw her eyes were dancing; that her face was flushed with happiness.

"Will they let you come, Phœbe?"

"They'll have to."

"You're not quite twenty yet. They might say . . ."

"I'll run away with you if they try to stop me."

"I hope it doesn't have to come to that."

Presently they found themselves in the drawing-room having tea. David, who was spending the weekend with Grace in Mrs. Dermott's lately acquired house in Kelvinside, had come across to pay Henry his respects.

Grace was doing splendidly, he told Henry. But did not much care to be out of the immediate reach of her mother and the best professional attention now.

Talk at once turned to the disaster. Yes, it was fully confirmed. David had special information. The papers would tell everything in the morning.

Now Henry was all questions. What had happened? Where had the weakness been? What was the speed of the train as it crossed the bridge? What was the force of the wind? Questions that David could not answer.

"I think I'll run through to Newport tomorrow and have a look at the damage myself," Henry said.

Bel looked at Phœbe. She did not seem to mind.

V

Bel had come to call upon her mother for several reasons this morning. The first one was filial. The old lady had a sharp attack of gout, and had, at the last moment, sent apologies and regrets that she felt unable to attend the wedding of Phœbe to Henry Hayburn, which, hastily arranged, had taken place in the drawing-room of Grosvenor Terrace yesterday. Bel had felt that it would be the next thing to cruelty not to drop down to Monteith Row, on this the morning after, to enquire for her mother's health and give her the gossip.

Again, having assured herself that the tradesmen had already done their part in restoring her house to its usual, Bel had felt it more tactful to leave her maid-servants, tired and out of temper, to take their own time to dust, sweep and add the final polish.

But there was yet another reason for coming out this morning; one she had not yet defined to herself. There had been a feeling of emptiness in the house; a feeling that Phœbe was gone. Presently, when she got back for lunch, she would have to face this fact. But here, sitting drinking tea in her mother's familiar room, the truth could be pushed away for a little longer.

Bel sat, willingly telling the old lady what she expected to hear. Yes, Phœbe had made a beautiful bride. Mrs. Barrowfield's own grandchildren had been the best behaved. Mary McNairn was getting ridiculously fat. George McNairn must have something organically wrong with him. If Bel were Mary, she would have George thoroughly examined again. Sophia had actually brought that dreadful muff. And in other respects had looked quite inexcusably shabby. After all, William was not a pauper. Yes, Mrs. Dermott had come too, having shed mourning for the occasion. She had been majestic, but amiable, and had renewed her Christmas-dinner friendship with Margaret Ruanthorpe-Moorhouse, which had been all to the good, as they had mopped each other up. David had come with his mother-in-law, Grace being indisposed and disinclined to come. Stephen Hayburn, looking more settled and sensible than formerly, had been his brother's best man.

"And Henry himself would be looking gey glaikit?"

Bel stiffened a little. Really, her mother used some very old-fashioned expressions sometimes. Why couldn't she say "rather stupid"? Her daughter wished she wouldn't. The children would be picking them up, and their little school friends in Kelvinside simply wouldn't know what they meant. Broad Scotch was so unrefined. But she knew that remonstrance would merely rouse opposition, and contented herself by saying primly: "No. I don't think Henry *did* look specially awkward. But his work has changed him, you know. He's much more of a man than he used to be."

The old woman sat ruminating for a moment. She was thinking of Henry's visits on those frustrated, impatient evenings last summer. It was odd how this young man, a comparative stranger to her, had made for himself a place in her affections. Odd, when she considered how set she was in her ways. Yet Henry's sudden need of her, coupled with his almost simple-minded honesty, had won her over. She looked at her daughter.

"Phœbe is very fond of Henry," she said at length.

Bel looked at the clock. She stood up. "Yes, I realised that for the first time on the night Henry came home." She drew on her gloves and took up her furs. "Still, Phœbe is so young, I dare say people will blame me. But I felt I was taking too much responsibility if I tried to stop it. Arthur felt the same. And Phœbe can be so self-willed. She might even have taken things into her own hands."

Mrs. Barrowfield smiled. This side of Phœbe appealed to her.

She kissed Bel, patted her on the shoulder, and assured her that, knowing the young people as she did, there was nothing else to be done; that they were good bairns; and that everything would turn out for the best.

VI

Little Isabel and Thomas Moorhouse were standing on the doorstep as their mother arrived back at Grosvenor Terrace. Sarah had, in spite of upheavals, found time to take them for their morning walk in the Botanic Gardens, and they were just come back. The children jumped and waved at the sight of the carriage, and at once begged Bel to allow them to climb up beside

McCrimmon into the driving-seat and drive round to the coach-house in the lane. Bel cautioned them that it must be nearly their dinner-time, told them to hurry and passed on into the house.

Everything was put back and in order. All the signs of Phœbe's wedding had been removed. Yet the house was strange. Bel caught herself humming a tune to keep her spirits up, as she went from room to room inspecting. The dining-room, the back parlour. And on the first floor, the drawing-room. Everything had been set aright. On the top floor she hesitated. Out of cowardice, she went into the children's rooms first. The nursery. Where, by the way, was her son Arthur? His school bag was lying in his room. She called his name but there was no reply.

At last she turned the handle of Phœbe's room and went in. It, too, had been put into some kind of order. Cardboard boxes and tissue paper had been stacked on the bed. On a chair there was an old dress, that seemed almost part of Phœbe herself. Bel took it up to shake it out, then, surprised by a quick emotion, laid it hurriedly down again, telling herself not to be a fool.

As she turned to go she was startled by a sound. She cast her eyes about her. There was nothing to be seen. She looked behind the window curtains. Then at last beneath the bed, where she found her eight-year-old son Arthur lying on his stomach.

"Arthur, what are you doing there, frightening the life out of me? Why didn't you answer when I called?"

The boy crawled out reluctantly. His face was swollen, grubby and tear-stained.

"Arthur, what's wrong?"

He did not answer.

"Did you get a whipping at school this morning?"

He shook his head.

"Are you ill with eating too much yesterday?"

Again he shook his head.

"Well, it must be something. What is it?"

Arthur did not reply. He stood looking red and sheepish. His mother examined him, puzzled. Arthur was getting a big boy now. He didn't often cry.

"Is it because your Aunt Phœbe's gone away?"

A fresh welling of tears gave Bel her answer. Really, this was ridiculous! She felt herself going, too, now! She held her son to her, and indulged herself for one long, luxurious minute. Suddenly she had an inward picture of Phœbe looking at them, glum and scornful, as only Phœbe could look. In the middle of her weeping, she began to laugh.

"Arthur," she said, "do you know what your Aunt Phœbe would say if she were here?"

"What, Mamma?"

"She would tell us both to stop being silly and go and wash our faces!"

Chapter Seven

THEY had arrived last night, and had come to this inexpensive little hotel in the Domgasse. It was after nine on their first morning in Vienna. Now, as they stood in their bedroom, they could hear the outside wings of the double doors open, and then a knock. Henry Hayburn, engineer, of Glasgow, Scotland, not quite loath to show off his accomplishments before this, his newly acquired wife, shouted in German: "Come in!"

A homely young porter in a striped waistcoat and a green baize apron, with thick blond hair tumbling over his sweating, over-worked brow, begged pardon a thousand times, but might he inform the gracious gentleman that there was yet another gracious gentleman awaiting his pleasure in the hall downstairs.

All this fine speech, rendered less formal by the slovenly, endearing dialect of Vienna, conveyed nothing to Mrs. Henry Hayburn, but her husband took care to show her that it conveyed something to himself. He took the card the boy held out and read the name: "Maximilian Hirsch". The gentleman downstairs had said it would give him great pleasure to be presented likewise to the gracious lady, the porter added, quite unbashfully casting approving, friendly eyes over Phœbe.

"That's the boss. You had better come down and see him," Henry said, turning to his wife. "Immediately," he added, addressing the porter, who thereupon bowed himself out.

As Henry and Phœbe made their way downstairs, Maximilian Hirsch came forward, to greet them. He had not seen Phœbe on the day of his visit to Duntrafford. The sight of this beautiful child Henry had brought back filled him with interest.

"Mrs. Hayburn!" He bent over Phœbe's hand and raised it to his lips.

Phœbe blushed scarlet. This behaviour was so very foreign. Her look sought help from Henry. Henry shut one eye.

Like many of her race, Phœbe was suspicious of extreme politeness. But this dark-skinned man of fifty, with his shock of black hair, his coat with its astrakhan collar, and his carefully pronounced, foreign English, seemed friendly enough. Besides, Henry's employer must be shown respect. Awakening to her responsibilities as a married woman, Phœbe did her best.

Yes, they had arrived late last night at the Nordwest Bahnhof, she told him. It had been a somewhat cold journey, but interesting. They had sailed from Leith. They had spent a night in Hamburg and a night in Berlin. Yes, it was all very new to her indeed. No, Phœbe had never been out of Scotland before.

She seemed a very direct sort of young woman, this, Herr Hirsch decided. Her first embarrassment had passed at once. It had, obviously, been superficial. There was no need to set her at her ease. She was at her ease already. Her figure was girlish and appealing in the close-shaped dress of dark green stuff with its prim little cuffs and collars. Her beauty was unusual. She seemed neither forward nor reserved. And she had charm. Not the warm, sophisticated charm of Vienna, but rather the cool, inconsequent charm of a half-wild thing.

"I am sorry, Mrs. Hayburn, I must take your husband away with me now. But it will give me great pleasure if you and he will have supper with me some evening soon."

Phœbe smiled assent.

Mrs. Hayburn was not overtired after her long journey?

Mrs. Hayburn laughed. Of course not. Everything was far too interesting for her to be tired.

Well, very soon, then. Herr Hirsch bent down and raised her hand once more to his lips.

Henry kissed her. "You're sure you'll be all right, dear?" he said possessively.

Again Phœbe laughed. "Of course! What would you do if I said I wouldn't be all right? Take me back home?"

Maximilian Hirsch had already swung himself through the outer glass door into the street. Henry hurried after him. As they went, Phœbe, much to the surprise of the head porter, turned, and, forgetting she was a married lady with a dignity to maintain, caught her skirts and bounded upstairs with the agility of a cat.

Back in her room in a matter of seconds, she stood in the centre of it humming to herself. Then she turned to the double windows, flung them open, and stepped out on the crisp, dry snow which lay on the little balcony outside. She was in time to see Henry striding round the corner, out of the Domgasse.

Standing there in the glittering snow and sunshine, Phœbe was suddenly, astonishingly, caught up in a flame of tenderness—tenderness for the young man she had just seen disappearing. She had never felt so light, so uplifted. With surprise it came to her that, for this instant in time, she was completely happy. That a joy, new, yearning and radiant, had taken possession of her.

She loved Henry, then. She had never before been quite sure. She had been sorry for Henry; had faith in Henry; fought for Henry. But now all these feelings were as nothing to this shining, consecrated joy, that was to stamp itself upon her memory and remain with her for ever.

For a time she stood in the blinding, winter sunshine, taking in nothing of what she saw about her, wrapped in this unexpected ecstasy. But at last the sting of the cold air brought her back to the world. She returned to her room, flung her long travelling coat round her, and came out again to see what was to be seen.

She leant on the balustrade looking up and down the street. It seemed strangely quiet here, to be in the heart of a great city. One or two children hurried along chattering; as little understandable as monkeys. Strange little children, in unfamiliar clothes. She could see a fat woman in the house opposite, with her hair in curl-papers, plumping just such another feather-balloon as they had on their own bed here. From a passage-way at the top of the street a man appeared. He must certainly be an officer. He came down towards her. What a magnificent creature he looked in his long black cloak, swinging open to reveal his green uniform, his slim-drawn waist, and his trousers cut so tight that they revealed his leg muscles! He might have been a figure in an operetta. But he had too much of an air; too much insolent distinction. As he passed beneath her he cast up black, questing eyes.

Bells that seemed to come from the sky joined themselves to the jangle from other churches, then struck ten. Phœbe twisted herself about, and just managed to see a tall spire almost above her. Filled with curiosity, she withdrew from the balcony to find out her whereabouts in a guide-book Henry had left with her. That must be the spire of the Church of Saint Stephen. Now the cobweb-patterned map of this new city had become a challenge in her hands. She must go out! Out into Vienna!

II

She must go out into this snow-clad, glittering city, into the sunshine to meet the new life that was to give her so much happiness!

But first she must set their luggage to rights. They had come late last night, and gone to bed very tired. She must tidy up this queer room, with its red plush sofa, its worn carpet, its shabby gilt chairs, its stove instead of a fireplace, which was to be their home until they could make better arrangements. An odd room, but not unfriendly; and the centre now of her universe.

She picked up the clothes that Henry had thrown off after his journey. They were new—hastily bought while he was at home. But already they were redolent of Henry's soap, Henry's tobacco, Henry's person. Already they had taken on creases from Henry's body. It pleased her to touch them, to fold them away. Life must go on like this. Things must never change. But with the thought of change, a breath of doubt blew through her mind. No, that was ridiculous. Of course things must change. Yet they need not change for the worse. Besides, no one expected to live on pinnacles for ever.

But she must hurry into her outdoor clothes, and have a first glance at this city she had come to live in. As she descended, the porter came round from behind his desk in the entrance, and asked in halting English if he might call a *Komfortable* for Madame. A *Komfortable*, he condescended to inform Madame's ignorance, was a one-horse cab. Madame thanked him—no. She was just going out for a walk. He bowed, held the door open for her, then returned to his desk.

She was charming, this girl, with her good but not quite fashionable clothes, and her fearless eyes, he said to himself, conducting one of his many little one-sided conversations, as was his habit to alleviate boredom. Now, if she were Viennese, what couldn't she look like? But, then, British women seemed to take a delight in throwing away their assets.

In a few moments Phœbe had found herself in the square surrounding the Cathedral of Saint Stephen. People were hurrying across it. Some two or three were going into the great church itself. Was a service beginning, or did the churches here, quite unlike the churches at home, remain open all the time? She must ask, because she wanted to have a look inside. What beautiful flowers in that window, still half-clouded with morning frost! Hothouse flowers they must be. Presently she was examining with rapture the shops, some of them world famous for their elegance, first in the Graben and then in the Kärntnerstrasse. She went from one window to the other, her face glowing with cold, her heart singing within her. She was young, she was feminine, she was having her first sight of Vienna. And in an hour or two she was going back to have lunch with her husband.

Now what was this great building on her right? She crossed and walked round to the front of it. She looked at her plan. It was the Opera House. Sometime she and Henry must go to a performance, just to see the inside of the building. She looked at a playbill and was able to deduce the words "Lohengrin" and "Wagner" from the angular Gothic scrip. "The new music," she said to herself, feeling gaily erudite.

And this must be the Ringstrasse, if she were following her book aright. What a great, beautiful street! How wide and imposing, with its fine buildings and its young trees sparkling in the snow!

What a strange little tram-trolley, with the bells of the horses jingling all the time! It was stopping near her. Should she get in and let it take her where it chose? No. Her husband had warned her not to lose herself. She must, she told herself demurely, do what her husband told her. And there was more than enough to see if she merely walked about.

Tingling with adventure, Phœbe went along the Opernring. The air was cold but exhilarating. The snow flew up in a dry powder at the touch of her foot. Presently she came to the Hofgarten. The wintry branches of its trees stood up like white coral.

The new palace was still only on paper, and thus Phœbe, looking across the immense open space made by Palace Gardens, parks and squares, to the distant heights of Kahlenberg, wondered if she had suddenly come to the edge of the city. But glimpses of other, distant buildings through the snowy trees prompted her to continue along the Burgring through that quarter of the city which, more than any other, had but lately come to be the final expression of Habsburg magnificence.

Even now, as she passed along, Phœbe could see that some of the public buildings were not yet completed. There was scaffolding, but little work appeared to be going on. Winter must have brought it to a standstill. But what grandeur! There was so much to see! To explore!

It was strange Henry had said so little of all this. But then, of course, Henry had been preoccupied. And who, better than herself, knew just how preoccupied Henry could be? That was a part of his make-up. And on this shining morning she would not have changed a hair of her husband's head.

At the corner of the Volksgarten she halted for a moment to look about her. Inside the garden itself old women were sweeping the paths clear of their latest powdering of snow. In the stillness she could hear the voices of children playing. She would go in, cut across it, and get back to her hotel through the Inner City.

The air was so still that the slenderest twigs stood motionless, each one bearing upon it its feathery burden of snow. Their pale tracery glittered against the blue of the sky. Brought to life by the burst of sunshine, starlings chattered in the evergreens, and among the fir-trees whose dark branches sagged beneath their white burden. Now and then a bird would fly into the open, making a little cloud of silver dust, as the powdered, displaced snow hung for an instant in the sunlight.

Here in this magic garden it was almost hot. Would she be crazy if she brushed away the snow from one of these seats and sat down for a moment? Three pale, over-disciplined little boys, in dark green coats with sable collars, passed her walking hand-in-hand beside a fashionable governess. A young man, who might be a student, arm-in-arm with a young girl, both of them smiling as they went. A soldier of some cavalry regiment, in long coat and spurred boots. He turned to look at the young woman, sitting here unattended in the winter sunshine, and permitted himself the homage of a smile. The strange, blue eyes remained cool and impersonal as he passed on. Then two women, very elegantly dressed, deep in gossip.

It was beautiful in this hushed, foreign garden, with its strange, snow-covered temple. Beautiful. Far away. Unreal and strange. What was she, Phœbe Moorhouse, doing here? No, not Phœbe Moorhouse, Phœbe Hayburn. At this time exactly a week ago she was dressing for her wedding. All the familiar faces had been about her then. Now, in this place of white stillness, Phœbe asked herself if she would choose that the past week—the week during which she had been Henry's wife—should be taken back and forgotten. She smiled to herself. Her strange moment of ecstasy on the balcony this morning came back to her. No. Something would snap now, if Henry were taken from her. Her husband. The impetuous, yet oddly sensitive male creature, who took her into his arms in the darkness; who was grateful to her for being a woman. A new Henry. But one she would not change. He had shown forbearance and a great tenderness, and out of these things her love for him had put forth a hot, Maytime bud, and burst—it would seem suddenly—into full bloom.

A puff of wind brushed the garden, blowing a light cloud of dry snow before it. She must not risk taking cold through sitting here any longer. She passed by the Ballhaus Platz and the Michaeler Platz into the Kohlmarkt. Here there were still more fine shops to be examined. Italian silk. Bohemian glass. Hungarian leather. Everything that was rich, elegant, unusual. And now here she was in the Graben once more! Phœbe laughed to herself. She had actually recognised it. She was getting to know Vienna! The pealing of bells warned her that it was midday. Henry had said he hoped to get back early. Another look at those shops she had already seen. That fine china. That strange embroidery. Those flowers.

But Henry might have come back, and would be wondering where she had gone to. As she turned into the quiet of the Domgasse, she saw her husband at the front door of their little hotel, waiting for her, bareheaded in the sunshine.

Chapter Eight

IT was a quarter to seven in the evening two days later. Maximilian Hirsch pushed his way through the glass doors of a restaurant in the Kärntnerring. He stood for a moment, blinking in the light, while a waiting doorman hastened to relieve him of his heavy fur coat. He thanked the man with what would have been stiff formality, had his thanks not been spoken in the Viennese dialect which proclaimed him one with the fellow-citizen he was addressing. Was the restaurant full? he asked. There was still room for the gracious gentleman in this dining-room, the man said, indicating a door.

Maximilian thanked him. And there was just one other thing. A foreign young lady and gentleman would ask for him about seven. Would the man be so good as to let him know when they arrived? Meantime he would see about a table.

Maximilian came here only when he had people to entertain. At other times he ate at a restaurant of long standing in the Griechengasse, where he was a *Stammgast* or regular diner. There he found comfort, pleasant familiarity, his own table, and cooking to turn the brain. But this town-man's restaurant was no place for strangers. Indeed, a young lady like Frau Hayburn, who, along with her husband, was to be his guest tonight, would have been more than out of place among the sybarites of the Griechengasse.

Besides, this here, was one of the famous restaurants of Vienna. It was a place for Frau Hayburn to see. He called for an aperitif—a pleasant, un-Viennese custom he had learnt in Paris—and sat holding it in his plump white hand, sipping it now and then and looking about him. Yes, all these mirrors, this gilt, brocaded furniture, these glittering gaseliers, that soft music, was far more for a young woman than the subtleties of cooking.

As he sat waiting, his black eyes met the eyes of one or two acquaintances, and each inclined towards the other with conventional bows. This place was the restaurant of finance and wealthy business. It was of the first class, but the aristocracy did not haunt it, as they haunted Hopfners in the Kärntnerstrasse or Sacher's near the Opera. Here Maximilian was on his own social level, and, as a typical man of Vienna—that city of so many sharply defined grades of society—it had never occurred to him to risk the unpleasantness of a snub. His wealthy, middle-class bachelorhood suited him excellently. He much preferred savouring life to wrestling with it.

The strong waters he was tasting gave him a comfortable glow. The hidden orchestra was playing a homely, old-fashioned waltz. It might have been written by Lanner, or his partner the elder Strauss, Maximilian reflected. At any rate, it wasn't a waltz such as, in these days, the younger Strauss was writing—heady, compelling stuff, that was sweeping the town. No; it had the heavy, simple rhythm of a peasants' round dance. Maximilian beat a finger thoughtfully on the damask table-cover. He encouraged the music to rouse the pleasant ache of memory.

Thirty years ago. He had been twenty, and he had gone with fellow-students to Grinzing to drink the fresh-pressed grape, mix with the workpeople, and dance with the girls. Perhaps they had played this tune then. It seemed elusively familiar, and brought things back. It had been early autumn, and he and his girl of the evening had stayed all night in the woods. He remembered the dawn as it came up out of Russia. He remembered the early morning birds, and the sunshine beginning to strike through the beech leaves. He even remembered the face of his blonde companion. Why did that music bring back these things so clearly?

And yet he had had a very good fifty years of it. During the first forty of these he had stayed with his mother in a villa in Penzing near the Palace of Schönbrunn. At her death, and now being a man of substance, he had removed his easy existence to an expensive flat in the Inner City. His windows had a view of the Minoriten Church and the open space that surrounded it. In addition to being within walking distance of the bank, he was now within walking distance of the Opera and most of the theatres. Like most educated Viennese, his interest in these places was fanatical.

Thus he had fashioned the pattern of his life—a pattern easy for an intelligent, wealthy citizen to weave in this graceful, culture-loving, pleasure-mongering city. Some imperial pride; a real and perceptive interest in the art of the opera singer and the actor; much excellent eating; some selective drinking. Kindness and good manners; some cynicism; much self-indulgence. No attempt to pierce the iron defences of circles, intellectual or aristocratic, to which he did not belong. Pleasant affairs—a sin hidden is quite forgiven—and just as much work as would keep him going.

The band had finished its nostalgic music. Maximilian Hirsch pulled out his fine gold watch, flicked it open, and looked at the time. It was after seven now. What had happened to the Hayburns? Oh, there they were! He jumped to his feet. As they were led towards him, he saw that they had seen him and were grinning, a little gauchely, as they came.

A broad smile of welcome overspread his smooth, dark face as he advanced to greet these two denizens of another world.

II

Maximilian liked to think of himself as a taster of life. He liked to see himself, a highly civilised citizen of a highly civilised city, sampling, appraising, measuring—places, peoples and manners—with his own urbane, tolerant yardstick; savouring the bouquet of them as he would savour the bouquet of a wine he did not know.

Tonight he was enjoying himself. They were something fresh for him, these two. The quality of the young man he already knew. He was quick and decisive in his work. He had enterprise, and that strange, British seriousness that had no play-acting about it. So far as young Herr Hayburn's work was concerned, Maximilian was receiving what he paid for. He had been no dilettante when he had engaged this young man. But Maximilian had long satisfied himself about this. It was not Henry's constructive talents that filled his mind now.

He sat in his corner smiling genially upon his guests, rotating the stem of his wine-glass with his finger and thumb, and looking on the luxurious stir in the room beyond. At a nearby table, a party which had dined early in order to reach their box in the

Opera before the first act was over was rising to go. Laughter. Perfume. The rustle of silks. The aroma from long Viennese cigars. Discreet music. Waiters hurrying to and fro. Stacked plates. Service wagons. Pails of ice. Flowers. Well-dressed men, prosperous and polite. Their women; charming, young, and dependent; or old, influential and bedizened. If, like Maximilian, you understood some of the relationships behind these good manners, it was all the more entertaining. No; his business relationship with the Hayburns did not concern him tonight. He saw them as a new and amusing type, lit with a flame that gave forth, somehow, a different light from the brilliance around them. They did not conform to the Anglo-Saxon pattern he was accustomed to. Particularly the girl, with her dark blue, strangely set eyes, that were avidly taking in everything around her. He must find out what she was thinking.

And they seemed so simple, so artless. At their naïve request that he should choose for them, he had ordered a meal of *Backhendl* followed by *Salzburger Nockerl.* They were eating these things with appetite, but no special show of interest. Their glasses of *Voeslauer* were scarcely touched.

The orchestra was playing snatches from a Mozart opera. Unconsciously, Mrs. Hayburn was beating time as her hand lay on the table.

"Do you like Mozart, Mrs. Hayburn?"

"I beg your pardon? Do I like—?"

"Do you like the music of Mozart?"

"Yes, I like all music."

He saw that she did not recognise the composer of this fragment. "Perhaps you did not hear much music in Glasgow? But now that you have come to Vienna—"

"Oh yes, we had splendid concerts in Glasgow. We used to go sometimes."

"But here, in Vienna, you can hear everything! The best! Opera, concerts—!" Maximilian shrugged and cast eyes of wonder and appreciation heavenwards.

"Yes, I hope we'll have time."

Time! Would a young woman with a single drop of Vienna running in her veins have talked about having time? "My dear young lady! It is your duty!"

For reply Phœbe smiled with respectful indulgence. After all, she could not be expected to argue with Henry's employer. Besides, foreign though Mr. Hirsch might be, he could not possibly be quite serious.

Maximilian drained his glass, asked them if their food and wine were to their taste, received quite formal assurances, and decided it was no easy matter putting himself into accord with these strange young people.

And yet she was lovely, this child. Put her in the hands of a good dressmaker, teach her to moderate, to mix with graciousness the suddenness of her manners, let her pick up the small change of conversation, and she would become enchanting.

He was following this train of thought when he made his next remark. "I must present you to my aunts, Mrs. Hayburn. They are much older than you, of course, but they can teach you about our wonderful Vienna."

Phœbe murmured that she would be very pleased.

No. A strange, gauche creature, who had everything to learn. "And where are you going to stay, Mr. Hayburn? You are still in your little hotel, yes?"

Phœbe answered for him. "Henry had quite a nice room before he was married. He thinks we might go back there."

"What! To the Quellengasse in the Favoriten? Impossible!"

She was looking at him directly now—regarding him gaily with those strange eyes of hers. "Why?"

"But it is a workmen's quarter! You have your lives to live! The shops! The theatres! You will make friends! You cannot receive in the Favoriten!"

"But, Mr. Hirsch, Henry and I are here to work, not to play!" She was so earnest, so charmingly young, that he leant over and patted her hand.

"But you must play, too, my dear child. It would be much waste for you only to be serious, here in Vienna."

A cloud he did not understand passed across her face. "Henry has his way to make," was all she said in reply.

But her host was quick to note that, a moment afterwards, her eyes were full of eager amusement as a bejewelled woman entered the room flaunting a scarlet ostrich fan.

"Henry! Would you look at the size of that fan!"

At last she was understandably charming. Her eyes were sparkling now like those of any other young woman. He wondered what she would say if she knew this woman's history, and the aristocratic names of those who had given her her finery. Yes. He must do something about the education of this lovely barbarian.

III

It was a very few days after this that Phœbe had an envelope handed her by the porter of her hotel. She had just come back from one of her many solitary walks of exploration. It was time for lunch, she was very cold and hungry and, remembering that Henry had said he would be too busy to have his midday meal with her, rather more lonely than she cared to admit.

The envelope was addressed to her in a strange, spidery hand. She tore it open. For a moment it was difficult for her to make out the writing. But reading it through more than once, the full sense became plain. It was a message in stiffly phrased, imperfect English, inviting her to come to the Paulanergasse in the Wieden on the following day. The writer signed herself Stephanie Hirsch, described herself as the aunt of Maximilian Hirsch, and hoped that Mrs. Hayburn would do her sister and herself the honour of taking the midday meal with them. Further, the writer asked Mrs. Hayburn's pardon for inviting her thus informally, and might she assure her that no disrespect was meant? But, as her sister was no longer young, and as she, the writer, was inclined in winter to a chest complaint, they neither of them went out any more than was quite unavoidable. Being "English", perhaps Mrs. Hayburn would find it easier to overlook this unconventionality, and dispense with the ladies' failing to pay a first ceremonial call upon her. If Mrs. Hayburn accepted, the carriage would be sent for her tomorrow.

Mrs. Hayburn had no difficulty whatever in overlooking the daring unconventionality of the aunts of Maximilian Hirsch. From the letter, she suspected that the ladies might be somewhat alarming, but already she was becoming tired of being left so much to herself. She sat down, then, to write them a note of grateful acceptance, which her friend the porter undertook to have delivered.

At half-past eleven next morning a carriage, drawn by handsome Russian horses, came to a standstill before the door of the hotel in the Domgasse, and Phœbe was conveyed to the apartments in the Wieden.

An avuncular house-porter, middle-aged and benign, and treating her with that combination of respect and approval which is one of the charms of simpler Vienna, led Phœbe up the old-fashioned stone stairs to the flat on the first floor.

Presently Phœbe found herself in an ante-room, the window of which overlooked the street. Being alone, she gazed about her. It was a very strange sort of place indeed. More a museum than anything else, she decided, and certainly the last sort of room she had expected two elderly ladies to possess.

It was essentially a male room. Apart from the curtains at the window of double glass—the inner ones elaborately looped-up lace, the main ones of plain red baize—there was little that would not have been appropriate in a mountain hunting-box. The chairs were stretched with worn leather, and studded with many brass nails. A skin took the place of a rug on the floor of polished hardwood. But most amazing of all to Phœbe were the heads of foxes, the heads of chamois, the antlers of stags, and even the head of a wild boar, which hung from the walls. There were several daguerreotypes in plush or gilt frames, depicting an old, but apparently vigorous gentleman in Tyrolese costume. Occupying the place of honour in the midst of these was an oleograph of the young Emperor Franz Joseph himself, wearing a Styrian hunter's hat, with its shining black-cock plumes, and a long grey hunter's cape, from beneath the fold of which the muzzle of a sporting gun protruded.

Phœbe was examining these things with curiosity, when she became aware of the rustle of silk behind her. She turned in confusion. A tall, thin lady of sixty-five was standing very erect, holding out her hand and smiling.

"Mrs. Hayburn, no? It is a pleasure that you come!"

She was surely the most civilised human being Phœbe had ever seen. Her stiff black dress was bustled, although this was not the fashion of the year; it was severe and unadorned—unless the little crucifix on a fine gold chain might be called an adornment. Her poised head, with the well-tended grey hair cut to a fringe that came low on her brow. Her smile that seemed just to have won the battle for kindly tolerance against instinctive disdain. Her white hands. Phœbe felt uncouth and provincial.

"You look at the picture of our dear father, yes? He is dead already twenty years. He hunted very much. He arranged this room, and we do not change it. This is the Kaiser, Franz Joseph, no? My dear father had allowance to hunt several times in his private lands."

The tall lady seemed inordinately proud of this fact, as she led the way through the door, whence, presumably, she had come. As she followed her, Phœbe did her best to respond by making appropriate, awestruck noises.

Now they were in a larger room, carpeted and more feminine. At a round cherry-wood table, a little bent lady, who seemed much older, was sewing.

"My sister, Helene, Mrs. Hayburn."

The elder lady did not get up. She merely gave Phœbe her hand, and bestowed upon her a smile of benignity resembling her sister's. "Do you speak German, please?" she asked in a voice of great gentleness using the German tongue.

Phœbe shook her head.

"Tell her I can't speak English, Stephanie," Fräulein Hirsch said to her sister, once again taking up her embroidery. "You must be our interpreter."

"You look at this room, too, Mrs. Hayburn?" Fräulein Stephanie asked, seeing Phœbe look about her.

"It's beautiful!" Phœbe's eyes went everywhere. The cherry-wood furniture, elegant and frail; the faded striped coverings; the china and bric-à-brac; the coloured glass in its special cabinet; the silhouette portraits and miniatures hung in thin gilt frames against striped walls; the faded carpet of lime green with garlands of roses; the white porcelain stove. It was a room of pale tones, but, with many fresh spring flowers, it was friendly and charming.

"I am glad that you like it." The Viennese woman was pleased. "It is old. Our mother was young in the Biedermeier times. Except for photographs and piano, we keep this room old, too. Most young people who come—" She shrugged and smiled with sad indulgence. "*Na?* You will come now, please?"

Lunch had been announced.

IV

Phœbe found herself in the dining-room of the flat. It, too, was old-fashioned, but elegant, and there was no doubt about its dignity. A very old man, who had been their father's personal servant, waited upon the ladies. She noted with interest his blue tail-coat, his brass buttons and the white cotton gloves he wore as he handed dishes.

All this was old, established and strange. But Phœbe found herself responding; enjoying this new adventure; taking pleasure in the company of these stiff, but not uncharming women. The yellow muscatel wine, that the man-servant had poured out for her unasked, expanded her senses.

"I'm very new to Vienna," she found herself saying. "If I make mistakes, you must tell me."

"No. A young lady so charming is not able to make mistakes, Mrs. Hayburn."

She was beautiful, this girl, Stephanie Hirsch decided. Beautiful, and likeable. And although her manners seemed casual, they were not rude, neither were they quite English. Did the Scots, then, differ from the English in these things? Phœbe's youth moved her as she had not been moved for long. It would give her pleasure to take her guest under her wing, help her, if she would allow it. Max, their nephew, had been quite right to ask them to receive her.

"No, please! You do things so differently. It would be very kind of you to tell me." (What would Bel have said to this? Phœbe begging to be taught manners!) "You see, there are so many things I don't know. You could help me so much."

It is flattering to be asked for guidance. And none the less so if one is old and conventional, with the best of life beyond recall. And especially when she who asks for guidance is young, quick and full of red blood. Fräulein Stephanie knew that most Viennese young women of Phœbe's looks and age would have taken little pleasure in coming here to her backwater in the Paulanergasse. But she guessed that this foreign girl might be somewhat lonely, somewhat bewildered, somewhat directionless, despite—or perhaps, indeed, because of—her very recent marriage, and the great changes it had brought her.

And thus an unlikely friendship between Phœbe and Stephanie Hirsch sprang up. After their meal the elder sister went to rest, while Phœbe, pressed to remain, sat with the younger, listening and learning.

The relatives at home would not have known this Phœbe. And yet it was the same Phœbe, impelled by a sudden new enthusiasm, enjoying a new experience—a feeling of play-acting, perhaps, a feeling that now she was doing something that those at home would never do.

She had drunk her afternoon coffee, said her farewell, and promised to come soon again and bring her husband with her. Now she found herself once more sitting in the well-preserved, old-fashioned carriage.

As it clattered over the snowy cobbles, Phœbe smiled to herself. She was delighted—childishly gleeful, indeed—over her visit. Her husband did not know everything about Vienna! She was opening up ground on her own account now, learning customs she had known nothing of. Her long talk with Stephanie Hirsch had been warm and instructive.

In the last days she had been secretly doubtful of what the future would hold for her. It was very well to be brave and spirited. But these things did not make up for lack of experience, nor, for that matter, for quite blank ignorance. Today she had found another woman she could turn to. A strange, rather stiff foreign woman, perhaps, but one with whom she found herself in sympathy. And she was grateful. The thought, indeed, gave more comfort than Phœbe's courage liked to admit to Phœbe's nineteen years.

Chapter Nine

THEIR first quarrel since their marriage. Before it, Henry and Phœbe had spent much of their time together in adolescent bickerings, as two much attached school friends might bicker.

But now their new awareness of each other made disagreement different. These hot young people were now so much of one flesh that the inevitable divergences which, sooner or later, must arise from the clash of their strong wills could not but cause them surprise and pain.

The quarrel took place after Phœbe's return from the Hirsch ladies. Henry had come back to the hotel in the Domgasse with news. His tutor and interpreter, Willi Pommer, had appeared this morning, and he had gone out to lunch with him. Herr Pommer had brought word from the Quellengasse. The good Herr and Frau Klem were well; and Pepi, despite some show of what Willi was solemnly pleased to call high spirits, had, at last, consented to become formally betrothed to himself.

Even Henry, who was no reader of other people's hearts, wondered a little at the point of view Willi was taking; at the Austrian's strange, and what seemed almost insensitive satisfaction over his now nearly certain hopes of becoming the possessor of a modest dowry, and the pretty little wife that went along with it. But Henry had long since learnt to accept divergences of outlook in this unaccountable city, and if they did not directly concern himself, he saw no reason to harass his mind with them.

And Herr Pommer had brought a message from the Klems to Herr Hayburn. They hoped that he would do them the great honour of coming to see them, and of bringing the gracious lady with him. The Klems had become very attached to Henry Hayburn, Willi assured him—rather to Henry's surprise—and naturally they would be much interested to meet the wife he had so recently brought back. In addition, there were books, papers and clothes belonging to Herr Hayburn at the Quellengasse. Frau Klem was a little surprised he had not been to see after these, and would be glad to know what he intended to do about them.

Henry now took the opportunity of asking Herr Pommer's advice. Would it not, didn't he think, be a good idea if he and Phœbe went back to the Quellengasse to live for a time? Since he had returned to Vienna, Henry had been so much occupied with his work at the factory, with showing his wife Vienna, and in settling down to marriage generally, that he had had little time to think of more permanent lodgings. Now he had come to a point where everything must be sacrificed to his work. His wife understood this perfectly; and did not Herr Pommer think that she would do better to be under Frau Klem's wing, than struggling alone, or more doubtfully befriended, in unknown rooms elsewhere?

Herr Pommer certainly thought so. The gracious lady had the language to study. He would find her a suitable teacher, and Pepi, of course, would help while she was still there, which would not be—his face flushed with complacent self-consciousness—for very long, he hoped. And when she was gone, perhaps they could have Pepi's room as well. He was sure that his future mother-in-law was anything but grasping. She would be glad to let them have it for very little more.

If Willi seemed, at this point, rather to have taken upon himself the role of calculating son-in-law, Henry was too well aware of the advantages he was setting forth to let this disturb him. Yes, Frau Klem's was certainly the place for Phœbe and himself. He was in no doubt about this whatever. Though the room he had occupied would be somewhat cramped, Phœbe was as anxious to save money as he was. Indeed, she, herself, had already spoken of going to the Klems. If the good Frau Klem would but have them, Henry was certain his wife would be as delighted with the idea as he was.

But in that certainty he was wrong. And this was not the reason for their quarrel.

He had no sooner suggested that they should, this very evening, settle their permanent headquarters, than he was made aware of the fact that Phœbe had been having ideas put into her head by the aunts of Maximilian Hirsch.

"But, Henry, the younger Miss Hirsch says that only working people live out in the Favoriten."

"Well, we're working people, aren't we? We're here to work, anyway."

"Oh, you're trying not to understand me! You know perfectly well what I mean." Phœbe, flushed and angry, turned from the long glass in front of which she was brushing her hair before going down to supper.

Henry was on the edge of their bed, still in the thick, fur-lined coat the Viennese winter had forced him to buy. He got up and began to struggle out of it moodily. "We haven't come out here to live like swells, anyway," he grumbled. His wife's unexpected opposition in this, his new world of tenderness, shocked his senses more than he cared to admit. But that was no reason for giving way.

"Of course not, Henry. But after all, as Miss Hirsch says, we're young and have our lives to live."

"Lives to live? What does she mean?"

"Well, enjoy ourselves a little, and cultivate our minds, Henry!"

"I never heard such rubbish! The way to live your life is to do the work you have to do—properly and well!"

Phœbe turned back to the mirror, brushing her hair savagely. At another time she might have smiled at her own glum reflection. But now she was too angry. She knew that when Henry spoke of his work, he was speaking of something that was his obsession. So long as he was left to that, he did not care where he—or she—lived. It was his enjoyment. But what about herself? What did she get out of it? No. This was downright hypocrisy. As his wife, she must not allow it. He had no right to treat her like this; pushing her into the house in the Quellengasse so that he could conveniently forget about her!

Phœbe was not yet twenty. Rights and wrongs were still black and white. She had not yet learnt that the colour of compromise is grey. And she had come back so uplifted, so enchanted, as only a young girl can be, with the new friend she had found today—a friend who must know so much more about life in Vienna than Henry possibly could. She turned to Henry once again: "But, Henry, surely we can afford—"

"How do you know what we can afford?"

"You told me yourself before we were married that we were earning enough to live comfortably."

"But not enough to squander!"

"Oh, of course not! But Miss Hirsch says—"

"Damn Miss Hirsch!"

"Henry! Don't you dare!" Phœbe stamped her foot. Arthur and David would never use language like that! She stood close in front of him, her hair down, her colour high, her eyes blazing.

Suddenly this new facet of her strange beauty, joined to his own trembling feelings, overcame him. He caught his wife's lonely unwillingness into his arms—unwillingness which did not last.

And when they came to descend for their evening meal, Phœbe, a hand through Henry's arm, had promised she would go with him to visit the Klems that evening. They would decide everything after they had been there.

II

Like many who glory in the adventures of the mind, who are inventive and bold in their vocation, Henry felt a timidity, a dislike of change in the background of everyday things. His homing instinct was strong. It had been a wrench, an uprooting, for him to come to Vienna in the autumn. Only the strongest pressure of circumstances could have forced him to the step. But, having got himself there, and having found a room in the Quellengasse, his homing instinct had reasserted itself. It was there he had managed to settle down.

Frau Klem had been kind. She had looked to his comfort almost fanatically. Recognising him to be eccentric, she had cooked his meals at whatever times of the day or night he had chosen to appear, regardless of the fact that he might have spared her by eating at the suburban restaurant nearby. She had looked to his mending and his linen. And, when the cold came, seen that the fire in his stove burned brightly. It is doubtful if Henry noticed any of these attentions. But it had made him aware that the Klems' was a very good sort of place to have a room in.

Besides, there had been Pepi. Gay, light-headed and ridiculously pretty, she had run about, serving him as her mother did; helping him with his German when he asked her; teasing him when she thought his mood was dark. Deep in his preoccupations,

Henry had taken almost as little notice of her as he had of her blond, leonine father. They were, one and all of them, part of a convenient background—nothing more. If Pepi had conceived an interest in the gesticulating, innocent young stranger, the last person who had been aware of this was the stranger himself.

What, then, could be better than the Quellengasse, if Frau Klem would have them? Thus, in the evening, after their meal, Henry set out with Phœbe.

The night was cold and brilliant. There had been a powdering of snow earlier. As they crossed the Stephansplatz, they could see smooth drifts, new, white and unsullied, blown into corners of the great cathedral's walls. Looking down the Graben, they saw that a full moon was flooding the white roofs of the central booths and the straw-covering of the rococo fountain, with a light that seemed almost blue, against the yellow warmth of flaring, gas-lit windows. Overhead there were stars.

Despite the cold, the evening promenade in the Kärntnerstrasse was in full swing. Shops and restaurants were blazing with light. Even on this winter night, the street was teeming. Men and women wrapped in heavy furs. Officers of line regiments. Demi-mondaines in the height of winter fashion. Personal servants brought from the further parts of the Empire, bearing themselves proudly in the full consciousness of their magnificent regional clothes. A Slavonian woman, her many petticoats ballooning out beneath her heavy sheepskin coat, and wearing hessian boots and a turban. A Polish woman, seen through the plate-glass windows of a famous coffee-house, wearing a white skirt braided with gold, red-leather boots, a white fur-lined attila and a lancer's square-topped cap. Hungarians. Bohemians. Transylvanians. All of them aware of the spectacle they made in this incredible, glittering street. All of them adding to the brittle brilliance of their Empire.

Phœbe hung on Henry's arm. Her heart was singing. It was a far cry from here to Grosvenor Terrace. Tonight Henry and she were very near to each other. The storm had blown up between them, changed to a tempest of the feelings, found its appeasement, and now there was a tender, shining calm. She stopped at one of the several toy-shops in the Kärntnerstrasse. There were dolls dressed in the absurd peasant costumes of these men and women here in the street. She must buy one and send it home to little Isabel.

It was typical of them that they did not think to hire a *Fiaker* or a *Komfortable* to take them out to the Quellengasse. A cab was an expense, a luxury in Glasgow. Unless you were old, or ill, had much luggage or were very self-indulgent indeed. Phœbe and Henry were none of these things, so why hire one, even in Vienna? A tram ran from the top of the Kärntnerstrasse at the Opera house up into the Favoritenstrasse, and they could walk the rest of the way.

All entertainment was early in Vienna, and the opera made no exception to this rule. Thus an hour of the performance must already have passed as they reached the stopping-place near the Opera House and stood waiting. Yet even now fashionable people were arriving, alighting from hired *Fiakers* or private carriages, and passing on into the lighted building.

It would have pleased Maximilian Hirsch to see Phœbe now, as she stood, her shining eyes taking in the extravagance of this lovely, flaunting city. She hugged her husband's arm. It was all so strange, so unreal, so enchanting! Everything was new, everything adventure. If there was another side to Vienna's glamour, Phœbe had not yet even thought about it.

Now the little horse-tram was coming, the many bells on the horses' collars emitting a continuous metallic sound, a cascade of brassy rustlings, as the steaming horses came along the moonlit Ring. Now she was sitting close to Henry in the dim, oil-lit car. Now they had turned and were heading uphill towards the Favoriten suburb.

III

The Klem family made a picture of domesticity this evening. Joseph Klem lay, stretching his comfortable and corpulent length, on the plush sofa, that stood to one side of the stove. Now and then he withdrew a plump hand from behind his head to stroke his side-whiskers, smooth back his thick, blond mane, or remove from between his teeth for a moment the carved meerschaum pipe he was ruminatively engaged in smoking. He wore a patched jacket and embroidered slippers, that had once been worked for him by his schoolgirl daughter, Pepi. The colours of these had been of a child's bright choosing, but a homely dinginess had long since claimed them, and now they were merely comfortable. A shaded lamp stood on the round, baize-covered table, where Pepi and her mother sat sewing. Their busy hands, and the rough, coloured table-linen they were hemming, were caught in the circle of bright lamplight. Their faces, as they bent over their work, were thrown into the warm glow made by the coloured shade.

Though her hands continued steadily occupied, now and then Pepi's mother raised her eyes to look at her daughter. Pepi's behaviour was somewhat unaccountable these days. The child was so demure, so well-behaved. Was her daughter, Frau Klem wondered, feeling the weight of the responsibility betrothal had brought with it? Joseph and Martha Klem were well aware that they had rather forced this betrothal to Willi Pommer. But they did not take blame to themselves for that. Pepi's future had to be provided for. And Willi, if he was not the Apollo Belvedere, was at least diligent, honest and, they judged, sufficiently in love, or at all events, good-natured enough to put up with Pepi's tantrums.

But now, almost alarmingly, there were no tantrums. Almost alarmingly, for it was so unlike Pepi. What had happened to the child? What did all this docility mean? Pepi—their temperamental, sparkling, naughty little Pepi—had, since Christmas, turned herself into an obedient mouse. Frau Klem's plump face wrinkled with anxiety, and she scratched her greying head with a thimbled finger. No. She knew Pepi too well. She could be a deep little creature when she liked. Now the waters of the girl's behaviour were running so smooth that her mother could not but think they must be running deep.

Yet what could Pepi be hiding? What was she up to? But she must stop indulging these maternal fears. The child was growing up, that was all—accepting the unexciting life they had chosen for her; persuading herself, at last, that thus she would find happiness.

"I see, from a bill, that Lisa Fischer has been given a part at the Karl Theatre," Joseph said, taking his pipe out of his mouth and staring placidly at the ceiling. And, as no one replied to this, he added: "I didn't know she had a voice for anything but the chorus. She must be getting on with her singing."

"She must be getting on with somebody who has paid down the money for the part," his wife said tartly.

"Oh, I don't know." Joseph stretched himself comfortably.

"Well I *do* know!" Frau Klem was not at all averse to talking scandal, especially such scandal as diligently and shamelessly generated by this black sheep of her husband's family. Only yesterday she had caught a glimpse of Lisa skating on a flooded lawn of the Stadtpark, her hands crossed with those of an elegant, slim young man who wore fair, cascading side-whiskers, a light beige bowler hat and a modish, short overcoat of much the same colour. Lisa herself had been flaunting a wax-red cashmere skirt, the pleats of which flared becomingly as she skated. And how her sable bonnet and the sable muff she carried on her arm had been come by, the good, but gossipy Frau Klem did not dare to think! She would have been more than glad to discuss with her husband all that this implied; been glad, indeed, to invent further implications if necessary; but she was not prepared to do this in in front of their daughter. The seeming success of her cousin Lisa Fischer had in times past had its unsettling effect upon Pepi. The less Pepi knew about toilettes that must certainly have come from Maison Spitzer, Drecoll or Marsch, the better.

"Oh, but Lisa is singing much better. She's gone to a new teacher." For a sudden, eager instant Pepi looked up to say this, then she quickly dropped her eyes again, and went on with her sewing.

Her mother put her work down on the table, and turned to her daughter. Had Pepi been in secret contact with this, quite literally, scarlet woman? Anxiety made Frau Klem's voice severe. "Will you please tell me who told you about Lisa Fischer's voice?"

For the fraction of a second Pepi's expression might have seemed to betray confusion. But it was only a fraction. And her face was so much in the shade that it was hard to tell if her colour had risen. "Really, Mama! Why are you looking at me like that? *I'm* not Lisa Fischer! It was the little Schani Fischer who told me. I met him in the Stubenring the other day. I see no reason to walk past him just because he's her brother! The boy can't help that, can he?"

If this was intended as a red herring, Pepi's mother followed it obediently. "The Fischers would do much better not to talk about Lisa to their younger children," she said, taking up her sewing and masking her relieved anxiety in righteous indignation. "The children will learn all the whys and the wherefores soon enough."

Pepi did not reply to this. When, in a moment, her mother ventured to glance at her from the corner of an eye, she appeared to be sewing, as quietly diligent as ever.

On his sofa Joseph Klem had fallen asleep.

IV

Presently they were roused by a knocking at the door. Frau Klem went. There was the noise of welcome.

Pepi dropped her work and rushed to rouse her sleeping father. "Quick! Quick, Papa! Visitors." She shook his shoulder in her agitation. "It's Herr Hayburn's voice!"

Joseph had only time to rise to his feet before Phœbe and Henry came into the cheerful little room. Martha Klem was genuinely pleased to see them. She had come to feel almost maternal towards Henry while he was with her in the autumn. And, even making allowance for his preoccupations, she had been a little hurt that he had not come back to see her. But now the warm-hearted Viennese woman had forgotten everything but the excitement of his arrival with his wife. She fluttered about, taking their coats, scolding her husband for looking untidy, bidding him change his jacket and brush his hair, smiling encouragingly at the young lady, asking her in dumb show where she would like to sit, calling to Pepi to clear up the table, and telling her to go at once and make coffee.

Pepi did as she was told. She was glad to be in the kitchen by herself. As she put the beans into the coffee-mill and turned the handle, she could feel the sullen beating of her heart. She had dreaded this. And it had come. So that was the other girl he had gone to fetch. Her eyes had told her that Frau Hayburn was beautiful. And they had told her that Herr Hayburn was conscious of his wife's beauty. This was a marriage of love; it was no marriage of convenience.

As she bent over the cooking-stove a tear fell, and was turned by the heat into a puff of sizzling steam. There was little of reason in Pepi's make-up. She was a thing of instinct and emotion. She could not have defined what Henry had brought her in the last few months. A strange, gauche friendliness. A vivid interest in his troubles at the works. An absurd masculine helplessness that was, somehow, engaging. And, above all, his foreignness; the novelty of him. He came from a golden, outside world, far beyond the confines of the Favoriten. He was young. He was clever. One day he would be rich. He had made no love to her. But that, perhaps, only added to his interest, in this city where love was almost a matter of politeness; where pretty girls like Pepi could find amorous young men two for a *Kreutzer*, and reject or accept their advances as the mood took them.

And so, with a young girl's light-headedness, Pepi had woven her fantasies and dreamt her dreams. She had always known that Henry was betrothed, but that might be a mere loveless arrangement. Such betrothals were the rule in Vienna. Here, in this gay city, it was the custom for love rather to overflow its banks than to remain within them. It was dull and stupid to go without adventure, if adventure was yours for the taking.

Why she had accepted her own betrothal to Willi Pommer, Pepi could not have said. It had been pressed upon her, and for the sake of peace, perhaps, she had allowed it. Perhaps she had been waiting to find out if Henry loved his wife; to see if there was still hope of intrigue. By the illogical, frivolous standards of this, the most seductive of cities, it did not strike this light-hearted little moth, dazzled by the brightness of her native candles, that the feelings she allowed herself were wrong. But, right or wrong, the sight of Henry together with his wife had given her her answer. And it was an answer she did not like.

Pepi wiped her eyes, examined her face in the kitchen mirror, and picked up the coffee-tray. Life was a thing to be lived. If you could not live it in one way, then you must live it in another. She had nearly given herself away tonight about Lisa Fischer. What a fool she had been!

She kicked the sitting-room door open with one foot and went in with the coffee-tray. Frau Hayburn, first to see that she was heavily laden, jumped up to help her.

Phœbe, still in her mood of honeymoon pliability, felt herself forced to admit that this was a pleasant place. Mr. and Mrs. Klem seemed so pleased to see her husband and herself. Their kind faces were overflowing with interest and pleasure. Henry was interpreter, and, with his three-months-old German, things went slowly. But they had turned this slowness into a good-natured game, and there was friendly laughter, and much dumb show. As, this afternoon, she had been uplifted by the distinction of the Misses Hirsch, now she was uplifted by the warm simplicity of the Klems.

She began to wonder why she had been so silly as to quarrel with Henry about their coming to live here. Henry, of course, had been much wiser than she. She must, she told herself, remember this in future when she felt like opposing him. Her friend Stephanie Hirsch would understand when she explained to her more thoroughly just what their circumstances were. (Phœbe had a very hazy idea of them herself, but this did not now occur to her.) And their stay here would not last for ever. She would have time to learn to speak a little, and Mrs. Klem would teach her to keep house in the Austrian way. And perhaps in some months Henry and she would have an apartment of their own.

Thus, before they left, their stay was arranged. In a week's time they were to come out here from the Domgasse. The spring would be coming, Frau Klem said, smiling, and out here the gracious lady would find herself almost in the country, which would be very healthy for her. The room that Herr Hayburn had occupied this autumn was a little small for two, she was afraid, but the gracious lady did not, perhaps, mind. Besides, they could have Pepi's room before so very long, she added, giving her daughter's arm a brisk little pat. In the springtime? Was that not so, Pepi?

But when Phœbe and Henry, together with their belongings, arrived in the Quellengasse at the end of eight days, Pepi's room was already empty.

Chapter Ten

A RELENTLESS day in mid-March. The east wind, crossing Scotland from Edinburgh to Glasgow, blew steadily as though it blew from a fan. Smoke trailed from the chimneys horizontally. In the streets, dust and torn paper played games. Warmth and comfort were difficult to find.

But Bel had found them. The fire in the back-parlour of Grosvenor Terrace was stacked high. She sat with her feet on the fender, busying herself over family mending, and watching her six-year-old daughter Isabel, who was occupied in cutting out scraps. Every now and then Bel took her eyes from her work to look down upon the little girl's industry.

Isabel was crouched on a stool set on the hearthrug, her fair ringlets dangling in front of her, her protruding tongue following the twisting scissors this way and that, cutting and snipping in an ecstasy of concentration. In addition to her little serge dress, she was wound in an old nursery shawl, the ends of which had been secured behind her small shoulders by one of Sarah's, the nurse-housemaid's, hairpins.

For a moment the child stopped, straightened her back, sighed, pushed away those troublesome ringlets that Sarah was forever re-shaping with a hairbrush round her large, red fingers, then she bent down again and went on with her snipping. But she had given her mother a glimpse of a flushed face.

"Don't you think you should stop and have a rest now, dear?" Bel said, a little anxiously.

Isabel had been allowed to get up only this afternoon. For a week she had been in bed with fever and cold. Perhaps it was not good for her to occupy herself so intensely.

"But I want to finish this," came non-committally from the tangle of fair hair.

This highly-coloured sheet of the members of the Royal Family had been a stealthy gift from Cook, who had her own ways of worming herself into the children's affection behind Sarah's somewhat jealous back. She had waited until Sarah had wrapped up little Thomas and marched him off for a bleak afternoon walk in the chill, unblossoming Botanic Gardens, then she had appeared above-stairs, plump, affectionate and triumphant, and handed over this present she had secured to celebrate Isabel's convalescence.

Isabel had received it with a child's solemn radiance, thanked Bessie demurely, promised rather pompously to kiss her later on, when there was no chance of giving her infection, then gone off to cut out the scraps before the parlour fire. Cook had returned to her kitchen, glowing with the sense of her own generosity, her importance, and her ability to demonstrate her attachment to the children, Sarah or no Sarah.

"Well, after you've finished that one, I think you should go on the couch for a little and play with the Austrian doll your Aunt Phœbe sent you. I'll get it for you," Bel continued, in answer to her daughter's last remark.

Isabel did not see any point in replying to this. She wished, indeed, that her mother would stop trying to carry on a conversation. It hindered concentration. As a result of this last interruption her somewhat inexpert scissors had cut off the late Prince Consort's nose. That meant cutting out the nose and pasting it separately, which would be a great nuisance, and very difficult to do properly so that it did not show.

Isabel was not pursuing art quite for art's sake. She was hoping to have something really remarkable to show her brother Arthur when he got back from school this afternoon. Her six years were ever anxious to measure themselves against Arthur's nine, her femininity against his masculinity. Isabel adored Arthur. Now this misfortune with the nose. It was most provoking. If only her mother—

The front door banged. Could that be Arthur home from school already? Should she hide her unfortunate slip away, or should she ask him to help her to patch the poor Prince Consort?

II

But before she had time to decide, her Aunt Sophia came into the room.

"Bel, dear! And wee Isabel! How are you, lovey? Your Auntie Sophia has just come in to see how you are. Wil told me just this morning at breakfast that Isabel had been ill, Bel. And he said he had known for days! Aren't boys awful? Someone had told him. I forget who it was. Now, had he met Arthur? Or did he tell me he had run into Sarah buying a newspaper? No. No, I'm sure it was Arthur. But, then, why should I think of Sarah? Or am I thinking of her in connection with something else? Well, anyway, I'm glad to see you up again, dearie. And what are you busy with?"

Isabel, having bestowed just as hurried a greeting upon her aunt as her mother's ideas of a little girl's politeness would permit, continued with her scissors contemptuously. If her Aunt Sophia had any sort of eyes in her head, it must be perfectly obvious to her that she, Isabel, was cutting out scraps. There were times when grown-up people asked the most nonsensical questions.

Bel was not displeased at seeing Sophia. The searing winds had kept her in this afternoon. Sophia was, at least, an excuse for early tea. Sarah's second-in-command could bring it, or Cook, indeed, if it came to that. There was no need to split ceremonious hairs over Sophia. She pulled the bell-cord, invited her to lay aside her bonnet, the singed muff, and her outer wrappings and bade her pull the arm-chair opposite close to the fire.

"And what's the news, Bel dear?" Sophia, now in full certainty of the cup of tea, which had been one of the stronger strands among the tangle of motives for her coming, bent forward and warmed her hands at the fire.

"Nothing very much," Bel answered, intent once again upon her mending. Then, as though she had found a crumb to throw to her guest, she added: "We had David here last night. He begged a bed. He had to attend some meeting that kept him too late to get home to Aucheneame."

Bel was little surprised that Sophia received this information with no great show of interest. The smallest piece of family news usually set her tongue wagging. But now, she was merely leaning forward, holding out her hands and gazing expressionlessly into the fire. "How are Grace and the baby?" she asked presently.

"Oh, very well. Grace is up and about again." Bel's surprise increased. The mention of a new baby, especially a new Moorhouse baby, was the topic of all topics to open the floodgates of Sophia's chatter. But Sophia still sat silent, her face, middle-aged and moody, glowing red in the firelight. "He seems very proud of his son," Bel added, throwing the bait yet again.

"That's good." Sophia sat back in her chair, her eyebrows raised defensively.

Bel was mystified. Had Sophia something to tell her? She gave her another chance. "Have *you* seen anything of David lately?" she said, looking up from her sewing.

A motion from Sophia gave Bel to understand that she had no wish to say what was to be said while sharp little ears concealed by tangled ringlets sat between them.

But at this moment the door was thrown open, and Cook, who, having admitted Sophia to the house, had gone to make tea unbidden, brought in the tray and set it down on the parlour table with a self-satisfied smile—a smile that demanded of the ladies where they could find a better anticipator of their wishes than herself? And, following on this, Sarah arrived back with little Tom. And on their heels came Arthur home from school. There were handshakes and boyish, March-cold kisses on Aunt Sophia's hot, fire-baked face, then Sarah, having added Isabel and her scraps to the cavalcade, swept all the children upstairs to their nursery tea.

In the wake of the storm Bel rose to pour out for Sophia. She was still wondering about David and the Butter family. "Two lumps, isn't it? Did you say you *had* seen David, Sophia?"

Sophia stirred her tea reflectively. "No. But William went to see him. Oh, I shouldn't be telling you this, Bel dear; it's really nothing, but I know you won't repeat it. You see, dear, William and I are just a little disappointed with David. Now, I wouldn't dare to say anything about this if David wasn't my own brother. But you know you can say things about your own people, without anything—anything very—well, serious, dear, being meant. You see what I mean, don't you?"

There was really nothing yet for Bel to see. But, as curiosity was now thoroughly aroused, she hastened to encourage Sophia by assuring her that, of course, she saw everything.

"Well, it was this, dear. You see, Wil is more than sixteen-and-a-half, and we've been thinking about his business training. He's been getting splendid reports from the Glasgow Academy. Oh, I know it's not as—well—fashionable, dear, as the new Kelvinside Academy, where you're sending Arthur, dear—but some quite important people send their sons there."

As there was a momentary pause here, Bel, all ears now, further encouraged her by saying: "Of course, Sophia, very important people."

"Well, you see, dear, William wrote to David and told him all this, and asked him if he couldn't possibly make a place for Wil in Dermott Ships. He explained our own business wasn't suitable for a boy to have a training in, and a shipping office like David's would be so wonderful and everything. And that it wasn't a case of a large salary, or a permanent appointment. And that times were so bad, it was difficult to get a young man into anything nice. It was a beautiful letter. William showed it to me before he posted it. And you know, dear, William is the least well-off of all the brothers-in-law. Not that I am complaining about that, of course." Sophia stopped. Her face was flushed with vexation.

"But what happened, Sophia? What was David's reply?"

"He sent no reply. And then William went to see him."

"But David's not like that, Sophia. There must have been—What did he say to William?"

"He made an excuse about his mind being taken up with Grace. It was at the time of the baby's birth. But he must have come to the office every day. He must have written other letters."

"But what did he say to William about giving Wil his training?"

"He put on a far-away look and said that times were so difficult that he couldn't make any promises just now. That perhaps later on—" Sophia put down her cup, pulled a handkerchief from her belt, blew her nose and added: "There won't be any later on, Bel. If it had been the son of one of David's grand friends—" To recover her poise she took up her cup once more.

"Do you think Grace knows about this, Sophia?" Bel asked after a pause of bewilderment.

"Oh no. I don't suppose so. Besides, Grace is not like that."

"No, Grace is not like that."

There was a silence for a moment, then Sophia burst out: "Do you know what about my brother David, Bel? He is getting mean and pompous! I would never have believed it! All Grace's money has been bad for him!"

"I've always been very fond of David."

"I know you have."

"He was quite like his old self last night, Sophia," Bel said rather lamely, pouring out fresh tea for both of them.

She sat herself down by the table, reflecting. It was difficult to judge the rights and wrongs of this. It did seem a little thing for David to take his sister's boy into a great office where there were already so many. Was it true, what Sophia said of David? Was a large fortune taking away the gift of understanding? Blunting him to the hopes and fears of others? Robbing him of the common touch? It was a pity if the rudimental weakness of his character should betray him in this way; should destroy the quick sympathy she, Bel, had always loved in him. Could he really be afraid that his coltish nephew should not seem presentable enough to do him credit? Was snobbery sapping David's courage?

She felt a self-accusing pang. In this respect she, too, was not without stain. She had to admit it. But now her own snobbery—a snobbery that was constantly breaking down before her womanliness—allowed her to understand David and be sorry for him. No. It would be a great pity if, with his large way of life, he should begin to grow small.

"Perhaps if Arthur spoke to David, Sophia—" she began, coming once more to the surface.

"No, Bel dear. If David can't do that for his own flesh and blood—"

"But perhaps there was some mistake."

"I don't see how there could be. No, dear, please leave it."

"Or Grace, Sophia?"

"Not for the world, Bel! We are not proud. You know that very well, dear. But there are limits."

"I'm sorry, Sophia. I do hope it will come right."

For reply, Sophia held out her cup. "But it *is* all right. We've forgotten already. Don't bother any more about it. I shouldn't have told you, Bel dear. And we're not going to make a family quarrel out of it." She took her cup back from Bel, thanked her, then asked: "And when did you have a letter from Vienna last?"

III

Bel was glad that Sophia had changed the subject. There was nothing more she herself could say without appearing to take sides. And she had no wish to do this. She was grateful to her that she had not tried to engage her sympathies more deeply. Later, when she had Arthur to himself, she would ask him what he thought.

"We had a letter from Phœbe this morning," she said, following Sophia's example and having a third cup of tea. "We were glad to get it. She doesn't write very regularly. We were beginning to wonder."

"And how is poor Phœbe getting on?" The adjective "poor" as applied by Sophia to the Phœbe of these days denoted a regret that her sister should have married so rashly and so young, should have attached herself to such an odd, erratic husband, and that she should be forced to live anywhere that was not Glasgow.

"Oh, she's getting on very well—in a way." Bel looked about her. "I should have the letter somewhere."

"Why 'in a way', Bel dear? She's in rooms, isn't she? I was very pleased to hear it. How could poor Phœbe keep house for herself? And with all these foreigners about! I was glad to hear she was being looked after."

The thought crossed Bel's mind that Phœbe's wit might, with little trouble, quickly bring her skill in housekeeping well above Sophia's. But she merely went on: "I say 'in a way', Sophia, because I'm not too sure about the people she and Henry are staying with."

"I thought he was a respectable bank clerk."

"Yes. But there's a daughter. Phœbe mentions her in this letter. She ran away from home just before Phœbe and Henry went to stay. Her parents had no idea where she had gone. It was a week or two before she was found singing in a theatre in some small

Austrian town. I don't like houses that daughters run away from, Sophia."

"No, indeed, Bel dear. They must be light-minded sort of people. Have they brought the girl home?"

"No. She wouldn't come."

"Better not."

"Much better not, Sophia."

"There could have been no question of Phœbe staying on if she had come, Bel."

"No."

"Especially running away to a theatre," Sophia added.

Bel *had* heard that there were worse places than theatres for daughters to run off to. But, according to Moorhouse ways of thinking, not much. "Well, anyway," she said, "they're talking of finding a place for themselves before long, and that would be best. Oh, here is the letter." She had found it in her work-basket.

Sophia took it and settled down to read. She read slowly, punctuating her reading with mild exclamations of sympathy, surprise and bewilderment. Once she laid it down on her knee, looked across at Bel and exclaimed: "You would wonder from all this what kind of place Vienna is, at all," then picked it up and went on reading.

The part about seeking a place of their own came at the end of the letter. Sophia re-read it aloud:

"It's all right here. But Henry's books and papers take up a great deal of room. And we may want more accommodation for all kinds of reasons later this year."

Sophia folded the letter, and, looking at Bel, repeated the words: "All kinds of reasons." She was surprised. For once, her own pedestrian wit had moved more quickly than Bel's. "So there's to be a Hayburn baby, is there?"

"What do you say, Sophia?"

"Well, it looks like it, doesn't it? That's what Phœbe's trying to tell you."

"I didn't think of that."

"Well, I must say you surprise me, Bel dear. Remember, Phœbe's very young, and it will be the first. I remember I didn't know how to tell anybody when Wil was coming. And if I had

had to write it! Poor Phœbe! So far away! Dear me! It's that o'clock already? How the time flies!" Sophia got up and began putting on her things without breaking the flow. "Well, it's been lovely, just what I needed to cheer me up. And you won't say a word to anybody about our little difficulty with David, will you, Bel dear? You see, William was just saying he couldn't bear—" Bel accompanied her to the door. If Sophia had remained sensible she would have discussed Phœbe's letter further with her. But the sluices looked like opening. And there was nothing now to do but bid Sophia and her flood of chatter good afternoon.

IV

She shuddered as she closed the door behind her. The wind cut like a knife. Bel bent down and stirred the hall fire. Its reflection jumped and glittered on polished brass and varnish. But even here it was chilly.

She hurried back to the warmth of the parlour, her mind full of Phœbe's letter. She took it up and read the end of it once again.

Yes, almost certainly Sophia was right. Odd, that she had missed the sense of it when she had read it this morning. Now she must write to the child at once to make sure.

Bel crossed to the parlour window and looked out thoughtfully upon her own back garden. The door in the wall by the side of the coach-house leading to the lane had been left off its catch and was blowing back and forth. The grass was powdered with March dust. Bleak, shrivelled leaves eddied against a corner of the garden wall. There were shouts of children playing. They must be McCrimmon the coachman's, children playing with their kind in the lane. Presently a half-grown kitten ran into the garden, and was immediately followed by the eldest McCrimmon child, who caught it up in her little purple hands, clutched it to her, and carried it out of the back garden, shutting the door behind her. Bel wondered that the child could bear to play so gaily in this cold wind. But, except for her hands, she was warmly, if somewhat miscellaneously clad, and health rounded her cheeks. A different child from the pale little creature Phœbe and Henry had brought from the slums that Saturday afternoon over a year ago.

Phœbe. Bel realised now that she had really been thinking about Phœbe all the time she had been standing here; that she had been apprehending what she saw at the merest surface level.

Phœbe to have a baby without herself being with her? It was unthinkable. Had this been her fear from the beginning? Yet what could she have done with this headstrong couple? And it might be that Sophia was wrong. She must write to Phœbe at once, demanding an immediate answer.

But, if Phœbe said yes? How could she go to her? With this house, a husband and three children? Gazing before her, Bel twisted the blind-cord in her fingers, her eyes gazing out on the walls, roofs, and swaying naked trees, all of them a monotonous grey in the bleak evening light.

But her heart held the glowing picture of the stormy girl who, now that she had gone from her, Bel was coming to miss more and more.

Her mother had told her just the other day that she, Bel, was too possessive; that she tried to manage everybody; that she was too sure of her own judgments. That might be, Bel muttered, tangling the blind-cord and arguing with herself defensively, but Phœbe wasn't everybody. She was almost her daughter. She was someone very dear. And she was young and foolish. And Bel didn't even know if she was with respectable people.

The walls and windows began to tremble in Bel's vision. She dropped the tangled blind-cord, and, coming back to the fire-place, leant her brow on the mantelpiece, gazing into the fire.

No. She must write to Phœbe tonight, and if things were as she suspected, Phœbe must come home. She was having no nonsense. Henry would have to bring her. Or, if that was impossible, she could join with some other woman who might be travelling. Phœbe had written that she and Henry had taken to going of a Sunday to a Presbyterian service conducted by a missionary of the Free Church of Scotland. Bel had regretted that it was the Free Church and not the Established Church of Scotland. Moorhouses were all Established Church people. Still, on the whole she had been glad. Surely Phœbe could find a respectable companion among the congregation.

Bel was a planner, and this burst of planning soothed her. Now she felt she was getting things into some kind of order in her mind. Her sense of tidiness reasserted itself. She rang for tea to be removed, went to the window, disentangled the cord, pulled down the blind, then drew the heavy curtains. The afternoon was almost gone. Arthur would presently be home, and, anyhow, she had had enough of the cold, comfortless light of the long March day.

Now the darkened room glowed in the firelight. That was better. She took a taper from the mantelpiece, held it to the fire, lit a wall-bracket beside her chair and sat down once again to her mending.

Tonight, when things were quiet, she would write to Phœbe.

Chapter Eleven

MRS. ROBERT DERMOTT was so enchanted to find herself a grandmother that her friends were beginning to think her a menace. Even at the committee table, where it was her habit to assume a manner that was forthright, purposeful and stern, she had, more than once, softened, changed colour and, catching at the straws of her importance, referred to the fact that it had been somewhat difficult for her to see to everything just recently on account of family ties. After that she would look around her with an expression which proclaimed that of course she couldn't go into that sort of thing here, thrust her spectacles back on her nose, and sharply demand of the secretary what was the next item on the agenda.

Outside of her committee work, Mrs. Dermott's obsession was completed. If she were not at Aucheneame instructing the monthly nurse in her duties, and explaining to her just how she herself had felt when Grace was born; then she was visiting friends, and even mere acquaintances, in order to keep them posted in the progress of the new Robert David Dermott-Moorhouse. With a flash of his old humour, David had taken to teasing his mother-in-law about the baby. He was forever pretending to receive letters from his brother Mungo reporting the progress of the Ruanthorpe-Moorhouse baby, and how surprisingly his mind and body were developing. But Mrs. Dermott would have none of it. She affected to meet David's teasing with the coldest of disinterest, and returned his rally by telling him that, if his nephews were going to matter more to him than a son of his own, then it was a pity Providence had bothered to send him one.

All these pleasantries pleased Grace. Everything about the advent of this child was a matter for gratification. And not least that her mother had taken a new lease of life, and was beginning to find some compensation for the loss of her father.

But if there was endless patience for the new Robert Moorhouse at Aucheneame and at the smart little house in Hamilton

Drive, where his grandmother now had her home, patience was not quite so endless in other quarters.

Bel had had rather a lot of Mrs. Dermott. Being in the process of successfully rearing three children of her own, she was not without the necessary small talk on the subject of babies. But she had long since learnt to take her family, its ailments and its nourishment, in her stride, and the infatuated grandmother, however important Bel might consider her to be, was in danger of becoming a bore.

When, therefore, on the day following Sophia's visit, Mrs. Robert Dermott's card was brought to Bel, together with the information that Mrs. Dermott's carriage was standing at her front door, and would Mrs. Arthur Moorhouse drive into town with her, Bel, catching still the overtones of command in Mrs. Dermott's invitation, could not but feel a sense of persecution.

But she had planned to visit her mother this afternoon to discuss the problem of Phœbe. And as her own carriage was at the coach-builders having Arthur's monogram painted discreetly in yellow on its shining doors—there had been a battle with Arthur's modesty about this—Bel decided to take the line of least resistance and accept Mrs. Dermott's offer.

It was as cold as it had been on the previous afternoon. Mrs. Dermott's hackneys stamped the ground impatiently as Bel mounted the carriage-stone and entered the carriage.

"Oh, there you are, Bel, my dear. I am so glad you were able to come with me. Bitter weather for late March, isn't it? Now, take this spare rug all to yourself, Mrs. Moorhouse. You mustn't get chilled." Since Grace's marriage, her mother had announced that she was going to call all Grace's brothers and sisters-in-law by their Christian names—a gesture which, on the whole, pleased everybody. But Mrs. Dermott's memory was like a defective fly-paper. Sometimes things stuck; and sometimes they didn't.

By this time Bel was well used to being pulled forward into a first-name intimacy, only to be thrust back later to the level of plain Mrs. Moorhouse. She thanked Mrs. Dermott, and wound the rug about her as the horses swung round into Great Western Road.

"I'm just going down to Albany Place to visit Mary," Mrs.

Dermott said, triumphantly remembering Mrs. George McNairn's name. "She sent me a very nice letter the other day, with a little subscription I had asked her for, and also hoping the baby was thriving. I acknowledged it at once, of course; but I suddenly felt I ought to drop down and pay her a little visit, and tell her just how the baby was. I really must say, Bel, everybody has been most kind and interested about Grace and David's child."

Bel dug her hands into her muff, smiled a misty, elegant smile, and said: "Such a dear little baby!"

"Yes, indeed, my dear. Now, Mrs. Moorhouse, when your children were as young as that, did you—?"

Bel was engulfed until the horses were standing before Mary's house in Albany Terrace.

"You know, I'm a terrible old woman! I've never even asked you where you were going!" Mrs. Dermott said, preparing to descend herself. "But of course you'll come in to see Mrs. McNairn, too, before I take you anywhere else?"

But Bel stood firm. She had no wish to see Mary's embarrassment at Mrs. Dermott's sudden descent. And, in addition, she felt she had paid for her drive handsomely in pandering to Mrs. Dermott's pride and interest in her grandson. The least Grace's mother could now do was to send her to her destination. She hastened to tell her, therefore, that her mother expected her at Monteith Row at the earliest possible moment this afternoon—a lie which was not, perhaps, white enough to leave Bel's conscience quite in peace—and that she could easily get out here and pick up a hansom.

Mrs. Dermott gave her coachman instructions to take Mrs. Moorhouse to Monteith Row and call back here for herself at a stated time later.

II

There are many reasons for gossiping. And not all of them are bad. Sophia was sitting comfortably with her sister Mary this afternoon gossiping over David's unhelpfulness with young Wil, all unconscious that David's formidable mother-in-law was about to descend upon them. Sophia was not ill-natured. She was gossiping to distract her sister Mary's anxiety, quite as much as to relieve her own feelings.

For this afternoon Mary's spirits were low. Her husband was ill with an illness that was becoming more and more evident. It was beginning to show itself in the diminishing plumpness of his naturally heavy body, in his sallow skin, in the lack of spring in his gait. In his forty-fifth year, George McNairn was quickly turning into an old man. And the worst of it was, as Mary had just told her sister, George would admit none of it; would not even discuss it with her. But his placidity had given place to a very uneven temper, and he had taken to working at his business like a fanatic, spending his diminishing energies in a way that distressed his wife acutely.

Having heard Mary's recital of her troubles, therefore, Sophia's good-nature, rather than her reason, had prompted her to apply David and his iniquities as a counter-irritant. She was thus in full flood when David's mother-in-law broke in upon her.

If it had been anyone other than Mrs. Dermott, she must have wondered why Sophia's face was bright scarlet, why it wore an unmistakable expression of guilt. But Grace's mother, large in body and mind, had little proficiency in subtle deduction—prided herself, indeed, in the lack of it.

She advanced into Mary's stuffy drawing-room beaming with pleasure. "My dear Mrs. McNairn, how cosy it is in here! And Sophia! How nice to see you! I've just taken the liberty of coming in for a moment to thank you for your very kind letter about the baby, Mary, and to tell you how he was getting on. And how is your family, Mrs. Butter? I seem to hear of nobody but ourselves these days."

The two sisters did not see so much of Mrs. Dermott as Bel did, but even they were becoming accustomed to her confusing modes of address. They stood up, received Mrs. Dermott with the best grace their embarrassment would allow them, and Mary, leading her to the fire, insisted that she should take tea and making the excuse of giving orders, hurried from the room, leaving her over-powering visitor with Sophia.

To be left alone with Mrs. Dermott was like being left alone with a friendly battleship. She sat leaning forward warming a large, red, diamond-ringed hand at the fire, and launching benevolent broadsides at Sophia.

"I'm so pleased to find you here, too, my dear. How is your nice husband?"

"William's very well, thank you, Mrs. Dermott. I wish I could say the same for Mary's husband. She's just been telling me that poor George—"

"I brought your sister-in-law, Bel Moorhouse, down into town with me in the carriage. Such a dear woman! So kind and straightforward!"

"We all like Bel, Mrs. Dermott." Then, feeling she must, however guilty her feelings, Sophia added: "And how are Grace and her wonderful baby?"

Mrs. Dermott went solemn at this, a little. "Oh, I don't know that he should be called a *wonderful* baby, Sophia," she said, almost stiffly. "Indeed, only the other day I was giving Grace and David a lecture: telling them they must keep some kind of proportion; that the baby might be everything to them, but they must really remember not to bore other people about him." And, still further to Sophia's amazement, she added: "But why did you say *poor* George? Is Mary's husband ill?" The reference to George McNairn had, after all, become stuck to the fly-paper of Mrs. Dermott's mind.

Sophia had just time to tell her of Mary's apprehensions before her sister's step was heard outside the door. For a moment Mrs. Dermott's eyes filled, and her large face took on a soft uncertainty that gave her, of a sudden, a strong likeness to her daughter Grace. "Poor Mrs. McNairn," she said. "I know what that is. It's just over a year—" and then, as she saw Mary, she added with a heartiness that could deceive nobody: "There you are, Mary! Taking all sorts of trouble about me."

And thereafter her behaviour was odd. Her sympathy seemed to keep wheeling round Mary in strange, wide circles. As was to be expected, she spoke much of her grandchild as she drank tea. But every now and then her mind swooped down to ask Mary questions. How did her boys do? How were the little twin girls? Were they at home, and might she see them? When they came, she kissed them majestically, bestowed half-crowns, gave each a pat of dismissal and a far-off smile as they scampered off giggling, then she turned as though they had never existed to go on with what she had been saying. Of George McNairn, it seemed, she could say nothing whatever to his wife.

III

Suddenly the door was thrown open and Mary's schoolboy sons came in, bringing with them their cousin, Wil Butter. And as suddenly the noise of their entrance was muted at the sight of their Aunt Grace's formidable mother. At the unexpected appearance of Wil a feeling of guilt returned to Sophia. She well understood her own son's heightened colour. She stood up to say she must go, and demanded of Wil if he were coming with her.

Wil's cousins claimed him. They had brought him to show him a model steam-engine they were attempting to build, and they begged their aunt to allow him to stay and share their schoolroom tea.

"I'll take you home, Sophia. I want to talk to you. See if my carriage is there, will you?" Mrs. Dermott said, turning to Sophia's son and smiling to herself at his Moorhouse good looks that so much reminded her of David—looks that even grubby adolescence could not quite extinguish.

"I'm distressed to hear about Baillie McNairn's illness," she said to Sophia, as they settled back in the carriage some minutes later. "I felt I couldn't say much to his wife, but if there's anything I can do, you'll tell me, won't you, Mrs. Butter?"

Sophia, a little overcome at finding herself alone with Mrs. Dermott, and touched, perhaps, at what she had just said, told her, with rather less periphrasis than usual, that she would certainly let her know, and that she was being very kind indeed.

With a "Don't talk nonsense, Mrs. Butter," said with what sounded so like rudeness that Sophia blushed once more, wondering what now she had said to offend, Mrs. Dermott turned her head away, and seemed for a moment to have found some object in the street at which to gaze intently.

Sophia waited. For a time there was nothing but the movement of the carriage and the trotting of the horses.

Suddenly Mrs. Dermott turned. "That's a handsome boy of yours, Sophia. What are you going to do with him?"

Sophia found herself forced to collect her wits before she answered. Obviously David's mother-in-law knew nothing of David's refusal. "Well, Mrs. Dermott, you see, William has been trying to place him in a nice office. Oh, just for training. After that, of course, he'll—"

"Then why on earth doesn't he go into Dermott Ships? Surely that's good enough for him?" The tone of her voice sounded in Sophia's ears almost like insolence.

"Well, we thought of that, but—"

"I'll speak to David."

"Oh no! Please!"

Mrs. Dermott turned her bulk round and looked at Sophia's confusion. "My dear Sophia! Why ever not?"

"Please, Mrs. Dermott! I don't think William would like it."

"But why? My husband's office is the best in Glasgow!"

"Oh yes, we know that. But—"

"Well, then, Mrs. Butter! Isn't your own brother, now that he—? My dear girl! What's upsetting you?"

Sophia, beaten, had extracted her handkerchief from her shabby muff and was wiping her eyes. Her companion sat looking down at her, as much at a loss as she was. Again there was a pause. The carriage swayed and rattled.

"I wish you would tell me, Sophia," Mrs. Dermott said at last. Now her voice was not so peremptory.

"William did ask David. But there wasn't any room."

"Room? Room for his own nephew!"

Sophia did not answer. How could she accuse David to his wife's mother. How could she explain her own humble, good-natured estimate of herself and hers, to this commanding, wealthy woman?

"David must have misunderstood."

Sophia merely shook her head and blew her nose.

The horses had come to a standstill before Sophia's house in Rosebery Terrace. The footman had jumped down to open the door for her. His mistress motioned him to re-close it.

She sat contemplating David's sister. She was used to managing people, and here was a situation to be managed high-handedly.

It was very well for David to be carrying on a quarrel with Sophia, or Sophia with David, or however it was. But all that must be nothing to her. She was forever dealing with contention on her committees. She had better deal with this family one, or young Wil Butter would lose the chance of the best business training in Glasgow. In the eyes of Robert Dermott's widow, there could be nowhere like Robert Dermott's office.

She laid a hand on Sophia's arm. "I'll speak to David, and get it all arranged for you at once."

"Oh no! David doesn't want him!"

"Doesn't want him, Mrs. Butter? I don't think it's very nice of you to say anything so unkind about your own brother. Of course David must want a splendid boy like that! Who wouldn't? I'm proud to have him as a relative. Why shouldn't David be? I never heard such nonsense!"

Sophia's wits were confused with this alternative slapping and patting. But her modest pride held. "We couldn't have David think for a minute that we had come to you."

"And why not? I belong to your family, don't I?"

"But William and I are not asking favours!"

"Asking fiddlesticks! It seems to me the favour is to David. And even if it were a favour, surely I, at least, may ask a favour in the business I watched my own husband build up?" She paused for a moment, then she added: "I don't think David will want to refuse me."

Sophia brightened enough to smile. "It's very kind, Mrs. Dermott," she said. "But I don't like the idea of my boy going into Dermott Ships, then feeling uncomfortable because he's forced his way there."

"Really, Mrs. Butter, you talk as if your brother David was a monster! You know very well that if *I* ask him he won't have the—well, anyway, my dear, the horses are getting cold. I'll have this all seen to, and let you know."

In another moment Sophia found herself standing on the windy pavement waving her muff at the retreating carriage and wondering if the word Mrs. Dermott had omitted to say was "courage".

IV

For a terrible moment old Mrs. Barrowfield, looking down by chance from a window in Monteith Row, thought that Mrs. Robert Dermott had come to call. She knew her carriage, for she had seen it more than once at Bel's. But, strong-minded herself, she had no wish for closer acquaintance with Mrs. Dermott's forcefulness. Bel's mother thought she was doing quite enough if, when she met her by chance in Bel's drawing-room, she managed to be civil. Once, indeed, calling spades spades, she had bluntly said to her daughter: "Now, Bel, see that ye don't bring that upsettin' old body here!"

Bel had promised; smiling to herself a little, that her mother had called Mrs. Dermott old, despite the fact that she, herself, was eight years older.

Behind the lace curtains of her sitting-room window, however, Mrs. Barrowfield's perturbation faded as she saw that her daughter's fashionable bonnet was the only one to emerge from the carriage. Indignation, alarm and thoughts of a hasty change into her best shawl subsided pleasantly, and now she was standing, a poker in her hand, stirring flames of welcome from the fire.

Seated opposite her mother now, Bel answered questions. She gave the reasons for coming as she had; how little Isabel's cold was keeping, and how everybody else at Grosvenor Terrace fared. These preliminaries having been got through, Mrs. Barrowfield rang for the tea-tray and astonished her daughter by saying:

"So Phœbe's expecting?"

"Now, Mother, how on earth did you know that?" Bel jumped up, and leant against the mantelpiece.

Mrs. Barrowfield was delighted with the effect she had made. It gave her a feeling of still being in things; of not being laid aside. She smiled triumphantly. "How do you think? I had a letter."

"From Phœbe?" There was a ring of jealousy in Bel's voice.

"No. Henry."

"From Henry!"

"You forget that Henry's a friend o' mine."

"Has he been writing to you regularly, Mother?"

"Well, I wouldna say regularly."

"And you never told me."

For reply, Mrs. Barrowfield gave a chuckle that her daughter considered both offensive and sly. "Am I not to get keepin' anything to myself?"

Bel's colour rose a little. "No, really, Mother! A thing like that!"

"But I just got it yesterday," the old lady said, by way of laying a resentment she had naughtily striven to arouse.

"I had one from Phœbe. I've got it here," Bel said, feeling there was much too much of importance to talk about to indulge in childish annoyance with her mother. They compared letters. Henry's was the more explicit.

Phœbe's child was expected in October. Presently they laid down the letters they had exchanged and looked at each other.

"She's young," was Mrs. Barrowfield's comment.

"She's far too far away!"

Old Maggie, who had come in with the tea-tray, wondered who was far too far away, and why Miss Bel had spoken the words in tones of vexed exasperation, standing, flushed, before the fireplace, her bonnet thrown carelessly down, a strand of her smooth, fair hair straggling out of place.

"Listen, Mother. Phœbe must come home."

Mrs. Barrowfield said nothing. She rose heavily to her feet and began pouring out tea, forgetting in her abstraction that her daughter might very well have done this for her. She liked Phœbe Moorhouse; always had liked her—ever since, indeed, she had seen her, a little girl of ten, help to push her own luggage up the hill to Ure Pace. But Phœbe could look after herself.

In a drawer in her bedroom she had a little pile of letters written in Henry Hayburn's strangely adolescent hand. Letters written before his marriage. Letters of homesickness, of self-distrust, of crushing loneliness; or again, of self-praise, of over-confidence, of boyish boasting—according to his mood. She had held her tongue about them. Why should she expose these raw confessions of his heart? Better than anyone, she felt she had understood his arrogance at Christmas. It was an armour his half-developed poise had forced upon him before the family.

Little did Bel and Arthur know that it was she who had urged him to come home and marry Phœbe. She had guessed from his letters that his loneliness in Vienna was stretching him to breaking-point. And she had felt responsible. She had told him to go. His marriage was, as she saw it, the remedy. And the happy and few letters he had written since had told her she was right.

She sat gazing into the fire, her tea untasted. Why had she, an old woman, become so attached to this young man? It was strange and unusual, but it was so. Was it because he needed her?

And now here was Bel, her own daughter, but yet in very essence a Moorhouse, proposing to take his wife once more from him. She raised her eyes to meet Bel's.

"Well, Mother?"

"Phœbe had better stay with her man."

"What? And have her baby in Vienna?"

"Well? What for not?"

"Oh, how can she, Mother? The girl's not quite twenty!"

"And what about Henry?"

"Henry will want his wife to have the best of attention."

Mrs. Barrowfield looked again at her daughter glumly. This was Bel back at her high falutin. Carried away by her own fine phrases. Taking upon herself the right to arrange for everybody. Never for once doubting the soundness of her own judgment.

"And what do the other women in Vienna do?" she asked. "I havena heard that they all come to Glasgow."

"Oh, Mother! What am I to say to you? I thought you would be reasonable about this! I came down for your advice."

"Well, you're gettin' it! Leave man and wife alone. Don't interfere. They're young, but it's their business. Not yours. Don't try to be a Providence for everybody, Bel!"

"But don't you understand that Phœbe will be quite alone?"

"Dear me, Bel, she'll have her man!"

"A lot of use he'll be, Mother."

"Well, it was *your* father I wanted when you were coming."

"But you were at home, Mother! And father was a doctor!" Bel was almost shouting now. And there were tears. "And don't you understand, her life may be in danger?"

"I was forty-one when you were born. So was *my* life in danger. And yer father was ower old-fashioned to let them use chloroform!"

Oh, it was no use talking to a woman of seventy-five about these things. Bel smoothed her hair, wiped her eyes and sat down to drink her tea. For the remainder of her visit her demeanour towards her mother was sweet, tactful and controlled, as though she were talking to a child of twelve.

And presently, when she rose to say goodbye, the old lady found great difficulty in withstanding the temptation to box her daughter's ears.

Chapter Twelve

A FINE, unusually warm morning in Holy Week. Henry Hayburn sat in one of the great coffee-houses on the Ring. On account of the unexpectedly warm weather, the large plate-glass window near which he found himself was thrown open. From where he was, Henry could have put out his hand and touched the shoulders of those who passed him down there on the pavement.

It was not yet April. Easter was early. But today there was bright sunshine. Already there were one or two straw hats and parasols in the street.

Mrs. Barrowfield had been right. Henry's marriage had given him the background his work demanded. Now that he had a wife to accompany his scanty leisure, to listen to him, to fulfil his manhood, Henry's mind was free.

His work fascinated and engrossed him. The adventure of setting up a factory in a strange land, employing foreign workers and meeting new technical difficulties, filled him with a keen sense of romance. An odd kind of romance, perhaps, and one little known in this, the romantic city. But romance nevertheless.

A light wind blowing down from the Vienna Woods ruffled the fringe of the striped awning that hung out over the sunny pavement. To Henry it was just a breeze. But to the natives—to those tarock players at the table behind him, to that old man with the Barbary organ over there on the far side of the Ring, to that stiff dowager sitting in her carriage beneath her tussore parasol—it was a promise and a harbinger. All of them breathed a little more deeply, caught, or imagined they caught, the scent of damp earth and rising sap from the sprouting woodlands up there in the blue distance, and told themselves that spring was about to invade their city.

Somewhere a clock struck eleven. Henry looked about him. Maximilian Hirsch had given him this place of meeting, and eleven was the time. Henry, from his point of vantage, leant forward and cast an eye up and down the pavement. Maximilian was not yet to be seen. The morning was growing warmer, the scene more animated. Shop-girls in bright colours. Plump City men, hats in hand, mopping warm brows and looking about them for a table where they might sit and cool themselves. A flower-seller passed by, her basket laden with Parma violets and mimosa arrived from Italy overnight. Out in the expanse of the Ring itself, carriages, hired and private, were becoming more numerous. Many of them were moving in the direction of the Aspern Bridge on their way to the Prater. Some of the trams had open trolleys now, and, as the stocky little horses trotted back and forth along the Ring in the sunshine, their bells added a joyful noise to the other sounds of the City. It was difficult to believe that the passengers were everyday people merely going about their business. They wore an air of gaiety as though they were holiday-makers, out to see the sights.

Henry ordered his coffee, and when it came sat sipping it moodily. What had happened to his employer? Why was he keeping him waiting? He had more than enough to see to when he got back to the factory. It was maddening that he should have to waste the morning like this, merely to see some papers that he could just as easily have seen in Herr Hirsch's private office at the bank. Herr Hirsch knew very well that he, Henry, hated wasting time. Why then had he asked him to waste this morning dawdling in a coffee-house?

II

As he sat stirring his coffee, stroking his beard and mechanically following the come and go of the traffic, Henry became aware that his eye had fixed itself on the figure of a young woman sitting in an open tramcar. As she came nearer, he saw that there were parcels on her knee, together with a bunch of flowers that might be mimosa or yellow tulips.

Suddenly he came to his senses. The girl was Phœbe. His own wife. As she passed him by, he could see her sitting, sunk in her own thoughts, far away from the animation about her, pensive and tired, perhaps, with her morning shopping.

A quick uprush of tenderness, of passionate excitement, took hold of him. He waved to her but she did not see him. Now he felt that he must run out into the street, race after the trotting horses, and climb into the car beside her. But already the tram had gone on. He would never catch up. He would only look ridiculous. He sat back regretfully, and took another sip of his coffee.

Why this excitement, when he had seen her at breakfast, only a few short hours ago? She had sat out there, unconscious that his eyes were upon her. Why should this sudden glimpse of her thus, unattainable, pensive and alone, stir him so deeply? Was his conscience chiding him with neglect of this wife of his, who was now to bear his child? Should he have given her more of his companionship? Of his support? Had he been taking all and giving little?

He was glad that Hirsch was not yet with him. He wanted to sit here alone, examine himself and think.

After their first quarrel, there had been strangely little friction between them. Knowing Phœbe and his moods as he did, her patience had been remarkable. She had told him not to worry, that she did very well meantime, that he must give everything to his work. But had he any right to take her at her word? Did not his wife come before all else? Phœbe could be so remote, so independent, that it was easy to forget she must need him, as any other woman must need her husband. Especially in this foreign place.

For a newly married couple, his wife and he had spent far too little time together. On many days he was so busy that he saw nothing of her until late in the evening. But Phœbe had not complained. And her time seemed full. She seemed to be occupying herself picking up Austrian marketing and housekeeping; in learning the language; in amusing herself with the shops and the sights of this endlessly amusing city. That she should be exerting patience until such time as he should find himself established, had not before entered his mind.

Now Henry was stricken with a sense of guilt. His feelings rose, quick and hot, to blame him bitterly. He had failed Phœbe! It was no use trying to find excuses in his inexperience! He was nothing but a thoughtless monster!

An old man in a moleskin cap, with a tray of primroses hanging from his neck by a string, stopped and held up a bunch. Henry, in his agitation, was quite unaware that the man was there. The old creature shuffled off, muttering to himself that the strange young man in the coffee-house was, as the Austrians say, "heavily" in love.

He was not wrong. Henry was "heavily" in love with his lawful wife. And he was full of youthful doubt and a sudden sharp self-criticism of his conduct towards her.

He drained his cup and drank some of the fresh water that, after the Viennese custom, stood in a glass beside it. Yes, he would talk to Phœbe tonight.

But where the devil was Maximilian Hirsch? The precious morning was almost gone. He leant out once more and looked about him. Why were people standing gaping by the edge of the pavement?

The ring of distant hoofs on granite slabs told him. A squadron of Hussars were coming back from morning exercise in the Prater. Now they were in front of him, coming down the Ring. The horses were dark and gleaming with sweat. Each rider, in his blue tunic with its yellow frogging and his fur cap, held himself proudly, in the knowledge that Imperial Vienna was watching him go by. Brass buttons sparkled in the sunshine as attilas, hanging from square shoulders, swayed to the rhythm of the walking horses, as they passed, row by row.

And, good heavens! There was Maximilian Hirsch standing among the mob watching the horsemen—a sight he must have seen hundreds of times. Watching them with the innocent interest of a child! Truly, the Austrians were an unaccountable, time-wasting people!

III

Now the last row of mounted Hussars had passed. The watchers by the kerb were breaking up and moving off. The pavement in front of Henry regained its spring-time animation. Gaily dressed ladies. Fashionable men. Milliners' girls. Flower-women. Clerks in shabby, light-brown overcoats. Peasants' wives in vivid regional colours. Officers in bright uniforms. Countrymen in chamois shorts and short jackets. Bareheaded porters in striped waistcoats and baize aprons. The cheerful, surging, colourful mob that might be seen in Vienna on any sunny morning.

Maximilian Hirsch had turned, too. In a moment he had spied Henry, given him a signal of greeting, and presently he stood beside him, offering him his hand.

"Good morning, Herr von Hayburn. Wonderful morning, isn't it?" He said in the Viennese dialect, at the same time sitting down and looking about him, hot and smiling. He took of his hat, wiped his brow, and looked at Henry quizzically. This young man was altogether too solemn. Maximilian knew that Henry hated to be called von Hayburn. It was ridiculous to be so young and yet so serious. Henry needed teasing.

"You will have a quarter with me?" he asked, raising his finger to attract a waiter. "I can't drink coffee now: it's too near lunch-time."

Henry drank little wine, and it was part of his creed that he must drink nothing at a time of day when there was still work to be done. But he did not dare to offend Maximilian.

While the wine and mineral water were being brought, Maximilian gave him the papers to look through. As the young man was doing so, the other took out a long Viennese "Virginia", drew the straw from it, lit it and sat puffing contentedly, following the passing show outside the window. After a moment his eyes wandered back to Henry.

"Understand?" he asked, indicating by his question that Henry might still have some difficulty with German.

"Yes, thanks."

A clever boy this. There was little that he did not grasp. Henry was bent forward, reading the sheets with concentration. Maximilian examined him afresh. His straight black hair straggled over his sallow brow. His young beard needed trimming. His hands were rough and stained with oil like a workman's. The nails were closely cut, and none too clean. How did his young wife like this? What sort of life was he giving her?

Henry laid down the papers.

"All right?" Maximilian asked him.

"Yes, I think so."

"You'll manage to deliver on time?"

"I'll see that we do."

"Good." Maximilian gathered up the papers out of the way of the waiter who was waiting to put down the little tray of wine and mineral water, and thrust them back into his pocket.

He picked up the carafe, poured out for both of them, touched glasses with Henry and sat back once more. "How's your wife?" he asked, after a sip or two.

"Quite well, thank you."

But Maximilian wanted to know more than that. "How is she liking Vienna?"

"Very well."

Maximilian regarded Henry for an instant, the beginnings of a smile just showing; then, with no unfriendliness in his tone, he asked his next question. "How do you know? Do you ever ask her?"

Henry's colour deepened. "Well—she seems all right. She knows I'm too busy to go out much. She understands. The landlady we're staying with takes her about."

Still Maximilian's eyes were upon him. Still the teasing smile. "Von Hayburn, you're a hypocrite. I don't believe you're looking after her! It would serve you right if she took a lover!"

This was the kind of Austrian joke that Henry's Puritanism did not think funny. But Hirsch had touched on a sore spot. Had he not, as he sat here ten minutes ago, blamed himself bitterly for neglecting Phœbe? He sat now confused and silent.

"Where are you going to live during the heat of the summer?"

"We don't know yet. Where we are, probably. For a time, at least." Then, answering a question in Maximilian's eyes, he added: "You see, it's all uncertain. She's going to have a child in the autumn."

The elder man leant across the table, took his hand and shook it warmly; thus merely adding to Henry's confusion. "But, my dear boy, she must be looked after! Why hasn't she seen more of my aunts? They were horrified when they heard she had gone to a district like the Favoriten. Oh, I dare say the old ladies in the Paulanergasse are not very interesting. But a young woman in that condition must have women friends!"

Maximilian swallowed down the dregs of his wine and again

looked at Henry. This was ridiculous! Preposterous! Indeed, it made him angry! He set down his glass on the marble table and launched forth. Henry was behaving like a thoughtless boy. Why had he brought this girl from Scotland if he were going to treat her thus? She must see his aunts at once, and have their help and friendship!

And why should not the Hayburns spend their summer in a little house on the edge of the Vienna Woods where it would be cool and pleasant for Phœbe, yet not too far for Henry to come to work?

This he said, and much more. And, as he spoke, he was glad—if a little surprised—to see that Henry looked ashamed of himself. But well he might! It was not before time! He did not deserve that beautiful child for a wife!

Maximilian finished his tirade and stood up. "Now, you'll look after your wife, von Hayburn, won't you?"

Henry's reply was the ashamed grin of a schoolboy who has been scolded and forgiven.

Herr Hirsch handed the waiter a coin and drew out his watch. It was a quarter past twelve. He had invited a crony to lunch with him in his pet restaurant, the "Reichenberger Beisel", in the Griechengasse, at twelve o'clock. But a quarter of an hour in Vienna was neither here nor there.

He gave Henry his hand, saying he must go, and took his leisurely way across the Inner City.

IV

A few minutes later, Henry also found himself in the Inner City. Like Maximilian, he, too, could call himself the *Stammgast* of a Viennese restaurant, although it had never occurred to him to do so. But Maximilian's restaurant in the Griechengasse and Henry's restaurant in a passage-way off the Herrengasse were very different places. Henry had come upon his one day quite by chance, as he was taking a short cut through one of the rights-of-way or *Durchhäuser* which abounded in the Inner City; relics of earlier days when Vienna was a closely crowded labyrinth inside protecting walls; when much time and inconvenience were saved to those who went on foot, that they were given rights to pass through other people's courtyards.

In one such passage-way off the Herrengasse, Henry had found a little eating-house. He had come here in the first place merely because he was hungry, because it looked cheap and because he happened to be passing by. It consisted of one large stuffy room, constantly lit by gas-flares, since, from its position, there was never enough daylight. If the regulars—clerks, students and *Fiaker* drivers—had at first resented a foreigner's presence, Henry had certainly not noticed this, any more than he had noticed the grease-spots on the checked cloths or the all-pervading smell of *Gulasch*. But in a short time custom had set aside a table for him, and "der Mister", as he came to be called, was to be seen sitting solitary in his accustomed corner, papers or a book propped against a carafe of untouched wine, deep in his reading, and munching abstractedly anything that happened to be put before him.

But today Henry had no reading propped up in front of him. He felt unhappy, and his conscience was not clear. The sight of his wife passing him by in the tramcar. The scolding he had just had from Herr Hirsch. The thought of the child that was to be.

Henry was a simple creature. Now that he had thought of it, he was filled with self-reproach at his treatment of Phœbe. She had been too much alone, too little with him. He had been very busy, of course, but, in the full flood of his penitence, he could look back and think of many times he might easily have spent in her company.

The elderly restaurant-keeper, having served everybody for the moment, leant against his little service counter watching his customers eat, and conversing with the plump lady who combined the occupations of wife, cook and cashier. Now he gave it out as his firm opinion that something was on "der Mister's" mind. She nodded sympathetically. Yes, he looked troubled as he sat there, forgetting his soup, looking about him, and crumbling rye bread with his long, stained fingers, his bony wrists protruding from his sleeves.

Should he apologise to Phœbe? Henry wondered. No. Somehow that would merely be awkward and unnatural. But tonight he would talk to her and put things right.

And now, having reassured himself a little, Henry remembered the vegetable soup that stood before him, took up his spoon and allowed his eyes to range about the room while he ate.

In a far corner, dim in the gas-light, there was a table of young people, most of them regular customers, who came and went, making this their common meeting-place—students from the music or medical schools, judging from an occasional fiddle-case, or from the fact that at more hilarious moments stethoscopes were brandished, and even, on more than one occasion, amid the screaming of the girls, a human skull. Today the din was at its height. There was gaiety and laughter, and, as was the unself-conscious custom of Viennese youths, bursts of song.

Henry, well used to this behaviour, sat watching them, incuriously. But now a single voice piped up. In some way it sounded familiar. He looked across, and saw that it came from a young woman who sat conducting herself with a fork as she sang. He had heard this voice many times singing about the house in the Quellengasse. It belonged to Pepi Klem.

She finished, bowed exaggerated acknowledgement of her companions' applause, then her eyes caught Henry's. She smiled and waved her fork. Henry, surprised and embarrassed, smiled in return.

So Pepi was back in Vienna? He fell to wondering about her. Her mother, he knew, had been much troubled at her disappearance. Willi Pommer had for a time been inconsolable. But Henry had, just then, had more than enough to think of on his own account. Having heard that she had been found working in some provincial theatre, and that her parents had accepted the inevitable, Fräulein Klem and her problems had passed from his mind.

Now the party in the corner was standing up to go. They were teasing their host as they paid—or begged him to mark up—their modest reckonings. There was laughter, banter between young men and women, and noise. Presently Pepi said goodbye to her friends, came across to Henry, and sat down facing him, her elbows on the table.

V

"Well, Herr Hayburn? Aren't you pleased to see me?" She was laughing at his surprise, his flushed face, his obvious embarrassment as he stammered out:

"Oh, how are you?"

His innocence amused her now, as it had always amused her. But now there was recklessness in her amusement—recklessness born of the jealousy that had driven her from home, of the careless informality of her life in the theatre, of her new, defiant independence.

She offered her hand in a formal handshake across the table, rather with the affected air of a prima donna.

"I suppose you are still in the Quellengasse?"

"Yes, we are."

"And how is the gracious lady?"

"My wife is very well."

"She must be quite Viennese now."

"Oh, no. I wouldn't say that."

"No? Well, she had better learn. If she doesn't want to be hurt in Vienna."

"I don't understand."

Pepi shrugged. She had picked the bundle of wooden toothpicks out of the glass that contained them, and was making squares and triangles on the table-cloth.

Henry watched her, puzzled. Here was a Pepi he had not expected. She was gaily dressed, confident and full of high spirits. There had been tears, tragic predictions and endless talk in the Quellengasse at the time of her going. Phœbe and he, when they had mentioned her to each other, had spoken of her as a brand gone to the burning. Now here she was, delighted with herself. His artlessness could not believe that she was in any way changed. She seemed the same friendly little Pepi she had always been. He was glad. Last autumn she had been a very good friend to him.

"I've been in Lemberg, in Galicia," she said at length, looking up from her game with the toothpicks. "The Mama has probably told you. It wasn't much of a place, but I got an offer of work in the theatre there. I had to start somewhere."

And, as Henry had no comment to make, she added, with a

glint of mischief: "Besides, it might have been worse. It's the Headquarters of an Army Corps. The officers helped to amuse us." Her eyes dropped to the table once more, and she continued with her squares and triangles.

"And what exactly were you doing?" he asked for the sake of saying something.

"Singing in the chorus. Doing anything. Studying."

What would he have expected, had he been told he was going to meet her? A weeping magdalen? A broken creature who could not raise her eyes to those of an honest man? But now her eyes as she raised them regarded him humorously and calmly—the eyes of a young woman who is no longer afraid; who has taken the measure of emotion and knows where it leads.

But she wasn't establishing the old friendship with him. She must try again.

"Were the poor Papa and Mama very anxious when I went away, Herr Hayburn?" she asked, with exaggerated sympathy.

"Yes, they were. They thought you were murdered or something."

She laughed. "Well, it didn't last long. I wrote whenever I could. I had always wanted to make a career on the stage. But they would never hear of it. Now they realise that I'm in earnest."

"Then you'll come to see them?"

"Of course! I only got back to Vienna yesterday. I'm staying with my cousin for a few days. I've got a summer job in the Prater. It's only the chorus again, but I want to be in Vienna to have singing lessons. You see, I want to study and turn into a real artist." She looked at Henry, sighed and added: "The poor Mama! If I don't manage to see her today, please give her all my love and say I'll come tomorrow." She stood up, tied the green ribbons of her bonnet, pulled on her gloves and held out her hand. "Well, then, dear Herr Hayburn. Until very soon."

Henry had risen, too. He stood now at the door of the little eating-house, watching her as she took her way across the paving-stones of the shadowy passage towards the arch of white sunshine at the open street. Now he could see her standing framed in the light for an instant, as though she were halted by the sudden brightness. Now she had flicked open her frivolous green parasol, gathered her skirts in one hand and tripped off up the Herrengasse out of sight.

Henry turned back, paid his bill and looked at his watch. Already he was a little later than he liked to be. It was bad for discipline to give the impression that he had allowed himself a leisurely lunch.

He made his way towards the Neubau, walking fast and taking as many short cuts as possible.

So that was Pepi? He had not disliked seeing her again. She had always been a friendly little thing, and had helped him through those first lonely months when he had not had Phœbe. He would be glad to tell her mother she was in Vienna once more, if she herself had not already appeared and done so. And he could assure Frau Klem, too, that she looked very well and seemed rather the better than the worse for her adventure.

Chapter Thirteen

TO Phœbe it seemed as though in the last day or two a curtain had been lifted—as though the strange, dull veil of commonplace that had, somehow, so quickly fallen between herself and Henry—between herself and the first, shining happiness of her marriage—had suddenly been torn asunder and they were back once more in the radiance of their first days in Vienna.

How had it come about? From the sudden burst of warmth and sunshine that had taken possession of the city as though the weather knew what was expected of it in Easter Week? From the extravagance of joy that now was reigning in the Quellengasse? From the fact that the simple father and mother Klem, having had a visit from Pepi, and having received her assurances that she was really studying and would one day be a great prima donna, had—rather inconsequently, the Hayburns thought—turned right about and, instead of making a tragedy of Pepi, had decided to make an idol of their prodigal daughter?

Or was it merely that Phœbe felt, during these bright days, that there was now no need to be jealous of her husband's work? For a change had taken place in Henry. He had become boyishly tender towards her; gauchely apologetic. The mask of self-importance that Vienna had given him fell from him now when he was with her. Once again they had come very near.

Phœbe found herself wondering how this had come about. Even when, some days ago, she had told him she hoped to be the mother of his child, Henry had not perhaps responded with the tenderness she had expected. Now in his own way he sought to serve her lightest wish, as though he were seeking to right some wrong he had done her. To Phœbe it was incomprehensible. But it was pleasant, and she was uplifted and happy.

And this Eastertide in Vienna enchanted her. It was as though this ancient capital of the Holy Roman Empire had set aside her frivolity, and let herself be washed clean for the festival of Death and Resurrection. Her church spires stood up, hard and pure against the pale Easter sky. Behind them the outline of the mountains. And in the streets everywhere, the Viennese in their holiday clothes. Some mere promenaders; others going to church. Fashionable men and women. Comfortable burghers with their wives. Harassed mothers with worn prayer-books. Children with gleaming, holiday faces. Officers and soldiers wearing their white linen tunics for the first time this year. A cheerful crowd of high and humble. Shop-windows full of coloured Easter eggs, Easter presents, Easter food.

Sometimes by herself, sometimes in the company of Henry, Phœbe visited the churches. She had, in these months abroad, lost her Puritan and provincial hesitation—almost fear—of entering a popish building. And, though it never crossed her mind to question the rightness of her own faith, she found herself taking pleasure in these foreign churches; even in their ritual. She had come to love the smell of incense, the guttering candles, the sacristans with their keys, the dim, praying women, the solemn bursts of music. Even the beggars at the church doors holding back the leather curtains and begging alms. To her it did not mean religion; it meant romance.

And now for Easter, that the simpler people might better remember the story of the Agony, each church had set aside a chapel, and there had arranged, in effigy, the Holy Tomb. In the great churches, in the Votive Church, the *Hofkapelle*, the Church of Saint Stephen, the arrangement was elaborate and rich. In lesser churches it was simple. But each, according to its resources, had its Tomb, its plaster Roman soldiers and angels watching over the effigy of the weary, bloodstained Redeemer who now, His agony over, lay at rest.

It seemed strange to these young Presbyterians that sometimes people could be seen turning away from these stiff images, the tears shining in their eyes. These Holy Tombs appeared to the Hayburns unreal, foreign and strange.

Henry had told Phœbe of his plans for finding a little house somewhere on the edge of the Vienna Woods. He had mentioned it as though the idea were quite his own. He did not tell her of the scolding he had received from Maximilian Hirsch, and his consequent feelings of penitence. And with this planning for her, Henry was pleased with his own new-found sense of responsibility, his protective masculinity. The Klems might be sorry to lose them, he argued; but, after all, Pepi had reappeared in Vienna, had made her peace.

Further, he suggested that Phœbe should call once more upon the ladies Hirsch, tell them of her condition, and beg their very kind advice. At this Phœbe was really astonished. She had taken Henry to call on the ladies some weeks ago, and when, after a very formal cup of coffee, they had found themselves once again in the street, he had told her bluntly that she must not expect him to visit these "old tabbies" any more.

Phœbe was almost as little a reader of hearts as was her husband. But now even she began to suspect that someone had intervened to change his mind.

II

It was into this pool of re-established happiness that Bel's letter, bidding Phœbe come home to Scotland, dropped like a stone. But they did not allow it to do more than ruffle the surface. There was nothing now quite real to the young couple except each other.

She held out the letter to him one evening as he arrived home.

"Here's a letter from Bel."

"Any news?"

"Nothing much. Except that she wants me to go home if there's to be a baby."

"Why?"

She was surprised at the rush of colour to Henry's face; at the quick, angry question. It was as though she had touched the trigger of a gun.

"It's all right, dear! I'm not going! Do you want to read the letter?"

"No."

She folded it up, and that, for the time, was the end of the matter. She would write later and tell Bel how they both felt about it. It was natural enough, perhaps, that Henry should not see things through Bel's eyes; that he should want to keep his wife by him. She would say no more about it.

And now, in and around Vienna, the tide of spring was rising—fresh, sprouting days that had little to do with the springtime of her comic operettas. The thrushes were singing in the Volksgarten and Votivpark. In all green places, flowering shrubs were budding. Presently there would be laburnum—golden rain, as the citizens call it—and lilac in profusion. When the fitful sunshine appeared for long enough to make its presence felt, there was the scent of lime and elder. In the Haupt Allee—the great main drive of the Prater—with its double row of giant chestnut-trees stretching, as it seemed to Phœbe, to infinity, the pale green leaves had begun to fan themselves out above the now-emerging fashionable world, whose ritual it was to drive in their elegance beneath them. In the People's Prater the booths and merry-go-rounds had received their yearly coat of paint. The voices of showmen—good-natured, crude and coarse—could be heard insisting that all and sundry should walk up and try their luck or find amusement.

Times had been bad this winter here in Vienna, as in most other towns in Europe. But what was that to a young Viennese, who could find *Kreutzers* enough to take a girl to have fun in the Volks Prater?

On more than one fine April Sunday, the young couple, having done their duty by attending the Scotch service in the morning, had gaily agreed that in Rome one must live as the Romans, and had spent the remainder of their day in the Prater. If their behaviour towards each other was a little ashamed, a little conscience-stricken, a little indulgent towards the reckless, laughing inhabitants of this carefree city that had not seen the Presbyterian light, it did, perhaps, no harm to anyone, and may even have given spice to their own enjoyment.

On one of these occasions they encountered Pepi Klem. She was in the company of a spirited young man, whom she was pleased to introduce to the Hayburns as her cousin. He seemed a gay, affectionate sort of cousin, and, on Henry's suggestion that they should drink a cup of coffee together, readily assented. Before the Hayburns had done with them, they had made the round of the People's Prater. They saw the traditional Viennese Punch-and-Judy show, made up of two clowns and a rabbit. They had visited fat women and strong men. They saw "the lady without a body"—a young and cheerful head and shoulders on a stand; like an animated barber's dummy. They saw the ladies of an Eastern harem. Henry had swung Pepi so high in a red, plush-lined swing-boat that she had screamed to Phœbe and her "cousin" to stop him. On a merry-go-round they had rotated to the Miserere music from "Trovatore", Pepi riding side-saddle on a spirited wooden horse painted and harnessed to look like one of the Emperor's Lippizaner horses from the Spanish Riding-School; Henry was seated on a pig; the "cousin" occupied a large and comfortably upholstered giant model of a teacup; while Phœbe rotated demurely in a comfortable seat set between the wings of a giant swan.

It pleased Phœbe to see Henry in this mad mood. This crazy, dare-devil Henry. It was a Henry she had never seen before, a Henry she had not even suspected. Pepi Klem and he behaved like children. The switchback railway. The spiral slide. The house of mystery. Where she judged it was prudent for herself, she took part; where not, she stood by and laughed. It was as though her husband had opened a safety-valve of high spirits. Phœbe welcomed it. The weight of the winter seemed to be lifted from him. She was grateful to this madcap girl for breaking down his seriousness; for releasing the boy that was still in him. If they were all a little above themselves; even a little hysterical; then that, indeed, didn't matter.

That night they lay in the darkness side by side, still too excited to sleep. After a time Phœbe spoke:

"Henry."

"What, dear?"

"Today was Sunday. Isn't it awful to think!"

"Think what, dear?"

"How we've both been behaving."

"Awful, wasn't it!"

But she could feel the bed shaking as he laughed silently to himself.

III

The Hirsch ladies' reception of her was a little stiff, Phœbe felt, when next she went to call in the Wieden. The younger Hirsch sister had been so ready to open her formal heart to this foreign girl her nephew had begged her to befriend, that Phœbe's casual treatment of her, Phœbe's disregard of her advice over such matters as lodging and a language teacher, had looked like a rebuff.

And young Frau Hayburn's husband had made none too favourable an impression either. His awkwardness of person, his pronouncements on matters Viennese about which he could not possibly know, his British off-handedness—all these things together did not recommend him. And his table manners were deplorable. He did not seem to have the faintest idea how to manage his coffee-cup, the little cakes or the thimble-glass of cognac, which were provided for his entertainment. Max said he was clever, and this Max's aunts were quite ready to believe. Herr Hayburn's knowledge of German, if it were gained in the short months he had been in Vienna, was quite astounding, mixed though it might be, here and there, with the language of his workmen. Even his grasp of Austrian politics, if unconventional, was remarkable. But he was an odd, angular sort of young man to have paying a visit, and the ladies had been glad when his wife had taken him away again.

But now Phœbe's condition and her need of their help held an appeal that was irresistible. Of course dear Frau Hayburn must come to them whenever she felt like it! Yes, a little house on the edge of the Vienna Woods was just the place for her to spend the summer waiting for her baby! That was to say, if her dear husband really insisted that he was unable to leave Vienna for a proper holiday, because of all this new and very important work he was organising.

Besides, they themselves would only be out of town for four weeks. They had quiet rooms in Gastein where they went each year, so that Helene might take the cure. For the rest of the summer they lived very well and much more quietly staying at home, taking the air in the Prater, or even, if they felt adventurous, driving out into the surrounding country. If fashionable

Vienna was pleased to disport itself in the Salzkammergut, on Tyrolese mountains, or by the Adriatic, that was fashionable Vienna's affair. And so, for the greater part of the summer, these well-intentioned and rather sentimental ladies would be at dear Frau Hayburn's disposal.

Left alone with Fräulein Stephanie, Phœbe spoke of doctors. She told her of Bel's letter insisting she had much better go home.

Her friend called the proposal ridiculous. Why, she demanded, should dear Frau Hayburn leave the city where the most famous specialists in Europe were to be found. Did not the whole world of medicine come here to learn? Where could Frau Hayburn better be looked after? Had she never heard of the great medical school and hospital founded long ago in the time of Maria-Theresa by the great Queen herself? And was there not at this moment an excellent maternity hospital in the Alsergrund?

Phœbe did not know that she had done the one thing that no Viennese would allow. She had implied a criticism of Vienna. She had an idea that doctors in Glasgow were not quite ignorant, that the city in the Clyde had contributed more than its share to the store of medical knowledge; but never having had much interest in these things, she was unable to find names and facts to set against those of Stephanie.

And yet she was glad her friend was so insistent; glad that everything she said supported Henry. For Bel's influence with Phœbe was strong. Stronger, indeed, than Phœbe knew.

Though a week or more had passed, she had not yet brought herself to answer Bel's letter. It was nothing to run counter to Bel's advice in unimportant things. But in this, a great happening in her life, all Phœbe's instinct turned towards Bel's judgment.

She was happy in Vienna. The tenderness that had somehow been re-born between herself and Henry was everything to her. She loved her husband, and had no wish to leave him. Yet, she had kept Bel's letter, wondering.

Now her decision was taken. Tonight she would write to say she was staying where she was. That she had good friends. That everything was available for her well-being. That Henry could not possibly do without her.

Presently she realised that her friend was sitting watching her,

her white hands slowly smoothing out the folds of her stiff black silk.

"*Na?* Frau Hayburn? You have come back?" Stephanie Hirsch was smiling with quizzical affection.

"Back?"

"You were not here. You were lost? No?"

For reply Phœbe stood up, smiling herself in turn, embarrassment adding colour to her face. She held out her hand.

With a quick gesture Stephanie put a hand on each of her shoulders, turned her to the light and regarded her for a time with admiration.

"You are a dear and beautiful child!" she said, speaking in her own language, and, taking Phœbe into her arms, kissed her first on one cheek and then the other.

Phœbe blushed scarlet and took her leave. Austrians were perhaps sentimental, she told herself, as she made her way down the worn stone staircase. But she would go back soon. For Stephanie Hirsch was kind.

Chapter Fourteen

THE Hayburns were present at Pepi Klem's reunion with her parents. Behind a set smile of politeness the Scotch couple considered the episode over-acted.

Pepi threw herself first into her mother's, then into her father's arms. She begged their forgiveness, implored them not to scorn her, and told them her love had brought her back. But she had not, it seemed, retracted one whit from the stand she was taking over becoming a singer and leading an independent life of her own.

Her simple, kindly parents, loving, in the Austrian fashion, this dramatic situation, were delighted. Her father offered, now he was convinced, as he put it, that music really called her, to pay out a portion of what had been intended as her dowry, for the proper training of her voice. The mention of the word dowry caused Pepi to demand in stricken tones: How was poor, poor Willi Pommer? Willi Pommer, it seemed, felt rather a dull dog these days, on account, no doubt, of herself; but apart from that he was very much as usual. This last was the only part of this scene of reunion that did not quite come up to the emotional level of the rest, the Hayburns felt, forgetting that Pepi had merely broken an agreement, and not Willi Pommer's heart.

But it was not for these two young people from an Island where the show of feeling is counted a weakness, to judge this reunion in a land where quick emotion is part of the currency of daily expression. That the Klems exaggerated their joy did not mean that their feelings were hollow.

Pepi, then, was to continue with her cousin Lisa Fischer until such time as the young Herr and Frau Hayburn should be gone. Pepi, greatly daring, had told her parents where she was living at present, guessing rightly that even Fräulein Fischer would be caught up in the present wave of emotion—other aspects of her existence forgotten—and clothed with a halo as a handmaid of song. Thereafter she, Pepi, would return to her father's roof, hire a piano, and add arpeggios and distinction to her home in the Quellengasse.

It was on account of the arpeggios that Frau Klem looked to the Hayburns' going with so little concern. For would not Pepi presently be a famous prima donna and fully compensate them?

If Phœbe and Henry could not, perhaps, read the future with the Klems' eyes, they were, none the less, pleased that the matter should be so pleasantly settled.

II

The month of April was, indeed, to be among the most pleasant Phœbe had known. When it was some days old she wrote to Bel telling her that she intended to stay with her husband in Vienna; that here there was more than the necessary skill—in this she quoted Stephanie Hirsch pompously—and that they were now looking for a little house near the woods in which to spend the summer. When she had posted the letter she felt misgivings. It was not easy for her seriously to flaunt Bel.

But now, with her husband and the Hirsch ladies supporting her own strong inclinations, Phœbe decided that her decision must be right.

She was seeing much of Stephanie Hirsch now. Henry had taken Maximilian's lecture to heart; and, busy though he was, he made time to visit the "old tabbies" in the Paulanergasse, present them with a bouquet of Italian roses with a formality that sat so ill upon him that they were touched, and thank them for all the kind interest they were taking in his wife.

And so, with the best of goodwill fully restored, Stephanie Hirsch put herself and her carriage at Phœbe's disposal and spent many radiant April days with her, exploring Vienna's lovely surroundings. These were days unique in Phœbe's life. In her memory they were to take on the quality of a dream, long since dreamt. Even as she lived them, she was assailed at times with a sense of their unreality.

The soft air of an unusually mild spring. The shining Russian horses. The much-polished, old-fashioned carriage. The grey-haired, elderly woman in the carriage beside her, whose mid-

European elegance owed little to the fashion of her time; whose dignity did not rob her friendliness of warmth. The triumphant consciousness of her own young body, and the magic that her love for Henry was working within it.

More than once their carriage took them up into the woods out of sight of any dwelling, following, perhaps, an alley road by some rushing stream. They drove through regions of pine-trees where squirrels scurried out of sight, disappearing into the gloom of the brown, needle-covered forest floor; through bright regions of sprouting beech, oak or birch, where there were April violets, pale fresh grass and patches of white sunshine. Then suddenly they might come upon an opening and find all Vienna lying over yonder in the crystal distance; its gardens, its palaces, its church spires all to be distinguished in the clear spring light. Days of rapture, of expectation, of young fulfilment, of sharp awareness of the romance and beauty that fed her avid senses.

By mid-April they had found a little house. It had not been altogether easy for Phœbe to persuade Stephanie that she and her husband were seeking anything so simple. Like most other Continentals of her day, the younger Fräulein Hirsch took for granted that the Hayburns, like all the other "English", were made of money.

It was a house, its upper storey of timber, situated in the forest near Ober Döbling, a miniature Tyrolean chalet, gay with fresh paint, with an upper balcony from which you could touch the pine-trees, a little rose-garden, a motherly landlady, who was, at once, intimately interested in Phœbe, and a benign St. Bernard dog, that bore with sleepy dignity the malicious slander painted on a board nailed to the garden gate, that here there was a fierce creature on the watch ready to tear all tramps and vagrants to pieces.

On the following Sunday Henry went alone to see this house. He grumbled, as a formal show of his authority, at the price demanded for the season, decided, however, that it was healthy and at a distance that could easily be covered twice a day on his "Kangaroo", and so it was taken.

Phœbe seemed to herself to be moving through this Viennese April on a strange rising wave of happiness. Her heart kept bursting into an ever-brighter blooming, like the lilac and the laburnum in the parks around her. She ran to the Paulanergasse to tell Stephanie that Henry had taken the house, and that they were moving out on the first of May.

Stephanie Hirsch bent to kiss Phœbe, and as she did so, there were tears in her eyes. At no time in her own life had it been given to her to know ecstasy. The sight of it in Phœbe aroused in her a strange, unnamed compassion.

"But, my dearest," she said, "the first of May you cannot go. You are coming in the carriage with me." And as Phœbe looked blank, she added: "On the first of May is the May Corso in the Prater. It is very important that you see these things, if you will live in Vienna." And she went on to explain to Phœbe the nature of this May Day ceremony. Nothing would make her sister Helene and herself happier, than that Phœbe and Herr Hayburn should drive in the Prater with them.

They accepted the invitation, and Phœbe's month of April moved on joyfully to this fitting end.

III

The first of May dawned serene and misty, promising a full continuation of the fine weather. Henry, accustomed to early rising, awoke at his usual time. It was almost with a sense of annoyance that, as full consciousness returned, he came to remember what day it was. He was an industrious young man, with work to do, and a day of holiday seemed to him at this cool hour of the morning, nothing but a needless and frivolous interruption.

He turned to look at his wife. She lay beside him, still breathing deeply and steadily. Her face was rosy with sleep. The black plaits of her hair were straggling on the pillow beside her. That he might not wake her, he slid gently from his side of the bed, crossed to the open window and stood in his nightshirt looking about him.

The Quellengasse beneath was almost empty. No workmen, it seemed, would be working on the unfinished buildings today; but further down he could see a woman on her knees scrubbing an entrance. Nearer by, a peasant woman was delivering milk from a cart drawn by a great, yellow ox. A small baker's boy, in a white coat, passed beneath, bearing so large a tray on his head that, for a time, it seemed to Henry, as he looked down, as though this tray of *Kaisersemmel*, salt sticks and *Gipfel* moved along the pavement of its own accord. In a kitchen near at hand someone was roasting coffee. Its sharp aroma mixed itself with the smell of last night's *Gulasch* and the May-time scents of lime and plane-trees.

He gave a sudden start as he became aware that his wife was standing in her nightdress beside him.

"Oh, hullo. I thought you were asleep."

"So I was. But you've been standing here for hours, Henry. What are you looking at?"

"Nothing much. The weather."

"It's going to be glorious today!" She looked about her eagerly.

"Happy?"

She turned to him and nodded, her eyes dancing like a child's. Suddenly her face flushed, and as though to cover some other feeling, she laid a hand on her husband's arm.

"You silly boy," she said quickly, "you've let yourself get as cold as a puddock. Go back to bed and warm yourself."

As they sat up in bed, Phœbe talked with animation of the day that lay before them. He had never seen her so uplifted. He watched her, wondering. She lay propped against her pillow looking at a beam of morning sunshine as it crept across Frau Klem's coarse window-curtains.

"If our baby's a boy," she said presently, "he's going to be called Robert Hayburn after your father. Just that. Robert Hayburn. None of your Ruanthorpe-Moorhouses or Dermott-Moorhouses or any of that nonsense."

Henry laughed. It was impossible to follow the train of her thinking.

"I don't see what there is to laugh at," Phœbe said, turning to look at him. "And, by the way, this morning I must go out and find some flowers for the Hirschs. I meant to order them yesterday." And, as he had protested at her extravagance, she added: "We really must, Henry; they've been so kind."

While Phœbe was buying flowers, Frau Klem brought Henry a letter. It was in the handwriting of Bel Moorhouse. To his surprise, it was addressed to himself. He tore it open with curiosity. As he read it his face darkened. So Bel was writing to *him* now? To tell him it was his duty to send Phœbe home! But his wife wasn't going! What business had Bel to interfere? He folded the letter angrily and thrust it into his pocket. He would not mention this to Phœbe today.

IV

Stephanie Hirsch felt inclined to laugh at Henry as, along with his wife, he presented himself in the Paulanergasse at three o'clock. He wore his best clothes as though they belonged to someone else, and his dutiful, self-conscious bearing suggested anything but lightness of heart. But his wife, with her arms full of roses, her glowing cheeks, and her summer dress, seemed to bring with her everything that was young into the old-fashioned room of the Paulanergasse.

The Hayburns were given sweet wine and the inevitable chocolate cakes with cinnamon, while the Hirsch ladies put the finishing touches to their stiff finery. At last, with an amount of fuss that was a severe trial to the young man of the party, they were seated behind cockaded flunkeys in the family landau.

Stephanie had looked forward to this year's Corso with keen anticipation. It is always pleasant to show off what one has known and loved to the young and the eager. And to this Viennese woman there was nothing so precious as Vienna and its pageantry. She sat beside Herr Hayburn facing Phœbe, who was in the place of honour on her sister Helene's right hand.

The carriage made its way out of the Wieden and down that part of the Ring that leads to the Aspern Bridge. Already it was noticeable that all the smarter traffic was making in the same direction. As they passed the Stadtpark, with its shrubs hanging heavy with blossom, they noticed it was unusually empty. The fineness of the weather was drawing everybody to the Prater to see the world go by.

Presently they had crossed the Danube Canal and found themselves in the Praterstrasse, the wide and handsome street that leads to the entrance of the Prater itself. Here carriages were coming in from all sides, and the traffic was heavy as it moved down towards the famous pleasure-grounds.

Workpeople on holiday crowded the side-walks; some of them standing, hoping to see a celebrity pass; more of them walking towards the Prater, where they would see the parade in full swing. There were many families, the plump fathers and mothers carrying baskets of food to be eaten later. Even if times were bad, and there was no money for the roundabout or even a cheap restaurant in the People's Prater, you could always take the children's bread and sausage to the Prater meadows, and have all the fun of watching and criticising the rich and the aristocratic, as they displayed their finery to each other in the Haupt Allee—or main drive. The weather of the first of May was kind this year. Little children trotted, chattering and excited, after their parents.

Now the Hirschs' landau was at the Prater Stern, where seven streets meet and the great park begins. Here the press of carriages was so thick that they could move round the circle only slowly, almost completing it before they reached the entrance to the Haupt Allee. Now they had passed under the railway bridge and were in the great carriage-drive itself, with its double rows of giant chestnut-trees, planted three and a half centuries before, in the days when the Prater was an island of the Danube, and the private hunting-grounds of Austria's rulers.

As they found their place in the glittering stream of carriages, Phœbe looked at her companions. The elder Fräulein Hirsch had taken on a quite special dignity, now that she found herself in this parade of Vienna's society. She sat like royalty, alert and stiff, ready to return the formal salutations of acquaintances as they passed her coming back down the Haupt Allee in the opposite direction. Henry was sitting, glum and unhappy-seeming, as many Scots do when they are excited. Stephanie made weak attempts to appear dignified like her sister, but she was flushed and happy, and intent on pointing out everything.

Phœbe had seen the parade of carriages in the Prater many times already, but never thus, at its height. And it would have taken someone who was much less avid of life, much less eager, to remain cold before this astonishing spectacle.

Now, leaving the entrance, they were passing the Kaisergarten, where the Court, ever conscious of the spectacle it must provide for the people, had come to be seen and to take a ceremonial luncheon. Now their coachman had cracked his whip, the horses had dropped into a trot, and the landau was holding its place in this river of vehicles that flowed between towering, leafy banks of fresh green chestnut-trees with the candles on them bursting into bloom—banks that seemed to stretch into infinity in front of them.

Thousands of *Fiakers*. Poor and prosperous. Cabriolets. Phætons. A four-in-hand driven by some sensation-mongering grandee. A closed carriage with a regal old man looking through its windows. A shabby *Komfortable* with its single tired horse, lumbering along, bearing a numerous and vulgarly joyful City family. An open landau with a French governess and three young children in white, holding coloured balloons. One or two featherweights, with officers driving high-stepping English hackneys tearing back towards town from the May Day races in the Freudenau at a showy speed that was very dangerous in this traffic. A famous actor with his wife in a discreet, blue coupé. Aristocrats, financiers, men-about-town, demi-mondaines, gourmets, foreign ambassadors, artists, actresses—a swaying, garish flood of elegant humanity.

There were high spirits and laughing salutes. There were women dressed in the best of taste, and women whose every garment was an exaggeration. There were feathers and parasols; elegant, light-coloured top-hats and carefully trimmed whiskers. There were faces thick with paint, and faces lined with sorrow. There were carefree, reckless faces, and faces stiff with ambition.

It was astonishing how Stephanie seemed to know everyone, although she came out so little. Her eyes went everywhere, seeing everyone, seeming to miss no one. There, on the riding-track beneath the trees, was the Count Egon Taxis. And with him was the Archduke Franz Salvator. There, in her carriage with a friend, was the prima donna Pauline Lucca. And there, coming down in the other direction, was the Princess Metternich, sitting in a coupé with an elderly woman, who looked like a professional companion. And look! Over there, being greeted by Sonnenthal, the actor, was Fräulein Charlotte Wolter of the Imperial Theatre. And the fair young lady who was with her was Fräulein Kathi

Schratt! And there again, on horseback in the riding-track, were the Barons Albert and Nathaniel Rothschild.

Stephanie mentioned the names of many famous figures as they passed them by. Counts and princes. Fashionable singers and artists. Nobles and aristocrats from the Crown lands and the Empire. But she did not mention the great hinterland of struggling peoples inside the ring of Habsburg influence, whose labours went to build up this unique three miles of glittering pageantry. Peasants from the Hungarian Puszta. Sub-Carpathian gypsies. Jewish artificers from Galicia. Swabian tobacco-planters from the Bacska. Horse-dealers from Moravia. Bohemian weavers. Mohammedan trinket merchants from Servia. Podolian shepherds. And many more. All contributing to the display in this, their Emperor's capital city. A city that was, in the main, only hazily conscious of their remote existence.

But it was not the names of celebrities, of which she knew nothing, this brilliant froth, floating on a sea of some fifty million souls, that made the shining afternoon for Phœbe. It was the perfume of the trees, the low-hanging blossoms, the glimpses of green meadows and sunlit ponds, the carriages with their freights of elegance and colour, the flunkeys in traditional family uniforms, even the moving forest of whips, the smell of harness and of foaming, high-mettled horses.

And, when at last they had come to the end of the seemingly endless Haupt Allee, and their horses, rounding the Lusthaus, dropped to the traditional walk for the beginning of the return journey, the glimpses of the distant town through the green, the circle of blue mountains behind it, with the Habsburgwarte standing plumb above the centre of the Haupt Allee like the sight on a rifle, and the spire of Saint Stephen's dreaming in the sunshine a little on the left.

As again she lay in the darkness that night, sleep did not come at once. Still she was milling in the colourful traffic. Still she saw fashionable gloved hands raised in salutation. Still the endless line of giant trees bearing their candles. Still the perfume. Still a brassy phrase of distant music from the People's Prater.

Henry, from his breathing, did not seem to be asleep either.

"Henry."

"What is it, dear?"

"Wouldn't Bel have enjoyed seeing everything today?"

But Bel's letter was still in the pocket of the jacket he had not so long since taken off. Tonight he did not feel particularly well disposed towards Bel.

"Yes, I dare say she would," was his only comment. Then he added: "I must get to sleep. I want to be at the works early tomorrow."

Chapter Fifteen

THE beginning of June found Bel unsettled. Things were not going as she would have them go.

In the first place there was the question of holidays. Both the Arthurs, father and son, clamoured to go back to Arran. Her mother, who seemed, these days, to be determined to go against her, took their side. This year Bel had wanted somewhere more conventional. The freedom of Arran was demoralising. Each September, when she got the children home to Grosvenor Terrace after two months of running wild, it took her some weeks, and a strictness she had no pleasure in exerting, to bring them back to the ways of gentility.

Then there was George McNairn. Now, when he did go to business, it was only to drive down in a cab for a couple of hours, and come back utterly exhausted. Bel had never liked Mary and George much; but Mary was her husband's sister, and very much a part of her life. Mary must be helped. George could not leave Glasgow this summer, and Mary would not, of course, leave George. That meant seeing to the children, providing for their holiday and taking them off Mary's full and sorrowful hands. Sophia was too muddle-headed to help. Good-natured though she might be, she was no rock for Mary to cling to.

No. Mary's children must be removed, kept well and happy and forgotten about during this unhappy summer of their father's illness.

Arran, then, was the place. So the farmhouse was retaken; and Mrs. Barrowfield stoutly undertook to keep house throughout the two months of occupancy, bringing with her her own old and none too willing maids. Sarah would go down to look to Bel's children and also the little McNairn twin girls. Grosvenor Terrace and Albany Place must remain open. If the Arran contingent were packed together like sardines; if young cousins and maids from different households fought with each other like wild cats, then that was quite in the Arran tradition. Her mother, Bel assured herself a little callously, was more placid than she was, and would survive.

Sophia, having heard of this arrangement, announced, irresponsibly, that she thought she would like to go to Arran too. "You see, Bel dear, I'll be able to help with the children when you have to be in town. The only thing is, of course, that if I take my little maid with me, I don't know what I'll do with William. I don't suppose Arthur would like his company when he's by himself in Grosvenor Terrace?"

Bel had looked to having Grosvenor Terrace as a sanctuary to which she might run from the pandemonium of Brodick. Now even the sanctuary was to be invaded. But if the summer was to be ruined, let it be ruined thoroughly. Yes, William and everybody else might come to Grosvenor Terrace!

When she told Arthur, he was furious; which did not improve her own temper. She pointed out to her husband, not without some heat, that she had made all these arrangements to help his relatives—not hers; that the thought of this summer made her sick; and that the least he could do was to hold his tongue and go through with it.

But something quite other than these things lay at the source of Bel's discontent. It was her anxiety over Phœbe. Not content with Phœbe's reply, that she intended to stay in Austria with her husband, Bel had written to Henry, lecturing him on his responsibility towards so young a wife. She had waited for more than two weeks, then had received this reply:

"Dear Bel,

"I would have written to you sooner, but both of us have been very busy getting into this small house. We have taken it for the summer. Our friends say that it is the right place for Phœbe to be, and that the heat is never too much up here in the woods. But Phœbe will have told you that already. About her coming home. There is no question of it. There is every kind of help in Vienna when the time comes. It is said they are further advanced in these things than we are. So please do not write to us about this again. Our minds are made up. We both join in sending our love to everybody."

"Yours affectionately,

"Henry Hayburn."

This letter made Bel very angry. She, the centre and pivot of the Moorhouses, did not like to find herself thrust back into her place, and told to stay there, by this, the newest and certainly the least-loved member of the family. No, Henry was adding impertinence to Phœbe's stubbornness.

Bel rang for the carriage. She would show this letter to her mother. Wounded self-importance and baffled anxiety heaped themselves high upon her already blazing annoyance. She thrust the letter under Mrs. Barrowfield's nose.

"There, Mother. What do you think of that?"

"Dear me, Bel. What is it?" Mrs. Barrowfield took up her spectacles and rubbed them with deliberation. What was Bel in such a to-do about now?

Bel watched her as she stood reading the letter. When the old woman looked up, there was actually a grin of mischief in her face. Her daughter could hardly believe her eyes.

"That's one in the eye for you, my lady," she said, handing Bel back the letter. "Did I not tell ye to let them alone?—No! Here! Stop!"

But Bel had flounced out of the house again. Now her mother, looking down, could see her getting back into the carriage! Silly girl! She might have stayed for a cup of tea. But Mrs. Barrowfield was not unduly troubled. In her teens Bel had done this kind of thing quite often. And she had always come back repentant. She wasn't a really bad-tempered lassie. The old lady called to Maggie to bring only one cup.

II

On the same evening Arthur came, bringing his brother Mungo with him. Mungo, following upon a visit of compassion to Mary McNairn, had appeared at the office this afternoon. Arthur, who wanted to talk over the McNairn situation, had persuaded him to send a telegram saying he would remain at Grosvenor Terrace for the night.

Bel, dark as her mood was, was not displeased to see him. He brought with him an air of the country. He was solemn, responsible and friendly. Mungo, at least, was neither troubling her spirit nor needing her help. His good-natured simplicity, combined with his dignity and his solid bank balance, recommended him to her. His coming tonight and his preparedness to do what he could to help poor Mary in her difficulty was a great comfort. Bel felt that everything was not being left to Arthur and herself. Mungo, in this family of plaguey relatives, was one relative who did not plague.

He had scarcely arrived before he brought out a letter from Margaret addressed to herself. On edge, Bel opened it a little apprehensively. The other letter she had opened today had brought her no pleasure. This one ran:

"MY DEAR BEL,

"I give this to Mungo to hand over to Arthur if he does not see yourself. I do hope he remembers. I am writing to say what a great pleasure it would be if you could come down here to the Dower House for some days; indeed, for as long as you can. You have shown me so much kindness, which I have never yet had any opportunity to repay. I know you are a busy person, but *do* try to find time to come. If Arthur can manage a weekend, that will make it perfect. At least we can offer you a rest. I shall see to it that our noisy son is not allowed to disturb you. The gardens are beginning to look lovely. I should so much like you to see them. We are most distressed to hear about George McNairn. He is the reason for Mungo's coming to Glasgow. I hope your family is well.

"Your affectionate sister,
"MARGARET RUANTHORPE-MOORHOUSE."

Normally, going by herself to the Dower House to spend some days would not have appealed to Bel. She had never reached intimacy with Margaret. But just at present Bel was sick of intimacies. Margaret's cool good-nature, her unpossessiveness, even the fact that she could write of her year-old-son, Charles Mungo, without doting, appealed to Bel. The idea of well-bred simplicity and rest at the Duntrafford Dower House suddenly enchanted her.

Mungo added his invitation to Margaret's. She had told him to bring Bel back with him if, by chance, it could be managed. To Arthur's surprise, Bel accepted.

Bel, immaculate as always, was astonished a little at Margaret's appearance next evening. She had driven the pony-trap to the station herself. She wore a helmet-shaped fishing-cap of faded tweed that had originally belonged to Sir Charles. It was skewered to her somewhat untidy head by several formidable hatpins. Fishing-flies clung to it. Her Inverness cape was patched and faded, too, and her strong gauntlet gloves looked as though she had used them for weeding. Her handsome red face became even redder, and her fine teeth flashed resplendent, as she bent to give Bel one hand, while she held the reins in the other.

Clearly, here in the country Margaret was in her own element. Her manners were much more warm and not nearly so stiff. Could she be shy, and at some loss, when she came among her husband's relatives in the City?

"My dear Bel, how are you? This is very nice of you indeed! I'm so glad Mungo has persuaded you!" And as Mungo got Bel into the trap and followed after her himself, Margaret went on: "I'm afraid you're going to have a very dull time with us! Still, I've got one or two surprises for you. And tonight I am taking you over to the House to have dinner. Mother would be furious if she thought I was keeping you to myself. I promise you, it's only the family! I won't say any more!" She looked slyly at Mungo now. Bel wondered why. "Oh, is this your luggage the porter is bringing? Thank you, Macmillan. Yes, pile it all in here. That's splendid! What a lot of people we know at the station tonight, Mungo! Of course, it's Friday. Oh, hullo! How are you? On Sunday afternoon? Well, I think we'd like to very much. Oh, this is my sister-in-law, Mrs. Arthur Moorhouse. Oh, hullo! And how are you? When? On Monday to dinner? No, we've nothing."

And so it went on. Margaret seemed to be holding court in the pony-trap—presenting Bel, announcing triumphantly that she could not possibly let her go for a week at least, as she would miss this invitation and that. Bel wondered if this was the country's idea of a rest. But it was impossible for her to refuse, with the givers of the invitations standing there hanging upon her reply.

At last Margaret turned the pony's head and they were off. As she did so she laughed. "The thing is," she said gaily, "I don't often drive to the station like this. And when I do, I seem to run into everybody. And they all seem ready to pounce. You see, Mungo and I are frightful recluses really. And it makes it worse when we do appear. Still, we have to go sometime, and I'm so pleased we have you here to go with us. I was afraid Duntrafford might be dreadfully dull for you after Glasgow."

As the pony trotted downhill in the warm June evening, Bel sat silent, fatigued and apprehensive. Must she go the round of all these grand people she did not know, whose loud voices and high falutin manners seemed to her genteel, City Scotchness, as though they were all acting—rather self-consciously, but much delighted with themselves—in some charade? She had been lured down here with the promise of peace, rest and a garden. Now it would seem she was in the middle of a whirl such as she did not know at home. She was glad she had packed her best evening dress, just on chance. It would be put, it seemed, to much use.

III

There was a chatter of voices as Bel, following Margaret, and attended by Mungo, ascended the staircase to the drawing-room of Duntrafford House some hours later.

"Now, my dear," Margaret announced as they stood aside to have the door thrown open, "this is surprise number one."

And a surprise it indeed was. For, as Bel advanced to take Lady Ruanthorpe's hand, she saw that the room held David, Grace and Mrs. Dermott.

"Look who's with me!" Margaret called triumphantly.

Bel, as ever, rose to the occasion. Her sudden shyness gave her cheeks colour, and to her confident, somewhat provincial manners, a charming—almost a young girl's hesitancy. For a moment as he watched her, David caught a glimpse of the young Bel Barrowfield his brother Arthur had presented to him more than ten years ago. Her close-fitting dress of lace and lilac satin. Her fair, carefully arranged hair. Her fine eyes and elegant mouth. Her clear skin. The effect she made was excellent.

Bel, sensing the surprise and pleasure at her unexpected appearance, paid back this friendly homage with a full measure of charm.

Lady Ruanthorpe kissed her for the first time in her life. "This is wonderful, my dear! But why didn't you tell us, Margaret? Charles, ring for Campbell. He must lay another place."

But old Sir Charles paid no attention. He left arrangements to his daughter. He was advancing to meet the lovely Mrs. Arthur Moorhouse. A smart girl, this sister-in-law of Margaret's. He wished his own women could get the same kind of spit and polish on themselves. He gave her both hands, and likewise, quite unexpectedly, bestowed upon Bel an avuncular kiss. Thereafter he called to Margaret to order up champagne.

Mrs. Dermott, too, hailed her with pleasure. "You didn't expect to find me here, did you, Bel? But Lady Ruanthorpe very kindly asked me with David and Grace. You see, Mrs. Moorhouse, we've been writing to each other about the Indigent Mothers for years, and we both felt it would be such a good thing if we could really meet and thrash them out. I promised not to quarrel with Sir Charles about our grandsons." Mrs. Dermott manœuvred herself round in her chair to look slyly—if anything so large as Mrs. Dermott could look slyly—at her host.

But Sir Charles did not hear. He was delightedly filling a glass of sherry to give to his beautiful guest.

Had Bel known these relatives would be at Duntrafford, she certainly would not have come. But now their presence—as the familiar so often does in an unfamiliar setting—reassured and pleased her. To meet Grace and David, smiling and affectionate, seemed to her like suddenly meeting her own children.

And as she sat at Sir Charles's right hand at dinner, basking in his approval, even Mrs. Dermott did not seem so dogmatic and tiresome.

It was hard work responding to the flatteries of her host. But it was a pleasant labour. For so long now, no one else had required a like effort of her. Her beloved Arthur merely grunted at her and accepted her as part of the furniture. She was grateful to the old man for bothering to remind her that, conscientious mother and busy housewife though she might be, she still had a reasonable measure of good looks and charm. Yes, tonight she would indulge herself. She would allow herself to be as wilful and petted as she pleased.

During a pause in the conversation Mrs. Dermott bent forward to ask her: "Did you know, Bel, that David has just taken Sophia's boy into Dermott Ships?"

Bel was amazed. She could only repeat: "Dermott Ships?"

"Yes. Sophia spoke to me about it, and I mentioned it to David. He was delighted to have his own nephew, of course. And he says young William has made a very good start."

Had Bel been less anxious to keep up the façade of charm before Sir Charles, she would have asked questions. But her tired and flattered head was swimming a little from the unaccustomed glass of sherry, and now at the table a sip or two of champagne.

She had spoken to Arthur about David's behaviour, and Arthur had said it was neither for himself nor Bel to interfere. Now it seemed Mrs. Dermott had taken things in hand and the matter was settled! In spite of herself, Bel wondered how. For a moment she felt a stab of jealousy; a shaft of resentment piercing the glowing cloud of well-being that enveloped her. She must ask Sophia about this later. But almost at once her thoughts, rather inconsequently, floated off yet again into her rosy surroundings.

"I'm certain he's a clever boy," Mrs. Dermott said after a moment, puzzled, a little, at Bel's smiling unresponsiveness.

"Oh!—Wil? Yes, I'm sure he is."

But Sir Charles felt the ladies had said enough about their own affairs. He frowned a little, swallowed some champagne, and turned to Mrs. Dermott, demanding:

"What school have you put your grandson down for? We've put Charlie down for Eton."

IV

In the drawing-room before the men came, Bel found herself alone with Mrs. Dermott and Lady Ruanthorpe. Grace had carried Margaret off to see the rival baby, Robert David, now asleep upstairs.

If, thanks to black coffee, her thoughts were rather less misted than they had been at the dinner-table, Bel was still a little above herself; a little drunk with unaccustomed flattery; a little too confident that Bel Moorhouse could do no wrong.

For a moment, as they talked, the nagging pain which was Phœbe pulled at her heart-strings. She sat silent, watching Mrs. Dermott and Lady Ruanthorpe: the forceful, shipping prince's widow, and the sharp old lady of the county with her natural habit of command. They were strong personalities, both of them; more informed, more travelled, better bred than herself. Bel's snobbery was prepared to think them wiser than they were.

Should she not ask their help about Phœbe? Beg them to advise her what she must do? Had not Mrs. Dermott straightened out the difficulty between David and young Wil Butter, in a way that could only leave her astonished?

As though in answer to her thinking, Mrs. Dermott turned. "And how are the young people in Vienna, Mrs. Moorhouse? I hear Mrs. Hayburn is expecting a baby."

Bel blushed as though she had been detected in some misdeed. "So far as I know, they're very well."

"Are you talking about anybody I know?" Lady Ruanthorpe demanded, her hands clasped over her ebony stick.

"Yes, Lady Ruanthorpe. We are talking about Mungo's sister, Phœbe." Bel raised her voice a little.

"Oh, Phœbe? I know Phœbe. Nice child. She's a friend of mine. How does she like Vienna?"

"She's going to have a baby." Mrs. Dermott repeated this information with unnecessary loudness.

Her hostess was not deaf. Like many of the old, she was given merely to indulging herself in fits of inattention. She stabbed an immense lump of coal in the fireplace. It fell to pieces, flaming brightly. She looked at the end of her stick. "Charles is always scolding me for doing that. He says it will ruin the end of this. But I don't care." She settled back, looked at the others and said, "Now what were we talking about. Oh yes, Phœbe. So she's having a baby? Dear me! What a lot of babies! My daughter, your daughter, and now Phœbe." And, as no one had anything to say to this, she added: "She's coming home to have it, of course?"

"No, I don't think she is," Bel said, delighted that the subject had thus opened itself.

"I don't see how she can have it there. Her husband ought to send her." Lady Ruanthorpe said, with indignation.

"They have been writing to say that everything is better arranged in Vienna."

"Everything fiddlesticks! What do *you* think, Mrs. Dermott?"

"If it had been my daughter, I would never have considered such nonsense for a moment!" Mrs. Dermott breathed all the indignation of a Victorian matron.

"Phœbe isn't my daughter, unfortunately," Bel said. "I've been terribly worried about it. You see, I brought her up."

The old women looked at Bel. She had spoken with emotion. There were tears in her eyes. Lady Ruanthorpe blinked like an old parrot. Mrs. Dermott's face went red, a little, and she said: "I know, my dear. Of course you have."

They were all three quiet for a time. The large ormolu clock on the white marble mantelpiece ticked quietly under its glass dome.

"Mungo is her eldest brother. He had better write to her husband," Lady Ruanthorpe said with decision. She believed in the direct attack.

"Henry Hayburn is very stubborn," Bel said elegantly, wiping her eyes, and pleasantly aware that the sight of her tears had had its effect on the others.

In reply, Lady Ruanthorpe merely grunted.

Bel looked at Mrs. Dermott, the planner of campaigns, the skilful shepherdess of committees.

"I've been thinking," Grace's mother said presently. "And it has just struck me that it would be a good thing if Henry's brother Stephen went on holiday to Austria this summer. You see, I've known these boys all my life. Their father was my husband's friend. Henry was brought up to worship his brother Stephen. Stupidly, my husband always thought. Stephen was older, and much more of a success—to his mother's way of thinking, anyway."

Bel caught her meaning. "You mean that Stephen could persuade Henry?"

"Persuade Henry and bring Phœbe home. You see, Bel, she's terribly young. And perhaps a little reckless. She won't want to have her second baby so far away, I do assure you."

"No."

"And David will be delighted to give Stephen the time off and what money he needs. After all, Phœbe is David's sister. I'll make a point of seeing Stephen whenever I get home."

Bel expressed appreciation. But now that it looked as though she might have her way, she was filled, perversely, with misgiving and a sense of guilt. She knew how angry her mother would be with this. Perhaps, after all, Mrs. Barrowfield's counsel was right. Should not they all forbear from interfering? Had her emotions, her tenacious love for this sister of Arthur's who had once done so much for herself, betrayed her reason?

But, after all, what did it come to? A child brought safely into the world among its own kind. Some months of separation for the young couple, at the most. A triumphant Phœbe returning to rejoin her husband with their baby. And yet Bel knew she would not, when next she found herself at Monteith Row, admit just what part she had taken in this affair. She hoped Mrs. Dermott might arrange it so that it would look as though it had been settled between Henry and his brother Stephen.

The men were joining them now, and Grace and Margaret were appearing.

Bel's eyes met David's, and she threw him a smile. But if the smile was elegant, it was likewise artificial. She was not so sure now that she liked David as much as usual. Mrs. Dermott had said that David was delighted about Wil Butter. Now she was quite certain he would be delighted to send Stephen Hayburn to Austria.

Bel decided that she liked men who were not always so easily made delighted.

V

Now Phœbe seemed to be all by herself in a swing-boat in the People's Prater, clinging to its sides for dear life, as it swung up infinitely high, then crashed back with a sickening shudder, amid the roar of the people who had gathered round to look at her. Why didn't it stop? Why couldn't she get out? Why did it always tremble so shockingly when it reached the bottom of the swing? As though at any moment it would fall to pieces and kill her? And why did the people always roar each time it fell back? She must get out at once!

But where was Henry? Why wasn't he here with her? Oh, there he was, standing among the roaring crowd, looking up expressionless, as though she did not belong to him! She would give him a good scolding for this when they let her out! Didn't he know that she was going to have a child? His child? That all this horrible swinging was the worst thing possible for her now?

But who was it that was pushing her like a madman? She must try to turn round and shout to him to stop it at once! She could hear him howl with laughter every time he swung her! Yes! Just as she thought. Stephen—Henry's brother. Stephen's behaviour was amiable and good up there with them in the little house in the forest. They had spent several gay weeks together. But now, in the Prater, he looked like a maniac, a demon, as he hurled himself laughing against this dreadful swing!

Again there was a crash and a shudder as the swing descended. If the people would only stop roaring, she might make herself heard. Oh, there was Bel, pushing her way determinedly through the middle of them, trying to get to her! Bel would stop Stephen's mad behaviour! Force him to see reason! Make him understand that she was going to have a child; that she must be careful, just now. Bel was always self-possessed. Always knew exactly what to do. Even now she looked calm, almost complacent. But wasn't she too complacent? Didn't Bel, even, grasp the danger of this mad joke?

Now she was swinging down to the ground again. The swing was shuddering dreadfully. This time it would certainly fall to pieces! And what a roar the people were making! But all the same she must shout. Bel *must* be made to hear her!

"Bel! Bel! Stop him! Stephen must stop!"

"It's all right, Mrs. Hayburn, I'm here beside you. Just keep calm. The captain says we'll be in the Firth of Forth in about an hour. Then we'll be in sheltered water."

Was she coming back to consciousness? Had she been dreaming? Or drugged by that silly student who was the only doctor on board ship? Or had fever made her delirious? Now, at any rate, she was in her senses again, and knew she was on her way from Hamburg to Leith. Coming home into Bel's care to have her baby. And who was this beside her now? Of course, the stewardess.

Once more a wave struck the side of the little steamer, causing it to rear, shudder and fall back again like a stricken animal. Spray struck the glass of her port-hole, like a handful of sharp pebbles; then the wave rose against it, filling her cabin with green darkness. Her tortured body could feel the engines chugging, vibrating, then racing as the propeller left the water. As the ship rolled back she could hear the water rushing from the deck above her, the roaring of the wind; and now her port-hole showed a disk of grey sky once more.

Must she be sick again? Must she rack her exhausted, pregnant body yet more?

"I'm sorry, stewardess."

"It's all right, Mrs. Hayburn. Don't mind about me. Is that better? Wait a moment. Now lie back and rest. A drink of water?"

"Thank you. Did the captain say an hour?"

"Yes, Mrs. Hayburn. Just about an hour."

In an hour this heaving torment would have ceased; this racking sickness would have stopped adding itself to the fevered chill, or worse, she had so foolishly given herself, sitting with Stephen, lightly clad, much too late, in the garden of a Hamburg restaurant. The day had been hot. They had dragged round the sights. She had stupidly overtired herself. Merely to sit on and on in the cool night air had been delicious.

But now she was paying for her folly. Her throat was on fire. There was a cannon-ball in her head. Her limbs ached with fever, and there was other, more ominous pain. If only the storm would stop! But in an hour. Just about an hour, the captain had said.

But she smiled gamely as another wave struck them, and said: "Stormy."

"Yes. It's one of the worst late August storms I've known, Mrs. Hayburn. I've been on this trip a good many years."

But the pale girl had closed her eyes again, and consciousness seemed once more to have receded.

Sometime over an hour later Stephen Hayburn crawled from his cabin. The steamer was still swinging back and forth, but this was heaven to the last two days. He knocked gently on Phœbe's door.

"Mr. Hayburn?"

"Yes; how is my sister-in-law?"

For answer the student doctor opened Phœbe's door, closed it behind him, and stood supporting himself against the handrail in the passage. Was there sweat upon his brow because he too had been sick? Or was it the condition of the patient he had just left?

"How is she, Doctor?"

"Oh, she'll be all right. It's just this storm, and the other things coming together." He was still callow. His reassurances did not yet have quite the professional ring.

It was dark now as Phœbe came back again—dark, except for the light of the candle in its hanging socket. She opened her eyes and lay looking at the white-painted boards of the ceiling reflecting the dim yellow light. Her sleeping-bunk was quite miraculously still. Now and then on the deck above her there were footsteps. The port-hole must be open a little, for at intervals a light breeze made the flame flicker, and there were dockland smells of tar, smoke and seaweed. Far-off shouts came across the water, and the horn of some distant vessel on the move.

She closed her eyes again. How strangely still it was! She could hear the water of the dock lapping gently against the iron sides of the boat. Now she could rest. If only this shivering would leave her; this rawness all the way down her throat. She would try to fall asleep; perhaps she might wake up better.

But now she caught a faint perfume in the cabin. What was it? Why was it so familiar? Of course. It reminded her of the soap they used at home in Grosvenor Terrace. She had forgotten. Viennese soap smelt quite differently. The stewardess must use this soap, too.

And the stewardess was good. She was still sitting, holding her hand. By way of thanks, Phœbe pressed her hand in return.

But the hand was soft. It was not any more the workworn hand of a ship's stewardess. And why was her own hand now being lifted up and pressed to someone's lips? Phœbe raised her head and looked down. In the candlelight she could see a familiar, fair head bending over her; a fair head that was bowed in an agony of love and contrition.

Chapter Sixteen

IT was warm work toiling uphill on his "Kangaroo". Even now, in this first week of September, as Henry headed towards the little house in Ober Döbling, the air was still and sultry. He pedalled laboriously. His long, loose body sweated profusely. When he got in he would take off his clothes and stand under the spray he had arranged for himself in a corner of the garden. That would be cool and pleasant. And after his outdoor meal he would sit on for a little, inhaling the evening breath of the forest and the scent of wet earth, as his old landlord, Herr Weigel, moved about in the dusk, watering his garden.

But he must not linger long. He was resolved that all his time should be taken up with work while Phœbe was away. He had let himself get behind with things. It had been too pleasant up here this summer. Every night, almost, they had sat outside talking.

Now Henry was puffing along a dusty, suburban boulevard. Children on the pavement called to each other. They had come to look for this long-legged foreigner, mounted so strangely on two revolving wheels; for at this time the new "safety" bicycle was a novelty. Some of the bolder ran alongside, shouting. Young women sewing and gossiping together, as they sat on public benches beneath dusty chestnut-trees, looked up and smiled as he passed them by. But Henry was used to all this—so well used that he did not even notice.

No. There was much for him to do. There was no need for the loneliness he shrank away from. Phœbe and Stephen had been gone almost a week and he had managed very well. He had kept himself occupied with his books and his drawing-board.

He was passing villas now—villas separated from the street by high railings, hanging with dusty bougainvilia and parched rambler roses. Beyond, in their gardens, beneath umbrella-shaped trees, housewives were sitting at little metal tables set on the white gravel, occupying themselves with embroidery. In some gardens the evening meal had been laid out and was already in progress.

This being alone, this letting Phœbe go home with Stephen, was, after all, the right thing for him to do, surely. Was it not for the sake of their child?

It had flattered Henry's simplicity that Stephen had come out here to them. He had always looked up to Stephen, envied him his easy manners, his knowledge of the world. His coming had been a pleasant surprise, and his companionship just what Phœbe had needed during these summer days of waiting.

And Stephen, primed with David's money and Mrs. Dermott's arguments, had set them thinking. After all, their child's welfare must come before all else. If the chances of its arriving safely into the world were better at home, then home, as they both at last came to see, Phœbe must be sent. Now that Stephen would be able to take her with him, Henry had felt he must let her go.

Their Viennese friends had been bewildered. The disappointment of Stephanie Hirsch knew no bounds. That she should not be near Phœbe at the coming of the child, had been a blow to this gentle-hearted woman who had so much time and affection to throw away. She had begged her nephew Max to intervene. But it was all of no avail. And so Stephanie, and even the elder Fräulein Hirsch, had come with tears and roses to the Nordbahnhof to see Stephen and Phœbe go.

Now Henry had jumped from his bicycle, and was pushing it uphill. The way was steep and dusty. But for an occasional wine-garden, where heady, year-old wine was on sale, he was now quite in the country. To his left and right stretched the wine-lands. The clusters of grapes looked ripe already, as they hung in the evening sunshine, gold-green and matt blue, drinking in the last of the warm rays that slanted down upon them over the western forest. Their blue-sprayed leaves were limp with the long day or heat.

Now he had mounted again. In a short time he would be home. He pushed on with determination. Perhaps tonight there would be a letter. He had received an electric telegram saying Phœbe had arrived in Scotland. It had merely given that information; nothing more. But this evening there might be a letter giving him the details of her journey.

Now he had turned off the main road, and was walking once more, up towards the little house. The Saint Bernard dog had spied him, and was stirring up the dust with his great, soft paws as he gambolled down to meet him. Old Weigel was working among his tomato plants. As he pushed his "Kangaroo" through the gate, the old man heard Henry. He shouted an evening greeting, and told him that letters had come.

II

Two hours later Henry was still in the garden, sitting motionless, staring before him. They had brought out his supper to him. Later they had taken it away again.

The old couple took counsel with each other. Something had happened to him. He had received bad news. They were afraid to ask him. But something must be done.

It was getting dark. Old Weigel lit a candle, set it inside its glass funnel and carried it out into the garden.

Was Herr Hayburn quite well?

Henry's eyes wandered up to his face and he nodded.

Was Herr Hayburn's letter from the gracious lady?

The eyes that looked up at him were wild. "My wife is very ill. The child was born dead."

The old man winced. He stood by the little garden table unable to speak.

A cool breeze blew down from the woods. It brought with it a scent of pine resin. Here and there, down in the village, lights had begun to twinkle. In the distance there was the sound of a woman's laughter.

Herr Weigel came to Henry, laid a hand for a moment on his shoulder, then took his old, fat and sympathetic body into the house. There was nothing he could do in the face of this. Nothing he could say.

Some little time later the Weigels looked out once more into the garden. It had become quite dark. They could see him still bent forward, his arms resting on the checked table-cloth, his strained face caught in the circle of light. In one hand were the folded letters.

The great dog ranging in the garden came and brushed against Henry, bringing him back to life a little. So there was to be no child. And Phœbe was dangerously ill. No child. Even with all his young anticipation, he had not fully known how much he had looked to having this child.

But Phœbe? Supposing there was to be no Phœbe either?

He didn't know. He wasn't the kind of man who could manage himself, who could command his stunned feelings.

Now there might be no Phœbe.

His landlady came from the house. She had a glass of cognac in her hand. She sat down at the table beside him.

"Take that, Herr Hayburn."

He took it from her and swallowed it obediently.

The good woman was encouraged. "It's getting cold, Herr Hayburn; come inside." She led Henry into her kitchen. "I'll make you some coffee. You've eaten nothing." He came with her, obediently, like a boy.

Now he was sitting warming himself by the stove and drinking the coffee she had given him.

"*Na?* Herr Hayburn? Better?"

He nodded. She was a motherly woman, this, with the kindliness of peasant Austria.

He began talking, his year-old German stumbling here and there. His wife had caught a severe chill, bringing on high fever. Following on that, she had crossed the North Sea in an August gale. She had been very sick. They had taken her straight to hospital in Edinburgh where her baby was stillborn and where she, herself, now lay in danger.

It seemed to give him relief to tell them; to loosen the tension.

The old man tried to encourage him. The gracious lady would be well soon. She was young. Many young people had lost a first child. Their married life was only beginning. Would it not be better now that Herr Hayburn should go and lie down?

Henry went. Their wooden bedroom was still redolent of Phœbe. Of her clothes; of scent Stephen had bought her; of herself. There were one or two odd belongings she had left behind. Some ribbon. A handkerchief. Some books.

He sat down on his bed and re-read his letters. One from Arthur Moorhouse. One from Mrs. Barrowfield. Arthur's was a formal letter, stiff, sympathetic and put together with difficulty. Henry must believe Arthur when he wrote that Bel had acted out of her great affection for Phœbe. Bel and he were deeply sorry. Bel was refusing to leave Phœbe's side.

Mrs. Barrowfield had taken upon herself to write to Henry, too. Her letter was full of an old woman's love, and—if Henry's wit could have read beyond the restraint she had imposed upon herself—rage, at what had happened. She, too, had come to Edinburgh. And while the doctor had assured her that Phœbe would recover, she thought it would be wise for Henry to come home.

III

It was four o'clock in the afternoon some weeks later. Vienna lay drowsing beneath a late September sun that was bland and golden. Fashionable streets were beginning to give signs of life. Show windows had begun to display the novelties of the early winter.

In the many public gardens there were riots in the flower-beds. Trees and shrubbery were beginning to take on the brilliant reds and yellows of the autumn. The City was shaking itself free from the dust and heat of the summer.

Next week the Emperor Franz Joseph would have returned from his hunting-box at Ischl; the Crown Prince Rudolf from boar-hunting in Moravia; and it was believed that the Empress Elizabeth, who was somewhere on the Adriatic, would be returning to the capital shortly.

The autumn season was beginning. Everywhere friends met friends. Where had they been? In the Tyrol? In the Carpathians? On the Baltic coast? In Carlsbad or Gastein? At all events, it was splendid to see everybody again, and to look to the excitements, artistic, musical, and social, that their City had in store for them.

Maximilian Hirsch came down the Kärntnerstrasse humming to himself. A pleasant lunch-party, the weather and Vienna were having their effects upon him. For a moment he stopped before a flower shop to look at its triumphant display of colour. He meditated for a time as to whether he should commit himself, just at present, by bestowing these dark red roses in a certain quarter. But he decided with a chuckle, which interrupted but did not stop his humming, that, much as these wonderful flowers were crying out to be sent somewhere, it would be better, perhaps, just at the moment, if he avoided new complications. Having made up his mind thus momentously, he continued humming on his way.

Suddenly he became aware that he was being hailed from a carriage.

"Max! Max!"

"Aunt Steffi!"

"You bad boy. Were you trying to walk past me?"

"Of course not!" It was nice to be called a boy at fifty.

"Jump in beside me. I want to talk to you."

"Do you want to scold me for something?" He stepped up into the carriage, and put her hand to his lips.

"Not this afternoon, Maxerl, although you look as if you needed it. Next time, perhaps. No. I want to ask you about that poor child."

"Who? The little Hayburn?"

"Yes. Have you got an hour to spare?"

"No. But I shall spare it."

"That's a good boy. I'll drive you across to the Krieau, and you can give me a cup of chocolate."

"But with great pleasure! Oh! One moment! What about the silk stockings you were going to buy?"

"I wasn't going to buy any silk stockings. I won't tell you what I was going to buy."

"I'm quite sure it was silk stockings. Never mind. I'll buy a pair, and send them to you."

"Please, Johann. To the Creamery in the Krieau. Oh, I dare say you'll buy the silk stockings. But you won't send them to anyone so old and ugly as your Aunt Steffi."

The old coachman drove off laughing. The young Herr Maximilian had so much fun about him! He always had the effect of making his old ladies quite witty.

Maximilian was pleased with this encounter. It suited his mood. It was just right to go driving on this golden autumn afternoon with a fond and flattering woman, who, being old and a relative, did not make any claims upon him, other than those of family affection. "Tell me," Stephanie began presently, "has her husband come back?"

"Oh yes. Two or three days ago."

"He might have come to see me, Maxi. He knows I love his wife."

"He has been very busy. Actually, it was very difficult to let him go. But of course, I had to."

"Of course. And what did he say?"

"She has been very ill, but now she is out of danger."

"Thank God!"

Maximilian turned and smiled at the facile tears in his aunt's eyes, as, ranging from one side of the Ring to the other, they seemed to be seeking solace, at one moment in the Stadtpark, at another in the high buildings that faced it. "Was the child she lost a boy or a girl?"

"A boy."

"What a tragedy!" The loss of a male child was, of course, more serious.

"Yes." Maximilian said nothing more for a time. He sat back comfortably in the sunshine, letting himself be lulled by the motion of the carriage.

"Poor young people!" Stephanie said after a time, wiping her eyes with a handkerchief. Then, by way of taking comfort to herself, she added: "But there will be more children and they will forget."

"The young Hayburn told me there will be no more children."

She hesitated for a moment, then asked: "Maxi, do you mean he is afraid for her to have them?"

"No, not that. They told him it would be very unlikely."

Stephanie did not ask anything more for a time. Her misted eyes looked about them unseeing as they made their way down the Praterstrasse. She loved this odd, foreign young woman.

Oh, if they had taken her advice, and the little Hayburn had remained here in Vienna, where there were the best doctors in the world! Why had her relatives forced her to go home to that cold land, where no one knew anything! And that sister-in-law! She must be hard and possessive, as she had heard so many Lutheran women could be!

Now they had passed the Prater Stern and were in that part of the Haupt Allee which lay on the way to the Krieau. The memory of the May Corso and Henry's comically gloomy face brought her back.

"What about Herr Hayburn?" she asked.

"He's very unhappy. He's stupid with unhappiness."

"Poor boy!"

For reply, her nephew Max shrugged, casting his eyes around at the very considerable press of fashionable traffic about them, and the high, yellowing chestnut-trees.

"Is he still in the little house in the forest?" she asked.

A smile played round Maximilian's mouth. He was certain that what he was going to say next would make her very angry. "No," he said, "he has gone back to the apartments in the Favoriten. He says he can work there."

Much to Maximilian's surprise, Stephanie did not explode. She merely turned round and looked at him with interest. "Tell me, Maxi," she said, "there's a young girl there—a music student—isn't there? I seem to remember the little Hayburn telling me. Do you think he has—a friendship?"

Again he shrugged, and threw his eyes upwards. "Who knows? These British people are so strange! One can guess nothing!"

Chapter Seventeen

ON the first of October, 1880, Baillie George McNairn died. The news found Bel at the breakfast table after everyone else had gone out. She sat wearily, leaning on her elbows, swallowing tea and staring before her out of the window. Sarah had come to her with a note, and Bel had directed her to tell the messenger she would come down to Albany Place this morning.

Bel poured herself yet another cup and leant forward pondering. Sophia, who had written her the note she had just received, was with Mary, so there was no need for her to go to Albany Place at once.

George's end had been expected for some days now. Bel's grief was not deep. But she was sorry for Mary, that her husband should be taken from her at so early an age as forty-five; she was sorry for Mary's children; she was sorry for Arthur, upon whose shoulders the worries of Mary's affairs would certainly fall; and she was a little sorry for herself.

Bel went on swallowing and staring in front of her, putting off the moment when something must be done. Whatever happened, she reflected, whatever blunders she might make, it was always herself and Arthur to whom the family turned.

She thought of Phœbe. That had been her great blunder this autumn. Those weeks in an Edinburgh hospital when she had scarcely left Phœbe's side. It had been so exhausting, and she, Bel, had felt so repentant. When Henry Hayburn had come, she had wept and blamed herself to him. But Henry had been stony and bewildered. He had not shown her whether he forgave her or not.

Yet it was herself, Bel, who sat yearning by Henry's wife through the days her life was in danger; herself whom Phœbe had wanted. And, knowing that the young couple's purse could be none too long, it was her husband, Arthur, who had defrayed the expenses of Henry's journey from and back to Vienna.

And yet, when at last Phœbe was out of danger, and she, Bel, had come back to Glasgow, she discovered that Henry had been to see her mother, and unburdened his outraged heart in Monteith Row. The old lady was now waiting, armed and ready with accusation and reproof, for Bel's long-suffering self.

Bel had not, of course, intended to tell Mrs. Barrowfield of the Duntrafford conspiracy. The old woman, knowing her daughter, had got it out of her. And thereafter Bel had to stand naked and ashamed before her mother's fury, forced to account for her actions towards a young woman about whom she need never have bothered, on whom she need never have expended any affection whatever.

Well, she supposed she and Arthur would always go on being like that. Always taking responsibility, and often receiving blame for the responsibility they took. Always being asked for help and advice, and often having their help and advice called interference.

Bel sighed, set down her cup and prepared for action. Thank goodness Phœbe was now safely in the Duntrafford Dower House, whither her convalescence had now allowed her to travel. Margaret had been insistent that she should come to her at the earliest moment possible; that she would find health in her native countryside more quickly than elsewhere. Bel, occupied with Mary, had relinquished her grasp of the beloved invalid.

But what was there to do now?

Mary's boys—Georgie and Jackie McNairn—were staying here in Grosvenor Terrace at present. Only half an hour ago she had packed them off to their school at the same time she had seen young Arthur off to his. She had better call for them, she supposed, and take them down to Albany Place.

She would need the carriage for that. Indeed, the carriage would be needed all day. To fetch Arthur and David. To take clothes to be dyed black, and to take herself to buy not unbecoming mourning. To take Arthur—it would, of course, be Arthur—to make the funeral arrangements. To do endless errands.

While she waited for it to come, Bel wrote to Grace at Aucheneame, who had in her charge the little twin girls, Anne and Polly. Bel offered to see to their clothes. George McNairn's daughters, who were not yet quite six, must appear at his funeral in all the black correctness of Victorian mourning.

II

A strange, unfamiliar Mungo stood at the door of Duntrafford Dower House looking about him at the rich autumn beauty of this quiet, sunless morning. His sturdy body was clad in the formality of a black frock-coat. On his head was a tall hat, and in one hand he carried black kid-gloves. The merest onlooker would have known that this was not a dress to which he was accustomed. It was the day of George McNairn's funeral, and in a moment he and his wife Margaret must leave for the City.

His other hand was given to his fifteen-month-old son, Charles Mungo Ruanthorpe-Moorhouse, a person of much importance, in spite of his childish petticoats and his still inarticulate tongue.

He was not a beautiful baby. As yet, there were none of the Moorhouse good looks about him. His little snub face and popping eyes gave him a strong resemblance to his grandfather, old Sir Charles—a resemblance which became quite remarkable when the baby laughed, as he was now doing at a yellowhammer that had alighted for an instant on the gravel of the drive only a few yards in front of him. As he pointed and looked into his father's face, Mungo was seized—not for the first time—with an odd feeling that, somehow, he was bending to hold the hand of a strange, miniature Sir Charles, with little dark curls and a pink face.

"That's a yella yite, son," he said, giving the yellowhammer its Scotch name.

In reply, the baby laughed louder, and the bird flew away.

Mungo turned to find Phœbe standing beside him. "Hullo. What are you doing out of yer bed at this time of day?"

"It's after ten."

"Well, that's early for you. Has Margaret allowed ye?"

"I didn't ask her." Phœbe bent down and put her arms about the baby.

"Now, Phœbe, don't try to lift up that bairn. He's ower heavy for ye." Mungo spoke sternly.

"It's all right. I won't."

Mungo watched his sister as she supported Charlie's steps across the gravel of the drive in the direction of a wicker chair that had been placed for her on the lawn beyond.

"Will ye be quite warm?"

"Of course. It's stuffy this morning. When do you go?"

"In two or three minutes."

He looked across at Phœbe. His countryman's eye did not approve of the thinness that gave her body too much elegance nor of her pale face with the dark rings about her eyes. But in spite of these, or indeed because of them, Mungo—at most times slow to notice—did not fail to remark the unreal, almost ethereal quality that suffering and a great disappointment had given his sister. She looked fragile and lovely as she sat there bending over the little boy.

Too fragile. For a moment Mungo felt misgivings. But immediately he reminded himself that once before, as a child, Phœbe had suffered a great shock and that her country stamina had stood by her.

Now his wife had appeared.

"Hullo, Mungo. Where's the trap? If it doesn't come now, we'll miss the train."

"I think I hear it."

"Oh, hullo, Phœbe. I didn't know you were down. Are you all right over there? They've been told what to give you for lunch. And don't let that child worry you. Call Mrs. Crawford and hand him over the moment you get tired."

Now a groom had come with the pony-trap. Margaret crossed to her son, gave him a purposeful kiss, patted Phœbe, then took herself, her black finery and her husband into it.

"See you at dinner," she called as the pony trotted out of sight.

III

Now her nephew was quiet in her lap, pulling a spray of Michaelmas daisies to pieces.

"Don't, Charlie. Don't put them in your mouth."

It was comforting to sit here on this warm, sunless morning, pressing this little creature against her. And Margaret was good. Her kind brusqueness suited Phœbe. She didn't nag or insist. And yet her attentions did not falter. Phœbe was glad she had come here almost directly from hospital.

She had received a letter from Stephanie Hirsch this morning—a foreign letter full of bad English, love and regret. Had it been from anyone other than Stephanie, she would have despised its sentimentality. But Phœbe was learning. She had begun to realise that even the sentimental, even those who expressed themselves too easily and too much, could feel as deeply as the stern and the reticent.

Stephanie had seen little of Henry. She thought it was a pity that he had gone back to the Quellengasse. But Phœbe did not think so. Her husband was a lonely, vague sort of creature. Frau Klem, she knew, would look after him.

She lay back in her chair thinking of Henry. The two days he had spent with her in Edinburgh had been a wordless misery. Neither of them had Stephanie Hirsch's ease in expressing their feelings. She had been glad when Henry had gone away again.

But she must get well and go back to him. Now that she only had Henry, would always only have Henry, the thought of him seldom left her.

As she sat thinking of him, tears of weakness sprang to Phœbe's eyes. But at once contempt sprang after them. These were not Phœbe Hayburn's tears. They were the maudlin tears of a foolish invalid.

She became aware that she was pressing the child so tightly to her that he was kicking to be set down. "Poor Charlie! Was I squeezing the life out of you?"

Mrs. Crawford appeared at the door with something she must take.

"Oh, Mrs. Crawford, is it time for that already?"

Phœbe swallowed what she was given, handed over the child to his nurse and went inside to write letters to her husband and Stephanie.

IV

Today Sophia's chatter helped rather than hindered. And it was unceasing.

"Now, Mary, I don't think you feel well enough to come downstairs to the service. You've been wonderfully brave, dear;

but remember, it has been a long strain for you. Well, if you feel you ought, there's no more to be said. I'll sit beside you.

"Oh, Bel dear, there you are! Are you all here? Only the two Arthurs and yourself? Yes, of course. The other children are too small. Still, I thought, maybe Isabel—But what about Phœbe? No. Of course. She's at Duntrafford.

"Don't bother about that, Mary. I'll do it.

"Good morning, Margaret. We were just talking about Phœbe. How is she, poor child? Well, of course. When you think what she has just come through. And how is that wonderful son of yours? The image of his grandfather? Fancy!

"Oh, Grace dear, there you are! Yes. Poor Mary! It's terrible, isn't it? Oh, of course, yes. I was just saying that to William this morning. We must all make sacrifices according to our ability, to help Mary through. It was very kind of you to keep Anne and Polly. Hullo, dears! How are you? How nice you look in your new dresses! Your Auntie Bel *did* get neat ones for you, didn't she? David! Come and kiss your old sister! You're not too grand for that, are you? How's little Robert? Wil says he's just terrified of you in the office. You're so great and important!

"Oh, here you are, William, and the children! William, have you got the black gloves I bought for you? What do you say's coming down, Margy? Wait a minute. I think I have a pin. There, that's better. Remind me to sew it. Now, children, go and kiss your Aunt Mary and say how sorry you are.

"Oh, Arthur, are you coming back here to read George's will? Yes, I thought you would. Well, of course we'll help as much as we can. But remember, William is a poor man! He hasn't got what you and Mungo and David have. Isn't that so, William?"

William Butter said nothing.

"Oh, here's the minister! Now are you sure you feel quite up to the service, Mary dear? Very well. But I'll sit with you at the end of the front row, so that we can just slip out if it is too trying. Georgie, Jackie, you're the chief mourners. You had better sit with Anne and Polly in the front row, too. That's right."

And so, in Mary's darkened dining-room, the service was read over the remains of her husband. And when that had come to an end, Baillie George McNairn was followed by the men of the family to his last resting-place.

Later in the afternoon, Mary's brothers, together with William Butter, sat round the dining-table while George's lawyer read his will.

Only the tongue of flattery could possibly have called George McNairn clever. And he had died at the early age of forty-five. But, after his kind, he had been shrewd and acquisitive. His affairs were in good order. In the time that was given him he had been able to save a sum which, if it seemed small now, to David's and Mungo's magnificence, would provide for his widow the necessary upkeep of the house in Albany Place.

There was, then, Arthur said, looking round the table, only the education of the children to be considered. Georgie was fifteen and would soon be earning. But Jackie was twelve. And there were the little twin girls, whose education had not yet begun. But girls did not need much education. They had only to grow up, stay at home, learn to dust and find husbands.

What, then, Arthur asked, was everybody prepared to do? For his part, he would see to all the immediate payments, thus saving Mary embarrassment in her first distress. And thereafter he was ready to take his full share.

Mungo said Arthur had better find out exactly how things worked out as they went along, and promised he would not see Mary and her children stuck.

David pointed to the fact that times were bad, and that his mother-in-law still drew a very substantial income from Dermott Ships, in addition to Grace and himself. But, yes, certainly they could count upon him putting his hand into his pocket for Mary and her children when necessity arose.

If anybody had been looking at William Butter, they would perhaps have noticed that the colour in such parts of his face as happened not to be covered with black hair had deepened a little at these declarations of generosity; that his lips had parted for a moment as though he might even bring himself to some kind of articulate utterance. But as no one *was* looking at him, his lips closed again, his colour receded once more, and William did not feel himself called upon to make any more definite gesture.

When they joined the women upstairs for tea, Sophia was still voluble. "Oh, there you are, boys," she said, presiding at the tea-table in place of the afflicted Mary. "Now you must tell me how you like your tea. I *should* know, but I keep forgetting. And I've just been saying to Mary how she had nothing in the world to worry about, Arthur. You and William are really just on her doorstep, ready to help at any minute, and Mungo and David are not really so very much further away."

Bel turned from the window where she had been standing, cup in hand. "There's McCrimmon with the carriage, Arthur."

As the horses trotted westward, Bel's curiosity overcame her. "How did things go downstairs, Arthur?" It was difficult to ask questions with their small, sharp-eared son sitting opposite, but she could not help herself.

In reply Arthur grunted.

"I suppose you've offered to pay everything and take the responsibility?"

Again Arthur grunted. But his grunt contained a note of assent.

Bel sighed, looked out of the window and said: "I suppose you and I are like that. We just can't help it."

The eyes of Arthur the Second remained deceptively innocent. But what he had heard had done him no harm.

V

It was the first week in December. Bel sat looking at Phœbe as they drank tea together before a blazing fire in the drawing-room of Grosvenor Terrace. Phœbe was recovering—but slowly. Her disastrous journey had occurred at the end of August, but still, even now, there were the marks of her ordeal upon her.

Phœbe folded a letter she had been re-reading, put it back in her workbox and took up her cup of tea. Her eyes met Bel's.

"How is Henry, dear? You never give me any news."

"Oh, Henry's all right, I suppose."

"You suppose? Doesn't he write to you regularly?"

"Not regularly. But he writes."

Bel laughed.

"That letter I was reading wasn't from Henry, if that's what you mean. It was from a friend in London. I met her at the Mission Church in Vienna. She's going back there at the end of the year."

"Who is she, Phœbe?"

"A governess. She wants me to travel back with her."

"You can only do that if you're well enough."

"I'll be all right."

"But is she quite a nice person, Phœbe?"

"She's at least sixty."

Bel gave a satisfied "Oh." Age and niceness went, apparently, together.

"I was hoping Henry would come home for you."

"He's very busy."

"Still." Bel looked at the fog outside the window for a minute, then turned her eyes to the fire.

"I've been thinking," she began. "Arthur says things are getting better. Wouldn't it be a good thing for Henry to try to get something here at home? Surely with all the experience he's had—"

"But how can he? He's too far away to look for anything."

"Arthur would help. And look at David. He knows everybody now. You don't want to stay in Vienna all your life, do you?"

Phœbe considered this for a time, then said: "I don't know." For a moment her thoughts carried her back to the Imperial City. She had known rapture there. Her eyes had been taught to see, her senses given a new awareness. Whatever her outward seeming, she was a different young woman from the one who had gone there less than a year ago. Now, once more, they were standing, she and Henry together, in the cool magic of an early May morning. They were in their nightdresses by the window in the Quellengasse. Over there in the mist, the Prater. And there the Arsenal. And there the Karlskirche. And further off the spire of Saint Stephen's. There had been nothing more to ask of life that morning. The universe was bursting into bloom.

Deliberately, Phœbe drew out the dagger of grief and disappointment that was stabbing her. She examined it calmly. She was even a little proud that she could find strength now to perform this trick.

Bel wondered why she was biting her lip. "Don't bother about these things now, dear," she said. "Only, I thought it would be nice to have you both at home."

Phœbe paid no attention. She put back the dagger. Things must go on.

Yes, there was Henry. So long as they were together it didn't much matter where they were. She would write to this woman, in London and tell her she would travel back to Austria in her company.

Chapter Eighteen

FRAU KLEM was at her wits' end with Herr Hayburn this autumn. She had not meant to have a lodger in the Quellengasse now that Pepi was at home again and contributing something to the household from odd work in the theatres. But on his return from Scotland the young man had come, told her of his misfortunes and begged her to let him have his old room once more.

The good woman had been moved and flattered. Moved by his loss. Flattered that he should look to her and hers for comfort. She did her best for him. She saw that he was fed; that he was kept warm; that his clothes were looked to. There was little else she could do. But, together with her daughter, she held many a conference about him.

Pepi grew hot at Phœbe's treatment of Henry. Frau Hayburn had been a fool to go back to Scotland to have her child; and now, having lost it, to leave him all alone like this. It would serve her right if Henry—

No. Pepi must not talk like that. You had only to look at Herr Hayburn with his wife to know that there was only one woman in the world for him. And these Scottish people were very strict, Frau Klem had heard; as strict as—well, any decent persons ought to be. But she noticed a toss of Pepi's head, and wondered if, after all, life in the theatre was good for a young girl. Besides, Pepi must remember what poor Frau Hayburn had been through.

But Pepi did not seem to be much touched by the thought of poor Frau Hayburn.

After these discussions Frau Klem would end with a sigh and go back to her housework; while Pepi went back to her singing practice, taking her scales as high and as loud as she could, until her simple mother was driven to wonder if these slate-pencil sounds could really have anything to do with music.

But in the first weeks he had come back to her, Herr Hayburn seemed a poor creature enough. Frau Klem had seen him one day by chance in the Favoritenstrasse. As he passed her by, his eyes had the same look of suffering witlessness that she had seen in the eyes of the oxen as they were driven down this same street on their way to the slaughter-house. But presently, as better news of Phœbe came, things turned more bearable for Henry. He was glad now that his homing instinct had brought him back to the Quellengasse. These people were kind. They helped him to keep going. To take a hold of himself.

Once more he allowed himself to become one of themselves, as he had done in his first months in Vienna. On Sundays they went together on little jaunts. Often Henry stood treat in some suburban wine-garden, where, in the splendour of the dying Austrian autumn, they ate their *Schnitzel* and drank the year-old wine.

He began to take long walks. Often Pepi Klem would go with him, chirping along by his side, talking good-naturedly of anything that might distract him. Henry readily fell into the habit of having her with him. Soon he was paying no more heed to her than he would to his brother Stephen. She asked him to talk English. They began to call these walks her English lessons.

October, November. Still Phœbe's letters did not say when she would be with him. What was wrong? She had assured him she was recovering. Very well, then. It was impossible for him to go back to Scotland to fetch her, but her coming could be arranged. He had written about her coming, many times, and she had replied that she would come soon. Why, then, didn't she do it?

He was a man now. Fully awake. He longed to hold his wife once more in his arms. This thought, indeed, had become an obsession that blinded him, in part, to what his wife had suffered. He began to nurse a grievance. He began to forget she must be given time.

In the second week of December he wrote, telling her yet again of his loneliness, and begging her to return to him. Phœbe replied with a letter that was gay and teasing. Sending him all her love, telling him nothing definite, wishing him a Merry Christmas, and saying she would see him soon.

From her letter he did not guess that she planned to surprise him.

II

It was twelve o'clock on the last day of the year. Henry crossed from his office in the Neubau, making for his usual mid-day eating-house in the passage off the Herrengasse.

Vienna lay under snow. It had been swept up into great heaps on either side of the Ring. A silver sun had broken through, and its glitter upon the snow, in the Volksgarten, on the Burg Platz, on the palace roofs, threw back reflections that forced Henry to contract his eyes to mere slits.

But presently he was in his little restaurant, bidding his usual vague good-day, and waiting to have his meal set before him. Except for himself the room was almost empty. It contained Christmas decorations, but few customers. The *habitués*, it seemed, were elsewhere. Most of them were not at work today, and thus they had not sought their usual eating-place. Henry, too, was finished now.

"Der Mister" seemed out of spirits, the rotund proprietor said to his wife; out of spirits, and downright bad-tempered. They watched him as he sat, slumped in his chair, tugging his beard and staring at the glowing ribs of the tiled oven, the door of which had been left open. The good woman gave it as her opinion that he looked ill.

Henry had been living in daily expectation of news telling of Phœbe's return. She had not written for a fortnight. Yet since Christmas he had got a letter from Mrs. Barrowfield saying she had seen her, and that she looked very well. He could not understand it. With the prospect of nothing to do, either this afternoon or tomorrow, bitter loneliness had fallen upon Henry like a beast of prey. The Klems, he had been told, would be little at home. Pepi was not in work just at present, and able to go visiting with her parents.

There were many things he might have done, acquaintances he might have seen. Even the ladies in the Paulanergasse would have been glad to see him, for his wife's sake. But in these last weeks Henry had clung to the routine of his work. He had tried to think of little else. It had been his lifebelt. Now, for the next days, there would be no work for him to do.

As the old man brought him his soup, he asked if the gracious gentleman felt well? Henry said he did. His host said that it was very cold, but sunny. Henry admitted that this was so. The old man asked what the gracious gentleman did on Sylvester Day in England. The gracious gentleman snapped ungraciously that he didn't know, as he did not come from England. Defeated, the old man retired.

Shortly he came back, however, professionally cheerful, with Henry's meat, fried potatoes—and a bottle of wine, which he begged Henry to drink with his own and his wife's compliments. It gave them pleasure, the good man said, to make a present of this bottle of Hungarian red wine to one who patronised their modest house so regularly.

Henry unbent a little. The determined friendliness of the couple had penetrated. He thanked the man and, remembering some kind of manners, bade him bring two more glasses. His host and hostess must drink with him to the New Year. The man did as he was told. His wife came from behind, wiping her hands on her apron, and beaming. The glass of wine warmed Henry.

He was inventing yet another toast, and filling up their glasses once again, when Pepi Klem came in. Coming from the dazzling sunshine, for a moment she could see nothing in the dim gas-light. He had seen her in this place only once before. That had been last spring, when she had just returned to Vienna. In his desperate, mock heartiness, Henry called to her:

"Hullo, Pepi! Come and drink to the New Year."

She gave a little start, then smiled in recognition. "Oh! I didn't know you still came here. I expected to find some friends."

Another glass was brought and another toast drunk. The couple were pleased to see that so bright a companion had come to chase away "der Mister's" glumness.

The old man laid a place for her, smiling; taking it for granted that this was Henry's girl for whom he had been waiting, impatient and angry.

Henry's loneliness responded to Pepi at once. Here was someone he knew who was gay and friendly. For the time, at least, he need not be miserable. He bade her choose her lunch, and ordered another bottle of wine.

Now it was pleasant in the little warm restaurant. Pepi talked nonsense, hummed snatches of songs and laughed at nothing.

He watched her; half smiling, half bewildered. But she was cheerful and feminine, and her presence soothed him.

She asked him if he were working this afternoon and what he intended to do. He told her he was not working and had no plans.

She said nothing to this—merely went on humming dreamily. One or two others came in; along with them two students, friends of Pepi's. But they only nodded in recognition, and crossed to their own table.

Henry asked her if she did not want to join them. She smiled vaguely and said that the wine had made her sleepy. He said that he felt sleepy, too. They could hear, somewhere, a church clock strike two.

"I didn't know it was so late," she said, looking round her.

"It doesn't matter to me. I've nothing to do."

"Neither have I." Suddenly she sat up and looked at him. "Herr Hayburn! Shall we go for a sleigh-drive in the woods? It would be wonderful today! We can drink coffee somewhere."

Henry was surprised to find himself assenting.

III

They had hired a horse-sleigh in the suburbs, and were speeding out towards the Vienna Woods.

Now, as Henry sat thickly wrapped beside his companion, he took the trouble, British fashion, to assure himself that this was just the thing his health and spirits needed. That a run in the sharp winter air would clear his head, disperse the cobwebs and render him fit to begin the work of the New Year.

His companion saw that he was cheerful, that he was pleased to find himself with her.

Their way took them up through Döbling and in the direction of Weidlingbach. It was some time before Henry realised they were coming out in the direction of the house that he and Phœbe had rented last summer. They passed the end of the path that led up to it. Now, in the snow, everything seemed unfamiliarly familiar.

Memory forced itself upon him. The still evenings in the garden up there. The roses and the pine-trees. Their hopes. Stephen's companionship. Phœbe's last descent through these trees, when at last they were persuaded it was right for her to go. The evening he had received the news.

Seeing his solemnity, Pepi spoke. "You lived up here in the summer, didn't you?"

"Yes."

"Where?"

"Oh, quite near here."

But she wanted him to stay in the present, to be merry and think of herself.

"Oh, look! Isn't it beautiful!"

The snow was just right for a sleigh-drive. It was dry, powdery and not deep enough to make running difficult. There was no wind to blow it into drifts. The sun had been bright as they started out, but now it was obscured by clouds hanging so low that it looked as though they might run into them as the road climbed higher. The meadows, lit by the grey winter light, lay flat, white and monotonous around them. Now in the woods the pine-trees stood motionless, each branch bearing its heavy burden. On other trees, too, the frailest twigs were rimed with powder.

Everywhere they turned there was beauty, peace and mystery. Even the hoof-claps of their horse were muffled as he drew them on and upward, his breathing changing to little clouds that floated past them. For a time the only sounds came from the sleigh-bells.

The valley was narrowing. The road was taking them up one side of it. Down there was the stream. Now they could catch, here and there, the bickering of such water as still ran over the black stones and under frail bridges of ice. Yet further up, where the rock had been cut to make the road, dropping water had formed grottos of icicles.

Presently they were on the top and almost in the clouds. It was becoming misty. They could only see the nearer trees, the road, and the huddled back of the driver's sheepskin coat, as he sat in front of them, cracking his whip and calling to his horse. Their universe of whiteness had turned suddenly clammy—menacing and unfriendly.

Under the rug, Pepi came closer to Henry, grasping his hand as though in fear.

Presently they had passed the top and were dropping down. The sleigh was running easily, the bells playing a different tune. Now the mist had parted and they could see the snow-covered roofs of a village beneath them.

Pepi gave a little cry of pleasure. She called to the driver. Down there was a room where they could drink coffee. The man replied that he could do with it.

The inn parlour was warm and friendly with its decorated Christmas tree; the innkeeper welcoming. Today he had expected no one. The young man, he saw, was foreign. But he knew better than to ask about a couple who had so plainly escaped beyond the frontiers of convention. It was natural with young people. Who was he that he should blame them?

Henry drank his coffee morosely. In the sleigh, the touch of Pepi's hand, the nearness of her, had brought a sudden excitement. Longings had risen within him—longings that clouded his reason. Now Pepi's voice as she talked to the inn-keeper moved him strangely and brought him near to despair. What was it she was talking of? He did not know.

The man had left them alone. He poured himself fresh coffee and threw it, scalding, down his throat. Now he was ready. He must get out. Out of here. He reached for his coat.

"But what's wrong?" She asked.

He turned at the door, dazed. He spoke hoarsely. "It's time we were getting back."

"But why? I haven't finished yet."

"I'll go out and speak to the driver."

"The driver? I sent him away. I thought it would be nice to wait here for supper and go back in the moonlight. Didn't you hear me talking about it just now? You must have been far away! When you said nothing, I thought it was all right. The innkeeper said there was someone here who could take us."

He looked down at her, beaten.

She came to him. "My dear, are you sure you feel all right? Has anything happened?" She took the lapels of his jacket in her hands.

He caught her to him.

It was the next afternoon when Henry returned with Pepi to Vienna.

IV

"And your dear husband will be at the station to meet you?" The elderly English woman with whom Phœbe had travelled from London smiled across the carriage at her with a prim, tired smile. The carriage was stuffy. Neither of them had slept much.

"No, he won't. I'm giving him a surprise. That's why I planned to arrive on New Year's Day. I knew I would catch him in his rooms."

"When did you leave Vienna?"

"August."

"He will be surprised!"

Mrs. Hayburn had lost a child, her companion gathered. Poor little thing! And she was so young! But now she was going back to her husband, to her youth, to all the intoxication of this city that held so many foreigners in its thrall.

The older woman envied her. To be coming back to a steady, British husband, and, at the same time, to the gaiety of Vienna, was a thing any woman might envy. Phœbe's companion sighed, as she straightened her veil and buttoned her mended gloves.

Like so many other governesses, French and English, she had come at first to Vienna for a year, merely to gain experience. Now, after more than thirty, the Imperial City still held her. She could not leave it for longer than a few weeks at a time. In common with others of her kind, she had spent her days moving from one noble family to another, educating daughters, helping worldly mothers to sell them to the highest bidders in the Empire's glittering marriage market; a mine of gossip about the intrigues and scandals that raged perpetually in Austro-Hungarian society.

Phœbe looked from the window. The train had almost passed through the mountains to the west of Vienna. In a short time they would be in the Westbahnhof.

On hills and forests the snow lay thickly. The sky was grey and leaden. Now the suburbs were beginning—the familiar villas and gardens of Vienna, taking their New Year's morning rest under the blanket of whiteness. There were few people to be seen. Everywhere there was peace and stillness. Now the City itself. The train was slowing down. Now the rush and confusion that went with the arrival of the morning express from Western Europe.

Her heart was beating as a *Komfortable* took her towards the Klems'. She could see Henry already. He would be newly awake and dishevelled, his eyes staring like a boy's. She laughed at the thought of him.

Her excitement mounted as the *Komfortable* entered the Quellengasse. She had no eyes to notice that some of the buildings, half-finished in the spring, were now complete and occupied. And here was the Klems', and there was the old house-porter, beaming broadly and ready to help her with her luggage.

And had the gracious lady brought the gracious gentleman with her?

What did he mean?

Merely that he thought that he was not upstairs. He could not, of course, be sure.

Phœbe laughed. He must be there. Where else could he be?

The Klems' outer door on the staircase was still closed.

Phœbe rang with determination, once, twice, many times. At last she heard Herr Klem himself grumbling behind it. Now he was standing, leonine, unkempt and angry, in his shirt and trousers. But at the sight of her his colour mounted and his face took on a grin of confused welcome. How was she? Had she just come? And what had she done with Herr Hayburn?

He led her into Henry's room. It was as she would have expected. His books and papers were scattered on his work-table. A suit of clothes, folded no doubt by Frau Klem, lay upon a chair. Her own photograph stood by his bedside along with one of his mother. His other belongings were everywhere.

But the bed had not been slept in. Phœbe turned.

"Where *is* my husband Herr Klem? He must have gone somewhere."

The man shook his head uncertainly. He asked if Herr Hayburn had known the gracious lady was coming this morning.

"No. It was a surprise. But Henry *must* have said where he was going."

Herr Klem shrugged. He knew nothing of it. Perhaps his wife—

And now Frau Klem, flustered and untidy, came to add her greeting. She was genuinely pleased to see Phœbe. She would bring her hot water and make coffee at once. And was the gracious lady quite well and glad to be back? It was a pity Herr Hayburn was not at home to greet her.

This time Phœbe's eyes filled with anger. "But *where* is he?" Couldn't the woman stop gabbling and tell her where he was?

At once Frau Klem was humble. Didn't the gracious lady herself know? She had taken that for granted.

"How can I? I've only just come from Scotland."

"He must be with friends."

"What friends?"

"*Na?* The gracious lady must know Herr Hayburn's friends."

They stood bewildered for some moments longer, then Frau Klem went to make coffee, followed by her husband. He shut the kitchen door behind him.

Together they agreed that this was very unlike Herr Hayburn. But really, if his wife wanted her husband to confine his escapades to such times as she was not arriving back in Vienna, it would be much better if she told him when to expect her.

"Perhaps Pepi knows," Herr Klem suggested.

"Go and see if she is there. I didn't hear her come in last night."

But Pepi's room was empty, too.

"I don't think that child should be going so much to Lisa Fischer's," Pepi's mother went on, preparing breakfast. "Oh, I know Pepi's an artiste, too, now. But I don't think mixing with Lisa's friends is doing her any good."

Chapter Nineteen

HENRY'S transparent honesty would neither allow of apology nor concealment. He had sinned against his wife. And at once he hastened to admit the enormity of his sin. Let Phœbe do what she liked with him! Leave him! Divorce him! Anything! No punishment could be bad enough!

His conscience, consumed for a time in a flame of madness, sprang up once again, sharp and more vigorous from its roots, sprouting thorns to torment him. Thorns of tradition; of background; of the rigid code by which he and his kind lived.

Now they were having it out in their room in the Quellengasse. It is difficult to tell which of them suffered more.

Shocked and bewildered, Phœbe sat watching her husband pacing up and down; dishevelled, broken and ashamed. In any other circumstance the sight of his unhappiness would have melted her. If ever Henry was a lame duck, he was a lame duck now—lamed by his own hot folly.

But this folly had been committed against herself, against their own past intimacies, against her own body, so nearly broken by the disastrous, stillborn birth of his child. Her young, burning pride could find no forgiveness.

Flushed, expressionless and silent, she watched him, as he went back and forth, blurting out his misery, his loneliness, his weakness. She could not answer him, throw him a crumb of comfort. Had she not suffered, too? Had not she made that dreadful journey home? Been ill? Suffered these weary months of convalescence?

Had it been to amuse herself? Did he imagine she *liked* losing his baby?

At the thought of her child, Phœbe felt the tears fighting to come. But she dug her fingernails into the palms of her hands and bit her cheek until she could taste blood in her mouth. Her eyes followed him, dry and hard, as he moved about the room. She could not forgive him.

They were living in a foreign land, she knew, where such things were looked upon differently. But this had nothing whatsoever to do with herself and Henry; nothing whatever to do with their own strict ways. That they had learnt to live among the people here, to understand and like them, to find toleration, even, could not condone Henry's behaviour.

But what was she to do?

Henry was asking her. She must, she supposed, find an answer.

"The first thing we must do, Henry," she said, speaking evenly, and with no show of emotion, "is to get out of here."

Henry clutched at the word "we".

"Then you've made up your mind to stay?"

Phœbe did not reply to this at once. Stay with him? What else?

Go home to Bel lamenting that she had insisted upon marrying a waster? No. That was a thing she could never bring herself to do! Her mother's Highland pride flamed up white within her. She would rather go down to the Franzjosefskai and pitch herself into the Danube Canal!

As yet she had no idea of her feelings—no idea if she loved or hated her husband. But one thing she did know. She must fight out her battle here in Vienna alone. Alone and apart. Free from leering gossip, from over-eager sympathy. The family at home must know nothing until, at least, her decisions were taken.

"I've made up my mind to stay in Vienna in the meantime. I don't suppose you're any more anxious than I am that this should reach home. But I am leaving this house at once. You can come with me. I haven't unpacked. We can go back to our old hotel, and take two bedrooms. One for you and one for me."

II

"Well, Maxi?"

Maximilian bent over his aunt's hand and raised it to his lips; then, this salutation being too formal, he kissed her on both cheeks.

"How are you?"

"Very well, my dear. But your Aunt Helene is in bed. Nothing. A little cold."

"I'll see her before I go."

"Yes. You must."

Stephanie rang for coffee and led her nephew to a seat. "We haven't seen you since Christmas Day, and that was only for ten minutes. And now it's the middle of February."

"I've been very busy."

"Amusing yourself, Maxerl?"

"Working, Aunt Steffi."

"*Na?* A little of both, perhaps?" Maximilian looked about his aunt's pleasant old-fashioned room. The February sun was casting pale, slanting rays through the double windows with their draped lace curtains, catching silver dust-particles, and throwing patterns of light on the floor. The room was warm from the stove, and heavy with the scent of spring flowers.

"It's nice here," he said.

"Then why don't you come oftener?"

Maximilian did not reply to this. He had got up and was wandering about, looking at familiar pictures and photographs. Aunts and uncles. His own parents. Suddenly he stopped and held up a filigree frame.

"Hullo! This is new."

"Which, Maxi?"

"This photograph of the little Hayburn."

Stephanie laughed. "You take a great interest in the little Hayburn, don't you?"

"Of course. An uncle's interest, my dearest aunt."

"I'm glad. Do you know, Max, I believe you only come to see me when you want to talk about the little Hayburn!"

Maximilian was still examining Phœbe's photograph. "I say!" He exclaimed. "She's very smart, isn't she?"

"Yes. I sent her to a place in the Kohlmarkt."

"I was sure her clothes were Viennese!" He continued to admire Phœbe. Her close-fitting jacket. Her slim waist. Her modish bonnet. And the expression of her face had a new elegance, somehow. A little harder, perhaps. A little more sophisticated. But it pleased his sense of style. He looked up. "That young woman could almost be called a raving beauty. 'Mister Henry' had better look after her."

"They've just taken a small flat quite near here," Stephanie said after a moment.

"The Hayburn told me. Much more sensible."

Stephanie signed to the servant, who had come in with the tray, that she would pour coffee herself. She did not want him in the room.

"Maxerl," she asked as she gave her nephew his cup, "has anything gone wrong between these children?"

Maximilian sat down. He shrugged. "I took them to "Lohengrin" at the Opera a few weeks ago. It's the only time I've seen her since she came back." He thought for a moment, then added: "She seemed a little more artificial; a little older; a little more—what shall I say?—remote. It's easy to understand—losing her child."

In turn, Stephanie took her cup and sat down beside him. "Do you think the Hayburns are still in love with each other? It was a marriage of love, you know."

Maximilian considered. "I should say he is. I don't know about her."

"What do you mean, Max?"

"Well, that night at the Opera he behaved as if he were her servant. Holding things for her. Running for this and that. Watching her expression to see if what he said pleased her. I wanted to laugh. And if you could see him in the factory! He's getting more and more bad-tempered!"

"What do you think it means?"

Again Maximilian shrugged. "Who can tell? The English are strange animals. But it seems to me the Scotch are stranger!"

They sat silent for a time, drinking coffee and following the train of their thoughts. At length Stephanie turned to her nephew.

"Do you know what I think, Maxi? I think the poor child is trying to grow a shell."

Her nephew smiled. That was nothing new in Vienna.

III

Yes, Phœbe was growing a shell. A shell of elegance. A shell of fine manners. A shell of social interests. Things that might have been good in themselves, if all else had been well with her; but now they were anodynes for her sharp unhappiness.

Henry, ashamed and obsequious, allowed her to do what she

liked. In the rented flat in the Wieden she had taken to receiving such of the English and American colony as she chose to invite—wealthy students mostly, and one or two Viennese. She learnt to chatter of music, of the theatres, of the doings at Court.

Her husband watched her, troubled. This was not Phœbe. Not the girl he had married. But he blamed himself, left her alone, and found his own anodyne in more and yet more work.

But daily, Phœbe found herself face to face with her misery. Lying in the darkness of her lonely bedroom, she fought her battle, time and time again. Why had Henry done this to her? They were not of the same clay as those people here. They could not take things lightly.

But by degrees the mists of intolerance began to clear a little. She began to wonder about this patient, untidy, lost young man who left the flat early each morning and usually came back in time only to go to bed.

Towards the end of March, Henry, exhausted and ill with overwork, was at home for some days.

She nursed him with devotion, though she showed him no affection. When he thanked her, she turned his thanks aside with hard, impersonal brightness. But when he had gone back to work, the house seemed empty. And so, through this unhappy year, Phœbe and Henry blundered on. Contrition and distress on the one hand; pride and bitterness on the other.

A sharp old woman of their own kind—Mrs. Barrowfield, for instance—might have brought them back to reason, and a measure of happiness. But here, in their exile, there was no one. And the colourless letters they sent home gave no inkling of their distresses.

IV

And meantime Imperial Vienna continued on her brilliant way. More brilliant than ever; for in May the Emperor's son, the Crown Prince Rudolf, was to be married to the Princess Stephanie of Belgium.

By April, at many points in the Ring and at such other places as the royal processions would be seen to advantage, scaffoldings for seats were being placed. No trouble would be spared. That the Princess might not see the waters of the Wien river, muddy and full of factory refuse, as she crossed the Elizabeth Bridge coming from the Palace of Schönbrunn, the entire bridge was to be turned into a bower of flowers in which young girls would stand and throw rose-petals at her carriage. On a tribune opposite the Burgtor the mayor and dignitaries of Vienna would present addresses of welcome. The spire of Saint Stephen's itself was to be outlined during the nights of celebration with glass bulbs containing electric lights.

The month of April was cold and wet. The scaffoldings, undecorated, looked bare and forbidding. People kept telling Phœbe how wonderful they would look with all their garnishings. These things chimed, somehow, with Phœbe's mood of cynicism; with her feeling that all was vanity; that reality's scaffolding could never long be hidden.

At first she had thought of Pepi Klem merely as a wanton, who had set a cruel barrier between herself and Henry. But now, as time went on, she found herself possessed by an unnamed urge to see her. She had caught sight of her in January in the chorus of an operetta. Henry had not been there, and she was glad. But although her curiosity had sent her back to the same theatre, Phœbe had not seen Pepi again. What had become of her? Phœbe did not want to meet her face to face, but the desire to see her amounted to morbidity.

And meanwhile preparations for the Imperial marriage continued. The first of May, a Sunday, was wet and cold. The yearly Prater Corso fell flat. In the afternoon it rained, and there was little of the customary glitter. The Hirsch ladies, ever conventional, drove the length of the Haupt Allee but they did not invite the Hayburns to accompany them.

Now, however, the weather had changed, as though by Imperial command. There was warmth and brilliant sunshine. With luck, it would continue until the wedding-day, which was the tenth.

Vienna thrilled with interest at the news of each important arrival. Gossip and surmise flew. The Prince of Wales was here. He had been greeted on the platform by the Archdukes and by Sir Henry Elliot, the British Ambassador. The Belgian King and Queen were at Schönbrunn Palace holding their own temporary

Court, and giving out that their daughter already felt more at home in Vienna than in Brussels. Prince and Princess William of Prussia had arrived in the royal train from Berlin. Regal and imperial blood was flowing to Vienna from all parts of Europe.

And humbler Vienna was kept carefully and properly informed. It must be entertained by the doings of the great. It heard that the Prince of Wales had dined with the Archduke Karl Ludwig. That two thousand five hundred of the Empire's aristocracy had been to a ball in the Imperial Palace, where the Emperor and the Empress had shown themselves particularly gracious.

And now, on the day before her wedding, the Princess Stephanie was to show herself to the people over whom one day, she would be Empress. Her future Emperor, the Crown Prince Rudolf, had, to increase his worthiness of her and to prepare himself for matrimony, just returned from a pilgrimage to the Holy Shrine in Jerusalem.

On a seat in one of the stands erected on the Ring, Phœbe sat with Henry, waiting for the Princess Stephanie's procession to pass her by.

She had been surprised when Henry, who cared little for such things, had come to her with place tickets. But Henry had become like that. He thought, now, of things to please her.

She sat looking about her, while her husband sat woodenly beside her. The Ring was dense with people, most of them carrying bunches of lily-of-the-valley, for this, it had been said, was the favourite flower of the Princess.

Now there was no longer any bare scaffolding. There was bunting everywhere. The black and yellow of the Empire. The yellow, red and blue of Belgium. The white and blue of Bavaria; as a compliment to the Empress. Where there was no bunting, there were festoons and garlands.

Now the Princess Stephanie was coming. There was shouting in the distance that could be heard above the pealing of church bells and the firing of artillery. Down there on the pavement below them, people were struggling for a better view; darting out, only to be pushed back by the soldiers cordoning the street.

Suddenly, as the procession was nearing them, Phœbe saw a young woman dart forward, trip and stumble, laughing into the arms of a gendarme, who roughly ordered her back. It was Pepi Klem. To show her composure, Pepi made him some reply and did not return to the pavement until the man had commanded her yet more harshly. Then she walked unhurriedly back, giving Phœbe time to look at her.

Now the splendour of the Austro-Spanish Habsburgs was passing Phœbe by. Red trumpeters mounted on black horses. Court servants in seventeenth-century uniforms. Horse-guard. Foot-guard. Carriages with the suite of the Princess drawn by black thoroughbreds harnessed in gold. More soldiery. And now the fair young Princess with her mother in a carriage drawn by milk-white stallions of the Imperial stud, their heads nodding with ostrich plumes, the postillions in mediæval white and gold. Bells rang. Guns fired. People shouted. Flowers were thrown.

But Phœbe had no eyes for a Habsburg exhibition. She had seen that Pepi Klem was going to have a child.

V

Somewhere about midsummer Henry received this letter from Mrs. Barrowfield:

"DEAR HENRY,

"It vexes me sore that it should have come to this. You may well be miserable! If you are, as you say, repenting in sorrow, it is no more than you should be doing. I am glad to hear the Lord has given you that much grace, anyway.

"Your letter says that 'sheer desperation' is making you tell me everything. Well, my dear boy, maybe you might have done a worse thing than write and tell Granny Barrowfield. She has always been fond of you and your wife, and would do anything to help the both of you. And I may just tell you, that two or three minutes—since just before she went to look for her ink-bottle—she was down on her knees asking her Maker to put some common sense into her old head, so that, with His help, she would maybe write and give you some of His Divine Guidance.

"You are not a bad young man, Henry. You never have been, and never will be. There is nothing vicious in the build of you. You are just a great big innocent. But, if I know you at all, your blood runs twice as quick as most young men's, and your feelings are strong. It may be hard for an old woman of seventy-six to judge the strength of a young man's temptation. But what is wrong is wrong.

"All the same, I never thought it was right, the way they took Phœbe away from you last August. It was against nature and against common sense. When Bel told me what she and Mrs. Dermott and Lady Ruanthorpe had done, I could have taken a stick to the three of them. I could never abide the Dermott woman anyway, and I dare say the other old cat is worse.

"I was very, very sorry for you at the time, dear Henry. I nearly came out to see you. But at seventy-five, and me not used with the travelling, how could I do it? And mind you, I think these three women—and I am sorry to say my own daughter was one of them—sinned against you, just about as much as you sinned yourself. Only their sin is not listed in the Ten Commandments, so maybe it is harder to put a label on it, and not so awkward for their consciences. But you can take it from me, that conscience or no conscience, Bel heard all about it from her mother!

"I doubt you will just have to put up with what you call Phœbe's hardness. And if you think she has got harder since this woman is to have your bairn, surely you can see the reason for that, too? As your wife, Phœbe can only see the whole thing as a terrible affront. (By the way, how do you know this bairn will be yours? If the besom is anybody's girl, then it may be anybody's bairn. Be sure to write about this. Don't forget.)

"I wish I could give you more comfort, Henry. But remember this: Phœbe's blood runs quick, just the way yours does, and if you give her time, I think things will get better. She would not be staying on with you if there was no love for you left in her. Have patience, ask help on your knees, Henry, and brighter days will dawn!

"I hear from Arthur that he can get you the offer of a good job here at home. But he will be writing to you himself, I dare say. That would be far the best for you both.

"This has been a long letter for an old woman to write. I hope the Lord has made me put down everything I should. But anyway, now I must stop. As you ask, I am sending it to your office.

"Yours lovingly,

"ISABELLA BARROWFIELD."

Chapter Twenty

THE Volksgarten was quite still this morning—still and autumnal. From the Franzensring outside, the traffic sounded far-off and muted. When, some minutes ago, the clocks of the City had announced the hour of eleven, their peal had come to Frau Klem, sitting here in the garden, with the unreality of those strange bells said to come to the ears of becalmed sailors from belfries long since sunk beneath the sea.

The children near her went about their games quietly; throwing dead leaves into the pond and watching them thoughtfully, as they floated on the glassy surface; or hiding from each other noiselessly and without enthusiasm behind the pillars of the Theseus temple, while governesses and nursemaids sewed and gossiped in whispers on the seats around.

Frau Klem sighed, looked into the face of her sleeping grandson, adjusted the shabby shawl that was wrapped about him, decided that her seat was hard, and wished that Pepi would come back to fetch them.

She must have been gone almost two hours now. Surely they must have reached a decision about her by this time. The letter from the Director had said half-past nine. But theatres were go-as-you-please places, she had always heard. Still, Pepi was only seeking student work in the chorus to earn some now very necessary money, and her voice was true and strong.

A trio of tiny children passed. They were richly dressed in little velvet coats, and attended by a nurse in Bohemian peasant costume. The children of some nobleman, perhaps. Frau Klem stroked back a wisp of untidy fair hair, and her eyes followed them until they had passed from sight among the shrubbery. A pang of jealousy and regret caused her to hold the bundle in her arms yet closer.

No. She had never expected to have grandchildren so rich and well tended as those three. And yet, if Pepi had married a respectable burgher—like, say, Willi Pommer—it would have been the delight of her heart to make and contrive small clothes for them, and lead them out—a proud grandmother—before the world.

Not that she did not love this child; but its coming had been unfortunate, look at it as you would. Oh, she had been assured that Pepi would be a great singer, that she would one day earn enough money for all of them and bring up her son to be a gentleman; that you had to make all kinds of allowances for people as highly gifted as Pepi's teacher declared her to be. And, of course, young people were highly inflammable.

But Frau Klem did not like it. She liked things straight and settled. Herr Hayburn had been very good. He had been to see his son, and had been helpful. But he was a stern, remote young man; and he couldn't be Pepi's husband. And say what you would, a husband and a ring on the right finger was better than a weekly allowance. Even for a young woman who was going to be a great opera star.

The little creature in her arms was awake now. He was looking up at her with wide, dazed eyes.

As though she blamed herself for these thoughts, Frau Klem gave rein to her instincts. She kissed him; she talked nonsense to him; told him he was the sweetest baby in Vienna and that she would not change him for all the other children in the Volksgarten, however grand they might be.

For a moment, one or two elegant nurses raised their eyes to look at the rather shabby woman fussing with the untidy infant over there on that seat by herself.

But she was sorry that Pepi had needed to look for work so soon after the baby's coming. Whatever the doctor had told her, it couldn't be good, either for herself or for the child. Still, if she got this work in the new season of operetta at the Ring Theatre—as the Comic Opera House was coming to be called—she would be able to pay for her lessons, and help with other expenses, too. It had been nice of her cousin Lisa to put in a word for her. More people were coming into the garden now. A young man with a roll of music in his hand passed near her. She wondered if he had been to have his voice tried, too. A staid old gentleman in a black frock-coat, a grey cravat with a pearl pin, and whiskers cut like the Emperor's. One or two women of fashion.

Suddenly a modish young woman emerged briskly from a side-alley. She was almost standing over Frau Klem before they recognised each other.

Colour flooded to the roots of the elder woman's hair. It was Frau Hayburn. Frau Klem smiled stupidly.

For reply, Phœbe responded with the coldest of nods, turned her back and walked on quickly up the gardens.

Frau Klem watched her as she went. The encounter had been uncomfortable. Frau Klem's heart was beating. But poor Frau Hayburn! You could hardly blame her, when you remembered she had lost her own child!

Now she saw that Phœbe's steps had slackened. That she had stopped. That she was coming back. Now again she stood before her.

"I'm sorry, Frau Klem. I was rude to you just now. I apologise."

How beautiful, how elegant Frau Hayburn had become since last she had seen her in January! Elegant, and strangely bright, like a diamond.

Frau Klem was friendly and humble. "Please, Frau Hayburn. But I understand!"

Phœbe said nothing to this. But she did not move. The woman could see that she had lost colour; that her strange, dark blue eyes were ranging about the gardens as though they were seeking help.

For a moment Frau Klem wondered if she were going to faint. But now the blood had come back hot into her face, and she was looking down at the child.

Her voice, as she spoke, was low and controlled. "Is that your daughter's child?"

"But, yes. You see, Frau Hayburn—"

"My husband's child?"

For reply, and finding no words, the grandmother uncovered the child's face. As she held him up for Phœbe to see, he opened his eyes once more and looked about him.

She wondered at Frau Hayburn's quick, low cry. She did not guess that a familiar twitch of the tiny mouth, a hovering frown about the dazed, scarcely focused eyes, had almost torn the heart out of her.

"I must go now."

Frau Hayburn turned and went away without another word.

II

December the seventh.

Henry Hayburn sat at the back of a box in the Ring Theatre taking no part in the conversation.

Some time ago Maximilian Hirsch had come to him saying that he had, by good fortune, been allotted a box for the first performance of Offenbach's "Tales of Hoffmann", and would Herr and Frau Hayburn care to join his party? The presentation of this, the only serious opera the dead German-Parisian composer had written, was being awaited with excitement in Vienna. Maximilian was sure Frau Hayburn would be interested.

Henry had accepted. Not because he wanted to go in the least. But because he thought it might please Phœbe. This was a rule with him now. Helpless, he was forever seeking to make amends.

He looked at Phœbe. She was sitting in the front of the box, talking with the other young woman of the party. Together, they were discussing the many well-known people who were appearing at this important premiere, pointing them out to each other, as they came in. An Archduke, one or two ambassadors, stars from other theatres, a society beauty.

Phœbe was brilliant—lovely. And quite detached now from himself. It was as though she had encased herself in sophistication that he might not come near her. He did not know, any more, what Phœbe was thinking. They occupied the same house; ate meals at the same table. But they had fallen into a dull politeness, the one towards the other. Sympathy, emotion, between them was, it seemed, dead.

Maximilian turned to say a word to Henry, to draw him into the conversation he was having with the husband of Phœbe's friend. But as he did so applause broke in the theatre. The conductor had come in, and was taking up his baton. Herr Hirsch turned back to listen to the opening music of the new opera.

There was little overture, apparently, for almost at once the curtain had risen on Luther's wine-cellar in Nuremberg, lit only by beams of moonlight, while the voices of the Spirits of Good Cheer could be heard singing their opening chorus behind the scenes.

Henry was glad to be left alone. Let them sit listening to this tomfoolery, and leave him in peace!

Now the innkeeper had come in, carrying a lamp. Obediently the light on the stage jumped up to reinforce the effect of brightness. The engineer in Henry was puzzled. How could so many gas-burners jump into flame at once? But he was forgetting. He remembered having read that the new Director had installed a system of electric contacts near each gas-jet. By merely switching on the current of electricity and the flow of gas at the same time, immediate and full illumination would result. It was ingenious and interesting. But they had better take care. People, these days, were rushing into all kinds of new uses for electricity without taking enough thought.

Now the prologue was over. People whispered that Herr Ferenczy was singing this new part well. There was applause while the curtain descended slowly on Hoffmann, as he began to tell of his unhappy loves. Presently it had risen on the first of the Tales.

Henry watched the traffic of the stage without bothering to take it in. The chorus of Spalanzani's guests were coming in to hear the song sung by Olympia, the wonderful mechanical doll.

Suddenly his eyes were caught by a little, plump lady of the chorus. Her paint, patches and high marquise wig merely underlined her identity. It was Pepi Klem. Sweat broke upon him. He looked at Phœbe. Had she, too, seen Pepi? Would she think he had brought her here, knowing, yet caring nothing?

But the fixed, charming smile remained on Phœbe's face. Now the human doll had been brought from its cabinet. Spalanzani's guests passed down before it, one after another, to admire its finery. Now for a moment Pepi was right in the front of the stage. Phœbe could not miss her.

But Phœbe's expression did not change.

This was horrible to him, this iron control! It was well that she did nothing now. But when once they were home again, he knew she would smile, say what a pleasant evening it had been, bid him a bright goodnight, and go off to her own room.

Doing what he conceived to be his duty, he visited his child regularly. He had learnt from Frau Klem that Phœbe had seen the child in the Volksgarten. That it had upset her. But not by the flicker of an eyelid had Phœbe betrayed any of this to himself.

And he loved Phœbe. He always would love Phœbe, he supposed. Yet this coldness would kill him! In her heart she would blame his callousness for bringing her here tonight. But he hadn't known. Pepi had said something about work again, but he had, typically, taken little notice.

Down on the stage the doll was singing her elaborate, high-pitched song. Sitting among Spalanzani's guests, Pepi was simulating an elaborate, coquettish interest.

Crude rage took hold of Henry—crude rage and revulsion. That young woman was a slut! She should be at home. What right had she to flaunt herself thus brazenly, with a child little more than two months old? He was glad that soon he would shake the dust of this terrible strumpet city from beneath his feet!

But now, in the flash of his rage, a dark place was illuminated. *Would* he be glad to leave Vienna? What of the child he would leave behind him in the Quellengasse? He knew now that his son had entangled his affections.

His desperate eyes again sought his wife. The fixed smile was still upon her lips.

A great bitterness flooded Henry—bitterness and dark bewilderment. The doll had finished her song. He could see Pepi down there on the stage clapping in mock applause.

He must get out of here! Out, to walk by himself and think. Real applause had broken in the auditorium at Fräulein Jiona's singing of the doll's music. Under cover of the noise he opened the door of the box, signed to Maximilian and went. Outside, rudderless and distracted, he fought himself back to some kind of composure, striding up and down the empty foyer.

When he reappeared in the box at the end of the act, Phœbe hoped, with every show of elegant concern, that there was nothing wrong with Henry.

III

December the eighth.

It was after half-past six. Pepi Klem sat in her corner of the chorus gazing into the mirror and trying to decide just where, on her cheek, she should place the dab of black paint, which from the auditorium would look like a beauty spot. At last she decided upon the top of her cheekbone, just a little beneath the corner of her right eye, took up her paint-stick, made the spot and sat back to examine the effect.

All about her in the large room was light, laughter, noise and comedy, half-dressed women. This was no hack, ageing chorus. The Director, Herr Jauner, had been determined to have everything and everyone of the best—soloists, chorus, orchestra. The posthumous masterpiece of Offenbach must be rendered with all the care and reverence due to it, and in accordance with the traditions of this, the most musical of cities. In February the dead composer's work had been acclaimed in Paris. Now in December it must be still more acclaimed in Vienna.

Several of the girls were clearing their throats, singing snatches. Pepi did the same, hoping that those nearby would note the fineness of her voice. But as nobody showed any interest, she stopped, gave her pert little face an additional dusting of rice-powder, and decided that she was enjoying herself.

She was grateful to her cousin, Lisa, for getting her this work. It had come very soon after the birth of her baby. But work with this management was a chance not to miss, and she needed money. If she made a somewhat plump little guest in Spalanzani's house and Giuletta's palace, the chorus-master had been pleased with her voice, and she would soon regain the slimness of twenty-one. Besides, her mother helped with the child, and a neighbour, a good woman who had borne a child at much the same time as herself, had been glad, for a consideration, to undertake the nursing of it.

Last night, on the part of the dressing-table assigned to her, she had placed photographs of her father and mother. The other girls had photographs. She must give herself the importance of having photographs, too. Now, tonight, she remembered she had another. She took it from her bag and wedged it between the glass and the frame of the mirror. It was of herself, holding the baby—a thin little card, of which she had only one copy, done cheaply and inexpertly in the Favoriten. The baby was not very clear—he had not stayed quite still—but it wasn't bad of herself, she thought, as she looked at it now.

"Whose child is that?" the girl next to her was asking.

"My child."

"How sweet!" The girl smiled. Experience had taught her not to ask too many questions.

But time was getting on. A call came for the ladies of the chorus to go down. Pepi stood up and gathered her loose dressing-wrap about her. As a Spirit of Good Cheer, she had only to stand behind the scenes and sing. When that was over, there was ample time to come back up here and finish dressing for the first of Hoffmann's Tales.

She found the large stage milling with people. Discipline in the Ring Theatre was not as strict as might be. This presentation, it was said, took more than two hundred, and most of them seemed to be here—men and women of the chorus, dancers, soloists, carpenters, scene-shifters, men in charge of the lighting.

She pushed her way through them to the front of the stage and the closed curtain. To Pepi, as to any other stage-struck girl, this great wall of cloth, which would presently rise and disappear out of sight, was the very essence of excitement, of romance.

Another girl was examining the audience through a peep-hole. Pepi touched her arm. "Please, will you allow me for a moment? I want to find my mother and father."

Yes! There they were, high up, right in front on the fourth gallery.

She had wanted them to come last night, but the first night demands of the more influential had made that impossible. Besides, today was a Roman Catholic holiday, and her mother and father had been able to join the newly formed queue just after four o'clock. Pepi herself had left the Quellengasse long after they had. She had waved to them pompously as she passed them outside just before six.

At the peep-hole she laughed affectionately at her blonde, untidy mother hanging over the brass rail, scanning the auditorium beneath her with the excitement of a young girl. Her father was sitting back in a typical attitude, running his hand through his fair mane, looking cross and impatient for the performance to begin.

Still at the peep-hole Pepi became aware of a hissing of gas. For a moment she did not bother to turn round. They were testing the lighting apparatus. They had done so last night.

But now there was an excited shout! She turned round.

By the new mechanism, the gas had been turned on, but the electric contacts had not lighted all the jets. Gas was streaming everywhere and rising to the hanging scenery above. All at once a darting flame set one of the side-pieces alight.

The mob on the stage turned and ran, Pepi with them. But because of her distance from the entrance, most of the people on the stage were before her. She could hear a girl screaming as she fell and was bruised by the others on the stone stair leading down from the stage to the street. She would wait for a moment and keep calm. The men would control the fire presently.

Suddenly she remembered she had foolishly left some money in her bag. She must take time to rush up to her dressing-room—it was only a step or two—seize her bag and bring it out to safety.

Now she found herself standing, panting, before her mirror.

Two other girls were there—fetching their valuables, too, perhaps.

She took her bag and turned to go.

Suddenly the lights went out.

Down on the stage no one was at his post, and hysteria vied with folly. An excited scene-shifter drew the burning side-pieces up above the stage to where the other scenery was hanging, and worse—to where escaping gas kept collecting. The gas exploded; the scenery caught fire and began to fall down upon the stage. No one opened the cocks of the safety water-tank above. No one lowered the iron curtain. The cloth curtain was blown outwards, revealing the blazing stage to the waiting audience, who had, as yet, suspected nothing.

There was panic and a rush to escape. But the same hand that had turned off the gas in Pepi's dressing-room had turned it off on the stairs and in the passages. Only from the stage, which was supplied from a private gasometer on the roof, did gas continue to pour itself into the theatre, asphyxiating many more people than were burnt.

Folly piled itself still higher. Cloakroom attendants had the keys of emergency doors in their pockets. It was nobody's business to call the fire brigade. When the firemen came at last, they fought their way to the floor of the theatre, only to have their lamps extinguished by roaring draughts and their lungs choked by gas and dense smoke.

But folly was not yet finished. In spite of the choking smoke, the firemen called out to ask if anyone were still in the theatre. There was no reply. They came out to say that everyone was safe, and took to removing furniture from reception-rooms and records from the office.

Yet hardly any from the third and fourth galleries had been able to leave the theatre! The one or two who had fought their way to safety gave this terrible news! When the firemen returned at last to the help of the upper galleries, the narrow staircases were so much blocked with the crushed and the suffocated, that by the time these were removed, the galleries were collapsing into the inferno beneath.

The windows of the chorus-room were few and high. They were shuttered against the December weather. Neither light nor air could come to the three girls that way. There was black darkness—black darkness, an increasing smell of smoke and, above all, the stupefying, giddy smell of gas.

They called to each other, groping until their hands touched: then they clung together. Pepi could feel the others shuddering, sobbing with terror and coughing convulsively.

She must try to keep her head. "We must feel our way round the wall until we find the door," she said, as firmly as her voice would let her.

They advanced until they touched a wall, then began to feel their way along it. They went slowly. The hands they felt with trembled.

But the sickening smell of gas, combined with the acrid smell of smoke, made Pepi's head spin. Now she needed all her resolution to keep upon her feet.

"Here's the door!" Her voice did not seem to belong to her. It came from far away. Unreal. She had felt like this once at the dentist's. Bells rang in her ears. She seemed to feel herself fling the door open.

No! That made it much worse!

This smoke and gas! But was it, after all, a real door? Or was she—? If only this smoke and gas—! And was she on her knees—? Or was she imagining that, too?

Her baby's face seemed to be suspended above her, expanding and contracting like a reflection on glassy water.

The Hayburn. But the Hayburn couldn't help her here!

Her mother. Her mother could help her. If only her mother, leaning up there on the rail of the gallery, would—Oh, this smoke! She must keep her eyes tight shut. And this coughing! So bad for her voice, too! How could they expect her to sing if—? Yes, her mother could—

But Pepi Klem no longer thought what her mother could do.

The little moth had flown into the flame.

IV

Phœbe had waited in the night once before—when, as a child of fourteen, a fierce instinct had held her until she could snatch to safety the little boy she loved. Reason had fallen away from her then. It had fallen away from her now. Once again she was nothing but an instinct; but this time an instinct blinded by hurt pride.

Bareheaded and dishevelled, she thrust her way through the surging crowd, pushing back and forth among them; dodging policemen, soldiers and firemen; jostled, shouted at, insulted—caring for none of them, in this red world of flame, smoke and embers.

What did she seek? An escape from her own jealous sufferings? Appeasement for the heart Henry had come so near to breaking?

But why was she seeking these things here?

Or was she standing, primitively, crudely paying unholy homage to the gods of this dreadful holocaust?

It was only when she found herself before the burning theatre that this strange madness came upon her. She had been waiting for Henry to return for his meal in their rooms in the Wieden.

He was late, as he so often was these days. He had much to hand over, he said, before he returned to Scotland. But tonight he might be hanging back. The sight of the Klem girl on the stage last night must have increased his embarrassment.

Then the house-porter's wife had come up, fat and breathless, to tell Phœbe that the Ring Theatre was burning; that you could see the glow in the sky. Phœbe threw on her fur jacket, took up her gloves and went out to look.

Everything around lay ominously quiet. Silver snow and moonlight. Somewhere a clock struck half-past seven.

Yes. Just over there to the left of the Karlskirche there was a red glare in the sky. And was that a distant shouting? Phœbe made her way into the Wiedner Hauptstrasse to get a better view.

Here she found excited people streaming towards the Opernring. She followed with them. As she passed the Opera House she saw the audience in their finery leaving hurriedly, or standing on the steps distractedly seeking *Fiakers*. The performance had been stopped. As she cut behind the Opera and thence along the Herrengasse, all the sky in front of her glowed red and angry. Her heart beat in her throat. Now she was in the Schottengasse. And now in the Schottenring among the mob before the theatre itself.

It was after eight. But she had taken no account of time or exertion. She stood, panting. The flaming theatre lit up the Schottenring as though it were broad day.

About her the agonised citizens of this emotional city were standing, weeping aloud, imploring one another to do something. Some of them, as was obvious from their holiday clothes, had been in the theatre—people in poorer circumstances, most of them, who had gone early to cheap seats. This young girl cried that she had left her mother behind. She had hoped to return with help. This man—a wife and two half-grown children. This woman—her lame husband. If the firemen would only run their ladders up to that window there—she was sure it was that window—her husband had said he would wait. Oh, why didn't they do it! The woman tried to tear her way through the crowd, fighting like a wild cat.

A burst of sparks shot upwards from the roof. A gust of wind caught them and blew them towards the crowd. Police and soldiers shouted at the people to stand back. They paid little heed, brushing hot cinders from their clothes. Flames blazed up now—blue gas-flames.

Phœbe moved again, struggling forward; her Highland eyes wide open, gleaming and possessed.

They were suffering, these people around her. But she had suffered, too! Suffered when she lost her child! They were suffering and lamenting, for those who were suffering still more in that monstrous, burning trap.

She was plunged in an ocean of suffering. Tossed hither and thither in buffeting waves of suffering. It filled her with a sullen exaltation.

Another burst of sparks drove the crowd back for a moment. The licking fire roared and crackled. Again Phœbe thrust her way forward. What was that wild screaming. People at upper windows shrieking for help? They were suffering, too! She had suffered when she learned that Henry had been unfaithful to her; had touched, as she thought, the bottom of the pit. But when she had seen the Klem girl at the Crown Prince's wedding celebrations—! No. It had been too much!

What was that man doing? Going to jump into the stretched canvas the soldiers were holding? Now there was a string of them, jumping one after the other, like sheep through a gap. Why couldn't the fools wait? They would be killed if they jumped down, one on top of the other! No wonder firemen were shouting at them to stop! That was right! Play the hose on them and stop them!

Was that woman crazy—out of her senses? Was she actually going to hurl her child down without waiting for the men to spread the cloth for it? Oh—! A groan had gone up from the crowd in front. Good thing she could not see! Even in this black exaltation she could not have borne it.

No, she, Phœbe, had not had *her* child. But if she had, she would never have pitched it from a window! She would have pitched herself first! And that child she had seen in the gardens? What of it?

But what—? Had the crazed mother thrown herself from the window after her child? But she was quite right. She wouldn't mind losing it now.

Phœbe did not know that she was shuddering; that her eyes were mad and staring.

These people should stop gesticulating and howling at the windows! It wouldn't do them any good! The firemen were getting people from the building as fast as they could. Those at the windows might still have a chance. Though how the heat didn't finish them off, she couldn't understand. Even out here in front it was hot!

But the howling at the windows was stopping. The white faces were disappearing—falling away—and in their place red, cruel squares of fire! The fire must be coming to the front now. Driven by the heat, policemen, soldiers, firemen, crowd were falling back.

Why didn't these people about her stop this senseless moaning? This senseless wringing of the hands? Queer to think she had been in there with Henry last night! What if they—? But she would have kept her head and done something. Or perhaps not. And her suffering would be finished and done with.

But she must move from here. The heat was unbearable.

Suddenly there was the sound of an explosion. An eruption of flames to the sky. Now a crash. Myriad sparks rose with them. A man shouted that the gasometer which fed the stage had exploded and fallen, taking the roof of the theatre with it. People stumbled back in terror. Phœbe with them.

V

Why didn't she leave all this? Why didn't she go home? Hadn't she had enough?

But now, for the first time, having reached the edge of the crowd again, she saw the Sanitary corps at work. Laying down the bodies they had brought out. Piling them on carts that would take their shocking loads to the General Hospital to await identification. Some of the bodies were burnt past recognition. Others—by far the most—untouched by the flames, were dead of gas-poisoning or suffocation from the smoke.

Why was she staring at them? What was she seeking? These horrid shapes were no concern of hers.

A young woman was sobbing beside her—searching among

the dead as the soldiers set them down. Phœbe turned to look at her. She saw she was half-dressed; that her teeth were chattering with cold. But why was her colour so absurdly bright? Phœbe looked more closely. Her face was painted. Of course; she must be one of the singers.

"You'll get pneumonia," Phœbe said sharply.

The girl continued to sob. Her brother and sister had been in the fourth gallery.

"You should go home. If they're safe, they're safe. And if not, you can't help by standing here getting your death of cold. Look. Take this and put it on. My dress is thick." Phœbe took off her fur jacket and forced the girl to wear it.

The girl stopped sobbing. "A foreigner?"

"Yes." What could it possibly matter to the girl what she was?

Suddenly a new, quivering urgency was shaking Phœbe. "You're one of the singers, aren't you?"

"In the chorus."

"Are you all safe?"

"Most of us. But one or two—"

"Did you know Josephine Klem?—Pepi Klem?"

The girl looked up without at once replying. The paint upon her face did not conceal her strange expression. "Did the gracious lady know Pepi Klem?"

"Is Pepi Klem safe, Fräulein?"

The girl looked away in distress. Why did this foreign woman speak so sharply. What did the tone of her voice mean? Why was her look so crazed?

"Tell me if you know anything of Pepi Klem."

The girl raised a hand and pointed. "They brought her out, just before the explosion. I was looking for my brother and sister. She's lying over there."

Phœbe turned and ran. Now she knew why she had come! She would see the body of this woman before they carted it away. The body of this harlot who had taken Henry from her. She stumbled forward, her eyes staring, her lips parted.

Yes. Here was another cart. And here the bodies waiting to be loaded.

"Get out of the way, please! Haven't you been told already to keep back?"

Firemen, soldiers, men of the Sanitary Corps were working, perspiring, smoke-black and grim. And hardened, it would seem, to the awful bundles they must carry.

Phœbe stopped with a cry, as though some hand had struck her! Pepi Klem was lying at her feet!

She stepped backwards. Her eyes looked stupidly about her. The night spun round. The street—the crowd—the sparks—the roaring, burning building.

Were her senses slipping? Was she going to faint? What was happening?

No. She was still here—still in this world of terror. And the woman she detested was lying at her feet.

Detested?

She looked again at Pepi Klem. In the brilliant fire-light she saw that Pepi's eyes were closed as though in sleep, that Pepi, too, was painted. She had not been put down roughly; she lay easily—round-faced and artificial—pert and childish. A beauty spot was set high up on her cheek. Her thin wrap had fallen back, exposing her neck, circled by a ribbon of velvet. Her full bosom was pushed high by the lacing of her corsets.

Pepi Klem. Or a little rococo archduchess peacefully asleep among the laurels of Schönbrunn?

Phœbe stood over her, shaken and appalled. Appalled that she herself had had it in her to nurse so great a hatred against this silly, pretty child! And now Pepi Klem was dead! She could never trouble her any more!

Shame took hold of Phœbe—shame and a storm of weeping. This wilful girl who had so many times despised the tears of others stood now, heedless of the tragic rabble, crying out her heart, in abandonment and wild hysteria.

How long she stood thus, Phœbe did not know. But now a hand was laid upon her shoulder. "This body must go to the General Hospital. You can identify it there."

The men had gone with Pepi. Phœbe pushed herself free of the crowd, hoping to find some kind of cab to take her home. Why should she wait here any longer in this place of burning death?

Had she not found the release she had been seeking?

VI

A little later Phœbe jumped from a *Komfortable*.

No, Herr Hayburn was not at home, the house-porter told her. Yes, he had been to the fire, but he had come back some time ago and gone away again. He had asked where the gracious lady was, and left the key for her. She had run out, leaving it on her dressing-table. But wasn't the gracious lady very cold? Hadn't she gone out in her fur jacket?

Phœbe said she must get some money to pay the driver, and went upstairs. In the sitting-room she struck a match, lit the gas and looked about her. The evening meal had not been touched.

A shiver ran through her. Yes, she was cold, she supposed, and hungry. And certainly she was very tired.

But what must she do now? Where was Henry? She could not stay here, quiet and alone. The excitement of the night, the tumult in her senses, would not allow it, tiredness or no. She must find her husband. But where? If only her throbbing head would let her think! She could think of nothing but the raging fire and the face of Pepi Klem.

Pepi Klem. Now she knew.

Impatiently, Phœbe tore off a piece of dry bread and stuffed it into her mouth. She poured herself a glass of wine and took it with her to her bedroom to drink while she found warm clothes. In a few moments she was downstairs, placating the *Komfortable* driver, who was grumbling at being kept from his trade on such a profitable night.

But why was this foreign woman jumping into his *Komfortable* again? Was she going back to the fire?

"To the Quellengasse, please."

"The Quellengasse in the Favoriten?" Why should he drag out to a suburb, when trade was so brisk in town? He shrugged his regrets. "Impossible."

"Double fare."

The man hesitated, for a moment. Then he shook his head. "Not tonight. The gracious lady must see that my horse—"

"Treble fare."

The man slammed the door and jumped up.

The familiar staircase in the Quellengasse was alight tonight, as was, indeed, every staircase in Vienna. Women with whom she had often passed the time of day were hanging, chattering and anxious, at the entrance. They ran forward.

"Is that the little Klem? Oh—the gracious lady!"

They fell back disappointed.

Phœbe jumped out. "Can you tell me if Herr Hayburn is here?"

They looked at each other doubtfully, then one of them, seeming to decide that on such a night nothing should be concealed, said, "Yes."

Phœbe paid the driver and turned back to them. "Are the Herr and Frau Klem upstairs?"

They chattered round her like tragic magpies.

The gracious lady could not know, of course!

The Klems were in the theatre tonight!

To see Pepi!

They were going to the fourth gallery!

No one was saved from the fourth gallery, except one or two who jumped!

They had gone early, and would be trapped near the front!

The fourth gallery had crashed some time after nine o'clock! Where were they, if they were safe? Frau Klem would certainly have come back to the child.

But Pepi? Why hadn't Pepi come? All the singers and stage-hands had escaped, they had heard.

Phœbe looked at them blankly. She would not waste time giving the news now.

The Klems' door was opened by a woman with a child of her own in her arms. Again the quick look of hope, followed by disappointment.

"Where is Herr Hayburn?"

The woman, who knew Phœbe by sight, tried to look bewildered. But her distress allowed her to dissemble no better than the women downstairs.

"Please. Where is he?"

"In there."

VII

He was sitting in a chair, his back to her, bending forward, as once before she had seen him bending forward in her brother David's room. This time he held a bundle in his arms.

She was afraid, for the child's sake, to startle him. She crossed the room and stood, looking down upon them. Lame ducks.

He did not raise his head. He thought it was the woman she had just seen.

"Henry!"

He looked up quickly. But her voice held tones he had not heard for many months.

"Phœbe!"

"My love!" She went to him, pushed back his hair and kissed his brow.

Now she stood beside him, gripping his shoulder to steady herself. But she must tell him somehow.

"Henry, I saw the baby's mother tonight."

He did not answer at once.

As she waited, she saw from a window that no one had bothered to shutter, how the sky, far away to the left, was alight with evil smouldering red. She felt him move uneasily.

"When? If she's safe, then why—"

"She isn't safe, Henry. The poor child won't see her baby any more."

"Dead?"

"Dead."

She took her hand from his shoulder and moved towards the window.

He looked up once again. "But what am I to do? The child's grandmother must have been killed, too!"

She turned.

"Henry!" Her tone was accusing.

He looked away again, distraught and shiftless.

But Phœbe had dropped on her knees in front of him and was taking the child into her arms.

Chapter Twenty-One

ON Saturday, December 24th, 1881, the family, being Scotch, held their Christmas dinners.

Mrs. Robert Dermott's, given in her house in Hamilton Drive, was truly astonishing. And the most astonishing thing about it was that the chief guests should be Sir Charles and Lady Ruanthorpe, who were, astonishingly, staying with her.

The news that this formidable couple had accepted Mrs. Dermott's invitation, and were coming to Glasgow, had shaken Bel a little. Would she, too, now be expected to invite them? Bel was far from unenterprising, but the thought of having the strong-minded baronet and his lady to stay at Grosvenor Terrace alarmed her. Their daughter, Margaret, had, at first, been bad enough. In the secret places of her heart, Bel found comfort in the thought that Sir Charles was old, delicate and might soon—although she dare not admit this hope even to herself—be dead. Besides, she was receiving him, along with the others, in Grosvenor Terrace tonight after dinner. Perhaps that could be counted as gesture enough.

Now, in the presence of her guests, Mrs. Dermott's ample hospitality, quite unlike Bel's, was in no way clouded by foolish fears or murderous hopes. Indeed, she regarded having induced her new friends, the Ruanthorpes, to leave Ayrshire for the Christmas weekend as a triumph of friendly persuasion.

She looked down her lavish dinner-table, very much as she was used to looking down her committee tables, beaming good-will and practical, strong-minded encouragement; conveying somehow to her incongruous guests that she expected them all to enjoy themselves, get on with each other, and see life—for the time being at least—from the same angle as herself.

And the party *was* incongruous. In addition to Sir Charles and Lady Ruanthorpe, all the four Butters were there; David and Grace, of course; Mungo and Margaret; and, to make even numbers, Stephen Hayburn. But Mrs. Dermott's firm gentility was holding everything together splendidly.

Sophia's tongue, halted a little by the presence of the laird and his lady, and also by the fact that she was eating the dinner of her life, was really not too hard to keep in check. The Davids, the Mungos and Stephen Hayburn could be depended upon to take their share of rational conversation. William Butter could be counted upon to say nothing whatever. That was why she had put him between his own daughter and Grace. And Wil and Margy were nice young things, whose bright, adolescent intelligences counselled good behaviour when occasion demanded.

Old Sir Charles upon her right hand and firmly under her eye, an eye which saw that he should lack in nothing—found himself doing very well. The dinner was good, his hostess had got hold of some quite reasonable wine, and really everything was very jolly. All that was lacking was a pretty woman to look at. Mrs. David on his other side wasn't bad; still, he had always found her a bit colourless. But they were driving across to Arthur Moorhouse's for an hour or so after dinner—somebody's sentimental idea that the whole family should be united tonight—and there he would see Mrs. Arthur herself, who was always damned handsome. And Phœbe Hayburn, he had heard, was just back from Vienna, in which city, unless she were more of a fool than he took her to be, she would have found a dressmaker with the wit effectively to underline her odd, but definite beauty.

"So there's to be quite a number at Arthur Moorhouse's tonight?" he said addressing no one in particular; attempting, a little consciously, perhaps, to be genial. Further down the table his daughter, Margaret, caught the tone of his voice. She knew it for the one her father used at servants'-hall and tenants' entertainments.

Grace answered him. "Oh yes, Sir Charles. You'll see Phœbe and Henry just home from Vienna. And Bel and Arthur themselves, of course. And Mary McNairn and her two boys. Her twin girls will be in bed, I expect. A great family reunion, really. Mary didn't want to come. But Bel insisted. She couldn't bear the idea of Mary being left alone. So like Bel! She's the kindest person I know!"

Sir Charles grunted, not an ungenial grunt, then returned in silence to his turkey. He did not know about Mrs. Arthur's kindness, but he knew she could look deuced smart.

"Mamma." Margy's fifteen-year-old modesty was addressing her mother further down the table.

"What is it, dear?"

"Can I see Aunt Phœbe's baby, tonight?"

"I don't know. You'll have to ask her."

"I can at least go up and see him sleeping." Margy gave herself up to an exquisite anticipation.

Craning her neck round an epergne, stuck with maidenhair fern and hothouse carnations from Aucheneame, Sophia caught her daughter's eye, smiled upon her with foolish indulgence and shook her head.

Margy had become, as only adolescent girlhood could, maniacal about this Austrian child. Her life was made up of the moments she was with him, and the barren stretches of time which must elapse until she should be with him once again.

No one else took up the theme of this orphan baby, whose parents had been burned in that dreadful theatre fire. Innocently, Margy had laid a constraint upon the tongues of these doting parents and grandparents—the constraint of primitive jealousy.

Babies of Moorhouse blood came into the world red and unattractive. Good looks might come later. But for many months they continued ugly and uncomfortably like young birds. At three months the Austrian foundling was perfect. He had none of this Northern lack of finish. In spite of early upheavals, in spite of change in home, nurse and diet, the new Robert Hayburn was thriving like a mushroom. He bore now no noticeable resemblance to his father. His small limbs were rounding out to a dimpled perfection, that caused those aunts of his adoption, who came to see him bathed, to force such rapture as common politeness demanded from throats that were become dry with envy. When he was a little older, there would be nothing left for him but to sprout dove's wings, shoulder a rope of roses, and help the *amorini* and the dolphins to draw the fluted barge-shell of the Venus Aphrodite across the painted waves.

As they put on their wraps to go across to Bel's, Sophia, released from the constraint of the dinner-table and Sir Charles's presence, expressed herself to Grace.

"Of course, in a way, I think Phœbe and Henry were awfully good, Grace dear, to adopt this little boy. Especially as he has lost both his parents in that dreadful fire. Do you know, I missed reading about it properly. Wasn't it annoying? My silly maid has used that morning's newspaper to crumb fish on, and the bit got soaked with egg! And then, of course, with Phœbe losing her own baby and everything— But, as William was just saying this morning, you never know what kind of wild blood, these adopted children have in their veins. It's a terrible risk! And foreign blood too! And I think, in a way, it was foolish of them to give him Henry's father's name. They should have kept his own, if they knew it. But, then, I dare say it was too difficult to pronounce. Oh, Grace dear, don't think I'm being unsympathetic! He's a lovely wee thing! Margy's crazy about him! But I just hope he'll grow up to be a good and righteous man, and be a credit to us all!"

Grace hastened to say that she had no doubt the Hayburn foundling would grow up without flaw. But the jealousy that troubled Sophia had not left even Grace's gentle heart untouched. As she descended to the carriage she found herself seeking comfort in the fact that her own baby—disappointingly plain at almost a year old—had nothing but good, West of Scotland blood in his veins.

II

It was not a large gathering, by Grosvenor Terrace standards. Bel and Arthur, with Arthur the Second, who was now ten. Mary and her two sons. Phœbe, Henry and old Mrs. Barrowfield. But it had been homely and pleasant, and when the time came for tea to be set out and Mrs. Dermott and her party to arrive, there was no one who did not regret their coming a little. Bel and her guests felt they could have been very happy left to themselves.

But now here they were, filling the room with noise and fussing. Kissing, shaking hands, giving and receiving greetings. Admiring Bel's decorations, asking how each other did, welcoming Phœbe and Henry home. Insulting already overloaded stomachs with currant bun, and behaving in all things with a Christmas spirit.

Mrs. Barrowfield had found refuge in a corner. She sat with

Mary, unobtrusive and apart, drinking tea and looking on. She had no wish to be nearer the formidable Lady Ruanthorpe, who sat holding court by the fire. Still less did she want to be near Mrs. Dermott, whom, for reasons known only to herself, Mrs. Barrowfield detested. Yet, illogically, she was pleased with her own daughter, that she could move among these grand people with so much calm assurance. Tonight Bel's fairness profited from the simplicity of black satin.

Called now to Lady Ruanthorpe's side, Henry and Phœbe were crossing the floor. Mrs. Barrowfield watched them with affection. She felt a link with them. She was the only one here, or indeed anywhere, who knew their story. Henry looked tired and older. Tonight he seemed aloof; a little arrogant; as though he didn't care whether the Moorhouse clan liked him or not. Which, when she came to think, was probably true. But his maturity suited him. He would now, at last, develop, Mrs. Barrowfield hoped fondly, into that paragon of paragons, a successful businessman.

Phœbe was elegant in a dress of unrelieved white. She had bought it in the Kohlmarkt. She looked beautiful, the old woman thought; although there were signs of strain in her face. And a suggestion of that look she had once had as a child, after she had brought young Arthur from the slums. It seemed, almost, as though Phœbe were seeing things that others could not see.

But Mrs. Barrowfield was pleased with her. She had, after all, refused to quit Henry, and thus, once more, their ship was safe in open water.

For a moment Bel's crowded drawing-room swam before Bel's mother's eyes.

Now she heard Phœbe's voice. "Bel, Lady Ruanthorpe wants me to bring down Robert. Do you think I ought?"

Margy Butter was running forward. "Oh, Aunt Phœbe, let me come, too!"

Bel gave her consent.

III

The child had been inspected and admired. And now, for a moment, they were isolated, all three of them, under the gaselier in Bel's drawing-room. Phœbe, Henry and the child in Phœbe's arms.

The new Robert Hayburn had been sleepy, but now he opened his eyes wide and looked about him; as though he, in his turn, were inspecting this strange race of Northerners, with their bland self-satisfaction, their benign importance-seeking, their innocent, provincial shrewdness.

The ghost of a gay little smile passed across the baby's face—the mere suggestion of a smile; but it was enough to cause Sir Charles to put his hands behind his back, bend forward, scrutinise the infant, and remark: "If you ask me, you won't have your sorrows to seek with that young man!"

And then, his eyes catching the bright lights above him, the child stretched up one of the small, rosy starfish that served him for hands, and, being a son of Vienna, seemed to be trying to reach their glitter.

Sophia came forward. "Oh, Phœbe dear! I was just saying to Grace tonight, how *good* we all think it is of you and Henry to take this wee man! And we all think—"

With one of those quick gestures that bewildered even her nearest and most beloved, Phœbe turned, the child still in her arms, and left the room.

On the landing, behind the closed door, she halted. What was it that had stung her? Did she sense Sophia's insincerity? Had she become intolerant of family judgments?

Good?

Was it because they persisted in measuring goodness and badness with their own smug yardstick? Phœbe now had learnt that there were things that would not let themselves be gauged by cautious Moorhouse standards.

As for this child of Henry's: she had followed her instinct. That was all. And the family could think what they liked about it! Find out what they liked!

But after a time the flame died down within her. Had she been unjust? Or was she still a little overwrought? She stood now, remembering things that would not let her be.

A young woman lying dead at her feet, lit by the light of a savage fire. The tolling of bells, and a great city bowed in mourning. A Mass said in a suburban chapel for the souls of a departed family, a family that was kind and simple, according to its own, too easy ways. The Mass attended by two young strangers, who knelt in humility, knowing nothing of its ritual.

The same strangers standing by a graveside—the graveside of her child's mother.

These memories were near, and as yet she could hardly bear them. Later on, perhaps, their outlines would be softened.

But why was she standing here? She looked at the child in her arms. His eyes again were heavy.

Phœbe mounted the stairs, laid him in his cot and turned the gas low. For a time she lingered. Presently she bent forward to assure herself that he was settling to sleep. Then, leaving the room quietly, she went back to join the others in Bel's drawing-room downstairs.